A Postcard from the Volcano

LUCY BECKETT

A Postcard from the Volcano

A Novel of Pre-War Germany

IGNATIUS PRESS   SAN FRANCISCO

Cover art by Chris Pelicano

Cover design by Roxanne Mei Lum

© 2009 Ignatius Press, San Francisco
All rights reserved
ISBN: 978-1-58617-269-5
Library of Congress Control Number 2008933490
Printed in the United States of America ∞

IN MEMORY OF
MY PARENTS

AND FOR MY GRANDCHILDREN
ISABEL AND HARRY ROSENBAUM

Children picking up our bones
Will never know that these were once
As quick as foxes on the hill;

And that in autumn, when the grapes
Made sharp air sharper by their smell
These had a being, breathing frost;

And least will guess that with our bones
We left much more, left what still is
The look of things, left what we felt

At what we saw.

Wallace Stevens,
"A Postcard from the Volcano" (1935)

Aus der Heimat hinter den Blitzen rot
Da kommen die Wolken her,
Aber Vater und Mutter sind lange tot,
Es kennt mich dort keiner mehr.
Wie bald, ach wie bald kommt die stille Zeit,
Da ruhe ich auch; und über mir
Rauscht die schöne Waldeinsamkeit,
Und keiner kennt mich mehr hier?

Joseph, Freiherr von Eichendorff,
"In der Fremde"
(Silesia, ca. 1835)

Prologue

In the winter of 1961 Max Hofmann was dying. No one said so, not even the doctor, who seemed to think that the promise of improvement, however empty, was kinder than the truth. But Max knew. At least from time to time, he was quite certain he was dying.

On some days, if he stayed downstairs and sat upright at his desk instead of in a comfortable chair out of which it would be difficult to get, or walked for a few minutes in the garden, he could persuade himself that he was getting better, that ordinary years lay ahead. The leafless garden with its pinched grass and dirty London brick walls: would he see spring arrive there? The purple crocuses? The brash yellow flowers of the forsythia, the brash pink flowers of the cherry? He didn't like town gardens, especially town gardens planted with English enthusiasm for colour, any colour, the brighter the better. He didn't think he would see the cherry blossom or the crocuses again. Actually, he knew that he wouldn't. And that was fine.

His wife fussed in the daytime, and in the evening, as if to hold him back from death, hugged him before he went by himself to bed. His clever, careful son and his high-spirited daughter stopped bickering when he came into the kitchen and from the narrow hall watched him with embarrassed anxiety when he stopped on the stairs to gather a little breath to go up another step.

His favourite pupil came on Thursday at six o'clock, as she used to come for her violin lesson. She was seventeen. She knew. To realism he had accustomed her.

"Where is your fiddle?"

By now he was in bed, sitting upright against four pillows.

"I didn't bring it."

"I see. A bad decision. Fetch mine."

She found it downstairs, tuned it downstairs, carried it up slowly as if it were heavy.

"Play a little."

"Are you sure? What shall I play?"

"The Bach."

She was learning one of the solo parts in the double violin concerto. Two weeks ago he played the other part with her, stopping every so often to growl objections to her playing. "Stay on the beat. Most of all when the beat is slow." "Ach! The top F was sharp." "Listen for me. So, you will not race ahead."

She played, by heart, for a few minutes with her back to him, standing at the window looking out over two dark gardens at the lit kitchen window of the house opposite. She reached a cadence and paused.

"That is better", he said. "Bach is for the end. Good."

She saw a cat jump onto the sill of the lit window. She took the fiddle from her shoulder but didn't turn round. Standing with violin in one hand, bow in the other, she watched a woman open the kitchen window, let in the cat, shut the window.

"You're too young to die. People aren't supposed to die at fifty-five."

"No. There you are wrong. I am too old already to die. By many years I have outlived my life."

"You shouldn't say that. It's not fair."

"Probably not. All the same it is the truth. Later you will understand this. Now close the curtains. Come here."

She shut out the London night and sat on his bed, the violin on her lap. The silence in the room was close and warm, broken only by the soft popping of the gas fire.

"I brought you some flowers."

"Quite right. Where are they?"

"Jane took them, to put in water. She'll bring them up with your supper."

"What kind of flowers?"

"Freesias."

"From a shop."

"It's January."

"Too expensive."

He closed his eyes.

"I'm tiring you. Shall I go?"

"I am the one who goes." He did not open his eyes. "No. Stay. Two things I have to say to you."

She looked at his hands resting on the eiderdown and wondered again how the broad, blunt fingers of his left hand could fly over and stop with absolute precision the thin strings over the thin fingerboard of his violin. His violin, silent on her lap.

"The fiddle I want you to have. It is what I carried with me. The fiddle I brought and a little satchel of books. But you are not reading German. Nor are my own children, half-German though they may be. Never mind the books. It is a good fiddle. Much better than yours. Many years ago it belonged to a good man. It will improve your playing."

Her eyes filled with tears. His remained closed. She saw his hands tense, then relax.

"The fiddle. This is simple. It does not matter so much. A violin is just a violin. The other thing is not for you to have. It is for you to do."

"Anything. Tell me. Anything."

He looked at her, with a penetrating blue-eyed look she knew well.

"It will be too much for you. Too difficult. You will have your own life. I cannot imagine how your life will be. But it must be your own."

"Tell me what you want me to do. I'll try. I really will try my best. I promise."

He shifted uncomfortably and she moved his pillows so that he could sit up a little. He regained his breath.

"Listen to me. When I left Germany I left my own life. Of course I have not all this time been dead. I came, as you know, in 1933 to my friend the canon and his wife. I was the tutor in the holidays, for their grandsons. I was a terrible tutor at first. These good grandsons taught me English. At the school I was teaching violin to little boys who had no patience. One or two could learn. I am no teacher but what can I do? Who will employ a Prussian lawyer? Then the war, and the camp. For enemy aliens. I am an alien. I am not an enemy. After the beginning this camp is not so bad. There is music. There is German to speak. There is also Jane. She is a nurse in this camp.

"Then some of us are offered to fight Hitler after all. Not as real soldiers but digging latrines, loading trucks. After the war more teaching. Better teaching. Better pupils. You, for example. Jane of course. A home. The children. All this you know. A life. OK. For twenty-seven years I have lived, but—how to say it?—with the left hand. No bowing arm. No sound. Half a life. My own life Hitler took away. That life is only now here." He tapped his forehead with a thick middle finger. "And even memory is not reliable—how does one *know*? And will very soon be gone. Pff! Blown out just like that, as one would blow out a candle."

"No, that's not true!"

He looked at her sharply. "Isn't it? God, you mean. God does remember, does know. Well, perhaps. Perhaps indeed. Either way," he said, "there you are. This is what I give you to do."

She met his look, but shook her head.

"I don't understand."

His face was pale, glistening from the effort of talking. He closed his eyes.

At last he said, "You do. You will. This life that is lost, that will be altogether, finally lost, or not, when I die. You will find it, discover it, even invent it. What is the difference? I leave it to you, what to do to find it, because you have the application and the imagination and the sense for truth. Perhaps imagination and the sense for truth are even after all the same thing."

"But . . ."

She sat still, thinking.

"I don't know enough. I will never know enough."

"Who ever does? You will learn. You will learn enough for what I am giving you to do."

"But I didn't know you then, when you were young."

"You know me now. It is the same."

"But it's not, is it? Surely your friends . . ."

"My friends. There is the whole point. They are dead. As, very soon, I also will be dead. There were five of us. Perhaps six, but that you will have to decide. And an old schoolmaster. All of them died. I did not. Only now I die. Open the top drawer, on the left. Yes. Under the socks, and then under the paper. There is a postcard. That's it. That is for you, to help you, one day when you have grown up and have time for me. It will be many years, but that does not matter. I should have done this myself if I had been by any chance a writer. But I am not, and now after so many years I have no language left to use for what is not simple."

She was looking at the card. On it was a list of names—seven lines, seven names—with dates and places of birth and death. Only the last name had no date or place of death. "Max Ernst, Count von Hofmannswaldau, born Waldau, Silesia, March 1905."

He watched her closely as she read the list. When she looked at him he nodded, and smiled.

"That's it. That's what you have to start from. Don't worry. Forget about it now. But don't lose it. When the right time is arrived, that postcard is all you will need."

"Is it really a kind of game you want me to play?"

"Of course, silly girl. It is a game and not a game. A story to make up and a story that is true. Listen to me. Those names, they were people. They were alive. They died. And now there is no one to tell their stories, our story, how we were at one place at one time, from different countries, cities, ruined empires. It was partly for the music we made that we were friends. Friends, lovers, rivals, what have you. Then one way or the other, Hitler killed all of us. Or Stalin. Even me. I lived, but was I alive? From time to time perhaps." Another smile. "The story will be a good one. Quite complicated. The world was a complicated place for us. The story you tell will not have so many facts, but it will have as much truth as if I had been myself the writer, perhaps more because you were not there. Or not yet. Do you understand?"

"I don't know. I think so." She saw that it mattered very much that she understood. "Yes, I do understand. I will try. One day I'll try to do what you want me to do, what you think I can do. I will."

"Good."

His eyes closed. His head sank back on the pillows. His face was paler than before and looked both smoother and thinner.

"Now go", he said very quietly. "I shall sleep now. Good. You are a good child."

She didn't see him again. Nine days later, he died.

The funeral service was a Requiem Mass in a nearby Catholic church. His family, a few of Jane's relations and some pupils and colleagues from the school, none of them Catholic, found the Latin service impossible to follow. There was no sermon, no eulogy; nothing was said about Max or about his life. Strangers carried the coffin down the aisle, and then Jane and the children and three or four others got into cars to follow the hearse to the cemetery. At the house, when the family came back, those of the pupils and colleagues who hadn't gone home stood about awkwardly with glasses of sherry or cups of tea.

13

There were sandwiches and slices of fruitcake. An elderly woman, perhaps an aunt, said to Jane, "I never knew Max was a Roman Catholic."

"Nor did I till a few days before he died. He asked me to fetch a priest. I had no idea how to find one. But there's a Roman Catholic family two doors down. Five or six children—you know. They brought the local priest to the house that same afternoon. He spent nearly an hour with Max. Goodness knows what they talked about. Yes, the priest was the same one who did the service. Quite a nice man. Very Irish, of course."

After a few months, Jane sold the house at a good price, for it was in a part of London that was becoming fashionable. She moved with the children to a cottage in Norfolk close to her brother's house, where she had grown up. Knowing nothing of Max's wish, she also sold his violin, for a good deal of money.

A violin is just a violin.

PART ONE

Chapter 1

Like the heroes in children's stories (who, he noticed, turned out best), Max was the youngest of three sons. He was much the youngest. His brother Carl Friedrich, named after their father, was eleven when Max was born, his brother Heinrich eight. Both of them were already out of the nursery, presided over by their Polish nanny Emilia. Carl Friedrich had his lessons in the library with his tutor Dr Mendel. Heinrich struggled mutinously in the schoolroom with Miss Wilson, his governess. Miss Wilson called him Harry, which he so much disliked that no one else in the house ever used the name. Carl Friedrich, sunnier and more amenable, had been called Freddy since Miss Wilson's arrival when he was six, by everyone except his father, who called him Fritz, and Dr Mendel, who for the time being called him Carl Friedrich.

Max's name could not be anglicized or altered, though ever since he could remember, the "Ernst" had disappeared from everyday family life.

The late, the unexpected, child was his mother's favourite always. Therefore, and for other reasons too, he was much of the time more or less resented by his brothers, and from time to time also by his father. From the day of his birth, there was a particularly strong connexion between Max and his mother. She was not surprised when, as the years passed, he was quicker and brighter than his brothers had been at the same age, quicker to talk, to sing, to joke, to read. He was as a small child more ingeniously naughty than they had been. When he was four or five, he would hide Miss Wilson's purse or spectacles or gloves, so as to produce them as if by magic when she had searched for a satisfactory amount of time. This was not so much in order to bask in her praise for cleverly finding her things as to make her feel less in command of everything than she liked to make sure everyone acknowledged her to be. He spaced these deceptions carefully so as not to be discovered, and perhaps never was.

When he was seven, he found in the big wood of oak and ash and chestnut and birch, the wood beyond the cattle pasture at the back of the house, a hollow oak, once struck scorch-black by lightning. Inside this tree it was possible to disappear completely and sit down comfortably, protected from rain, snow, and wind. Here he hoarded one of everything he thought a house should have, one plate, one cup, one knife, one spoon, one book at a time so that he could sit in his tree and read a few pages, and one picture, a sepia postcard of the bay of Naples that his grandmother had sent him. He had never seen the sea, but he knew the names of several volcanoes, including Vesuvius. His house in the hollow tree required a certain amount of borrowing and dissembling, or, as he knew quite well, stealing and lying. On the day after his eighth birthday, he found in his hollow tree a small tin box with a painted castle on its lid. Inside were three ginger biscuits, which he loved to eat, and a slip of paper wishing him a happy year. So his mother knew. The same day, he took everything out of his tree and returned each object to its proper place, except for the badly tarnished silver spoon and fork, which he hid among pan lids in a deep drawer of the kitchen dresser. The cook, Frau Stock, was his friend and didn't mind him playing in her kitchen unless she was cooking for company. Neither he nor his mother ever mentioned the tree.

By the time he was eight and a half, Max was doing his lessons for several hours every day with Dr Mendel in the large, light schoolroom upstairs. The library with its leather-bound books behind glass in heavy bookcases, had been returned to his father's world. His brothers were seldom at home. Freddy was a junior officer in a cavalry regiment, posted to the garrison town of Thorn not far from the Russian frontier. When he came home on leave, he spent much of his time talking to their father with a lot of laughter, mostly, as far as Max could gather, about horses, girls, money, comic or admirable senior officers, and the iniquities of lazy Polish soldiers in the regiment and crooked Jewish traders making more than they deserved out of the army's presence in Thorn. Heinrich was in cadet school at Lichterfelde and was away for months at a time. Miss Wilson, having taught little Max to read, write, do sums, and recite a number of English poems by heart, had left to be governess to a grand family in Saint Petersburg. "I am going to teach two little princesses, Max. They have had a French governess, but now their mother wishes them to learn English." On the day she set off in the carriage for the railway station, with her two trunks and four hatboxes and a new leather valise with her initials in gold, a present from Max's parents, she said to his mother, "Max is an exceptionally intelligent little boy. He will do very well." But earlier Max had heard her say to Dr Mendel, in English he understood easily, "That child's so sharp he'll cut himself. He needs watching, I can tell you." Max, as he waved dutifully from the steps, was delighted to see the carriage disappear round the bend of the long drive with its avenue of lime trees.

Dr Mendel was teaching him Latin and French and geometry, which he loved because he liked the fine wooden ruler, protractor, and triangle and the pair of brass compasses with which Dr Mendel taught him how to draw neat figures. He also loved Dr Mendel's history and geography lessons. These were not separate, because they always began with a map and often ended with a battle, which meant a battle plan that altered as Dr Mendel told the story. Lines in different colours represented the starting positions of soldiers or ships. Arrows in the appropriate colours showed the lines colliding, advancing victorious, or retreating in ignominy. Max's favourites were Hannibal's march with elephants (grey crayon) over the Alps, the Carthaginian victory over the Romans at Lake Trasimene (because of the Carthaginian arrows creeping round the lake in the fog), and the Greeks' defeat of Xerxes's Persian fleet at Salamis (because the Persians had six times as many ships as the Greeks and still lost the battle).

After Dr Mendel had been persuaded to retell the stories of these battles, with newly drawn battle plans, four or five times at the end of Latin lessons, he one morning refused to do Lake Trasimene again. "No, my boy. Not today. It's time you understood a little of what war means." He tidied away the atlas, the battle plans, the crayons, and the picture book with engravings of Greek and Roman soldiers in different kinds of armour. When the red plush cloth on the old schoolroom table was bare, Dr Mendel laid his fists a long way apart on the table and looked earnestly at Max.

"Listen to me carefully, Max", he said. "War is a terrible thing, always a terrrible thing. Thousands of soldiers are killed, young men, most of them, who will never grow old, never even grow up, never become the men God intended them to be. Thousands more are wounded, damaged perhaps for the rest of their lives. They might lose a leg, or an arm. They might be blinded by the flash of guns, or they might be deafened by explosions. I know there were no guns in these battles of the Greeks and Romans, but there were swords and javelins and arrows and daggers, and there is always fire, burning people's houses and crops, burning next winter's food and fuel so that people will be hungry and cold. It is never only the soldiers who suffer in war. War is a terrible thing."

"But my father says there will soon be a war and a war will be good, because we shall win it. We have really good generals, just as good as Hannibal and Themistocles, and anyway, we always win wars since Frederick the Great, my father says."

"Your father is right. Very likely there will be a war. Very likely Prussia will win because—you remember the map and the war of 1870—Prussia is Germany now, the whole of Germany except for Austria, and Austria will fight alongside Germany if there is a war. Of course, the Prussian soldiers are well trained, well disciplined, and also brave. Soldiers who are both obedient and brave are difficult to defeat. The Romans were difficult to defeat because they treated their soldiers well and trained them well. Your brother Carl Friedrich is a fine young man. He will do his duty, and so will all his friends. And so, one day, no doubt, will Heinrich. But we should be sad, you and I with our books here, and our violins and our piano, if there is a war. We should not be happy. War is always a terrible thing."

"But it's not. It's not! You only say that because you're French, Dr Mendel, and the French always lose wars in the end. They win for a bit. Napoleon won a lot of battles. But then he lost. And the other Napoleon didn't even win for a bit. He just lost."

"I am not French, Max. Not truly French. One day you will understand. The French love war, like the Prussians. *La gloire*, that was what Napoleon gave them, and Louis XIV, of course. The French like to win, as the Prussians do. And you are quite right: forty years ago, the French lost, with the second Napoleon—yes, I know he was called Napoleon III—who was indeed a bad general, really not a general at all. They lost a big battle and many small battles, and they lost Alsace, my home, which is now part of Germany. Poor Strasbourg, my city, was told that it was all of a sudden a German city."

"Is that why you live here, in our house?"

"It is perhaps one reason. There are more important reasons. But that's another story, for when you are older. For now, while you are still a small boy, it is enough if you understand that the French hate the Prussians, the Germans, all of us here, because they lost that war. They think that if there is another war, this time they will win, especially if they can persuade England to be on their side. England has hardly ever been on the same side as France in a thousand years, but this time the French might persuade them, and if they do, it will be Germany's fault. The French hate us, you see, because forty years ago we humiliated them. Do you know what that means?"

"I'm not sure. That we made everyone think what bad soldiers they were? That we made them look silly?"

"That's right. That's another reason that war is a terrible thing. The people who lose are full of hate and resentment. They feel humiliated in the eyes of the world, particularly if the winning side makes a great spectacle of its victory. The beaten people know they are the best people—nowadays, every nation is taught to think itself the best—so they are sure it was not fair that they lost. Their generals must have made bad decisions. Next time, they will win. On the other hand, the people who win become proud, arrogant. They are sure no one will ever beat them. Everyone knows they are the best people; they won, didn't they? This also is a terrible thing."

"But what about heroes? Don't they make all the difference? Frederick the Great was a hero, my father says. My father says if it wasn't for Frederick the Great, we would be in Austria instead of in Germany, and that would be very bad for us because the Austrians are old and tired and their soldiers are only good for parades and not enough of them are German. Is that right?"

"Perhaps. It is at least what many people in Prussia think."

"Well, heroes, then. Napoleon was a hero too, because he beat nearly everybody till the end. Like Hannibal. And Field-Marshal Count von Moltke was a hero because he beat the other Napoleon, Napoleon III, and that was good for us. You told me when I was seven, when I had my first lesson with you but Miss Wilson was still here, that we would learn about heroes, like Hector and Achilles and Aeneas and Turnus and their battles, so war can't always have been a terrible thing. What about Hannibal, anyway? And Themistocles, who was so clever at Salamis? They were great heroes, weren't they?"

"Calm down, child. There's no need to get so excited. Yes, they were great heroes. But shall I tell you what happened to them? Hannibal and Themistocles died in foreign countries a long way from home, not like heroes in battle but old and sad, so sad that both of them swallowed poison. That means they chose to die and did not let death come to them in God's good time."

"Poison? Actual poison? So none of what they did was any good? Why didn't you tell me that before? It's not fair."

"Don't cry, Max. I'm sorry. I have said too much for one day. Hannibal and Themistocles lived a long time ago, and Hector and Achilles and Aeneas an even longer time ago. You shouldn't be worrying about the deaths of heroes at eight years old in peaceful Waldau. Perhaps there will not, after all, be a war. If there is a war, perhaps it will be quickly over. Here."

Dr Mendel produced a snow-white handkerchief, crisply ironed, from his pocket, shook it out, and gave it to Max, who blew his nose fiercely. This was not the first time he had cried in a lesson with his tutor. He scrubbed at his eyes and gave back the handkerchief.

"Max, you are a good boy. You talk a lot. But you think a lot also, which in a little boy is very good, because there is much in this world to think about. That's enough, now. Go and find Rolf and play out of doors for half an hour while I see if Frau Stock has ready my coffee and cake. Then we will practise the violin for an hour or so before your mother will want you in the salon."

"No more lessons this morning?"

"No more lessons this morning."

Rolf was an English golden retriever, much the same age as Max. At this period of Max's life, Rolf was his best friend, and except in the schoolroom, where dogs were not allowed, was his constant companion. Rolf would be waiting for him, lying on the stone flags of the hall, his head between his paws. As Max skidded down the stairs, the big dog stood, stretched his front paws out straight, and then bounded out with the boy through the open door into the sunshine. If it was raining or snowing too hard for there to be any fun to be had out of doors, Max would call Rolf from the landing, and he and his dog would go up the narrow wooden stairs to the long, low attic with its four square windows where Max arranged on the floorboards armies of lead soldiers according to Dr Mendel's battle plans and Rolf watched, his head again between his paws. Rolf never knocked the soldiers over, not even with his tail.

A violin practice after Dr Mendel's coffee and cake was a treat. Usually Max had to wait until after tea—his mother had tea at four o'clock every day, a habit picked up from Miss Wilson, and liked to hear Max's account of his day as she sipped her English Earl Grey with its slice of lemon—before he was packed off back to the schoolroom, where Dr Mendel would be waiting for him, reading his newspaper. Then he was allowed to take his violin from its case, unwrap the piece of silk in which he had folded it the day before, and take his bow from the green baize-covered slots that held it in the case. He loved everything about his violin: the magically shaped and gleamingly polished wood; the taut catgut of the strings, the tension of each exactly the right amount different from the other three; the stretched fine horsehair of the bow and the circle of mother-of-pearl in the end he held between his right thumb and fingers; and the silk that wrapped the fiddle and was arranged neatly on his left shoulder by Dr Mendel before he touched the A string with his bow. Dr Mendel gave him an A from a tuning fork and then made him tune all four strings by himself with no help from the piano, so that he was used to listening with all his attention to the sounds he was making before he played even a scale. He wanted more than anything in the world to play as well one day as Dr Mendel played, perhaps even better, and he listened with passionate concentration to everything his tutor told him and every note, phrase, or whole piece he played for him to copy.

This was always called "practice", not a lesson. Every day, there was practice, and both of them, the pupil and the teacher, worked harder at it than at any of the other things they studied. No one else in the house ever came into the schoolroom when this practice was taking place. If anyone had, probably neither Max nor his tutor would have noticed.

Dr Mendel at this period seemed to Max to be an old man, though not as old as his grandfather the professor in Breslau, whom Max revered as the source of wisdom and jokes on any topic under the sun. Dr Mendel, in fact, was a few years older than Max's father, but when Max was eight, Dr Mendel was not much more than fifty.

On Saturdays, after a short schoolroom morning of stories and poems in German and French and an hour of violin practice, Dr Mendel would disappear from Max's life for the rest of the day. Sometimes in fine weather he changed into old breeches, stockings, and boots and walked for many hours in the hills to the south of Waldau. Sometimes he went to Breslau, forty miles away, on the train, and came back on Sunday afternoon with a new book or two for Max, and often some new music for them to learn. On Sundays after tea, in Max's favourite hour of the week, looked forward to and worked towards for the six and a half other days of every week, he left Dr Mendel in the schoolroom with a formal bow of his head at the school room door, and went downstairs to play his violin in the salon with his mother accompanying him.

The connexion between Max and his mother had become most of all a matter of music. He loved to stand in the angle of the big black Blüthner piano, his fiddle to his chin, facing her as she played. There was a carved wooden stand for his music. But once he knew the piece— and he never played a piece with his mother until he had learnt the notes thoroughly by heart—he looked at her rather than at the music, though he thought it grown-up to turn the page at the right place with the point of his bow as Dr Mendel did. His mother accompanied him as if he were himself playing the piano as well as the violin, or that was how it seemed to him.

If Max's father were in the salon when the child appeared with his fiddle and his music on a Sunday after tea, he got up quickly and left the room. As if he were angry, Max thought, or as if he hated music. Yet Max knew that after dinner, when he himself was in bed and supposed to be asleep, his mother would often play to his father in the warm, candlelit salon, Schubert or Chopin or Liszt.

Much later he understood that his mother's music, like his mother's beauty, seemed to his father to be his very own, his possession, his pride, what he had wanted, married, acquired in her. Before Max was born, his father had tried to learn the flute, to play to his wife's accompaniment. Unable to cope with doing anything badly, he had given up the attempt long before he was able to play well. No wonder he resented his youngest son's music, the gift and the persistence he had inherited from his mother and shared with her so deeply and happily.

But the portrait of Bach, which before they were married he had sent his steward to Leipzig to find and buy at considerable expense for his bride, remained over the wide mantelpiece of the salon fireplace. Nearly all the other pictures on the walls at Waldau were dark engravings of paintings of Prussian battles and German cities. On Max's ninth birthday, in March 1914, Dr Mendel took him downstairs after the nursery breakfast they shared with Emilia. His father was out on his horse, his mother still in bed and not to be disturbed until nine o'clock. In the salon Dr Mendel stood Max in front of him, opposite the fireplace and the portrait, put his hands on the child's shoulders, and said most seriously, "Whatever becomes of us all, Max, never forget that face. It is a face that tells of faith, patience, and hard work. We cannot all be Bach, but we can all hope for faith, practise patience, and work hard. This I would like you to remember."

"Mother," Max said as they walked home from church—his father had stayed to talk to the pastor—on the Sunday following his birthday, "why doesn't Dr Mendel come to church with us? Or go to the other church with Emilia and the maids? He never does, not even at Christmas." Max that morning, because of what Dr Mendel had said in front of the portrait of Bach, had tried hard to listen carefully to the pastor's long sermon and understand every word. He soon gave up. The sermon seemed to be mostly about how there were too many ships in the English navy, though the pastor ended with a resounding promise that whatever happened, God would be on the side of Germany. So Max found himself wondering, instead, about Dr Mendel. Had he talked about hoping for faith because faith was something he didn't have? What, in any case, was faith? Max thought it was something you belonged to. His parents and Frau Stock and Hans the groom and one of the farmers and Miss Wilson belonged to the Protestant faith; Emilia and the maids and Tadeusz the gardener and the other farmer belonged to the Catholic faith and on Sundays went to the other church. If faith was something you belonged to, why would you hope for it?

"Is it because he doesn't belong to our church or the other church? Is it because he doesn't believe in God? It can't be that, because he does. Believe in God, I mean. He talks about God as if he knows him."

"Max!" His mother laughed but not, he was sure, because he had said something funny by mistake as he sometimes did. "You do ask a lot of questions", she said, meaning she was wondering how to answer this one. He kept quiet.

"No. It's not because he doesn't believe in God. You see, he's a Jew."

"A *Jew*!" Max stopped on the drive and stared at his mother. All his devotion to Dr Mendel, the absolute trust with which he listened to everything he said, and the passionate attention with which he followed every movement of fingers and bow as he played the violin, shook and cracked inside him as if the ground had shaken and cracked under his feet.

"He can't be! He absolutely can't be!" he said furiously. "I've seen the Jews in the big market in Breslau. And in the station when we went to Berlin that time. They have different clothes and everything. They have long curls by their ears sticking out of black hats, and long black coats. And they don't talk proper German or French. They don't look like Dr Mendel, not in the least bit like him, or talk like him. And I've heard Freddy telling Father about the Jews in Thorn, how they make money out of the soldiers and get the officers into debt on purpose. Dr Mendel *can't* be a Jew. I don't believe you!"

"Oh, Max, my dearest child. Life is so much more complicated than you know."

"How is it complicated? Tell me. Dr Mendel says I can understand quite complicated things. He says . . ."

Max was now in tears. How could he any longer believe what Dr Mendel said?

"Don't cry, my darling. I don't know why you're crying about a thing like this." Realizing that she didn't understand, he cried more bitterly. "It's nothing, I promise you. Nothing for you to get upset about. It's only a name, really, like a label. It doesn't make any difference, you know, not any more, not in Germany. Dr Mendel isn't like the Jews you see in the market, or the ones in Thorn, I expect, that Freddy talks about. Or the poor families in the station. I know it's sad to see them, looking lost and hungry. I've seen them too. Those are Russian Jews. They're very poor, and in their villages nobody treats them properly, and sometimes soldiers come and attack them. That's why they leave Russia, because they're afraid. They're trying to reach America, where they will be safe. Lots of people try to help them. Your grandfather organizes help for them and finds money for their passage on the ships to America. But first they have to get all the way to Bremen or Hamburg, and it's a long, difficult journey for them. Next time we go to Breslau, you should ask Grandpapa about all this. He'll explain it all much better than I can.

"But Dr Mendel isn't a Russian Jew. Of course not. It's quite different. He was a Frenchman when he was young, and not poor at all. His father was a doctor like Grandpapa, and Dr Mendel went to the Sorbonne—that's the university in Paris—and to the Conservatoire. He's a very good musician, as you know, and now he's a German as we all are. If he were not, your father would never have allowed me to find him to teach Freddy and Heinrich. Of course, I hoped that

26

they would learn music with him as you have, but neither of them had any talent, so it is very nice for me, and for Dr Mendel too, that you have some talent and also that you are a good boy and work so hard at your violin."

"It isn't nice for Father, is it? He never stops to hear us play on Sundays." Max had managed to stop crying. "But Mother," he went on, "if Dr Mendel was French, why did he leave France? He nearly told me one day, but then he didn't. The usual reason: he thought I wasn't old enough. Do you know why he left France?"

'Well, yes, I do. The part of France where he was born became part of Germany after the last war, and the French people didn't like that, and it made them sometimes unkind to the Jews who lived there because they thought they were on the side of the Germans. And then some other things happened that made things very difficult for Jewish people everywhere in France. Also, because Dr Mendel is a musician and there is more music played in Germany and more parents wanting someone to teach their children violin and piano, he thought he would perhaps be happier in Germany."

"Do you think he is? Happy, I mean."

"Oh, I think so. He enjoys teaching you. And he has friends in Breslau. He plays quartets with them sometimes, which is important to him. And there are good bookshops and music shops that he likes to visit. I hope he is happy."

"Hope for faith", Max said.

"What did you say, darling?"

"Nothing."

"Now cheer up, please, Max. It's Sunday, after all, and I'm so much looking forward to hearing your Mozart after tea. Have you learnt another whole movement?"

'Yes, but . . ." He almost began to cry again and just managed not to.

"And we must go home", his mother said, taking his hand as if he were four years old and not nine. "Frau Stock will be very cross if we're late for lunch." They walked for a few minutes in silence.

Max thought.

"But Mother", he said.

"What is it?"

"I still don't understand about Dr Mendel and God. If he's a German now and lives with us, why doesn't he come to church with us, like Miss Wilson did? Or go to the other church with Emilia?"

"Because Jews don't go to any church. If he lived in Breslau, he might go to the synagogue, which is like the Jews' own church. But here in the country, there isn't a synagogue for him to go to. And lots of German Jews don't go to the synagogue, even in the cities. But don't worry about it. Talk to Grandpapa about it when we go to see him. He'll explain properly. Now"—they had reached the steps of the front door—"run upstairs and wash your hands, and your face too, and when your father comes back, we'll have lunch. Perhaps he'll have time to take you for a ride this afternoon. Gretel must be very bored in her field."

Gretel was Max's pony. He loved her, though not as much as he loved Rolf, and a ride with his father was always a treat, not only because he enjoyed cantering through the fields and woods and jumping easily over fallen trees when his father allowed him to, but because he rode well and this pleased his father. Sometimes he fell off Gretel because she shied at a bird clattering out of the bracken or stopped dead in front of a jump, and his father praised him if he managed not to cry, quickly caught his pony, checked that she was not lame, and remounted. "Well done, Max. We'll make a dragoon of you yet. A cavalry officer always takes care of his horse before he worries about himself." When they got back to the stable yard, his father handed the reins of his own horse to the groom but watched critically while Max unsaddled Gretel, rubbed her down, and put on the halter to take her to her field. "Good boy." From his father, this was high praise.

That summer, the war did begin. On a Friday morning in the holidays, his father had set off down the drive on his horse before breakfast to fetch a newspaper from the railway station. His mother, up and dressed much earlier than usual, was waiting for him to come back. She was so anxious that she could not sit still in her favourite rattan chair on the terrace but went into the rose garden, where she snipped off dead heads with her garden scissors and, when there were no more to snip, began to cut a bunch of not-quite-opened flowers. It was very hot. Max had no lessons because Dr Mendel had gone away for a fortnight to stay with his sister in Alsace. Freddy should have been at home, but a week earlier he had been recalled from leave and was now back with his regiment in Thorn. They had all gone to the station in Breslau to see him off, and Max didn't understand why his mother had cried almost all the way back in the local train. Heinrich was at home on summer leave from cadet school. He was still asleep while their mother waited for their father to bring the newspaper. Max, not knowing what to do with himself, sat on the terrace steps with his hand on Rolf's neck and watched his mother. It was already too hot for the retriever to want to play, even if Max hadn't realized that it was not a morning for rushing about the garden or throwing sticks for Rolf to fetch.

At last he heard a horse cantering up the drive. His father jumped down, flung the reins at the waiting groom, and bounded up the steps into the hall. Max met him.

"Mother's in the rose garden."

"We're at war!" his father shouted, as if the words were "We've won!" He ran across the terrace and into the rose garden, where he swept Max's mother off her feet and swung her round. "It's war!" he shouted again as he put her down. "We've declared war on Russia. Don't worry, don't worry, my dearest"—Max's mother was white, open-mouthed, holding both her husband's hands, looking up at him—"it'll all be over in a few weeks. Don't worry about Fritz. This is the greatest day of his life. There's no possibility of the Russians defeating us. We have a modern army, modern guns, soldiers far better trained than theirs. We shall win, I tell you, and in a very short time."

But she flung herself into his arms again, and they walked back into the house, his arm round her shoulders, supporting, almost carrying, her. She was crying. He settled her gently in a comfortable chair in the hall and then noticed Max.

"Where's Heinrich?"

"Still in bed, I think."

"Wake him up! Wake him up! This is no day for a cadet to be asleep! I expect they'll order him back. Can't have soldiers lazing about at home when we're at war, even if they're too young to fight. Poor boy—he's going to miss this war, just as I missed the last one. And so are you, little Max. It's bad luck, but it's wonderful news for Fritz and his friends. And in Thorn too, practically in Russia. Good marching country, though I expect nowadays they'll be moved up to the front by train—they're bound to be in the first battle with the Russians. Go on, Max! Wake up your brother and get him down here. Quickly now!"

Later that day, his mother sent Max to look for her garden scissors. He found them on the grass, the opening roses she had cut scattered and wilted where she had dropped them.

On Monday morning the telegram came, summoning Heinrich back to Lichterfelde. More packing. Their mother and Emilia dashing about upstairs, reminding each other of things that might be forgotten. A pile of new shirts for Heinrich, each one wrapped in tissue paper. Emilia ironing old ones in such haste that she scorched one with an iron left too long to heat and cried as she threw it on the rag pile in the laundry room. Another farewell, at Waldau station. More tears.

On Tuesday an officer in an unfamiliar uniform came to Waldau and had lunch in the dining room, discussing with Max's father the weight of field guns, the length of trains carrying troops eastwards, the quantities of fodder needed for so many horses for so many weeks. After lunch his father and the officer set off on foot for the farm, the second farm, the stable yard at home. When the officer had gone, Max discovered that most of the horses were to be taken for the war. On Wednesday soldiers came and rode away, leading two horses each. Only two draught horses were left at each farm, and most of the boxes in the stable yard were empty. His father's favourite horse had gone, and his mother's chestnut mare. Two old horses were left for them to ride, and two more for the carriage. Gretel, too small to be of any use, was left in her field. Max made sure she was still there, took her some carrots Frau Stock gave him, stroked her friendly nose, and then combed her mane and tail carefully with the curry comb he had brought in his pocket. He was close to crying, at the idea of her being taken to pull a gun across a battlefield—he thought of Hannibal's elephants and of Russian wolves howling in the snowy forests—but his mother had done enough crying for everyone.

On Friday Dr Mendel arrived at the house in the carrier's cart from the station. The carrier helped him down and put his old leather bag on the ground beside him. He stood, looking more lined and greyer than two weeks ago, searching his pockets for some coins for the carrier. Max ran towards him as the carrier climbed into his cart and took the reins, and Dr Mendel hugged him. He had never done this before.

At lunch Dr Mendel told Max's parents of his journey, of how he had begged and bribed his way onto one train after another all the way from Strasbourg, and of how the roads and railways across Germany were full of soldiers, guns, and horses travelling both east and west.

"They are so happy, these young men, singing, laughing. It is a game to them. But it is terrible, terrible. They are not even afraid."

Max's mother listened, wide-eyed, a hand to her throat. But his father interrupted. "Dr Mendel, I beg you. These are days of heroism, of glory. I want Max always to remember them. I want him to remember Fritz, going bravely to war. You are not to speak of fear in this house."

Dr Mendel said nothing further at lunch and nothing about the war to Max as, the next day, they went back to work on violin scales and arpeggios and a new sonata, and on Monday morning to ordinary lessons. Latin verbs. The ablative absolute. The correct position in a sentence of a prepositional phrase. Mathematics. A short poem of Goethe for Max to learn by heart.

For two weeks there was no history, no geography; there were no maps and no battles. Then, at the end of yet another hot, sunny morning, when Max had pleased Dr Mendel by reciting correctly an ode of Horace and by correctly scanning the lines in his exercise book, he looked searchingly at his tutor and decided he was almost back to his old self.

"Dr Mendel?" he said.

"Yes, Max?"

"Please, will you tell me about the war?"

"But Max, you know very well your father has forbidden me ..."

"He only said he didn't want you to talk about fear. But surely the war is history, and geography as well. I don't understand anything about it, why it started, where the battles are, what's happening anywhere. And my own brother is in the war, so don't you think I need to understand it, just a bit? If you don't explain it to me, nobody will. I can't ask Mother. She cries too much. And Father just tells me I'm too young to understand. But I'm not. I'm not—you know I can understand things when you explain them."

"Dear child." But Dr Mendel closed the Horace, the Latin grammar, and the exercise book and pushed them in a neat pile to the middle of the table. Max saw that he was going to do some explaining after all.

"Your father in this case is actually right. I'm not sure that even the old and wise, even the most experienced ministers and generals, even the Emperors—and there are four Emperors fighting this war—really understand what it is about, or why it began. Certainly nobody knows where it will lead."

"*Four* Emperors? How can there be four? In Rome there was only one Emperor. We've only got one Emperor, the Kaiser, named after

Caesar. You told me. And the Russians have got only one too, the Tsar, named after Caesar in Russian. They're fighting against each other, so where are the other two?"

"A little patience, Max. This is going to be a history lesson, so we'll have to have a map, won't we? Fetch me the big atlas."

Max fetched the big atlas, so heavy he could scarcely carry it. Dr Mendel turned to a double-page map of Europe at the end of the atlas.

"Find me Breslau. Good boy. Berlin? That's right. Saint Petersburg? Further north. Further east. That's it. Now here"—he put a finger in the middle of the map—"is another great city you have heard of, Vienna, no further away from us here in Waldau than is Berlin. Vienna is the capital city of another German empire, very old and very complicated. Once upon a time, as you know, Waldau and Breslau and all Silesia were in that empire, the Habsburg empire. But that was long before there was a Kaiser in Berlin. There's still an Emperor, a different Kaiser, in Vienna. He's a very old man, and his empire is so old and so muddled that it's difficult for him to hold all its peoples together. Our Kaiser in Berlin rules over some Polish people, as you know very well because of Emilia and Tadeusz and the Poles in the village and on the farms. But almost all of our Kaiser's subjects are Germans. The Habsburg Emperor has a much harder job. He rules over a lot of different peoples, speaking a lot of different languages, and though his rule is mostly good and mostly fair and has been peaceful for a long, long time, some of these peoples are not happy to be in his empire. Some of them want to rule themselves—they have no idea, I think, how difficult this would be—and some of them are more like Russians than they are like Germans and prefer the Tsar in Saint Petersburg to the Emperor in Vienna."

The finger made a curved sweep from right to left over the southeast of the Austro-Hungarian empire—Max read the names Transylvania, Serbia, and Bosnia after the finger had passed them—and came to rest pointing at a smaller city.

"You see this city. Its name is Sarajevo. I believe it is a beautiful city. It is the capital of Bosnia. A few weeks ago, some foolish young men, Serbs, plotted to kill the heir to the old Emperor's throne as he was driven in a procession through the streets of this city. Such young men, you know, in Russia have before now killed the Tsar, government ministers, people they don't like. These plotters in Sarajevo almost failed. They threw a bomb. It missed the car with the Emperor's heir in it. It went off all the same, of course, and other people were hurt. Later in the day, one of the young men found himself very close to the right car. He had a gun in his pocket, so he shot the Emperor's heir and his wife and killed them."

"That was the archduke", said Max, who had heard the grown-ups talking about "the poor archduke".

"That's right."

"Was he a bad man?"

"No, not a bad man. I think he would have done his best for all his people and tried to keep them in peace."

"So why did they kill him?"

"They killed him because they wanted Bosnia to be in Serbia instead of in the empire. There are lots of Serbs in Bosnia, but lots of other people as well, Croats and Moslems and Jews and Germans, who don't mind being in the empire. These boys killed the archduke for the glory of Serbia, and of course for their own glory, to be heroes of Serbia."

"Are they really boys? How old are they?"

"They are nineteen, younger than your brother Carl Friedrich."

"So are they good, like heroes are good? Or bad, like murderers are bad?"

"They are murderers, not heroes. They thought what they were doing was brave, which it was. They also thought it was noble, which it was not. Some Serbs may think them heroes for a while, but they will be wrong. The lives they have given up would have been more use to Serbia than their deaths will be."

"Are they dead?"

"I don't know. If they're still alive, they're sure to be executed soon."

"But they could still be heroes when they're dead? Like martyrs?"

"A martyr is a witness to the truth. Whether Bosnia is part of Serbia or part of the Empire is not a matter of truth but a matter of politics. Politics is about power, not about truth. And now nearly all of Europe is at war because of these foolish boys."

"But why?"

"Why indeed. I think it is one of those great events in history that happen without any single person deciding that they should happen. Serbia has to be punished for the archduke's death. Serbia looks to Russia for protection. Austria has a huge army, which it mobilizes to

33

punish Serbia. Russia has a huge army, which it mobilizes to protect Serbia. Our Kaiser mobilizes our army to help Austria and to attack France because France sees there may be a chance to win back her own lands lost to Germany forty years ago. England is the friend of Russia and France, so England also declares war on Austria and Germany. So in one week Europe is at war, when her Emperors and their ministers all wish to rule in peace."

"What does 'mobilize' mean?"

"It means to set in motion, to set going, as you might set going a clockwork toy you have already wound up. Austria and Germany, Russia and France and England, they have huge armies, hundreds of thousands of soldiers with nothing to do but practise for battles that may never happen. They are wound up but not set going. The order comes to move. They move. They are delighted. I saw them on the trains in those days when I travelled back here. It is hardly surprising. What are soldiers for? War. Here is a war. No wonder the soldiers are happy. But once they are set going, these hundreds of thousands of men, who will be able to stop them?"

"Who is the other Emperor?"

"The other Emperor is the King of England. But he is different. The King of England has the biggest empire of all, but none of it is in Europe. Great Britain is very rich and powerful because of its empire. At the same time, Great Britain has no frontiers in Europe. Great Britain has only the sea because it is an island, which makes the British less worried by this war than we are. The Germans, the French, the Austrians, and the Russians all have frontiers with each other to defend, battles to fight on their own fields, lands to keep or lose or win, but the British don't have to worry about all that. They will cross the sea and fight, and then they will go home again. Let me show you the British empire."

Dr Mendel turned back a few pages of the atlas and smoothed out a map of the world. His finger pointed to New Zealand and Australia, then up to Burma and India; it swept across nearly half of Africa, then went across to the West Indies and up to the great expanse of Canada.

"You can see how small Europe and its troubles must look to an Englishman."

Max was looking at the map.

"Russia is bigger than all those places put together. If we fight the British empire *and* Russia, won't we lose the war?"

"Well, we shall see. Your father, who knows the Prussian army and knows some important people in Berlin, is quite sure that Germany will win and that the war will be over before Christmas."

"What do you think, Dr Mendel?"

"It is not for me to think about such things. I am a foreigner, a guest in your father's house as well as his servant in the task of educating you, Max, and he does not wish me to speculate about the war. Now let us put the atlas and the Latin books away and do a little geometry before it is time for my coffee and cake."

Ten days later, on a bright Monday morning with the hot weather still holding and Max and Dr Mendel eating their breakfast with Emilia in the nursery, there was suddenly a shocking, terrible wail from downstairs, then another, and another. Emilia scraped back her chair and ran to the door, along the passage, and down the stairs to Max's mother's bedroom. Max sat frozen. Dr Mendel, looking down at his plate, would not meet his eye. The wailing stopped. Max listened. Two or three fields away, a cow mooed. Silence. Footsteps. Emilia was coming back, up the stairs, along the passage.

"Max, your brother has been killed, God rest his soul." She crossed herself as Max rushed to her and clung to her in a desperate hug like a much-younger child. Dr Mendel got up and quietly left the nursery, resting his hand for a moment on Max's head as he went.

In the days and weeks that followed, Max consciously practised becoming accustomed to the idea that Freddy would never come back. He loved and admired his elder brother, but Freddy, ever since Max was very young, had been mostly away from home, coming back only from time to time, always in uniform, as a cheerful, indulged visitor. When, on the day following the telegram, Emilia took Max to the Catholic church, where the priest celebrated a Requiem Mass for Freddy, he tried to pray, as Emilia told him to, for the peace for Freddy's soul that the Latin of the Mass seemed to be all about. He could not imagine Freddy, lively, energetic Freddy, bounding upstairs or vaulting onto his horse and making his horse rear to show off in the drive, in eternal peace. So he gave up and prayed for peace for his mother instead. With his father, who had put on his old dragoon uniform, he went two days later to the service for Freddy in the Protestant church. There were flags and marching hymns and a sermon about heroes dying for the fatherland and hardly any prayers. Max thought this a much better send-off for his soldier brother.

As far as Max could tell, Freddy had been his father's favourite son, his father's friend, a grown-up to talk to about grown-up male things when Heinrich was still a boy and Max still a child. So Max was now surprised to see how badly, with how very much more grief than his father, his mother had taken the news of Freddy's death. For a week, she stayed in her bedroom. Emilia went in and out with trays and cups of tisane but shook her head when Dr Mendel asked from time to time: "How is the countess today?" One day, Emilia said, "What she needs is a funeral. But of course, in war, it's impossible. My poor lady—there'll be no grave for her to visit with her flowers." Max, who had never been to a funeral, was glad that Freddy would not be brought home in a coffin and dug into a hole in the village cemetery but that he had been buried on the battlefield like the heroes of Greece and Rome.

Eventually his mother emerged from her room and picked up her familiar habits, eating lunch in the dining room, drinking tea in the salon, and accompanying Max at the piano on Sundays, but not for many months playing in the evening to Max's father. She was very quiet and never spoke of Freddy. For the first time in his life, Max found it easier to talk to his father than to his mother. More than a month after the telegram, a letter arrived from Freddy's colonel saying that Carl Friedrich, Count von Hofmannswaldau, had been killed outright in the first cavalry charge of the battle of Tannenberg, a German victory over immense Russian forces that would live forever in the annals of the Prussian army. The colonel was certain that the battle would be decisive in the successful outcome of the war on the eastern front and trusted that Lieutenant von Hofmannswaldau's parents, assured that their son had died nobly in a noble cause, would before too long find that pride in his heroic death would overcome their natural grief at their sad loss. Max's mother left the dining room in tears when his father read the letter aloud at the end of lunch on the day it arrived.

That afternoon, Max's father took him for a walk and told him that, though it was perhaps impossible for a mother to understand that her son's death in battle could be a splendid thing for the family, Max must never forget that Fritz was a hero who had brought credit to them all.

"There was the poet, of course. But he was a long time ago, and, they tell me, not a very good poet, though you will find him in all the histories of German literature. There was one Hofmannswaldau who was killed in battle in Frederick the Great's time. The battle of Liegnitz, in 1760, not far away from here. He was fighting for Austria—can you imagine?—fighting against Prussia! But that was his duty, then. He was a subject of the empress in Vienna, and in those days our family was Catholic. His son, and all of us since, have been proud to be subjects of Prussia, and proud to be Protestant too. Your grandfather fought in the last war, the war against France, but he came home safe and sound. And now Fritz has been killed in a great battle against the Russians, and that makes me very proud."

"Will Heinrich have to fight in a battle?" Max asked.

"Poor Heinrich, I'm afraid, is too young. The war is sure to be over before he's old enough to fight. They don't send the cadets to their regiments until they're eighteen. He'll be very disappointed, and so will all his friends."

"That will be good for Mother. That Heinrich is too young."

"Of course. But ..."

They walked on in silence. Max waited.

"It's time you realized that your mother's family is not ... doesn't have the same tradition as ours. It is not a military family. Nor is it accustomed to responsibility for land and the people who live and work on the land. This—"

Max's father waved an arm at the fields and woods that stretched away to the mountains in the south.

"Your mother is happy here, I hope. Happier in her garden, perhaps, than out in the country. She doesn't care for shooting or riding, though I bought her a beautiful, gentle mare. But none of it comes easily to her, so I'm afraid it's very difficult for her to accept Fritz's death as right and good, a sacrifice for his country, his life laid down for Prussia and the Kaiser in the noble tradition of this family."

That night, when he went to bed, Max thought about what his father had said. He knew that it had been somehow a criticism of his mother's family, almost a warning. Max thought of his beloved grandfather in Breslau, the old professor of medicine with his neat, pointed beard, his gold-rimmed spectacles on the end of his nose, his smile, and his acute look at whomever he was talking to. His grandparents never visited Waldau. Sometimes his mother took him to Breslau on the train, and they would stay in her parents' flat for a week or two. The flat was full of books, but the books were quite different from those in the library at Waldau, its dark leather volumes with faint gold titles all looking the same and never touched behind the glass of tall mahogany bookcases. At his grandparents' flat, the books were on white painted shelves with no glass, or left about on tables or on the piano. Some were bound in leather, but even they were different sizes and colours. Many more were unbound, with just white or yellow paper outside their pages or with grey boards with stiffened corners in another colour. On Grandpapa's desk, there was a bone-handled paper knife with a straight steel blade. When Max was five or six, he would play on the study floor with toy building bricks made of dark red and blue stone, in shapes of cubes, oblongs, and arches with ashlar lines. These bricks, if you spent long enough and worked it out carefully, would all fit exactly back into their heavy wooden box with a sliding lid. But Max would stop playing with them and watch his grandfather in his armchair reading a new book. He watched him for the concentration on his face and for the accurate upward glide and outward turn of the knife in his right hand as he neatly sliced open the folded edge of each uncut page. To Max, it seemed as if his grandfather were cutting into the secrets of the book itself, as if no one had ever before seen what the next page had written on it. Sometimes he would put down the knife, pick up a pencil from the velvet cloth on the round table beside his chair, and write a note in tiny, neat writing on a page of the book. When Max was allowed to try the paper knife on the uncut pages of a book his grandfather disliked enough not to want to finish it, he found achieving a clean cut much harder than it looked. He practised his way through the rest of the pages, acquiring the knack by the last few, when his grandfather threw the whiskery book away. "That was a better fate than the man who wrote such rubbish deserved."

In what was supposed to be the flat's pantry, a narrow room with a sink beyond the kitchen, Grandpapa had a workbench with a row of chisels of different sizes hanging above it, an oiled grey-blue stone on the bench for sharpening them, a heavy iron vice fastened to the edge of the bench, a lathe, and chunks of precious wood—walnut, box-wood, and cherry—waiting to be carved into spoons, inlaid boxes, bowls, perhaps a set of chessmen for an inlaid chess board. Max loved the tools and the wood and the smell of French polish almost as much as he loved his violin.

Other people—friends of his grandparents, teachers from the university, or young doctors his grandfather had taught, and their wives—would come to visit. They were delighted to see Max's mother. They talked and talked, and many of them played one instrument or another so that chamber music, with his mother playing the piano, would often end the evening. Max was allowed to stay up to listen, sometimes to turn the pages for his mother. His grandfather had a beautiful chest with many wide, shallow drawers full of music, the parts of each piece in a cardboard folder, and the names of the composers in his grandfather's writing on labels in little brass frames on the outside of each drawer. There were two drawers for Mozart and three each for Beethoven and Schubert.

As the war went on, past Christmas, past Max's tenth birthday, and then on and on for months and years, with news, often, that made his father angry and silent for days, Max and his mother travelled to Breslau more and more often, though they usually stayed only for a day or two. Max's grandmother was not well and most of the day sat on a comfortable chair by the window with a pretty shawl round her shoulders and another over her knees, and with some embroidery on her lap to which she hardly ever added another few stitches. Max and his mother brought from Waldau eggs and butter, sausage and ham, poppy seed cake, and in the summer cherries and raspberries and roses with their stems wrapped in damp cotton wool, because there were wartime shortages in the city and his grandmother's eyes lit up at the sight of fresh fruit and flowers. Earlier in the war, they had packed these things in big baskets and carried them from the station. By the summer of 1918, rationing in the city was so strict and poor people in the streets so hungry that they packed the food among clothes and papers in old suitcases and brought no flowers. There were still hens and cows on the farms but only one pig on each, being fattened on scraps for the winter, so there was no more ham or sausage to bring.

"I watch the war from this window", Grandmama said. "I see the young men with their crutches and their bandaged eyes. I see the widows with their little children, and the mothers of lost sons going to early Mass every morning to pray that they may be found alive. I see people half-starved, searching the rubbish in the streets for something to eat. And you, Toni, with poor Freddy killed so young and now Heinrich on the western front, where nothing goes well. . . . How old is Heinrich? Nineteen? He should be a student, enjoying himself in the summertime. What is it all for? What does Carl Friedrich say?"

"Carl Friedrich is furious, and very worried too. He's angry because he thinks the war has been badly managed almost from the beginning.

He says we won the war in the east in spite of the Austrians, whose soldiers were no use to us because half of them were traitors, and we won it long before the revolution in Russia. At the start of the war, he says, the Russians were fifty miles away, and we beat them back a thousand miles. We should have made peace years ago with the Russians, let them get on with their revolution, with the whole of Poland under German rule between us and them, and moved all our armies west to defeat the British. Now we do have a treaty with the Russians, a very good treaty for us, he says, but he thinks it's too late. The navy—you should hear him on the subject of the navy—provoked the Americans into joining the war, and now we have no more food and no more soldiers and we can't win in the west. Carl Friedrich was so proud of Freddy, but now he calls the war dishonourable, as if Freddy's death was for a bad cause. And people have been so starved and desperate these last few months that he thinks the Communists will have it all their own way when the war is over. He may be right. I don't know."

Max's grandfather had come into the room while his mother was saying all this. He put an arm round Max's shoulders and said: "Come, now, Toni. I don't believe it will be so bad. To begin with, it will be a great blessing for everyone in Germany when the war is over. Perhaps that will be very soon now. Things will not be the same after the war, of course. But perhaps they will be better. Perhaps we will have learnt some useful lessons. Perhaps we will have learnt that a Prussian empire, one man's invention, is not the way to govern Germany. There has been too much complacency, too much self-satisfaction, too much of what some people call philistinism, but we can call it Prussian pride, pride in soldiers and pride in efficiency, pride in larger and larger steelworks and coalmines and factories. Perhaps Germany needs to remember its true greatness, the greatness of Schiller and Goethe and Heine, of Bach and Mozart and Beethoven. The greatness also of science, of mathematics, physics, and medicine, which will make the world a better place for many, many people. This is a greatness neither victory nor defeat in war can take away from us."

"How can you say that, Father?" Max's mother's voice was high, despairing. "On our farms, there are no young men left to do the heavy work. They're all at the front, or dead. If they send them home because they're too badly wounded to fight, they're too badly wounded to work. Their mothers and sisters and young boys Max's age do their best, but they haven't enough to eat. When things are so bad, music and poetry are just another kind of complacency, don't you see? And your science has only made the war more dreadful. That's what Carl Friedrich means by dishonour. Look what happened to Frau Haber."

"My dear child", said Max's grandfather, his level voice steadying Max as well as his mother, who seemed to her youngest son not at all a child but quite old. "Let's not confuse one thing with another because the times are hard. When the war is over, the men will come home, and hard work will put things to rights in a year or two. You mustn't think—I know you don't really, when you are yourself—that music and poetry are a kind of complacency. Never should they feed pride; they feed the soul. A person who loves them is humbled by their beauty until, almost, he himself disappears. That is not complacency. And the same is true of science, which reveals the beauty of the workings of things to people, who, also, disappear into the rigour of their search. Never should they let themselves be used, by the people who have power, to deliver what is ugly and destructive from what they have discovered of God's creation."

"But they do. They have. They always will. War and greed and selfish advantage—"

"Toni, Toni", said Max's grandmother from her chair by the window. "Don't upset yourself. We must stay calm and hopeful, however deeply we feel all this misery and loss. You have Carl Friedrich, and Heinrich, God willing, and Max here, who has his whole life ahead of him. And you have your poor families on the estate, who depend on you and Carl Friedrich. There is much to work for, much always to do."

Max's mother, shaking her head as if to shake it free of a circling wasp, went over to Grandmama, who was too frail to do more than three or four stitches of embroidery in any hour. She kissed her. "Yes, Mama, of course you're right."

As Max and his mother walked home from the station that evening, their suitcases light, the swallows wheeled in the warm sky, preparing to leave.

"Mother, what happened to Frau Haber?"

"She died. Professor Haber was a very clever student. Grandpapa taught him chemistry a long time ago when he was just a boy. He went to Berlin. Frau Haber became a teacher in the university too. She was a lovely girl, a little older than I. Her name was Clara. She was one of the first women who studied chemistry seriously—very few women when I was young studied at the university at all. She played the violin, and when I was growing up, she was happy to play second violin in quartets at Grandpapa's, though she was a better player than Dr Herschl. You remember him."

"How was it because of the war that she died?"

"Oh, Max. But perhaps you are old enough . . . You are old enough to see what this war has done to so many people. Professor Haber is now a very distinguished chemist. A lot of people have heard of him. He has his own scientific institute in Berlin. I suppose he thought the institute should help the army win the war. Anyway, it was Professor Haber who invented poison gas—you have heard your father talk about it—and when the army used it in 1915 and many, many soldiers died or were blinded, our soldiers as well as the enemy's, Frau Haber couldn't bear it. She killed herself. So she too, in a way, was a casualty of this war. Though I think—I used to know her quite well, and I admired her very much—it was not only the deaths of the soldiers that made her so unhappy. There have been thousands and thousands of soldiers killed in other ways . . . I think it was probably more painful to her that her own husband couldn't understand that to use his knowledge and his talent, his inventiveness, in such a way was a terrible betrayal of—"

"How was it a betrayal if it would help us to win the war? Surely everyone ought to invent anything they possibly can to help win the war. I don't understand why Father is so against poison gas if it will bring a proper victory."

"Even if it did, and now they say it won't, it would still be a horrible thing. Your father thinks it isn't a fair weapon, and that's why it should never have been used. You see, there are other things that can be betrayed besides the country itself. You can betray what is right—perhaps that's it—what is always right, no matter what is happening."

"How did she kill herself? Did she swallow poison, like Hannibal?"

"I don't know, Max. I really don't know."

"Perhaps she did. Poison because of the poison gas."

"Max! That's a horrible idea. No, she didn't poison herself. In any case, you're too young to think about such things. If it weren't for the war . . ."

They walked on through the summer evening. At the end of the Waldau drive, his mother stopped.

"There's another thing we must talk about, Max. You will be fourteen next March. Of course, your father wants you to go to Lichterfelde, like Freddy and Heinrich. But I don't think I can bear another child of mine . . . And what about your violin? Your own talent, which you have from me. What will become of all the work you have done with Dr Mendel? In cadet school, you won't be able to practise every day. The other boys will laugh at you for wasting time."

"Dr Mendel says—"

"What does he say? He's said nothing to me."

"He doesn't want to make difficulties. That's what he says. But he does say he's nearly at the end of what he can teach me in ordinary lessons and that he'd like me to go to the Gymnasium to learn from better teachers in a proper class with other boys like me. He says I need competition or I'll think I'm cleverer than I really am, and that's bad because it's not realistic. You know how keen he is on being realistic."

"Oh Max, it would be wonderful if you could go to the Gymnasium. You could live with Grandpapa and Grandmama, and Dr Mendel could be in Breslau too, so that you could have your violin lesson every day after school. But your father . . . Would you like me to try to persuade your father? That two soldier sons is enough? That you need to learn more, and be with boys of your own age? That the violin is also important?"

Max ran his finger along a bar of the field gate, always open at the bottom of the drive. A big splinter caught in his finger. He took it out carefully.

"No, Mother. I'll talk to him. He won't like it if he thinks it's your idea, to keep me safe when Freddy was killed in a great battle and Heinrich is still in danger. And he won't like it a bit if he thinks it's Dr Mendel's idea because he thinks Dr Mendel doesn't understand about the army. He's right. He doesn't. Perhaps I can tell him that I know I can be of more real use not as a soldier but as something else—maybe as a doctor, like Grandpapa. Then perhaps he'll change his mind about Lichterfelde."

"You're a good boy, Max. You can try. Of course you must try. But don't be too hopeful. Your father doesn't change his mind easily. And don't talk to him about what's useful. That's exactly what he thinks has gone wrong with everything."

He tried, once, a week or two later when he had spent a hot Saturday out in the harvest fields with his father, helping the old Polish farmer and his granddaughters gather, tie, and make shocks or bundles of mown barley. They had worked all day at the same task and in the shade of a tree at noon shared the bread and cheese and thin beer Emilia had given them to take out for lunch. Frau Stock had gone to help her widowed daughter look after her children and run her draper's shop in Breslau, and in any case there was little cooking to be done now in the big kitchen at Waldau. Emilia did her best with the rations; there was always bread and plenty of potatoes. There was real coffee for breakfast only on Sundays, and for two years there had been no Earl Grey tea and no lemons.

All day, Max and his father had exchanged scarcely a word. Their hands were sore from the stalks of the barley and from pulling and tying the hairy binder twine. They walked home along a cart track with deep, dried ruts and coarse weeds gone to seed in the centre between the ruts.

"Father, can I ask you something?"

"What is it?"

"I should like very much to go to the Gymnasium in Breslau next year."

His father stopped and turned to face him with cold blue eyes.

"What is this?"

"I should like to learn more mathematics, and biology and chemistry properly, because I should like, when I'm grown up, to be a doctor."

"Is this your mother's plan?"

"No. No ... it's my own idea."

"Mendel's plan, then. He thinks you're too clever to be a soldier. Too clever to be a Prussian gentleman. Is that it?"

"No, Father. Please ... I thought ..."

"You are a child still. While you are a child, you do what I say. No son of mine is going to the Gymnasium with the sons of tradesmen and tailors to be a doctor, or anything else. You will go to Lichterfelde like your brothers and be an officer in the Prussian cavalry. What's left of it. That is my decision. You hear me?"

"Yes, Father."

Max reported this conversation neither to his mother nor to Dr Mendel, and neither of them in the months that followed mentioned the Gymnasium or Lichterfelde to Max.

Less than a year later, and three months before he was to go to Lichterfelde, his childhood and the authority of his father came, together, to an end.

44

Chapter 2

Even at seven in the morning, although the sun was shining and the sky was cloudless, the air was dense and still, the start of an early July day that was going to be very hot. Max got up before anyone else in the house. He put on his shirt, shorts, and tennis shoes. He went downstairs without a sound and out of the back door, across the yard with its stone water trough and long washing line propped up with a wooden pole, round the house to the garden, over the mown grass, through his mother's roses heavy with scent and with many petals already fallen to the ground, and down to the small river that flowed between the lawn and the meadow, now deep in flowery hay, on the other side. Because it was past midsummer, not many birds were singing; there were pigeons somewhere; an occasional pheasant clanked from the wood beyond the meadow. Alders and willows grew on the banks of the stream, and a spreading silver poplar, its leaves scarcely stirring.

Max was alone. Rolf, his golden dog, old and stiff, white-muzzled, had died in the winter, and he had turned down the mongrel puppy Tadeusz the gardener had brought him from the village wrapped in a piece of sacking. "I can't have a new dog, Tadeusz. I have to go away to cadet school in October, and they wouldn't allow me to take him with me. You keep him." So the puppy became Tadeusz's dog and followed him about the garden, lying in the shade, his muzzle between his paws, to watch the old man hoeing between the rows of beans and peas as Rolf used to watch Max arranging his toy soldiers. "So fortunate", Max's mother would say quite often, "that Tadeusz was nearly seventy when the war started. If he'd been a bit younger, he'd have been a soldier by now, and then what would we have done?"

Max sat in the grass between a willow and the silver poplar, their branches meeting over his head, and watched the water. The sun was behind him and to his left, already high in the eastern sky. The light caught the long willow leaves and the smaller, rounder leaves of the

45

poplar with their pale undersides, and caught also the slight ripples in the gently moving stream. Tiny flies danced above the surface of the water, and Max waited for a fish to rise. Then he noticed green leaves under the water, leaves not moving as the stream flowed through them. Weeds, he thought, but surely the river here was too deep for such beautiful weeds to be growing so close to the surface. As he looked more carefully, scarcely breathing, he saw that the leaves were reflections, reflections of the willow leaves and the poplar leaves with the sun shining behind them, and he saw that the stream was indeed flowing through them because the water was moving, and the leaves, in the windless light, were not. The stream goes by; the reflections stay. It reminded him of something. Some music? Yes. Schubert. In his mind's eye, he saw the fingers of his mother's left hand softly rocking over the piano keys. But it also reminded him of something else, something more puzzling, something he had read with Dr Mendel. They had read some difficult books in the last year—"the beginnings of philosophy", according to Dr Mendel, "perhaps all you will ever come across"—and he had found some of them impossible to understand, though not at all boring. "Never mind, Max. Remember to come back to these pages one day when you are older."

He got to his feet and walked a short distance, only three or four yards, along the riverbank. He looked back. As he knew they would have, the motionless reflections of the sunlit leaves had disappeared: the quietly flowing water where he had watched them flowed on, brownish, only the little ripples shining each for a fraction of an instant. Perhaps he would try to explain it, this curious thing of the moving water, real, and the steady reflections, just as real yet not real at all, to Dr Mendel. No. He would do it badly, and spoil it with words. He went back to the squashed patch of grass where he had been sitting, and watched the still leaves and the passing water for minutes and minutes. They reminded him of his grandmother, sitting in her chair by the window, watching the flow of the world in the street outside her flat in Breslau. She had died two weeks after the armistice, as quietly as she had lived, sitting in her chair one afternoon, happy that at last the war was over. His parents had gone to Breslau for her funeral, leaving him at home with Dr Mendel and Emilia. He was pleased to have connected the reflections and the river with her. He would come back, on sunny summer mornings, and remember her here.

He gazed on at the reflected leaves, his own reflected leaves. How could he bear to go away? How could he desert his river, his trees, the quiet of the Waldau summer, and go away to Lichterfelde with hundreds of other boys, and nervous horses clattering in stable yards, and the shouts of a parade ground? How could his father make him go? Should he have one more try at persuading his father to change his mind? What would be a good way to begin?

But then he imagined the conversation, his father's anger, his scornful blue eyes. With all that had happened, wouldn't it be even more difficult than it had been last summer at harvest time? And as he admitted to himself how badly a confrontation with his father was likely to go, he understood that now it might actually be easier, more peaceful, for him to leave Waldau and deal with cadet school as best he could. His mother, he knew, would miss him very much, but if he had been allowed to go to the Gymnasium in Breslau, she would have been mostly alone at Waldau with his father in any case. And Heinrich?

One day in October, before the armistice, Heinrich had suddenly appeared at Waldau, thin and looking much older, with his left arm in a sling. He had told them almost nothing about his year on the western front. He was on his way back to the east. "We're done for in the west. It's the Americans. It's not a fair fight any more. But the Americans don't care about the east. The high command's sending us back there, what's left of us, so we can hang on to what we won in the war. Otherwise the Poles will grab the lot."

"How can you fight with your injured arm? How can you even ride your horse? Surely you've done enough! Three years at the front— isn't that more than enough? Look at you—you need proper meals and proper rest. Carl Friedrich, can't you tell somebody he's not fit to go back?"

"Mother, you don't understand. We don't use horses any more. The war's quite different now. There are tanks and motorbikes and aeroplanes. And I'm perfectly well. My hands don't even shake, and my ears and eyes are fine. You should see some of the fellows who are still at the front. In the east, they need officers to keep some sort of order. Do you want us to lose the war in the east as well as the war in the west? For Waldau, the war in the east is the war that counts."

"The boy's right, Toni. And no Prussian officer looks for excuses for leave when the regiment needs him."

47

So Heinrich disappeared again into the war. In the weeks after the armistice, more than seven months ago now, Max and his mother expected Heinrich to come home any day. But there was no news of him. In March a letter arrived, the address blurred by rain and almost illegible. It had been posted in Riga at the end of January. The remains of his dragoon regiment were fighting the Red Army along the Baltic coast with the blessing of the British navy. "The English should have been on our side all along", he had scribbled. But in May, the son of a neighbouring family, a friend of Heinrich's from cadet school, had been brought home on a hospital train from somewhere near Warsaw with his leg blown off, and his father had told the count that Heinrich was now fighting with the Russians against the Poles, who were struggling to establish an independent Poland. "Quite right", the count said, telling his wife and Max of this. "Of course the Poles can't be allowed to govern themselves. Hopeless people. The peasants will work if they're organized properly, but the nobility are quite useless and always have been. All drunk by lunchtime and balls in Vienna their only idea of responsibility—not that there'll be any more of that kind of thing. I hear Vienna is starving. At least the Russians have some idea of how to rule an empire, and there'll be plenty of people left who know what they're doing even if they've dispensed with the Tsar. If we can manage to govern Germany without a Kaiser—I've yet to be convinced that we can, but for the time being we have to try—no doubt they can manage to govern Russia without a Tsar. Anything efficient in Russia has always been German, in any case. Now that the Austrians have finally lost everything, Emperor, empire, the lot, we need to take over Vienna, save what's worth saving, and decide on a sensible frontier with Russia. We should have the whip hand in the east at least."

All this was before the news came, in the middle of May, of the peace terms laid down in Paris by France, England, and America for the representatives of the German republic to sign. Max had never seen his father in a rage to equal that which broke on them all at Waldau on the day the newspaper set out these terms. The count had ridden early to the station for the paper, as he had every morning throughout the war. Max, his mother, and Dr Mendel, at breakfast in the kitchen with Emilia, heard a distant roar of fury from the little business room beyond the library, where his father had taken the newspaper. Then a silence. Then a louder roar, and the crash of two doors,

48

three, being flung open and slammed as his father marched across the library, then the hall and the dining room, and burst into the kitchen.

"Look at this! Look at it!"

The count held up the newspaper with one hand and hit it with the furious forefinger of the other. "GERMANY SURRENDERS ALL CLAIMS TO ITS EXISTENCE", the paper said on its black-bordered front page. The words, Max discovered when he read the crumpled paper later, were those of the old ambassador leading the German delegation in Paris.

"It's a scandal! A wicked, devilish plot! A conspiracy against us! Such a treaty has never before been devised in the whole history of Europe! The French, the French are to blame! President Wilson promised us open discussion, but we are presented with a fait accompli, a punishing peace as if we alone had begun the war. We're told we have to pay what they call 'reparations', huge sums of money that we haven't got. What is Austria paying? And Russia? They started the war, not us. And, even worse, we're told we have to sign away great tracts of Germany. Alsace-Lorraine, of course—no doubt you'll be delighted by that, Mendel, as if the hated Prussians hadn't fed you and housed you in comfort all through the war—but West Prussia and Posnania as well. Both are down to be part of what the negotiators choose to call 'Poland', though the only reason anyone wants these lands is that they're German. German government, German hard work, German honesty, for all these years. And worst of all—you won't believe this, Toni—Silesia, our beloved Silesia, German for hundreds of years, is to be divided as if it were an orange, and half of it is to go to this invented Poland. So they sit there in Paris drawing lines on maps of places they know nothing about, and we at Waldau may end up being governed by Poles! We won't stand for it! This must be fought, and I mean *fought*, fought with soldiers and guns. If only Fritz were alive! If only Heinrich were here! What can I do? There are only Poles left—though our Poles will never want to live in this ridiculous new Poland. They'll want to stay in Prussia for certain! There! That's important. If people are to choose which nation they wish to belong to, ask the Poles in Germany! But they won't get the chance to choose. We're all being told what will become of us by western politicians in frock coats in Paris. What do they know of Germany east of the Elbe? What do they know of the Poles, of the Russians? What do they care? All they want to do is to punish Germany, as if we wanted such a terrible

49

war, as if we alone armed and built ships and competed. I shall tele-graph the President of this preposterous republic—in Weimar, of all places! What is Weimar to the world? A little town in Thuringia, with the tombs of poets. It's not even in Prussia. As if we are to be ashamed of Berlin! I shall telegraph the President and tell him these terms are impossible. Impossible! The Prussian nobility will never, never accept them, nor will the Prussian army!"

"But Carl Friedrich, what good will it do? Out here in the coun-try, there's nothing we can possibly do. The Allies won the war. We lost it. We are hardly in a position to—"

"What war did we lose in the east? The Austrians lost, the Austri-ans for whose sake we waged war in the first place. But we never lost. We defeated the Russians. We gave them a peace they had to agree to. All signed and correct. No problems. After their revolution, they couldn't have fought against us with any hope of winning. That treaty was torn up by us, under compulsion from the Allies, not by the Russians. There've been no Russians at the conference in Paris, not a single one. How is that just? How can that be called an open peace openly discussed? How dare the Allies force on us and on Russia this fabri-cated Poland that'll never be able to govern itself? How dare they? It's not truthful, it's not honourable, it's a treacherous French plot, and the British and the Americans have been too weak and too ignorant to stop it happening. The French love the Poles; they always have. What they've always wanted is to surround us with enemies. There's only one thing we can do now. We must declare a German frontier in the east and defend it against anyone prepared to fight us over it. The Russians won't fight us; they don't want this invented Poland any more than we do. And is it likely that France and England, as worn out by the war as we are, will want to come and fight for Poland? Or Amer-ica? Will American soldiers cross Europe to fight for Poland? They're all terrified of Bolshevism, terrified of Lenin, terrified of intellectual Jews bringing revolution to their countries. Very good. Excellent. Who do they think will hold the line against Bolshevism more effectively? The Germans or the Poles?"

This had all taken place two months ago. The count had tele-graphed the President. For days, for weeks, he waited for a reply. He seemed to Max to get angrier every day, white-faced, his jaw set. He rode over the estate on the only horse that remained in the stables, galloping down the overgrown rides in the forest, until the horse was lamed jumping a fallen birch into a warren of rabbit holes hidden under brambles. At meals, everyone ate in silence. If Max's mother asked a question or said something harmless to Max or Dr Mendel, his father snapped at her as if she had spoken only to irritate him.

No reply came to the telegram. The newspaper said that the negotiators in Paris were doing their best to persuade the Allies to modify the terms of the peace treaty. Max's father ground his teeth at the feebleness of this, the only response to what he kept saying was the deepest insult offered to a great state since the fall of Rome. The cabinet in Weimar resigned. As June went on, the news became more and more confused. The President was resigning. The President had not resigned. At last the newspaper said, to the count's renewed disgust, that the President had put together a fresh government just in time to sign the treaty.

"Who is this Ebert? He told the soldiers marching back from the western front that nobody had defeated them. Somebody has defeated them now. Their own President—their own government—has defeated them. How can the army have agreed to this disgrace? How can they?"

At the end of June, by the time that the newspaper described the actual signing of the treaty in the Hall of Mirrors at Versailles, the shameful treatment of the German delegation, the rejoicing all over France, the firing of cannon, and the ringing of bells, Max's father had passed through rage to grim, clenched despair. There had been one concession to Germany achieved in the negotiations: Lower Silesia would stay in Germany, while the people of Upper Silesia were to decide for themselves by plebiscite whether their part of the province was to be included in Poland.

"Carl Friedrich, surely this at least is good news?"

"The Poles want the coal and steel. They'll win the plebiscite. There are more of them than there are of us, and they're being fed nationalist nonsense from Warsaw every day. They're being told we've oppressed them all these years, kept them down, taught them German, made them work. We have. Of course we have. Kept them in order. Taught them German. Taught them to obey the law. Given them work. That's why they're the only Poles who've prospered ever since Poland was abolished."

"Well, there you are. They're bound to vote to stay in Germany. You've said so yourself. And we'll be all right, here in Lower Silesia, won't we?"

51

"No. We shall not be all right. The world's moving too fast. No one understands what's happening, how quickly Prussia is falling to pieces. This new Poland, and Czechoslovakia, an invented country! Independence, self-determination—only words, modern, fashionable, American words. It's nothing but a way of destroying Prussia, destroying us, giving to the Poles all the victories of Frederick the Great, all we rescued from Napoleon, all we conquered from the Russians in 1914 and 1915. As soon as this new Poland is as big as it can be, the Bolsheviks will attack it and defeat it—what sort of an army have the Poles got?—and we'll all be living under Lenin. You mark my words."

Max tried to get Dr Mendel, who through these last weeks had sustained his resolute refusal to speak about the negotiations, the government, the treaty, or the plebiscite, to explain to him what was going on so that he could decide for himself whether his father's rage and despair were well-founded. He loved his tutor too much to badger him every day, but he knew Dr Mendel knew that he keenly looked forward to the moment when he would think it possible to give Max his own account of it all without betraying his father's trust.

It was a chance in a lesson that at last, one morning, persuaded Dr Mendel to talk to him about the news.

For several months, Max, with great delight, had been learning Greek, although Dr Mendel said that his own Greek was rusty and that Max needed a better teacher. In the hot schoolroom with all the windows open, they were reading slowly through a couple of pages of the *Iliad*, with the help of a German translation and Dr Autenrieth's special dictionary for Homer that seemed to know exactly which lines you were struggling to understand.

In the middle of a truce in the war with Troy, a treacherous arrow from an enemy bowman had wounded the Greek King Menelaus. Dark blood flowed from the wound, but a doctor came and pulled the arrow out and sucked the wound clean so that Menelaus was not going to die. Agamemnon, seeing his brother's blood flowing, went raging about the Greek army, rousing his captains to fight, and the soldiers of Ajax gathered like a storm cloud. When, the poem said, a shepherd sees such a cloud, black and far out over the sea, with flashes of lightning along its edge, he drives his sheep into a cave for shelter. Dr Mendel collected the books together and put them in a neat pile on the table.

"Well, Max. You see how there is nothing new under the sun. It is rage that keeps war going, and fear is its consequence. Some people thought, or hoped, that the armistice was a truce, only a pause in the fighting, like the truce in the Trojan war. But now we have peace, and a treaty that all the countries have signed to secure it, and a peace is much more than an armistice. We must rejoice that there is peace. We must. The killing of our young men, the young men of nearly all the nations of Europe, at last has stopped. Those who are still alive will come home to their families, to their mothers and their sweethearts. They will come back to the farms and the mines and the factories. The blockade will be lifted: people have been hungry for more than a year because of the blockade, but now it will be lifted. I expect it already has been. Trade will begin again. Food will be brought to the markets and the shops. For all this we should rejoice."

"Then why is my father so angry?"

"Your father is angry—and I've no doubt many thousands more are just as angry—because he feels let down by his own country and his own army he has always been so proud of. Not, I think, because the war was lost—he knows it was lost in the west, though of course he doesn't accept it was lost in the east—but because we were lied to for years. We were told the war was being won, that there would be total victory, soon, soon, all the way up to the very end, when suddenly we were told that we had asked for an armistice because we could fight no longer. That was a terrible shock for your father. Why had the nation not been told the truth? Your father is too honest and too realistic to suppose, as many now do, that we were being told the truth all that time—which would mean that the request for an armistice was not necessary, that it was some kind of treacherous device to harm Germany from within. Another shock for your father was the undignified manner of the Kaiser's departure. The army put up no fight to defend him or to save him from humiliation. He went away. They let him go, and then they agreed to serve this new republic, which to your father is an insult in itself. What does a Prussian nobleman have to do with a republic? Prussia has been ruled by a single man ever since the Great Elector. What is this kind of rule called, when one man governs a nation?"

"Autocracy?"

"That's right. And what is the rule of the people called?"

"A republic?"

"Well, not necessarily. A republic can be the rule of a few people. Then it's called an oligarchy. *Oligos* in Greek means "a few", as *autos* means one person by himself. What is the Greek word for the people, all the people?"

"*Demos?*"

"Good boy. So the rule of the people, who vote to elect the government, is called democracy. America is a democracy, and so is France, and so is England, even though England still has a King. In England, the King has no real power. These are the countries that won the war in the west, so democracy has defeated autocracy, and our new republic is to be a democracy once it has got itself sorted out."

"Is that good?"

"It may be. It may be. But it will need much goodwill and trust if it is to be good for everyone. And I'm afraid that many people will find it difficult even to hope that it will work well."

"Like my father?"

"Like your father. He does not believe that democracy will ever suit the Germans. And in any case, it takes a long time for a nation to adjust to a sudden change such as this. The newspapers have called what happened in November a revolution, because it was a sudden change. But it wasn't a real revolution, thank God. In a real revolution, there is much bloodshed—the class of people who have always held power, the nobility, are done away with, and there is a civil war. That is what happened in France at the end of the eighteenth century. That is what is happening in Russia now. In both countries, most of the people were peasants. Nothing like that has happened here. Nor, I think, is it likely to, because Germany is too prosperous and its government is too complicated. People will go on doing what they always do. The only difference is that the Kaiser has slipped quietly away. Some of the names of institutions and the machinery of government will change, but the realities will be much as usual even after properly democratic elections."

"That's why I must still go to cadet school?"

"That's why you must still go to cadet school."

Dr Mendel picked up the pile of books on the table and moved it a little farther away. He cleared his throat.

"When you get there, Max, you will meet a lot of boys who have been infected with hatred and rage and with the irrational idea that we never lost the war at all, that we or the army or the government or the Kaiser were betrayed—'stabbed in the back' is the phrase—by wicked people who wanted to bring Germany as low as possible. There are no such people, Max, and it's important that you don't believe anyone who tells you such people exist. Your father doesn't hold to this 'stab in the back' theory any more than I do, and no sensible person in this country does or ever will."

"Who is my father so angry with, then?"

"He is angry with the men who drafted the peace terms in Paris and forced those terms, without discussion, on the German people. He is angry because the peace terms imply that this country alone was responsible for starting the war, which is not true. He is angry with the French for exacting vengeance so crudely and stupidly for what happened in 1870. In all these respects, your father has good—or anyway, very understandable—reasons for his anger. But ..."

"But what?"

There was a silence, as if Dr Mendel were organizing his thoughts carefully before he spoke.

"It is most important that this anger does not continue among the young, among people of your age, Max, or one day there will be another war. This last war has been so terrible that nothing like it must ever be allowed to happen again. It began, at least in the west, because of the war of 1870, because of the humiliation of France and the crowing of Germany. Now we have the humiliation of Germany and the crowing of France. It was Prince Bismarck who invented war reparations to punish the French, and now the French are using his invention to punish the Germans. And look where the French made the Germans sign this treaty! The Hall of Mirrors at Versailles is a room for gloating in. I have seen it. A great, vulgar, glittering room where the King of France could lord it over his visitors from the rest of Europe, to make them feel small and insignificant and embarrassed. That is why in 1871 Prince Bismarck chose it for Prussia to humiliate France in France's own palace, for the world to take notice that the Kaiser was an Emperor too—like Franz Joseph in Vienna or like the Tsar in Saint Petersburg, as glorious as Louis XIV or as Napoleon once had been. What could be a more perfect revenge for the French than to choose the Hall of Mirrors again, to show that the tables are turned, to show that the great defeat has become a great victory? Yet what is revenge? An action of the primitive, the uncivilized. We have the law and justice so that we do not have revenge, vendetta. What took place in the Hall of Mirrors was as barbarous as a Corsican knife between the ribs. It was also exceedingly stupid."

"Why was it stupid?"

"It was stupid because a vendetta, a blood feud, is almost impossible to stop."

"So what should we do now, in Germany, in Prussia? Is there anything we can do?"

"If our enemies are stupid, we should be intelligent. If our enemies are bullies, we should be gentle. When the victors behave with childish cruelty, it is the task of the vanquished to behave with grace, with magnanimity. We should be harmless as doves and wise as serpents. Or there will be another war. I do not want you to fight and die as Freddy did. I do not want you to fight and live as Heinrich has. Poor Heinrich. He will not recover soon from where he has been, from what he has seen."

"Can the government do anything? My father says the government is useless, 'invented', he says, like Poland. He says it won't last and it can't do any good because it's not strong enough."

"While the army is willing to support the government, there is hope. Hope of a return to order and prosperity for people prepared to work hard. Certainly, both the government and the army must decide not to fight anyone, anywhere, with any weapons whatsoever, for a long, long time to come. The peace terms seem very harsh, I know. But the politicians in Paris in their frock coats, as your father would say, have done their best, I believe, to give as many people as possible what they want, or what, at present, they think they want. Your father may be right about these new countries. It is quite possible that the Poles and the Bohemians and the southern Slavs with their patched-together countries, after so much suffering and so much destruction, may find it more difficult than they expect, perhaps even impossible, to govern people who have been accustomed for generations to blame distant imperial capitals for everything that is harsh and difficult in their lives. Some of the people in these countries don't belong to the nations that are now becoming states. They may find themselves worse treated than they were before the war by the empires on whose graves everyone is dancing. The Jews, for example. The Jews in Russia were so poor and so afraid of the Cossacks and the Tsar's officials that they could not be worse off in this new Poland than they have long been. But the Jews whose towns and villages used to be in Prussia and Austria may find that in this new Poland, they are more unjustly treated than they used to be. The people at the bottom of the heap may be worse treated by those next up in the order of ignominy than by those at the top. Germans despise Russians, who despise Poles, who despise Jews. The prospects for the Jews are not good. We shall see."

"Dr Mendel—"

"Max, I am sorry. I have been talking too much, trying to explain things too difficult for a boy of your age to understand. I apologise. It is time for you to go outside for a little break, and I will see if Emilia has a cup of tea for me. Perhaps you would like a quick swim in the river on such a hot day?"

"No. I wanted to ask you something."

"Of course."

"Does it make any difference, being a Jew?"

Dr Mendel looked down at the tablecloth, the plush tablecloth that had been there all of Max's life, and smoothed it with his familiar hand. He did not answer for some time.

"Ah", he said. "At last we come to it. Yes, Max, it does. It makes a great deal of difference. A Jew does not ever quite belong to the country in which he lives. I have been a French Jew, and I have been a German Jew, but I have never been a Frenchman or a German. The Jews are a people who carry their homeland with them wherever they go because it is in their souls and not in the streets of cities or in the villages and fields and woods where other people allow them to live."

"Is their homeland where God is?"

Dr Mendel raised his head and looked searchingly at Max.

"It should be, Max, it should always be, perhaps for everyone. But it is not always so, even with Jews. They also, as other people do, often make another homeland for their souls. Perhaps it is France, or Germany, or science, or music, or the making of much money. Then, because they have lost God, they have lost the distance that should be precious to them, the distance from which it should be easier to look calmly at all these passions, the loves and hatreds and fears, which drive wars and draw frontiers and arm people to fight over them."

"You haven't."

"What have I not?"

"You haven't lost the distance."

"Perhaps I have not. Not, at any rate, all the time. But I have been most fortunate. To be permitted to live in your parents' house. To be

57

permitted to teach all these years a talented child who has worked hard and practised not just the violin but reading and thinking and paying attention to whatever I have suggested to him. I have been most fortunate, and I thank God every day for my good fortune."

Max was struck, almost stricken, by a question that had not occurred to him before.

"What will you do when I go to Lichterfelde? Will you go back to Strasbourg?"

"I think not, Max. It is now too late for me to return to France. There I would be thought a German by now. Also, I have become fond of Silesia. I have friends here, friends in Breslau. Breslau is a city that has been, on the whole, just to the Jews. Perhaps I will find another boy to teach violin. Perhaps you will visit me when you are on leave."

"Of course I will. I don't want to go to cadet school. I don't want to leave Waldau. I don't want to leave you. Or Mother."

"Steady, Max." These two words, and a look, were enough. "I know. But you are old enough to leave your childhood behind. You will make friends of your own age. Not many, but they will be important to you. And as time goes by, you will meet girls. One of them perhaps will be your sweetheart. That will be also important. Very important. And in any case, a boy of your age must still do as his father wishes. It will not always be so. One day, you will be grown up and free to do as you decide for yourself. That is when you must be very careful to decide well, because only you and God will know what is possible for you, what you are able to choose and what you cannot choose. The reasons for these things are so complicated that no one else will ever know them all. You may not know them all yourself. Most likely, you will not."

There was a long silence while Max thought about this.

"Dr Mendel?" he said at last.

"Yes, Max?"

"Can a person choose to be a Jew?"

"No, Max. A person is or is not a Jew. It is possible to choose to be a Christian, but a Jew will be a Christian as well as being a Jew, not instead of being a Jew. But it is not possible to choose to be a Jew. Although ..."

"Although what?"

"Never mind. This is something for you to ask your grandfather about. When you are older. He will explain."

"Then it's not fair. If you can't choose to be a Jew even if you really want to be one, it's not fair."

Dr Mendel laughed. Max was astonished.

"Max, it really is time you left Waldau and found some new teachers, some friends to talk to who are not old foreigners like me. The life we lead here is very quiet, very far away from the world."

"Does that help to keep the distance? The Jewish distance?"

Dr Mendel laughed again.

"Well, in my case perhaps, though I try to pay some attention to the world and what goes on in it, and your father pays it even more attention, as you know. But listen to me, Max. This is important. As soon as you are in the world, you will discover that it is a great disadvantage, a great difficulty, to be a Jew. Many people hate Jews, without thinking, just because they are Jews."

"Like Heinrich does. Or anyway, he used to. Perhaps he doesn't any more. But that's stupid."

"Indeed it is. But one of the things you will learn as you get older is that many of the strongest feelings people have are stupid. They don't think about them. They collect them from other people, and the words of hatred or contempt—or, come to that, the words of adoration and hope—that they share with these other people make them feel strong and united, and that in turn makes them feel as if they counted for something. When there's not much to adore or hope for, they fall back on hatred and contempt, and very often they will pick on the Jews, hating or blaming them for things that have gone badly. The people who believe Germany was 'stabbed in the back' last year are inclined also to believe that 'the Jews', whatever that means, did the stabbing. Which is altogether quite ridiculous and comes from blind hatred."

"But why? Why all this hatred? Is it because it's really better to be Jewish but you can't choose to be, so people mind that other people are Jewish?"

"No, almost the exact opposite. Or, nowadays, perhaps yes. Nowadays perhaps you are right. Let me try to explain. For many hundreds of years, people hated the Jews because the Jews were not Christian and because Christians were taught that the Jews killed Jesus."

"But wasn't Jesus a Jew?"

"Yes, he was, and so were his friends. His enemies and his friends. All Jews, with the odd Roman on either side. All human beings. If no Jews had become Christians, there would have been no Christians at all, no Church, no Christians now, anywhere in the world. So Christians owe all they believe to the Jews."

"So it's stupid for Christians to hate them? As well as unfair?"

"For most of the time that the Christians hated the Jews, the Jews were made to live in separate districts of cities, sometimes in different clothes from everyone else so that people could tell at once who was a Jew, and Jews were not allowed to go to the same schools as Christians or learn the same things. But about a hundred years ago, Christians, or some of them, stopped hating Jews and decided that perhaps, after all, Jews were human beings like everyone else. Then Jews were allowed to join the life of Christians in schools and universities and hospitals and even government offices, and people have found that Jews do many things very well, better than anyone expected, and so they are hated all over again."

"Why do they do things well? Are they just cleverer?"

"Not really. There are lots of stupid Jews, just as there are lots of stupid Christians. But Jews have an ancient tradition of learning. Jews have always taught their children to read, while until quite recently, and still in Russia, most of the Christians around them couldn't read. There are books and stories from long ago that all Jews know and remember, and some teachers and scholars spend all their lives, even in the poorest villages, studying those books and stories. So Jews are good at learning. And when they were given the chance to learn other things, subjects that the Christians had developed without the Jews, things like physics and chemistry and medicine and philosophy and economics, the Jews turned out to learn quickly and think well. As for music, there has always been much music in Jewish life. When I was a boy, there were famous violinists in Russia who couldn't even play from written-down music. Probably there still are. But as soon as Jews were allowed to join the conservatories and the orchestras, everyone could hear how rich in skill those long centuries of isolation had been. So the Jews were resented, of course. First they were hated for being "outside" and of no use, except at the one thing they were allowed to do, trading and lending money, which made all the people who depended on them hate them more. Then they were hated for being "inside" and of a great deal of use. Educated Christians don't much care any more whether Christianity is true. In fact, the more educated they are, the less they care. So nowadays, they don't bother to accuse the Jews of killing Jesus because they don't bother enough about Jesus for it to matter who killed him. But they do mind being overtaken by Jews in things they thought they were best at. It's as if the Christians were saying to us now, 'Very well, Jews. Do what you like, as long as you do it badly.' "

"But that's not fair either, not fair at all."

"It's not. You are right. But it's how things are. Most people have deep inside them a sense of justice, as you have. But nothing is more easily overcome by hatred, fear, or greed—or whipped-up solidarity against other people. When you grow up and find out how the world goes, Max, you will be glad, I have no doubt, to be a Prussian boy."

"But—"

"Enough, Max. Enough for one morning. Probably too much. Now off you go and have a swim. Get dried properly before you get dressed. Then we shall practise the Bach sonata. He will put things to rights. He always does."

That was yesterday. Max sat in the soft grass on the river bank and watched the water flowing through the reflections of the willow leaves, remembering it all. He was sad. He didn't see how he was going to manage without Dr Mendel to explain things to him. He knew there was a great deal more he had to learn if he was ever to become as wise and good as Dr Mendel, and how was he to learn enough unless he had Dr Mendel to teach him? On the other hand, as he thought about everything his old tutor had told him the day before, he saw more and more clearly that it was out of the question to ask his father again if he might be allowed to go to the Gymnasium in Breslau instead of the cadet school. Everything was bad enough for his father at the moment; Max didn't want to make it worse. And perhaps Dr Mendel was right: cadet school would be new and exciting. There would be lots of boys of his own age, among them perhaps a real friend such as he had never had. He had played with the farm boys when he was younger, but that was different—it was only play, sliding down stacks of corn (which was not allowed), building a robbers' lair in the woods (which wouldn't have been allowed if anyone had known about it), and damming the river with boulders, downstream from the garden, to make a fishing lake. This last escapade had got them into serious trouble; his father had made them shift every boulder and stone to return the stream to its proper course. So a friend, perhaps, to talk to. And one day a sweetheart: this was the single word from yesterday that stuck in his mind, a kind of promise from the future, stopping his thinking every time he remembered it.

He sighed and looked at his wristwatch, his present from his mother on his fourteenth birthday. Ten to eight. Important not to be late for breakfast. He spent another three or four minutes looking at the still leaves in the moving water. Then he ran up to the house.

The schoolroom morning was ordinary. Neither he nor Dr Mendel referred to the conversation of the day before. They worked on algebra, which was becoming seriously difficult. Max struggled with a Latin prose, a dictionary beside him, crossing out, rubbing out, and rewriting as he tried to make each sentence both shorter and grander than the German sentences he was trying to translate. This was a favourite exercise of Dr Mendel's when he thought Max needed some solid work to pin him to the schoolroom table for a silent hour. He would open a German translation of a Cicero speech or a passage of Tacitus, find Max a knotty paragraph to translate, and—at the end, of course—compare Max's effort with the original Latin. Max enjoyed the puzzle, enjoyed knowing that there was, in the same room and to be looked at with laughter once he had done the best job he could, the answer, or at least what a great writer long ago had written. If he had produced a phrase or two, occasionally a whole clause or sentence, that was there in the original, he and Dr Mendel were equally delighted; the further away from the original his version was, the funnier it looked. Today, he couldn't concentrate properly. "*De officiis* II.xi", he had written carefully at the top of the page. He rearranged his Latin version of four sentences for an hour and then put down his pencil, baffled by the fifth.

"I can't do it today. I'm not sure what he's saying even in German."

"Let me see. The first two sentences are good, quite close to Cicero. Look. 'No man can be just if he is afraid of death, pain, exile, or poverty, or prefers their contraries to justice': you have got that almost exactly. Never mind the last sentence. Cicero himself has lost the clarity of what he is saying there. That's not at all a bad try, Max. Now we'll do something easier. A little more Lamartine?"

"All right."

Max thought Lamartine almost as boring as Cicero, but at least all he had to do was understand him in French and perhaps write a German translation. That was nowhere near as difficult as a Latin prose.

The poem Dr Mendel chose for that day was called "The Lake". It had the usual gloomy sort of beginning, the poet moping about some woman, but the French wasn't hard, and Max was translating it without paying much attention when he was surprised by two lines. "L'homme n'a point de port, le temps n'a point de rive: Il coule, et nous passons."

"But that's just like by the river this morning!"

"What did you say, Max?"

"It doesn't matter. It's too difficult to explain."

Max translated the rest of the poem, his sadness of the morning returning with the poet's words. "Man has no harbour, time has no shore: It flows and we pass." How could he have thought Lamartine boring only ten minutes ago?

His father did not appear at lunch. This was not unusual.

"I've no idea where the count is", Max's mother said to Dr Mendel. "We'll start lunch without him."

"He was sent for from the village", Emilia said, carrying a tureen full of soup into the dining room. "Half an hour ago, a lad came to the kitchen door and said please, could the count come. Trouble in the village, he said. Quite agitated, he was. The count said he must go but he wouldn't be long."

"I see. Well, I'm sure he'll be back soon."

By two o'clock, Max was in his attic practising the Bach. He practised in the attic so that neither Dr Mendel nor his mother could hear him play. He stood with his back to the line of low, square windows, all open as far as they would go. On the dusty boards under the sloping ceiling, his lead soldiers were arranged in the formation of the Prussian infantry and cavalry before the battle of Leipzig. He hadn't touched them for two years.

Although he hadn't bothered to fasten the pages under the brass clips, not a breath of air stirred the music on the stand. The heavy stillness of the hot day outside was broken by scarcely a sound. When he stopped at the end of the difficult fast second movement of the sonata, letting the notes fade quickly into the whitewashed walls of the attic, he heard a duck score the river in a faint splash of spray. He didn't turn to look but sensed the duck bobbing on the water, refolding its feathers. He thought of his reflected leaves breaking and recovering. "Le temps n'a point de rive: Il coule, et nous passons." With the point of his bow, he turned back the pages of the fast movement he had just played and stood for a moment listening in his head to the adagio beginning of the sonata, a single page of long, slow notes. It flows. He rested the bow on the strings of his violin. But music makes patterns in time, like the reflected leaves on the flowing water. He played the first five bars of the adagio, with a gentle vibrato from his left hand, the notes sweet, even, exactly in tune, exactly in tune with each other and with the motionless stillness of the summer day in the garden, in the meadow, in the woods, on the blue, hazy hills to the south.

A door slammed somewhere downstairs. The bang was followed at once by a lot of noise: a high wail—that was Emilia—more doors opening and shutting, the barking of Tadeusz's dog—what was he doing inside the house?—then Dr Mendel's stiff footsteps on the wooden stairs up to the attic.

Max put his violin and his bow down carefully on the open case on the floor. There was urgent knocking on the door.

"Max, Max, come quickly. Your poor mother—there has been a tragedy. Come to your mother!"

"My mother! What's happened?"

He ran down the wooden stairs, looked up and down the passage on the first floor.

"Max! Max!"

His mother's voice. He ran down the stone stairs to the hall. His mother, white-faced, was standing in the hall, clasping to her Emilia, who was shaking with sobs. Tadeusz was in the open doorway, twisting his cap round and round in his hands; his dog was whimpering at his feet as if he had been hit.

"Mother, what's happened?"

"O Max, your father ..."

Her face crumpled. She bent her head, hiding her face on Emilia's scarfed head.

"Max", Dr Mendel had followed him downstairs and, standing behind him, put his hand on his shoulder. "Your father has been shot. There has been a battle in the village."

"A battle? Is he all right? Is he wounded?"

"Your father is dead, Max. Tadeusz says there was nothing anyone could do."

"Dead? *Dead?* How can he be dead? It must be a mistake. The war's over. The war's been over for months. How could there be a battle in the village? Who is there to fight? Is it the Russians? The Poles? I don't understand."

His mother, through her tears, said: "Germans shot him, Max, German soldiers in uniform, Tadeusz says. Emilia, sit down, there's a dear." She disentangled herself from the still-weeping Emilia and settled her gently down into the chair in which she herself, also weeping, had been left by the count on the morning the war began.

"We don't know how it happened. We don't know—" She broke off at the sight of something beyond the open door, clasped her throat with both her hands, turned and ran up the stairs.

Max looked out into the sunshine and then, the old gardener standing back for him to pass, walked outside and stood on the top step.

A long way down the drive, through bars of light and shadow cast by the avenue of lime trees, a haycart drawn by two horses was coming at a plodding pace towards the house. As he watched the swaying cart slowly approach, with the blinkered draught horses tossing their heads now and then at the flies, and saw the small, silent crowd of peasants following the wagon, he no longer heard Emilia's subsiding sobs or Tadeusz's heavy breathing or the creak of harness and wheels. He heard only the long, sweet phrases of the Bach sonata's first movement, the steady adagio become a threnody.

At last the horses emerged from the avenue into the white, stony space in front of the house. The horses turned, the cart's wheels scraping on the stones, came alongside the steps, and were pulled up. The crowd of peasants fell back and stood motionless in a semicircle. The carter laid down his reins and whip, jumped to the ground with what seemed a clumsily loud thud, walked round behind the half load of hay, and unfastened the backboard. Max's father lay on the hay as if asleep, a white cloth over his face. When the carter and a peasant from among the bystanders pulled the body downwards, and two more came forward to help carry it up the steps, Max moved to one side to let them go into the house. Before he followed them, he saw a dark patch of blood on the hay where his father's head had lain. Menelaus, he thought. But Menelaus was still alive.

In the hall, they paused. "The library", Max said, and led them down the passage opposite the one that led to the salon. He looked up the stairs to the landing. There was no sign of his mother, nor of Emilia, who must have gone up to be with her.

They laid his father on the brown leather sofa under the dark books in the glass-fronted bookcases.

"Please go now. Thank you. My mother will be most grateful. Thank you."

Three of them were Poles and crossed themselves as they stood for a moment in front of the body. Then they left, shutting the door carefully behind them.

For a few minutes, Max stood alone in the library, wondering what he should do, what Freddy or Heinrich would do. He was afraid to lift the cloth that covered his father's face. He was afraid to go upstairs to his mother. For the first time in his life, he understood that he could not ask Dr Mendel for help. The echoing absence of his father, the weight of silence in the library where his father's body lay while his father had altogether gone, presented him, he knew, with a family responsibility that was his alone.

So he stood. Then he thought of what his father would have done, and went into the little business room beyond the library and sat in his father's chair at his father's work table. There was a big mahogany desk in the library with an elaborate old lamp on it (there was no electricity at Waldau), which Max had not often seen lit since Dr Mendel had taken over the schoolroom from Miss Wilson. But this table was where his father worked at papers to do with the house and the estate, and this much smaller, lighter room was where his father used to see his steward when, before the war, he had one, and now talked to the farmers or to anyone who came up from the village to ask him for help.

Max had very rarely set foot in this room. Occasionally his mother had sent him to ask his father a question about arrangements, or horses, or trains: Max would stand, aware of interrupting his father's work or solitude or both, and, having got his answer, would go away as quickly and quietly as possible. He had never before sat down in the business room.

Now he looked at his father's things instead of looking at his father's body.

The table was old, square, and solid, with worn leather set into its surface. The chair he was sitting in was equally solid, equally old, with a cracked leather seat. On the table, neatly arranged, were a shagreen and silver inkstand with pens in it, and a blotter to match; a large black tin box with *Schloss Waldau* written on an ancient label that was curled at one corner and stuck to the box's top; and a silver-framed photograph of Max's mother with a baby who must have been Freddy—she looked very young—in her arms, the baby in a long white dress.

The count's chair faced the door, with its back to the window, so that whoever came to visit him—there was one other chair on the opposite side of the table—could see the count less clearly than the count could see the visitor. There was one painting on the wall beside the door, of Max's mother as a girl of about eighteen, dressed in the stiff, corseted fashion of the 1890s, with a high-necked dress, sleeves wide at the top and tight down to the wrist, and a skirt to the floor. She was sitting dreamily at a velvet-draped piano, one elbow beside some music open on the piano's reading desk, one hand supporting her cheek, the other hand resting on the keys. On the piano in a black frame was a hazily suggested portrait of Liszt as an old man, with his straight white hair and handsome face. It was a fact famous in the family that Max's mother as a child had been taught by a pupil of Liszt.

On the wall to the right of the desk was a large, unframed map of the Prussia of Frederick the Great. The battlefields were marked with crossed swords in gold, and the Waldau estate with a small, irregular circle in black. Tannenberg was marked with red crossed swords, and its date, 1914, was also in red. Under the map was an unglazed oak bookcase, two shelves high, with a pile of papers on top held in place by a creamy marble paperweight with a rearing bronze horse decorating it. Max got up to look at the books in the bookcase: Ranke's *Hardenberg and the History of the Prussian State*, five volumes; Mommsen's *Roman History*, three volumes; and *The History of Frederick II of Prussia, Called Frederick the Great* by Thomas Carlyle, in six volumes, in English. Max had never heard of this last work. On the bottom shelf were the works of Goethe in six beautiful green leather volumes; Schiller's plays in two; nine volumes of Shakespeare's plays in the Schlegel-Tieck translation; and four volumes, in English, called *Trout Fishing*. Max took one of the fishing books to the table and sat down again. There was a fine, detailed painting of a trout as the frontispiece to the book, with the Latin name of the fish in copperplate underneath. He shut it—what was he doing?—and resumed his study of this unfamiliar room.

Against the wall opposite the map and the books, to his left, was a heavy oak cupboard with four doors. Above it, high on the wall, were an elk's head and the antlered skulls of two stags; beneath them, all in their places on a cast-iron rack, were two shotguns, a rifle, and a heavy pistol. All in their places. How had his father gone without a gun to deal with a battle? Max remembered sharply what lay on the sofa next door.

He sat a moment longer with his head in his hands, then got up and left his father's room, closing the door behind him. It seemed dark in the library. He went to the sofa and removed with some difficulty, because it was stuck, the white handkerchief covering his father's face. He replaced it quickly. He ran outside through the still-open front door and was sick at the bottom of the steps. Then he went to find Emilia.

She was sitting quietly in her old easy chair by the kitchen stove. She held out her arms to him and hugged him close.

"Mother mustn't see him. It's terrible. His face is—"

"It's all right, Max. It's all right." Emilia was now quite calm. "Maria will help me. She knows what to do. She always lays them out, people who've died. Tadeusz has gone to fetch her. She'll be here soon. Now go upstairs to your mother and stay with her. She didn't want me there. We won't let her see your father till we've tidied him up."

Heavily, as if he had been ill, Max went up the stairs. He knocked on his mother's bedroom door.

"Come in, Max." Her voice sounded almost normal.

He found her, to his relief, not so much grieving as desperately anxious to find out exactly what had happened in the village.

"I'm sure he died a hero's death. He would have died bravely, wouldn't he have, Max? Defending Waldau. He would have. In a way, it's what he always wanted. We must find out. Who can we send? There's no one left to send. You can't go down to the village—you're too young, and we don't know what's happening there. Oh, I wish Heinrich were here. How can we let him know his father is . . . Who can we ask to find Heinrich?"

She wasn't expecting him to answer. And for the next hour, while she kept talking and crying, crying and talking, she said nothing about seeing the body. While she was talking, Max heard sounds of voices in the hall, then several people coming slowly and awkwardly upstairs, then his father's dressing room door shutting, then a long silence.

At last, his mother said:

"I'm so tired. I think I'll lie down for a little while. Max, would you go and see if Emilia could make me a cup of tea? We need to think about what we should do next."

Emilia wasn't in the kitchen. He made his mother tea and put everything on the tray: the little teapot with roses, the cup and saucer, the small milk jug. He took the tray upstairs. It was surprisingly difficult to keep it steady. His mother was asleep, so he put the tray on the dressing table, beside a framed photograph of his father in hussar uniform with a sword, and another of Freddy looking very young in the same uniform.

Silence in the house. Back downstairs. No one was in the hall, the kitchen, the dining room, the salon. The library door was closed. He paused, braced himself, then opened it. The library was empty and exactly as usual, the sofa empty and tidy, as if no corpse with half a face had ever lain on it. He shut the door. As he did so, he thought he heard the distant rattle of hooves and wheels. Through the still-open front door, he saw the pastor's pony and trap briskly trotting up the drive.

"Max, my poor boy. I hear there's been an accident. I'm so very sorry. Has everything been attended to? Where is your father now? How has your poor mother taken it?"

"She's asleep now. My father . . . I'm not sure. Upstairs in his room, I think."

Max took the pastor up to the count's dressing room. The door was now open. The curtains were drawn, so that the room was dark except for the soft light of four candles, in the silver candlesticks from the dining room placed on chairs at the four corners of the bed. The count's body was lying on the bed, his head turned to one side on the pillow so that the shot half of his face was scarcely noticeable in the darkness. His hands were outside the covers, folded on his chest with a rosary twined in them. At the end of the bed, Emilia and old Maria were kneeling side by side, each with a rosary in her fingers.

Max was so impressed with what the two women had achieved that he almost knelt himself. Then he heard a sharp, disapproving intake of breath from the pastor standing behind him in the doorway.

"What is this? The count would not wish . . . By no means. These superstitions are not appropriate. Not at all."

His voice was harsh, quiet but not a whisper, and therefore seemed very loud. The two women got awkwardly to their feet. Maria bobbed a little old-fashioned curtsy. The pastor took Max by the shoulders and set him aside. He went to the window and drew the curtains swiftly back. Light, like a noise, dispelled the mysteriousness of the room, and the broken half of the count's face became clearly visible. The pastor blew out the candles. Then he carefully untwined the rosary from the dead fingers and held it out to Emilia. She took it and, now in silent tears, left the room. Old Maria knelt again, closed her eyes, passed her rosary one bead forward and moved her lips in prayer.

"That's better", the pastor said, surveying his alterations to the room. He stood in silence for a moment.

"What a terrible wound. What a shock for your poor mother."

"She hasn't . . . she hasn't seen him yet."

"Oh, I understand."

The pastor went back to the window and half-closed the curtains.

"Now take me to her. I should say a few words. Perhaps you would wake her?"

Max knocked at his mother's door. When there was no sound from inside the room, he gently opened the door. She was not asleep. She was sitting at her dressing table, looking vacantly at her face in the glass, the teacup in her hand.

"Mother, the pastor has come."

"Oh." Her voice was distant, dazed. She put the cup down on the saucer. "Of course. Come in. How kind of you. Yes."

She got up and came towards the door, holding out her hand, which the pastor bent to kiss. Max closed the door and went downstairs to look for Emilia.

The next morning, while men nailed the lid onto the count's coffin— Max never knew whether or not his mother had visited his father among the candles, relit after the pastor had gone—Dr Mendel set off to walk to the village. Several hours later, he returned, having talked to his friend the Waldau doctor and to enough other people among the shocked families to have put together a more-or-less coherent account of what had happened.

There were too many people in Waldau looking for too little work. Returned soldiers, poor Germans who had left their homes in the east because they didn't want to live in the new Poland, and Polish peasants from across the new border who could find no work at home were competing with each other and with the few able-bodied labourers left in the area for summer jobs, for haymaking and fruit picking and next month's harvest, on the local farms. There was neither enough work nor enough food to go round. The day before, in the heat, a group of discharged soldiers, hungry and in rags, had turned up at a Polish farmer's barn outside the village, where a dozen Poles, equally hungry and equally in rags, had spent the night drinking the last of the vodka they had brought with them, singing boisterously and then sleeping. A fight developed in no time, the barn was set alight, and soon most of the men in the village were brawling in the streets, some with the vagabond Poles, some with the discharged soldiers. There were even fights between German and Polish neighbours who had lived side by side all their lives. Someone had gone for the police in the nearest town, but, instead of police, twenty Freikorps soldiers, still in uniform, still with guns, had ridden into Waldau, shooting to restore order. The count, on foot in the melee of people shouting and hitting each other in the main street, had been killed by a Freikorps shot. News of his death, spreading in seconds, stopped all the fighting in the village, and the people, calming down quickly, were horrified to find that, besides the count, three Poles and two Germans had been killed and that five Poles and three Germans, one a woman, had been wounded. The Freikorps detachment, commanded by a boy who, according to Dr Mendel's informants, looked no more than eighteen, had galloped out of the village, and no one knew where they had gone. The doctor expected one of the wounded Poles and the German woman also to die.

"So Carl Friedrich's death was an accident, a meaningless accident. Why did he go to Waldau? *Why?* There was no need for him to go, and he wasn't even any use! He would have so hated to die for nothing in a brawl in the village street. Oh, I can't bear it for him that his death was so stupid—not a hero's death, not a death in a proper battle. Just a muddle because people are so hungry and so poor ..."

"The count was trying to help them, dear lady," Dr Mendel said, "trying to calm things down so that people wouldn't be hurt. It was very brave, not stupid at all, and his death may have saved a number of lives."

"Oh Dr Mendel, you are so good. You always see the best in everything. But Carl Friedrich would have thought it stupid, unnecessary, all because of the treaty and the new frontier. And who are these Freikorps soldiers? So young and not under anyone's control— imagine shooting at wretched peasants who have nothing—no homes, no food, no work, no country, half of them! What does "Freikorps" mean?"

"They are soldiers of the German army who have been demobilized but who have volunteered to stay under arms. They are permitted, at present, to keep control all through the border regions, because the government is afraid of serious riots."

"Wasn't this a serious riot? And all they did was shoot people. It's a disgrace! What would Carl Friedrich say? Oh! Oh, what shall I do without him?"

She went out, slamming the door. Max and Dr Mendel were left alone in the salon.

"Mobilized meant being set going. So demobilized means being stopped. Is that right? And these Freikorps soldiers don't want to stop because the clockwork hasn't run down yet."

"That's right, Max. It would be very much better if all the soldiers who fought in the war handed in their guns and went home, but I'm afraid that will not happen."

"Do you think Heinrich is part of a Freikorps?"

"Very possibly."

"How can we tell him about my father's death?"

"With your mother's permission, I have written to the Ministry of War in Berlin. They will be able to let him know, I'm sure. No doubt he will come home as soon as he can."

For the funeral, on the following morning, they brought back the cart, empty now of hay, and carefully loaded the coffin onto it. This was difficult to do smoothly. Max saw the six men—one was Tadeusz, but he didn't know the others—sweating in the hot sun as they tried to keep the coffin level, and was embarrassed rather than sad. A car had materialised from somewhere to take his mother and him, and his grandfather, who had arrived that morning from Breslau, at walking pace down the drive behind the cart. The bearers, Emilia, and Dr Mendel were joined by others as the procession reached the village. Most of the small crowd, but not Dr Mendel or Emilia or Tadeusz or several others who waited outside, followed Max and his mother into the church.

There were hymns and prayers, and the pastor spoke at length about the count's faithful stewardship of his estate, his patriotic sacrifice of his eldest son for the fatherland, his loyalty to the best traditions of Prussia, and his generosity to the church and the Waldau school. Max soon gave up trying to match this peaceful description to the angry man he knew, and so he looked, as he had done every Sunday of his conscious life, at the tablets on the walls recording the dates of birth and death of former counts, with those of their wives and children in smaller lettering under the capitals for the heads of the family. The style of the tablets altered according to the period. The earlier ones, from the eighteenth century, aimed for elegant, factual dignity, their lettering plain and Roman like the lettering of the Latin inscriptions photographed in Max's *History of the Caesars*. The nineteenth-century tablets were in old-fashioned German script, two of them with lines from Goethe. The east window, over the plain stone communion table with its plain silver-gilt cross, had the Hofmannswaldau coat of arms in red and gold stained glass.

He looked at the coffin, draped in the black, white, and red flag of Prussia with its imperial eagle. On the flag was a bunch of white roses. Where was his father? Not there, for certain. Not here among the stone memorials and the coats of arms. Where was he, then? For he was not nowhere either. What did that mean? Max gave up.

The last hymn was sung: "A safe stronghold our God is still / A trusty shield and weapon ..." This hymn was the pastor's favourite, and it was sung in this church nearly every Sunday. Is our God a safe stronghold? *Was* he a safe stronghold? Max wondered as he looked sideways at his mother but could not, through her black veil, tell whether or not she was crying. As the bearers came up the aisle to shoulder the coffin again, the organ played "Now Thank We All Our God" and continued to play it, softly and slowly, as the pastor, then Max and his mother and grandfather, and then everyone else followed the coffin outside and down a long path to where a fresh, tidy grave had been dug. As the coffin was lowered, Max felt nothing except anxiety for his mother, that the coffin might jolt against the sides of the grave. Once it was lowered, his mother, and then Max, copying her, and followed by his grandfather and other people, took a handful of soil from beside the grave and threw it down onto the coffin. Max thought he would never forget the noise each handful made.

After lunch, the guests all left at the same time. The pastor in his trap took Grandpapa, who wanted to catch the afternoon train back to Breslau. Three elderly couples and a widow from neighbouring estates were packed, with lap robes, into two cars.

Max sat in the salon with his mother. The effort of the day over and her veil lifted, she looked pale and tired but calm. She smiled at him.

73

"Thank you, Max. Your father would be proud of you." She looked down at her hands, folded in her lap. "I'm sorry Grandpapa wouldn't stay. I thought perhaps now . . . But he has never found it easy here. It was kind of him to come today."

"Mother?"

"What is it?"

"Emilia says there will be a Requiem Mass in the other church for Father tomorrow. Like there was for Freddy. May I go with her?"

"Certainly not. What would your father think?"

"But I went with her for Freddy. We lit a candle for his soul."

"There you are. Your father would have been horrified. I expect he didn't know you went. I don't think I did either. You were only a little boy then—what were you? Eight or nine. That doesn't count. It wasn't your fault."

"My *fault*? But surely it isn't bad to go to Mass. It's beautiful. I remember. A lot of candles and the priest in black and gold bowing to God and walking round and round the altar with his swinging smoke, a peculiar sweet smell, not like anything else."

"Max! Listen to me. Of course it isn't bad to go to Mass. For the Poles, it's good, very good, for Emilia and Tadeusz and all the others. But it's not German, not Prussian. Compared to our services, like the one we had this morning, a Mass is, well, primitive and superstitious, a kind of magic ritual. Prussians, your father would say, long ago grew out of such things. The Catholic Church is all very well for peasants; they are like children who need to be told what to think, what to do. But Prussians, particularly the Prussian nobility, are adults. They don't need such leading by the hand."

"Couldn't I still be counted as a child, just for tomorrow?"

"Come here, Max." She laughed as she hugged him.

"Yes, all right. You could. Even your father would think that a fair point. And Emilia would like it if you went with her. Yes, you go. Where would be the harm?"

She thought for a moment.

"When I was very young, Max, not much older than you are now, there was a professor in the university, a friend of Grandpapa's, who sometimes came to our house. I was very much impressed by him. He was a Catholic priest as well as a professor—I suppose he was a professor of theology—and he was good and kind and very, very clever. Quick-witted, like Grandpapa, and funny. He was a musician too and liked to hear me play. He seemed to me to know everything, and he made Grandpapa laugh as no one else did. And, *mirabile dictu*, as Grandpapa would say, he was a Prussian, not a Bavarian or an Austrian as you might have expected. Your father never met him. He died soon after your father and I were married. I have sometimes been sorry I never asked him about his faith ... But probably it was just as well that I didn't have the chance."

"Why?"

"Well, it might have made complications. Marriage, as you will discover one day, Max, has enough complications of its own. There are things now that I so much wish I had said to your father, before it was too late. But now ..."

For the first time, she looked simply sad as she broke off, and Max went to her and hugged her again.

"Now run along and find Dr Mendel. Some practice would do you both good, and he's been so thoughtful. Don't worry about me. I shall have a little rest now. Perhaps after tea we might try a piece neither of us has played before. It's been a long time since I tested my sight-reading on something really difficult."

The Requiem Mass the next morning was, to begin with, only confusing. The two things Max remembered as so beautiful, the priest's robes and the incense, now struck him as silly. He had seen the priest several times in his everyday black clothes in Waldau: why did he dress up so grandly in church when he was only an ordinary middle-aged Pole? And why fill the church with so much smoke that it almost made you cough? The magic he remembered had vanished: it was like moving away from his reflections in the river.

And another thing: he'd expected that, now that he knew Latin, he would be able to understand properly what the priest was saying. But the priest's Latin sounded quite different from Dr Mendel's. Some of the time, the priest muttered or bent his head and moved his lips so that he couldn't be heard at all, and mostly his back was turned to the people so that his face couldn't be seen. There wasn't a prayer book to help Max follow what was going on, nor could he ask Emilia, kneeling beside him, to explain anything; every time he glanced at her, her head was bowed and her eyes were shut.

Not that anyone in the church seemed to be following the service very attentively. The church was full—there were a number of men and boys standing at the back—but most of the people seemed to be concentrating on their own prayers, and there was also a good deal of whispering and hushing of small children. Max tried to think about his father, but neither his father alive, with his blue eyes and his restlessness and his disappointed anger, nor his father dead on the dressing room bed seemed to have anything to do with what was happening in the church.

He gave up the effort and watched the Mass more carefully.

A boy a year or two younger than he, in a long black robe with a white overgarment, was kneeling near the priest. The boy rang a little bell three times. This seemed to draw people's attention briefly. A little later, one ring of the boy's bell stilled the congregation a bit more. Soon afterwards, the boy rang his bell again. The priest was standing at the altar. He held up first a flat, white circle—was it bread?—and then a silver cup, no doubt of wine, as he did so saying very quietly obviously solemn words, and then kneeling on one knee, down and then up, several times. The boy rang the little bell three times for the bread and three times for the wine, and as he did this, the whole church was absolutely quiet. Max caught the first words for the bread. "Hoc est enim corpus meum." "For this is my body": of course; this was Jesus speaking at the Last Supper. The words for the wine, more complicated, he mostly missed, but he heard the first few: "Hoc est enim calix sanguinis mei." "For this is the *calix*"—chalice, cup?—"of my blood." As the priest held up the cup, Max properly noticed for the first time the long picture made of carved wooden figures in a heavy gold frame on the wall above the altar. There were people gathered, all looking upwards, as most of the people in the church were at that moment looking upwards at the cup. The carved figures were looking up at Jesus, who was hanging dead on the cross high above them, exactly in the centre of the whole carving, exactly above the priest's hands holding up the cup. "My blood." Max thought of his father's bloody face, with a white cheekbone splintered in the blood, and felt sick again. He bent his head and prayed to forget the blood and the bone that wouldn't leave the shadows of his mind. He shook his head, as if he could shake them away. When he looked up, the priest was bowing before the altar and striking his chest three times with his fist as he said some more words Max understood.

"Dona eis requiem", he said three times. "Give them rest." "Dona eis requiem sempiternam." "Give them everlasting rest." That was what this Mass, after all, was for. For his father, and all the dead.

Max looked round the part of the church that he could see without turning his head. Candles everywhere. Big candles on the altar. Little candles in groups under statues and paintings. A statue of Mary with a crown and a blue dress, carrying the baby Jesus. A statue of a thin-faced man in a brown robe with a rope, painted paler than the robe, round his waist. A painting of a Roman soldier, without a helmet, but with a sword and a breastplate, and bare legs under his tunic. A painting of an old man with a beard, a book in his hands, and a lion at his feet. Max had no idea who they were, except for Mary, but people had lit candles, on rickety iron stands, in front of each of them. He remembered the Mass for Freddy all those years ago. "You must light a candle for his soul." Were each of these candles lit for someone's soul? He remembered Freddy in his polished boots, his polished spurs, his brilliant white breeches, climbing into the train as he set off for the war. Perhaps the Roman soldier would be looking after Freddy's soul, and the soul of his father too, who had thought the war so glorious then. Perhaps Freddy and his father were now together somewhere, talking and laughing as they used to. And perhaps his gentle grandmother—should he ask the thin-faced man in brown, with his gentle expression, to look after her soul?

At the end of the Mass they all stood up, and Max expected the priest to go, but instead he moved to the left side of the altar, where he had read a long piece of Latin earlier in the Mass. Now he started reading again. "In principio erat Verbum." Max didn't recognize the passage and quickly gave up trying to understand it. When everyone suddenly knelt on one knee and stood up again as the priest was reading, he did the same, a little late. At last the Mass really was finished. The priest had gone, following the boy through a side door, and the people were leaving the church, some talking quite loudly. When a few of them noticed Max with Emilia, they fell silent, and one or two gave him a respectful nod.

"Emilia", Max whispered. "Can we light a candle for Father, and one for Freddy too, and one for Grandmama?"

"Of course we can. And you can say a prayer for each of them."

Emilia produced a few coppers, and Max lit two candles at the foot of the soldier, and one before the brown-robed saint. Max knelt for a moment in front of his candles. "Please take care of Father and Freddy. Please take care of Grandmama."

Walking home with Emilia, he wished he had known enough to pray in a more grown-up way. But he was pleased at least to have lit the candles.

"Well, Max", said his mother later. "How was the Mass?"

"I didn't understand it very well."

"Of course not. You're a Protestant boy. But it won't have hurt you to be there, just this once. When Heinrich comes home, don't tell him you went to the Catholic church. He wouldn't like it. And he's the head of the family now."

Max stared at his mother as the future he had become accustomed to suddenly dissolved and reassembled itself.

"Mother?"

"What is it, darling? How pale you look. Are you feeling all right?"

"I'm feeling ... I don't know. Not ill at all. Mother, that doesn't mean I have to do everything Heinrich says, does it?"

"No, no, of course not. It's just that Heinrich will be responsible, when he comes back, for Waldau and, I suppose, for you and me as well. But there's no way of telling what he'll want, or what he'll think about anything. We haven't seen him properly for so long. He hardly knows you now, so of course it will be for me rather than for him to make decisions about you."

There was a long, laden silence between them, which Max remembered for many years. He was sitting on the Turkish carpet in front of the fireplace, empty for summer, in the salon. He traced a dark blue pattern, something like a formalised tree, against a red and black larger pattern, over and over with his finger. At last he said:

"So I needn't go to Lichterfelde any more?"

"No, I don't see that you need to. I know how much your father wanted you to, but ... I think he wanted you to be a soldier in a different world. Everything is changing—the border, what will become of Germany, the new countries—it's difficult to imagine a soldier's life in ten years' time, or even five ... Those were Prussian soldiers in Waldau on Thursday, and the boy in charge no doubt went to Lichterfelde, and they ...

"And then Heinrich, when he does come home, is going to have problems enough. It is important that you should be able to stand on your own feet, to live your life independently of the estate. Things are not as they used to be when your father was a boy. After all, you are

the clever one. I'm sure you will pass the Gymnasium examination—
you must ask Dr Mendel about that—and then there is nothing that
has to be paid. What you need now is to go to Breslau and work hard
at your lessons with boys of your own age. Your grandfather will keep
an eye on you, and you will keep him company in the evenings now
that he's by himself."

"And you, Mother?"

"I must stay here to look after things for Heinrich. Herr von Zie-
bitz, who was here yesterday, will help me; he was a friend of your
father's, and I know he has many of the same difficulties."

Max didn't know what "same difficulties" meant nor how this red-
faced old man with his tremendous white moustache could help his
mother. But he understood a little more when he read a short report
in the next day's local paper, left by Emilia on her chair in the kitchen:

"The funeral took place on Saturday of Major Count von Hofmannswaldau, killed by a stray bullet during the disturbance in Waldau
on Thursday. We learn that the Freikorps detachment that suppressed
the riot has been commended by the high command in Berlin. Armed
risings of the Polish population in the border areas are officially regarded
as acts of insurrection, and German citizens, for their own safety, are
recommended by the authorities not to interfere in the restoration of
order when such acts take place.

"The count's eldest son died for the fatherland in the battle of Tannenberg in 1914. The Schloss Waldau estate, which is rumoured to be
burdened with very considerable debt, passes to the late count's second son, Captain Count Heinrich von Hofmannswaldau, who is at
present on active service in Poland."

He took the paper upstairs to Dr Mendel.

"It's not right, is it, what they say about my father's death? They're
saying it was his fault, that he shouldn't have interfered. That's not
true."

Dr Mendel read the account and then laid down the paper on the
schoolroom table.

"It's what they need to say at present. They need the Freikorps to
be heroes. Your mother, on the other hand, needs to think your father
is a hero. It does not suit anyone for your father's death to have been
an accident. And in a way, it was not. Your father's sense of responsibility and his courage took him down there on Thursday. So your
mother is closer to the truth than the government is. Even an

accident is a complicated thing. And the truth—well, the whole truth is not for us to know."

"Is it for God, then?"

"If it is anywhere, it is with God."

"But yesterday, at the Mass with Emilia ..."

"Yes?"

"I don't know. I didn't understand it."

"I wish you hadn't gone to the Catholic church, Max. But there, you are a boy who is capable of thinking for himself. And now you will be able to go to the Gymnasium."

"So you know that?"

"I know. Your mother and I discussed it last night."

"Oh. I see. I thought ..."

"I'm sorry, Max. Remember that you are not yet grown up. And something else. Whatever you will learn, from better teachers than I will ever be, keep thinking. Don't let anyone else make up your mind for you. About anything. Now it is practice time. Go upstairs and do some work on the last movement of the Bach."

Max went up the wooden stairs to his attic. He looked out of the open window at the hot, still evening, the long shadows of the trees, the river gleaming here and there between the willows. Poor Waldau, burdened with very considerable debt. What did that mean for Heinrich, for their mother? For himself, it meant that he was to study properly, in a school, and to work properly, to earn a living like his grandfather. That was good. And—the word came back to him— there might be a sweetheart too, a girl he hadn't met, whose name he didn't know, but who already was somewhere, somewhere in Breslau perhaps, thinking at this moment of the boy who would one day be her sweetheart. Would he love her instead of Waldau?

He turned away from the window. Before he picked up his violin, he knelt down and bent his head almost to the dusty floorboards, to look, on their level, through the ranks of the faithful lead soldiers waiting for the battle of Leipzig to begin.

He stood up. There was a long wooden box in a corner. It had croquet mallets and hoops inside. No balls. He stood the mallets and hoops against the wall. They would come to no harm. Then, one by one and very carefully because they broke easily, he laid all the soldiers in the box, for some boy, one day, to find.

Chapter 3

The cleverest boy in Max's class was a Pole. Six months older than Max, Adam Zapolski had arrived in Breslau a few weeks after the beginning of the school year in the autumn of 1921. He was even cleverer than Hans Mackelroth, Max's rival for the last two years at the top of their class.

Mackelroth was an earnest, silent boy, tall, thin, and shortsighted. He worked with imperturbable concentration, never said a word in lessons, and had very small, very neat handwriting, covering every page to precisely sustained margins so that his exercise books looked almost as if they were in print. He was better than Max at mathematics and the sciences, slower but more methodical, accurate, and almost always correct in the answers he had patiently arrived at. Dr Strauss, who this year taught their class mathematics and physics, regarded Mackelroth as the best pupil he had come across since before the war. Mackelroth's father, also tall, thin, and shortsighted but surprisingly old—Max had seen him once, talking to Dr Strauss after school—was a district judge in Breslau, and Mackelroth was to be a lawyer like his father. Mackelroth had listened politely when Dr Strauss told him that he owed it to Breslau, "second only to Berlin, my boy, as a city of scientific distinction", to study physics and mathematics at the university. Or perhaps, if he found it more interesting (the tone of voice implying that no sane person could), chemistry. "You have the makings of an excellent scientist, Mackelroth. Germany itself may require your gifts in the future. And we need more good Germans among our professors."

"My father wishes me to study law."

Zapolski was a lithe, good-looking boy, not as tall as Mackelroth, with pale skin, high cheekbones, black hair, and amused blue eyes. His brilliance in mathematics astonished the rest of the class but did not impress Dr Strauss.

"You jump to conclusions, Zapolski. They are often correct, I grant you, but I'm sure I'm not mistaken in supposing that, on most occasions, you have no notion of how you have reached them."

"Intuition, sir."

"Jumping to conclusions, Zapolski. Scientists are defined by their careful use of rational, indeed of logical, method. In mathematics, certainly in schoolboy mathematics—and, Zapolski, I feel you need to be reminded from time to time that you are still no more than a schoolboy—the workings are as important as the answer, as I have reminded you more than once."

"Newton jumped. Einstein jumps."

"That may be. You are not Newton or Einstein. You have not yet taken your final school examinations and will for the time being do as you are told."

"Sir."

The laughing eyes established for the class the victor in this exchange.

"Who is Einstein?" Max asked Zapolski later. They were walking side by side along the street after school, Max on the sidewalk edge pushing his bicycle on the road with one hand on the centre of the handlebars.

"He's a great physicist. He works in Berlin. He's upset Newton's applecart so the apples are all rolling about on the ground."

"What do you mean?"

"The theory of relativity, it's called. Brand-new. Revolutionary stuff. Time and space and matter are all different now. So is light. Mixed up together so you can't tell which is which. I don't suppose old Strauss has come across it. When he does, knowing him, he'll probably call it a Jewish fraud. Don't worry." He laughed. "I don't understand it myself. But it's the most exciting idea for centuries according to a friend of my mother's. A young professor in Vienna."

They walked for a bit in silence. Then Max ventured to ask a question of a kind neither of them had so far approached.

"Why did you leave Vienna?"

"Oh, there were reasons. Various reasons. I'm a count, you know, like you, but unlike you, a count of nowhere and nothing, so I've chucked the title. We had an estate—a small town, villages, farms—my family owned it for centuries. In East Galicia. Very poor, you know, the people. Actually, you probably don't know. There's nothing like it in Germany, certainly not in Prussia. The peasants are Ruthenes. Simple people, and very poor. Drunk, but not quite as drunk as Russians. Superstitious. It's more magic than it's Christian, their religion. Which days are lucky, which are the devil's days, so unlucky you shouldn't move from the stove. An icon corner in every hut, a Russian stove and an icon corner and precious little else beyond a chair or two, a lot of bedding, and a huge cooking pot. They just about understand simple Polish, but not German, unless they have a son to spare who joins the army. Then he has to, had to, I should say, learn German to understand orders. And a lot of Jews, of course. You'd have better luck with German there, because of Yiddish. Most of them no better off than the peasants, though some do well enough. Innkeepers, shopkeepers, traders in what the peasants grow. The Jews write things down for the peasants. Letters. Wills. IOUs. Keep track of their debts. One reason the peasants hate them: they depend on them. Some of the Jews had left before the war—they scraped together a bit of money and made it to Germany, or even to America. Hundreds were murdered at the beginning of the war, when the Russians invaded."

"What do the peasants grow?"

"Potatoes, sugar beets, rye. The farming's poor because the land is poor. Turn your back on it for five minutes, and it's back to swamp and forest. Anyway, it's all gone now. I don't suppose I'll ever see it again."

"Why not? How do you mean, gone?"

"Just gone. It's in another country now, for one thing."

"Isn't it in Poland? You're Polish—I would have thought you'd be pleased. Waldau, my home, is still in Germany, barely, and I'm pleased. The plebiscite—for Upper Silesia, you know—was a shambles. Maybe you heard about it? A lot of Poles voted to stay in Germany, but they said we had put unfair pressure on them. So we lost the mines and the steelworks. But don't most Poles want Poland to be a country again?"

Zapolski stopped in the street and looked at Max.

"I'm surprised you know that. The Silesians one comes across don't seem to realize that Poland was ever a country. You're right in a way, of course. But the government in Warsaw has very little idea of who a Galician peasant is, and less of what a Galician count might be. And they don't care. Or, to be fair, they haven't had an opportunity yet to get round to caring. They think all Poles must be better off now that the empires have gone, and since most of them lived in Russia, you

83

can see their point. But where I come from, Habsburg Poland—well, case not yet proved.

"My cousin went home in the spring to see. My mother wouldn't let me go. She said I was too young and all she had left and all that. Not true, by the way. By no means true. So my cousin went, and came back. There's nothing left. A few walls instead of a house. Burnt out. Looted. Everything gone—books, pictures, music, the piano. The lot. Wine. My father had a cellar full of wine. Probably things were stolen first, before the fire. The wine would have been, for sure. We don't know who set fire to the house. The peasants told my cousin the Red Army, but it could just as well have been the peasants. They were starving in the war. It was winter when the house burnt down. Deep snow. So probably they began by breaking up the furniture for firewood."

"What will happen to the estate?"

"Who knows? In theory, it's still ours. But in practice—I don't know. My mother won't go back there; she's always hated it. And now, well, there's been a lot of fighting since the war, Bolsheviks against Poles, Ukrainians—that's what the Ruthenes are calling themselves these days—against Bolsheviks, Poles against Ukrainians. Something called the republic of western Ukraine with Lemberg as its capital city lasted no time at all. Soldiers fighting soldiers, mobs fighting mobs—there are pogroms too—any or all of them attacking the Jews. Horrible. And then Bolshevik agitators tell the wretched peasants that now they can be free. Freer than when they just got on with their lives? Freer now that soldiers on the loose, Red, White, Polish, Ukrainian—what's the difference when they're stealing your hens and raping your daughters?—are frightening them to death? I don't think so.

"They loved the Emperor, you know, old Franz Josef. When I was small, I had him all mixed up with God in my mind because my nanny used to talk about him in the same way. "If you're good, the Emperor will look after you." Well, I wasn't and he didn't, so there you are. Nearly all the peasants had a picture of him, hanging on a nail on the wall, a postcard in a frame, almost as holy as the icons. I expect they still have. In his white uniform. I think they quite liked us too. Not my mother, perhaps. To a Ruthene peasant a Viennese German lady is more or less from the moon. But they liked my father. He made them laugh, and he listened to them. He helped them when he could. He paid for a nurse to help the doctor in our town. He paid for the odd bright boy to go to school in Lemberg. They liked me because I look like my father and my grandmother. They really loved my grandmother because she was always there. When their children were ill, she appeared in her pony trap with custards and plum jam and beef tea. And teddy bears. She made the teddy bears herself, out of plush, with boot buttons for eyes and long wool stitches for noses. I used to help her stuff them."

"Did she take jam and teddy bears to the Jewish children as well?"

"Of course. Why not? They're poor too. My father paid the wages of the heder teacher in the town. That's the school for Jewish children. It's all quite different from the west. There aren't rich Jews in Galicia to take care of the poor Jews. Or not. Before the war, there was a sort of town council that met every so often to look after the drains and write a letter to the Imperial Railways asking if a train could stop with the post and the newspapers more than twice a week. It never made any difference. Twice a week was all we ever got. This town council consisted of the mayor, who was a Ruthene ironmonger who couldn't read and write; my father; the rabbi; and both priests. Can you imagine such a thing in the west?"

"Both priests?"

"The Polish priest and the Ruthene priest. One Roman Catholic, one Greek Catholic, though actually the Ruthenes are neither Greek nor Catholic—they're Russian Orthodox who obey the Pope, though most of them have never heard of him."

They waited at a crossroads for a tram and several loaded carts pulled by slow horses to go by. Then an impatient car overtook all of them. They crossed.

"Do you think of Silesia as the west?"

"To me it's the west. It depends on where you start from, like left and right."

They walked in silence for a few minutes. Max finally couldn't resist a hesitant question.

"Your grandmother and your father—are they . . . ?"

"My grandmother died before the war. It was probably best for her that she did. My parents were in Vienna. I was at school. They didn't tell me she was ill. I never got a chance to say good-bye."

More silence. Max didn't look at Zapolski.

For several weeks, they had walked this way after school, through the wide streets and big squares near the Gymnasium, towards Cathedral

Island, where Zapolski lodged in an ancient house with, according to him, an ancient widow, a friend of his grandmother. After shaking hands with Zapolski at his door, Max would bicycle back to his grandfather's flat, not far from the university, on the other side of the city's old moat and across a branch of the river, retracing some of the streets they had walked. Until today, they had talked only about the school day, and not even much about that.

"My father was killed in the first big battle of the war."

"At Tannenberg? My——"

"Certainly not. Tannenberg was a Prussian battle. The Prussians won, of course. Good for them. No. My father's battle was at a place called Krasnoe-Busk. It's two places, actually. It's not far from our estate—fifty or sixty miles. You won't have heard of it. The Russians won. My father was a reserve colonel in a cavalry regiment, in the imperial army. The war was a complete muddle at the beginning. No one had any idea of how big the Russian army was. It was still August, and both sides were trying to avoid riding through standing crops. Some of the peasant soldiers, especially the Russians, were trying to avoid killing anyone because killing people is a sin. Chaos and cavalry charges. Lances. Horrible weapons. And the parade-ground saddles were useless in battle. Too light. Slipped round too easily."

They crossed another road.

"I was supposed to go to cavalry school the year after the war ended", Max said.

"Oh, so was I. But that's all finished, thank the Lord. Too silly for words, all that dressing up and prancing about in riding schools. Look where it got us. That was the nineteenth century's way of doing things. Tanks and aeroplanes finished off the nineteenth century, and a good thing too. Now they say they've given us a new world, a world without armies. Tanks and aeroplanes strictly rationed. Hardly any soldiers."

"They?"

"The Americans. The English. The French. The people who drew lines round the new countries and said, 'That's the end of empires.' Instead we'll have little countries, little republics—Poland, Czechoslovakia, Hungary. Old countries reinvented, and completely invented new countries. Austria, my mother's country, is the most ridiculous of the lot. It never was a country. It was always really Vienna and some mountains, a big grand city ruling an empire, or the Habsburgs' private estate. Now it's a big wretched city which would like to be grand but has no reason to exist any more. Millions of people. No work. The rich hysterically enjoying themselves because the war is over. The poor looking for scraps of food in the rubbish outside the restaurants. And far too many priests.

"We'll see how these little countries get on between Russia and Germany. I know Poland, my country, isn't small, but it might as well be, poor and weak as it is. As if Russia and Germany, having lost their Emperors, have lost the idea of bullying everyone else. Threatening them, invading them, taking them over. Poland was invaded by the Bolsheviks last year. We defeated the Red Army outside Warsaw. But just barely, with a great deal of luck. What happens to Poland if Russia attacks it again? Or if Germany attacks again, one of these days? But they tell us there can't ever be another war. Europe has learnt its lesson at last. Like it did after the Thirty Years' War. Like it did after Napoleon. For a bit. Universal peace is the order of the day, the brotherhood of man, all of us in our nice tidy new nations on excellent terms with everyone else in theirs. I don't think that's likely. Do you? Not without some kind of system to hold it all together. Even something not too different from dear old Franz Josef in his white uniform."

"You wouldn't want the Emperors back?"

"Well, there were Emperors and there were Emperors. The cleverest people in Vienna think it would have been better to keep a Habsburg Emperor as a kind of figurehead for a federation of all the nationalities. All the little countries on an equal basis. Apparently, the last emperor, Karl—you've probably never heard of him; he lasted about five minutes—had a plan on those lines before the end of the war, and it was wrecked by the Germans in Vienna, who preferred to be tied to Berlin. Stupid, stupid. As usual."

"But there'd still have to be armies, wouldn't there? Poland couldn't have defeated the Bolsheviks unless it had an army."

"That's true. But soldiers have to do what they're told, or they're an absolute menace. German soldiers are supposed to be the best disciplined, and look at what's going on here! The government's ordered the Freikorps off the streets. Disbanded them. And what's happened? The very same thugs, soldiers with not enough to do when some government they don't believe in tells them they're not soldiers any more, are still roaming about looking for trouble, making trouble if they can't find any, only now they're in different clothes and calling themselves Stormtroopers."

"Isn't all that a good reason for having a proper army?"

"Of course . . . if the proper army were able to control the thugs. You're right. There have to be real soldiers, to do what they're told by governments, to back up the police if people try to start violent revolutions, like they did here when the workers rioted and let the big Communists out of prison. I wish I'd seen that. Rosa Luxemburg—what a woman."

"You don't admire the Bolsheviks, do you?"

"In some ways, I do. They've made things happen—the will to power, you know. One can't help admiring effectiveness. But no, I don't admire Marx. So dull, the world would be, if he were right. If revolution's inevitable, all we have to do is sit about and wait for it to happen. But of course it isn't inevitable. Nothing is. Everything depends on what people actually choose to do. What do you think you'll choose to do, now you're not going to be a soldier?"

"I don't know. Perhaps . . ."

"You don't need brains to be a soldier. Soldiers are better, actually—more reliable—if they're not clever enough to question what governments decide. You're too intelligent to be a soldier, and so am I."

"I'm not sure. Wouldn't it have been better if the generals had questioned the governments in 1914? Don't governments sometimes make seriously bad decisions?"

"Of course they do. But the answer to that is to be in the government, now that we have these republics—even here there's a republic—trying to make sure government decisions are good ones, not to be a general trying to make the government see sense when his only weapon is a mutiny."

"Would you like to be in the government? In Vienna? In Warsaw? What do you think you will do, yourself?"

"Ah, well. That depends."

"On what? On your mother?"

"Certainly not. My mother is not a truthful person. She says one thing and means another and does a third, and has no idea that that's what she's doing. She has never read a real book in her life, though she thinks she has. She has a lot of money. How she still has, after the war, I can't imagine, but her father and now her brother are still rich. They have steel mills near Cracow. And now that the plebiscite's given your coal and steel to Poland, they'll probably be richer than ever. Also she sings. Rather well."

"Sings?"

"Yes. If she hadn't been spoilt by too much money, which made her lazy, she might have been an opera singer, even quite a good one. She has a big voice, and she has looks. She certainly has a sense of drama. But you'll see when you meet her. She's perhaps not quite Brünnhilde, but Sieglinde, say, once upon a time. She would see herself as Isolde, no doubt about that. Nowadays, Kundry would suit her perfectly. Do her good as well."

Max knew that these were characters in Wagner operas. He wasn't going to admit to Zapolski that he had never heard a Wagner opera. Zapolski went on talking. They were nearly at his house.

"So she just sings drawing room songs, the more dramatic the better. 'Erlkönig' and 'Der Zwerg', the big Brahms songs, the Wesendonck songs, Mahler of course ... Here we are. See you tomorrow, Hofmannswaldau. Ah! Tomorrow's Thursday. We'll see if we can't take a few shots at old Fischer."

"Good-bye, Zapolski. Thank you."

Max pedalled away very fast, furious with himself for that "thank you". He knew why he had said it. Not only because Zapolski had suddenly, after so long, told him something about himself, but also, and more, because he had said, "You'll see when you meet her."

"Damn. Damn. Damn." He swore to himself as he swerved through the carts and wagons on Blücher Square, following a large car with two solid figures in uniform on the back seat. Perhaps Zapolski, his back to the narrow street as he opened the carved door with his key, hadn't heard the thank you. But Max knew he had. Zapolski never missed anything. That was one of the things that made Zapolski so—what? He quickly abandoned looking for the right word because he didn't want to find it.

Dr Fischer taught the class Latin and Greek every day, ancient history twice a week—this history lesson often became, as had history lessons in the schoolroom at Waldau, more modern than ancient—and on Thursday mornings what he called "a little of this and that, some philosophy, perhaps some Shakespeare". Philosophy and Shakespeare, never mind "this and that", were not part of the official school curriculum on which the boys would be examined at the end of the following year, and the Thursday morning lessons were therefore resented by the more earnest and ambitious boys in the class, probably including

Mackelroth, who considered them a waste of time. German literature was taught by a very serious young schoolmaster whose reverence for Goethe was such that he buried wild and wonderful passages of *Faust* under mounds of laboriously shovelled commentary. French literature, which was also on the curriculum, was taught by an irascible Frenchman who refused to speak German in class in any circumstances: his lessons were resented for patriotic reasons.

Dr Fischer was always allotted the best students for their last two years in the Gymnasium and so was allowed by the school authorities his Thursday morning classes "to exercise, gentlemen, parts of your minds that you may one day need more urgently than you need your capacity to employ the iussive subjunctive correctly". He had told them this at the beginning of the school year, in a silence that, since he was famous in the school, was partly intrigued and partly mutinous. Max, already two years in the school, better than Mackelroth at Latin and Greek and therefore usually at the top of the class in these subjects ("You have been well taught, Hofmannswaldau, very well taught. Most unusual for a boy educated at home"), was among the intrigued. Soon he was enthralled and found himself looking forward to Thursday morning as the high point of each week.

In the first month or so, he had tried to explain to Dr Mendel, at the end of his Monday afternoon violin lesson, what he had found interesting or difficult to understand, usually both, in Dr Fischer's Thursday morning class.

When Max left home to stay with his grandfather and go to school in the Gymnasium, Dr Mendel had also come to live in Breslau. He lodged with the first cellist of the opera house orchestra, Herr Rosenthal, with whom he had played quartets on his weekends away from Waldau. Herr Rosenthal's flat was small, neat, and sunny, at the top of a tall house in a terraced street not far from the opera house. An upright piano and four chairs and music stands arranged for a quartet took up much of the space in the living room where Max came for his lessons. There were piles of music on the piano, on the floor, and on some low wooden shelves on two walls, but no sense of disorder. Over the fireplace was the room's single picture, a big bold sketch, in sweeping black brushstrokes, of a Jewish violinist standing, swaying to the music he was playing, his hat on the back of his head. Years later, Max realized that it must have been painted by Chagall. The picture, the absent quartet, and the tidy piles of music gave the sunny silence in the room, when you opened the door, a laden, sweet quality all its own. Herr Rosenthal, a good deal younger than Dr Mendel, was also a bachelor. Max met him once and was impressed by his dapper appearance, his keen glance, and his old-fashioned politeness. "Herr von Hofmannswaldau, I am delighted to meet you. It is a privilege." After a few months, Dr Mendel, too, was employed to play in the opera house orchestra. He had collected a few private pupils and of course continued to teach Max, who practised every evening in his grandfather's flat out of loyalty to Dr Mendel and to his mother, though with less enthusiasm now that his head was full of so much more than music.

Quite soon, Max saw that Dr Mendel was listening only politely to his descriptions of Dr Fischer's classes. This unfamiliar chill was surely his own fault: he must be making a mess of things (that week's lesson had been about Socrates's death and what it had meant to Plato) that were entirely new to him. But the next Monday, Dr Mendel said, "Do you know where he comes from, this Dr Fischer? Is he a Silesian?"

"No. I think he's a Rhinelander. Someone said he comes from Cologne."

"Ah, in that case he's definitely a Catholic."

"Perhaps he is. I don't know."

"Be careful, Max. Be very careful. Remember what your father used to say about Catholics."

"But my father was only talking about Polish people, poor people like Emilia and Tadeusz. He didn't know any other kind of Catholic. My mother told me that once."

"No, I don't expect he did. But he was right about Catholics all the same. It is important for you to understand that the Catholic Church is part of the past, and not a happy past either. It has been cruel at many periods in its history to people who for one reason or another have found themselves outside what it has always seen as its own circle of light, outside, therefore, in the dark. And it has been friend to many cruel rulers. The Pope himself from time to time has been a cruel ruler."

"But Dr Fischer—"

"Listen to me, Max. The Catholic Church requires its members to think certain things. It does not allow them to think for themselves, to make up their own minds. It took hundreds of years to free people from the constriction, the oppression of the Catholic Church. To free the Jews, for example, from the hatred and contempt that the Church had encouraged. I could tell you things about the Jews in Spain ... and in France before the war, which, after all, I remember well. But what you must realize is that Catholics are not permitted to use their brains freely and rationally. I have brought you up, Max, I hope, to use your brain, since you have one, for yourself, to be a free man, an independent person, to be able to discriminate, to judge on the basis of the evidence whatever you happen to encounter. Don't lose that freedom. Above all, don't be persuaded by anyone to throw it away."

"But I don't even know that Dr Fischer is a Catholic."

"Whether he is or not, no doubt he has a great deal to teach you. But keep your head, Max, keep your balance. That's all I'm saying."

Max did not mention Dr Fischer or his lessons to Dr Mendel again.

At school, he found out as much as he could about Dr Fischer from the boys in the class who made it their business to know everything about everyone. He was indeed a Catholic. He had taught in Breslau for nearly thirty years, moving twenty years ago from a less distinguished Gymnasium to this one, which had long been regarded as the best in the city. His wife had died in the great influenza epidemic in the year after the war. His son had lost a leg on the western front and was a lawyer in Berlin. His daughter was a nun in a Carmelite convent in Bavaria. This last piece of information disturbed Max, who had so far, if he thought of them at all, thought of nuns as old ladies in starched wimples occasionally to be seen in trams or pushing wounded soldiers in wheelchairs in the street. But this was a nun who was young, perhaps beautiful, the daughter of someone he saw every day.

"What a waste", said one of the news gatherers.

"How do you know?" said another. "Old Fischer's no oil painting. She may be hideous. Kinder to hide her from the eyes of the world."

"I bet she's pretty. Old Fischer adored his wife, you know. He puts flowers on her grave every Sunday."

"How on earth do you know that?"

"A friend of my mother's told me. She goes to the same Mass as old Fischer."

Max had for two years been vaguely aware that there were Catholics in his class and that there were three or four Jews. But since religion was not a topic ever discussed in lessons or by the boys among themselves, he had paid the distinctions no attention. He thought of himself, after all, as a Silesian, a Prussian of course, now and then as a Junker, but hardly ever as a Protestant.

After Dr Mendel's warning, he observed Dr Fischer more closely. He was an untidy man of about fifty-five, large, and always dressed in a baggy brown suit that suggested he had once been larger. He wore a wide-brimmed hat and a floppy bow tie of a kind that no one under fifty would have dreamed of wearing, and gold-rimmed spectacles that he frequently took off and polished with a big silk handkerchief. He used this handkerchief to blow his nose, to mop his brow, and, when he looked round and failed to see the official duster, also to wipe his flowing, always legible, Greek or Latin script off the blackboard. He had, altogether, the neglected look of a widower still expecting his wife to come home and put him to rights. He was merciless with the idle or badly prepared ("You may waste your own time, Herr Müller, if you are foolish enough to regard time as your own, but not mine or that of the rest of this class" or merely, "This is a truly terrible piece of work"), but he was generous in his praise of an exercise well done or bravely tried by a less clever boy. His voice was deep and quiet, except when he roared with assumed anguish at an elementary mistake. His presence in the classroom was heavy and only distantly threatening, like that of a bear tamed and gentle but a bear nevertheless. Max, sitting at his desk in the second row while Dr Fischer explained the syntax of an exceedingly tricky passage in a speech in Thucydides's account of the debate on Mytilene, decided that he was not looking at a sinister man who wished to take away anyone's capacity to think for himself. He decided this—and made a mental note to Dr Mendel—on the basis of the evidence.

Max, by now, was very competent in the classical languages, and on a good day, more than competent. His Latin proses and verses were fluent, ambitious and generally correct, usually earning a high mark and a "very well done" from Dr Fischer. But Zapolski, now always top of the class at the end of each fortnight, was better than Max at composing Greek, and much better than Max, not to mention better than Mackelroth and all the other boys in the class, at reading to its depths the densest poetry in both languages. Dr Fischer might spend an hour shedding new light on a chorus of Sophocles or a passage of Virgil that Max discovered he was wrong to think he had understood perfectly well, preparing it the night before. Then Dr Fischer might ask Zapolski to read the passage to the class. That was all. "Herr Zapolski, would you be so good as to read aloud from line 187 to line 264." Again and again, Max was astonished at what then happened.

The class was entirely still, most of the boys because they were really concentrating, following the lines in their books, but two or three because the first time Zapolski read aloud, they had exchanged mocking glances and been quelled by a terrifying look from Dr Fischer.

Zapolski read without raising his voice and without anything histrionic or explicitly emotional in his manner. What transformed for Max each passage that he read was the security of his hold on the rhythm of the verse together with his flexible phrasing, altering according to the sense of the words and of whole sections of the passage, so that life and feeling spread from the lines on the page into what felt to Max like his own soul. Music, he thought, looking at his Virgil, a mere page of print with pencilled translations of difficult words in the margins and pencilled quantity signs, long or short, like slurs, over a few syllables. Zapolski read aloud as a violinist plays a sonata movement from the notes printed on a page. Not just any violinist. Not just any sonata. Yet this was not music. Was the poem more than music, on account of its words? Or, on account of its words, less than music?

It was a mystery. And now that he was seventeen and being taught by someone else, someone he didn't know and someone who was resented by Dr Mendel, there was no one he could try to explain the mystery to.

Arguments between Dr Fischer and Zapolski were more likely to take place on Thursday mornings than in ordinary lessons.

One Thursday morning towards the end of April, Dr Fischer read with the class the passage in Plato's *Republic* where Socrates discusses the difficulty of educating someone to be a truly good ruler if he has to carry the people with him to be effective. He attacks the idea that the ruler who will be obeyed needs to be no more than clever at understanding the masses and therefore able to give them what they want, as a lion tamer becomes effective only by learning what the lion likes and dislikes, "calling what pleases it good and what annoys it bad". But what people want is not necessarily either just or right.

Dr Fischer put down his Plato and looked along the rows of boys at their desks.

"Well?" he said. "What do you gather from this warning?"

Silence. One raised hand.

"Herr Zapolski?"

Zapolski stood up. "That Plato didn't think much of democracy, sir."

94

"You are quite right. So, given his doubts as to the merits of democracy, what does he hope that the good ruler—the philosopher-king, as he calls him in this book of the *Republic*—may nevertheless be able to achieve?"

"To persuade the people that what pleases them may be bad, and what they don't like may be good?"

"That's right. And on what would such an enterprise depend?"

"On the ruler himself being certain about what's good and what's bad. Which is hopeless, because nobody knows. I'd have thought the lion tamer approach the only logical one. People know what they like and what they don't like, and the only way you can get them to do what you want is to give them what they like when they obey you and what they don't like when they don't. Galleys and shackles or bread and circuses."

A murmur of appreciation from the class, who recognized the last phrase, though most of them were probably not following the argument.

"Your cynicism, Herr Zapolski, has long philosophical antecedents, as indeed this passage of Plato, an attack on the sophists of his time, demonstrates quite clearly. Would you agree, however, that the distinction between a good ruler and a bad ruler is one that has some validity?"

"I would prefer to say that an effective ruler is not the same animal as an ineffective one."

"So might, in your view, is always right?"

"Of course. Politics, sir, is always about power—how to get it, how to keep it, how to use it."

"For?"

"Sir?"

"What would an effective ruler use his power for?"

"To consolidate his rule. To acquire more power. To extend the territory over which he rules. To become famous forever."

Dr Fischer laughed.

"What a Roman you are, Zapolski. First bread and circuses and then Cicero, Cicero at his worst, of course. How to impress the centuries! Be just only if justice will be good for your reputation. Machiavelli comes to mind, and Thomas Hobbes. Sit down, Zapolski. Now listen, all of you."

The class relaxed. They enjoyed old Fischer's little speeches and knew that for a few minutes, no one was going to be asked a question he was likely not to be able to answer.

"Plato suggested that it was possible, very difficult but possible, for a ruler to be just for justice's sake, to be good for the sake of goodness. As a young man, he had lived, as you know, through a peculiarly unpleasant period in the history of Athens, so he was well acquainted with the dangers of democracy when a people is treated by its masters as a wild beast that has to be alternately soothed and goaded. His philosopher-king is not a figure of report but a figure of aspiration, and the very idea of him supposes that there is indeed, in reality, goodness, that there is truth, that there is beauty, and that these are one—a set of propositions that, we know, Herr Zapolski regards as absurd."

"Sir!"

"Zapolski?'

"Sir, it's not that I don't think there's such a thing as truth, but truth in reality has nothing to do with goodness, and absolutely nothing to do with beauty. Truth's neither good nor bad, because those words don't mean anything, but it's certainly ugly, bleak, and grim and has nothing in it to cheer us up."

Dr Fischer picked up his copy of the *Republic*, turned back a couple of pages, and read, translating as he went: "Listen: 'Our true lover of knowledge naturally strives for truth'—he turned over a page—'and where truth gives the lead, we shall not expect a company of evils to follow but a good, sound character, and self-discipline as well.' That's not a bad description of some of you boys at your best, and I would include you, Zapolski, at your best. But since you think the connexion Plato makes between truth and goodness mere fantasy … Never mind for the moment.

"My intention this morning was to provoke—I have already provoked Herr Zapolski, or rather, Plato has—some thought about the pressing need of our new republic (a worthy enterprise, I hope you will agree) for thoughtful and well-informed young men, such as I trust you all to become, to aspire to work for it one of these days, as perhaps members of the Reichstag, even, eventually, as government ministers. It's becoming more and more important in these difficult times that men of sound education, good judgement, and moderate political views should stand ready to counter those of less education, weak judgement, and extreme political views, who say they are only waiting for the republic to collapse to replace it with a bullying, marching version of the Kaiser's empire or, even worse, with a Communist state that will take its instructions from Herr Lenin in Moscow. Never forget, gentlemen, that the centre is not less good, less interesting, or less powerful than the extremes because it makes less noise.

"Now, since the whole of Germany has been subjected to Prussian order—no bad thing in itself, I am the first to admit—we have become, or had become until the war, most excellent administrators. But administration is not the same thing as government, and although we have a strong tradition of obedience, we have no tradition of government. We do what we are told, but we leave the telling to someone else, to the prince, the King, the duke, the Bishop. Eventually to the Kaiser and his Chancellor. But now at last we have what perhaps was intended all those years ago in Frankfurt, a parliament, a cabinet, a Chancellor who must earn and keep the support of all these people because he has no Kaiser behind him to keep him upright, to keep him in his job. He must take responsibility, they must take responsibility, and answer to all of us for what they do, and perhaps, silently, also to God. If democratic government is to work in Germany, we must have good people who are also clever and brave to take responsibility. Or things will go from bad to worse.

"Perhaps a few of you boys will, as time goes by, take politics seriously. The republic will not survive unless, to take responsibility for it, there are good men who know some history and are able to keep their balance when all about them irrational voices cry of treachery and vengeance.

"Germany educates many very well. They become professors and doctors and lawyers. They make scientific discoveries, write books, and deliver notable lectures. But they wash their hands of the government of the country because they think it full of anger and bad faith, and while they wash their hands of it, it will remain full of anger and bad faith. Fifty years after the invention of the United States of America, Alexis de Tocqueville, a very brilliant Frenchman—yes, indeed, and there have been many brilliant Frenchmen, I would have you remember—observed the same phenomenon there: many good and clever men, disdaining politics. We are fifty years from the uniting of Germany by Prince von Bismarck, and we are in exactly the same case.

"But there are brave and noble exceptions, and you should take to heart the example they set. Dr Rathenau, our present foreign minister, is one such. A wise man, a man of experience and skill, and a man of the centre who does not cry treachery or preach vengeance.

He hopes to build the republic, for all the problems that have first to be overcome, into a safe and fair *commonwealth*—an English word, and one with an honourable sense—where the poor are helped and the rich contribute to that help, and which is able to sustain friendly relations with the other countries and peoples of Europe. Take note of what he says and does, for he is the kind of statesman I should very much like one or two of you to become in due course."

"Sir?"

"Herr Kolberg?"

"Sir, Silesia wouldn't have him as a candidate for the Reichstag because he's a Jew. I know because my father belongs to the Democratic Party."

"That is indeed the case, Herr Kolberg, and it is very much to the discredit of Silesia that it should have been so."

This produced a ripple of protest in the classroom, suppressed by a look from Dr Fischer.

"What's more, the Chancellor of the republic, who appointed Dr Rathenau to his present position, is a Catholic, which some people in Silesia find almost as difficult to stomach. Nevertheless, Dr Rathenau is closer than anyone else in Germany at present to Plato's idea of a philsopher-king, and this I should like you to remember."

That afternoon, Max and Zapolski left the Gymnasium together as usual. It occurred to Max to say that Zapolski actually agreed with Dr Fischer much more often than he wanted to think, but he didn't say it. He didn't know Zapolski well enough.

They were crossing Blücher Square in the sunshine when Zapolski said:

"It's spring, and about time too. Breslau in the spring. Not quite Vienna, let alone Paris. But spring all the same. Everything feels different today. Better. Perhaps just warmer. Look, the awnings are out over the shop windows, and there are café tables on the sidewalk over there. Shall we have a coffee? I wonder if there's any chocolate cake in Breslau cafés."

They sat down, and Zapolski ordered coffee, cake, and brandy. For something to say to his host—at least he hoped Zapolski intended to pay since the order struck him as the height of extravagance—Max asked:

"How did you get to be so good at Latin and Greek? Did you have a very good tutor?"

"Monks", Zapolski said. "I went to school in a monastery. On the Danube, not far from Vienna. They are a brainy lot, Benedictine monks. They worked us like slaves. So we learnt. Also, I suppose I'm used to languages. I've been in and out of languages ever since I can remember. We always had German and Polish at home, and my mother goes in for a good deal of French. Then Latin in the monastery—just part of the air one breathed."

"I thought there weren't any monks nowadays. I thought some hung on after the Middle Ages, a few rattling about in buildings too big for them, and then Napoleon swept them all away. At least I must have read that somewhere."

"What a Prussian you are! Napoleon had a go at it, certainly. In Prussia, Bismarck had a more effective go. But it would take more than either of them to get rid of monks in Austria. They're not a bad lot, as a matter of fact. Of course, the whole basis of their lives is nonsense, but given that, they could be a great deal worse. Strict, of course, but quite kind and patient underneath the strictness, most of them. I would be much less kind and much less patient than they were, faced with classrooms full of ghastly children to teach when what I had signed up for was a life with God."

Max was thinking of Dr Fischer's daughter, the nun in Bavaria. "When you say the whole basis of their lives is nonsense, do you mean their being shut away from the world, the vows of poverty and chastity—"

"Chastity, as far as one could see, they more or less stuck to. It probably did some of them a good deal of harm. Freud, you know: the dire consequences of repression. But poverty was a joke. They had very comfortable lives indeed on the fat fees they charged the parents of the boys in the school. No, I didn't mean all that when I said the whole basis of their lives is nonsense. I meant the whole of Christianity, the supposed life with God."

"All of Christianity? Or just Catholicism?"

"All of it, of course. Once the central plank gives way—'God so loved the world' and all that—the whole lot crashes into the river, and away it goes. Bits of a bridge from nowhere to nowhere. For a start, only an idiot could believe nowadays that God exists. No, Hofmannswaldau. We are a chemical accident in a meaningless universe. Everyone who knows anything knows that, though plenty of people don't want to admit it. It's frightening in a way, I suppose. But exhilarating too. And in any case, if God did exist, how could he love the world? Look at it!"

"What about Jesus Christ?"

"What about him?"

"Do you think he ever lived? Was he a real, historical person? Or is he just a story?"

"Oh, both. Both, of course."

"How can he be both? Surely he's either fact or fiction."

"Don't you know Strauss?—no, not our Strauss; how could he ever have said a single interesting thing?—David Friedrich Strauss. The book's called *The Life of Jesus*. First fact, then fiction. There was this fellow called Jesus, who did and said—particularly said—some extraordinary things, in Palestine, at the right time, the time it says in the Bible. The Romans executed him because he was causing trouble. Then a collection of Jewish myth makers got hold of the story of his life and turned him into something quite different: the Son of God, or God himself in human form, the redeemer, the saviour of the world, all that nonsense. In one word, they turned him into Christ. So you see, first fact, then fiction. More coffee? More brandy?"

"Just coffee, please."

"Oh, come on. Brandy's good for the brain."

Max thought while a waiter came and went and came back with more coffee and more brandy. He had never drunk spirits before and was feeling hot and oddly calm. He decided he would sip his brandy so slowly that his body wouldn't notice he was drinking it. When the waiter had gone again, he said:

"But what about the things Jesus said? The Sermon on the Mount and all that. Doesn't that leave Christianity with quite a lot, even if the stuff about him being God and the saviour isn't true?"

"It does leave Christianity with quite a lot, yes. But it's done much more harm than good. Never mind the ridiculous pretensions of the Church down the ages, all based on the myth, the fiction bit, of course, the part about Jesus being the Christ. The Church calls itself the body of *Christ*: the Church never calls itself the body of *Jesus*. But what Jesus himself said has done a lot of harm as well. What he said weakened the will. Recommended submission in all circumstances. The Roman empire lost its nerve as a result. Christianity. Slave morality, Nietzsche calls it. Sitting about and waiting for God to do something for you when you could be doing something for yourself. Everyone has the chance to choose his own character, his own life, to use his own will. To rise above the way things happen to be. To use passion and force to break free of circumstances, to break free of history and family and all that. Above all, one has the chance to use one's brain, one's capacity to reason, to understand how things really are and to think through them to where one wants to get. One chance, and that's it. Look at the people who have been the most Christian, the most submissive, the most faithful in waiting for God to provide: the Poles and the Jews—oddly enough, the Jews have been the most Christian of anyone; perhaps that's why the Poles hate them so much—and what's God done for them? Nothing whatsoever. What did God do for poor old Franz Josef, who put the ramshackle empire into God's hands day after day at Mass? On the other hand, the Prussians, at least since Frederick the Great, have given up on God and gone for power, efficiency, and getting things done themselves, like the English. And the Americans."

"You're wrong about the Prussians. They think of themselves, mostly, as very Christian. They go to church every Sunday and listen to long sermons, even people like my father. They think of themselves as adult rational Christians and of the Poles as superstitious children who have to be told by priests exactly what to do and what to think. That might be your slave morality, I suppose. But isn't it possible to be powerful and efficient and Christian as well?"

"No, it's not. You can't be *really* Christian. Look at Frederick the Great. He loathed Prussian piety. He loathed devout Jews. He thought all religion nonsense. French Enlightenment atheism was how to get things done, he thought. And he was absolutely right. But I'm not talking about whole countries. I'm talking about people one by one. You. Me. We're young. The world's a mess. The war was a disaster. The empires are finished—the real one and the sham Prussian one. So what are we going to do? Fall back on Christianity and the will of God? Or use our own brains, our own strength, to make something great, something beautiful and significant, of our own lives? Have another drink."

"No, really not, Zapolski. I think we ought to go home now. My grandfather will be worried if I'm back much later than usual."

"Oh what a good boy you are! Perhaps you're a Christian yourself, and I've offended you. I'm sorry. I thought you were far too intelligent to believe any of it's true—you know, really true. Waiter! Two more brandies, please!"

Max knew he should get up, thank Zapolski for his invitation and his hospitality, push in his chair, shake hands, take his bicycle from the plane tree against which he had leant it, and go home. But he felt so strange that he wasn't sure he could do any of these things properly. So he stayed where he was and even picked up the new glass of brandy when it arrived.

"Cigarette?" Zapolski held out a leather cigarette case with gold corners.

"No. Thank you." Max had tried a cigarette before, last year on the playground at the Gymnasium. It had made him feel sick, and the very thought of smoking one now almost made him ill. There was something he wanted to ask Zapolski. Sitting very still, after one more sip of brandy, he made himself remember what it was.

"Who is Nietzsche?"

"You mean to say you've never heard of Nietzsche? My poor child—what have you been doing all this time? 'God is dead, and we have killed him.' Tremendous stuff. Nietzsche is by far the most important writer of our time—well, not quite our time, but everything he said was going to happen is happening, faster and faster as you look. He's a philosopher, but not like Kant and Hegel: everyone pretends to have read them, but no one really has. Nietzsche's not difficult to read. In fact, he's intoxicating to read, actually makes you feel drunk. He's more of a prophet, I suppose, than a philosopher, if a prophet is someone who tells the truth to the people of his own time, which is what they told us in the monastery a prophet is."

"Is he dead? When did he die?"

"Oh, about twenty years ago. But he'd been mad for years when he died."

"*Mad?* How could he be such a wonderful prophet if he was mad?"

"Visionaries, you know, can seem mad to other people, when they're actually closer to the truth than an everyday sane person could ever get. That may have been true in Nietzsche's case for a while, but I have to admit that in the end he was really mad. Perhaps he sacrificed his mind to clear the minds of the rest of us."

"What should one read?"

"Well, *Zarathustra* is the Nietzsche Bible. *Thus Spake Zarathustra*—the prophet, you see, is Zarathustra, but he talks for Nietzsche instead of talking for God like the Old Testament prophets. But it's a very long book. You might do better starting with something shorter, *Daybreak* perhaps, or *Beyond Good and Evil*. The *Will to Power* is a muddle, and a very long muddle too, but there are some extraordinary things in it. 'We have art so as not to perish of the truth.' Think about it."

"But that would mean that the truth is . . . that the truth is all . . ."

Max knew he was now too drunk to talk, let alone think, sensibly. He was also frightened by how he felt and by how, once he got home (which meant walking, not bicycling, and would therefore make him even later), he was going to prevent his grandfather from realizing that he was drunk. But he was frightened even more, now, by Zapolski and what he was saying, so airily and yet with such conviction. If art was only to protect people from the truth, then art was obviously false, lies, a sham thing. How was the poetry read so beautifully by Zapolski false? How was a Bach sonata something *sham*? And why wasn't Zapolski drunk?

"So . . . what do you think", Zapolski said with perfect clarity, "it would mean?"

There was a word, an obvious, ordinary word that was the answer to the question, but Max couldn't remember it, couldn't find it in his fuddled mind.

"Zapolski, why aren't you . . . I'm sorry. What I mean is I must go home. It's really important that I go home."

Zapolski laughed, but not in an unfriendly way. "Yes, of course you must. You'll have to push your bike, I'm afraid. But that might be just as well. Off you go—I'll deal with the bill."

"Thank you . . . I'm sorry. Yes, I must go."

When he got back to the flat, his grandfather opened the door as he was trying to find his key in his pocket.

"My dear boy", he began. Then he stopped. "Ah!"

"I'm late, I know. I'm sorry. I was talking to a friend and . . . and then I had to walk. I'm a bit tired. Would you mind if I . . ."

"Go to bed, Max. Sleep it off. Did you bring your bicycle home?"

"Yes, I did. It's downstairs."

"Good. Go to bed now."

In the morning—Max had had a long, rough night, which he hoped, without much confidence, his grandfather had not been aware of—his grandfather said:

"Do you think you can cope with school today?"

"Oh yes, of course. I must, even though I did no preparation last night. I might be lucky and not be asked to translate, or to solve one of Dr Strauss's equations. If I'm asked, I shall have to say I was ill."

"Well, that's not far from the truth. Drink this tea. Don't try to eat anything. Take care on your bicycle."

That was all.

Chapter 4

A week later, on a sunny afternoon, Dr Fischer closed his copy of the *Aeneid* with a sharp snap and said:

"Gentlemen, we have had enough of bloodshed and misery. Look at the beautiful spring day. Will you be so good as to open your copies of the *Bucolics*: we shall return—I assume that the *Bucolics* have been well known to you all for several years—to the fourth poem in the cycle, one of the most remarkable works ever to flow from the pen even of Virgil. Now, is there anyone in the class to whom this poem is not already familiar?"

A look along the rows of desks, the rows of boys. No one will admit to not knowing it, Max thought. If they've never seen it before, they'll just hope for the best.

"No one? Very good. Now first, to dispel the reek of the battlefield and the anguish of Aeneas as the young men die, we shall read this poem straight through. Herr von Hofmannswaldau, would you be so good?"

Max shut his eyes and opened them again. He had read the *Bucolics* with Dr Mendel when he was twelve or thirteen and remembered an atmosphere of nymphs and shepherds, a good deal of moping about love, a lot of names of flowers and plants he had never heard of, and Dr Mendel explaining that the poems also had to do with the politics of the time Virgil was writing—the civil wars still going on and generals taking peasants' land for their soldiers. That was about all he remembered. However, perhaps if old Fischer had asked him to read, he wouldn't then ask him to explain anything in the poem.

He sat up straight and launched himself into the hexameters. With his now much better Latin, he realized as he read that the poem was much odder than he remembered any of the *Bucolics* being. It was not about nymphs and shepherds and forlorn love at all but was a kind of prophecy about a child who was going to bring in a golden age and make the whole world a peaceful, fruitful, magical place. A prophecy, he thought as he reached the last lines, about the newborn baby smiling at his mother: who had been talking to him about prophecy just the other day? He couldn't remember.

"Thank you, Hofmannswaldau. That was well read." He never says that to Zapolski, Max thought. Because it's obvious.

"Now, does any of you have a question about the vocabulary or the syntax of these remarkable lines?"

There were a few questions, answered by other boys with better Latin or better memories or better notes in the margin than the questioners; one or two questions, having drawn a blank in the class, were answered by Dr Fischer. Then he put down the book, took off his spectacles, polished them, and put them on again.

"What do you suppose is the meaning of this poem?"

Silence in the classroom.

"Does any of you know in which year it was written? Herr Mackelroth, do you happen to remember?"

"Sir, it was written in 40 B.C."

"Good. So, what was the political situation in the Roman world in the year 40 B.C.? Herr Zapolski?"

"There was a pause in the civil war. Mark Antony and Octavian had carved up the world between them and made a truce. Both of them got married, Antony to Octavian's sister. But—"

"Stop there. You are correct. But Virgil could, during that year, have had no sense of your 'but', of what was soon to come. So who, in your opinion, is the child foretold in the poem?"

"The son of either of the marriages. A chancy business, childbirth. Or the son might have been a daughter. So Virgil is hedging his bets. He wants to be on the right side of whoever produces a son."

"Very possibly, Zapolski, you are correct again. But, as I am sure you can all see, we remain, so far, only on the surface of these lines. Let us dive a little deeper. The birth of what other child might be thought, with hindsight, to have been prophesied in this poem?"

"The birth of Christ?" someone suggested.

"Thank you, Herr Gerhardt. But how, no doubt you will be wondering, could Virgil be writing of the birth of Christ in the year 40 B.C.?"

"He couldn't. The idea is ridiculous. Sir."

"Herr Zapolski, if you regard the idea as ridiculous, perhaps you would honour the rest of us with your explanation."

The bear was growling a little, but everyone knew that Zapolski would take the growl as a challenge rather than as a warning.

"Well, sir, in the first place, how could a poet writing forty years before the birth of Christ—or of Jesus, one should say—a child born to obscure parents in an obscure province, have any notion of what might be made of this birth by Jewish writers a century later or more? In the second place, the poem is clearly a utopian fantasy, nothing to do with Christianity. Even the Church has never promised us that sheep would change colour by themselves to save us the trouble of dyeing wool. In the third place, if Virgil is having a vision of history repeating itself indefinitely"—Zapolski looked down at his book and translated "And great Achilles will be sent again to Troy"—"then you might as well say that Virgil is prophesying the birth of Nietzsche. Eternal recurrence, according to Zarathustra—"

"That's quite enough, Zapolski, thank you very much. Now listen to me, if you would. In the first place, it is by no means impossible that Virgil read parts of the Old Testament in Greek: he read a great deal, and the Greek translation of the Jewish Bible—which, by the way, was known as—yes, Herr Geyer?"

"The Septuagint, sir."

"Thank you, Geyer." He would know that, thought Max, and he would have to say it. Dr Fischer continued:

"So, if Virgil came across the Septuagint and read, say, the prophet Isaiah, it would not be surprising if he echoed the Jewish longing for a saviour of the world. In the second place, if a poet is imagining the unimaginable, his imagery may well be fanciful. In the third place, it is not truly 'eternal recurrence'—a hope, if it is a hope, to which Nietzsche, I would beg you to observe, was driven by sheer despair—that Virgil acknowledges here but original sin. 'Pauca tamen suberunt priscae vestigia fraudis', you see, line 31: 'A few traces, however, endure of the ancient crime.' When he wrote the poem, there was peace. There would again be war. He knew it. I fear that this is the human condition."

Two hands shot up in the classroom.

"Herr Weil?"

"Do you think there's going to be another war, sir?"

"Alas, I do. But this is not the time to explain why. Yes, Herr Zapolski?"

107

"Sir, do you really expect us to believe not only that Virgil prophesied the birth of Jesus but also that he knew what Saint Augustine would say about original sin four centuries in the future?"

"Ah."

Dr Fischer clasped his hands in front of his large stomach and, head down, paced heavily back and forth, twice, in front of his desk. This almost-ritual walk always made the boys who were in any case interested in what he had to say listen more carefully when, at the end of his walk, he stopped and, standing at his high oak lectern with both hands gripping its sides, finally spoke.

"In the Middle Ages," he began, looking not at Zapolski or anyone else but over all their heads, as if there were a message to be deciphered on the far wall of the room, "they said of Virgil that there dwelt in him 'anima naturaliter Christiana', a soul that was Christian by nature. What they meant by that, I would suggest, is that he had such an acute sense of the sorrow of the world, the trouble to which man is born, the sinfulness that persists in every human undertaking, however powerful and successful men become—and gentlemen, remember that Virgil stood on the brink of the most successful empire yet established—that he hoped and believed, insofar as a poet of pagan Rome could, in a rescue for the human race that could come only from God, from, as this poem suggests, the birth of the divine into the human world. Of course he could not have known, and here Herr Zapolski is quite correct, that Christ would be born in Judaea nineteen years after his own death. But of the meaning of Christ's birth, he had an intuition that itself perhaps was a gift of God. What have we, as Saint Augustine was fond of asking, that we have not received? Yes?"

Zapolski's hand was up. He stood to say, politely:

"But if there is no God and Jesus was only a man, then Virgil's hope was a shot in the dark, like Isaiah's. No target for the shot. An arrow flying into nowhere."

"You are right, of course, Zapolski. Sit down, if you would."

Zapolski, looking surprised, sat. The class was absolutely still. Dr Fischer went on:

"Herr Zapolski deserves congratulation for understanding with unusual clarity the central question. The central question is the one that Jesus put to Saint Peter: 'Who do you say that I am?' If we reply only, as many who call themselves Christians now do, 'A good man who recommends that we should behave unselfishly and with compassion', then indeed we are saying that, even if God exists—and the God of the philosophers, of Kant and Hegel, for example, is so remote from us, so unconcerned with our affairs, with our broken hearts, that he can in no way be said to have loved the world—his identity in trinity with Christ is no more than a fairy story, and a fairy story so hard to comprehend that it appears to be a waste of time even to try. Is this how you would describe your present position, Herr Zapolski?"

Max had kept track of Dr Fischer's long sentence with difficulty and knew he hadn't grasped it completely. He looked at Zapolski, who had no doubt understood it. In a Thursday lesson a few weeks earlier, it had become clear that Zapolski, if he hadn't actually read Kant, at least had an accurate sense of what Kant had thought, about God and about our duty to behave unselfishly and with compassion. Zapolski stood up.

"My position, sir, to which I'm quite certain I shall stick"—he had been offended, as Max knew he would be, by Dr Fischer's use of the phrase "present position"—"is, as you say, that Jesus was no more than a man and that God doesn't exist. God doesn't exist at all, here or in the minds of Kant and Hegel, or anywhere else. He never has. So the philosophers who try to keep him somewhere, somehow, to make the rest of what they're saying more respectable, are just as wrong, just as much aiming their arrows into the dark, as the Christians are. We have to manage without God, because that's where we are, in a world without God, a world God didn't make, a world that just happened to evolve out of matter in a universe of atoms and chance. To admit that this is how things are, really *are*, and not just how they seem, which of course they do to us all in the twentieth century, is at least honest and truthful. And we ought, if we think it out properly, to be able to make less of a mess of things than all the people who believed in God have made. After all," Zapolski looked round the class as if to gather support for his clinching statement, or perhaps, it struck Max as Zapolski spoke, to present, with some scorn, the class as evidence for what he was saying, "what rescue did there turn out to be?"

There was an almost imperceptible movement, rather than sound, of approval from some of the class. Most, Max was sure, hadn't really followed the debate but admired the conviction with which Zapolski had delivered his concluding point. Max knew that Dr Fischer wouldn't allow Zapolski this apparent victory.

"There turned out, Herr Zapolski, to be no rescue as a magic trick performed by God for the human race as a whole, no rescue, at least in this world, this mortal life, for fallible human beings floundering in the consequences of their wilfulness, greed, envy, and cruelty. But there did turn out to be something else, rescue into the grace of God, which belongs not to this world but to eternity, offered as a gift to each of us. The offer, of course, like the offer of the gift of faith, may be ignored or refused. Or a gift may be misused. It has been known for the gift of intelligence to be very seriously misused, particularly by some of those who have received it in great abundance."

Zapolski's hand went up. Dr Fischer paid no attention.

"I was thinking of Professor Nietzsche. But in all cases, it is true to point out, or perhaps to warn, that the greater the gift, the greater is the obligation to make of it what one hopes to be able to answer to God for. In offering us something, God asks for our answer. Answerability is what makes us human."

Zapolski stood up, said quickly, "Only if there is a God", and sat down again. But his moment of triumph was plainly over, and the class had relaxed.

"However," Dr Fischer continued, "I would like you all to remember that someone who describes for the first time something that already exists has not created it. Columbus did not create America, nor did Copernicus cause the planets to revolve about the sun. America was there before Columbus, as was the solar system before Copernicus. Original sin was there before Saint Augustine described it. It is still there for those who have eyes to see, even for some who believe there is no God. Herr Zapolski?"

"Sir, how is it possible to believe in original sin unless you believe that God commands and we disobey?"

"That, Herr Zapolski, is a very pertinent question, to which I myself consider that there is no satisfactory reply. However, if you read Schopenhauer's *World as Will and Idea*, the book, Zapolski, upon which Nietzsche cut his philosophical teeth, you will find an extensive and penetrating description of original sin."

Zapolski was again on his feet.

"But sir, I thought Schopenhauer was an atheist."

"That is precisely my point. He was. But his description of the will to life as the pitiless force that drives the universe is also, as it happens, in its application to the human world, a description of original sin. For him, of course, there is no rescue, only a noble withdrawal from the will to life, the very opposite, Herr Zapolski, of Professor Nietzsche's enthusiastic embrace of the will to power."

This time, Zapolski remained quietly in his seat, looking down at his desk. Even he, it was clear, had not read Schopenhauer.

Dr Fischer was not in the habit of drawing attention to his winning of an argument. "We seem to have travelled far, gentlemen," he said, as he began again to walk to and fro, "from the fourth *Bucolic*. But not so far, in fact, as you might imagine. On Thursday I shall tell you a little more about Schopenhauer. Like Virgil, he lived in a pagan world. Schopenhauer's world, however, is very largely our own—Herr Zapolski's views are not quite as unusual as he supposes—and it is important that all of you acquire some sense of Schopenhauer's world before you are asked—I would suggest, by God—to confront its assumptions. You will be asked, that is certain, though you may refuse to answer. One may always refuse to answer. Now"—he looked at the clock on the wall facing him, behind the boys—"two minutes remain before the end of this afternoon's classes, and I think we have all had quite enough. Good day, gentlemen."

They stood as he left the classroom.

Zapolski never discussed with Max these set-tos with Dr Fischer, who, Max could tell, allowed them to develop only when he chose and only rarely, perhaps once every four or five weeks.

That day, a day of warm sunshine in early May, with the leaves beginning to break from the grey twigs of the plane trees in the streets and the willows along the water of the moat, they walked in silence to Zapolski's door. Max bicycled slowly home to his grandfather's flat.

He found the old man kneeling on the sitting room floor surrounded by large sheets of paper that had clearly been unrolled. Brass weights of different sizes from the kitchen scales were holding down their corners. On the sheets of paper were ruled pencilled lines and small neat figures in ink.

"Look at these, my boy", his grandfather said as Max came in and stopped by the door in order not to tread on the paper. "I've been waiting for months for these to arrive from Paris, and now at last they've come."

"What are they, Grandpapa?"

"The working drawings for making a harpsichord. I think I told you. Perhaps I didn't. It's time we were able to hear Bach's music as he himself heard it. There are a few pianists who now play Bach and even Mozart on the harpsichord, and the sound is very fine, both old and new to modern ears. And wonderfully crisp, with no opportunity for the self-indulgence of the pedal. I have wanted to build a harpsichord since before the war, but it's been difficult to find the help I needed, and your grandmother thought there wasn't enough space here for such a project to be possible. But now—you won't mind stepping round my carpentry for a while, will you, Max?—I'm determined to try. One day this will be a present for your mother. I so very much want her to play again. I know she would play a harpsichord most beautifully, and if you played your violin with her, you would find the sound altogether new and fresh. Violins, after all, haven't changed, while the pianoforte is a very different thing from a harpsichord."

Max thought of what Dr Fischer had said about gifts. "Grandpapa," he said, "you are a great man."

His grandfather looked up and gave him a sharp glance.

"My dear boy, I am not. I'm an old man who enjoys a small challenge. That's all. Now help me up, or I may be on the floor till bedtime. Thank you. And could you roll up the drawings for me? That's it. There's some tape to tie them with. I shall have to get the large pieces of wood for the instrument's case cut for me at the sawmill. Then I shall get the strings, the keys, and the plectra sent from Paris. Perhaps this will be the first harpsichord built in Breslau since the eighteenth century. Most of all, I hope it might cheer your mother."

After supper, left for them as always by Frau Gärtner, a war widow who came every day to clean the flat, do the washing, and give his grandfather his lunch, Max thought the excitement over the harpsichord had subsided enough for him to ask a question or two.

"Grandpapa, have you read Schopenhauer?"

"Oh yes, indeed I have. When I was young, we all read him. Medical students, you know, don't normally read much philosophy; there isn't time to learn how to understand it. But Schopenhauer isn't difficult to understand, and we loved him because what he was saying matched so well what we'd learnt from Darwin. He was scientifically sound—he matches, by the way, even better what Freud has recently taught us—but at the same time there was so much passion in his work: sadness, which always appeals to the young, and passion, particularly for music, where we found so much that was beautiful in our lives. But now ..."

He struck a match, lit his pipe, and leant back in his armchair.

"Now?" Max said.

"Now I think him a dangerous influence. All that unrestrained emotion, licensed, as it were, by being apparently described as all there is in life, has done a great deal of harm. Wagner, for example. Look at what he's done to music. Unrestrained emotion, on the stage, in the orchestra. Enough to make you seasick, like a rich meal followed by a stormy voyage. It's a misuse of music, to load it with so much specific passion. What's become of the power of the mind, the reason, so strong and clear in Haydn and Mozart, in Beethoven, and above all, in Bach? Wagner's music is a morass, a swamp of feeling into which people love to sink, leaving their minds behind on dry ground with, as it were, their clothes. But of course you don't know Wagner's music. A good thing too. I shall build my harpsichord as a personal protest against Wagner."

"What about Nietzsche?"

"Ah. Where have you come across Nietzsche? Not, surely, at the Gymnasium?"

"Well, not exactly. My friend Zapolski, the Polish boy who arrived this year, has read Nietzsche. Zapolski seems to have read nearly everything. He very much admires Nietzsche. He seems to think of him as a kind of liberation ..."

"A liberation from what?"

"From Christianity, mainly. But Zapolski went to school in a monastery near Vienna, so I suppose ..."

"I'm sure you suppose correctly. An intelligent young man strictly brought up as a Catholic is very likely to find Nietzsche most attractive. But I would say Nietzsche is even more dangerous than Schopenhauer. The will to power instead of the will to life. At least Schopenhauer thought the will to life horrifying, whereas Nietzsche thought the will to power wonderful, exciting, exhilarating. Do you remember the first weeks of the war? I know you were only a child, so probably you don't, but that was like a kind of national epidemic of the will to power. And what was it but a will to kill, a will to die? Terrible, terrible, and look at what became of the war. Your brother, and your father, and poor Toni ..."

Max tried not to think too much of his mother. Since he had left home, more than two and a half years ago, she had lost her spirit, her vitality, even almost her smile. She stayed at Waldau. Very occasionally she travelled to Breslau on the train, but when she came, she didn't want to see people, or play chamber music, or go to the shops when, a few months after the treaty, they began again to have pretty clothes, rich fabrics, things that before the war she used to enjoy, if only to look at and touch. Now that Heinrich was back at Waldau—Max had seen him once, when he went home for Christmas—their mother was looking after him. She had written in the spring to say that Heinrich was soon to be married to a girl called Elisabeth Grauer. The letter told Max and his grandfather only her name, which meant nothing to either of them. Max hoped that the wedding and perhaps a kind daughter-in-law in the house, and in due course grandchildren, would help his mother to feel that life still held some promise, some hope. Every single time he thought of her, he felt guilty about leaving her, though his grandfather told him firmly that it was entirely right for him to be at the Gymnasium, that he had been at home in the country quite long enough, without proper teachers and without friends of his own age, and that the troubles of adults were not the responsibility of their children.

"I could have stayed at home, at least till Heinrich came back. Dr Mendel is a proper teacher."

"No. That wouldn't have been good for you, and it wouldn't have been good for your mother either. Your mother received a series of shocks that summer—your father's death was not the only one—and the entirely sensible thing was for you to come to Breslau and discover at the Gymnasium what it is you want to make of your life."

"She seemed happy for a while, that summer after Father's death. I'm sure my coming here was what—"

"No, Max, you are not to blame yourself. I promise you your mother's sadness is not on account of you."

Because this was seriously said, and because Max trusted his grandfather, he accepted most of the time that there was something here, perhaps something to do with women's health, that he couldn't understand and that his grandfather was not going to explain. But the thought of his mother, mixed up, as he recognized it was, with his sense of exile from Waldau itself, always gave him a twinge of pain nevertheless.

"Schopenhauer, Nietzsche—I should have thought you would be too busy, at your age, with Greek and Latin and mathematics and history to be worrying about these big, seductive ideas. Playing with fire, I'd say. They won't be asking you questions on Schopenhauer and Nietzsche in the examinations, will they?"

"No, of course not. But don't you think, in a way, the big ideas matter more than all the subjects we have to do for the exams? Dr Fischer, who teaches us Latin and Greek and some other things as well, says it's no good for us to learn history, for instance, as if Germany were the only country in Europe and as if its history began with Frederick the Great and Goethe. Grandpapa?"

"Yes, Max?"

"Do you believe in God?"

The acute look, over the spectacles, across the pipe.

"Ah. So Dr Fischer tells you that Frederick the Great and Goethe didn't believe in God."

"Well, they didn't, did they?"

"Frederick the Great certainly didn't. Goethe both did and didn't—like many people, I'm afraid. Like me, since you ask."

"Could you explain, Grandpapa, if it's not too late? I don't understand how you can both believe in God and not believe in God. I thought it would make much more difference than that, so that you, or anyone, would have to decide one way or the other."

"That sounds like Nietzsche and your friend Zapolski." His grandfather laughed. "No, Max, it's not too late, or at least not too late in the evening. I'm too old to have to go to bed at a set time, you know, and so are you. It may, on the other hand, be too late in my life—I'm afraid I haven't thought these things out as clearly as you would obviously like me to have done. But I will try to explain; of course I will. I may not do it very well.

"When I was young, your age or perhaps a bit older, in the seventies, I believed above all in the power of the mind. I was a scientist, remember, training to be a physician. Medicine had just begun to make astonishing progress here—that was why I came to Breslau—and it seemed to me that to join this work would be the most exciting challenge I could find anywhere. There was excellent work going on in biochemistry, immunology, and the study of bacteria. We were making real advances in dealing with some serious diseases that had seemed quite incurable, quite beyond the possible reach of science, only a very few years before. Perhaps you can imagine how exciting it was to see that careful, methodical work in laboratories might soon be able to rescue people, especially children, from entirely undeserved suffering and early death. Scientific progress was what we believed in, I suppose, as other people believed in God. It was what made our lives worth living. We got up in the morning full of enthusiasm for that day's work and went to bed exhausted but satisfied with perhaps a tiny piece of secure knowledge established, or another possible idea abandoned as definitely useless. We were pleased—proud, I have to admit—to find we happened to have the talent and happened to have the opportunity to do this work."

"What have we that we have not received?"

"What?"

"I wondered if you sometimes thought it wasn't chance that gave you the talent and the opportunity but perhaps God?"

The professor leant forward, knocked out his pipe into the fireplace, and began slowly to refill it from his leather tobacco pouch.

"It's a good question, a most unusual question, I must say. No. I don't honestly think it would have occurred to any of us to think of God in connexion with our work. God, you see, was for us entirely a matter of religion, and all of us had left religion behind. It was Goethe, now that I come to think of it, who said somewhere: 'He who possesses art and science has religion; he who does not possess them needs religion.' Our grandparents were religious in the proper, old-fashioned sense; perhaps in some cases, our parents were too. But for us, religion was something we'd grown out of, something the academic world we lived in was no longer concerned with or had simply replaced. There were scholars in the university studying theology, of course, but we regarded them as historians, or philosophers, or something between the two. Religion in their case was something to be studied, but genuine religion was something people *did*, or, as far as we were concerned, used to do. We didn't do it, and if the theologians or other people in the university still did, it was no business of ours. We believed, as I say, in the mind and in what it could achieve for the good of humanity, and what we did, every day, was to work with our minds towards that good. You could say that then, and perhaps in all the years up to the war, we were full of faith in what we were doing, but it wasn't a faith that had anything to do with God."

"And then—the war?"

"Yes, the war. The war destroyed our faith in science. The horrors of the war, on both sides. The scientific world was one, united, you know, before the war. I remember London in 1912, the celebration for 250 years of the Royal Society. That was only ten years ago, but now it seems to have been another age, another world . . .

"Yes, well, the war showed us, or some of us, that what we were doing, all this new knowledge of the chemical components of matter that we were assembling, wasn't, after all, good in itself as we had thought, as we had believed. It wasn't bad either; it was merely useful, and powerful. It could be put to good ends, such as the curing of disease or the manufacture of artificial forms of valuable substances, like fertilizers. But it could also be put to bad ends, wicked and destructive ends, and it was the discovery that this was not only possible but required—required by the state, which paid our salaries—and then much praised, that destroyed our faith in science. Or that destroyed *my* faith in science, perhaps I should say, since there are still many, particularly in the younger generation, who believe that scientific progress should command the kind of absolute obedience and dedication given in religion to God. And many believe that it's perfectly legitimate to use the power it brings for political ends, to wage war, to prolong war. Ach!"

"Was it poison gas that destroyed your faith?"

"Poison gas, yes. What a dreadful weapon. Poor Fritz Haber, and poor Clara. I see you know about her death. But as well as poison gas, Fritz Haber's manufacture of nitroglycerine provided our army with the basic means of fighting for years of the war. Without his work, who knows? The war might have ended much earlier. Millions of lives might have been spared."

Max said nothing and waited for his grandfather to relight his pipe, which had gone out.

"So you see, if the power of the mind is no more than exactly that, a human adventure that can as well lead to death as to life, is there anything, anywhere, in which an intelligent man can put his trust, his faith? I don't think so. And yet there is beauty and some kind of truth—what kind precisely, I don't know, and I'm not sure anyone does—in great music, great painting, great poetry. *Art* and science, Goethe said. I think I believe in the great works of art now, and only in them, not as God of course, but as telling us about something *else*, something outside us and beyond our comprehension that somehow makes our lives worth living. That's why I said I both don't and do believe—not in God as religious people understand the word but perhaps in something that might be called God because it is mysterious, because it seems to be truly good, because it demands loyalty and dedication as I once thought science did."

"But music and painting and poetry are also us, aren't they? I mean, they're just the power of the mind again, different from science but still the power of the mind, another human adventure."

"But can they be used for evil purposes? To kill? To prolong war? No, they can't. *Not if they're any good.* So that makes them different. I'm not saying they are God, in any sense, only that they point us towards something beyond ourselves . . ."

"Couldn't that just be wishful thinking? Couldn't music, even great music, just be something we invent and play, play with like a baby with a rattle, to cheer ourselves up? Zapolski told me Nietzsche said we have art so that we don't perish of the truth."

"Did he, by God! That's a truly terrifying statement. There's no way of refuting it except by saying, 'I don't believe it.' That's precisely why I'm hesitant to say I have any faith in anything at all. I was trained to use my mind cautiously, rationally, never to commit myself to anything that couldn't be proved. So my answer to your original question should, I fear, be, 'No. I don't believe in God.'"

"Hope for faith."

"What did you say?"

"Oh, just something Dr Mendel said to me when I was younger. Hope for faith, he said. But I don't know. Perhaps it's more honest to decide to manage without it, because of the evidence. Because there's no proof, I mean."

"As Zapolski does. You admire him, don't you?"

"Well, he's made up his own mind, on the evidence. He's independent and clear. And he thinks life is really exciting, challenging, like you said about the harpsichord. We can decide, each of us, who to be, what to do, what to make of our lives."

"I hope that will be true, for you of course, and for him. For all the clever boys in the Gymnasium. But I wish it could be true for everyone. If you read Nietzsche, you'll see that he leaves almost everyone—everyone else, that is—out of account altogether, as if they weren't human beings at all. That's why I regard him as dangerous."

"Science and art leave out an awful lot of people too."

"They do. They do. And Nietzsche approved of both. What does your Dr Fischer say about him?"

"Oh, nothing really, but I'm sure he'd agree with you."

"Has Dr Fischer said anything about what he thinks you should do with your life?"

"Not at all. He doesn't talk to us one by one. He would like us to believe in God. He wants us to be interested in all sorts of things, in philosophy, in literature, in the past. He has said he'd like some of us to try to get into the Reichstag, perhaps into the government, one day. Zapolski thinks that too. But not because he agrees with Dr Fischer. As a matter of fact, Dr Fischer's a Catholic."

Max said this tentatively, afraid that his grandfather would react as Dr Mendel had done to the idea of a Catholic schoolmaster in Max's life.

"I see", his grandfather said. "That means that religion, in his case, is probably something he still does. I've often envied Catholics that habit, that discipline. In a curious way, I think it frees them rather than binds them. One less thing to have to decide about. There's Mass on Sunday. You have to be there, so you are. No need to think it out every time. Did you know Catholics have something called holy days of obligation? It sounds nonsensical. Yet perhaps it would do us all good."

"But then why . . . ?"

"Why did I never become a Catholic? Oh, Max. Such a long story. Because I was trained to the discipline of proof. Another thing altogether. But also because I start from far too far outside. Perhaps this is as good a time as any to tell you something you don't know and are going to have to know sooner or later. First I shall make some coffee. What's the time? Not yet midnight. Good. The fire's nearly out. See if you can bring it back to life while I make the coffee."

Max remade the fire on the embers. He was, unaccountably, afraid of what his grandfather, in higher spirits than Max had seen him for months, was going to tell him.

The old man reappeared with a tray, coffee, cups, sugar, and a plate of little biscuits, favourites of Max's grandmother. He hadn't seen them for years. They were expensive: his grandfather must have asked Frau Gärtner to buy some in case of a special occasion. He felt more afraid. Grandpapa poured the coffee and offered Max the biscuits. Max took one and put it on his saucer.

"Now, Max, listen carefully. I am a German, of course. I have been proud all my life to be a German, to live in Germany, to speak, as my only language, apart from some bits and pieces of Latin and English, the language of Schiller and Goethe and Heine, to have been always a citizen of German cities of great renown and high culture, first Frankfurt and then Berlin and then Breslau. I am also, officially, a Protestant. I was baptized as a small baby by my Protestant parents. I married your grandmother in a Protestant church. Your mother was also baptized as a small baby, as were you and your brothers at Waldau. Of course. But I am a Jew. Perhaps I should say, '*And* I am a Jew', or 'I am *also* a Jew': it would be better if I could. I know, however, that what has to be said is: '*But* I am a Jew.' "

Max put down his cup and saucer on the floor. There was a long silence.

"Grandpapa, I think I knew that. I think I've known for a long time, though no one told me." He added quickly, "No one lied to me either. Of course not. No one told me you weren't . . . it wasn't . . . What about Grandmama?"

"She also. A rather different story. Hers was a Breslau family. Her father was a timber merchant. She had no brothers, so the family has now disappeared. It was a prosperous family. You and I are fortunate, now, when so many people have lost so much, to be able, for instance, to stay in this flat, which belongs to us, and to have Frau Gärtner to help us. Though how much longer all this will be possible, I don't know. The inflation is getting very alarming."

"What about your family? You said you came to Breslau because the medical work in the university was so interesting. Was it in Frankfurt that you grew up?"

"I was born in Frankfurt, the city of Goethe, the city of the springtime of the nations. Also the city of the most crowded and squalid and poor and confined ghetto in the whole of Germany. But that was over, that life, when I was born. The Jews were free at last, at least in theory, to do anything, to study anything, that anyone else could do or study. And in any case, my parents were Protestants, weren't they?"

"What was the springtime of the nations?"

"Ah, you Prussian boy—you've never heard of it? That's because it was a failure. Prussians don't like to think about failure. That's why the war, the only great failure the Prussians have ever had, has left them so confused. In 1848, the year of revolutions—you'll have been told about the revolutions, but only probably that they came to nothing—there was a German parliament in Frankfurt."

"I've just heard of that. Dr Fischer mentioned it."

"Good. Its members came from all the German lands—the members called themselves delegates, not exactly elected but cast up, you might say, by rioting workers in the cities—to meet in a big Frankfurt church and discuss the future of a united, enlightened, liberal Germany. Very serious they were, very well-intentioned, full of hope, these bourgeois intellectuals planning Germany, which didn't then exist. A free country, with free Jews, free Poles even—though they weren't sure about the Poles—and a new flag, black, gold, and red, and a new song, *Deutschland über alles*, which would inspire a liberal country as the Marseillaise inspires France. Wonderful. A working drawing with all the right forms and measurements for beautiful music to be played on the instrument when it was built. It came to nothing, nothing whatsoever. It was a ghost before it was born."

"What happened?"

"There were no soldiers. The Frankfurt parliament had no army. The Prussians, of course, had an army, but the King of Prussia didn't want to preside over a liberal constitution, and in the end, Prussian soldiers shut the whole thing down. It was the end of that future for Germany. The instrument was never built, and the music died away into silence, or rather into military marches. Instead of the Germany planned in Frankfurt, we had Bismarck and 1870 and the Kaiser, and then we had the war."

"Might it have worked, if it had been built, that kind of Germany?"

"Who can tell? Human beings have a limitless capacity for making a mess of the best plans and the best intentions. Look at America. Slavery, and terrible brutality, in the land of the free. Look at our new republic, with the same flag and the same song as in 1848: I was so delighted that its constitution was agreed on in Weimar rather than in Potsdam, with the blessing of Goethe and Schiller instead of the vulgar strutting of the Kaiser. But I'm afraid the republic is already weak and divided. Democracy, its defenders would say, is bound to be divided. But in England or America, democracy is divided and at the same time strong. Why not here?

"But what I wanted to tell you is that my father, your great-grandfather, was one of those who drew up the constitution. He was part of the effort, part of the dream. He always thought the Frankfurt plan was full of real hope, real possibility. Its failure broke his heart."

"What was his work?"

"Oh, he worked in the city hall in Frankfurt. Frankfurt wasn't in Prussia then: it was a free city, governing itself. It was once a free city of the Habsburg empire. My father's work was dull. But politics was his life. He was a clever man, a thoughtful man. He became one of the delegates in the Frankfurt parliament. If the plan had come to anything, he would have been a minister in the new government. There were several baptized Jews in the parliament, and he was one, the first in our family. His father—I never met my grandfather; he died before I was born—had his children baptized just after the defeat of Napoleon, in 1816 or 1817, when freedom for the Jews was set back all over again. My father was his eldest son. Since then, my family have been Protestants, at least in name, though I don't think any of us—certainly not my father, or my brother who went to America in the seventies to make his fortune and died instead, or I myself—have ever been Christian in any religious sense. Or, naturally, Jewish.

"I was born in 1850, only a year after the collapse of the Frankfurt parliament. I was the youngest in the family. I had two sisters, both dead now, as well as a brother. I'm not sure my father really had the energy to concentrate on another child, but my mother was ambitious for me. I went to elementary school, Gymnasium, and medical school in Berlin. Then there was the hospital and university work here. Gradually through my life, an ordinary successful German bourgeois life, my sense of Jewishness wore off. When Toni married your father, it seemed to your grandmother that we had left even the distant memory of the ghetto far behind. A Junker family, a Prussian count: what could be more respectable? What, above all, could be more German? Yet one can't forget one's Jewishness; nor can anyone else. Colleagues, friends, patients, students: the acknowledgement of a difference, a difference that isolates and estranges the Jew, is always there, like a bad smell no one mentions in a beautiful room. Fellow Jews—there are plenty of them, of course, in science, in medicine, in music—become one's closest colleagues and dearest friends, just because in their company the bad smell goes away. It's come and gone during my lifetime, the pressure, the strain of being a Jew. It was bad when I was a boy, but medicine was not closed, at least to baptized Jews—at school, I thought I would perhaps be a country doctor. Then it got better.

Bismarck, who didn't like Jews unless they were very rich and useful to the state, disliked Catholics even more than he disliked Jews. In his new Prussian Germany, Jews were in theory completely emancipated. I never wanted to accept a position that was closed to a religious Jew; it seemed wrong. But at that time, Jews could become even judges, even professors. So I became a professor, here in Breslau.

"Then it got worse again, but worse in a subtler way. A theory, pretending to be scientific and so all the more dangerous, appeared in France and was adopted by a lot of people in Germany who should have known better. The theory was that Jews are worse, intrinsically, unalterably and forever, than other people because they belong to a race, the Semitic race, which is intrinsically, unalterably, and forever inferior to other races. So it's natural and right for the superior races to despise Jews, to exclude them from power and privilege, to mock and bully them as if they were not actually human beings at all. It's a ludicrous theory. It has no basis in science or history, let alone philosophy or ethics. It has no basis, either, in Christianity, which, if it hadn't at the very beginning accepted converted Jews as Christians, would have had no beginning, no history, no philosophy or ethics. But people have taken to this theory because they want a scientific reason to hate and despise the Jews. It's reappeared in a most unpleasant fashion since the war, and I fear it's now taken hold among the uneducated, where it certainly didn't start. These young thugs only need some kind of excuse to humiliate others because they feel humiliated themselves, by the defeat and by the treaty; and the idea that all Jews can be bullied just because they're Jews gives them their excuse. They're already picking on easily identifiable Jews, poor families from the east who speak only Yiddish, and it will get worse, unless the government and the police make sure that all terrorising of people for nothing more than who they happen to be is a crime that will be properly and strictly punished. Have you noticed anything of this kind in the Gymnasium?"

"No. Well, not really. Sometimes you hear a boy call someone else a 'Yid'—just as a general insult, or because he's being selfish and stingy about something. But there are some Jewish boys in my class, and no one treats them any differently from the rest, though one or two of the teachers might like to, I think."

"That doesn't sound too bad. If the brightest and best of the young are not infected by this nonsense, there's some hope that it will fade away in time, as it's faded away before."

"I've seen posters in the streets, not many, saying 'Jews Out' and the same thing painted on the windows of one or two shops."

"Bullies. The Stormtroopers most likely."

Max got out of his chair, poured some more coffee into his grandfather's empty cup, knelt on the floor, and put two more logs and some lumps of coal carefully onto the fire. He stayed on the floor, kneeling on the rug and looking into the fire.

"Grandpapa?"

"Yes, Max?"

"It means . . . all you've told me means I'm half-Jewish, doesn't it?"

"Well, yes and no. You are half-Jewish in the sense that the racial theorists favour. But, as I've said, their theory is nonsense. According to their theory, you're only half-German, but that's absurd. You're wholly German in every sense that matters. So is your mother. So am I. I know no Hebrew, and a bit of Yiddish only because much of the Yiddish language is a primitive German dialect from long ago when the Jews moved east because the Poles were more tolerant than the Germans. That's no longer the case, I'm afraid. I've never been inside a synagogue or been present at a Sabbath meal in a Jewish home. So while I may not be a Christian in any religious sense, as I've tried to explain this evening, I'm certainly not a real Jew. And yet . . ."

"And yet?"

"I don't know. Perhaps there are instincts collected from the long past. Swallows emerge from eggs in a Breslau street, learn to fly in a few weeks, and a few weeks later set off for Africa and know how to get there. That's an instinct collected from the long past. Jews have an instinct for keeping out of trouble, for submission—you could dignify it by calling it an instinct for peace. For many generations, they weren't required or allowed to carry weapons, to fight in the armies of any of the countries that gave them refuge, gave them homes. When they were told to join imperial armies because they were at last being treated like normal citizens, sometimes in the east, though not in Germany, the young men killed themselves rather than fight, because their instinct and the law of Moses told them they were not permitted to kill other human beings. When your brother was killed at Tannenberg, your mother and your grandmother and I felt it differently from your father. He was sad, of course, at his loss, but so proud too. To him, the war was a wonderful thing. At last Germany's turn had come. After Spain and France and England and their empires, with the Germans always on the edge, without a proper country until so late, now at last, with Germany richer than England, it was Germany's turn for triumph, not just over France but over England, over the world. 'Each people has its day in history, but the day of the Germans is the harvest of all times.' "

"Who wrote that, Grandpapa?"

"I can't remember. Schiller, I think. Anyway, it's what your father and thousands like him thought in 1914. Let the young men ride into battle in their polished boots and their snow-white breeches. Let their blood pour out into the Prussian earth, sacrificial blood shed for the greater glory of Germany. But Freddy's blood wasn't only your father's, the blood of generations of soldiers; it was your mother's too. It was mine. The blood of different generations, of those who down the centuries studied the Torah in the ghettos and lit the Sabbath candles. And never held a weapon."

Stiff, kneeling on the floor, Max stood up and sat down again in his chair. Now he looked at his grandfather.

"Grandpapa, what do you think I should do? With my life, I mean."

He saw the old man's face clear, his glance come back from remote distances to meet his own.

"Well, I thought you were going to be a doctor."

"So did I. At least, Mother wants me to study medicine, like you, or perhaps to be a violinist. But now, I don't know. The work that really interests me at school isn't in mathematics or physics or chemistry. I can do my work in those subjects, but I'm much more interested in history and philosophy, in understanding how everything has become so tangled up and cruel—the war and so on—and what we should do now to make sure there isn't another war and that things get better for people."

"Ah. Dr Fischer's plan perhaps. Doctors, you know, do try to make things better for people. That's the point of all their work, in universities and laboratories as well as in hospital wards and at home, where people fall ill and die, children and the old, and women, worn out too soon. People need help. They'll always need help, whatever else is happening in the world. The wounded soldiers need help too—whatever you think of the war—the blind and the amputees, and most of all, those with broken minds, the ones who saw and heard more than they had the strength to bear."

"Yes, of course, of course. Perhaps it's the best, the noblest . . . But I'd like . . . Never mind, I'm not sure even what I mean. But don't you think that in politics, perhaps, it might be possible to change things, really change things for the better, especially now in the new republic?"

"Perhaps you'll be the next Walther Rathenau, particularly if he's a success in the government."

"I don't know much about him. I know he's the foreign minister. Dr Fischer admires him very much. He thinks he's a kind of philosopher-king like in Plato. I did see a horrible poster, 'Death to Walther Rathenau, the—'"

"Yes, I've seen it too. It's the bad smell in the room again. I met Walther Rathenau once, at a conference in Berlin before the war. A most remarkable man. His mother was a Frankfurt lady, a very fine pianist, as I believe he is too. He should become our Disraeli, but I'm not sure he has the toughness, the thick skin, to cope with the rough and tumble of political life—he is almost too noble, too much of an idealist, perhaps."

"Who is Disraeli?"

"Disraeli? Benjamin Disraeli. With a name like that, he was the English Prime Minister fifty years ago—what an achievement. He was baptized as a boy, like my father, and I don't think he was any more a religious Christian than I am. But England isn't Germany—it's easier for a Jew to be Prime Minister in England than it is for a Catholic. And Disraeli wasn't the same kind of Jew as Walther Rathenau. There are two kinds of Jew, head in the air or feet on the ground, as the English would say, and Disraeli's feet were on the ground."

"Which kind do you think you are, Grandpapa?"

"Oh, head in the air, no doubt. But you—you are your father's son, Max, and the Junkers have their feet on the stony fields of Prussia. Now, it's nearly one o'clock. I think we should go to bed, don't you?"

"Just one more thing, Grandpapa. Does Heinrich know . . . all that you've told me tonight?"

"Heinrich? I've no idea. I would think not, unless your mother has told him, which is most unlikely. It wasn't something your father ever referred to. Perhaps he wasn't altogether happy with it himself. That was why I was never entirely at home at Waldau—something to do with instincts collected from the long past, I daresay. Of course, I don't know Heinrich as I know you—I haven't seen him since before the war, and now he's a grown man and has been through a very great deal. He has experience of a kind he knows I've never had, and of a kind that separates for the rest of their lives those who've had it from those who haven't. These boys who put up the 'Jews Out' posters and shout insults are mostly too young to have been soldiers in the war. They're jealous of those who were old enough to have had to fight and kill and risk death, so they try to generate the experience for themselves on the streets. The same is true of this new passion for sport among the young, athletics, tennis, swimming, what have you— but at least that's healthy and does no one any harm. I wouldn't say anything to Heinrich if I were you, when you go home. He might be very angry with all of us, but particularly with your father, and what good would that do anyone, most of all your poor mother?

"Now, Max, we must go to bed. I hope you'll sleep—I've given you a lot to think about. Perhaps too much. But you're an intelligent boy, and old enough now to think your way through facts you certainly deserve to know. Try not to think too much tonight. It's late, and the best thing to do is to sleep on it all. You have school in the morning. Dr Fischer won't appreciate a half-asleep pupil in his class. I should like to meet this man one day."

Max tidied up, put a guard in front of the fire, and took the coffee cups on the tray to the kitchen, his own cup full of cold coffee, with an untouched biscuit on the saucer. He stood in the kitchen, looking out of the window at the dark backs of houses in the next street, and wondered what the biscuit reminded him of. It took him a few minutes to remember the roses his mother had dropped on the ground on the morning they heard the war had begun. Then he went to bed.

It was just as well, Max thought several times in the next few weeks, that Zapolski seemed not in the least interested in him, in who he was or where he came from. Zapolski never asked questions, and Max was too much in awe of him to volunteer information that might seem "banal", one of Zapolski's favourite words, or, worse, given in order to exact sympathy. So while he struggled to get accustomed to what his grandfather had told him that night, he was glad to walk to Cathedral Island nearly every afternoon with Zapolski, talking about the day's lessons, the peculiarities of other boys in their class, books they were reading (especially Nietzsche), and sometimes the state of the country and the news in the papers, but never the subject that was really preoccupying him.

Sometimes, as the weather got warmer, they stopped in a café for half an hour or so, but there was no more brandy on these occasions. As they drank their coffee, they watched the people go by, Zapolski pointing out to Max the most fashionable girls, with the shortest, brightest hair and the shortest skirts as they approached in the passing crowd. Max preferred to look—not obviously, he hoped—at a different kind of girl, those with dark hair in old-fashioned chignons and longer dresses. Perhaps such girls were just younger than the sort Zapolski picked out and still in their school clothes. Max knew almost nothing about girls. One day, Zapolski said:

"Have you ever . . . you know . . . with a real girl?"

Max was shocked.

"No, of course not."

"Well, I think we're getting too old for this, watching the girls go by like dirty-minded schoolboys. We'll have to do something about it. I'll think of something."

Max hoped he wouldn't. He had a very hazy idea of a night world of dance clubs and brothels that existed in a quarter of the city he had heard talk of at school but never been to. He suspected Zapolski knew no more about this world than he did but was much keener to find out. Zapolski sometimes talked about jazz as if he knew what it sounded like. Max had heard no jazz—only from Zapolski and a couple of other boys in the class had he heard even the word—and he was sure that his grandfather and Dr Mendel would be appalled at the idea of him seeking out this new, barbaric kind of music. On the other hand, if he went out in the evening with Zapolski, perhaps they need never know where he'd been?

But it wasn't to a jazz club that Zapolski invited Max one afternoon in June as they walked under the willows by the old moat, though Max knew his grandfather and Dr Mendel, who would certainly have to be told, would be almost as disapproving as if it had been.

"My mother's coming to Breslau next week. She's got a box for the opera, *Tristan*, the Friday performance. How she does it I don't know, but she always manages to get a box wherever she goes. She said I could bring a friend. Would you like to come?"

"Of course I would. Thank you, Zapolski, very much."

Tristan, Zapolski said, was very long, and the performance was to start at seven; he told Max to come to the White Eagle to join him and his mother's party at six for a cocktail, a word Max had never heard, and something to eat before the opera.

The White Eagle was the most expensive hotel in the city. Max had never been inside it. As soon as the hotel footman opened the door of the private sitting room with the loud words "Count von Hofmannswaldau", Max wished he had refused the invitation. He was wearing the newer of his two student uniforms, which had been suitable and inconspicuous when he'd been to the opera house before, with his grandfather, to dress rehearsals of *The Marriage of Figaro, Der Freischütz*, and *The Bartered Bride*. Dr Mendel had got them tickets. Now here were Zapolski and another man in white tie and tails, and a look of surprise on the beautiful face of Zapolski's mother, who was dressed in black with diamonds, when Zapolski introduced him. Max clicked his heels and bowed his head stiffly, immediately feeling like an idiot to find himself saying not "Good evening", as he should have, but "I'm sorry not to—" He was cut short by a dazzling smile of a kind he'd never met before, a smile into his eyes, and the words, in a voice so low that no one else in the room would hear them, "Don't worry, Max; of what importance are clothes? It's wonderful to meet Adam's friend at last." And then, louder, "What will you have to drink? Adam!"

Zapolski had never called Max by his first name, and didn't now, taking him to a table on which various drinks in glasses of different kinds were arranged on gleaming white linen. "I'd have a Sekt if I were you, Hofmannswaldau", he said. So he did, sipping the tingling wine so slowly that it lasted all of the half hour that went by before they left the hotel for the opera house. There were also plates of small sandwiches. "Foie gras or caviar?" Max had never tasted either before, thought them equally delicious, and remained unsure which was which.

For most of the time, during which a middle-aged couple arrived, were greeted, and were talked to, he was able to stand in silence by the table with the drinks on it, hoping to be forgotten about. Then Adam's mother came towards him, preceded by a scent as exotic and delicious to Max as the food he was eating.

"My dear boy! Adam has told me too little about you. So like him, don't you think? He deals in mystery. Tell me. Do your parents live in Breslau?"

"No, not in Breslau", Max said, very politely. "My mother lives at Waldau, in the country, about forty miles away. My father is dead. I stay in Breslau with my—"

"Oh, my poor child! Killed in the war, I suppose, like Adam's father. Well, life has to go on, doesn't it? Are you the eldest son—or the only son, perhaps?"

"No, my brother Carl Friedrich was—"

"I see. Well, never mind. Adam says you're very clever. What do you propose to do with your life? Not waste it in the country, I hope, with horses and shooting and town councils?"

"I'm not sure. I might be a doctor if—"

"Very worthy, no doubt. Adam says he's going to be a philosopher, but I don't like to think of him shut away in a university. So bourgeois, don't you agree? But then, I'd rather he were in Breslau—however bourgeois—a good, sober German town, than in Vienna for his education. Vienna's gone mad since the war. Have you heard *Tristan* before? No? I'm so glad. Every young man should hear his first *Tristan* in very special circumstances. I believe tonight's performance will be excellent, even though we're only in Breslau. The conductor's come from Berlin, just for four performances, I'm told. A Jew of course, but then all the best conductors nowadays seem to be Jews. Naturally, they convert, but that doesn't make any difference, does it? Klemperer converted the other day. So talented. So modern. He became a Catholic—would you believe it? We're so lucky in Vienna—we have Richard Strauss running the opera house. In fact, his *Tristan* was the last I heard. Wonderful. He's a wonderful musician. Have you heard *Salome*? No? You will. You will. Come, you must meet Hans Christian, my special friend, you know."

Max took in very little of this, though he remembered all of it later. The impact on him of Zapolski's mother, her blonde hair short but heavy each side of her face, her diamond earrings and necklace, and the white, soft skin of her neck, shoulders, and bosom above her low-cut black dress made him feel drunk and dizzy as his few sips of white wine had certainly not. Now he was shaking hands with a tall, fair man of about thirty, with very broad shoulders and an easy laugh.

"Hello, Count. So you're the clever schoolfriend, are you? What do you make of Adam? A difficult fellow to get to know, isn't he?"

"Look out, Hofmannswaldau. Hans Christian's fishing for information about me. Don't you dare tell him anything!"

Before Max could think of something to say, he was rescued by the door of the sitting room opening and a footman saying, "The countess's cars are at the door." After a flurry of servants, coats, and politeness, he found himself sitting beside a chauffeur for the five-minute drive to the opera house. Then he was sitting in the depths of one of the best boxes, on a little gilt chair behind Zapolski's mother and her friend and the middle-aged couple, and next to Zapolski who was looking carefully at the grandly dressed audience settling itself in the seats below. Max saw the reassuring grey head of Dr Mendel in the orchestra pit towards the back of the first violins, and Herr Rosenthal in the front desk of the cellos. The house lights went down. The conductor appeared, was greeted with applause, bowed to the audience, turned towards the orchestra, and raised his arms. Silence.

The first bars of the overture were like no music Max had ever heard before. He sat transfixed, forgetting the other people in the box, the embarrassments of the evening so far, his grandfather's disapproval of Wagner, everything else but this music, now and now and now, which stirred him to what felt like the very depths of his soul. When the overture died away to quietness and the curtain rose, he had forgotten that he was in a theatre and that this was an opera, so that it was as if he alone in a magical dream had arrived on the deck of a ship where two women in long dark velvet dresses were surrounded by rich hangings and, somewhere out of sight, a sailor was singing a wistful ballad about an Irish girl. He moved scarcely at all during the whole of the first act. He didn't understand, and didn't entirely hear, all the words that were sung, but the music held him so securely that he knew, as if he had always known, that Tristan and Isolde were bound together by a passion so deep and so secret that only an accident, the drink they thought to be deadly poison, could have brought it to expression. When the curtain fell quickly and the orchestra reached a feverish stop, he was astonished that people clapped, even cheered. He was amazed that the house lights went up and everyone in the theatre began to talk, stand up, look for their wraps and handbags, and smile and wave across the seats. He couldn't clap, couldn't move, couldn't speak. Clearly, however, he had to do all these things. So he did.

At the intermission, people came to the box to greet the countess. There was a lot of talking and laughing and no room, so Zapolski and Max went out into the red plush corridor.

"Well?" Zapolski said, his eyes laughing.

"I don't ... I can't ... It isn't like anything I've ever heard ... ever."

"Good."

And, side by side, they leant with their backs against a polished wooden shelf that ran the length of the red corridor, and said nothing else until the bell rang to warn of the start of the next act. They stood outside the box door to let the visitors, still talking, leave, and got back to their little gilt chairs as the house lights went down.

The chattering of the audience subsided, and the orchestral prelude began. When the hunting horns died away and the curtain rose, Max was instantly back in his own magical dream, now among the trees of a summer garden under a castle wall as night was falling. The music, the passion of Tristan and Isolde in the moonlit garden, was even more absorbing and strange than in the first act. After a stretch of time that was long but always felt doomed to be not long enough, the dawn and King Mark's hunting knights crashed into the lovers' trance like the intermission's interruption from the noisy world of the theatre, the clapping, the talking, and the people in evening dress and diamonds. But before the curtain fell for the second intermission, the music of King Mark's wounded sadness at his betrayal by Tristan, whom he loved, carried Max even further down into a depth of feeling he didn't know was possible. Zapolski's mother turned round as the din of the interval began and levelled her smile at Max.

"So, Max, what do you think of Emmy Krüger?"

He had no idea what the question meant.

"I ... that is ..."

"A fine voice, of course, but in my opinion, not as ... My dear boy, you're as white as a sheet. Are you feeling all right? Adam! Take Max outside for some fresh air—he doesn't look at all well."

They went out through the milling audience, who were looking for glasses of wine and plates of food, arranged on small tables each with a named flag in the centre. In the street, among the coachmen, the horses, and the chauffeurs of big cars, they walked round the corner of the opera house into a quiet side street and stopped under a lamp. Zapolski lit a cigarette. When he had smoked it slowly and thrown the butt some distance into the gutter, he said:

"You'll get over it. It's only music."

Then he stood, looking away from Max along the quiet side of the opera house towards the busy street, the lamplight on his face. He was not seeing the traffic and the passers-by; his eyes were distant, his attention somewhere else.

Max had a sick sensation of falling, as if in a nightmare. But it didn't wake him up because he was awake. I love him, he thought. I love Adam Zapolski. He was shocked as if by a shot from a gun he hadn't seen. He backed away a step or two and shook his head hard.

"Perhaps we should go back", he said. "Do you know how long the intermission lasts?"

"Not all that long, and I need a pee. Let's go."

They went, and Max waited alone in the red plush corridor until the visitors left the box. He refused himself permission to think about what he had just discovered. There's another act, more music. It'll start again soon, very soon. Thank God.

He was back in his seat before Zapolski slipped into the box and sat down on the chair beside him. Max didn't look at him.

The curtain rose on a desolate castle by the sea, the wounded Tristan lying asleep with his devoted Kurwenal guarding him. The saddest tune Max had ever heard drifted across the knight and his squire. The tune was played not in the orchestra but somewhere else, somewhere out of sight altogether, on a reedy cor anglais. His whole head was suddenly full of tears. He sat completely still, swallowing and blinking, forcing back his tears.

The music was as beautiful and strange as before, pulling him towards its complexities and its meanings, but he had lost his connexion with it. Preoccupied with the presence of Zapolski so close to him, sitting with his chin in his hand listening and watching attentively, Max could feel only the chaos inside him. When Tristan came to and began to sing of the sorrows of his life, Max suddenly saw him as a middle-aged tenor in medieval costume looking much too stout and healthy to be close to death. The music turned to celebration, Isolde arrived, Tristan died in her arms, there was a fight between Kurwenal and King Mark's black knight, and King Mark forgave everyone. It all now seemed rather absurd: Max looked at the orchestra pit, where the players, hot and tired in their evening dress, were playing hard, staring at the notes in front of them with occasional glances at the conductor, mopping their brows with white handkerchiefs when they had a few bars' rest. Max could think only of whether there might be some arrangement of cars and guests that would allow him to travel with Zapolski as far as Cathedral Island after the opera. But before the end, Isolde, singing over the body of the dead Tristan, drew Max back into the dream, and for a few minutes of her rapturous farewell, everything was possible—love was possible, consummation was possible, it was possible for the chaos of passion to be resolved, resolved in calm, in death, in peace. Then the curtain fell, and the audience, on its feet, roared and stamped applause, and bunches of flowers were in the singers' arms and at their feet.

Max, dazed and exhausted, managed, on the sidewalk by the chauffeurs, to thank the countess politely for inviting him, and then found that he was indeed to be in the back of a car with Zapolski, who would be dropped at Cathedral Island before he himself was taken home to his grandfather's flat. It was late. There was no traffic in the streets. The journey took only a few minutes. They said nothing. As Zapolski got out of the car, he said:

"Goodnight, Hofmannswaldau. I'm glad you came."

Damn him, damn him, Max thought as the chauffeur drove him on. Why didn't he mock as he always does?

Max got through Saturday and Sunday, mostly walking by himself under the June trees in the Scheitniger park. He had said very little to his grandfather about his evening at the opera. ("*Tristan* was extraordinary. Quite different from anything else. No, of course not better than Mozart or Beethoven or Bach. Just quite different.") On Sunday afternoon, he had sat for a long time on a fold-up wooden chair in the park, among the old people and the young mothers with children, listening to the military band playing marches and tunes from operettas in the bandstand. He thought the music might banish the Wagner from his memory. But once he was out of earshot of the band, he knew it hadn't.

Monday was an ordinary day at school. On Mondays Max never walked to Cathedral Island with Zapolski because, his violin slung across his back, he had to bicycle quickly in the opposite direction for his lesson with Dr Mendel.

"Well, Max, what did you make of your first Wagner opera?"

"I don't know. It was wonderful, a bit frightening, very sad. I thought it was more like Virgil than like other music."

"Like Virgil? That's an interesting thing to say. Can you explain what you mean?"

"It's difficult to explain. It's something to do with the music behaving like words—I know there are words being sung, but it's not them I mean. It's that the music becomes a kind of language. Music is always a language, I know. But this is a language you could translate, which music usually isn't. It's not just the mixture of the beat and the phrasing that makes it like Virgil, but it's that you're being told the story, being given the meaning, at the same time, actually in the music. There's a boy in my class who reads poetry aloud so that you ... Well, it's a bit like the *Tristan* music."

"It's very tiring to play, I can tell you. And there are Wagner operas even longer than *Tristan*. He was a remarkable composer, of course. A genius in his own way. But you must never think he was the greatest composer of all, as many people do now, because that he certainly was not. Now, Max, we shall do some work."

The next day after lunch, Dr Fischer came into the classroom for their Greek lesson a few minutes late. He was never late. They stood, as always; he plodded, more heavily than usual, down the side of their rows of desks to his lectern. When he turned to face them, he looked older, crushed.

"Sit down, gentlemen."

There's a new war, Max thought.

"Gentlemen, I have just learnt that Dr Rathenau was shot and killed this morning on his way to the foreign ministry. His assassins were young Prussian officers of the Freikorps, only a few years older than you. Things are not going well, it's true, for the government or for the country. But Dr Rathenau was our best hope for the improvement of our country's condition, both at home and in the eyes of our neighbours. He has not been murdered because he was a bad man or a bad minister, not even because he was a good man and a good minister. He has been murdered because he is—because he was a Jew. This is a disgrace from which it will take many years for Germany to recover, and you boys must never forget it. I would ask you to stand for a moment as a mark of respect for a brave and noble man."

Three boys remained in their seats long enough for Dr Fischer to have to compel them to their feet with a look of steel. When he left the classroom at the end of afternoon lessons, these three boys and four others cheered.

As Max and Zapolski approached Blücher Square on their way to Cathedral Island, they heard raw shouting and singing. Thirty or forty men, mostly young, a few the wounded soldiers in rags who always begged or sold matches in the square, were swaying together round the statue of Blücher and drunkenly singing, "Death to Walther Rathenau, the rotten, lousy Jewish sow" and then shouting an untidy cheer. Housewives and children going home from school were hurrying along the sidewalks, not looking at the crowd. Two policemen were standing on the corner of the square, their backs to a café, watching. Zapolski, his face alight with fury, left Max with his bicycle and marched to the swaying crowd.

"Stop that! Stop!" he yelled. Some of them stopped singing and looked blearily at him. The rest didn't notice him. Max let his bike fall with a clang onto the road and ran to Zapolski's side. A giant in the crowd shouted, "What's it to you? Rathenau's a filthy traitor." A cheer went up from the crowd: "A traitor, a traitor!" The giant went on, "Stabbed us in the back! We never lost the war!" The rest picked this up: "We never lost the war! We never lost the war! Death to Walther Rathenau . . ."

Zapolski now roared with a voice Max would never have suspected he had. "Shut up, all of you! Shut up!" Most of them did.

"You're wrong! Rathenau was a good man! There's no hope for this country if people like him get murdered and people like you dance on his grave."

"Oh, toffee-nosed, are we? People like us, indeed. We'll see about people like you! Milksop students! Mummy's boys!" The giant was at the back of the crowd, under the statue, Blücher's raised commanding arm immediately above his head. As he lunged forward, his way blocked by a dozen others, Zapolski said to Max, "Run!" They ran. What happened behind them in the square they couldn't tell, but when they stopped, out of breath, four streets and four corners away, no one was pursuing them.

"Well done!" Max said, almost putting an arm round Zapolski's shoulders, stopping himself in time. "Well done!"

"Useless. Completely useless. Stupid, too. We might have been lynched. You know something, Hofmannswaldau? I hate Germany. Perhaps I'll go back to Galicia and be a Polish count with no education and nothing to my name. Nothing *but* my name, more like. Ancient, and now completely absurd."

"Please don't."

"What?" Adam looked at him with laughing eyes. "Oh, all right. Perhaps not yet. But doesn't it make you sick, that kind of thing?"

"Of course it does. And the policemen just standing there. You know, old Fischer's got a point. The only hope is for some decent men to be in the government, to make the police enforce the law, to make sure things don't get even worse."

"Rathenau was a decent man in the government."

"Yes. But then ... I don't know. We can't just abandon Germany. At least I can't. Zapolski?"

"What?"

"Why do you argue all the time with Dr Fischer? There's so much you really agree with him about, or you wouldn't have been brave enough to—"

"I love the old boy. I really love him. But if he's right, he's completely right and Nietzsche's completely wrong. And Nietzsche's obviously the one who's right. Look at what was going on in the square just now—that's where we are, exactly where Nietzsche said we would be."

"But what he said we should do about it doesn't make any sense. At least it doesn't to me."

"You'll get there in the end, if you stick at it. Now, hadn't we better go back for your bike?"

The square was peaceful when they returned, the beggars quiet, the rest of the mob gone. One of the policemen had picked up Max's bike and was standing holding it, beside his colleague.

Max took the bike and nodded his thanks. The policeman touched his cap. Max looked at Zapolski, who shrugged.

"I must get home", Max said. "My grandfather will be upset about Dr Rathenau. Perhaps he doesn't even know yet."

"Of course. Thanks, Hofmannswaldau. *A demain.*"

These six words lit the rest of Max's week.

Chapter 5

That summer, Max discovered that love also, or perhaps instead, can be lived alone.

A couple of weeks after the assassination of Dr Rathenau, the school year ended. Zapolski's mother was in Italy, so he was staying in Breslau for a week after the end of term before going home to Vienna. At a formal ceremony on the last morning of the term, they received prizes, Max the Latin prize for the year, Zapolski the prizes both for Greek and for mathematics. "Poor old Strauss", Max said, as they walked from school towards Cathedral Island that afternoon, each carrying a heavy case full of books. "It must have stuck in his throat, having to read out your name for the mathematics prize instead of Mackelroth's."

"Mackelroth should have got it, really. He takes much more trouble than I do. Also, he minds, and no doubt his father the judge minds too, about prizes. Prizes, however, unless you happen to be a Mackelroth, are banal. No rational person could give a damn for a school prize—it depends on who else happens to be in the class, that's all."

Max was glad he had managed not to look pleased even for a moment with his Latin prize, though he had been proud of his two more marks than Zapolski in the examination. He knew perfectly well that Zapolski had in fact worked hard, as he always did, for all three examinations. His slight irritation with Zapolski's pretence not to care in the least about his school work suddenly, to his astonishment, gave him the courage to say:

"Zapolski, I wondered—since you're going to be here for a few more days—would you like to come to my grandfather's for a meal, perhaps for lunch on Sunday? I'd like you to meet him. He's an interesting man."

"Yes, I would, very much. Thank you. You didn't spring fully armed out of nowhere, Hofmannswaldau. I'd like to meet your family.

People's relations give you the shadows in the picture, so you get a three-dimensional idea. You've met my mother, so you see what I mean."

"Or the light. Perhaps, anyway."

On Sunday Zapolski arrived for lunch, punctual, polite, and charming, with a box of Belgian chocolates. They had only just reappeared, in one or two expensive shops.

Max had never invited a friend to the flat before, and his grandfather only rarely entertained an old colleague from the university or perhaps a former student, and then only to coffee. Today the professor, who had been cast down as Max had never before seen him by Dr Rathenau's murder, had insisted on going to a good deal of trouble: Max said there was no need but, to his mixed delight and anguish, was overruled.

Frau Gärtner came in specially, early on Sunday morning with her children, to prepare a cold summer meal of fish, mayonnaise, different kinds of salad, strawberries, raspberries, meringues, and cream. While she worked in the kitchen, Grandpapa took her children into his carpentry shop in the pantry and turned tops for them on his lathe. Open-mouthed, they watched the chips fly from the chisel and then the wood dust float from the sandpaper as each top became smooth. Max remembered watching the same operation with the same wonder when he was their age. When Frau Gärtner and the children had gone, Grandpapa looked critically at the laid table—he had tidied away all his harpsichord plans and exactly carved pieces of wood—and said, "Flowers. No, Max, I'll go. I don't seem to have been out for weeks." Twenty minutes later, he came back with half a dozen red roses, a bottle of Franconian wine, and a bag of ice from the fishmonger. He put the ice and the bottle in a bucket in the kitchen and, when he had cut down their stalks with a kitchen knife, the flowers in a little half-glazed earthenware jug he found at the back of a cupboard.

"There. I think your grandmother would call that a respectable table, don't you?"

Max hugged his grandfather.

"So, do you boys have any idea what you might do with the rest of your lives?"

Max looked across the table. Zapolski's face was almost as blank as his own would have been. The professor laughed.

"I'm sorry. That's the question the old always ask the young. It shouldn't be allowed. I think only a very few boys still at school are sure what they will become. I was one, but I think I was very lucky, and most of my friends were like you. In any case, there's no need to make up your minds yet, of course. I remember enough about being seventeen to know that even next year, at your age, looks very long and full of possibility. The drama of the unknown. It's good to be young. Perhaps rather alarming as well."

Lunch was over. They sat at the table in the sunshine, Max now relaxing because his grandfather and Zapolski had talked easily of this and that through the meal as if they had known each other a long time.

"Max tells me you are a philosopher, Count."

"Well, not yet. But there is some thinking to be done, don't you agree, Professor? The nineteenth century had such a grand opinion of itself, so much progress, so much wealth, so many ideas for the future. And what did the future deliver? The war. Now that so much has gone, the empires and the hopes, you might say, wiped away as if they had never been, we have to start again, think again. To see if we can avoid the mistakes that led to the war. Because they were mistakes in thought, mistakes in value—thinking the wrong things were important."

"There you are. It *is* good to be young, and capable of understanding that it's the hopes that need changing. And your Dr Fischer, Max says, is Socrates for you clever boys. You sit on the end of his bed as Plato sat on Socrates's bed, and he teaches you to think."

"Well, Dr Fischer isn't quite Socrates. For one thing, he's a Catholic. He knows answers. Socrates knew questions. Our Socrates ought to be Nietzsche, who questioned and questioned, and that's what we must do if we're going to free ourselves, let alone anyone else, from the clutter of the past."

"Nietzsche's questions made him a great destroyer. I see that's exhilarating for the young, especially now when my generation seems to have made such a dreadful world of guns and gas and death. You know, Dr Rathenau once said the war was the fault of two hundred old men who knew each other. I do understand how much your generation must want a fresh start, a clean slate. But if you clear the ground of clutter, you have to build with something more solid than debris. Don't you think Socrates's questions were designed to lead his students to something more positive than a cleared building site?"

"You mean Plato? And then God and all that? Nietzsche thought Plato was practically responsible for Christianity. So what we have to do is to go back to Socrates's questions and skip Plato's answers. Look where they've got us."

"No, I didn't mean Plato. Certainly not just Plato, or just Christianity. But the bricks you might be able to build your new world with—I don't know—the best, the most beautiful and the most rational things people have made—the discoveries of physics and chemistry if they can be used for good and not for wicked ends. Or great music. Bach, for example. I've been reading Dr Rathenau's books again since his death. He said that Bach and Goethe and Rembrandt and Shakespeare were the evangelists of the German soul. Not they themselves, or even the music, the poetry, or the paintings themselves, but what they tell us, what they mean to us, how they make life worth living."

"Ah, culture! Culture instead of God. But it's been tried, tried to its limits since the intelligentsia stopped believing in Christianity, and it hasn't worked. I read in one of the newspapers that Dr Rathenau said, last year I think, 'All Europe is heading for the abyss.' Culture just isn't enough to halt the slide, as it wasn't enough to prevent the war. Dr Rathenau's two hundred old men—I bet they all loved Bach and Goethe. At least those of them who were German or Austrian. And no doubt the Englishmen loved Shakespeare."

"I wouldn't be too sure of that. There are famous generals who are proud to claim they've never read a book. But you may be right. I don't know how much difference it would have made if they had. Max, what about some coffee?"

Max stood up and looked at the untidy table, covered with crumpled napkins, dirty plates, and glasses.

"Grandfather, why don't you and Zapolski go into the sitting room? It has comfortable chairs. I'll make the coffee and bring a tray."

Grandpapa looked at him quickly, amused, Max could see, at being called "Grandfather". But he said only, "Good idea. Thank you."

As Max heated the kettle in the kitchen, made the coffee, and prepared the tray with cups, saucers, spoons, and sugar, he heard his grandfather and Zapolski talking in the sitting room, but he was too far away to make out their words. Twice both of them laughed. He heard his grandfather ask something, and Zapolski answer. Then there was a silence and, after a minute or two, the delicate beginning of a Chopin prelude, most beautifully played. Max put the coffee pot on the tray, picked it up, and stood motionless in the kitchen, listening to every phrase. He had no idea Zapolski played the piano. That he was a musician as well as everything else he was came as no real surprise—look at the way he read poetry aloud—but, added to everything else, it seemed almost too much to bear. Max put the tray back on the kitchen table and bent over the sink with his eyes shut, as if he had been dizzy or faint, though he was neither. The prelude ended. He straightened up, shook his head, picked up the tray, and carried it carefully into the sitting room.

As he came in and pushed the door shut behind him with his heel, Zapolski looked at him with his laughing eyes over the length of the piano and launched into a noisy, passionate, pulsing mazurka. There was no music on the piano. Zapolski finished the mazurka with a flourish.

"Well played, Count", Grandpapa said, with a single clap of his hands. "It's been years since anyone got that much music out of that piano. And Chopin too. I don't think I've heard any Chopin since before the war. Extraordinary, his music, both so gentle and so fiercely energetic."

"We Poles, you know. We're famous for being mad, at least in Germany. We're always drunk, of course, and wild like the mazurka. We're not so famous for quietness. But we can do that too."

Max bent over the tray so that neither Zapolski nor his grandfather could see his face, and he poured coffee into the three cups as Zapolski played a Mozart minuet softly and with a lightness of touch that, after the mazurka, was astonishing. He played it at a tempo Max knew Dr Mendel, who was fussy about tempos in Mozart, would have regarded as exactly right for dancing a minuet. Max gave his grandfather a cup of coffee and the sugar. Zapolski finished the minuet and softly closed the lid over the keyboard. He turned on the piano stool as Max gave him his coffee. He took no sugar, which Max knew.

"Thanks, Hofmannswaldau."

Meanwhile, Grandpapa had opened the box of chocolates.

"Delicious. Just like before the war. What are your plans for the summer, Count? I expect the famous Dr Fischer has set you boys plenty of reading to do wherever you will be."

"I shall be in Vienna for a while, and then I don't know. My mother will probably have some plan. She likes the sun, the south, the Mediterranean. 'Do you know the land where the lemons bloom?'"

"Will you enjoy that?"

This wasn't the kind of question Max usually asked; it had surfaced because he was so aware that he had not yet seen even the sea, never mind the Mediterranean and the lemons.

"Not much—because of what my mother does all day. Life on the beach in front of a grand hotel is very dull. And it's too hot for reading the kind of thing Dr Fischer expects us to understand properly, with notes in a notebook and questions on the syntax for next term. As for casinos—there are few occupations in the world more depressing than watching other people gamble, even if they can afford it. I think perhaps this year I'll find something else to do instead of going with her."

"Later, in August, I'm going to Waldau." As Max said this, he felt light-headed, both brave and afraid, as if he had launched himself very fast from the snowy bank of a lake over empty ice that might or might not be thick enough to take his weight. "My mother will be there, and my brother and his new wife. I haven't met her yet. It's rather a beautiful place, a river, and mountains in the distance. Very quiet. Good for the kind of reading we're supposed to be doing. Would you like to come too?"

There. It was said. The silence that seemed so momentous to Max—had he offended Zapolski by presuming too much, by suggesting that he might want to come with him to Waldau when they were friends only because of school, only because Zapolski was alone in Breslau?—was short and perhaps not momentous at all. But he was grateful to his grandfather for saying nothing, and particularly for not saying, "What a good idea! Some company for you at Waldau!"

"I would. I'd like to very much. It's a long time since ... since I stayed somewhere real, somewhere that isn't a hotel, or a house that's opened up only for fun, for shooting or hunting or picnics with too many servants going ahead. Thank you. And if there's two of us trying to get through Dr Fischer's stuff, there might be a chance of us actually doing it."

Zapolski drank his coffee, accepted a second cup, talked to the professor for a little longer, and left after perhaps another half hour. Of that half hour Max remembered very little. He had invited Zapolski to Waldau, and Zapolski had accepted his invitation. It was enough for one day. Enough for one summer.

Zapolski, leaving the flat, shook hands with Max's grandfather with his swift bow of the head and thanked him for such an enjoyable visit.

Max saw him off at the street door downstairs. As he shook hands, Zapolski said, "Light, not shadow. Nathan the Wise."

Nearly six weeks later, in the middle of August, Max met Zapolski as he got off the Vienna train at noon one day in the main railway station. They had exchanged a note or two to make this plan, after Max's mother had written to say that his friend would be very welcome at Waldau. Max had asked Zapolski to bring plenty of books and anything else he liked to do because almost nothing happened at Waldau. In those empty weeks, Max had earned a little money copying orchestral parts for the opera house, had held bits of the harpsichord steady for his grandfather to measure this and drill that, and otherwise had walked in the hot city, becoming fonder and fonder of its tree-lined streets, of the cobbled old city, Cathedral Island, the moat, and the park as he wandered about thinking of Zapolski and stopping now and then in a café for a lemonade or a seltzer and to read a few pages of the book he carried in his pocket, usually Schopenhauer, his own task for the summer. He had worried that Waldau would bore Zapolski. He had worried more that another invitation would turn up in Vienna, something much more exciting and amusing than three weeks in the Silesian countryside, and that this day, here, now, would never happen. But the day had come. There had been no letter from Zapolski apologising for abandoning the plan. And there—here—he was, carrying a neat wind instrument case along with a large, heavy suitcase, and with a bag of books slung over his shoulder.

Max didn't have to ask the question.

"My clarinet. I ought to practise now and then."

"Your *clarinet*! I didn't know."

"Well—it was the monks' idea. There weren't enough clarinets for the school orchestra. I've often regretted playing the clarinet—there are no clarinets in Bach. The oboe or the flute would have been better. Especially the flute, like Frederick the Great. Such style, don't you think, Frederick the Great and the flute, like a carnation on a steel helmet. Do we have to go to a different station?"

They took a cab to the smaller station from which the local train left, talked during the hour's journey to Waldau as if they hadn't seen each other for much longer than six weeks, and were met at the village station by a chauffeur dressed in what looked like a soldier's uniform. They sat side by side in the back seat of a brand-new car, all their luggage stowed by the chauffeur, and tried not to laugh too obviously when Max signed his astonishment at the car. As they drove down the drive between the lime trees, Max was suddenly quiet at the sight of them, and Zapolski said, swiftly and softly, "Time for Christian names, don't you think?"

So it was with an ally at his side that Max met, in the hall—what had happened to the hall?—his new sister-in-law, and Heinrich, in plus fours, transformed into a married man and the master of the house.

"My little brother Max, and his schoolfriend. This is Betsy."

"How do you do? Where's Mother?"

"Max! How old are you? 'How do you do? Where's Mother?' You sound about six."

"I'm sorry."

Max shook hands with Heinrich's wife, clicking his heels and bending his head as he did so. He registered a pretty blonde with bobbed hair and unsmiling eyes. She was wearing a silk shirt and riding breeches.

"May I present my friend, Count Zapolski."

Handshake, clicked heels, polite bow of the head.

"It's so kind of you to allow me to accept Max's invitation."

"Not at all", she said, coolly.

"But Heinrich," Max said, "where is Mother?"

"I don't know. In the kitchen with Emilia, I expect. She's not well. Don't go upsetting her."

Zapolski, with his unfailing manners, said to Heinrich and his wife: "I had no idea that Waldau was such a beautiful house. The avenue—"

Max interrupted.

"I must find Mother. And you must meet her. Come with me. Please."

Zapolski made another brief bow to Heinrich's wife and then followed Max out of the hall and through the dining room, which looked different, grander than it used to. Max opened the kitchen door.

"Mother! Emilia!"

"Max! Ah!" The delighted cry was Emilia's. She was stirring with a long wooden spoon something in a big pan on the stove. She flung the spoon to the side of the pan, put both her hands to her apron to wipe them, and then stood still to allow Max to greet his mother first.

The countess was sitting in Emilia's old chair by the stove. She didn't get up.

"My darling boy. What a joy! They didn't tell me when you would arrive."

She looked frail, thin, much older. Max bent to kiss her forehead. She put up a hand to cup the back of his neck as he kissed her, as she had when he was a small boy.

"Mother, how are you?"

"Not very strong. As you can see. For some reason . . . I'm afraid it irritates Heinrich. I must try to get better, now that you're here. And who is this?"

"This is my friend Adam Zapolski. He's in my class in the Gymnasium, and he's met Grandpapa."

Adam bowed and kissed her hand.

"Countess, it's very kind of you to allow me to come to Waldau."

"It will be a pleasure to have a friend of Max's here. I'm so glad you could come."

Max was hugging Emilia, who kissed him on both cheeks and then held him at arm's length by his elbows—she was very much shorter—to give him a thorough inspection.

"You're looking very well. Not working too hard at school, then? And this is your friend?"

"This is Zapolski. He's Polish. Actually, he's a Polish count. He's come all the way from Vienna."

Handshake. Heel click. Bow. A bob from Emilia.

"You're making plum jam. How wonderful! My grandmother made plum jam every summer when I was little. How lucky we've arrived at just the right time."

"You can try some tomorrow, the pair of you. You can tell me, sir, whether my jam measures up to your grandmother's."

"Oh, it will. I know it will. It smells exactly right, bubbling away there. It's such a good smell, somewhere between almonds and vanilla."

"Max, I've got ready the room next to yours for your friend. Take him upstairs while I settle your mother in the salon and make her a cup of tea."

"Yes, Max. Do as Emilia says. I'm so sorry. I should be . . . But it's so good to see you both here."

Max kissed his mother again. She looked too much like Grandmama, sitting there, pale and old, which as she had never looked before, with a blanket over her knees.

"Max!" She called him back as they left the kitchen. "How is he?"

146

"Grandpapa? He's well. Very well. He would love to see you in Breslau."

"Oh. Yes, of course. Perhaps when I'm a little better. The journey, you know ... But I meant ... how is Dr Mendel?"

"He's fine. Very well too. I have my lesson every week, of course. I've brought my fiddle. And Adam's brought—"

"Has he enough work? Does he still lodge with—I can't remember his name."

"Yes. Herr Rosenthal. Dr Mendel plays in the opera house orchestra. And he has some other pupils. I think he's perfectly happy."

"I see."

Max caught a look of stricken sadness on his mother's face.

"Go on now, Max", said Emilia, stirring the jam with her back to the kitchen. "Take the count upstairs. He'll want to tidy up. He's had a long journey."

Upstairs, Adam looked out of the window of his bedroom. It had once been Heinrich's, and it had on the walls four large prints of an eighteenth-century squire shooting duck with a long muzzle-loading gun and a spaniel splashing in and out of reeds and water. Max as a child had keenly envied Heinrich these prints.

"What a beautiful view", Adam said, raising the sash window and leaning out. "Hills, almost mountains, over there. What are they called?"

"The Riesengebirge. I don't know why. They're not that high. Or not until you get into Bohemia."

"Giants live there, of course. Emilia was your nanny?"

"That's right."

"And now she looks after your mother?"

"Well, yes. I ..."

"You didn't know your mother was ill?"

"No. Not really."

"I'm so sorry, Max ..."

This was the first time Zapolski had called him by his Christian name. A little too much time went by before he answered.

"What?"

"If it's in any way difficult that I'm here, you must say. I can invent a reason for leaving very easily, anytime, tomorrow if you like."

"No. Please ... please don't think of going. Unless you want to, of course. I'm so glad you're here. I hardly know my brother, you see, and I don't know my sister-in-law at all. It will help a lot to have you here too."

It did help. At lunch that day, at dinner that evening, and in the salon after dinner when his mother had gone to bed—she climbed the stairs so slowly, leaning on Max's arm, that he wondered whether she might die during the night—it helped to have Zapolski, an actual stranger, to talk easily to Heinrich and his wife when Max could think of nothing easy to say. He wanted to ask Heinrich what was the matter with their mother, what the doctor had said, why she spent most of the day when she wasn't in bed in the kitchen with Emilia, and whether she liked or had been consulted about the many changes in the house: the new curtains and chairs in the dining room, the carpet with a brash red and green pattern covering the flagstones in the hall (Max thought of Rolf, once upon a time always waiting for him on the stone flags at the bottom of the stairs), the two long sofas upholstered in white silk in the salon and the big portrait of Betsy in a blue evening dress and diamonds over the mantelpiece, and the girl from the village who waited at table at lunch and dinner, dressed in black with a starched white apron and cap, and then, in an ordinary apron, helped Emilia wash up. He was probably being overcritical, he told himself. It was possibly wrong for him to resent Betsy on his mother's behalf. After all, the dining room looked better, the white sofas were very fine (though useless for a dog of any kind), and the girl from the village helping Emilia with the washing up was good, though being dolled up as a city parlourmaid was pretentious and silly. But the carpet in the hall was horrible, and worst of all was the portrait of Betsy.

After dinner, when even Zapolski was failing to think of anything to say and Betsy was looking at a shiny American magazine full of pictures of thin women in strange clothes—a kind of magazine Max had never seen before—Heinrich stood up.

"Well, if you boys have no objection, I think we'll go to bed."

"Heinrich?"

"What is it?"

"What's happened to Bach?"

"What do you mean?"

"The painting that used to be there, over the fireplace. Where is it now?"

"Oh, that. It's in the attic. I might find out if it's worth anything one of these days. If it is, I'll sell it and buy something a bit brighter."

"But it's Mother's."

"Yes, I suppose it is."

"You know it is. Father gave it to her when they got married."

"Well, I don't think she's noticing that sort of thing much now, do you?"

"Have you asked her?"

"I can't remember. Probably not. It's none of your business, in any case, Max. You're welcome to try to cheer her up while you're here, but you're not to interfere in our affairs. Don't make trouble. Understood?"

"But—"

"Is that understood?"

Heinrich looked and sounded like their father—younger, of course, than Max had ever seen his father, but very like. Max at the same instant was aware of the roused admiration on Betsy's face as she looked up from the white sofa to Heinrich standing there angry, in front of the fireplace, with his feet wide apart. His mother would have been looking not at his father, but with anxious eyes, at Max. But she was ill and weak and already in bed.

"All right", Max said.

"Good." Heinrich held out an imperious hand, palm downwards, to his wife. "Come, Betsy." He pulled her out of the sofa, and they left the salon, not shutting the door behind them.

Max and Adam looked at each other and waited for a door to close upstairs. Heinrich and Betsy's bedroom had been his mother's room. She had been given what had once been a room for visitors. Did she mind? He would have to have a serious talk with Emilia tomorrow.

"Sleep on it", Adam said. "I've got to go to bed anyway. All the frontiers you have to cross these days—the Austrian frontier, the Czech frontier, the Czech frontier again, then the German frontier—all with their passport police and their customs men in their shiny new uniforms. Never a minute's peace on the train."

They switched off the lights—there was a generator now at Waldau, clanking faintly in an outbuilding beyond the kitchen—and followed each other upstairs. There was carpet on the stairs as well as in the hall.

"Good night. Sleep tight", Zapolski said in the dark passage.

"Good night, Adam". There, he'd done it, and it sounded, he hoped, perfectly natural. "Thank you for coming."

The next day, Max did talk to Emilia, in the kitchen after lunch, when his mother had, slowly and painfully out of breath, climbed the stairs to her room with his help, and the girl from the village, whose name was Gisela, had gone home on her bicycle.

"What does Dr Loewenberg say? Has he seen her?"

"Oh yes, he's been very good. He comes every two or three weeks. He says her heart is failing. He told me he wrote to your grandfather to ask about your grandmother's illness. He says it's the same, what your mother has, and there's not much he can do. She must rest, which she does, and eat well, which she doesn't. I do my best with her, but, Max, she is too sad. I don't think she wants to get stronger. And now Dr Loewenberg is leaving, soon, in a few weeks, I believe."

"Why is he leaving? He's always been the Waldau doctor. He can't be too old—I remember him when I was little, and he was quite young then."

"He's leaving because the village has turned against him. He told me."

"But why? He's a good doctor, kind to everybody, even if they're too poor to pay him. He always has been . . ."

"Yes, but in the spring two families of poor Jews arrived from Poland, with lots of children, barefoot children the villagers don't want in the school—they've tried to drive them out. He's been defending them, finding them clothes, books for school, a bit of extra food. So now the village wants him to go too, because he's Jewish himself, though you'd never know. He's going to Berlin, where his daughter lives. He says he'll be able to work better there because he won't be so noticeable." Emilia was almost crying. "It's the same with me, Max."

"Emilia! What do you mean?"

"Your sister-in-law, Max, the new countess—she doesn't like me because I'm Polish. She doesn't want me to work here. I'll stay, of course I'll stay, to look after your mother. But if anything should happen to her . . ."

He hugged Emilia as she cried. But he couldn't think of anything to say.

The days were sunny and still long, the harvest fields golden. A few were already empty stubble. Where corn was being cut, there were lines of men toiling in the heat, and women and children binding sheaves and arranging them in shocks. In other fields, where sheaves were being loaded onto wagons by men with pitchforks, pairs of draught horses pulling the wagons stood patiently, lashing at the flies with their tails, and then moving forward a few yards at a time. The heavy boughs of the late summer trees and the shadows they cast were dark blue against the gold. Max and Adam spent most of each day out of the house, walking, Max with an old rucksack of his father's on his back. They walked till it was time to find the shade of a tree, near the river or a hill stream, to unpack bread and cheese and sausage and beer, and then read. They took a copy each of the *Phaedrus*, the book they had reached of those prescribed by Dr Fischer, and a lexicon and a German translation to rescue them if they couldn't sort out the Greek. Always they fell asleep under their tree long before they had completed the agreed number of pages. Often, because he so much wanted to, Max woke first and sat, with his arms round his knees and his Plato—open, a pencil between the pages—balanced on them, looking at Adam and hoping he wouldn't wake for a long, long time. Once they sat on a ledge of grass close to the water, an ancient oak a long way above them on the bank. The river was slow here, and quiet. Swifts skimmed the surface of the water for flies. Three times, as Max watched Adam's sleeping face, the shadow of a swift, a perfect swift-shaped shadow, crossed his face more quickly and silently than the beat of a wing.

The horses of the soul, he thought, the light and the dark, pulling for once exactly together. Passion and love not fighting each other but the same thing.

I will not forget this, ever.

As Adam opened his eyes, Max picked up the pencil with his right hand, steadied the book with his left, and hoped he appeared to be hard at work by the time Adam was fully conscious.

"What were you thinking?"

"Oh, nothing. It's too hot to think."

"Mmm. You weren't reading Plato, were you?"

"Yes and no. These horses. Plato's a poet."

Adam sat up, chose a round, flat pebble from the stony bank at their backs, and skimmed it across the river. It bounced three, four, five times.

"It's Schubert, isn't it?" he said.

"Schubert. Yes."

"'O river of my love, so full of mystery.' Poor fellow. Not Schubert. The miller's apprentice. Probably Schubert too. Anyone in that lovesick state. But the plodding over the fields and through the woods—that first *Schöne Müllerin* song, 'To wander is a miller's joy, to wander'—that's just like us. Exactly what students are meant to do during the summer holidays. A bit of Plato. A bit of bread and cheese. A lot of walking. It doesn't seem real, somehow, now. I suppose because of the war."

"You mean Heinrich? He never had holidays like this, because of cadet school; he's read no books to speak of; and because of the war, people of his age are either dead or won't recover from their wounds or are like he is now. Is that what you mean? So it isn't fair for us to be tramping about the countryside with nobody knowing where we are, and sitting by the river with our lunch and our books?"

"That's not quite what I meant. Heinrich would probably have been much as he is now if there hadn't been a war, or if Germany had won it. It's more that you and I, here and now, at Waldau, in the fields and woods, by the river, Count this and Count that, with Dr Fischer teaching us and the *Phaedrus* to read—it's all part of the past. And the past is finished and done with because of the war. Or, better, the war showed everyone how much had already been finished and done with for a long time, though not many people had noticed. So we are like ghosts, ghosts of seventeen who have been dead for years." He skimmed another pebble over the water. "Only four. Damn. Like the miller's boy in the songs, existing in words and music and nowhere else."

"Rubbish. You exist and I exist." Max hit Adam on the head, not hard, with his *Phaedrus*. "We occupy space and time. Not much, but some. And that's all a lot of Nietzsche, what you've just said. According to him, nobody had noticed anything till he told them, but he told them what he wanted to be true and then told them that that was all anyone ever did, all the truth there ever was. So in some weird way, Q.E.D. What I'm trying to say is that he actually *wanted* everything to be finished and done with. He *wanted* no more beauty, no more goodness, no more truth except the grimmest, bleakest view—his view—of everything. So he told us all that that's how things actually are, not just how he saw them. And that's why he would have *loved* the war, for being cruel and long and killing millions of soldiers, because it would have proved him right. But there've always been wars, some of them as horrible as people at the time could possibly make them—look at the Thirty Years' War. And there's also always been goodness—good people. And there's always been beauty—music, rivers, and hills. There's always been some idea that both goodness and beauty have something to do with each other and with truth. If we have to choose between Plato and Nietzsche, give me Plato every time. But my point is that we *can* still choose."

"Ghosts", Adam said, spinning one more pebble. "Six. That's better. But not stupid ghosts. And isn't choosing Plato instead of Nietzsche just choosing self-delusion? Let's pretend there's a God. So then the only difference between us and most people who call themselves Christians becomes that we know we're pretending. No thanks."

Max picked at the grass beside him. He saw a tiny yellow flower, with even tinier dark leaves, hidden in the grass. He didn't know its name. He tried to remember how and why he had felt so happy a few minutes ago, but couldn't. Something like despair rose in his throat. He said nothing and looked at the water silently flowing by.

"Max?"

"What?" He hoped that sounded ordinary.

"Your mother ..."

"What about her?"

"Does she believe in God?"

"I don't know. Perhaps. Probably not. She used to go to church with my father. We all did, every Sunday. Very dull, it was. Banal, you'd say. Patriotic sermons. Badly sung hymns. You're a Catholic, so you wouldn't know."

"Was. I was a Catholic. Not my fault."

"But now she's too ill. She didn't go to church with Heinrich and his wife"—Max couldn't say "Betsy"—"on Sunday, even though they went in the car."

"How old is she?"

"My mother? Forty-seven, I think."

"Not old at all. Three years older than my mother. But look at the difference. They're almost opposites, aren't they? Much easier to love, your mother, I'd say."

"She used to be—oh, quite different. Full of life. Laughing, you know. She was always on my side when ... well, when my father was disapproving. She plays—played—the piano really well. She was taught by ... it's hard even to remember, now."

"The war, I suppose. She must have been heartbroken by your brother's death, and then your father's when it was meant to be all over."

"Something else happened to her. That summer after my father was killed, she wasn't crushed, as she has been since. She was actually happy, freed almost, playing a great deal, learning new music. Something happened. I don't know what. Now I'll never know because she's too ill to be badgered with questions. She probably wouldn't have ever told me anyway."

"It would be good if she believed in God. In case she dies."

"But you think it's all nonsense."

"Some nonsense can help people."

That evening, Heinrich and his wife went out to dinner, driven by Dieter, the chauffeur, who turned out to have been Heinrich's batman on the eastern front. Heinrich was wearing a velvet smoking jacket, Betsy a low-cut orange satin dress with black sequins glittering on it.

Gisela from the village had the evening off, so Max, Adam, Max's mother, and Emilia ate early and in the kitchen. The countess smiled at both boys and at Emilia.

"How nice to be eating in the kitchen. Emilia, this is a really excellent stew. Max?"

"Mother?"

"You haven't told me anything about the Gymnasium this year. How is it going?"

"Well—"

"He won a prize, you know, the Latin prize," Adam said.

"Max! How splendid!"

"He's had me to distract him this year", Adam went on. "I expect he'd have done even better if I hadn't appeared on the scene."

"What nonsense. I'm sure both of you work very hard. Tell me about your teachers."

Adam caught Max's eye for permission and then launched into an only slightly exaggerated imitation of Dr Strauss teaching a chemistry class with equal scorn for the boys and the subject.

"And how, Herr Mackelroth, do you propose to account for the curious discoloration of this liquid under these conditions?" He picked up his glass of wine between finger and thumb as if it might bite him and peered at it with such distaste that Max and his mother and especially Emilia laughed and laughed. He peered at Max over non-existent spectacles and said, "I find your answer quite unaccountable, Herr von Hofmannswaldau. Have you studied page four hundred and fifty-three of the chemistry textbook as required for your preparation the week before last?"

"Oh, you poor boys", said the countess. "Can it really be as bad as that?"

"Much, much worse", said Adam. "But luckily, we do have other masters." He took off his nonexistent spectacles, polished them on his real handkerchief, and put them back on his nose, fixing his gaze on the far distance over Max's head. "It will not have escaped your notice, gentlemen, that this is one of the most incisively sarcastic passages in Cicero's attack on Verres. Here we have the moral authority of a great Roman advocate displayed at its noblest. Would you care to translate the second sentence, Herr von Hofmannswaldau?" He paused. "Aaagh!"—Dr Fischer's roar to a T—"That is a mistake I would not expect an eight-year-old to make!"

After supper, Max's mother, who, till this evening, had not truly laughed since he and Adam arrived at Waldau, asked Max to help her upstairs to her bedroom. They left Adam stacking dirty plates on the draining board for Emilia. But when they reached the landing halfway up the stairs, they stopped. At the salon piano, Adam had begun to play, at a perfect walking pace, the accompaniment to the first song of Schubert's *Die schöne Müllerin*. Then he began to sing: "To wander is the miller's joy, to wander . . ." For two, for three stanzas they listened.

"Let's go back down to the salon", Max's mother whispered. "No one has played that piano since—"

"Of course. Careful!"

Before they got to the open door of the salon, Adam was singing not the next song in Schubert's cycle, but a later, questioning one. "I can't ask any flower, I can't ask any star". They waited for the last stanza.

> "O river of my love,
> So full of mystery,
> I won't say it again,
> Say, river, loves she me?"

"Adam", Max's mother said. Zapolski turned on the piano stool and stood up as they came in, the countess leaning on Max's arm. "How lovely. I'd no idea you could play, and sing too."

"I can't sing. Not really. Only simple stuff."

"You play beautifully. I can tell. I used to play myself ... Max, get your violin. Couldn't you boys play something together? A little recital, since we're by ourselves tonight? Max, perhaps you could find me my lap quilt in the kitchen too?"

"I'll get your mother's blanket", Adam said. "Go on, Max. Fetch your fiddle. I've never heard you play. And find something not too difficult. My sight reading's a bit hit and miss."

Max went up to the schoolroom, where he had put his violin on the afternoon they arrived. He opened the chest of drawers where Dr Mendel had kept their music, and found a volume of Mozart sonatas. Downstairs, when he took the fiddle out of its case, he was careful to turn his back on his mother and Adam because his hands were shaking.

They played two whole sonatas. Adam accompanied him as his mother used to when he was a child.

"Thank you, oh, thank you, both of you. That was such a great pleasure. I never thought I would ... Now, Max, it must be really late. Would you help me with the stairs?"

She was looking younger, better, brighter than would have seemed possible a couple of hours earlier. As they went upstairs for the second time, she said, "Max, I would so like to see your grandfather. Do you think he would come here, just for lunch perhaps, one day? We'll have to ask Heinrich, I know."

"Of course, Mother, of course. Leave it to me."

Emilia, with the countess's dressing gown over her arm, appeared on the upstairs landing. As she put an arm round his mother's shoulders, taking charge of her, she winked her approval at Max.

He went back to the salon. Adam was sitting in an armchair reading the newspaper, nowadays fetched every morning from the station by Dieter.

"What a day! Adam ..."

"What?" He put the paper on the floor.

"Oh, never mind. Nothing. But thanks."

An evening four or five days later could hardly have been more different.

The day before, when Max and Adam were playing chess in the schoolroom because it was raining, three wooden crates had been delivered by the carrier, who brought them up to the house from the station in his old cart pulled by his old horse. Heinrich was out, seeing one of the estate farmers. Betsy, in the hall where the carrier had left the crates, shouted for Dieter. Then she came halfway up the stairs and shouted for Max.

"Damn. I'd better see what she wants. You've won anyway."

"Max! Get Dieter, will you? I want these unpacked before Heinrich gets back. It's a surprise for him. Quickly!"

Max found Dieter polishing the chrome on the car in what had once been the coach house.

"The countess would like you to unpack some crates for her. You'll need a chisel or a screwdriver."

"There's always something."

What emerged from the crates was a gramophone, in a square mahogany case with a lid, and a large curved horn to amplify the sound. The heaviest crate held a square box of records, most with labels in English—dance records, one called "Mississippi Rag", another called "Canal Street Blues"—and one set of records with German labels, songs from *The Merry Widow*. Dieter, under Betsy's impatient instruction, installed all this on an old oak chest under a window in the salon.

Max reported to Adam who, up in the schoolroom, was practising Brahms on his clarinet.

"Terrific! You wait till you hear some jazz. It's African music really, you know. The slaves in America, poor devils, never forgot how to play it, drums and banjos, and singing too. It kept their spirits up, or made them cry. Much the same, perhaps, if you're a slave." Adam played three or four melancholy, syncopated phrases on his clarinet. "I wonder what Heinrich will make of it."

Heinrich, when he came back from the farm on his handsome bay horse and jumped down from the saddle, throwing the reins to his new groom, was seized by Betsy.

"Come and look! I've got a present for you!"

Both boys were in the salon, waiting for the great inauguration.

"Listen, all of you!"

She wound up the gramophone, put a heavy black disc on the turntable, and when it was spinning well, set on the edge of the disc a metal arm with a needle screwed into it. There was a crackling sound and then the slow seductive beat of a band playing a dance, with a trumpet, drums, and a piano.

157

"It's a foxtrot!"

She started dancing by herself, gliding in front of Heinrich to the rhythm of the music, her feet moving expertly to the beat. She took Heinrich's hand, put her other hand onto his shoulder, and swayed. He shook her off.

"Not now, Betsy. Don't be silly. I'm wet and muddy."

"Spoilsport! Come on. Adam—I need somebody to dance with!"

She took Adam's hand and pulled him into the space behind the sofa. "It's not difficult. Look! Listen! I expect you only know how to waltz. Ah—that's it! You've got it! Wonderful!"

Heinrich turned his back on them, marched out, and slammed the salon door behind him.

"O dear! Temper! Serves him right!"

They danced for another minute and then the needle reached the end of the record. There was only a grating sound as the needle collected no more music from the grooves. Betsy jumped to the gramophone and took the arm from the disc.

"There you are! Isn't it a miracle? Real dance music, here in the back of beyond!"

"Well, it's not exactly real", Max said, sour with jealousy, like Heinrich—damn!—and then noticed that he sounded like Dr Mendel, Dr Fischer, and his grandfather rolled into one. "Sorry. No, it's extraordinary, of course. I'm sure Heinrich will be pleased, perhaps later . . ."

"He'd better be. We're having a little party tonight. That's why I was hoping it would arrive in time." And she ran out of the room, presumably to make her peace with her husband.

Max looked at Adam, who held out his hands, made a self-deprecating face and shrugged. Both of them laughed.

"Max?"

His mother was at the door, white and thin.

"What was that?"

"That was a gramophone record, Mother. A dance called a foxtrot."

"Was it? How strange! I hope they won't send the piano away now."

That evening, two couples arrived in cars for dinner. They were eight in the dining room—the countess had chosen to have an early supper on a tray in her bedroom—served by an evidently nervous Gisela and Dieter, dressed as a butler. Emilia had prepared roast duck, boiled potato dumplings, spiced red cabbage, and a fine pudding of apple cake, plum jam, and cream. ("We must get a proper cook as soon as possible", Max heard Betsy say to Heinrich the following morning. "One really can't have Polish food at a dinner party.")

The guests—Max and Adam sat on opposite sides of the table, with one husband and the other wife next to each of them—talked politely about nothing much for a while. The husbands had both fought in the war; the older of the two, a colonel, had a black patch over one eye and a long duelling scar on his cheekbone. Max, while he struggled to be agreeable to the other man's wife, who asked him questions she might have asked a ten-year-old, was aware of Betsy flirting with the colonel, without much success. When he turned towards Max and said, "Tell me, Count, what are the streets of Breslau like now? Have we got some sort of order back?" everyone at the table turned to talk to the person on the other side.

"Well, sir, it's difficult to say. Most of the time, the streets are quiet and perfectly safe, but there are a lot of beggars—soldiers without work, very poor people struggling in the slums. Trouble can blow up quickly, and the police are inclined to just stand back and watch. My friend and I"—he glanced across the table and saw Adam, animated and happy, talking to the dark, beautiful wife of the colonel, and missed a beat in what he was saying—"we ran into a nasty scene on the day Dr Rathenau was murdered. A mob in Blücher Square—"

"What does this joke government expect? A Chancellor—himself a Catholic, if you can believe that!—who's capable of making a Jew the foreign minister of Germany, and not just any Jew but a notorious defeatist, just waiting to roll over, paws in the air, and let the French and the English do exactly what they like with us—no wonder those boys took the law into their own hands. I'd have been proud to do the same if I were their age."

"But wasn't Dr Rathenau a hero of the war? Not the fighting, of course, but the organization. I read that without his work to supply the army in the middle of the war—"

"You believe everything you read in the Bolshevik press? My God! Jews and Bolsheviks, they've got us by the throat! Rathenau, let me tell you, young man, was responsible for the armistice. We could have won the war—did you know that? We *had* won the war in the east. The Bolsheviks surrendered. There was no need whatever to capitulate in November 1918—the November traitors, that's what they're called, and rightly so, and Rathenau was their leader."

"But wasn't it General Ludendorff who—"

"No, it most certainly was not. I won't have a word spoken against General Ludendorff, do you hear me? General Ludendorff was my commanding officer on the Russian front. He's a very fine soldier, I'll have you know, a very fine man, a German patriot of the old school. He would have fought the war right up to a total victory, and anyone who denies that he would have is a traitor. Stabbed in the back, he was—we all were—and Rathenau was the Hagen to his Siegfried."

The rest of the dinner party had fallen silent to listen. At the end of this speech, Heinrich said, "Hear, hear. Glad to have it said, loud and clear. These lads need telling. They weren't there, and they've no idea."

"Sir," Adam said in the silence, to the colonel, "don't you think there comes a point in any war when it's better to discuss terms than to lose more lives?"

The silence deepened. Max looked at his plate, proud of Adam, but also frightened of Heinrich.

"I'm not going to argue with you, my boy", the colonel said. "You are Polish, I gather, and in any case too young to understand anything about the war—you must have been still a child when it ended."

"My father was killed in 1914, fighting for his Emperor, as Count von Hofmannswaldau's brother was killed fighting for his. I'm not sure what was achieved by either of their deaths."

As the colonel furiously spluttered, Adam added, "I do know that Dr Rathenau's murder was a crime and a disgrace."

Heinrich got up, scraping his chair backwards.

"Enough! That's quite enough. I would remind you, Zapolski, that you are a guest in my house and that there are things it's extremely bad form even to suggest while you are under my roof."

Adam also got up.

"I apologize, Count. Colonel. I should have had the good manners to hold my tongue."

Adam bowed his head quickly, first to Heinrich and then to the offended guest.

"Since you are a foreigner, young man," the colonel said stiffly, "I accept your apology."

"Now," Betsy said, getting up herself, "let's forget politics and try our new gramophone. Dieter, will you bring the coffee and liqueurs into the salon?"

Max felt like a violin string that had been overtuned, screwed up and up, so taut, so sharp that it could snap at any second. Adam's courage and his apology that had been no apology were so mixed up with the apparently inevitable prospect of Adam dancing to Betsy's jazz with the wife of the now-furious colonel that Max thought he might faint. He excused himself with a mumble that no one noticed and went upstairs for a few minutes to the nursery bathroom, where he splashed cold water on his face, dried it, and stared in the mirror, telling himself he was being ridiculous until it was possible to go back to the salon looking, he hoped, perfectly ordinary.

All was calm. The *Merry Widow* records were played one after another, Betsy jumping up from the coffee tray to rewind the gramophone and reposition the needle for each one. After the guests, who were clearly familiar with gramophones, had expressed polite enthusiasm for the quality of the sound and had listened to one fast, catchy jazz tune ("This is called the Charleston. It's brand new") to which Betsy danced alone, Heinrich said, "Anyone for a game of poker? Small stakes, of course", and unfolded a card table on which Max, when he was about nine, had played bezique with his mother, with special cards and ivory counters for the score. Where were they now? He remembered the precise snap they made under his fingers.

Heinrich, both of his friends, and Adam, who had restored his credit with the dinner party by knowing how to play poker, sat round the card table with their brandy glasses and cigars, in an intent silence broken by single words and phrases now and then, while Max listened to the women, all smoking cigarettes, talking about clothes for tennis and for going to a fancy-dress ball in Berlin that was being given by a princess it was obvious they all knew only just well enough to have been invited. After about an hour, Betsy suddenly got up, went to the gramophone and put on the Charleston record again. She danced round the poker players.

"You are so *dull*—won't anyone dance with me?"

Heinrich threw his cards down on the table.

"Betsy! You've ruined the hand! One has to concentrate, you know."

The colonel stood up. "It's time we were going home, Count. We have a long drive, and it's important just now that Mitzi doesn't get too tired."

Shrieks of congratulation from the other two women.

On the following evening after dinner, when Max's mother was already upstairs, Betsy said she was bored and was going to have a bath. She put her hands on Heinrich's shoulders from behind as he sat on the white sofa, and kissed the top of his head.

"I'll see you later. Don't be too long."

Max and Adam stood as she left the salon. She didn't say good night to them. When she had gone, Heinrich got up and poured himself a whisky and soda.

"Where do you boys get these socialist ideas from? Last night—Rathenau a hero and all that. Is that what they teach you in the Gymnasium? Or is it still Mendel's influence? You spent too much time with that man, Max, and so did Mother. What do you think Father would say? Max?"

"Well, Father agreed with you about the armistice and the peace terms and all that. But he never blamed any of it on Dr Rathenau or on the Jews in general. He'd never have thought it right to murder the foreign minister, to shoot him in broad daylight in the street. Would he? He was all for order and authority and things being done properly. Old Prussia."

"That's all very well, but by 'authority' he'd always have meant a proper government, a King or Kaiser, proper decisions in Berlin, an incorruptible bureaucracy to carry the decisions out, and the whole thing backed by a disciplined, obedient army. That's what Prussia's always meant. Actually *meant*. How much of that has this thrown-together republic got left? Practically nothing. The bureaucrats, perhaps, still keen to obey orders and do the right thing, but where are they to look for orders? What's supposed to back the government now? Not the army but the people! So-called democracy. Nothing but division, compromise, indecisiveness. Mob rule and Bolshevism is what it will lead to. Already has. Look at Rathenau's funeral!"

Adam interrupted.

"Wasn't the funeral a sign that plenty of ordinary people were horrified at what had happened? Two million of them on the streets of Berlin just to watch, and no disorder at all. You could call that a triumph of peaceful democratic protest at a mindless criminal act."

"You could call it the result of Jewish propaganda. The Bolshevik press, as the colonel said. 'The Jewish prince' they were calling Rathenau—pernicious rubbish. When was there ever a Jewish prince? They cleverly had Siegfried's funeral march played for him in the Reichstag so that people would forget for the time being that he was Hagen and not Siegfried, that he'd done the stabbing, not been stabbed. And Wirth the so-called Chancellor saying the enemy stands on the right—preposterous! The enemy of Germany is on the left—but not outside, not in Russia, not even in France, but *within*, appeasers, reparations payers, defeatists, trade unionists. Jews. Rathenau, in a word. That's why he had to go. This country is being undermined, weakened, rotted *from within*—look at the inflation—deliberate, of course—so that the bankers can clean up while the country collapses."

"I think not", Adam said. "And it wasn't the left that called Rathenau the Jewish prince. It was the right. To make people hate him. It seems to have worked."

"It's not the people on the street who'll have the last word, funeral or no funeral. It'll be the army in the end, mark my words. The army's the only hope for this country, and the army will wait. You boys may think the army absurd, part of the past, something to be ashamed of—though how you can, Max, when Fritz was killed in a great battle, and Zapolski, with your father—but I'm telling you, its time will come. It's waiting. I'm waiting. Four thousand officers the wretched treaty allowed us, so all the rest of us have been sent home for now. But only for now. This republic can't possibly last. One of these days, somebody capable of restoring the honour of Germany is going to need soldiers. And we'll be ready to obey him."

"I wonder", Adam said, "whether the great man who will restore the honour of Germany is the kind of great man who will need soldiers. Perhaps he'll be more like Goethe, or Nietzsche. A great soul rather than an Emperor or a general."

"Culture", Max said. "Been tried and failed." Neither of the others, perhaps, heard.

"That's ridiculous!" Heinrich was losing his temper. "How could books restore the honour of Germany? What we need is a war, a war that we win, of course. And for that we need a leader, and the leader will need the army. Perhaps he'll have a great soul as well, to give us back our sense of direction, our purpose, our destiny, all that we had in 1914—that was only eight years ago, you know, and what's happened to us?"

"We lost the war", Max said, and wished he hadn't, because Heinrich roared with rage and planted himself in his place for holding forth, in front of the fire, lit for the early autumn evening.

"We never lost the war!" he shouted. "We mismanaged the last few months of it. That's all. And the Americans changed the rules of the game. Americans never fought in Europe before. It wasn't right. And in any case, on the day of the armistice, how many enemy troops were there on German soil? Not one. Not one single soldier. How near were the battle fronts to Berlin? Six hundred miles to the east. Six hundred miles to the west. Is that losing a war? How close was the Russian army to this house in 1914? Fifty miles away. Where is it now? How is that losing the war?"

"The Poles did help", Adam said, "to keep the Russians as far away from Germany as they are now. Two years ago, the battle for—"

"Warsaw. Yes, I know. I was there. And I wasn't fighting for the Poles, Zapolski."

"Heinrich!" cried Max.

"It's all right, Max. I'm not going to hurt your precious friend. He's a guest in my house, isn't he? And Mother's taken a shine to him. Anyway, he's an Austrian, aren't you, Zapolski? We would belong to the same country by now, if President Wilson had really done what he promised all along—nations for states, states for nations. Austria would have become part of Germany in 1919."

"I am a Pole."

"Living in Vienna. At school in Breslau. It's the same old story—become as German as you possibly can and then turn round and say you're Polish after all and you can't stand the Germans. It's exactly like the peasants, working for Germans, depending on Germans, being educated by Germans, and then voting for Poland in the plebiscite. And then, to cap it all, they're swarming all over Germany looking for work—not that there are many jobs here either, since the war—because they'd rather take our jobs and our wages than starve in Poland, and I can't say I blame them."

"But you do blame them, don't you? The Poles are poor. They always have been poor, and they're poorer now because of the war. Most of the war actually took place in Poland. Have you ever thought that because of the partition, because of the empires fighting each other, Poles in their own country had to fight each other all through the war? And that their land, their farms, their fields and roads and bridges were more wrecked by the war than any other nation's? You may not have had enemy soldiers on German soil. The Poles had millions. The Poles come across the frontier for work just to survive. You blame them for learning from Germany and then saying they're Polish. At the same time, you blame the Jews for learning from

Germany—learning much better than the Poles do, I grant you—and then saying they're German. You're very hard to please."

Heinrich looked at Adam, angry, muddled, even a little impressed. He poured himself another whisky.

"Whisky, Zapolski? Max?"

"No thank you", said Adam.

Max shook his head.

Heinrich drank, then sat down again and thought.

"Well, it's simple, really. Germany for the Germans is what I say. Poland for the Poles, perhaps—though it won't last."

"And the Jews?" Max said quietly. Heinrich swept on.

"Germany for the Germans should mean for all of them, though. Wouldn't the Viennese at least be better off forgetting an empire that doesn't exist any more and joining Germany, where they belong? What we have at the moment is two republics with no future—one big, one small—but once Germany has got rid of its republic, there'll be a future for Germany, you can be sure of that, and it ought to be the Austrian future too. If Prussia can cope with a whole lot of Bavarians being part of Germany, it can certainly cope with the Austrians, who are much the same."

"My mother would agree with you, that the best bet for Austria is to be joined to Germany. She would be entirely happy with that. Until a couple of months ago, I might have thought so too. Not any more. I find I have no great wish, now, to become a German."

"Good luck to you, Zapolski. Poland—how can you reinvent a country that hasn't existed for a hundred and fifty years? Of course, England and France have set it up as a buffer to protect the rest of Europe from the Bolsheviks. But that's no way to deal with the Bolsheviks. Over and over again, Russia has crushed Poland. Russia will always survive. Look at it! Look at the size of it! The way to prevent Lenin from doing too much harm is to treat him as we treated the Tsars: give him some respect, give him plenty of help—Russia needs German help; it always has—and stay on decent terms with his country. I can't help admiring the Russians in many ways. They did have a proper revolution. We couldn't manage even that. They got rid of the Tsar and came out of it with a strong leader, just as the French got rid of their King and came out of it with Napoleon. What happened to us? The Kaiser sneaked away; the Emperor in Vienna sneaked away. And now there's nobody capable of running anything either in Berlin or in Vienna, but in Moscow there's Lenin. If we stay on friendly terms with Lenin and let him get on with building utopia in Russia—he won't succeed, but trying will keep him busy—he's much less likely to turn into Napoleon and want to conquer everybody else."

"You don't, I imagine," said Adam, "want a Bolshevik government in Berlin."

"Certainly not. But I want a government that governs and doesn't just say, 'Yes, we must agree to reparations' and 'No, we mustn't get the army back on its feet because we have to be punished for the war'."

"The government you think so little of made a treaty with Russia in the spring, did you notice?"

"I did. The one constructive achievement since the war."

"Who signed it on behalf of Germany?"

"Rathenau did, I admit. Astonishing that a Jew should manage such a thing. Except, of course, that most of the big Bolsheviks are Jews. Much better than that treaty—and this wasn't Rathenau's doing; he was dead by then—there's an agreement between our army and theirs, made last month, very hush-hush, to do some joint training."

"Poor Poland."

"I'm sorry, Zapolski, but in the end it's a question of strength. Poland comes and Poland goes. Not to mention the countries that haven't even been reinvented but never existed before. Did you know that Lloyd George thought Silesia was in Ottoman Turkey, like Galatia? The epistle of St Paul to the Silesians! It was pure chance, for all he knew or cared, that Waldau ended up still in Germany. The only thing that'll sort it all out is another war."

"It might end in another defeat."

"Nonsense! Germany and Russia will survive. They survived 1918 and 1919: they would survive another war. They'll come out of it stronger and bigger. And they'll survive better if they make common cause. Bismarck said he would always rather deal with the Tsar than with the Polish nobility, and he was absolutely right. Do you realize that Prussia and Russia never fought each other from the middle of the eighteenth century till 1914? That's how it should have stayed. Bloody Serbia and the Habsburg empire—Why, *why* did we go to war for Franz Josef in 1914? Looking back on it, that's what it amounted to."

"A few minutes ago, Heinrich," Max said, "you were wanting 1914 back. Destiny and purpose and all that. Now you're saying the war was a mistake. And how could it possibly be good for Germany or good for any other country in Europe to have another war?"

"Because people need passion and uniforms and marching and hope, to make them feel proud of being alive, proud of being German. If we'd fought only the French and the English in 1914, we'd have won, easily. And now we'd be what the whole of the nineteenth century was preparing us to be, a great European imperial power, instead of this mess, this sheepish, cowardly, Jewish politicians' mess."

"What you're recommending, Count," Adam said, "is nationalism. But why should Germany have national glory—and perhaps Russia and France and England too—but not the Poles, not the Czechs, not the Croats or the Serbs or my poor Ruthene peasants at home who aren't even Polish? Or, come to that, the Jews?"

"Inferior races have to do what they're told by the stronger, by the races marked out for power. What made America rich and strong? Conquering the Wild West, colonizing it, pushing inferior races out of the way. Slave labor. We should do the same in the east. That's where the Habsburgs got it right—Germans to govern Slavs—and that's the problem in Berlin now, and probably in Vienna too for all I know. Jews in the government, Jews making laws the rest of us have to obey—it's against nature. It's all wrong, and something's going to have to be done about it."

"Out of humanity through nationality into brutality", Adam said.

"What?"

"It's a poem. Grillparzer. He was a Viennese, so you probably haven't heard of him. He wrote that poem fifty years ago. He called it 'The Path of Modern Man'. He saw nothing good ahead. He thought nationalism would be the end of civilization. Perhaps it will be."

The door of the salon opened. Betsy appeared, in a silk dressing gown with an empty glass in her hand.

"Heinrich! I thought you were coming to bed. If it's more interesting down here, can I have a whisky too?"

"Go to bed, Betsy. I'm coming now. I've been trying to knock some sense into these boys' heads. Without much success. They'll learn, one of these days, when they see some real life. Turn out the lights, will you, Max, when you've had enough of putting the world to rights?"

When Heinrich had taken Betsy by the hand and shut the door behind them, Max looked at Adam. His face was white, his hands clenched.

"Ach!" He relaxed and shook his head violently as if to shake Heinrich and everything he had said out of it. "If I were their guest, I would leave tonight, somehow or other, walk to the village, stay in the inn, I don't know, just not to be here in the morning. But I'm your guest, and your mother's. Thank God."

"I'm sorry. I'm so sorry. Some of that was horrible."

"It's wicked. Wickedly stupid and very dangerous. It's because people like Heinrich, officers in the army responsible for their men, have spread this pernicious rubbish that we had the Freikorps and now all the rest of them, Steel Helmets, Stormtroopers ... They're gangs of thugs, the lot of them, pretending to be soldiers and hardly being punished when they murder people because the judges are on the political right as well and hate the government. Naturally, Heinrich despises the Poles. Prussians always despise Poles. But how can he talk as he does about the Jews?"

"You mean, how can he since ... seeing that our mother's family ..."

"Yes, I do."

"Let me tell you something. My mother wants to see my grandfather. I'm so pleased about that. I've written to him and arranged it, for Saturday. Heinrich could hardly forbid my grandfather to come, but he's not pleased at all. He and Betsy are going to be out all day. Dieter's going to drive them to wherever they're going, then come back here, pick me up, and take me to the station to meet my grandfather. Once Grandpapa is safely back on the train to Breslau, Dieter will go and collect Heinrich and Betsy from their friends'. Can you believe it? To go to such lengths to avoid his own grandfather and to make sure his wife doesn't meet him—it's got to be for only one reason, I think, hasn't it? Could there be any other reason? You've met my grandfather."

"I'm afraid you're right. You heard the colonel last night. You heard Heinrich just now. But I expect Heinrich's real problem is his father-in-law."

"His father-in-law? Who is he?"

"Grauer, his name is. Siegfried Grauer—these Wagner names, you find them everywhere. He's a Breslau businessman. He made a great deal of money in the war—from the war, you might say."

"How do you know all this?"

"Emilia. I talked to her about the wedding. Put two and two together. Your mother didn't go to the wedding—I suppose she wasn't well enough. But you and your grandfather weren't even invited, were you? I've just heard of Grauer. He ran a huge clothes factory in Breslau, turning out hundreds of thousands of uniforms all through the war. He's got some house in the country that used to be a Junker estate. He's very rich indeed, and he has no other children. Only Betsy. A very considerable heiress, you see. He's also a famous anti-Semite. Won't employ Jews, or Poles for that matter, even right at the bottom of his heap doing the most miserable jobs."

"So that's why Heinrich suddenly seems to have so much money?"

"Of course."

"I thought perhaps he was running Waldau more efficiently than my father did."

"Max! No one's making any money out of land since the war. Learn some cynicism! No, don't. You're nicer without it. But Heinrich can't risk—"

"But how can one tell? How did you tell, come to that—Nathan the Wise—so late in the day, such a long time since my grandfather's family was religious or anything like that?"

"One can always tell. Your grandfather—I like him so much—is a wonderful example of the very best kind of German Jew. I've met such men in Vienna. No one who has not known, for example, the village Jews of Galicia can have any idea what a triumph of the human spirit, of ambition and application and brains, a man like your grandfather represents. They're wonderful too, in their way, the old Jews of Poland with their long beards and their red-rimmed eyes, haggard from decades of study at night by one tallow candle. But it's another world, completely different in every possible way from the world of university libraries and laboratories and modern surgery and trams and telegrams, and to have so competently made the leap between those worlds in just two or three generations is an extraordinary achievement. That's why it's so much resented, of course, by the old privileged classes, who've had all the opportunities for study and learning and progress for hundreds of years and have made so little of them. It's jealousy. Sheer jealousy."

"But people like Heinrich and the colonel", Max said. "Junkers, Prussian landowners, and soldiers who've never read a book—it was Hindenburg my grandfather was talking about, who was *boasting* that he'd never read a book—they don't want to be judges and doctors and university professors, so why should they mind if Jews make a success of professions they'd never touch themselves?"

"They mind because they feel threatened. They've got no real power any more. Actually, the Junkers never had much power; they just did what they were told by Electors and Kings and finally the Kaiser. But people like Heinrich don't want the professional middle classes to get above their station, to become powerful because they're clever and successful. And because now we live in a democracy, they actually *can* become powerful. Dr Rathenau was all those things. It's the same in Poland. The *szlachta*—that's the old aristocracy, me, in fact—wasted money, wasted education, wasted the land and the wretched peasants for generations. Now all the nobility can do is blame the Jews—or worse, encourage the peasants to blame the Jews—and put it about that all the sufferings of Poland are their fault. It's rubbish, of course. But if the *szlachta* could keep Jews out of the good schools and the universities, keep them out of the professions, they would, so as to hang onto any power and privilege for themselves. But they can't keep the Jews out of schools and universities. They bow the knee to France and the Enlightenment so they have to look as if they're treating the Jews fairly. But they'll bully them, mock them, make their lives miserable wherever they can. I hate it. It's the one thing about both Poland and Germany that I really hate, and the war's made it much worse, at least in Germany. Men like Grauer, Betsy's father, are the most rabid of the lot because they're too like the successful Jews. They've made a big class jump and a lot of money, and they want to establish that somehow they deserve it because they're good Germans, good Protestants, *Aryans*—that's the latest correct thing to be; did you ever hear such mumbo-jumbo?—and so they deserve what they've got while the Jews deserve to be back in the ghetto, back in the shtetl, hated and feared."

"But Adam"—Max got up, filled two glasses with soda water from Heinrich's syphon, gave one to Adam, and sat down again—"do you think it's possible that Betsy and her family will never find out?"

"It's perfectly possible if Heinrich makes sure she doesn't meet your grandfather. You might become a problem when you're a bit older. You look reasonably like a Prussian, but you're not really like one at all—you play the fiddle too well, and there's a kind of seriousness. Also a quickness on the uptake. Blood will out, as the anti-Semites say."

"But ... never mind." Max kept his eyes on the bubbles in his glass. "Heinrich needn't worry. Once my mother ... when my mother ... I shan't come back to Waldau. Ever."

"It's Heinrich himself who astonishes me. It must be really difficult for him, poor fellow, and he isn't too stupid to connect one thing with another, somewhere. Your grandfather, your mother—they're his grandfather, his mother too. He can't get round that, whatever he pretends to Betsy. Have you any idea what's going on in his head?"

"I think I can understand it, up to a point. He's ashamed of what he knows he is. Probably the thing he wishes most in the whole world is that it isn't so, that it isn't true. So everything he says and does is designed to hide the truth from himself and everyone else. Somewhere in him he's hoping that if he pretends for long enough, consistently enough, that he isn't half-Jewish, somehow or other he won't be. Look at his marriage. He must have known exactly what he was doing. If Betsy's father has plenty of money and no other children, it's perfect for Heinrich and for keeping Waldau going. It must have looked perfect to Betsy's family too. Heinrich's a count with an old Prussian name; Waldau's been in the family for God knows how long. But that Betsy's father is a famous anti-Semite must have been the cream on the cake for Heinrich. To make his alibi complete—to himself, I mean. As long as the Grauers never find out."

"How can he be your actual brother?"

"Oh, you never met my father. He was more intelligent than Heinrich, more independent-minded. He married my mother, after all, and he really loved her and loved to hear her play. But he thought no life in the world could be more honourable, more noble, than the life of a Prussian officer, and what he minded most, I think, is that he was too young to fight in Bismarck's war against France and too old to fight in 1914. He wouldn't hear of me not going to cadet school. Everything since his death—going to the Gymnasium, living with my grandfather, being taught by Dr Fischer—has been exactly the opposite of what he wanted me to be. But all the same I think he would have been shocked by how Heinrich is now. And if Betsy's father is the kind of man you describe, he'd have been even more shocked by Heinrich's marriage. For snobbish reasons, for a start."

"Well, there's nothing we can do about any of it. Certainly there's no hope of changing Heinrich's mind about anything. And probably he can't do much harm in Waldau. Perhaps having some children will soften him a bit, detach him from the army. Not that the army's where the worst of the thugs are. Meanwhile, I suppose we'd better go to bed."

Adam put the heavy wrought-iron fireguard in front of the still-burning logs as if he had lived in the house for years, and Max switched out the lights in the salon and bolted the front door.

As they went up the stairs side by side, Adam put an arm round Max's shoulders.

"Good night", he said outside their doors.

"Good night."

That night, not for the first time, Max dreamt of Adam and himself, this time together by some wide river, stripped, Adam's back bare—and woke exalted and ashamed. He jumped out of bed, flung open the window, and leant out, breathing deeply the chill of the dawn air. The rate at which his heart was beating slowed to normal. He thought of Plato's horses, pulling in opposite directions. Not controllable. Damn. Damn.

Did Adam feel as he did? Of couse he didn't, or he would never never have put an arm round his shoulders coming up the stairs.

Chapter 6

On Saturday morning, as arranged by Heinrich, Dieter took Max to the station to meet the Breslau train. When Max and his grandfather had got out of the car onto the warm white stone in front of the house, Dieter drove away to the stable yard. Silence. Sunshine. Pigeons somewhere in the trees. The old man looked back down the lime avenue.

"It is a beautiful place, when all's said. One forgets."

When they had climbed the steps together and gone through the open front door, they stopped in the hall and exchanged glances. The house was full of the rich, rolling, reflective sound of the first movement of a Schubert piano sonata. From the salon door, also open, came music and sunshine as if it were long ago. They went in and stood for a moment, until Max's mother noticed them.

"Papa!" Max's mother held out her arms to her father from where she sat in a corner of the sofa. Adam stopped playing and stood up.

"How lovely, Papa, how lovely to see you. And isn't it wonderful to have music here again? This is Max's friend Adam, who plays so well."

Grandpapa kissed his daughter's forehead. "We have met, in Breslau. It's a pleasure to see you here, Count."

Adam politely bowed his head. "Good morning, Professor."

"Shall we go upstairs, Toni? I want to have a proper look at you, now that I'm here."

He showed no surprise at how difficult it was for her to get up but gave her his hand and then his arm to hold onto as they set off.

They spent the hour before lunch upstairs and came down together, she leaning on his arm and smiling at Max, who was waiting for them at the bottom of the stairs. Grandpapa was serious and sad, with his stethoscope sticking out of his pocket.

"I feel much better. Grandpapa is so good for me", Max's mother said.

After lunch (Gisela was in the kitchen in her everyday apron, and Emilia was in and out of the dining room, beaming), they had coffee in the rose garden. The golden weather had returned after a few days of rain, and there was a new flush of roses, crimson, pink, and white, on a few of the old bushes. Adam collected the coffee tray from Emilia in the kitchen and brought it out to the garden, putting it down carefully on a slatted wooden table, grey from age and many winters outside.

"Countess, will you excuse me? I must do some reading. If I don't get a bit done, Max will be so far ahead of me I'll never catch up. Professor, good-bye. I'm so glad to have met you again."

Max's grandfather, without getting up from the garden bench where he was sitting beside his daughter, shook hands with Adam.

"Good-bye, Count. Thank you for keeping my family company."

When Adam had disappeared into the house, Max poured the coffee. They drank it in an awkward silence as if, Max thought, each of them had things to say to one of the others that he couldn't say in the presence of the third.

His grandfather, putting his empty cup back on the tray, sighed.

"So beautiful, Toni, your roses, even in September."

"They're untidy this year. I haven't been able to manage much myself, and since Tadeusz died, poor old man ... I do miss him, and so do the roses." She laughed. "But clever of him. I think he died at just the right time."

"Now, Max, I'm going to take your mother upstairs for her rest. Then I must have a word with Emilia. I'll be back in a little while. Perhaps you would wait for me here?"

"Of course, Grandpapa."

Max couldn't sit still for more than a few minutes. He took the coffee tray back to the empty kitchen and fetched his mother's pruning shears from the little garden room, where she used to arrange flowers for the house. For nearly half an hour, he snipped the dead heads and suckers and black-spotted leaves and scruffy died-back twigs off the roses until he saw his grandfather coming out of the house, white in the face and looking exhausted.

"What is it, Grandpapa?"

"My boy. Dear Max. You must be brave. I think I've seen your mother for the last time." He raised a calming hand. "No, she's no worse. Not at this moment. But I don't think she can last for more than a few weeks. Her heart ... Sit down, Max."

He sat himself, heavily, on the old bench by the table, and Max sat opposite him as before, on a rickety wicker chair.

"Her heart's in a dreadful state, worse than your grandmother's shortly before she died. It's not common in someone of her age, but it does happen. She had rheumatic fever as a child—you probably didn't know that—and it's a disease that does sometimes weaken the heart. She may also have inherited a specific weakness from your grandmother. I'm afraid ..."

The professional calm of the doctor talking to the patient's family suddenly deserted him.

"Max, I'm so sorry. You're too young to lose your mother."

"No, Grandpapa, It's you ... You are ... It's all wrong for you, as it was for Mother when Freddy was killed."

The old man looked at him. There were tears in his eyes, but they didn't flow.

"How like you, Max."

He had recovered his hospital manner. "All of that won't have helped your mother's condition. Freddy. The shock of your father's death. The sadness that summer three years ago. And now she feels she has lost Heinrich as well, to the war, although he came back. But she's happy about you. Really happy. She told me so, and I believe her. She knows it's right for you to be in Breslau and at the Gymnasium. She knows you and Heinrich have always been very different and always will be. She so much likes young Zapolski and is pleased that he's your friend. Now, Max, steady ... You need some of your father's Prussian courage here. And your mother's courage too. She's not afraid of death, you know. Far from it. I think she will ... almost welcome it. Certainly she knows it's approaching and is quite resigned. It shouldn't be painful, and I promise you that Dr Loewenberg—thank God he's still here—will be able to deal with the pain if she has any. Emilia is a wonderful nurse. I've explained to her exactly what to expect. I couldn't find anyone better and kinder to look after Toni in Breslau if she were well enough to travel, which she certainly isn't."

"It's too soon ... I never thought ... I should have been here, Grandpapa."

"No, Max. You should not have. It would have made your mother's illness more difficult, not easier, for her, if she'd thought you were staying here on her account through these years when it's so important for you to be at a good school. And you would have got bored and cross and resentful—yes, you would have. Any boy of your age would have, and entirely understandably. We've been lucky, all of us, and perhaps Toni feels it most of all, that I and my flat have both survived this long, so that you've had somewhere safe to stay. Ach!"

"What is it, Grandpapa?"

"My harpsichord."

Max hugged his grandfather long and hard among the late roses. Then Dieter drove them to the station in Heinrich's car, and Max waved the old man good-bye.

"Adam and I will be back in Breslau on Wednesday."

The next morning, Max went to find Heinrich in his father's business room. Nothing in it had been changed or moved, except that the old tin box with *Schloss Waldau* written on the curling label was now on the floor by the window and there were piles of typewritten letters and documents on the table. There was no sign of Betsy's modernizing hand in the business room. Perhaps she hadn't even seen it.

Heinrich looked up, not pleased.

"What is it? I'm working."

"I'm sorry to interrupt your work, but there's something you should know. Grandfather told me that Mother's heart is in a very bad way. He says she has only a few weeks more."

"I know. Dr Loewenberg said exactly the same thing the last time he was here. Not to her, of course, but to me."

"Heinrich. Mother's spirit is stronger than you think. Grandfather told me she's ready to die. They talked about it."

"That's good, I suppose. She certainly wouldn't talk to me, but then we were never close. You were always her favourite, with your wretched violin and that Mendel she was so keen on. I don't know how Father stood it all those years." He rearranged some papers on the table. "Do you think she'll want Grandfather to come back before she dies?"

"Don't worry."

Heinrich looked up sharply, then down again.

"They said good-bye. And Grandfather talked to Emilia. He's entirely happy with her looking after Mother."

"So I should hope. Not that it's any of his business."

"Heinrich, how can you say that? She's his daughter!"

"Of course. But this isn't even her house any more, let alone anything to do with him. If she hadn't been so ill, I'd have sent her to

176

Breslau to live with him when I brought Betsy here. But that wasn't possible, obviously, so we must make the best of it. Thank God for Emilia."

"What will happen to Emilia when ... after ... ?"

"I hope she'll go back to being a nanny. Betsy's pregnant, and she's keen to get a proper cook, so it seems a good solution. Don't say anything to Emilia, for heaven's sake. Betsy would be furious."

"Of course I won't. But ... you'll have to get her to treat Emilia ... well, less like a servant if you want that to happen. Or she won't want to stay."

"What are you talking about? Emilia *is* a servant, isn't she? And she's a Pole. And where would she go? She's lived in this house since Fritz was born. That's nearly thirty years. I don't think she's got any family."

"She's got a niece in the village; and the niece's husband died in the war. She has children. That's where Emilia would go. Don't you remember her afternoons off, always with her sister, when we were children?"

"Well, we'll see. That might be better. Betsy might prefer a trained nurse for the baby."

"Heinrich?"

"What?"

"Do you love Betsy? Did you fall in love with her? Is that why you married her?"

"You cheeky monkey! How dare you! Don't you want me to hold Waldau together? Keep the house? All father's things? The farms? This was the only way. Betsy's rich. Like Mother was when Father married her. Only Mother wasn't rich enough."

Max winced.

"Heinrich, how can you say that? Look at the things in this room, the painting of Mother. He adored her. It wasn't—"

"I'm not saying he didn't. But Waldau soaks up money, you know. It has ever since the nineties. Our grandfather—you don't remember him—spent money without thinking, all his life. Father had to struggle year after year to keep everything going. And he didn't succeed. The estate was broke when he died."

"You will be kind to her, won't you? During these few weeks?"

"Don't worry. She'll be looked after."

"One thing."

"What?"

"Emilia told me that the men came from the farm to measure the gate into Mother's rose garden. To see if they could get the plough in. What was that about?"

Heinrich laughed.

"Oh, yes. Betsy's tennis court. She's very keen on tennis. I've had to learn to play. The rose garden's just the right size. But don't worry, they won't plough it while Mother's alive. I've told Betsy. Now off you go. I've got estate business to do."

When Emilia went up to collect his mother's breakfast tray that morning, Max followed her into the bedroom.

"Mother?"

"Max, how nice to see you up here. Come and sit beside me."

He shut the door behind Emilia as she took the tray away, then came to his mother and kissed her.

"Max, did Grandpapa talk to you yesterday before he went back to Breslau?"

"Yes, he did."

"So you know my heart isn't going to last very much longer."

"Yes." He looked down at her hands, quite still on the quilt.

"It's all right, Max. You mustn't be too sad about me. My life, you know, is really over. There's only one thing I'm sorry I shan't see. I should like to meet your wife, your children. But you wouldn't be very often in Waldau, I daresay. I know you and Heinrich will never be friends, and Betsy—well."

She looked out the window. Her new room, facing east, didn't have the wide, green view of the lawn, the river, and the meadows stretching to the woods and hills to the south. But she could see a corner of her rose garden and a stand of silver birch trees whose leaves were just beginning to turn coppery. The morning sun lit all this with a clear gold light and poured like honey through the window into the room. She smiled.

"What a wonderful morning. You and Adam must go out and walk into the hills or perhaps ride. You should ask Heinrich if you can borrow horses. I do like Adam, Max. I'm so glad you have found such a delightful friend. Have you met his parents?"

"His father was killed at the beginning of the war. His mother—yes, I have met her. She is quite different from Adam."

She wasn't listening. She looked out the window again.

"I couldn't leave Waldau, you know, when Heinrich came home. Waldau, your father, my piano, and ... other things here ... have been my whole life, since I was a girl of nineteen, and Emilia has been so good. I couldn't have lived in Breslau. It's too sad there, and then all those stairs up to Grandpapa's flat, and looking after me would have been hard work, very hard, for him and for you. Grandpapa's too old for all that, even though he's a doctor, and you're definitely too young. And we couldn't have taken Emilia with us. She's hardly been to Breslau even for a day; she would have been miserable."

He took her hand, and she let it lie in his.

"So, it's better as it is. Now ..."

She leant back on her pillows, her hand still in his.

"Go and find Adam and enjoy your day. I know you are leaving on Wednesday, and today is already Monday."

Her eyes filled with tears.

"Go, Max. You are so young. Be full of hope."

Max kissed her hand and kissed her forehead, then left her.

At lunch, Max asked Heinrich if he and Adam could ride into the Riesengebirge on the following day, their last.

"Yes. Why not? Take care of my horses. No flat-out galloping and jumping gates. I want them back in one piece."

Heinrich's groom, whose name was Jan, was a Polish trooper from his regiment, lame because he had been shot in the knee by a Polish bullet outside Warsaw. He had worked for the regimental blacksmith and had set himself up a little forge in the Waldau stable yard to make shoes for Heinrich's horses. There were five horses now, in the paddock beyond the birch plantation. Two of them, not Heinrich's big bay but a chestnut gelding and a dappled grey mare, were saddled ready for them when Max and Adam went to the yard after breakfast.

"Morning, sir", the groom said to Max. "These two'll give you a good ride out. She's very quiet, very easy on the hand. The gelding's a bit more lively but a nice ride."

Adam said something to the groom in Polish. He beamed with pleasure and gave the reins of the gelding to Adam.

"Do you mind, Max? Hephaestus seems to have decided which we take. I only said, 'What a lovely day for an expedition.' "

"Of course I don't mind. You're bound to ride better than I do. And I like the mare's friendly face." He stroked her nose.

Adam asked the groom a question. The answer was "Liegnitz", in Polish "Legnica". So he had been a local boy.

He gave each of them a practised leg-up and fussed a little, tightening girths, looking at the stirrup lengths with an appraising eye, and then sending them off with a slap on the gelding's rump and a farewell in Polish.

They set off towards the mountains, cantering across the meadows, trotting for a while along the soft paths through the woods, and then letting the horses walk as the ground became steeper and stonier. Max hadn't ridden a horse for three years. He was astonished at how competent and alive he felt in the saddle.

"Isn't it good?" Adam said as he jumped down to open a gate tied up with twine at the end of a field they had cantered across. He looked up with bright eyes as Max rode through. "I've always loved riding. I'd forgotten."

For two or three hours, they said practically nothing else. Max rode in front of Adam: this was a ride he had often done with his father when he was a child, and he found he remembered at each moment of decision which way to go, where there was a gate, and even here and there where there was a fallen tree, now rotted and soft and looking unalarmingly low, which he and Gretel had been allowed to jump six or seven years ago.

They met almost no one. Harvest was still going on in a few fields, where men and boys, and girls too, were tying and making shocks of sheaves of barley and rye. When they had climbed higher than the cornfields, there were cows and goats here and there in the hill pastures, and once a boy herding some geese with a big stick opened a gate for them. Adam gave him a coin.

By the middle of the day, they reached a place Max remembered discovering with his father, a green, mossy platform beside a quiet, clear pool. The surface of the pool stirred slightly, constantly, and deep at its heart was a spring, bubbling without a sound. The path they had been following, through old woodland, mostly of ash, oak, and holly, crossed the stones of the shallow stream below the pool. On the other side, the meadow opened into a kind of amphitheatre, wide and grassy, with a few sheep on the skyline. The horses drank from the brown pool.

"Lunch", Max said, sliding down from the saddle and flipping the reins over the head of his mare to tie her to a thick oak branch.

Adam hitched his horse to the same branch and stood looking across the stream to the hollowed slopes of the hill, almost terraced for an audience. "What a place! What a perfectly wonderful place! It looks, over there, as if someone had made it, a Greek theatre almost, and yet it's much better than if someone had. And the spring—Greek too. Muses. Nymphs. Magical!"

They ate their picnic by the pool, drank cold water from their cupped hands, and lay on the grass looking at the shining sky.

"Max?" Adam said, after a long time when, though both of them were awake, neither had said anything.

"What?"

"Tomorrow we have to catch the train and go back to streets and trams and crowds of people and school. Think of it—Mackelroth and Gerhardt and Geyer and Dr Strauss."

"Please don't. I don't want to think about them today."

"Or ever. Sorry."

Adam propped himself up on an elbow and looked at Max, who stayed lying down and gazing at the sky, pretending to pay no attention.

"Max, I want to thank you. For inviting me. For allowing me to ... I don't exactly have a family and I don't exactly have a home either, any more. Vienna is other streets and trams, and somehow point-less now that there's no Emperor and no empire, though so pleased with itself as well, and there's my mother's life, which I don't much care for. So it has been ... well, the first time since I was ten years old ..."

Max sat up and looked at Adam.

"Don't. It's the other way round. I couldn't have done the last three weeks without your ... And anyway, look at my family. What a mess. Heinrich—turning into the worst kind of prejudiced idiot, full of theories he doesn't begin to understand and saying really awful things. And then Betsy! But my mother—it's been so good for my mother that you came. And not just because of the music and because Emilia thinks you're a hero and will talk about you for weeks. My grandfather says that a few weeks is all ... Well, also because, as you've gathered, my mother's heart is failing, and she needs to be sure that I shall be all right when ... when I get back to Breslau and the Gymnasium."

Was that too much? Max asked himself in sudden panic. But then Adam's voice showed he wasn't thinking about Max at all.

"Something that used to burn strong and clear in your mother is just flickering now, a little flame, and I don't mean her health. Something to do with music and Waldau. But it will be alight in her now, perhaps, for as long as she needs it to be. She is tremendously brave."

"How much you see. How much you notice."

Adam got his cigarette case out of his pocket, took a cigarette out of the case, struck a match, then threw it into the stream and watched it disappear among the stones as he blew smoke rings into the still air.

"Did we finish the *Phaedrus*?"

"Yes, of course we did. Three or four days ago."

"Plato's people talk too much. So when they stop, I can't remember what they've said."

"The wings of the soul."

"What?"

"Love. The wings of the soul. To take the soul to beauty and goodness and truth."

"Ah yes. Not what actually happens, I'm afraid."

Max thought about this.

"Could that be because what you've seen isn't really love?"

"My mother's goings-on, you mean? You could have a point. But in what sort of world could Plato be right?"

"This one. There's plenty in the *Phaedrus*, after all, about what drags love down so that it does harm rather than good: jealousy, possessiveness, sensuality for the sake of—well, for the sake of nothing but itself. I think Socrates—Plato, of course, really—knows what he's talking about. It rings true, all he says about what goes wrong with love. So why shouldn't he be right about what goes right with it? What it can be if it's not about power, not jealous, not stuck in physical self-indulgence? He says it's the most important thing of all not to miss. Doesn't he?"

"I suppose he does. I'm impressed. You've been really reading the wretched book. I've just been sorting out the Greek and thinking it's an old poem, an old dialogue, a lot of words, a few daft ideas about souls and the gods, about God even. But I liked the horses. Plato must have driven a pair of horses pulling a chariot, and pulling against each other; he tells you exactly what it's like."

"Is it because of Nietzsche that you can't take him seriously? Is it because Plato talks about love and God as if they must be connected and you think talking about God is nonsense, so talking about love in that kind of way must be nonsense too?"

"Yes, that's about it, I suppose. Unreal, you know. Ideal, beautiful in words, in dreams, and in poems, but unreal."

"I don't think so."

"Then you must believe. It can't be just thinking. It certainly can't be knowing, as one knows facts because somebody somewhere has shown, proved, them to be so. It's got to be belief. And I thought we'd agreed that those days are over, that it was belief that got the world into so much killing, so many men slaughtered, blinded, lamed, frightened for the rest of their lives. It was belief in Germany, in France, in the tsar, in the British empire—whatever it happened to be, and always belief that God was on its side. Disastrous: competition, aggression, war, hatred, revenge. Everything Nietzsche calls *ressentiment*."

"But if Plato is even a little right, even facing in the right direction, when he connects God and love, then the God that people connect with countries and empires and wars can't be God at all. Isn't that making something that's not God into God? It's idolatry. Isn't that what the word means? What I'm trying to say is that the real problem may be people, not God. If love gives a person the wings of the soul so that he can fly towards God, then God, or that idea of God, can't possibly have anything to do with war and killing. It must have been a different, an invented, God that inspired everyone in all the different countries in 1914 to believe that they were doing something holy and noble, marching off to war."

"The soldiers really were noble and brave, willing to die for something beyond themselves. It was Rathenau's two hundred old men who were to blame. Either they believed God was on their side, whichever side it was, or, much more likely, they *used* the idea of God being on their side to get the soldiers to march, to get the mothers and wives to give up their husbands and sons. To wave them off in stations, at roadsides, in city streets. They used all that stuff about sacrifice and redemption through blood shed for the fatherland. If the old men believed it, they were fools; if they didn't, they were criminals. Either way, belief in God comes out of it extremely badly, and you can't get away from that."

"I still think the idea of God Plato is trying to describe, with the wings and the horses and all that, is the opposite, is really noble, really beautiful. And if there's sacrifice in it somewhere, then it's sacrifice of what's selfish and out of control, like the black horse;

that kind of sacrifice has nothing to do with actual killing, actual death."

"All right, Max. Of course it's a beautiful idea. But is it *true*? Has it got anything whatever to do with anything that's *real*? Or is it just a fantasy to cheer us up? It's got to be one or the other, you know. There's no third possibility."

"Are you what Dr Fischer would call a thoroughgoing materialist?" Adam roared with laughter.

"Quick, Max, very quick. And plenty of Schopenhauer, I see. Well, yes. I suppose I am. The real is the physical, the measurable, even the predictable, except that so far we haven't enough knowledge to be able to predict the unruly—people, for example. But in theory, one day we shall have enough knowledge to predict even what people will do. And then every decision we think we've made will turn out to be an illusion as well. Which is good Schopenhauer too, incidentally."

"How can you be so cheerful about it? It's a horrible idea, and actually I don't believe you believe it any more than I do. Anyhow, even if it's going to be the case one day that free will is proved to be just as much an illusion as God, it hasn't happened yet. So in the meantime, I can decide that I believe in God. Can't I?"

"Oh, you *can*, of course. You can believe in God, in Plato, in love as the wings of the soul, the whole lot. *Fides voluntatis est.* The monks were very keen on that. But they were just as keen on faith being a gift of God. So you can choose whichever version you fancy. Or not, as the case may be."

"Dr Fischer said we will all have to choose whether or not—oh, never mind. You don't think it matters much, do you? Any of it."

"Perhaps it matters so much I haven't got the courage to think about it properly. Or perhaps it doesn't matter at all."

"*Adam!*"

More laughter.

"Come on, Max. Let's leave the horses here and explore the Greek theatre. And frighten the sheep."

They scrambled across the rocks downstream of the pool and emerged into the green bowl of the scooped-out hillside. On their right was a little grove of ancient oak trees, gnarled and bent, their green leaves just beginning to curl and dry towards russet in the September sun. On their left was an old stone sheepfold with a rough wooden gate leaning against the open gap in its wall.

"It's astonishing", Adam said softly. "This is the kind of place that must have given the Greeks the idea of a theatre at the very beginning. Look—the city on one side of the stage, the country on the other. Can't you see Oedipus himself, broken and blind, being led off into those oaks, and beyond, into the hills? The palace would be behind us, of course, but never mind that. I bet the acoustics are extraordinary."

"Let's test them. You stay here and do a speech. I'll go to the top where the sheep are and see what I can hear."

The grassy slope on the other side of the flat space where the chorus of the tragedy would have sung and stamped and where smoke would have risen from the altar of Dionysus, was quite steep, but he climbed it swiftly and easily. The wings of the soul, he thought. He reached the top as the sheep scattered, disappearing over what had been the skyline. The mountain rose beyond the bowl, beyond more grassy meadow and birches and pines, with the summit somewhere out of sight beyond the trees. He turned back. Adam, now a surprisingly small figure on the sheep-cropped turf with the wood behind him, waved. Max waved back.

He saw Adam stand absolutely still for a few seconds, his head up, thinking, remembering. Then he began to speak, in his ordinary voice, with every syllable perfectly audible from the rim of the bowl in the hills.

> "Look at me, men of my fatherland,
> setting out on the last road
> looking into the last light of day
> the last I will ever see.
> The god of death who puts us all to death
> takes me down to the banks of Acheron alive . . ."

It took Max two or three lines to recognize the Greek—Antigone's last scene, Oedipus's daughter preparing to be entombed in stone instead of being led to her wedding with Creon's son. He listened and watched, and the tears came easily. Adam in riding clothes with his clear baritone voice in the green theatre of the foothills of the Riesengebirge became the brave, doomed girl, became also Max's mother facing death.

Adam stopped in the middle of a line.

"Can't remember any more. How does it sound up there?"

Max waved. He knew he would have to shout to be heard at the bottom of the slope, and he couldn't shout. He stood for a moment longer, pulling himself together, and then ran down the slope, fast and out of control, his knees weak after the morning's riding. At the bottom, he would have fallen, but instead he fell into Adam's arms. Adam steadied him—didn't hug him—held him by the shoulders at arm's length, and looked at his face.

"Max! What—? Oh, I am so sorry. Your mother . . . What an idiot I am, what a clumsy, stupid oaf! It was the only speech I could remember. I was Antigone when I was twelve."

Max shook himself free, shook his head violently, sniffed violently, wiped the back of his hand across his face, and laughed.

"No, no. It wasn't just that. It was wonderful. Really. And the sound was extraordinary. I could hear you as clearly as if we'd been in the same room. What a place! I won't—"

"Come on. We'd better get back to the horses. We've got quite a long ride down to Waldau, and we'll have to walk most of it because it's downhill."

They returned to their picnic place by the pool, walking with a good two yards' distance between them, packed up the rucksack, untied the horses, and remounted. They rode all the way back with scarcely a word, in single file as before.

Max relived over and over what had just happened—the speech, the run, Adam breaking his fall, what each of them had said. Had Adam realized he was going to say, "I won't ever forget this day"? Of course he had. That was why he had interrupted, to save Max from some grand claim that would then be there, having been said, an embarrassment between them. Adam always realized everything. That was why it was complete rubbish for him to pretend to be a materialist, a person who believed that nothing intangible was real. This, however, belonged to the lengthening list of things that couldn't be said, so Max didn't say it.

They got back to Waldau in the blue dusk. As they crossed the last field before the river, they heard someone somewhere chopping wood, each blow sounding with a resonant distant knock across the meadows and the motionless evening air. They pulled up their horses and listened, until the sound ceased and there was deep stillness.

"Go out onto the mountain", Adam said. "And stand in the presence of the Lord."

"What?"

"Only a poem." The gelding walked on, and so did Max's mare.

They returned the horses safe and sound to Jan. The car wasn't in the coach house, and there was no sign of Dieter. They exchanged a look: no Heinrich and Betsy for their last evening?

It turned out to be so. No Heinrich and Betsy, no dining room, no parlourmaid, no gramophone, and no cards, but Max and Adam, Max's mother and Emilia, eating in the kitchen, managing to talk and laugh about nothing in particular.

After supper, they left Emilia in the kitchen and walked slowly, Max's mother on his arm, through the dining room and across the hall to the salon. Max made his mother comfortable on the corner of the white sofa next to the fire, with her blanket over her knees, then put on two more logs and blew the fire beneath them into a presentable blaze with the bellows.

"What would you like me to play, Countess?"

"Adam, you are a kind boy. What do you think? Perhaps some Bach. Bach, they say, is good for settling the soul."

"Mother . . ."

She smiled. "It's all right, Max. I should like to hear the echoes, when you've gone, and the echoes of Bach will last better than most. Don't look so alarmed, Adam. There's *The Well-Tempered Klavier* in the top drawer over there. That's right. Most of the pieces aren't too difficult, and they're so—clear. Such a comfort."

Adam played from the beginning, the preludes and fugues in one key after another, using no pedal, with a simple grace that made Max long for his grandfather's harpsichord to be finished. He watched Adam play and could imagine him playing the new instrument in the flat in Breslau, and his grandfather able to be pleased with the achievement of building something so complicated and fine. But then his mother wouldn't be there to hear. His mother wouldn't be there, here, anywhere. He looked at her instead. She smiled, catching his look, and he realized that she had been watching him.

When Adam had played for half an hour or so, she stopped him in the pause after the gentle end of a fugue.

"Thank you, Adam. I shall remember how beautifully you've played my old piano. Now, Max, for the second half of our concert, get your fiddle and see if you can find one of the Bach sonatas we used to play when we were both doing what we were told by . . ."

She failed to finish the sentence and, as Max looked at her, a great many things suddenly became clear to him.

187

She went on cheerfully, to cover the unprotected moment.

"Go on. See what you can unearth in the schoolroom."

He went upstairs as slowly as he reasonably could, wondering what exactly had happened that summer three years ago when he was—what?—fourteen. Too young to have any idea of anything. He and Dr Mendel were both about to leave Waldau, in the middle of September, to go to Breslau. As, now, he and Adam were to leave tomorrow. Dr Mendel had been at Waldau since—when? Since Freddy was six or seven, before he himself was born. Was it surprising that—what? Which of them had said something? Dr Mendel? His mother? Perhaps had said too much? Probably he would never know.

He came down with his violin and a volume of Bach sonatas, marked in pencil by Dr Mendel to help him, aged nine, with the phrasing.

He and Adam played a sonata, Max scarcely listening to what he was playing, aware that Adam was accompanying so well that something like a performance was being given.

At the end, his mother said, "I'm so grateful to you boys, both of you. These few weeks have made such a difference to me. Now, Max, I'm a little tired. Perhaps you could help me up the stairs. And Adam, I know you're both leaving quite early tomorrow, so we must say good-bye."

Max helped her out of the sofa corner, and she stood, out of breath, lighter and thinner, he felt, than ever, leaning on his arm, waiting for Adam to come from the piano. Before Adam could take her hand, she put it on his shoulder, reached up, pulled him towards her and kissed him on both cheeks.

"Good-bye, and thank you for coming to Waldau. Look after Max for me, won't you?"

"I'll do my best. I promise", he said, and kissed her hand anyway. "Thank you, Countess, for having me. It has been so good to be here. Good night."

The next morning, when their luggage was all ready in the hall for Dieter and the car, Max took his mother's breakfast tray from Emilia and carried it upstairs.

"Don't cry, Max. I won't. Somehow, now that it's nearly all over, the one thing I don't do any more is cry. Max?"

"Yes, Mother?"

"Adam. You love him, don't you?"

"I . . . he . . . he's a good friend."

"I was watching you last night when he was playing. I have noticed before ... Be careful, my darling. Don't frighten him away. I know how easy it is to do. I really know. I shouldn't like you to lose him as a friend. He's not as lighthearted as he wants us all to think."

"I know. He's like Nietzsche."

"Who? Oh, the writer. I wouldn't know about him."

She patted the quilt. He sat on her bed.

"Now, Max, you must be going. To catch your train. To go back to school. Work hard. Do well. I know you will. Have a happy life, which is more important."

"Mother ..."

He hid his face in her shoulder and felt her hand cupped round the back of his neck.

At the door, he turned to look back at her. She smiled.

"Look after Grandpapa for me."

He held up his hand because it was all he could do, and gently shut the door.

For her funeral, which was in the third week of October, they travelled in the train together, Max and Adam and Dr Mendel. Max's mother had written to his grandfather two weeks ago, in almost unrecognizable wandery handwriting, asking him to make sure that Dr Mendel was able to come to her funeral. This he had done. Grandpapa had also written a letter to Heinrich, which Max delivered as soon as they arrived at Waldau, explaining that he himself was not well enough to come—which was not true. Heinrich read the letter in the hall, nodded, and put it in his inside pocket.

During the service, the pastor spoke of her as a devoted wife and mother who had sacrificed her eldest son for the fatherland and suffered the loss of her husband in the unfortunate incident in Waldau, which of course the congregation had not forgotten. Her kindness to those in difficulties in the village would be much missed, and the pastor said he knew that the people of the parish would join him in extending deepest sympathy on this sad occasion to her two remaining sons, to her new daughter-in-law who was most welcome at Waldau, and to her father in Breslau who was sadly indisposed.

She was buried beside Max's father. Max stood at the graveside while the prayers of committal were read and felt absolutely nothing except a kind of tremor that ran through him as the pastor's handful of earth rattled on the lid of the coffin. His mother, somewhere beyond and more complete than his memory, his mother smiling, alive, full of responsiveness and affection and music, was safe and was entirely known. And what of his father, who had so loved her? I believe in God, Max said to himself. And not because I decide to. It happens that I do. He tried to remember something Adam had said to him about faith, but couldn't.

It was good to know that Adam was behind him—without being asked, he had offered to come—among the small gathering of neighbours and tenants who had walked round to the graveyard from the church.

He could hear Emilia sobbing. She had been waiting outside the church all through the service, with Dr Mendel, Dr Loewenberg, Jan the groom, old Tadeusz's daughter, and one or two others. It struck Max that Adam must have broken some Catholic rule to attend the Protestant service. But of course, Adam didn't regard himself as a Catholic any more.

After Heinrich and then Max had each added his own handful of earth, Emilia stepped forward to Max's side, threw a late rose into the grave, and crossed herself. She stayed at the edge of the grave, weeping, unsteady, her hands clasped on a rosary, until Dr Mendel also stepped forward and stood for a moment beside her, with bowed head. Then, with an arm round Emilia's shoulders, he helped her back to where she had been standing.

At the house afterwards Max went to find Emilia in the kitchen. When Gisela, looking very smart in her parlourmaid's uniform, had disappeared into the dining room with the last of the plates of food, Emilia clung to him in a long hug, and then wiped her eyes and blew her nose once more, and straightened her hat.

"It was just as your grandpapa said it would be. Very peaceful. No pain. She died in her sleep after a day, Wednesday it was, when she was so short of breath Dr Loewenberg said she couldn't last. I was with her—I was half-asleep in the chair—and she died so quietly you wouldn't have noticed her go. Four in the morning, it was."

"I'm glad. And thank you, Emilia, for everything you've done for her, and for all of us. What will you ... ?"

She hugged him again, laughing this time.

"Madam wants a fancy cook. So I'm off to my niece's. She's pleased to have me. I can help with the children when she's out to work. She cleans in the school, you know. And your brother's been very generous."

He went back to the salon, where he saw Adam across the room by the piano, standing beside Dr Mendel and talking to him quietly. Adam was protecting him, Max saw, from the cocktail party Betsy had created round herself in the salon. Before he could find his way through the strangers to join them, Heinrich appeared at his side.

"Mother wanted you to have that old picture of Bach. I got Dieter to wrap it for you—can you take it back to Breslau on the train?"

"Of course. Thank you. Could I ask you something else? There's quite a lot of music in the schoolroom. Old pieces I used to play. Would you mind if I took them too?"

"Help yourself. Mendel, by the way—what's he doing here?"

"Mother particularly wanted him to be here. She wrote to Grandpapa."

"Oh, well. It's the last we'll see of him, so I suppose it doesn't matter much. Mind you take him with you. I'll get Dieter to drive you to the station, you and Zapolski of course, and Mendel."

As they drove down the lime avenue an hour later, with the painting and an old valise full of music in the boot of the car, tears finally came. Not for his mother, about whom he felt actually happy, but because this time he could imagine no reason why he should ever see Waldau again.

Dr Mendel, sitting beside him, looked sadly at him. "Poor Max", he said, very quietly.

The leaves were falling now. Many of the roadside trees already had bare branches, stripped for the snow that would soon come. Adam was sitting in front, upright and silent, beside Dieter. Max looked at the back of Adam's neck and closed his eyes. It had been a summer he wanted to last for ever.

The next afternoon, Dr Fischer kept Max back for a moment as the boys filed out of the classroom after the last lesson of the day.

"I'm so very sorry, Hofmannswaldau, to hear of your mother's death. I shall pray for her."

"But she's not . . . she wasn't . . ."

Max was taken by surprise. What Dr Fischer had said meant that someone Max respected very much, someone who was evidently a rational and intelligent person, believed that his mother could be prayed for and therefore was not nowhere.

"Thank you, sir", he said.

On the way to Cathedral Island, pushing his bicycle as usual, he remembered—he wasn't sure why—Adam's words as they sat on their tired horses in the Waldau dusk and listened to the silence that gathered after the distant sound of someone chopping wood. "Go out onto the mountain and stand in the presence of the Lord." He looked sideways at Adam's face, thoughtful, occupied with something altogether else, and said nothing.

PART TWO

Chapter 7

Whichever of the three of them got up first would grind coffee beans in an old contraption of Grandpapa's that had been, no doubt, the top-of-the-line gadget in about 1910. Hard work, it was, and the squeak of its handle, accompanied by the smell of coffee and then the sound of the kettle rattling to the boil on the gas stove, was part of waking up in the flat for the other two, who were, that morning, still in bed. When the coffee was made, the slam of the flat door and the receding clatter of footsteps down the stairs, followed by the more distant bang of the street door shutting, meant that whoever it was had gone out to buy milk at the dairy, fresh rolls at the baker's at the end of the street, and the *Vossische Zeitung* from the newsagent on the corner. This was the signal for the other two to get out of bed, reach for dressing gowns, and try not to collide with each other at the lavatory door.

When Max was one of the two who had failed to get up first, he sometimes found himself hoping, in the very back of his mind, that it would be Adam who had made the coffee and that he would be there in the kitchen, back from the street and wide awake from the fresh air, in old flannels and an open-necked shirt. The passion of that summer five years ago had long quietened into a warm, reliable friendship. Human beings, Max occasionally and gratefully thought to himself, can get used to anything, particularly anything good. Adam, who never failed to notice things, must have had some idea of the storm of feeling that blew through Max that summer, but if it had ever reached words or, worse, actions of any kind, Max knew there would have been no saving the friendship.

Perhaps in something of the same way, he thought from time to time, Germany, as the distance from the war grew longer, was getting used to a moderate, sensible republican government, held together by a fractious coalition of the centre parties, changing its formation too often but being still strong enough to have warded off the danger of complete disintegration during the horrors of the inflation and the humiliation of the French invasion of the Ruhr. Or perhaps not.

The three of them discussed these things often. Max was the least optimistic, because he knew, from Emilia's letters, that Heinrich, leaving Betsy at Waldau with their two daughters, was back in Russia. This meant, no doubt, that he was training German soldiers who, under the peace treaty's terms, weren't supposed to be soldiers, and that he was training them to use weapons that weren't supposed to exist. For what? Another war. To restore the honour of Germany. Beginning with deception, lies, and a deal with the Red Army?

On this fine Friday morning in May 1927, Max knew it was Treuburg grinding the coffee because he heard him swear at the cutlery drawer in the kitchen table that stuck because, as was usual with him, he opened it too quickly and downwards.

Unlike Max and Adam, who were studying law at the university, Joachim von Treuburg was a medical student. He was a year or two older than they were. In fact, he was twenty-four, but he seemed even older because he had done a tough couple of years training to be an officer in the army after he left his modern Gymnasium in Königsberg. So he was now that rare bird in officially disarmed Germany, a reserve lieutenant. He knew nothing of the military enterprises in Russia and thought the German army much too weak for another war to be imaginable. He was a baron, although, like Adam, he pretended most of the time to have no title of nobility, and he came from deepest East Prussia, so far north and east in the snows and forests and bear-haunted lakes that Max imagined his family's estate to be practically Russian. He played the cello, which was how Max had met him, the year before, at rehearsals of the university orchestra. After a while, Max had invited him to share Grandpapa's flat with him and Adam. Max liked him; they needed someone else to share the expenses of the flat; and there was an empty room.

Max in his dressing gown came into the kitchen, poured himself some coffee, and fetched the butter and the cherry jam from the little larder. Treuburg was sitting at the table reading the paper and munching his jamless, butterless roll, dipping it into his black coffee before each mouthful.

"Anything interesting?"

"Not much. Plenty of arguments in Berlin. The usual sort of thing. But it looks as if there really might be a war up on the Baltic, between

Poland and Lithuania. Bad news, if it happens. The Poles would certainly win, and then East Prussia would be completely surrounded by Poland. All we need is more furious Germans being ruled by Poles—we've got quite enough of them already. Not that Lithuania is much protection against anything. It's a totally invented country, a bunch of Baltic peasants speaking a language no civilized person has ever known. But they reckon they should have Vilna. The Poles got blood to the head when they'd seen off the Red Army, so in the shambles after the war, they scooped in Vilna. Once upon a time, Poland and Lithuania weren't separate countries—that was the excuse—and anyway, Vilna's always been a Polish city."

"Vilna, mother Vilna, take me to your breast; Vilna, mother Vilna, give my spirit rest", Adam sang in Yiddish, coming into the kitchen in pyjamas and bare feet.

"Exactly", Treuburg said. "A Polish city and a Jewish city. I believe Vilna's very beautiful, by the way. At least if there's a war up there, it'll be rifles and old field guns, even cavalry and sabres. No tanks or aeroplanes, thank God, to smash everything to bits."

"There won't be a war", Adam said, pouring the last of the coffee into his cup. "Berlin won't want it. The Bolsheviks won't want it. Anything to stop the Poles mopping up another chunk of Russia—that's how they'll all see it. So it won't happen. Poor old Poles. Again."

"I don't know what you're complaining about, Zapolski. The Poles have done very nicely out of the peace, haven't they? If you consider that it was we, not the Allies, who beat the Russians, the Poles were lucky to end up with a country at all. Accidental beneficiaries of the western front. What that coffee grinder needs is a drop of oil. I expect there's something that would do in your grandfather's carpentry shop, Hofmannswaldau."

"I'll have a look. Or get some at the ironmonger's after this afternoon's class. Contract and tort in the import-export business. Why on earth did I choose commercial law?"

"Because", Adam said, pouring water from the kettle onto the ground coffee, "you had to pick something solid to balance your literature option. That's why I chose criminal law. I thought it would be more exciting than commercial law, but I promise you it's not."

"I'll have to do criminal law next year. Meanwhile, thank goodness for international law", Max said. "It's much the most interesting, and since we're both doing it, there's a bit of moral support."

197

"You mean Zapolski writes the notes", Treuburg said, not looking up from the paper.

"Only sometimes. But our theses have got to be quite different. In fact, before the end of next month, we've got to get our subjects accepted. Bright ideas would be very welcome."

Treuburg put the paper down and looked at his watch. "Does either of you mind if I bring Eva Grossmann back for dinner tonight? We're going to Prague on the early train in the morning. She's never seen it, and I want to show her a really fine city."

Max was so impressed by the implications of this question that he failed to answer it.

"A Habsburg city", Adam said. "Damn it. Why are the Bohemians doing so much better than the Poles?"

"They're steadier", Treuburg said. "And richer. They've had more Germans running things for centuries. Anyway, what about Eva?"

"Of course", Adam said. "Nothing but a pleasure. The fascinating Eva Grossmann. What shall we have to eat?"

"Don't worry. I'll get it this morning. I haven't got a lecture till eleven. And then lab stuff all afternoon. No ward rounds till Monday. Is that all right, Hofmannswaldau?"

"Yes, why not? Would you like us to be out? We could go to a film."

"Certainly not. I'd like you both to get to know Eva. She's a remarkable girl. Very modern in all her ideas."

"She must be", Adam said.

"Zapolski—are you going to disapprove?"

"Absolutely not. I'm entirely used to modern. Look at my mother."

"Exactly."

Adam looked sharply at Treuburg but bothered to answer him properly.

"No, really. Didn't I establish long ago—or, rather, Nietzsche established it, and I agreed with him—that there's no reason to prop up Christian morality in the absence of Christian belief? No reason at all. Bourgeois hypocrisy, conventional appearance at the expense of reality—what will the neighbours say?—but no actual reason. Except perhaps some aesthetic distaste for the consequences of heartlessness—people, women in particular, becoming thick-skinned to protect themselves from pain."

"Steady on, Adam", Max interrupted him. "We haven't even met Eva Grossmann properly, and if Treuburg is serious about her, we should."

"You can criticise when you know her", Treuburg said. "But not before. She's keen on music, though she's actually a painter."

"What does she play?"

"Piano. And she sings."

"That's a pity", Max said. "I wish we could find a violinist and a viola player we really like, for the quartet we keep meaning to organize and never get round to. Then we could play the piano quintets really well. I've asked Mendel. He has some good pupils, but they're still at school. They're not experienced enough for us, he says. I think he means he must protect them from our wicked student ways. And all those fiddlers in the orchestra, so dull and good. 'Good evening, Herr von Hofmannswaldau. Will you turn the pages, or shall I?'"

"There's a pretty viola player I noticed last week", Treuburg said. "New, in the back desk. Very dark hair in a chignon. A Jewish girl."

"Well," Adam said, "you can't suddenly invite her. It would frighten her to death. I'm glad they've given her a place in the orchestra, though, if she looks obviously Jewish. That'll be Wolf himself, not standing any nonsense from the students."

"They could hardly keep Jews out of the orchestra. Nearly half the players must be Jewish in one way or another."

"That's it. In one way or another. Where does the line get drawn? At the moment, it's still a question of appearance and surnames. But the worst of them can try to keep anyone they even suspect of being Jewish out of anything they're in themselves. I gather the duelling clubs look people up in the Almanac to deduce how Jewish their mothers and grandmothers might have been. Duelling scars are not de rigueur in the first violins. Thank God."

"On the contrary", Treuburg said. "In fact, it's the moral duty of barons and counts brought up on Bach and Beethoven not to join their beastly clubs. As we see. My father minds a great deal that I haven't. Every time I've been home in the last four years, he's looked for a scar before saying a single word to me. Well, he's going to have to get used to it. I think he minds more that I haven't acquired a scar than that I'm going to be a doctor. 'An occupation for Jews', he says. He would have much preferred law."

"I must get dressed", Adam said. "I ought to be at the ten o'clock lecture, and so ought you, Max."

"Yes, all right. I'll do a quick tidy-up of the kitchen and the sitting room while you're shaving. The whole place looks a mess, even though Frau Gärtner came yesterday, and if we've got company tonight ..."

"Thanks," Treuburg said. "Both of you."

Max and Adam walked together to their lecture. They were supposed to have read a considerable chunk of Grotius's *On the Law of War and Peace* (Adam: "Do you realize when this book was written? *1625!*") and hadn't. Mackelroth, whose reproachful, conscientious presence they had never shaken off because he was taking one or two of their courses, certainly would have.

The main university buildings were nearer the flat than the Gymnasium had been, across a footbridge over the moat, the oldest building a solid early eighteenth-century affair with tall windows, originally the Jesuit College. Dr Fischer had told them more than once of the proud Catholic past of the university, secularized in Napoleonic times when secularization was all the rage (Adam: "and a good thing too") and united with the university of Frankfurt-on-the-Oder, the next city downstream as the great river meandered its way from Breslau across the North German plain to the Baltic. Neither of them had been to Frankfurt or ever seen the Baltic, though they had been several times, separately and together, to Berlin, which they regarded as a thoroughly philistine place, "more like Chicago than a European city", an opinion Adam, who knew no more about Chicago than Max did, had picked up somewhere. Breslau, according to Dr Fischer, had been a city for a thousand years.

"I'm amazed Treuburg can get away with asking Eva Grossmann for the night and then taking her to Prague", Max said. "What about her parents? Won't they be horrified? Her father's a professor, here in the medical school, a famous surgeon. He was a student of Grandpapa's. It's not as if they were miles away not knowing what she's getting up to."

"Oh, there'll be a cover story of some sort. She's the kind of girl who doesn't let much get in the way of what she wants."

"How do you know?"

"I took her out a couple of times last year. She took the art history course. Actually, she practically asked me to take her out. We went to the jazz club you disliked so much. She dances very well."

"And?"

"And nothing. She's too tough for me—rich and careless. She's too like my mother, though much more intelligent."

200

"But Treuburg must be quite keen on her, to be ..."

"Treuburg can look after himself. They're two of a kind, I rather suspect. They'll keep each other at arm's length, not physically but emotionally. It's just as well, probably."

"Is that how you see him? I'm not so sure. Look at how he plays the cello, the Bach suites—I've never heard anything so formal and so passionate all at the same time. No arm's length there."

"Music and women are two different things. You know that perfectly well, Max. Music's easier, being—till you play it—only marks on paper. It allows you to love—to suffer; what's the difference?—without it suffering back."

Max thought of his mother and Dr Mendel but said nothing. It wasn't a topic he had ever discussed with Adam.

"That sounds like the voice of experience", he said. "Bitter experience, even."

"Not really bitter. Just tricky. Last summer—never mind. I like women, that's the trouble. And all this is so much more difficult for them than for us. Unless they're the Eva Grossmann type. And then there's something cynical, hedonistic, about it from the very start."

"Look out. You'll be deserting Nietzsche if you're not careful. The self-validating perspective of the individual—isn't it supposed to be enough to keep the modern person going?"

"No, Max. That's old Fischer describing Nietzsche, not Nietzsche himself."

"I'd like to see old Fischer again. We ought to invite him to Sunday tea sometime."

"Good idea. Goodness knows what Treuburg would make of him—he's probably never consciously met an intelligent German Catholic in his life."

They turned across the bridge towards the university buildings.

"Adam?" Max stopped.

"What?"

"Suppose Eva Grossmann gets pregnant."

Adam laughed. "Max! You're twenty-two. It's 1927. Do try to be your age. She won't. That kind of girl, nowadays, just doesn't. Come along. Don't worry about them. We'll be late for Professor Kahn, and you know how he stops and glares if anyone opens the door once he's started."

Max did his best to concentrate on the lecture. Though the topic really interested him—how far is it reasonable to assume a law of nature universal among human beings but not divine in origin?—the lecturer's delivery of his ancient pages of typescript, which he put slowly down on the lectern as he finished each one, was so flat that Max's attention constantly slipped, and he reassembled it only by guessing how many pages remained in the professor's hand.

He thought of Eva Grossmann. He had seen her at lectures, in classes, because she had taken some courses in law, though now she seemed to have stopped. She was thin and lively, with a mobile, comic face a bit like a monkey's, and copper-coloured hair cut in a neat, thick bob, almost a helmet, which it was difficult to imagine untidy or blown about. She wore lipstick and black stuff on her eyelashes and had a white, powdered face. She liked very short skirts and often had a kind of glitter in her clothes. Long beads in ropes hung round her neck, so long they nearly reached her waist. She was the kind of girl of which there was quite a number among the students at the university, all very—what would be the word?—evident, perhaps, proud to be holding their own among so many more men than women. Eva Grossmann was the most alarming example he had seen. How did one get near such a woman? Kiss her? The thought of the powder and the sticky red lipstick disgusted him. The thought of her naked in bed with Treuburg in the flat, later that very day, made him feel actually sick. He tried hard to listen to the lecturer.

". . . from which it is comparatively simple to deduce in the writing of this essentially Protestant philosopher a critical shift from the a priori assumptions of Thomas Aquinas . . ."

It was no good. He looked sideways at Adam's fine-boned face, which he loved. Adam was writing his usual crisp, accurate notes. He caught Max's glance and winked. The wink meant "this is the most boring lecture in the world, but don't worry, I'll do the notes." Max stopped even trying to follow what Professor Kahn was reading out to the silent, scribbling students.

How could Treuburg, so fastidious, with his clean shirt, clean underwear, and clean socks every single day, with his trips to the washerwoman down the street (while Max and Adam soaked their dirty clothes in the sink and rinsed them in the bath), and with his room so tidy that it looked as if no one lived in it, even contemplate Eva Grossmann with her lipstick in that neat, narrow, single bed?

The nausea returned, as did the question he had asked Adam. Max knew nothing at all of what "birth control" actually meant. He had gathered from *Anna Karenina*—which he had read with anguish a year or two ago, seeing his father in Vronsky, a romantic soldier with no war to fight, and his mother in sweet, gentle Kitty—that birth control was possible but that it was modern, selfish, and to be disapproved of as Tolstoy disapproved of it. But what it was in practice he had no idea. Adam had obviously guessed his ignorance, but he was too embarrassed to ask for enlightenment.

And what of Adam and girls? Max suspected that Adam had slept with a girl, perhaps with several girls. Adam had, last year, been on a number of occasions to the jazz club where he had once taken a miserable Max and where Adam played his clarinet with the band late at night. Several times he didn't come home at all, and said nothing when he eventually reappeared but seemed for a few days unlike himself, snappy and defensive. He was certainly not calm, satisfied, elated: but why did Max find himself hoping for a cheerful, open Adam after these escapades? To set him some kind of followable example? To show that it was possible, without unkindness or muddle or the sort of cynicism Adam had implied in Treuburg, to get from where they were now to being happy and relaxed in the company of a woman one loved? There were couples among the students, whose closeness, though demonstrations of affection were not the custom, was evident just from the way they walked side by side or exchanged glances. How did they achieve such closeness? Why did it evaporate? For often these couples would break up, no one knew why, and the man and the girl would return to the revolving crowd of people one by one in the lecture halls, classrooms, library, and corridors. Was a closeness that would last possible only in marriage and then with a great deal of luck? He thought of Heinrich and Betsy. And of his parents. Not exactly happy and relaxed, as far as he, too young to understand anything while his father was alive, could tell, looking back. Hadn't his father adored in his mother a woman she had actually grown out of being? Were his grandparents happy and relaxed? Perhaps. Although—or was it because?—they were already old before he knew them.

A familiar pang, this one. He missed his grandfather more than he had ever missed either of his parents. There was something almost every day, and not only because he was living in his flat among things familiar to him, that reminded him of the loss of his grandfather. He was the one person he could perhaps have talked to about all this. Why had he died? Why had he almost deliberately chosen death? No, that wasn't fair, wasn't true. Max was well used to these feelings and to his own criticism of them: he had been round and round this course so many times. It was only grief that made him angry like this, quite unreasonably angry with his grandfather. The idea of his own death, he knew perfectly well, never occurred for a moment to the old man when he responded, without hesitation, as he always would, to a straightforward appeal for his help.

It was in the freezing November of 1923. The inflation had reached its peak of crazy intoxication. For months the government had been printing paper money in greater and greater quantities, boasting week by week of the huge output of notes, as if it were somehow producing actual wealth when in reality the paper money was a kind of drug. Like a drug, or like the mad dancing to frenzied music that went on and on in the jazz clubs until daylight, it killed pain, numbed anxiety, and created a dizzy illusion that all was well. The only thing that had done anyone any real good, for more than a year, had been debt. Debt dissolved like soap bubbles, in days if not hours, because the numbers of marks owed meant less and less as you watched them. That was why, Max now realized, mortgaged landowners like Heinrich, even without the help of Betsy's father's real fortune in factories and machinery and cheap labour, had got richer, not poorer, through the inflation, whereas people like Grandpapa, with a university pension and some old securities, had got rapidly poorer. Frau Gärtner stopped coming in the spring because Grandpapa couldn't pay her, but he was so worried about the children that after a few weeks, he got her to come back twice a week to be paid with what food he could get in exchange for looking after sick shopkeepers and their families. By the autumn of 1923, the already-poor were actually starving. The farmers wouldn't bring their meat and eggs and butter, their potatoes and beets and cabbages, to the towns to sell because the money they were paid would buy nothing. So they stayed in the villages and bartered, while the city markets were almost empty except for people begging.

Early that November, Max's grandfather got a telegram from the association of retired doctors, which once a year assembled its members for a formal dinner in the great hall of the university medical school. Now the association was appealing for a few hours of the time of any retired doctor able to help: there was typhus in the slums to the east of the city, and malnourished children and old people were dying by the score every day. Grandpapa collected a bag of medicines and water-purification tablets from the hospital, found the old valise that had brought the music from Waldau, and packed it full of groats and dried fruit, dried milk, tea, sugar, biscuits, and brandy. It was heavy, and he took Max with him to carry it. What they found in the icy, filthy streets of wooden hovels thatched with frozen straw cut Max to the heart. He had no idea that in Germany in the twentieth century, in Breslau, his own much-loved city, and five years after the war, people could be living in such poverty. They were poor Jews from the east speaking nothing but Yiddish, poor Poles speaking nothing but Polish. They cried to see a doctor on their doorsteps. There were babies dead on their mothers' laps, fathers shaking with fever under thin, dirty blankets, and old people dying in chairs beside stoves cold for lack of fuel. Grandpapa did what he could for five days, returning to the hospital every morning for new supplies and sending Max to the shops with a sack of almost meaningless money to replenish the case. On the sixth day, Grandpapa was too tired to move from his bed. On the eighth day, he had a high fever, and Max sat beside him feeding him teaspoonfuls of sugared water on the instructions of another old doctor who had been to see him. On the tenth day, he died.

Not until a week later, after his grandfather had been quietly buried in the new Protestant cemetery at the edge of the city, and Max had stood, the reality of his loss still ahead, at the edge of yet another grave, with Heinrich beside him and Adam and a good number of colleagues and former students of his grandfather behind him, did he discover that Germany had very nearly fallen apart while his grandfather was dying.

Hundreds of miles away to the southwest, in the city of Munich, a ranting Austrian revolutionary called Adolf Hitler—along with General Ludendorff, so fiercely defended by Heinrich's colonel—had declared a putsch. They took advantage of the misery of inflation—which many people all over Germany were blaming on the Jews—and of the French occupation of the Ruhr, and of Communist agitators frightening property owners in Saxony, to announce the collapse of the republic. Their programme was to march to Berlin as Mussolini the year before had marched to Rome, make Hitler dictator, hang the cabinet and members of parliament, declare war on France, and get rid of the Jews. They thought the army would support them, but the generals' loyalty to the government in Berlin held firm, and within twenty-four hours the putsch was over and Hitler and Luden-dorff had been arrested.

Max knew almost nothing about Bavaria, where these dangerous histrionics took place. Adam had several times been to Munich, to the opera with his mother, and said it was like a provincial version of Vienna—Catholic, snobbish, right-wing, almost as keen on restoring its operetta monarchy as Vienna was on restoring the empire. There was a Habsburg painting in the Munich art gallery, a Titian portrait of Emperor Charles V sitting on an everyday chair in everyday black clothes, old and tired and sad and looking a bit like Dr Mendel. Adam had sent Max a postcard of this painting, on the back of which he had written, "How to be ruler of the world". It was still on a shelf of the kitchen dresser in Grandpapa's flat, propped against a Meissen teapot too good to use.

Apart from their vague notion of General Ludendorff, neither Adam nor Max knew much about the people who had tried to seize power in Munich. They called themselves the National Socialist party, Nazi for short. They had gangs of unofficial soldiers, Stormtroopers, in most cities, including Breslau. These were Freikorps types in brown shirts who marched and chanted and fought Communists and Social Dem-ocrats whenever they got the chance. They were most noticeable for the swastika symbol, which they wore on their armbands and waved on their banners and which, because it was meant to be an ancient Aryan sign, had become a gesture of menace to Jews, scrawled on their doors and shop windows, appearing on anti-Semitic posters, and even drawn on the corner of student notices pinned up in the uni-versity where Max and Adam had in the autumn of 1923 just begun their first term.

"Who is this Hitler?" Max asked Adam, as they both sat reading newspapers in a warm café, its windows misted against the frost out-side, a few days after Grandpapa's funeral.

"I've no idea. Well, I can guess a bit. If he was born an Austrian but fought in the German army in the war, which is what it says here, he'll be a rabid nationalist for sure. And a corporal, it says, so he won't have much education. I can picture the type. Vienna, you know— well, you don't, fortunately for you—could have been, should have been, the least nationalist city in the whole world. When poor old Franz Josef declared war in 1914, the posters to tell the soldiers what was going on went up in eight languages, one of them Yiddish. But even before the war, the city was full of nationalists hating each other and the Germans hating worst of all because of feeling superior to everyone else. So Hitler manages to become a proper German, a German German, fighting for the Kaiser, and hates the armistice, hates the peace, believes in Ludendorff's disgraceful stab-in-the-back lie, believes the Jews did the stabbing, and now wants power, war, and persecution of the Jews to save the soul of Germany. Well, it's failed, thank God—and thanks to the Prussian army doing its duty—so let's hope Hitler goes to prison for a long, long time and that all these boys in brown shirts get ordinary jobs, if the government can settle things down and burst the inflation bubble, and then we can forget about this ludicrous bully who thinks he ought to be running the country."

This was more or less how things turned out, with a steadier government and the stabilization of the currency, and with Hitler going to prison—though he was released after only a few months. But the brown shirts and the swastikas did not disappear from the streets of Breslau.

When Professor Kahn swept his pieces of paper together, the last one having been read and placed on the lectern, and sailed in his gown up the aisle between the students with their bent heads, Max came to and realized that he had registered hardly a sentence of the lecture.

"What's the matter with you today?" Adam said as they sat at a sidewalk table belonging to a nearby café. Their next lecture, on the history of treaties between European countries, was at noon, so they had an hour to kill. "I know what it is—it's Eva Grossmann coming to dinner, isn't it? It's one thing meeting these creatures at a student party or in a restaurant or even in a jazz club, but at home—in your flat, in your grandfather's flat—that's another thing altogether. Treuburg shouldn't have suggested it."

"Oh, that's ridiculous. I shouldn't mind. At least, there's no respectable reason to mind. It's his home too, after all. He can't very well invite her to East Prussia." He thanked the waiter, who had brought their coffee. "How do you mean—creatures?"

Adam roared with laughter. "Women."

"Don't laugh. It's not all women. It's—I don't know. The kind of girl who—Betsy's a good example. And Eva Grossmann even more so because she's a student."

"You mean modern girls, who know what they want and get it. I agree. They're frightening in a way. But you wouldn't want to box them in with governesses until someone comes along to marry them, would you? There's every reason to allow them to join in, to get a proper university education, to become doctors instead of just nurses, professors instead of just elementary school teachers. Particularly as every country lost so many clever men in the war. If clever women can do some of the work the men would have done, that must be a good thing. Don't you agree?"

"In theory, of course I do. In practice—well, we'll see what Eva Grossmann's really like tonight. Do you think she does ordinary things like help with the washing up?"

"The Grossmanns are rich. They live on the old moat, in one of the most beautiful houses in Breslau. He's a very successful surgeon. His wife must have been some kind of heiress. I don't suppose Eva's ever washed dishes in her life. But that's a different issue. You know . . ."

Adam, narrowing his eyes and looking at nothing in the far distance, had an expression on his face Max knew well. Something fresh had struck him.

"What?" Max said.

"I'm thinking about women like Eva Grossmann. The whole thing, the catching up, the tough overconfidence—'I can manage perfectly well on my own, thank you very much. I don't need you to patronize me, to give me a helping hand. Just let me get on with it and I'll show you'—is all exactly like the Jews, isn't it? And for the same reasons. They've been boxed in since time immemorial. Not allowed to go to universities. Not allowed to join the world. Not allowed by the men who ran the world but also not allowed by themselves. The rabbis were terrified that Jews would lose their religion, eat the wrong food, forget about the Sabbath, and say no prayers for their dead parents, while mothers and grandmothers were terrified that girls wouldn't want to have babies, wouldn't learn to cook and sew or at least run a house, would forget about going to church, or would say no prayers at all. Church, kitchen, children. All the old priorities would be lost in the worldly careers that used to be only for men, only for Christians. The net result is the same: pushy achievers. Jews no longer behave like Jews always have, obedient, obliging, apologizing for being alive; women no longer behave like women always have, obedient, obliging, out to please. Eva Grossmann is both a woman and a Jew—she proves the point."

"I suppose so. You may be right, but only about a few—a few women, a few Jews. There are many, many more who—well, who do things, the same things, but more quietly. Look at my mother, a woman, a Jewess, a good pianist, who got married very young, had children, and looked after her husband, her children, her house. She always played the piano well but was not famous. There were no concerts, no travelling, no notices in the papers. She wasn't pushy at all. She wasn't independent either, though, come to think of it."

"Of course. It's the ones who are obvious, the ones who make a lot of noise, who get resented, and then all the rest get resented on their account, so it becomes 'the woman question', or 'the Jewish question'—invented questions, both of them, since most women and most Jews have the tact and the common sense to make the most of new chances to do things, to join in, without irritating anyone else."

"But is that possible? Perhaps the old rabbis and the old grandmothers were right. Perhaps it isn't possible to catch up, to join in, as you put it, without stopping being properly Jewish, or without stopping being the kind of woman one could love and marry—I don't know. And by the way, I don't resent women like Eva Grossmann; I'm just scared by them."

"I know. I know. It's a very good thing Treuburg's asked her to dinner. You'll see. She's not really frightening. She's more of a case study in how difficult it is to survive being rich, clever, spoilt, and successful—in how difficult it is to survive as a human being, I mean. It's a bit like Germany."

"Like *Germany*? What on earth do you mean?"

This time Adam, delighted with another new idea, looked with his laughing eyes straight at Max.

"Imagine you're an Englishman, a hundred years ago, two hundred years ago. At any time, almost, up to 1870. What does Germany look like to you? An impossible patchwork of little states, the duchy of this, the margravate of that, princes and prince-Bishops, Electors, the odd King here and there—very odd, most of them—imperial cities, and, scattered about, hundreds of counts and barons with their castles and their medieval rights to this, that, and the other. A map no Englishman—or Frenchman, come to that—could make any sense of. And what would you have thought of Germans you'd heard of? Clever fellows, you'd have thought, Goethe, philosophers, composers cropping up all the time and even adopted by other countries, Handel every Englishman's favourite composer. There were some excellent soldiers in Prussia, useful to have on one's side. But you wouldn't have thought Germany a serious nation to be contended with. Not like France. No competition for England. The English loved the Germans, you know, in a condescending sort of way, thought them cosy, warm-hearted, unthreatening teddy bears. Then there was Bismarck, and Germany suddenly became a serious nation. Germany became a competitor, and a very efficient one. It copied all the English industrial inventions and then invented a lot more for itself. It overtook England, all in a single generation. So you see, if you go on imagining you're an Englishman, by 1900, by 1910—that's only seventeen years ago—the Germans are independent, ambitious, overconfident, and vulgar, in fact pushy achievers just like obvious modern Jews and obvious modern women. And how has Germany survived being rich, clever, spoilt, and successful? Remarkably badly, so far."

"Hubris and nemesis", Max said. "But there's a real difference. You can't have whole groups of people being tragic, women or Jews. But a nation can be tragic, pride going before a fall. A nation can even be comic—do you remember old Fischer telling us that the plots of tragedies and the plots of comedies are exactly the same? They're both about justice being restored."

"It was more chance than justice, the outcome of the war. And it was too untidy, too random, to be tragic. There were millions of meaningless deaths. No divine horizon there, which Fischer used to go on about. But nemesis for this country, yes. And who'll be next? The Americans? I wouldn't be surprised. Rich, clever, spoilt, and successful—the gods don't like it."

Max laughed with pleasure. "You are a brilliant fellow, you know."

"Nonsense. I'm just a foreigner. In Germany, it's a great help."

"International law should suit you perfectly."

"I don't know. It all seems a bit abstract to me, this year, too remote from the mess in which people actually have to live. Look at Grotius. It's all right; I know you haven't read the book, and I know you didn't hear a word of Kahn's lecture. But Grotius's book strikes me as too far away and long ago to have much bearing on how things are now. He speaks of noble ideals. But people aren't noble, and ideals don't work.

Look at the League of Nations. It all sounded wonderful last September when they let Germany in as a permanent member of the council, and even Poland as a temporary member. There was Stresemann making a noble speech about peace, and Briand making another. 'Away with rifles, machine guns, cannon!' It was all about beating swords into ploughshares, about Germans and Frenchmen becoming the best of friends. But if something goes wrong, if one powerful country goes mad and breaks the treaties—that could be France, could be Russia, which is quite mad already, could be Germany—then what? The League has no army to enforce anything, just bits of paper and good intentions. Nietzsche was right, you know. The will to power: it's all that counts in the end. Last year I thought perhaps work in Geneva, at the League, would be the thing. They must need people who can speak various languages—they might even think people with a Habsburg background would be particularly useful. And I'm not too nationalist. But I don't think it's real enough. Perhaps it has to be ordinary politics, closer to the mess. But where? How? I couldn't live in Warsaw. Or Vienna. Or Berlin. What shall we do with our lives, Max? Be city councillors in Breslau?"

"I don't think so. What party could we join? The Social Democrats wouldn't want us, and they have the only tolerable set of principles apart from the Centre Party. We can't join the Centre Party because neither of us is Catholic, one way or another. Wouldn't Heinrich be horrified if we joined the Social Democrats? It would almost be worth it just for that. And to see your mother's face too."

"Speaking of joining things, have you seen the notices up asking for people to audition for *Hamlet*? It's being staged by the university drama society—one of the very few that's not tied to one kind of Christianity or one kind of politics. I thought I might give it a shot."

"Can you act?"

Adam returned a laughing look.

"I don't know. There was *Antigone*, but that was in Greek. I was Götz von Berlichingen when I was fourteen. The monks were keen on plays. It was civilized of them to do *Götz*, considering the great enemy is the Bishop. 'Freedom, freedom!' I gasped as I died. My mother loved it. Would you come too if I went to the *Hamlet* audition?"

"I've never even thought of trying to act. But *Hamlet*—it's tempting. I could carry a spear on the battlements in the dark. Will it be in English?"

"German. Schlegel and Tieck's translation, no doubt. Not everyone's been brought up by Dr Fischer."

The clock in the bell tower of the university building across the river began to strike twelve. Adam threw a couple of coins on the café table, and they ran, just beating the lecturer to the door of the lecture room. Max took his own notes for the whole of the next hour.

Treuburg, having bought the food and laid the table in the morning, returned to the flat at six, set out the cold dinner neatly in the kitchen—what used to be the dining room had become Treuburg's bedroom—and left again, having looked critically at the sitting room (where Max was at the desk summarizing for himself Adam's Grotius notes) and having nodded his head with grudging approval. Adam was out. Max hoped he would be back before Treuburg returned with Eva Grossmann, and he was, bringing two bottles of Mosel.

"Well done", Max said. "You do remind me of Grandpapa sometimes."

"That", Adam said, not laughing, "is a serious compliment. Thank you. Now, chin up! We've got to make this go all right for Treuburg's sake. How many friends does he have?"

"He's friends with quite a lot of medics, I think. They do long-distance running and the pentathlon and all that. But quite a lot of friends can be the same as none."

"Exactly."

Eventually, in fact only twenty minutes later, they heard Treuburg's key in the lock and then Eva, out of breath—"What a lot of stairs you have." Then, "Thank you", as Treuburg took her coat and hung it in the hall. "I'll leave this here for now." A suitcase? In they came.

Eva was wearing a bright green silk dress, short and clinging, with gold and green and scarlet beads, pale green silk stockings—at least Max, taking all this in as she came into the sitting room glittering and exotic like a dragonfly, assumed they were silk—and gold shoes with a strap and a button like little girls' shoes.

"This is Max Hofmannswaldau", Treuburg said. "And this is Adam Zapolski."

"Adam and I ... have met", she said in her smoky voice, giving him her hand and suggesting rather more than Adam's account to Max warranted. Treuburg, Max gathered, was meant to notice this and meant to mind. It was impossible to tell whether he did either.

"Good evening, Max", she said, her scent reaching him as she shook his hand. There were rings on her thin, cool fingers. "I think I've seen you in lectures. Not that I go to lectures any more. I'm mostly at the Academy of Arts nowadays. I paint, you know."

She looked round the room.

"Is that somebody's ancestor?"

"It's Bach."

"I didn't know Bach looked like that. So very respectable. And what's *that*?"

"It's a harpsichord. My grandfather made it."

"How extraordinary. Does it work?"

"It's not mechanical. One plays it. Zapolski plays it."

"Adam! How wonderful! I'd no idea. Play it now!"

"Perhaps later", Adam said, while Treuburg at the same moment put a glass into Eva's hand.

"Would you like some wine?"

"Joachim, you're an angel. Of course I would", she said, but Max thought she was looking for something else, a cocktail perhaps.

She sat down and took out of her little gold bag a cigarette case and a black and gold cigarette holder. Adam lit her cigarette and then one of his own. Treuburg doesn't smoke, Max thought. Damn.

But when they each had a glass, she patted the sofa beside her for Treuburg to sit close to her, and she put her bare, braceleted arm round his shoulders.

"So Max," she said, "do you play too?"

"Only the violin."

"How convenient! A pianist, a violinist, and a cellist, all living together. I haven't heard Joachim play the cello yet. I'm sure he's a wonderful player. You should play trios. Do you?"

"Sometimes", Adam said.

"And what about quartets? Quintets? My father's surgical assistant is a violinist. You should meet him. He's a Russian or a Pole or something. Not a grand Pole like you, Adam. A Jew from the east, you know, but a brilliant surgeon in the making, my father says. I'll introduce him to Joachim."

She looked more carefully at the sitting room. Max saw he hadn't tidied it enough. There were piles of books on the desk and on the floor, piles of music on the piano, and a pullover of Adam's over the back of the chair by the harpsichord.

"What a nice, masculine room", she said. "So original, students living in a flat without anyone to look after them."

That's her mother talking, Max thought. He had never met her mother.

"Who does the cooking? Don't tell me ... Max, I bet."

"We take it in turns", Adam said. "We can all cook well enough to keep us alive."

"And a—what's it called?—a harpsichord as well as a piano. Remarkable. Surely you have a cleaning woman of some kind?"

"Yes, we do. She worked for my grandparents for many years. This was their flat."

"I see. Well, I suppose it's very convenient, being so close to the university."

"Shall we eat?" Treuburg said. "It's all ready."

"Marvellous! I'm starving. Pull me up, Joachim. I'm quite sunk in this sofa."

He pulled her up, and they walked toward the kitchen. Holding onto his hand, she stopped by the big bookcase. "Medical textbooks, just like at home. Are they all yours, Joachim?"

"They were my grandfather's", Max said. "He was a doctor. I think your father was one of his students."

"Really? What was your grandfather's name?"

"He was called Professor Meyer."

"Oh." She looked more carefully at Max. "Meyer. I see, Count von Hofmannswaldau. How aristocratic you all are, the three of you, to be slumming in the Jewish doctor's flat. Or were, perhaps."

"Eva!"

She lifted his hand to her lips. "I'm so sorry, Joachim. It was a joke. Jews are allowed to make jokes about Jews, you know, even if they mind ever so much when other people do."

"That wasn't a joke about Jews", Adam said. "But never mind. We're men of the left, are we not? Let's see what Treuburg has got for us to eat."

After dinner, at which most of the conversational work was done by Adam, and at which Eva, keeping Treuburg transfixed in a mesmerized silence, drank more than any of the men, they returned to the sitting room.

"Now, Adam", she said, "play the funny instrument for me."

"I don't think so. I'll play the piano if you like."

He sat at the piano and began a sequence of slow jazz chords, moving his hands over the keys without looking at them. She picked up the melody at once and began to sing, standing behind Adam and looking at Treuburg. "Basin Street ... is the street ... where all the dark and the light folks meet", in strongly accented American English.

Max left the room without a sound, pulled the door closed behind him, and then shut the kitchen door. He began furiously but very quietly to clear the table, to stack the plates, to throw the crumbs away. He wasn't sure which of the three of them was annoying him the most. He knew he couldn't actually run the water and start washing up, so when the kitchen was tidy, he went back to the sitting room door. She did have a good voice, and a rhythmic sense so firm, however much she played about with it, that even Dr Mendel would have been impressed.

He waited for the end of the song. He couldn't bear to go in and see her face, playing Adam and Treuburg off against each other. He heard Adam say, "Do you know this?" and set off with a fast, jazzy dance tune. Again she picked it up after a few bars and sang, "I wish I could shimmy like my sister Kate". She stopped singing—she didn't know any more of the words, Max deduced—and there were sounds of her dancing. He thought of Betsy years ago at Waldau, but he minded this more because he liked Treuburg much better than he liked Heinrich. When Adam stopped playing, Max went into the sitting room and shut the door noisily behind him. Eva had collapsed, giggling, into Treuburg's arms.

"I know," she said, looking tipsily into Treuburg's eyes, her hands on his shoulders, "I'll play some ragtime and Adam can get his clarinet."

"No, Eva. Not tonight. We have to get up at five if we're going to catch that train to Prague." And without looking at either of the others, he led Eva from the room.

Max went back to the kitchen and turned on the water in the sink. Adam followed him, shutting the door behind him.

When the sink was full, Max shut off the tap and turned to face Adam, who was standing, sheepishly, with a tea towel in his hand.

"How can he? How *can* he? And you—egging her on like that. I'm surprised he didn't hit you."

"Ah. It's all more complicated than you think. She's not a bad girl, you know. She's too tough for me, but she's not a bad girl. And after tonight, I suspect she's not so much genuinely tough as putting on a tough act. She's unsure of herself. Who isn't nowadays? And don't you agree that it's good for Treuburg to feel he's won some kind of competition? With Eva the prize. She's quite a prize too. If there's going to be a competition, there have to be competitors, don't there? Not to mention the fact that Treuburg is in full reaction against his father, the East Prussian baron. That's why he's here. That's why he's studying medicine: it's thoroughly middle-class, being a doctor. And a Jewish girlfriend fits the picture perfectly."

"That's all so cynical. I hate it. It makes the whole thing, women—men and women, I mean—just a matter of power."

"Precisely. Haven't I told you over and over again? Everything in human life is exactly that, a matter of power. How to get it, how to keep it. Masters and slaves. Men and women—or possibly women and men; it goes both ways. The survival of the fittest. Owners and workers. The ego and the id. And look out, because the slaves, the women, the less fit, the workers, and the id will rise up and get their own back one of these days. You see, they all agree—Marx, Darwin, Nietzsche, and Freud. Power is all there is. Strength, and, of course, if strength, weakness."

"You don't really believe that? Not *really*? Do you? You remember Dr Fischer on determinism: philosophers who spend the morning proving we have no free will and the afternoon choosing a new suit. Isn't it like that? You say these things, even do them, like just now, playing up to Eva for reasons so elaborate I can hardly follow them, but that's not who you actually are, is it?"

"Oh well, it was fun. That's probably more who I actually am."

"Adam!"

Both of them laughed, and they hugged each other.

"Come on. The washing up. Not to be faced at breakfast."

They went to the *Hamlet* auditions together, but Max, after watching half a dozen student actors deliver speeches with what struck him as embarrassing demonstrativeness, decided to stay at the back of the university theatre and see how Adam got on. Those trying for parts in the production had been asked to prepare a speech from the play: most of the men had learnt one of Hamlet's soliloquies, while more-modest or more-calculating students presented themselves with less competition by delivering speeches belonging to Claudius, Laertes, and Polonius. There were three Gertrudes and six Ophelias. The director was a fifth-year student who conducted the auditions with smouldering impatience, stopping most of the actors after a few lines, so that the choices he was making were obvious to all. He had let only three of the possible Hamlets finish their speeches when Adam was called, the last of the auditioners because the second-year student standing beside the director had a list in alphabetical order.

Max and Adam had learnt "O what a rogue and peasant slave am I" and had spent as much time discussing the complexity of the speech as memorizing the words. Here was Hamlet deliberately working himself up into a rage and then thinking yet again of a way of putting off doing anything. They tried to remember what Dr Fischer had said about this speech when they had read the play in English in their last year at the gymnasium. It didn't matter that they'd forgotten: every time they went through it, the speech got thicker with meaning, closer to the self-dramatizing adolescent each of them could understand more and more clearly.

Now Adam on the empty stage was at once Hamlet himself. He silenced the crowd of students, bored and tired after more than two hours in the theatre, and made them watch him. His comparison of his own real despair with the Player's rant about Hecuba became a comparison between himself and all the earlier Hamlets of the afternoon. At the hinge of the speech, the quiet decision to do something, anything, rather than nothing, the students waited, stock-still, as if they had no idea what he would say next. The director let him finish the speech. A dozen actors' names were read out by the second-year assistant; everyone else was asked to go. When Adam got home, an hour after Max, he had, of course, been given the part of Hamlet.

Chapter 8

Two weeks later, Max, Adam, and Treuburg were invited to a Sunday evening party at the Grossmanns'. Formal cards arrived, one for each of them, Frau Professor Friedrich Grossmann requesting the pleasure of their company to celebrate the birthday of her daughter Eva. Adam was now rehearsing every weekday evening and most of Saturday and Sunday but had a space on Sunday evening. "This is something not to be missed", he said to Max. They replied correctly, brushed their dinner jackets (the invitation said "Dress: Informal"), asked Frau Gärtner to iron their best white shirts, and set out together for the twenty-minute walk to the old house on the moat.

"How much do the Grossmanns know, Treuburg, about you and Eva?" Adam said. "We don't want to put our foot in our mouths."

"They don't know anything. I'm just an acquaintance from the university. The same as you."

"What about Prague?"

"Eva told her parents that she went with a girlfriend to see an exhibition. She stayed with the girlfriend's aunt."

There were perhaps thirty people in the Grossmanns' drawing room, most of them young, all of them standing with champagne glasses in their hands, their talk subdued by the heavy old-fashioned elegance of the room—dark books lining the walls; dark, thick, patterned carpets on the floor; a chandelier with candles rather than electric bulbs; dark velvet curtains at the long windows—and the June evening fading outside. The only clashing note was struck by a large, elaborately decorated cake on a silver stand, placed in the centre of a gleaming polished table with wrapped presents arranged around it. Max and Adam exchanged glances: no present . . . too late . . . never mind.

Eva, dressed in silver with diamond earrings glittering beneath her copper hair, came to greet them and introduce them to her parents, who were standing together in front of the mantelpiece. Behind them a huge arrangement of roses, carnations, and silvery leaves stood in the fireplace.

"Count von Hofmannswaldau, Baron von Treuburg, and Count Zapolski", Eva said. Each of them in turn clicked his heels and bowed twice, first taking Frau Grossmann's hand and raising it to his lips, then shaking the professor's large, white hand.

"We're delighted you could come", Eva's mother said once, to them all. "We're so pleased to welcome Eva's friends from the university."

The professor looked at them more carefully.

"Ah, Baron. You are studying medicine, I believe."

"Yes, sir."

"And in which branch of our noble science do you hope to specialize?"

"I hope simply to qualify in general medicine, sir. I come from East Prussia, and there are still country districts there much in need of a general practitioner with modern training. If there is another war, I would be proud to serve as an army doctor."

"More ambition, Baron, more ambition! I would have expected, with your advantages, that you would be aiming a good deal higher than that. And there's no reason to suppose there'll be another war, is there? Things have settled so well in the last two or three years, don't you agree?"

The professor, not waiting for an answer, turned his handsome attention to Max. "And what are you studying, Count?"

"Law, sir. In particular, at present, international law."

"Not a very German subject, I would have thought. Don't let the theoreticians destroy your patriotism, my boy. Our country is fast recovering its strength, its economic vigour. That's what will count in the struggle for power between the nations, you mark my words: what is practical rather than what is theoretical. That's why I chose surgery all those years ago, and I haven't regretted it."

He looked with satisfaction around his expensive room in his expensive house, and then said to Adam, "And you, Count?"

"Also law, sir. And literature, for love."

The professor gave him an acute look.

"I see. I imagine law is likely to be of more use to your nation than literature. Poland, I understand, has never been short of poets."

"I'm studying comparative literature, sir. The English, as it happens, come out of most comparisons rather well. As do the Russians."

Eva reappeared with some more guests to be introduced to her parents, and Max, Adam, and Treuburg politely faded into the crowded room, where they accepted glasses of champagne from a footman with a tray and stood close together observing the party. Eva, among her guests, was behaving with perfect decorum, though there was a kind of suppressed irony in her face, evident probably only to those who had seen her as she had been in the flat a fortnight ago.

After half an hour or so, the professor tapped on a glass with his fountain pen for silence and said in his resonant, somehow dangerous voice:

"Now, my friends, we are here to celebrate our beautiful Eva's twenty-first birthday, and before she cuts her cake and we all drink to her health, my dear wife and I have asked her to play for us. She and my distinguished surgical assistant, Doctor Jakob Halpern, will play Brahms's first violin sonata in G major. Do find somewhere to sit down. I'm afraid some of you will have to sit on the floor, but perhaps you're young enough not to find that too difficult."

Max was relieved to be able to stop trying to talk to people he didn't know. He and Adam, exchanging discreet disbelief in a quick look, sat on the floor by one of the tall windows, the velvet curtains now closed.

It was clear after a few pages of the sonata that Dr Halpern, a small, dark, bearded young man, his guarded expression unreadable behind his heavy spectacles, was a very good violinist indeed. His playing was precise, wonderfully in tune, and passionate but at the same time reticent, as if the music, given more freedom, would have been too much for him, for the room, for the occasion. It was also clear that, although she was attacking the keyboard and the pedals with a lot of panache, the Brahms was really too difficult for Eva. Almost all the notes were in place, and there was much emotion washing about on the surface of the music, but she had approached the piece as a technical challenge and was so keen to demonstrate her mastery of it that she wasn't actually listening to Halpern's playing, let alone accompanying it. So the piece was being given in two different performances, and its soul, the life particular to that composition and no other, was reaching the listeners in the hot, candlelit drawing room only fitfully, in some of Halpern's phrasing.

At the end, everyone clapped. Eva rose from the piano stool and graciously bowed to the applause. Halpern, unsmiling, tucked his violin under his arm and nodded briefly behind her, his acknowledgement of the audience much the same as that of the boy of about fifteen, apparently Eva's brother, who had turned the pages for her.

Professor Grossmann's speech about his daughter, the toast, and the cutting of the cake passed Max by because he wanted to ask Adam whether he thought they should approach Halpern and see if he might be interested in coming to the flat to play. There was no chance to say anything until everyone was eating cake and chattering again. Then Adam said:

"He's over there, not enjoying this. Go and ask him. He can always say no. Go on."

Max, holding his piece of cake untasted on a little plate, made his way through the backs of the groups of guests.

"Dr Halpern?"

The doctor, who was standing by the piano looking at a picture of a Chinese tureen in a book about porcelain, looked up, still unsmiling.

"Forgive me. My name is Max Hofmannswaldau. I'm a law student in the university. I'm a violinist myself, although ... You play beautifully. I have a friend who is a good cellist. We have been looking for a musician who might be interested in playing some chamber music with us from time to time, perhaps a quartet. We also have an excellent pianist who shares our flat."

"How do you do? You are most kind."

Max couldn't place the accent: Russian, perhaps?

Halpern looked down again at the porcelain book, and closed it. Then he looked straight at Max with dark brown, almost black, eyes through his spectacles.

"I have very little time. That is why I have not joined the university orchestra. But your invitation is tempting, I must say. I like to play chamber music. I am supposed to have two evenings in the week when I am allowed to be not present in the hospital. They are, unfortunately, not always the same evenings, which makes things difficult. But we could hope ... Where is your flat?"

"Very close to the medical school, the hospital. It's my grandfather's flat. He was professor of medicine some time ago. Professor Meyer. You may know his name."

"Of course. He has died, your grandfather?"

"Yes. More than three years ago."

"I am sorry. I should have liked to meet him."

"May I ask you something else?"

"Why not?"

"Do you by any chance know a good viola player?"

At last a smile, lighting the intense face.

"Indeed I do. To make the quartet complete. Of course. She is very young, eighteen, but a good player. She is studying music here in Breslau, so she has more time. Would you like me to bring her with me, when we try some music?"

"Please do."

The following Thursday morning, a note arrived from Halpern saying he was off duty that evening and would come at eight unless Max sent a message that it was not convenient. Adam was out by six, at his *Hamlet* rehearsal. Max and Treuburg got the sitting room ready, with chairs, music stands set low, and the parts of a Haydn quartet on the stands. Max, who no longer practised enough to have weekly lessons, often visited Dr Mendel and had asked his advice and borrowed from him the parts of several Haydn quartets. Grandpapa's music chest had a number of sonatas and trios but no quartets in the Haydn drawer.

"Start off with Haydn, Max", Dr Mendel said. "You'll soon see what they're like as players. This Dr Halpern is a fine fiddler, you say. That's all very well, but there have been great solo performers who can't play quartets because they don't listen. How much have you talked to him?"

"Hardly at all. I don't know him. I don't even know where he's from. Not Germany, certainly. But he seemed quite keen to join us. He likes playing chamber music, he said."

"Well. That's a good start. And the viola player?"

"A girl. A friend of Dr Halpern. I haven't met her yet."

Now Max felt nervous, as if he couldn't remember how to play his violin. It was five to eight. It's ridiculous to be nervous, he told himself. He fussed in the sitting room, straightening things. He wished Adam were there.

"Is he going to bring this girl he talked about?" Treuburg said.

"I'm sure he will. He knows we're trying to put together a quartet and haven't got a viola player here."

"Is she his girlfriend?"

"I don't know. Probably."

They arrived so punctually that the church clock at the end of the street was still striking eight as Dr Halpern knocked on the door of the flat.

Max opened the door.

"Good evening. Come in, please. I'm so glad you could spare an hour or two."

"This is my sister Anna."

"Good evening, Miss Halpern. How good of you to come. This is my friend Joachim Treuburg, who plays the cello."

Everyone shook hands and exchanged polite greetings.

"I think I have seen you, Herr Treuburg, playing in the university orchestra", Anna said.

She was dark, like her brother, with her hair in a chignon. She had a small, pale face, with brown eyes wide apart and a shy smile. She wore no makeup. How very good that she was his sister.

"It's a pleasure to meet you, Miss Halpern", Treuburg was saying. "Yes, I've seen you in the orchestra once or twice. Have you recently arrived in Breslau?"

"Thank you. Yes. Only two months ago. To join my brother. There are not any more such good teachers in Vilna, where we live, where our father lives."

"What have you chosen to play?" Halpern said.

"We thought we might try a Haydn quartet", Max said. "What do you think?"

"Excellent. One of my favourite composers always. No!" He was looking over Max's shoulder."You have a harpsichord here! What a wonderful thing." He crossed the room and ran his hand not over the keyboard, which was closed, but over the polished wood.

"How do you come to have this instrument? I have never seen one except in a book."

"My grandfather made it."

"Professor Meyer made it?"

"Yes. After he retired from the university."

"But the skill—that is a lifetime's skill. There, you see, Anna." Halpern turned to Max. "Our father does not believe it is possible to do more than one thing well. He thought I wasted study time practising German music on my violin. In Vilna, many musicians still play only Jewish music."

Halpern in Grandpapa's flat seemed quite different from the wary, unsmiling figure at the Grossmanns' party.

223

"Shall we begin?" Max said, moving a chair a little so that it was easy for Anna Halpern, in her longish dark skirt, to sit comfortably. She took her viola out of its case and also a pair of spectacles from a small case that she snapped open. With the spectacles on, she looked even more like her brother, her face younger of course than his, and also quicker to change, less serious, closer to laughing.

"Come on, Hofmannswaldau", Treuburg said, settling his cello between his knees. "Find your fiddle or we'll never get started."

"Oh", Halpern said, looking at the part on his music stand. "Do you really want me to lead?"

"Please", Max said. "I would much prefer to play second."

They tuned the instruments to Halpern's violin once he had tuned his strings; paused for a moment of silent attention, the other three watching his bow and his concentrated face; and then began to play at his nodded count.

After a few minutes of the first movement, Max, who before this had played quartets only with Dr Mendel and a couple of his elderly friends from the opera house orchestra, thought that he had never, ever, enjoyed any music so much. And Adam wasn't even in the room. When they finished the merry last movement of the quartet and put down their bows, Anna Halpern looked across the music stands, her spectacles still on, and gave Max the most beautiful smile he had ever seen in his life.

"Good, very good", Halpern said. "I hope we can do this often."

Max went into the kitchen to make coffee, leaving all the doors open.

"Do you have news from Vilna, Doctor?" he heard Treuburg say. "Are they afraid there will really be a war over the Lithuanian border?"

"In my opinion, or, rather, in the opinion of my father, since I have not been in Vilna for three years, there will be no war. To the Jews it is, perhaps, immaterial whether Vilna is in Poland or in Lithuania. Either is better than Russia, and we are accustomed to sustaining our own life in a city that ignores us but that is at the same time a little proud of us. Lithuania has simply been encouraged in its nationalism, an invention of the last hundred years, by the treaty of 1919. But it is too close to Russia to be truly free, even now, when the Russian government proclaims that Communism is freedom. Will Russia allow Lithuania to be an independent country for long? No. However, if the Russian government says there will be no war between Poland and Lithuania, there will be no war."

Max arranged on a plate a few of his grandmother's favourite biscuits and put the plate on the coffee tray: some impulse had made him buy them, for the first time for years, the week before. Now, providence, he thought, as he put the rest of the packet in the big tin, is on my side: there's something to celebrate I could never have foretold.

"Do you know Vilna?" Anna asked Treuburg as Max returned to the sitting room with the tray.

"I'm afraid not", Treuburg said. "I've heard it's a fine city with some magnificent buildings. It's not far, not much more than a hundred miles, from where my family lives, in East Prussia. But before the war—well, it was a Russian city. And now that it's Polish, I don't suppose visitors from East Prussia would be very welcome. There's an excellent university in Vilna, I believe."

"You are wondering why I came to Breslau to complete my medical studies?" Dr Halpern said. He sounded offended. Couldn't Treuburg be more careful?

"No, not in the least. The medical school here is probably the best in Germany, after Berlin. That's why I'm here myself."

"I am here because advanced study of any kind is easier for a Jew in Germany than in Poland. And easier in Breslau than in Königsberg, which my father would have preferred because of the length of the journey from Vilna to Breslau."

"Of couse. I understand. I do understand."

"I doubt it", Halpern said. "There is a chance, however, that Professor Meyer's grandson will understand."

"Please, Jakob", Anna said. "We have had such a lovely evening. There is no need to—"

"Isn't there? I hope not. I always hope not. But so often I am disappointed."

"Dr Halpern," Max said, "Treuburg and I have been hoping for a long time to put together a quartet to play here. The Haydn went well, I hope you agree. Not every good solo player, as we heard you were at Professor Grossmann's house, enjoys quartet playing, as it seems you do. Both Treuburg and I feel immensely lucky to have met you, and your sister too of course, who is also such a ... such a musical player. There are so many quartets for us to try. We have a good deal of music here, and a friend of mine, my old teacher in fact, Dr Mendel, has the parts of all the standard repertory and is happy to lend them."

"Jakob, say we may come again." Anna put a hand on her brother's shoulder.

"Yes, we shall come again. The Haydn was good, and we may perhaps try Beethoven in due course. And you said you have a friend who is a good pianist. I have never played the great piano quintets."

"Thank you, Dr Halpern. We'll wait to hear when you have a free evening, and we'll be delighted to see you both again."

"Truly we shall", said Treuburg. "Hofmannswaldau is entirely right." He came forward and offered Dr Halpern his hand. They shook hands, looking at each other with understanding.

When the Halperns had gone, Max said, "Well done, Treuburg. Worth winning him round, wouldn't you say?"

"If music can't break down these walls of suspicion, what can? Thank God my mother wanted me to learn to play the cello when I was a child. It was only because she'd inherited an old cello, her grandfather's I think, and she didn't know how to play it. There it is. It's an eighteenth-century cello. Its sound is better than I play it. My father, on the other hand . . . If my father had seen us tonight, playing Haydn with two Jews from Vilna, he would have been appalled. And very angry with me. Jews, in his view, are all very well in their place, which in East Prussia is one small step above the poorest Polish peasants. But when you see Jews in drawing rooms playing German music with the nobility—that's a sign that the world is falling apart."

"Like the Grossmanns?"

"Like the Grossmanns. Exactly. They're pushy, clever, successful, and very rich. I don't admire Grossmann himself. To have made so much money out of surgery can't be right. Abortions for the daughters of rich families, I wouldn't be surprised, while in the slums there are still people dying of appendicitis quite unnecessarily. But Eva: look at her! A free spirit if ever there was one. She's cut loose altogether from the constrictions of the past, from all these categories in which we've always lived. She never mentions being Jewish and has no sense of herself as a Jew. She hasn't collected from her father all that insistence about being a patriotic German. She doesn't even bore on about being a modern woman, though she is one, as you can see. And a painter too. I've seen some of her work. Very bright colours with thick outlines. Desperate-looking faces, distorted. It's called expressionism, she says, and I gather the professors at the Academy think highly of what she does."

"I saw an exhibition last summer at the Academy. Lots of pictures of that kind by different painters. It was like a nightmare, I thought. Everywhere you turned, there was something horrible. Have you asked Eva why what gets expressed in expressionism is always horrible? It's as if there were nothing inside these painters but terror and disgust."

"No, I haven't. If I did, I'd get no answer beyond a pitying look. Poor provincial landowner from East Prussia, only happy shooting elk. That kind of look. But the answer must be the war, don't you think?"

"I expect you're right. 'I have supp'd full with horrors' ", Max said in English.

"What?"

"*Macbeth*. Shakespeare. But this exhibition I went to had stuff in it from several years before the war. Did people sense it was going to happen? Did they sense it was going to be so horrific?"

"If they did, there were very few of them. The only thing I remember about 1914—I was eleven—was the tremendous excitement and how maddening it was to be too young to be a soldier because it was all going to be over in no time."

"What about your father?"

"Born in 1870. With the empire, he always says. So he was too old to fight."

"Like mine. Mine was born in 1865."

"Bitter it was, for my father. He had his hussar uniform all ready, the buttons polished. He loves uniforms. As a boy, he was an imperial page to the Kaiser. He volunteered at once, of course, in 1914. The regiment didn't want him. Reserve officers over forty were not required. He couldn't believe it."

"So . . . now?"

"He'll never get over the Kaiser scuttling away to Holland in 1918. He thinks it was plain cowardice, hopelessly un-Prussian. Actually, it probably saved a lot more lives. But death rather than dishonour is my father all over. So because the war was both death and dishonour, it thoroughly confuses him and only makes him angry. And I'm nothing but a disappointment to him."

The instant Max realized that Treuburg was talking as he never had before because Adam wasn't there, he heard Adam bounding up the stairs and clattering into the flat.

"Well! The rehearsal was fantastic, really fantastic. I haven't enjoyed anything so much in years as I'm enjoying this." Then he said, "I'm so sorry. I've interrupted you, tactless ass that I am. Overexcited like a ten-year-old. How was Halpern? And what of the girlfriend? Could she play?"

Max knew that Treuburg wouldn't say another word.

"She's his sister. She's a lovely girl, very young, and a good player. And he's terrific. A bit tricky as a character—touchy—but a seriously good fiddler, as we all heard at the Grossmanns', and what old Mendel would recognize at once as a real chamber music player."

"What did you play?"

"Haydn."

"I wish I'd heard you. Are they coming back?"

"Yes. It's unpredictable on account of Grossmann and the hospital—Halpern gets hardly any free time. But they'll be back."

"Good. Once this play's over, I'll be back too, in sane, sensible life. Compared to *Hamlet*, music is sanity itself."

"What do you mean?"

"Think of music. Order. Discipline. Getting it right first of all: right on the beat, right in the middle of the note. Shakespeare is wild liberation for a musician. Yes, you have to learn the lines. But then . . . You remember the play. Here's this fellow, pretending to be off his head because reality's too ghastly to be faced, and also as a disguise, and perhaps because it's all made him actually a bit crazy as well, and there's me pretending to be him pretending to be mad, and finding it intoxicating—really, like champagne—because he's both reckless and right. Max, we must get old Fischer here. I'd love to talk to him about *Hamlet*. I can't remember what he told us, and I know it was good."

"I'd like to see him too. I'll write and ask him to come, on a Sunday afternoon after your rehearsal. How soon's the play?"

"Four weeks on Saturday."

"I'd better get a move on, then. You'd like him", he said to Treuburg. "He's a wise old bird. He taught us for two years at the Gymnasium, and I don't remember him saying a stupid thing."

"Politics?"

"Centre. Centre Party. He's a Catholic. But he firmly believes in the actual centre. Dislikes the right and dislikes the left. It's how he brought us up."

"I see. But he didn't persuade you to hold onto your faith, Zapolski?"

"Too late, I'm afraid. Too late in history. Too late for me. All the other explanations are obviously closer to how things are."

"When I said something like that to my father," Treuburg said, "he was angrier than I've ever seen him. How can truth be left behind by history? How can an arrogant eighteen-year-old be too old for anything? But for my father, God and Prussia are much the same thing. And Bismarck too. All of them have let him down, but he'll go on believing in them out of sheer stubbornness. Corpse obedience. That's how he was brought up. It's how he tried to bring me up. It didn't work."

So Treuburg, this evening, would talk even to Adam. Perhaps it was the Haydn.

"Of course not", Adam said. "You're a clever fellow with a mind of your own. Like Hamlet."

"I don't know about that. And I'm not sure my father wasn't right about the centre in politics: too mushy, too many options, too many people pleasing themselves or jumping from one little compromise to the next while the floodwaters rise."

"That's not fair", Max said. "Look at what Stresemann's achieved by compromise, by keeping the centre together. Peace above all. Peace with France, peace with Russia. We have to have both, or Germany can't achieve anything good."

"What does that mean?" Adam said. "Industrial profits? The big capitalists getting bigger? They'd all prefer war to peace. But if you mean more work for people, more justice, more doctors and teachers for the poor, you're probably right. Such an unlikely hero, Stresemann. A bourgeois political fixer, and not even Chancellor. I don't know what Nietzsche would have made of him."

"Shows how unrealistic Nietzsche was, in spite of all that stuff about recognizing things as they are. The real problem with Stresemann is exactly the opposite of the one Nietzsche might have complained about. Grüber's lecture the other day on different models of democracy ... do you remember? The trouble with Stresemann isn't that he doesn't behave like Napoleon but that there's only one of him. One man who can make the system work isn't the same as a system that works. Grüber said that in England there are always two men, one on each side, and half the time the people don't even know their names. That's a system working."

"Sorry, Max. I'm too tired to think straight. Too tired to think at all. I've got to go to bed. I've got to learn hundreds more lines by tomorrow's rehearsal. A hundred, anyway. I'm as crazy as Hamlet to be doing this."

Max thought of Anna Halpern as he went to sleep, slept soundly, and woke up thinking of Anna Halpern. What could he do? Nothing but hope that she and her brother would come back to play another quartet.

They did, one evening the following week, and two evenings the week after that. A stiffness, not exactly hostile but certainly uncommunicative, connected Treuburg and Halpern. It was as if there were things between them that both knew and to which neither was willing to refer. It must be something to do with the history of the Baltic, Max thought, and perhaps something to do with Eva Grossmann as well. So friendliness was left to Max and Anna.

On their fourth evening, a Friday at the beginning of June, they played through one of Beethoven's *Razumovsky* quartets, from the music chest in the flat. "*Razumovsky?* You'll find them difficult", Dr Mendel had said. "And don't you dare try any later Beethoven until you know these people better, probably not until you're all a good deal older."

"That needs practice", Halpern said at the end.

"It's hard", Anna said. "Much the hardest thing we've tried. I need to learn the notes before we do it again. May I borrow the part?"

"Of course", Max said. "I need to work at the notes as well." Then, his courage taking him by surprise, he added, "Miss Halpern, I would very much like you to meet Adam Zapolski, who shares this flat with us, and also an old teacher of ours, Dr Fischer, who's coming to tea on Sunday at five o'clock. Would you by any chance like to come to tea as well?"

"That is kind. I should very much like to ..." She hesitated, looking at her brother.

"Why not?" Halpern said. "Perhaps Hofmannswaldau would be good enough to see you home afterwards. We lodge with Frau Schönfeld. Her flat is not far away, on the other side of the university. But she is old-fashioned. She would not like Anna to be in the streets alone after six o'clock."

"Naturally. I should be delighted", Max said, trying to sound merely polite.

Not much preparation was required for a tea party for four people: Treuburg said he was going out for the whole of Sunday, no doubt on some expedition with Eva. But Max spent most of Saturday not going to the law library, not writing up his notes on European treaties since the Peace of Westphalia, and not going to visit Dr Mendel to report on their partial success with the *Razumovsky* quartet. Treuburg was in the hospital, following a specialist on his Saturday ward round. Adam was at a rehearsal. Max went to the park, where he sat and listened to the band playing in the bandstand. He watched the neatly dressed children walking with their nannies and nursemaids, the boys sailing toy boats on the lake, and the old people alone, watching the children too. He thought about Anna Halpern. What did he know about her? Almost nothing. Not much more than a child herself, this girl from Vilna, being looked after by her brother—he must be seven or eight years older—so far from home, in her dark skirt and her white, high-necked blouse with the simple cameo brooch. He thought of her spectacles and how they changed her smile. He thought of her ringless hands, small and quick, one on her bow, one on the fingerboard of her viola. She played so musically, not always with every note in place, but always there, always listening to the other three, and with every phrase special to the viola given its proper due but never intrusive, never forced.

He stopped under some tall lime trees in the park, closed his eyes, and breathed in their scent because it reminded him of Waldau. He thought of how much he would like to take her to Waldau—but only if Heinrich and Betsy somehow didn't exist. As he thought this, he opened his eyes, struck suddenly by his own folly. How stupid, what a risk, to invite her so soon, too soon, to meet Adam, and without safe, quiet Treuburg, whom she was used to, even being there. Why had he thought he wanted Adam to meet her? Much better that he didn't, not yet in any case. But it was done. Impossible to undo it.

He walked back across the park, unable to decide if he were more afraid that Adam would dislike her, or like her. He couldn't say anything to Adam about her either. It was when he realized that this was so, and that it hadn't been the case about anything for years, that the strangeness, and the scale, of what was going on powerfully struck him. He stood still and actually stamped his foot on the last of the lawn near the park gate. No. It was all nonsense. He had asked a pretty girl he hardly knew to tea with Adam and Dr Fischer. That was absolutely all. Nothing to it. The sort of thing students did every day.

He went to the university library, found a book on the Peace of Westphalia, and sat at a table not reading it for an hour and a half. Then he walked home. No one was in. He ate some bread and cheese, spent another hour or two not reading another history book, and went to bed before Adam got home from his rehearsal.

On Sunday morning, he had a headache and felt he had hardly slept at all. Frau Gärtner had cleaned and tidied the flat on Thursday, as she did every Monday and Thursday afternoon when all of them were out. Max tidied the sitting room again and, more thoroughly, the kitchen in case Anna came in with a tray or helped with the washing up. There were plenty of his grandmother's favourite biscuits still in the tin. There were tea, sugar, and fresh milk from that morning. He stood in the kitchen and thought. Then he went out and bought Earl Grey tea, a small packet because it was very expensive, two lemons, and a bunch of white roses, which he put on the piano in the old pottery jug. He practised the second violin part of the *Razumovsky* for an hour, making himself repeat the difficult passages several times. At eleven thirty, Adam got up and came into the sitting room in pyjamas with a cup of coffee.

"Do I deduce that you're playing second fiddle in this quartet?"

"He's a better player. Also, I'm sure he's a better leader than I would be."

"Why's it so gleaming and shining in here? And why the roses? Ah, the tea party. I'm glad I'm not going to miss it. I could do with some light relief. We did the last scene four times last night. The boy who's playing Laertes is a half-wit. He can fence properly—that's why Kurt cast him, I suppose—but it's not enough."

"It's enough for Claudius."

"Max! *This is a play*. But I do keep having to remind myself. Anyway— roses, for old Fischer? Oh, of course, the girl. What's her name?"

"Anna Halpern."

"Are you in love, Max?"

"What a ridiculous idea. I hardly know her. We've spent four evenings playing quartets. And she's very young, only eighteen."

"Max! You're in love. I can tell. Did you buy a cake?"

"Damn. A cake—no, I didn't."

"Leave it to me. My contribution. I know about cakes. I'm half-Viennese, don't forget."

Perhaps it's just as well nothing gets past him, Max thought as Adam disappeared to shave and get dressed. I know I can rely on him. Exactly what Max meant by this, he didn't specify to himself.

"Hofmannswaldau, how delightful to see you again! I'm touched that you young people should think of inviting an ancient schoolmaster to tea. Thank you. I'll just leave my hat."

This was a dilapidated panama Max remembered from summers at the Gymnasium. He took Dr Fischer into the sitting room.

"Zapolski! I'm so pleased to see you after all these years. And you are playing Hamlet at the university, I hear. I would have expected no less of you. And—good afternoon, Miss. How nice to meet you."

"This is Anna Halpern", Max said as they shook hands. "She's studying music here in Breslau, and we play in a quartet together. Anna, this is Dr Fischer."

He realized he had called her by her first name, as if he'd known her for years, and, saying "I'll just go and make the tea", he disappeared into the kitchen, leaving his party in Adam's safe hands. How could he have wished Adam wasn't going to be here?

When he returned with a laden tray, Dr Fischer and Anna were sitting side by side on the sofa talking about the viola.

"You know, I've heard it said that the viola is the heart of any quartet. Not so conspicuous as the other parts, but if it's not quite right, the life of the piece doesn't work as it should."

"Those are beautiful words", Anna said. "My teacher says only to be very careful not to upset the balance of the music." As Dr Fischer said, "Well, there you are", and Max put the tray on the low table by his grandfather's armchair, she got up. "May I help you, please?" she said to Max.

"Thank you."

When each of them had a cup of tea and a piece of chocolate cake, Dr Fischer said:

"Now, Zapolski, *Hamlet*. I suppose you are giving it in German?"

"I'm afraid we are."

"That's a pity in a way, of course. On the other hand, it's most important that the audience should understand the words. As with opera. Though if you translate Shakespeare, it's some of the music that you lose because the music is in the poetry. Have you read any Shakespeare, Miss Anna?"

"A very little, in Polish. There are translations. My father said the German translations are better, but our Polish at home was better because we spoke it every day. German we had to learn."

"And now you speak German very well."

"Thank you, Doctor." She blushed and smiled. Max was aware of Adam noticing him noticing this.

"May I ask you three questions, Dr Fischer?" Adam said.

233

"You may, Zapolski, you may. I hope I shall be able to answer them."

"Why is Hamlet so cruel to Ophelia in the nunnery scene when he loves her—he is telling the truth at her grave, isn't he? Why does he decide for such a cruel reason not to kill Claudius when Claudius is praying? What's happened to him to make him so calm when he's sure he'll be killed in the last scene?"

"Well! What questions! You are asking me who is Hamlet, who is this sweet prince who has in him so many ideas and feelings in conflict. Scholars have worried over these questions for two hundred years. I'm no more than an amateur, but I'll do my best. Let me see ... Hofmannswaldau, this is most delicious tea. May I have another cup?"

Before Max could move, Anna got up and poured the old man another cup, deftly replacing his thin slice of lemon with a fresh one. Max allowed himself a smile of acknowledgement.

"Thank you, my dear. Now, I think there are two reasons for his cruelty in the nunnery scene, even three. He is, as it were, stamping on his feelings for Ophelia because his mother's behaviour has made him fearful of getting too close to a woman. Are all women unreliable, perhaps? Then he will decide to hate them."

"Yes, of course", Adam said. "Of course."

"He's heard Claudius and Polonius deciding to eavesdrop—I hope your producer will make sure the audience sees him hearing—and so describing himself as proud, revengeful, ambitious is meant as a warning to Claudius. If you think of the whole central section of the play as a duel between Hamlet and Claudius, you won't go far wrong. And, most importantly, he sees both Ophelia and himself as tangled up in original sin, in the sins in particular of their devious, weak parents, and he wants to escape somehow from the tangle, not pass it on. 'Why would'st thou be a breeder of sinners?' You see?"

"I do. I certainly do. Schopenhauer."

"Precisely. Schopenhauer was a great admirer of Shakespeare, you know. In very different ways, they both told the truth about how things are."

"A mess", Max said.

"A mess, of course. A sad mess. But God has given us hope. All of us." He looked kindly at Anna and smiled.

"Now, Zapolski. Your second question is more difficult. I think Hamlet doesn't kill Claudius while he's praying not for the reason he gives—that it isn't revenge to send Claudius to heaven—but because

234

actually, now that there's a real opportunity, he can't do it. Killing in cold blood is beyond him, so he produces an excuse to convince himself that he can put it off to another day. And that's connected to the real answer to your third question. Hamlet by nature can suffer, but he can't take action. That's what 'To be or not to be' is all about. 'Whether 'tis nobler in the mind to suffer the slings and arrows of outrageous fortune' or to *act*, 'to take arms against a sea of troubles'. By the end he's managed to take arms, to take action, once, on the ship, to deal with Rosencrantz and Guildenstern and Claudius's treachery. Now he can see that all he has to do is to suffer. So he's calm. What will happen is in the hands of God. You know, *Hamlet's* a deeply Catholic play."

"But then why is it set in Wittenberg?"

"Oh, that's local colour. We're supposed to be in Protestant Denmark. But really, we're inside Shakespeare's Catholic head, hell, purgatory, judgement, and all."

"Don't you think Hamlet himself is free of all that? Isn't he a modern man—or at least a Renaissance man? But I do see—perhaps he isn't. Perhaps he really is in the hands of God at the end. Or he believes he is. Is that the same thing?"

"Well, there's a question, Zapolski."

"Either he believes he's in the hands of God because it's 1600 or whatever, so it's just too early for him to hold onto the quintessence of dust idea. Or . . ."

"Or there is God, in whose hands we all are. It's the question you used to shake between your teeth like a little terrier when you were a schoolboy. It doesn't go away. If God is dead, as Nietzsche said, he has never been alive. If not—then not. Not now, and not ever. *Hamlet* does raise these questions. I'm so glad you are playing him, Zapolski. It will keep you awake. Students, I find, go to sleep more easily than schoolboys do."

"They do", Max said, thinking of Grotius. "But some of the lectures we have to go to, sir, are so dull you wouldn't believe . . ."

"Ah, I would. I was a student once, you know."

"Thank you", Adam said. "Thank you very much, sir. I knew I needed to ask you these questions. The producer—well, he's only keen to have the lines right and keep it moving."

"That's a good start. You won't get far without both of those. I hope I shall be allowed to come to a performance. Now . . . is there by chance a little more of that excellent cake?"

"Dr Fischer," Anna said as she cut him a piece of cake, "may I ask you a question?"

"Please."

"My father told us that Shakespeare is a very great writer but that the only Jew in his plays is a wicked man, a kind of monster. Is that true?"

Dr Fischer turned his bear's head to look properly at Anna with his friendly eyes.

"Many people think that," he said, "but it's not quite true. The Jews in Shakespeare's time were badly treated everywhere in Europe and were not allowed to live in England, so Shakespeare probably knew no Jews. But there was nothing human that Shakespeare could not imagine, and he imagined being a Jew, needed but scorned, as, in another play, he imagined being an African general, needed but scorned, both of them in the great city of Venice. The character of Shylock, a Jew, is allowed to show us the pain of being despised and bullied. He's also allowed to show us what may easily happen to the character of someone who's always been despised and bullied. He's not generous and humble, but is he likely to be? He's angry and clever and vengeful, but his forced conversion at the end strikes us not as good but as cruel. I think Shakespeare always regards contempt for other people as a grave sin—all his villains are scornful—and Shylock's character is the result of the Christians' contempt for him. So you see, to call him wicked and a monster is too simple."

"I see", she said. "I understand. That is different."

"Are you still teaching the boys in the last two years at the Gymnasium, sir?" Max said.

"Indeed I am. I'm not so old as I look, you know. I shall continue for a few years yet, God willing."

"I hope the boys realize how lucky they are to have you."

"I don't know about that. I fear the voice of moderation can seem quite dull to the young. Things are noisier in their world than when you were at school—films, jazz music, motorcars, sports clubs—though Germany is certainly in better shape, better order, than it was then, so soon after the war. Long may it last."

"Do you think it won't last?" asked Adam.

"I think it's fragile, Zapolski. There's still a great deal of hatred and rage about, and not enough confidence in the steady working of the republic. Look how many governments we've had, patched-together coalitions, just holding. There's a strong yearning for a single powerful leader, on the model of Signor Mussolini, and that I don't care for at all. Wagnerian *folie de grandeur*: a hero will put everything to rights. Or he'll burn the house down—I'm afraid he will more likely burn the house down. The truth is that the country has by no means recovered from defeat, and that's a dangerous condition. You know what Hegel said: 'World history is the court of world justice.' Nonsense, of course. But too many people believe it. So, either we deserved defeat, which can't be faced because it puts us in the wrong, or we didn't deserve defeat, which is even worse. Either way, Germany's been humiliated, and humiliation breeds resentment—your friend Nietzsche's *ressentiment*—and resentment drives much that is cruel and merciless in human life. A little like Shylock, now that I come to think of it. So I'm fearful still, even of another war. We shall see."

He looked at each of them in turn, smiling particularly at Anna.

"I'm sorry, children, to sound like a despondent old man. There's much that's good, much that's full of hope in this country, though it can seem hidden, buried. But it's there, and all of you are part of what is good and full of hope—which in due course you, Miss Anna, and you, Zapolski, should take home to your own country, your own people. Germany still has useful and beautiful things to teach, to people who can learn. Do you still play the clarinet, Zapolski?"

"Yes, though not as often as I should."

"Perhaps you will attempt the great clarinet quintets with Hofmannswaldau's quartet—the Mozart and the Brahms. Wonderful, both of them. How fortunate you are."

"After *Hamlet*", Adam said. "I can't do or think about a single other thing until this wretched play's over."

"We're all much looking forward to it", Dr Fischer said, and got up from the sofa with some difficulty. "Now I really must be going. I have a pile of Latin proses to mark before tomorrow morning. Poor boys. They do try, but so often they fail. I have very much enjoyed myself. Thank you, all of you, for having me to tea. Goodbye, Miss Anna. I hope Breslau treats you well. Goodbye, Zapolski, and good luck with the sweet prince. Now, what did I bring? Only my hat? Thank you, Hofmannswaldau, and good-bye."

Without asking if she could help, Anna stacked the cups and saucers and plates on the tray, picked it up, and stood waiting for Max to show her where the kitchen was. She washed the dishes while Max dried and put things away. She poured the cold tea from the pot through the strainer down the sink and asked him with her eyes what to do with the tea leaves. He took the strainer and threw the tea leaves into the bucket under the sink while she washed the teapot. They went back to the sitting room, where Adam was standing looking out of the window and eating a piece of cake without a plate.

"I'm going to walk Miss Halpern home. I shan't be long", Max said.

"Be as long as you like. I have speeches to practise. What I need is an empty flat. Not that there's enough room to walk about and talk at the same time. 'O God, I could be bounded in a nutshell and count myself a King of infinite space.'" He spread his arms wide, nearly knocking over the roses on the piano. "How does he do it? That's what I have to find out."

"Shut up, Adam."

"I'm sorry. It gets into the system. Good-bye, Miss Halpern. I'm so glad to have met you."

"Good-bye." They shook hands. "Thank you."

She had no hat but took a small scarf out of her pocket and tied it over her hair. It made her face look younger, like a child's, but from the back, as Max followed her down the stairs, she looked much older, like the Polish women or the Jewish women in the market.

"It's only a few minutes", she said as they emerged into the dusty warmth of the summer evening, "if we go through the university."

Trees, Max thought, water, leaves. When they got to the moat and the university footbridge, he said, "Shall we walk a little way, just to the next bridge or the one after?"

"What time is it?" She looked up at him, a little anxious.

He looked at his watch. "It's twenty past six. Will Frau Schönfeld be worried?"

She laughed. "It's Jakob who worries. He persuaded our father to let me come to Breslau, because the music teaching is much better, and to keep him company I think. But now he feels responsible for me in this dangerous modern city, so I must be careful to do what he expects. I teach some children piano, only beginners, but I must do it early in the afternoons, he says. But a few minutes by the water—why not? Jakob will be back from the hospital at seven."

They walked a little way, a decorous space always between them, along the footpath beside the moat, under the trees. There were ducks on the water and a pair of disdainful swans. Max knew, because he had often sat on it alone with a book, a cast-iron seat beside a willow, where you could watch the grey-green leaves trailing in the water. He wanted to sit there with her so that he could come back without her and remember.

"Shall we watch the ducks? Just for a few minutes?"

"All right. But not for long."

They sat side by side, not touching, in a silence that quickly became too full for Max.

"What did you think of Dr Fischer?"

She turned towards him and really smiled. "He is a very good man, I think, and also very intelligent, and kind. He was kind even to me."

"But of course he was. I hope no one has been unkind to you here?"

"No. Not yet. But I was surprised because Dr Fischer is a Catholic, yes?"

"Yes, he is."

"Vilna, where we live, is a most Catholic city. The university is Catholic, there are many Catholic schools, there are many priests and nuns. But they do not regard—no, they do not *notice*—the Jews. Although, you know, Vilna is also a most Jewish city. It is like two cities. You do not cross over the line from one to the other. I would never in Vilna meet a man like Dr Fischer. Or"—she laughed again—"like you and your friends, to play music with. There is something perhaps I should not tell you . . ."

"What is it? I won't tell anyone. I promise."

"Jakob accepted your invitation to play quartets because he had heard of Professor Meyer, your grandfather, and knew he was a Jew. Otherwise I think he would have refused. Politely of course, but he would have refused because of your Prussian names, and noble names also. So, your mother is a Jewess, and your father is a Christian. Is it often so in Germany? Is your father a Catholic like Dr Fischer? Are you a Catholic? I thought Prussians were always Protestant."

"What a lot of questions! In the first place, both of my parents are dead."

"I am so sorry." She put her hand on his knee for a fraction of a second. "I did not know."

"How could you know?"

"But I do know what it is to lose . . . Our mother died when I was seven years old. In 1915 in the middle of the war, the Vilna Jews were moved to Warsaw in trains. Sealed trains. Have you ever heard of such a thing? We were not allowed to get out, or even breathe fresh air. No water. Thousands of people. The Russians thought the Jews were helping the Germans, so they sent us away. Our mother and our little brother died. He was only two. His name was Akiba. When we got to Warsaw, the Poles hated us, and the Jews also, because there were already too many Jews in the city. The Russians closed even the beautiful park—the Saxony Gardens, it's called—to all Jews, because people with nowhere to go and no friends were trying to live there. It was not good. But our father took care of Jakob and me, and he is alive and well and allowed us to come here to study."

"Does he live alone?"

"My aunt looks after him. She's his sister. Her husband was an army doctor—in the Russian army, of course. He was killed in Galicia in the war."

"Is your father a doctor too?"

"Yes. He studied in Cracow in the 1890s. That was not easy for a Vilna Jew: he had to study in German, though when he went home he had to work in Russian and Polish. But at that time, Jews were not allowed to study medicine in Russia. In Cracow, he had the protection of a Jewish family with a large house. His father, our grandfather, was a rabbi in Vilna, and he was always sad that our father preferred to be a doctor. But if my father had been a rabbi, he would never have allowed me to come to Breslau. So that's good, isn't it?"

"Of course it's good. I'm so pleased you're here."

"Are you? Really?"

"Yes, really. Now"—he looked at his watch again—"we should be going if your brother's coming back at seven."

He got up. He almost held out his hand to pull her up from the iron seat, only because he so much wanted to hold her hand just for a moment, but he didn't.

They crossed a bridge.

"This way", she said. "It's not far from here."

"Tell me about Frau Schönfeld", he said. "Is she kind to you?"

"Oh yes. She is a nice old lady. Not so very old, perhaps fifty or sixty. Her husband was a colleague of Professor Grossmann. He died in the war, of blood poisoning, somewhere on the western front. She thinks it was because of the mud and the flies and the heat and that he would have been safer on the Russian front. But many doctors died there too, like my uncle. Frau Schönfeld is a good Jewish lady who keeps a kosher kitchen and bakes the Sabbath bread—she loves to have Jakob to say the prayers because before he came she was alone—and she goes to synagogue sometimes. I have been with her three times, but it's different from at home. I don't like it very much."

"How is it different?" He didn't want to say he knew absolutely nothing about Jewish services and prayers. If Jakob discovered his grandfather was a baptized Christian, there might be no more quartet playing. He might not see her ever again.

"At home the synagogue is small and old and rather crowded. Even a bit dirty. But warm, you know. Here the synagogue, at least the one Frau Schönfeld goes to, is new and grand and looks like a Russian church, with a dome and towers. On the inside it looks like a Protestant church—or that's what Jakob has told me. I've never been inside a Protestant church. But the people—they don't seem like Jews at all. The men have no beards, and the women sit with the men. And there's organ music and a choir with women in it. And most of the prayers are in German. It's all very strange to me, and I don't really like it."

"Have you ever been inside a Catholic church?"

"No. Certainly not. That would be quite impossible in Vilna. Are you a Catholic? You didn't answer my question, did you?" She laughed. "I'm sorry. That was not polite."

"That was true—better than polite. No. No, I'm not a Catholic, nor was my father. Just a Protestant."

"But do you believe in God? My father says Jews who convert always become Protestants because Protestants don't have to believe in God but Catholics do."

"I'm not sure that's fair to Protestants. Some of them certainly do believe in God. Ask Treuburg. Where he comes from, the Protestant church is very believing, very strict. God for them is very German, and that's why they don't like Catholics or Jews. My father was rather the same, though of course he didn't hate Jews or—"

"Or he wouldn't have married your mother. And Herr Treuburg? Does he agree with all that, the German God and not liking Catholics or Jews?"

"No. Not Treuburg. Certainly not. He's here, like your brother, to study medicine in a modern university, a modern city, where all this hating doesn't happen."

She stopped on the sidewalk and looked at him, her dark eyes unhappy. "But it does. It does. These notices telling Jews to get out. These men in brown shirts marching and singing. It's all horrible, and full of hate. Worse than Vilna. There are no notices, no marching in Vilna. My father didn't know, or he wouldn't have allowed us to come here. Even in the university, Jakob says, there are students who hate Jews because they think all Jews are Bolsheviks. And some are, of course, and then there's only more hate." She was in tears now. "And here we are, that's the house there, where I live, and I must go in. What is the time?"

"It's only ten to seven. Stop a minute. Anna—don't be afraid. This is Germany. It's safe here. These Stormtroopers, they're left over from the war either because they didn't fight in it or because they did. Now that there's more work and things are so much better, they'll all be gone soon. There are Jews in the government in Berlin now, and there are laws to protect everyone. You mustn't be frightened, not in Breslau. There've been Jews here for hundreds of years, living peacefully, with no one bullying them. I'll look after you. I promise you'll be safe."

"Will you, Max? May I call you Max?"

"Yes you may, of course you may. And yes, I will look after you. Now dry your eyes, or Frau Schönfeld will think I haven't taken care of you properly." Quickly remembering that it was clean, he took his handkerchief out of his pocket. She mopped her face and gave it back to him.

"Thank you. Thank you. Good-bye."

She held out her hand, and he took it briefly. This was just as well, he realized as he walked away, turning at the corner to wave—she was looking at him from the door, and waved back—because otherwise he would have kissed her.

"Well?" Adam said as he came into the sitting room.

"Well what?"

"Don't be silly. How was the respectable walk home?"

"Very respectable, thank you."

"Old Fischer loved her. Reminded him of his lost daughter the nun, I expect."

"His daughter's not lost at all. That's not how he'd see her, is it? Found, perhaps. Found by God."

"Max! Old Fischer really does bring out the buried Christian in you, even after all these years."

"Wasn't it good to see him? He's the same as ever. A bit more battered to look at but no sign whatever of him losing his—I don't know what it is exactly. He knows so much. But that's only part of it."

"It's certainly not just knowledge. He goes on thinking. What he said about *Hamlet*—some of it, I'm sure, was new to him as he said it. We read the whole play at school, after all, and I don't remember . . ."

"Well, we were struggling with the English, weren't we?"

"I wish this production were in English—think of it." He jumped up from Grandpapa's armchair and dropped to his knees by the hearth rug, staring into its faded pattern. "I loved Ophelia", he said, in English, with the shocked voice of sudden discovery, and then, looking up at Max with fierce, chilling eyes,

> "Forty thousand brothers
> Could not with all their quantity of love
> Make up my sum."

He got up and sank back in the armchair, his eyes laughing now.

"You see? And talking of brothers, you need to go very gently with this girl. Dr Halpern is a force to be reckoned with, I would guess. I know I've seen him only once, and you've played quartets with him."

"I like him. I think. I hardly know him, yet. But you're right. He's a force to be reckoned with. But what do you . . ." He couldn't finish this sentence.

"She's a sweet little thing. I love her laugh. She's only twelve, of course."

"Adam! She is only eighteen, it's true. Her brother said."

"You know what I mean. She's as innocent as a baby."

"Innocent—yes and no. She's been protected as far as is possible, I've no doubt, but she's familiar with horrors all the same. They had a dreadful time in the war, her family. Forced to leave Vilna in sealed trains because the Russians decided the Jews were helping the Germans. Dumped in Warsaw. Soldiers, guns, and abuse in Vilna, no doubt—she didn't say much. And you can imagine the warm welcome in Warsaw. Her mother and her two-year-old brother died."

Adam drew his breath sharply in through his teeth. "Ach—I'm sorry. Jokes are not in order. I had no idea."

"Of course you didn't."

"Max", Adam said, his voice and eyes serious, "she's a lovely girl, and I'm glad she's arrived in our lives. When flights of angels have sung Hamlet to his rest—I do see what old Fischer means about it being a Catholic play; that's practically from the Requiem Mass—I look forward to playing with your quartet. Even the clarinet quintets, if I practise. Now, I must go away and learn the scene with the gravedigger. I was more or less making up the lines as I went along yesterday, and clever Kurt wasn't pleased."

And he disappeared into his room and slammed the door.

Max looked at the roses in the pottery jug on the piano. He thought of Adam's very expensive cake. Forty thousand brothers, he thought, inconsequentially. He wished Adam hadn't said "I love her laugh" and "our lives". *Our* lives? Then he thought it would be more difficult if Adam hadn't liked her. Wouldn't it? Would it? He thought of Dr Halpern's contained strength, his concern for Anna, his misunderstanding about Max's grandfather. He thought of Treuburg and Eva Grossmann, at this moment in some hotel room perhaps; Anna mustn't discover all that. He saw complications ahead, and he felt energetic and resolved. I will take care of her. I won't upset Halpern. I trust Adam. All will be well.

The next day, he came back first, from an afternoon class at the university, and found a note that had been pushed under the door of the flat.

"I cannot any more clean the professor's flat. My son will not allow me because you have Jews visiting. I am sorry. M. Gärtner."

Chapter 9

Max took Anna to the first performance of Adam's *Hamlet* on a balmy summer evening. He collected her early from Frau Schönfeld's flat, and they walked the long way round to the other side of the university so as to sit for a few minutes by the moat. By now he hadn't needed to say he would be early; when he rang the bell twenty minutes before he had arranged to collect her, and shook hands with Frau Schönfeld with his Prussian bow, Anna was ready. Nor did he suggest the longer-than-necessary walk. They walked, saying nothing, and he remembered all over again, though it was only four days since they had played, with Treuburg and Halpern, two Haydn quartets because they had decided the *Razumovsky* was too difficult, how happy it made him to have her at his side.

Adam had refused to answer questions about clever Kurt's production. "What are you wearing?" "Is he doing naturalism or expressionism?" "Are there proper battlements?"

"Wait and see."

But clearly he approved of what was being put together in the last weeks of rehearsals: if he hadn't, he wouldn't have wanted it to be a surprise.

The university theatre, built just before the war, functional, plain, with wooden seats—no plush or gilding here—was full, the audience mostly students, with a very few older members of the university and some middle-aged couples and women alone, clearly parents of the cast.

Anna put on her spectacles and looked at the programme, a single sheet of paper with a cast list, ready on each seat.

"Three Jewish names. Do you think they are religious Jews?"

"Possibly, but probably not. Many Jewish families in Germany aren't religious at all nowadays. And many with Jewish names converted a long time ago."

"Like your mother's family?"

"That's right. You haven't told your brother, have you?"

"I promised. But I still don't understand. Is your mother's family Jewish or Christian?"

"Difficult to say. Either? Both? Properly speaking, neither. Certainly not religious."

"But ..." She looked thoroughly puzzled, and very young. "It is too complicated to understand", she said. "What does it mean, all this Aryan and non-Aryan you hear all the time, if some people are not sure themselves which they are? I don't understand Germany. At home it is not like this. A person is a Jew or a Christian. He knows, and so does everyone else. People may not be friendly, but they are clear." She shook her head and looked down again at the cast list.

"Do you know them all?" she asked.

"No. Two or three I know by sight. The fellow who's playing Claudius is quite famous in the university. He's a count from East Prussia—Treuburg knows his family—who started off very traditional when we were all in our first year, with duelling clubs, drinking songs, and the Eastern Marches Society. Not a kind of person you would like. Now he says he's a Communist and that we need a Bolshevik revolution instead of a democracy. Like Kurt—he's the producer. But I don't know how much is just a pose, put on to annoy his father."

"Who is Claudius?"

"The new King. Hamlet's uncle. And his stepfather. You'll see. Do you know the story at all?"

"Not really. I know Hamlet wonders if he should stay alive. That is all I know."

"Never mind. Actually, it's good not to know the story beforehand. Shakespeare's audience in London didn't know the story either."

She took off her spectacles and looked at him with shining eyes.

"It's so exciting. I've never been to a theatre before."

As so often, he wanted to kiss her. As always, he didn't, and not only because it was impossible here, with the audience chattering, finding seats, and looking round for friends. He was frightened of frightening her. He smiled into her eyes.

"That's good, too. *Hamlet* your first play in a theatre. Couldn't be better."

The house lights went down. The curtain rose. A cold draught came from the stage, as if it really were colder in Elsinore than in Breslau.

In near-darkness, two soldiers appeared in uniforms from the war, spiked helmets against the dawn sky, guns with bayonets. A third soldier appeared, then Horatio in student uniform. For a moment, Max wished he had stayed at that audition and tried hard for the part of Horatio, Hamlet's friend. "Give me that man that is not passion's slave." He looked sideways at the rapt face of Anna gazing at the stage. Idiot, he told himself.

The ghost of Hamlet's father, in old-fashioned armour and helmet, stalked twice across the back of the stage, the second time standing very still for a moment, leaning on a huge sword. The pose reminded Max of the statue of Bismarck he had seen in some book. Clever Kurt.

Trumpets sounded. A blaze of light revealed the court, two gilded thrones in front of tall tapestry hangings, with the courtiers in black frock coats and standing respectfully to either side of the royal pair. One of the courtiers was a small, grey-bearded man, clearly Polonius. The Queen was in crimson velvet, with a gold chain and a medallion round her neck; Claudius was dressed in a white and gold general's uniform with a sash. He was moustached and monocled, made up to look very like the Kaiser, even to the point of having one arm across his chest tucked into his uniform. There was a gasp from the audience and the beginning of a hiss, quelled by the power of the actor's ringing delivery of Claudius's opening speech.

Max looked for Adam and saw Hamlet. He had appeared from nowhere and stood at the foot of the stage, arms folded, head down. He was dressed as if for rowing or fencing, in everyday, 1927, soft black trousers and a black turtleneck sweater. He looked shockingly, insolently, out of place in the court.

Ambassadors were dispatched to Norway. Laertes—in a student uniform different from Horatio's, and with blond curls, and the face of a stupid son of a noble family, short upper lip and open mouth—was given permission to return to France. As soon as Hamlet spoke, in Adam's voice with a hard edge Max had never heard before, his slight Viennese accent making him seem foreign in Claudius's court, the atmosphere in the theatre changed. The audience was still, held in the wounded bitterness of the boy afflicted by his father's death and his mother's disloyalty. Ach! Max almost groaned: how was it possible that he hadn't realized how much of Hamlet was already there in Adam? He seemed younger than his age, as if he had far to go to catch up with the misery and disgust of his first speech alone on the stage, alone in the world. He pulled himself together to face Horatio and the idea of his father's ghost as if he were growing up before the audience's eyes. At the end of the scene, Max glanced at Anna. Her face was stricken as she looked to the wings into which Hamlet had just disappeared. He remembered that she hadn't seen Adam since the tea party with Dr Fischer. Why had he brought her? But then, how good to be able to give her *Hamlet* like a present. And in any case, Adam would be back in ordinary life next week, when the play was over. Then would come the clarinet quintet. He wished, violently, that Adam weren't a musician at all, on top of everything else he was. Max resolved not to look at Anna again until the intermission.

When the intermission came, after the players' performance and Hamlet's hectic high spirits at the proof of Claudius's guilt, she was full of questions. "Has he gone a little bit mad? Or just wild because of the ghost? Was he pretending to send Ophelia away because they were listening? Who are they, the two other students with German names? Are they friends or enemies?" She had understood a great deal, and Max saw she had almost forgotten she was only at a play, seeing a bunch of students pretending to be quite other people. It was real for her. Perhaps it was not much less real, by now, for Adam.

In the second half of the play, Max forgot Anna, sitting beside him transfixed with concentration. He watched Adam finding the fierce words to compel his mother to face the truth, killing Polonius without forethought or remorse, and pitting his wits against the King's. Machiavelli, Max thought. Then he thought of Nietzsche, when Hamlet, still in his black jersey and everyday trousers, watched Fortinbras's army set out for war, with kit bags and helmets, looking just like the soldiers everyone in the audience had seen in streets and stations over and over again from the summer of 1914. The quintessence of dust had become the will to power. He watched Hamlet catch courage from the nameless soldiers: if they can be brave for nothing, surely I can be brave for something?

The flame of the play died when Hamlet was offstage, though the girl playing Ophelia convincingly became a waif with glazed eyes singing bits of songs, a child destroyed in an adult game, and Laertes and the King, plotting Hamlet's death, seemed made for each other, corrupt members of a duelling club drunk with how easy it would be to organize a fight not for scars but for murder. Fooling in the graveyard, suddenly furious with grief over Ophelia's corpse, fooling again with the ludicrous Osric, Adam and Hamlet were one: Max felt he had never known Adam so well or loved him so much as now, when he was playing a character invented by Shakespeare, speaking words written on a page, translated into more words written on another page. That was it: playing what was written from his own soul. It was like playing the notes written by Bach or Mozart or Beethoven, from his own soul. How to know someone: hear him, watch him, play.

Thinking, Max lost for an instant what was happening on the stage. Then he heard, saw, something fresh in Adam. Anxiety. Resolve. Resignation. As Hamlet turned from Horatio to face the whole court sweeping with trumpets onto the stage, he crossed himself. What had happened to Machiavelli? Nietzsche? Hamlet was grown up now, ten years older than the injured adolescent he had been three hours ago. And what had he just done? Put his life in the hands of God. At last he took off his black sweater, giving it to Horatio without looking at him, and, in a white shirt with an open collar, he took the rapier from Osric without looking at him and flexed it against his other hand, talking as he did so to Laertes and then to Claudius, as if he were about to take part in a school fencing match.

The play rushed to its end, a rapid, brilliant fight all over the stage, with rapiers flying, clattering, and being picked up, with wounds, drinks, deaths, and explanations. The curtain came down. The audience stood, clapped, and roared approval. Max looked at Anna. There were tears on her cheeks, and she was standing, unable to clap, one hand over her mouth, the other looking for a handkerchief in the pocket of her dress. He gave her his, again.

They went to find Adam. There were no dressing rooms backstage, only a long, chaotic green room with a row of mirrors, sticks of greasepaint, tubs of cold cream, and clothes on the floor. Polonius was yelping as someone peeled his beard from his chin. Adam wasn't there. Clever Kurt was hugging Gertrude. Over Gertrude's shoulder he saw Max and Anna.

"Out!" he said. "No visitors in here. Can't you see?"

"Where's Zapolski?"

"Throwing up, I expect. He did last night and that was only the dress run. Go away. Please."

"Sorry."

It was late, after midnight, when they left the theatre. The streets were empty, still warm after the hot day. Max took Anna back to Frau Schönfeld's flat by the shortest way. Neither of them spoke, but the silence between them was different now, crowded with the weight of the play, of Adam's performance. Halfway across the old university footbridge over the river, Anna stopped and leant over the wooden railing, looking down into the water.

"What is it? Are you all right?"

"Yes. No. It was ... He was ... Thank you, Max, for taking me tonight. I will never ..."

She was still looking at the water. He put his arm round her shoulders, which he had never done before, but she straightened and shook her head.

"It's late. Frau Schönfeld will be waiting up for me. And Jakob too, probably. I shall tell Jakob he must see the play. Perhaps he will be able to take me to another performance."

When they reached Frau Schönfeld's door she said good-night and thanked him again but did not look at him.

He walked home with a discordant confusion of thoughts in his head; a low note he couldn't silence he identified as a sense of loss.

As he put his key in the lock, he heard music. At this time of night? What was it? Treuburg's cello. Bach. He shut the door quietly behind him. The sitting room door was open. Treuburg was playing by heart, his back to the door. Adam was lying on the sofa in a dressing gown and pyjamas, smoking a cigarette, his bare feet on the sofa arm. An untasted glass of wine was on the floor beside him, along with an ashtray and a telegram. He raised his other hand in salute when Max came in.

At the end of a slow sarabande that, with everything that had happened that evening colliding inside him, almost had Max in tears, Treuburg, without turning round, said, "By request. The artistic temperament—the romantic lead, I should say—needing a bit of classical order."

"Thanks", Adam said, stubbing out his cigarette. He sat up, swinging his feet to the floor. "Well, Max?"

"Wonderful—really wonderful. I had no idea you could act—though I suppose, if I'd thought, Hamlet ..."

"Is it acting, you mean? Or something else? I don't know myself. Was old Fischer there tonight?"

"I didn't see him, but ..."

"Ah. The girlfriend. Well, he may come another night. There are two more performances, I hope. What did she make of it?"

"She was bowled over. She's never been to the theatre before."

"Bowled over, eh? Good. There's a hell of a fuss brewing, Treuburg says. He heard it during the intermission. The clubs don't like the Kaiser as the villain. Of course they don't. Lèse-majesté. That was the whole point, of course, clever Kurt's main reason for wanting to do *Hamlet* at all. It works well, don't you think? The clubs will try to stop the show. No more wicked performances. They'll say it's treason. They won't succeed, I'm pleased to say. Shakespeare is Shakespeare, and the professors want to look as if they like living in a democracy. Freedom of expression and all that. And when you think of what goes on nowadays in Berlin, a student dressed up as the Kaiser in a production that will make the Breslau paper if it's lucky is hardly going to break any china. Oh, by the way ..."

He picked up the telegram. "Look. My mother says she's coming to the play on Saturday, without a boyfriend for once. I got two tickets for her. Will you take her? She couldn't possibly appear in a theatre without a man beside her, even if it's only a student show. You could collect her in a cab from the hotel, couldn't you, and get her back in one piece afterwards?"

"Yes. Of course. If it would help."

"Can't be done without you. I'm no use to anyone at the end of the play. Thanks. You have met her, after all."

"She won't remember me."

"Oh, she will. And she knows the three of us share this flat. She'll have long ago looked both of you up in the Gotha. I'm sorry, Max, but I don't know how else to deal with her. I'll go and see her on Sunday morning. That'll have to do."

"No. That's fine. Don't worry about her."

Some of the parents in the Thursday audience had been overdressed for the student theatre, so Max, suspecting Adam's mother would be too, put on his dinner jacket in order not to repeat the embarrassment of long ago. He took a bath, shaved for the second time that day, ironed his white shirt—there was no Frau Gärtner now but Katya, a Polish girl of about fifteen whom Adam had found somewhere and who didn't iron anything—and dressed carefully, frowning at himself in the bathroom mirror, trying a polite smile and a nodded bow.

He couldn't decide whether or not he was glad to have an ordinary reason to see the play again. There were only three performances—Saturday evening was his last chance—and here was Adam's mother to be looked after. There was no decision to be made. The experience had been so complicated that he half-wanted to repeat it, to see if he could, without Anna sitting beside him, sort out what he really thought of Adam and Hamlet, of Adam or Hamlet. Of Adam-Hamlet, the boy becoming a man in the course of a play full of absurdity, melodrama, and jokes, as well as of poetry. Not that the poetry was there any more, in the German translation. Dr Fischer had told them that at school: "Poetry is what does not survive translation." Someone famous had said that. He couldn't remember who.

He brushed his hair again. This was what his mind had been like since he woke up on Friday morning. That was only yesterday. Since then, he had been flitting about, distracted because he so badly needed distraction. Anything to think about would do, as long as it wasn't Anna. Next week perhaps, there would be an evening for music, when Halpern could get away from the hospital. Then things would be the same as they were before *Hamlet*. Wouldn't they? He knew they wouldn't. He didn't want to see the play again because he knew he would watch Adam through Anna's eyes this time and see why things wouldn't be the same. But he had to go. It was easier, at least, not to have to choose.

Although he was early, the countess was waiting for him—like Anna, he thought. But the countess was not at all like Anna—sitting in an armchair near the door of the White Eagle, a cocktail with ice in the glass on the little table beside her.

"Max! How wonderful to see you." She held out a scented, ringed hand. He raised it to his lips. "Sit down for a minute while I have a look at you. A drink? We have time, I'm sure."

"No, thank you so much. I have a cab outside."

"He can wait a moment. Now ..." She looked at him, smiling. She was wearing a short blue silk dress, the kind of dress Eva Grossmann wore. Her bobbed hair was more blonde than he remembered. She wore a long double string of pearls, and on her shoulder was a diamond brooch. Surely not—he looked again, trying to sustain a polite smile—yes, it was. The brooch was a swastika. Could he tell her to take it off? Could he tell her she might meet Kurt? That if she did, there would be a scene? That Adam would be ashamed? No, he couldn't possibly tell her. Tonight Adam wouldn't see her. He would take care to keep her away from Kurt. Would people think she was his own mother? He tried to listen to what she was saying.

"Grown up now, of course, like Adam. Well, you would be, wouldn't you? It was years ago, that *Tristan*, wasn't it? Let's not count how many years. Still the good-looking boy I remember, though. Adam's handsome friend in Breslau. I hear you share a flat near the university. How nice! And Baron von Treuburg as well. I haven't met him, of course. Will he be at Adam's play?"

"I don't think so. He has already seen it, and ... Countess, I'm so sorry, but I do think perhaps we should go to the theatre now."

"Of course, of course, my dear boy. Pay no attention to me. Let's go at once."

In the cab, Max tried to warn the countess about the university theatre not being like a real theatre, but she wasn't listening. She looked out of the window.

"I wish Adam would come back to Vienna. He could perfectly well finish his studies there. I should like him to meet ... Well, we shall see. Breslau, after all—it's only a provincial town, isn't it? Why don't you both come to Vienna?"

"I don't think ... Here we are. Allow me."

He jumped out of the cab, opened her door, and paid the driver with a note he had ready in his hand.

They found their seats, in the third row. Only the first few rows of seats had numbers, white cards with black figures, placed on top of the programme sheets.

"Oh dear. We should have brought cushions. One has to at Bayreuth, you know. Something to do with the acoustics. I expect you've been to Bayreuth, a musical boy like you. Let me see ..." She looked at her cast list. "Any other names I know? I think not."

The curtain rose. The dawn sky. The soldiers. The ghost.

There was a buzz in the audience when Claudius appeared: the Kaiser impersonation was now well known in the university. The countess gasped, and then laughed, high and loud. The actor glared at her after a couple of lines of his speech, to stop her. She stopped, but whispered in Max's ear: "What an amusing idea!" When Hamlet first spoke—perhaps she hadn't noticed him earlier—she hissed at Max:

"Has Adam lost his costume?" and when Ophelia came on, "Not bad at all. A pity about that frock."

With her beside him, restless, a bracelet jangling every time she moved, clearly much of the time bored, Max this time found, at first to his relief, the play more obviously a play. He was closer to the stage than he and Anna had been, and he caught moments of inattention in the actors; awkward movements; and Polonius looking much too young behind his beard and once failing to pick up a cue, Claudius filling the gap by repeating his last line. But Adam, the only person on the stage without makeup Max could now see, was more entirely Hamlet than even on Thursday. It was as if he alone were real and had strayed from reality into a world of costumes and greasepaint and unnaturally grand language. This explained his teasing, his manipulation of the other characters, even of Claudius who should have frightened him, even of Ophelia to whom he should have been kind. Towards the end of the first half, with the players set up by Hamlet to shame Claudius into self-revelation, Max was close to a whole new theory, and not just about the play. Only Hamlet, only Adam, and perhaps Horatio, watching, perhaps Max himself watching, understand it's a play, all a play, everyone pretending to be someone, something, else—he glanced sideways at Max's mother, catching her looking at her diamond watch—and only Hamlet knows that he's been given a part he can't play. He needs Horatio to help him play the wrong part, but at the end, dying and knowing he is dying, he wants Horatio only to tell the truth about him. What is the truth about him?

Watching Hamlet embarrassing Rosencrantz and Guildenstern by showing them he knows they're liars and spies, Max was thinking, "Hamlet cares only about the truth, or only *he* cares about the truth, and it's so hard to find, too hard for anyone to find. Where is it?" Then Polonius came and went, and the curtain fell. Applause broke out, the countess clapping with her hands raised so as to be noticed.

"Of course he gets it from me—acting", she said as they got to their feet. "I used to be an opera singer—you didn't know that, did you?—but then I married, and Adam was born. Sad, in a way, my career never rising as high as it should have. But there you are. Mothers must sacrifice themselves for their children, mustn't they? Is there a bar?"

"I'm afraid not. There's coffee, I think. But we could go to the café across the road if you would like a drink. There's a terrace. We'll have at least a quarter of an hour."

"Why not? A student café. Thank you, Max. I should enjoy that."

With any luck, no one he knew would leave the theatre. Certainly not Kurt.

"What do you think of the rest of the cast?" he asked as he pulled out a chair on the café terrace for her.

"Oh, well, not bad. Considering they're only students, not bad at all. It's not a play I care for, mind you. It's not heroic, like Schiller. Who are we supposed to admire? Not the Kaiser, obviously. And Hamlet has to talk so much. Adam must have worked very hard to learn all those lines."

They drank a glass of hock each. She smoked a cigarette.

"Excuse me a moment, won't you, Max", she said and disappeared into the café. He paid for the wine, left a tip for the waiter, and stood up with his back to the café.

He saw Anna and Halpern come round the corner on the other side of the street. He turned quickly, but it was too late.

"Max! Good evening! I brought Jakob. He is even better tonight, don't you think?"

Halpern followed her across the street.

"Anna, hello. Good evening, Halpern. Are you enjoying it?"

"Enjoying? No. But it is most interesting. A corrupt society. A young man lost. Most interesting, so old a play presented as if in our time."

Max was paralysed. Go, please go. Cross the road. Vanish into the theatre. But they stood, Anna saying something, expecting him to return to the theatre with them. Then the countess's scent, her bracelet jangle, her hand on his shoulder as she came up behind him. He turned, trying to make sure he was between her and Halpern.

"May I present Dr Halpern and his sister Anna? This is Countess Zapolska, Adam Zapolski's mother."

What else could he have done? As the countess and Anna were shaking hands—"Charming!" the countess said—he saw Halpern wince. "I beg your ..." he muttered, taking Anna's hand and pulling her away, crossing the street quickly.

"No manners, your friend the doctor", the countess said. "Well, Jews, what can you expect?"

Back in the play, Max was furious with Adam—how could he have landed him with his mother? This was surely the end of music with the Halperns. Anna would never be allowed to see them again. Max was almost too angry to notice that there, on the stage, was

Adam-Hamlet, furious with his mother. He caught the parallel in time to smile, in time to wonder whether the countess herself was picking up even the faintest echo from the scene being played in front of them. What she picked up was Max's glance. She leant towards him and whispered. "*Un peu exagéré*", she said.

Max pulled himself together. He was going to have to depend on Adam to straighten things out with Halpern. He could depend on Adam, couldn't he? Of course. The countess was his mother, after all, and he would know how to do it. But then there was Anna, and the effect Adam-Hamlet was having on her. Even now. The Queen on the stage was making the very most of Ophelia's death, but somewhere behind him in the audience there was Anna, longing for Hamlet to reappear, to leap from the shadows at Laertes by the grave, and to say, "I loved Ophelia. Forty thousand brothers . . ."

Max made himself concentrate. He didn't want to miss the change in Hamlet-Adam, the one moment when he wasn't outside the play, wasn't finding the part he had been allotted impossible to perform. There: "we defy augury". He knows there's something wrong with this duel, he knows his death is possible, likely, even certain. But if it is to be, it is to be, and the will is not his own but God's.

This time, when Hamlet-Adam died in Horatio's arms, Max felt the tears rising in his throat. He knew for certain that Adam would die before him, that he would never not suffer his loss.

The applause and the roar from the audience were even louder than they had been on Thursday. Students at the back of the theatre were stamping, in enthusiasm only, but the stamping quickly became rhythmical and a little alarming. It stopped, all the noise stopped, when Kurt, in dirty trousers and a red shirt, no tie, appeared in front of the bowing, smiling cast, Ophelia and the Queen holding bunches of flowers presented by a stagehand.

Kurt held up both arms, acknowledging the applause, which had begun again in more orderly fashion. Then he raised one hand for silence.

"Thank you. Thank you all for coming and for your appreciation of our show. Most of you know our production has been, let's say, somewhat controversial. We'd have been upset if it hadn't been." A roar of approval from the audience. "Shakespeare knew it all, didn't he? Tyranny, treachery, so-called sacrifice, so-called patriotism, the lot. We're grateful to him. We're grateful to the university authorities for not closing us down after Thursday's show. We're grateful to you for turning up. And I'm grateful to my cast and crew for the work they've put in." More noisy applause. Kurt backed into the line of actors, took the hands of Hamlet and Claudius, and all of them bowed once more before the curtain fell.

"Who was that young man?" the countess said as they joined the slow crush of people leaving the theatre. "The producer? He could have appeared properly dressed, don't you think? Now, can we go and see Adam?"

"I'm afraid not. They won't let us—there aren't real dressing rooms here. In fact, it's all pretty chaotic backstage, and Adam particularly asked me to tell you he'll come to the White Eagle in the morning to see you properly."

"Never mind. I expect there'll be a party anyway. They won't want outsiders, will they? Find us a cab, Max, there's a good boy. There's something I want to ask you on the way back."

He found a cab easily—most of the audience were walking away from the theatre—and again opened the door for her.

"Now listen." She settled in the back seat, lit a cigarette, and put her other hand on his knee. "We're going to Venice in a couple of weeks. I've invited Adam. I had to write him a letter—it's so tiresome that you don't have a telephone in your flat; everyone does now, you know—but of course, he hasn't answered. Have you anything planned for later in July and the first part of August?"

"I'm not sure. I shall be working in Breslau, I expect."

"Working? But it's the vacation, surely. You should have a holiday. I'm sure you deserve one."

"I shall probably be doing some teaching."

Last summer he had coached two boys, violin pupils of Dr Mendel, musical but not clever, who were behind in their Gymnasium classes. He taught them in the mornings, helped them with their violin practice, and then took them swimming or to the tennis club in the afternoons. Their parents paid him well. The family was going to the Baltic for July, but he had half-promised to tutor the boys again in August.

"Why? Oh, to earn some money, I suppose. Never mind that. If you come with us to Venice, of course it will be my treat. Have you been to Italy?"

"No, never. I should very much like—"

"Well, there you are. Persuade Adam. He might come if he knows you would be coming with him. Of course, you wouldn't have to stay with us all the time. You might find the Lido a little dull, though it's my favourite place of all. But you could explore the city and meet people, you and Adam. It would be fun for you, more fun than teaching in Breslau, anyhow. Oh, here we are. Keep the cab, Max. It's late. If you see Adam tonight, tell him I expect him at eleven tomorrow."

As soon as she had disappeared into the White Eagle, he paid the driver and began to walk home. She had said nothing about the play and nothing about Adam's performance. Did she somewhere resent its quality? It was impossible to know. Had she any idea who her son was? Had she thought about him, ever? She knew, at any rate, that Adam wouldn't want to go on any kind of holiday with her. And with who else? That "we" probably meant her and the current boyfriend.

But Venice, Italy, exploring with Adam ... He stopped walking and realized with a rush of feeling how much, how very much, he wanted to go. He had never been out of Germany. The idea of the Mediterranean, of white buildings and blue sea, of Vivaldi and Stradivarius and Titian—wasn't Titian a Venetian painter?—made him shout a "Yes!" to the empty street with the pressure of how much he wanted to go. It would be wonderful to get away for a few weeks, with Adam and no one else, from everything here that was so complicated and impossible to predict. He saw again Halpern's face as he noticed the diamond swastika on the countess's dress. He remembered that Halpern didn't yet know that his mother's family were converted three generations ago. Anna hadn't told her brother. He knew that once Halpern discovered the truth ... The swastika by itself might have been enough. And how, after watching Hamlet-Adam twice in three evenings, could Anna not have fallen in love with him? Any girl with some sensibility—he thought with anguish of Anna's smile, her spectacles, her fingers on the strings of her viola—was bound to have fallen in love with him.

He would persuade Adam to go to Venice.

It wasn't at all difficult.

Adam came in half an hour after Max got home. Treuburg was away. It was Saturday night. No doubt he had wangled some expedition with Eva. When he heard the door open, Max went into the hall and hugged Adam. Holding him at arm's length by the shoulders, he saw he was still wearing his black sweater and trousers and looked exhausted, with dark rings like bruises under his eyes. He smiled.

"Well? What did you think? Really?"

"It was wonderful. Really. Something extraordinary you've done."

"You know, I didn't do it. The whole thing's been very strange. Easy. Tiring, but easy. As if it were being done to me, not being done by me."

"Done by Shakespeare, you mean? Done by Kurt?"

He laughed. "Absolutely not by Kurt. In fact, we had a frightful row at the end of the dress rehearsal. We haven't been on speaking terms since."

"A row? What about?"

Adam, suddenly still, looked at him, or through him to Horatio. "If it be not now, yet it will come. The readiness is all", he said, and crossed himself slowly, deliberately. He laughed and returned to himself.

"About that. Kurt was furious. He's a Communist, of course. So, according to him, is Shakespeare. So is Hamlet. You can make quite a case for Hamlet's atheism, when you think about it. But he couldn't stop me. He's only the producer. I'm thirsty."

"What would you like? There's beer, I think. Wine? Seltzer?"

"Tea. Your Earl Grey. Is there any left? Did you see old Fischer tonight?"

"No. But he'll have come. He said he would."

Max lit the gas and put the kettle on.

"I had your mother tonight, remember?"

"My God, I'd completely forgotten. How was that?"

"Tricky in some ways. Never mind now. She's expecting you at the White Eagle at eleven in the morning. Adam ..."

"What?"

"She wants both of us to go to Venice with her. She says she wrote to you."

"She's asked you too? That's much better. I didn't want to go. That's why I didn't answer. And the play. But if you came too, it would be fine. We certainly need to get out of Breslau, and we've rather done walking in the mountains, haven't we? Something less German would be good for us. I haven't been to Venice since I was about fourteen. It's an extraordinary place."

"I'm broke. I'll have to work for some of the summer."

"Of course. But in Italy, she'll pay. Or I will. There still seems to be plenty of money, God knows how. Ill-gotten gains from something, I've no doubt. Thanks."

He took his cup of Earl Grey.

"Did she say anything about the play?"

"Practically nothing. She said you got acting from her and that you must have worked hard to learn all those lines. She made one or two remarks about the clothes. That was about it."

"What one would expect. Still ... This tea's good." He held out his cup, and Max refilled it. They were standing in the kitchen.

"You know," Adam said, "I'm glad it's over. Never again. Never anything like that. Safer to stick to music. I'm really looking forward to hearing your quartet. I'll start doing some work on my clarinet tomorrow."

"What do you mean 'safer to stick to music'?"

"It's contentless. Or rather, the content is the form, and that's all there is. Nothing to rattle the cage."

"What cage? What are you talking about?"

"I'll tell you another time. Perhaps. Unless it goes away. I'm going to bed. I have to deal with my mother in the morning. Let's go to Venice. On our terms. I'll tell her."

On Monday morning, there was a letter in the post for Adam from Dr Fischer, and a note for Max. "Hofmannswaldau", it said. "Unless Count Zapolski objects, Anna and I are able to play on Thursday this week. Jakob Halpern."

Max handed it to Adam across the remains of breakfast. Treuburg had already gone to the hospital.

"What's this? Of course I don't object. How could I? I haven't even met him. And Anna was only here that day for tea—a little duck. Old Fischer, by the way—he did come."

"And?"

"He liked it." Adam waved his letter but didn't show it to Max.

"I'm glad."

"But what's the problem with Halpern?"

"It was your mother, I'm afraid. During the intermission on Saturday."

"What did she say? I don't want to know. No: you'd better tell me."

"She didn't say anything. She shook hands with Anna. She was wearing a diamond brooch, a swastika. Halpern saw it."

"O God! Bloody Vienna! She's such a fool, my mother. She never thinks. She's actually quite incapable of thought. This'll be the influence of some dreadful man. We shall see when we get to Venice what the current man situation is. If swastikas are the form, we'll leave them on the Lido and do our own holiday, thank you very much. But it could be a fashionable knick-knack, a piece of expensive showing off—she may not have much idea what it means. On the other hand, I'm afraid she may. But how stupid, in a university, at a student show. It's just as well Kurt didn't see it. No wonder Halpern's being touchy."

"He's touchy anyway."

"Damn. I'll write to him myself. What can one decently say about my mother?"

Max didn't see what Adam wrote to Dr Halpern. On Wednesday morning, Adam had a letter, which he crumpled and threw away as soon as he had read it.

"They're coming. Thank goodness for that."

"Well done."

Max heard Adam practising the clarinet part of the Mozart quintet—the parts were borrowed from Dr Mendel—for hours on the rest of that day and the next.

Lectures were over for the summer, but there was work to be done on a thesis Max was writing on diplomatic immunity from the sixteenth to the nineteenth century, so he went to the history library, where it was a good deal easier to work than in the hot flat with fragments of the Mozart being repeated by Adam in his room, interrupted occasionally by a melancholy jazz tune. Adam was supposed to be writing about the constitution of the Polish commonwealth before the partitions, but he had so far made no detectable start on his thesis.

Max was pleased to find that much of the early material for his essay was about Venetian ambassadors, who seemed to have written books full of reports home from the capital cities of Europe. He daydreamed for a few minutes about Venice, then gave up on the ambassadors and wasted some time finding in the library an illustrated book about the constitution of the Venetian republic. He gazed at portraits of doges, the great council chamber of the doges' palace . . .

Halpern and Anna arrived punctually at eight on Thursday evening. Treuburg, after a long, sticky day at the hospital, was in the bath.

Max opened the door to the flat. Anna managed to smile at him but said nothing in greeting. Her eyes, bright with excitement, were on Adam. She shook hands with Adam, but was too overcome to manage a "good evening". Halpern shook Max's hand, and then Adam's.

"Good evening, Count. Thank you for writing as you did. You are not your mother's keeper. None of us is to be held responsible for our parents' prejudices, or how is the world to become any better?"

Even Adam was silenced for a moment by this.

"Treuburg's in the bath", he said. "He won't be long."

"The hospital becomes very hot at this time of year", Halpern said. "I know it well."

"Of course. Shall we do a little tuning while we wait for him? Woodwind instruments are the devil in hot weather. Are you and Miss Halpern happy to try the clarinet quintet tonight?"

"Naturally. I have heard the piece once. It is a most beautiful work. It will be sight-reading for us, but we shall do our best."

Except for Adam who had only to pick up his clarinet, ready assembled on the piano, they were still adjusting their instruments to their chins and shifting their chairs to the right positions in relation to the music stands when Treuburg appeared, neat as always, apologizing for keeping them waiting. He got his cello out of its case, sat down with the instrument between his knees, and played a long, powerful note on its bottom string; this broke the tension among the others, the reasons for which he couldn't have known.

They tuned up, Adam lengthening his clarinet a fraction because it was warm and a little sharp. All of them motionless, attentive, bows on strings, they looked at Halpern. "Two, three, four", he nodded and mouthed. They began. Six bars of the string introduction, then a liquid two-bar flourish from Adam's clarinet, and the first movement had properly started. The notes were easy, even at first sight, except for some rapid runs for the clarinet and the first violin, once or twice picked up by the lower instruments. Max, concentrating hard on his own part and listening to Halpern, was vaguely aware of one or two gaps in the texture of the music; he didn't know the piece well enough to be sure. But when they reached the end of the movement, with a couple of final arpeggios played exactly and without exaggeration by Adam, Halpern put down his bow and frowned.

"What is the matter with you, Anna? This music is not difficult. Difficult to perfect, yes. But not difficult to play. Twice you were lost.

The Beethoven quartet was very much harder, and you had no trouble, at least with remaining in the right place. Would you object", he looked at the others, "to playing the first movement again so that my sister can remember how to count?"

"Of course. I should like to", Adam said.

Max felt rather than saw Anna, beside him, in tears. She put her viola on the floor and left the sitting room, shutting the door behind her.

"Perhaps she's not feeling well", Max said.

"She is well. She must learn that when one plays, the music must come first. She will recover."

She came back, sat down, picked up her viola, and looked at Max, her eyes pleading. He winked at her. At least she knew he had understood. That was something.

They played through the first movement again, somehow rather less well, though Anna, her face tense with concentration, missed neither of her conspicuous entries, and Max thought, gratefully, that Treuburg, because the cello's line was almost always in conjunction with the viola's, was giving her special support.

"You know," Adam said at the end of the movement, "I think that's nearly enough for one evening. Or shall we just try the slow movement?"

"Please", Anna, who had not yet spoken, said softly.

"Ah", said Treuburg. "One of Mozart's great tunes. Have you got hold of the tricky passages, Zapolski?"

"Well, I've had a go at them. Turns and scales. They're not impossible. Is it all right with you, Miss Halpern, to try the slow movement?"

She blushed, looking at Adam, and nodded.

"You and I need mutes, Hofmannswaldau", Halpern said. "No, not you, Anna."

When they were all ready, Halpern again counted them in, and the lyrical clarinet line floated over the strings and, Max felt, out of the open window and on, out and out over the hot, dusty July city like summer rain. He felt Anna so much moved by the music that she was almost again in tears. He willed her to keep going, and was thankful to Mozart that the first violin had some complicated passagework of its own to negotiate, and the viola in this movement none.

They reached the end of the movement, with a rumble of triplets low on the viola and then lower on the cello, and a last note from the clarinet so deep it was hard to believe it came from the same instrument as the high, plaintive melody of two bars earlier. Max, in the silence, caught a mischievous glance, quelled, from Adam: he was going to play his bass note again, or joke about it, but thought better of it.

Anna took off her spectacles and cleaned them with the piece of silk she had taken from under her chin where her viola rested.

"Good", Halpern said. "That is very beautiful music. But it is not enough."

"Please, Jakob", Anna said. "It's enough for now. Perhaps later . . ."

"I'll make some coffee", Max said. "Or would anyone like beer? We have a jug in the larder, quite cold."

"That is not what I meant", Halpern said. "Beauty is not enough. That is what I meant."

"In that case," Adam said, "we need some beer."

"I should like some coffee, Max", Anna said, not meeting his eye as she put her viola on the piano and, on top of it, the folded piece of silk. "Thank you."

Max wanted to pick up the silk and lay it against his cheek. Instead, he went into the kitchen and noisily ground some coffee. Adam appeared, fetched the beer, and found the pewter mugs in the cupboard. These mugs—not Grandpapa's for he never drank beer—they had bought last summer: students must have beer mugs.

"You only need three. I'll have coffee", Max said.

"Quite right. Solidarity. Poor girl", Adam said, getting out a tray. "What's up with him?"

"I've no idea. He's a prickly character. No—she doesn't like sugar."

When they went back, Adam with the tray of mugs and cups, Max with beer jug in one hand and tin coffee pot in the other, things in the sitting room seemed more relaxed. Halpern was admiring Treuburg's cello.

"I should very much like one day to play a fine instrument such as yours. But there is little possibility."

"Beer, Halpern?"

"Thank you, Count." Why is he calling him Count? Blast him, Max thought. He never calls me Count or Treuburg Baron.

"That's good", Halpern said, drinking some of his beer and sitting down on the sofa beside Anna. "There, you see. Beer is good because one is thirsty. A bath is good because one is hot and dirty. Mozart is good because one needs beautiful music. But Shakespeare—for what, for when does one need Shakespeare? Your *Hamlet*, Count, a cruel and horrible story, is it not?"

So that was it. Max looked at Anna. She was sitting miserably on the edge of the sofa, looking down into her coffee. Both hands, tense, were holding her cup and saucer on her lap.

"Every tragedy", Adam said, "tells a cruel and horrible story. Look at Oedipus, or the Oresteia. But the great tragedies make us feel better, not worse. Justice prevails. There is a cleansing, a purging, of what human beings have spoilt. Some kind of order, made in heaven as they used to say, is restored."

Max recognized this as pure Dr Fischer. Was it just something to say to keep the peace?

"*Feel* better?" Halpern said, with scorn in his voice. "Of what importance is feeling?"

"Well, Nietzsche said we have art lest we perish of the truth. That makes it quite important."

"Oh, Nietzsche. Yes. But for how many people did he speak? For how many people did he trouble to think? And in any case, he was not talking about feeling. He was talking about filling a space, the space left by God. But the space terrified him. Perhaps God had not left it after all. Why should we perish of the truth? Only what we can establish with certainty as true can give us the power to cure, to heal, to make the lives of all people less terrible. Nietzsche said these things to shock, and not to shock only the readers of his words. He was shouting in that space, testing its emptiness, tempting God to reply, to be there, not after all to be dead. Nietzsche said things he hoped were not true, to see what would happen. Did a thunderbolt fall on him? No. So he said some more."

"A thunderbolt did fall on him", Max said. "He went mad."

"General paralysis of the insane. Not a thunderbolt. Syphilis. An avoidable disease." He drank some beer. Max could see he was going to go on. Was it only *Hamlet* that had had this effect on him? On the other evenings that they had played quartets, Halpern had said almost nothing.

"We must be grateful, in our generation. But not to Nietzsche. By no means. We must be grateful to all those who have helped to make acceptable the space Nietzsche was afraid of. This has been the great achievement of the last hundred years, the last hundred and fifty years. Something in our brains needs art. Nothing in our brains needs religion. When you talk about justice, you talk about religion, I think. The justice of heaven is an illusion, an unfounded hope. When I talk about justice, I talk about something that we have to make. The Greek tragedies I do not know. I have not been so fortunate to go to a classical Gymnasium, Count. In Vilna, such schools are for Christians only. But I have read some books. I have understood that in a tragedy the central character is to blame. That he makes a mistake, commits a sin, and so must be punished—as Nietzsche was punished by syphilis. But what did Hamlet do? He is just a romantic hero, a boy who is not happy. Vengeance is futile, and his death is only waste, like the rest. All those corpses at the end. Almost comical, I would say. I see nothing good in this story, only easy emotion, which is always dangerous." He glanced at his sister, his eyes cold. "Feeling better, feeling worse, feeling upset, feeling for the sake of feeling. We pay it too much attention. Are we ill? Are we well? Can we reason, deduce, test? That is what is important. That is why I am a doctor, a scientist."

"So am I", Treuburg said. "But for what do we make people well? Not just to be well but to live a life with at least the possibility of . . . well, what?"

"Of some kind of answer", Max said. "Some kind of response, to what is good. To what is given to us. Plenty of people would say Mozart has something to do with heaven. Or heaven has something to do with what is beautiful. Which anyone can understand if what's beautiful is a view of hills in the distance, say, or a river."

"Physiology", Halpern said. "The structure of the ear and the hearing function of the brain. Or the eye and sight. Plus mathematics, of course."

"Rubbish!" Adam said. "We're not automata. If that were true, a Mozart piece would have exactly the same effect on everyone who heard it. That's obviously not the case. And what about playing? You're far too good a fiddler, Halpern, not to know that for every ten people who can play the notes, there's only one who can play the music. What's that all about if music's no more than physiology?"

"Physiology and mathematics. Pythagoras knew that, at the beginning of science."

"Pythagoras believed in the soul. All sorts of souls, milling about in the universe, looking for bodies. That is nonsense, I grant you."

"So?" Halpern said. "So it is the brain that requires music, as thirst requires beer, or dirty skin requires a bath. Forget the soul, a meaningless concept. We do not yet understand the brain. But we shall. We shall. We shall one day, one day soon perhaps, discover the effect of

Mozart on the brain, or of Bach. Bach will be different, perhaps better. Or Wagner, different again, but certainly worse. Jazz, worse still. The marching songs of the Stormtroopers, worst of all."

"How?" Adam said. "How will you discover the effect on the brain of different kinds of music?"

"By experiment, naturally. How else does one discover anything?"

"Now that is frightening, don't you think? What would be the material for such experiments? People. Their brains. Dead or alive. Don't you agree that people discover more interesting things than any experiment can teach them? By intuition, by reflection, by allowing some kind of light to dawn? By using their intelligence, of course, but in a different way. The forward progress of science, knowledge, power, is like jumping from island to island of proof, fact, solid under the feet, while all about the islands the tides of the sea still flow, as mysterious as ever. Mozart belongs to the sea, not to the islands."

"So far."

"Please. I don't understand", Anna said, looking at Adam with her shining eyes. "What is the sea?"

Adam laughed. "We must be careful here. Your brother will think we are a bad influence on you."

"No. She is in Germany now. She cannot be protected from this belief in culture. She must understand it so as to judge it."

"I don't think Zapolski is talking about culture", Max said.

"Oh, really?" Adam said. "What is Zapolski talking about?"

"Anna", Max said, hoping she would look at him. She didn't. "Dr Fischer—you met him here, and you liked him, didn't you?—had a story he told us at school. One of his best. When Galileo discovered—through experiments, tests, proof—that the earth goes round the sun, the Church got in a panic and told him to recant. They thought he was a heretic, you see, because people had always believed that the sun goes round the earth, making the earth the centre of the universe. Anyway, they told him to recant or they might burn him as a heretic. So he said, 'All right. The sun goes round the earth', knowing perfectly well that the reverse is the case. His friends, his students, the people who had seen his proofs, were shocked. They called him a coward. But he said, 'One doesn't die for a fact. Science makes progress. Facts are discovered. If not by me, by someone else a little later. It doesn't matter who. Truth is worth dying for. A fact is not.' Facts make progress, pile up; there are always more of them. That's what

267

Adam meant. Truth doesn't. Truth belongs to the sea. So does art, great art anyway. If Mozart had died even sooner, no one else would have written the clarinet quintet. If Shakespeare had never been born, no one else would have written *Hamlet*."

Now she did look at him. "I'm too stupid. Or my German is too bad. I still don't understand." She looked back to Adam, as if only he could explain.

"Deep water, this", Adam said, and laughed again. "The sea. Don't worry, Miss Halpern. There are things none of us understands. Perhaps the difference between us—Max and I—and your brother is only that we are sure there always will be things no one understands, things we can only believe, or not."

"You mean God?" she said.

"Max might. I don't. Treuburg always says he doesn't."

"And Marx?" Halpern said. "Does Marx belong to fact or to truth? Many people have been willing to die for Communism as truth, to be believed in, instead of believing in God."

"Many more people have been killed in the name of Communism", Adam said. "And dying for something doesn't make it true."

"As with Christianity. Martyrdoms there have been. But also crusades, and pogroms. People willing to die are usually willing to kill. Marx filled the space left by God. He was a Jew, after all. Also a German. But at least he started from facts, and from wanting to change reality for the better. What use is Nietzsche, what use is culture, art lest we perish of the truth, to the wretched of the earth, to the people cut from the loom and thrown away? In the poor quarters of Vilna, of Breslau also, where they live ten or fifteen people to a room, in a cellar perhaps where no sunlight ever comes, where there are rats and lice and there is never enough to eat, they do not need Mozart. They need fresh air, clean beds, milk for the children. That people feel better because they go to plays about ghosts and treachery and murders is of no importance to them."

"Oh, I have taken too little care of this", Adam said.

"What is this?"

"Shakespeare. Do you remember, Max? A different play, another King. King Lear. Old and mad and tortured with guilt. Practically a Communist, in the sixteenth century. But Halpern, are the Bolsheviks going to deliver heaven on earth?"

"I don't know." Halpern looked suddenly exhausted. "It's too soon to say. I thought so once. When the revolution at last did happen. I was seventeen. A schoolboy. But we talked of nothing else. The Bund, you have heard of it? Yes? Yes. Jewish Communists in Russia. For a little while, it seemed as though the downtrodden, the persecuted, the poor, the workers, the peasants, the Jews, had at last a common cause, that the Jews, political at last, would be able to improve the lives of the oppressed in solidarity with the poor everywhere. The revolution was not Christian. The revolution was not Jewish. The people on the right, here in Germany as in Vilna, say it was, all the time. But it was not. Far from it. Jews as Jews the Bolsheviks hate as much as they hate Christians. They may hate Jews more, perhaps, from old Russian habit. But the revolution was at least for a better life in this world, not for reward in another. But very soon, in two years, it became clear—I was by now a student—that the revolution was to be very cruel and was to be only Russian. In result. In reality. In theory, Communists everywhere work for revolution everywhere. But if Marx had been correct, revolution would have occurred first in Germany and in England, in the most industrial, most capitalist countries. But where it occurred was Russia. In Russia, human lives have always been cheap, the lives of Jews and the lives of serfs equally cheap. Communism will not make them of value. Instead, Russia will make Communism a system of cheap lives, expendable lives, for a better future that may or may not come. About Russia Marx knew nothing. He was a man always entirely of the west."

Halpern stopped. "I am speaking too much", he said to Max. He always treated Max as his host in Grandpapa's flat.

"No. Not at all. Please go on", Max said.

"Thank you. I do not know how it is that I—it is perhaps the Shakespeare play. So, Russia is a cruel and terrible country. You do not understand, here in Germany. If there had been a real revolution here, after the war, if the grand capitalists and the grand landowners had been dispossessed and the farms, the mills, the factories, the mines had been taken over by the state and properly managed by honest officials—bureaucrats in this country are slow, they plod, but they are not corrupt; they have a sense of duty—then perhaps here the poor would have become less poor. But in Russia, always there are oppressors and there are the oppressed. There is no one else. It has always been so. It seems that only the oppressors have changed. When I was seventeen, I was willing to die for Communism. But I am not willing to die for Russia. In the civil war, there was nothing to choose between the armies. In Vilna we saw a good deal, but we heard more. The Whites allowed more pogroms; in fact, they not only allowed them but encouraged them, organized them. The soldiers were told that all Jews are Bolsheviks. In some parts of the pale of settlement, they rounded up all the people in every shtetl, the women, the old, the babies and children, and put them in a barn and burnt them. The Red Army was not much better. A Jew with a tavern, with a chandler's shop, with a string of mangy ponies was a filthy capitalist. They shot him, raped his wife and daughters, and set his shop on fire. The Hasidim in their long coats and sidelocks were religious. So they must die too. So much for the revolution being a Jewish affair."

Halpern stopped, looked round at Adam, Max, Treuburg, and drained his mug of beer.

"I apologize, Hofmannswaldau. You invited us to play Mozart. A civilized evening. Why not? I have spoilt it. This is Germany, not Russia."

"Please", Max said. "Don't apologize."

Halpern put his arm round his sister. She looked up at him and smiled, the first time in the evening she had smiled.

"Anna and I grew up in Russia. From our earliest childhood, we learnt to be afraid of the police, of soldiers, of anyone in uniform, of drunken workmen in the street. One of the reasons for the Haskalah was to hide from the men in uniform and the drunken workmen. We would come out of the study house, out of the ghetto, wear western clothes, shave our beards and our sidelocks, and nobody would notice us any more. For the fortunate, in Germany, it worked. Look at Grossmann. In Russia it was permitted only to a very few. But now, surely, with the revolution, it will be permitted? The revolution was supposed to be for the world, international, so Jews, who have always been compelled to be international, belonging nowhere so belonging everywhere, may disappear into a socialist future that does not distinguish? So you may think. But no. Jews are bourgeois capitalists by nature, are they not? So they cannot be Communists. Even Marx thought so. Deep in Marx, there is anti-Semitism. Where there is anti-Semitism, Jews give socialism a bad name, so socialism must get rid of them. They must be after their own ends—Jews always are—so in Russia the Bund is expelled from the Party. But in Poland, as usual, they think there is a conspiracy of Protestants, Freemasons, Jews, and Bolsheviks to take over the world. And behold, it is succeeding! In

Russia, in 1917, it had its first great success. Have you ever heard anything so stupid?"

Halpern suddenly looked at Adam with his intense, anguished eyes. "Where in Poland do you come from, Count?"

"From Galicia."

"Ah, Habsburg Poland. Not so terrible for the Jews as Russia. My father long ago was a medical student in Cracow. He has—he had—friends who were happy to live there. Now, who knows? Why, Count, were the Jews less despised in Habsburg Poland?"

"I remember well, when I was a child, in the middle of nowhere, on my father's estate, much goodwill", Adam said. "I think it was because the empire was such a mixture, so many peoples, so many languages. The treaty and its nations have made things worse for the Jews everywhere. Hundreds of Jews were murdered in Galicia in 1919."

"That is so. The better past was also because in the Habsburg empire the Poles were not themselves so much despised as they have always been by the Russians, and by the Prussians. The Poles after many hundreds of years should be accustomed to living with Jews. But after Poland was parcelled out among the empires, where they were treated with contempt themselves they treated the Jews with contempt. There was less contempt for Poles in Vienna than in Berlin or Petersburg. But you are also right that this is lost, this Habsburg easiness. Now that Poland is so proud to be again a nation, a country, it is everywhere in Poland that Jews are despised."

"Shall you return to Vilna when your medical training is complete?"

"There is my father. Anna and I, we are what he has left. We owe him very much. We owe him our company when he is old. He was pleased for me to come to Germany, to continue my medical studies in Breslau, and even allowed Anna to join me here, because he believed that in Germany we should not have to be afraid, that Jews have done well here and are accepted as equals in the universities, in the professions. Perhaps it was true once, before the war. I fear it is not true now. Someone like Professor Grossmann, who was established as a society doctor before the war, will no doubt be safe whatever happens. He is too like Germans of an exactly similar kind—rich, confident, and vulgar, making occasional religious gestures but only for show—for anyone even to remember that he is a Jew. Including himself. Oh ..." He suddenly leant towards Treuburg, who, from the depths of Grandpapa's armchair, was looking straight at him. "I apologize again. I had entirely forgotten your ... your connexion with Miss Grossmann. Forgive me, please."

"Think nothing of it", Treuburg said. "Your description of Grossmann couldn't be improved on."

"It was not ... discreet. Also, he is a good surgeon, and I am learning from him. But thank you. No. I am sorry. What I was attempting to say is that it is not the Grossmanns here in Breslau, or in Berlin, who need to worry, but the poor Jews who come to Germany from the east because they have heard things will be better for them here. It was true. It is now no longer true. Everyone hates them. Everyone— the Germans; the Poles, especially the very poor Poles; and most unfortunately also the German Jews, who do not wish to be associated with this oriental riffraff with their comical clothes and their bastard language. I feel most deeply for these Jews from the east because I am one of them and so is Anna. I wear western clothes and I speak German quite well, so I am not bullied in the street. But they are. Every day. Who is to help them? I do not believe that God looks after his people because I do not believe there is a God. But these are my people, and they are in danger here. America would be another thing for them. But most of them could never find the money for the passage, and America has recently decided that it has enough Jews. So what are they to do? Where are they to go? Even Stresemann wants to prevent the Jews from the east coming into Germany. They believe in God. Will God take care of them?"

"He won't", Treuburg said. "He never has. It's a paradox, isn't it? The people chosen by God, the people defined, identified, all these centuries, by their loyalty to God, have suffered more than any other people. Why?"

"But don't you see?" Adam said. "That's exactly why. The faithfulness of the Jews has been a reproach always to the Christians. The Jews's submission, their peacefulness, their not taking arms, the holiness of their sages—all of that's a reproach to Christians. Christian virtues are more evident in the Jews than in the Christians. That's why there's hatred. That's why there's contempt. The Jews were chosen to suffer. As Christ was."

"We suffer, yes", Halpern said. "Also we quarrel, bitterly, everywhere and all the time. You must not believe us to be so holy as you say."

"Better to be chosen to suffer than to be chosen to rule the world", Treuburg said.

"What?" Adam said.

"I'm speaking of Prussia. I mean the real Prussia. Not Breslau. In Breslau we are in the west, just as Halpern says. Look at us, in this room: a Pole who is half-Viennese, two Russian Jews, and a Silesian count who is half-Jewish. And one real Prussian, me. My father would be horrified. To my father and his friends, the Union of the Nobility, God chose Prussia in modern times exactly as God chose the Jews in ancient times. What is Prussia? Two centuries—the Great Elector to Bismarck—of the will of God, actually of the will of the state, compelled to be effective through discipline, obedience, and austerity, bringing history to a satisfactory conclusion. The triumph of Prussia over France was the final triumph of the will, but it was also the triumph of God over Voltaire and the Enlightenment, the triumph of aristocratic virtue over Napoleon the corporal from Corsica. It's impossible for people like my father to understand 1918. In old Prussia, there was no defeat. Why should thousands of good German Protestants now be ruled by Poles, by irresponsible, drunk, Catholic Poles? Meanwhile, the government in Berlin is a conspiracy of socialists and Jews. In Prussia, God and the King are as one, the King looks after the nobility, and the nobility looks after the land—rotten land, nearly all of it, by the way—and the peasants. The church belongs to the King, and the count or the baron or the Freiherr appoints the parson and keeps him in order, and all of them, barring a few Poles and a few Jews, are God's chosen people. Like the Jews, the Prussians are waiting for the Messiah, especially now, in this God-forsaken republic. Perhaps the Kaiser will return. Last year there was a plebiscite in Prussia about repossessing the Hohenzollern estates. There were practically no votes in favour. And if the Kaiser goes on sitting in Holland, not bothering to raise a finger against the conspiracy of socialists and Jews, there'll have to be another Messiah. A great leader chosen by God for the German people."

"The Reformation, the bloody Reformation", Adam said. "It's all Luther's fault. Giving Protestants the idea they're God's chosen people. He stole it from the Old Testament. And he was an anti-Semite if ever there was one. It all goes back to him, all this German this, German that, world this, world that. Look at them, the philosophers who've killed God: Leibniz, Kant, Hegel, Feuerbach, Nietzsche— Protestants to a man."

"Adam!" Max said. "I thought Nietzsche could do no wrong."

"I used to think that. You know I did. But I read some Nietzsche again while I was doing *Hamlet*. I thought Hamlet was like Nietzsche— the most intelligent fellow alone in a world of lies. I also thought a dose of Nietzsche would be a healthy antidote to—never mind. But— have you read *The Antichrist*? Wait a minute."

Adam disappeared to his bedroom and came back with a thin book. "Listen to this. I never noticed it before." He found the right page. "He's writing about the Gospels. 'One is among Jews—the first consideration if one is not to lose the thread completely. This self-pretence of holiness'—on he goes, such hatred, it's horrible—'is not the chance product of some individual talent, some exceptional nature. *Race* is required for it. In Christianity, as the art of holy lying, the whole of Judaism attains its ultimate perfection.' There's lots more. I marked it." He turned over a couple of pages. "Yes, here. 'One would no more choose to associate with the first Christians than one would with Polish Jews—neither of them smells very pleasant.' You see? Christianity is to be despised because it's Jewish. That's completely different from Jews being despised because they're not Christians. I'm not sure it isn't even worse."

"It is, it is." Halpern jumped to his feet and went to stand in front of the empty fireplace. "And I will tell you why." His quiet, intense voice became quieter, more intense. "It's there in what you have read to us, Count, in the single word *race*. For nineteen hundred years, we have been hated for not being Christian. In Poland we are still hated for not being Christian and always will be because the Poles are at least real Christians. But in Germany now there is something new. Here we are hated for being biologically inferior. Darwin, not Luther, not even the Pope, is responsible for this. Not Darwin himself—he was a great biologist, I have no doubt about that—but a cheap, perverted understanding of Darwin. Perhaps you have to work in a medical school to have seen this. Treuburg, you must have met it. 'The survival of the fittest.' A terrible phrase. Terrible because of what it can so easily be made to justify. It is used to justify the worst excesses of capitalism, of course. But also the designation of the so-called Aryan race as the fittest. The Slavs are less fit. Take care, Zapolski."

At last, Max thought.

"You may be a nobleman in your own country. You may have an Aryan mother who wears a swastika in diamonds—I am sorry, I did not intend even to remember that—but take care, because you are

274

half-Slav. Less fit. As for the Jews, we are the least fit. We are not meant to survive. Science says so. Or science will very soon be made to say so. Experiments are planned to prove that Jews are absolutely inferior to Germans. This is the work of the devil—so I would say if I believed in the devil, or in a God who watches the good and evil of the human race, whether we believe in him or not, and always judges. Our grandfather the rabbi—do you remember, Anna?—when we were little children used to say, 'The court of the Lord is never closed, in the here or in the hereafter.' When I was a child, that frightened me. Now I find I almost wish it were true."

"But nearly all the great German scientists are Jews", Treuburg said. "What do these pseudoscientific Aryans find to say about them? Ehrlich, Haber, Einstein, Freud, Born: where would German science be without Jews?"

"It would be almost nowhere. You are right, of course. For the moment, the Aryan pseudoscientists, those who are determined to deliver proof of the biological inferiority of the Jews, are counting these men as Germans. I do not believe this will last. Once it is decided to count them as Jews, those who are alive will go abroad. The loss will be Germany's. They are famous, so it will not be difficult for them to go abroad. It will not be difficult for the rich. But for most of us it will not be difficult; it will be impossible."

He laughed a harsh laugh, with no smile in it.

"Famous Jews. Another paradox. How much harm have they done? To the rest of us, they have done nothing but harm. We were safer, less hated, when Jews were less noticed, when they were allowed to get on with being religious, to lend a little money, to keep a little shop, to do a little writing for the peasants, and nothing more. In Russia—did you know this?—most Jews had no surnames until very recently. There was a time when very few Jews anywhere had surnames, names like yours that lasted through the generations. They had a name, and another name, perhaps the father's, perhaps not. Religious names. When they died, they vanished like drops of rain on a lake. Except for the occasional celebrated rabbi, no one heard of Jews. They lived with God, and they knew they lived with God, so they didn't care for the notice of the world. Then German bureaucrats, in Berlin, in Vienna, and eventually even in Petersburg, put them on lists, and found or invented surnames for them, so that they could be proper citizens of the empires, but above all so that they could be conscripted, made to carry guns and to kill for the Emperors. With surnames, a few of them became famous. Heinrich Heine, Karl Marx, Fritz Haber, Albert Einstein, Sigmund Freud, Theodor Herzl, Gustav Mahler: none of those first names is a Jewish name. Fritz! You know what Frederick the Great thought of the Jews. Are these people Jews, or are they famous? Are they Germans to be admired, or Jews to be despised? The question is becoming acute. I am glad we are, Anna and I, only Polish Jews. There is no doubt about us. Everyone knows we are to be despised. We do not smell very pleasant."

Halpern went to the open window and looked out. The midsummer evening sky was dark. The gas lamps in the city's streets, recently lit, gave the windless air a faint glow.

"That is why we shall return to Poland. We cannot stay in Germany, not for very long. We shall return to Vilna, wherever Vilna is said to be by then—Poland, or Lithuania, or Russia. The Jews in Vilna have suffered a good deal from the Poles, and from the Russians above all. They will suffer, I have no doubt, if the city is ever in Lithuania, from the Lithuanians. But everyone accepts that Vilna is also a Jewish city. There will always be patients for a competent Jewish surgeon in Vilna."

He turned back from the window towards the room.

Grandpapa's sitting room now felt like a classroom, with the teacher— the rabbi, Max thought, looking at Dr Halpern with his beard, his glowing eyes, his right hand over his heart as if to keep it from beating too loudly—holding the concentrated attention of his students, three of them, waiting for his next words. Max looked at Anna. It was impossible to tell whether she was listening, whether she was proud of her brother, or whether she wished she were somewhere else.

Adam got up. "More beer, anyone?" Treuburg shook his head. Max said, "No, thanks" very quietly. Halpern didn't notice the question. Adam poured himself more beer and lit a cigarette.

Halpern had returned to his place in front of the empty fireplace. He was looking down at Anna as if she were a precious child to be saved from illness or danger. As she was. Her head was still bent over her empty cup. Max took it from her and put it on the floor beside his chair, but she didn't look at him, or at her brother.

"You mentioned Herzl", Adam said. "Do you think of Palestine, perhaps, one day, for you and your sister?"

Anna looked up at Adam, astonishment on her face.

"You mean after our father has died? For a time when I was a student, yes, I thought of Palestine. As, before that, I thought of the revolution. We talked, we argued, about both, without end. But the more I have learnt about Palestine, the less I consider going there myself or hoping Anna might go there. We might, perhaps, be allowed by the British to go there because I am a doctor and because Anna will soon be qualified as a teacher. But there, already, you see one of the problems. The poor, the sick, the old—they are not permitted to go to Palestine. I do not wish to live in a place where only the young and fit and prosperous are permitted: that is not Jewish. It is not human. But even if the British allowed Palestine to help the helpless, to rescue the rejected from everywhere in Poland, I would be doubtful, even afraid, of what would become of this escape into an unknown future."

"Wouldn't it be a good thing for the Jews at last to have their own country?" Treuburg said. "Not to be always treated as foreigners in the countries of other nations?"

"I am a stranger in the earth", Adam said. "A pilgrim on the face of the land. A foreigner in a city not my own. Saint Augustine."

"But that is exactly the point, Zapolski. I am surprised you should understand. What Treuburg says sounds very fine, an ideal solution to what everyone in Germany calls the 'Jewish question', the 'Jewish problem'. Freedom. Independence. A country for the Jews. One day, perhaps, when the British decide the Jews are sufficiently grown up to govern Palestine for themselves. But here we have all three of the reasons for doubt, even for fear, about Zionism, as they insist on calling it although it has nothing to do with the Messiah's coming in Jerusalem at the end of time. Nothing at all, because it is not religious. Herzl was a Viennese Jew, assimilated, secular. A nationalist in the Habsburg empire, as if he had been a Hungarian, a Czech, a Romanian. His hero was Bismarck. He was more a German than a Jew, like the scientists. He knew very little about real Jews. He expected the language of Palestine to be German."

"You mentioned three reasons to doubt or fear Zionism. What are they?" Max said.

"The first is Zapolski's, the religious reason. The strength of the Jews for two thousand years has been strength of the soul, not of the state, not of power in the world, not of armies and weapons. We have lived here and there, everywhere detached a little, because, as I said, we have lived with God. I became a Zionist, as earlier I had become

277

a Communist, because I understood that there is no soul. No God. Of course, the rabbis in Poland are horrified by Zionism. They think it means the end of Jewish life. And of course the Zionists think the rabbis in Poland are ludicrous, almost a joke. They do not understand German. They are relics from a superstitious past that must be left behind. They and their people. I found I could not despise so many faithful souls."

"So religion", Adam said, "is still good for people not clever enough to understand that there is no God. You sound like Voltaire, Dr Halpern."

"Why not?"

"Why not indeed", Treuburg said. "Go on, please."

"Thank you. The second reason for fear is not spoken about among Zionists. Who encouraged Herzl? Who wanted the Jews to go to Palestine? Who thought there was a Jewish problem for which Palestine was the solution? The British government. The tsarist government. The Kaiser. Anti-Semites in France and other countries. The motive of all of them, although it is not admitted, is to get rid of the Jews. Send them to a desert where no one else wants to live, or so they say, and Europe can forget about them. How peaceful. And how soothing to the conscience.

"The third reason is the most difficult to talk about and is even difficult to understand completely. It is connected, I think, to the pseudoscience I was talking about earlier. If we become Zionists, if we replace religion, which has always identified us to ourselves, with nationalism, then we say to these bad Darwinian biologists, and to Nietzsche too, Yes, we are a race, an alien race. We agree with you that whatever we do, whether we become Bolsheviks or Zionists, or pretend to be Germans, or Russians, or Englishmen or Frenchmen, or even Christians because we have converted, we are nevertheless an alien race. Is such agreement with the so-called Aryans good? Is it sensible? Is it even sane? Is it not agreeing with our most cruel and most stupid enemies? And what of the Arabs who live in Palestine already? They are poor. People forget they are there. But there are hundreds of thousands of them. We must be careful that we do not end by regarding them as another alien race, inferior even to the Jews."

"Yasha," Anna suddenly said, altogether changing the quality of attention in the room, "are you saying that a Jew who becomes a Christian is no longer a Jew?"

"Yes. No." He smiled. He had not smiled all evening. "Is not that a perfect Jewish reply? The rabbis would say yes. The Aryan scientists would say no. I am inclined, if I have to choose, to agree with the rabbis."

Max thought of Dr Mendel, who had told him years ago that you couldn't choose to be a Jew. Did he agree with the pseudoscientists Halpern was talking about, with the swastika-daubing brown-shirted Nazi marchers, with Frau Gärtner's son? He thought of Grandpapa.

"Dr Halpern," Max said, "is it possible for a person who has been baptized a Christian but who doesn't go to church or believe in Christianity to become a Jew? If the person has some Jewish ancestors?"

Halpern looked at him, clearly surprised. "Why, now, with Jews so hard-pressed everywhere, would anyone wish to do such a thing? Ah ..." His glance rested for a second on Anna's bent head. "That is a question for the rabbis."

He knows, Max thought. He has guessed. Everything.

"I understand", Adam said, "why a Christian who becomes a Jew is no longer a Christian. He has changed his belief. For him, Jesus has become only a teacher, a good man who died. But I don't understand why a Jew who becomes a Christian is no longer a Jew. Perhaps in the past, when Christians were Christians, and Jews were defined precisely by not being Christian, this was easier to understand. But now, when many educated people called Christian, baptized as Christian, aren't actually Christian at all—and come to that, most educated Jews, at least in Germany, aren't religious either—a decision to become a Christian is one of two things. It's only a formality perhaps helpful towards a job or a position in society, in which case it can't make any difference. Or it's religious decision, in which case it's *adding* something, adding the belief that Jesus was—is—the Son of God, as the first Christians, all Jews, had to add belief in Jesus as the Messiah."

"No", Halpern said. "You are wrong, Count. From the Christian point of view, you may be right. From the Jewish point of view, you are wrong. To believe that Jesus was the Messiah is to take away the hope that the Messiah will come. That is the hope of religious Jews always. It is also to take away the detail of Jewish life, of what happens, of what people do, in a Jewish home every year, every Sabbath, every day. That is a lot to lose."

"Do you believe that the Messiah will come?"

"I do not. I am not religious. Do you believe that the Messiah has come?"

"No, I don't. I'm not religious."

"Then what's the difference between you?" Max said. "Both of you were brought up with a lot of stuff from the past, things you were told, things you did. Both of you are very well educated, very clever. Both of you have decided that the things you were told aren't true, that the things you did have no meaning. For you. But . . ."

"But?" Halpern said.

"I was brought up with much less, much less religion than either of you, and less than Treuburg too. I've been listening very carefully this evening, and I've learnt a lot, especially from you, Halpern. But I think both of you, you and Adam, have only *decided* you are not religious. You don't *know* none of it's true—as Galileo *knew* that the earth goes round the sun. And actually, I think both of you somewhere would like religion to be true, would like God to be there after all. And"—something else struck Max so forcibly that he brought both hands down flat on his knees—"suppose Christ does come at the end of time, for the first time for the Jews, for the second time for Christians. Isn't that possible?"

Anna suddenly said, "I think Max is right about you wanting religion to be true, Yasha. And perhaps"—she hesitated—"perhaps the count also."

"No. Absolutely not", Adam said. "I'm a rationalist, a humanist. I think you are too, Halpern. We proceed by using our brains. There's nothing else that thinks except human beings. The appalling mess the human race has so far made it's made because people haven't thought hard enough, clearly enough, because they are misled by emotion, tradition, prejudice, greed, jealousy. If they would clear their heads of rubbish and behave rationally, justly, life would be a great deal better for everyone."

"Aristotle", Max said. "John Stuart Mill. But they don't behave rationally, do they? Perhaps they can't."

"They could if they wanted to", Halpern said. "But they do not want to because they do not know enough. They have not been sufficiently taught. Education must be the way forward."

"It doesn't work", Max said. He was sure that Adam and Halpern were wrong, though he wasn't sure why. He blundered on. "It doesn't follow. Are the best-educated people the best people? Are they the most just, the most unselfish, the least prejudiced? I don't think they are, any more than the most-religious people are the best people. They can be, of course, but in either case it doesn't *follow*. I've known four good people—old enough for it to be sensible to call them good. With people of our age, you can't tell, can you? Two well-educated Jews, one with some religion, the other, baptized, with none. Two religious Catholics, one very well educated. The other can hardly read and write. What *follows* from that? Nothing. Or what follows is that it's something else that will make life less terrible—not education on its own, and not necessarily religion either."

"I'm sorry", Treuburg said, getting to his feet from the armchair in which he had been almost lying, his long legs stretched towards the fireplace where Halpern still stood. "But it's late. I have to be in the hospital at six in the morning. We're not going to finish the Mozart tonight, are we? Or settle the meaning of life. Why are we here? Nobody knows. Nobody *knows*. Anyway, I'm going to bed. I'm sorry, Halpern, Miss Halpern, but I'm three-quarters asleep."

"Of course", Halpern said. "We also must go. I also have to be early in the hospital. Tomorrow is not one of Professor Grossmann's days for visiting the post-operative patients. It has been a most interesting evening, Hofmannswaldau, and we thank you, and Treuburg and Count Zapolski too, naturally, for welcoming us and for the music, and for—I apologize again if I have spoken too much."

"Not at all", Adam said, getting up. "You talk, if I may say so, very well. It's been a good evening. You look sleepy, too, Miss Halpern. Here."

To Max's astonishment, Adam stretched out his hand to Anna and pulled her gently out of the sofa. Then he saw that he had been able to do it because her hand meant nothing to him.

"Thank you, Count", she said, and blushed again.

"Adam. You'll have to call me Adam, now that we've played music together."

Max saw that it was impossible for her to answer.

After they had gone and Treuburg had gone to bed, Max and Adam tidied up the music and the music stands and collected the beer mugs and coffee cups.

In the kitchen, drying the mugs and cups that Adam had washed, Max said, "She's right, isn't she?"

"Right about what?"

"You—or some part of you buried deep inside you—would like religion to be true."

"It wasn't Anna who said that. It was you."

"Was it? She picks things up. She's a bright girl."

"You need to go carefully there. I told you. He's very protective of her."

"Of course he is. Wouldn't you be? But I do go carefully. Very carefully. And in any case ..."

"In any case what?"

"Nothing. Just my imagination."

"He was very hard on her, I thought, when she missed a couple of entries. She was sight-reading, and doing very well."

"He's a perfectionist. For her as well as for himself. Entirely under-standable in the circumstances. What do you think of them, really?"

"She's a lovely girl. Very young. Very vulnerable. He's impressive. Clever. Thoughtful. He's also bitter, but that's hardly surprising. He seems to have fallen for several schemes for a better world—the Bund, Zionism—and come out the other side pinning his hopes on nothing but better education. Like the Jews of a hundred years ago."

"Well, it's what he's had himself, a good education. And it's always possible for doctors to see a purpose, a real use for what they've learned. Look at Treuburg. No doubts there. Sometimes I wish I'd—"

"No, Max, you don't. All that chemistry and biology for years and years, and following a monster like Grossmann round the wards, 'yes sir', 'no sir', 'I'm sure you're right sir'."

"Very few doctors are like Grossmann."

"I know. But think of how much more interesting the actual stuff we learn is. It's all old Fischer's fault, isn't it, for deflecting you from your grandfather's example? He's got a lot to answer for."

"Your Hamlet."

"Yes."

"And what was it that you thought Nietzsche would be a healthy antidote to?"

"Oh, a lot of nonsense, I expect."

Once more, six days later, the Halperns came to play the Mozart quin-tet. This time they played the whole work straight through. Anna made no obvious mistakes. Halpern led the minuet at an elegant, restrained tempo that Max knew Dr Mendel would have approved of, and played his trio—a short section of the movement with no clarinet part—with the held-back passion that always marked his playing. The last movement swung along, fast but not difficult except for some swapping of rapid passage work between Halpern and Adam. At the end, they all exchanged smiles of pleasure and, in Anna's case, Max thought, relief.

Over their coffee they said very little, as if the talk of the week before had built not bridges but walls between them. They exchanged information about their summer plans. The Halperns were visiting their father in Vilna when Halpern, in August, was to have two weeks' leave from the hospital. Treuburg was staying in Breslau. He had an important examination in September. Adam and Max were setting off for Italy the following week. When Adam said this, Anna looked as if she might cry.

"So", Halpern said. "I hope we shall play again in September. But nothing is certain."

At this, Anna's eyes did fill with tears. No one noticed except Max. He smiled at her.

"We'll all be back, I'm sure", he said. "We've got work to do, after all."

She shook the tears away.

"Shall we play the quintet once more?" Adam said. "To last us through the summer?"

"Why not?" Halpern said. "It is a great pleasure, to make such music."

They played it again, better than before, Adam's melody in the slow movement so beautiful that Max thought Anna might fail to keep playing. Not at all: she looked steady, concentrated, entirely calm when he shot her a sideways glance.

"Thank you", Adam said after a short silence. "Perhaps we should offer it to the Century Hall. No, of course not; don't worry"—he had caught the appalled expression on Anna's face—"it was only a joke. Much better to play just for ourselves. Perhaps after the summer, we might try the Brahms. More-difficult notes, but easier to play."

"I know exactly what you mean", Halpern said. "Brahms, the untidy heart. More allowance for the amateur player."

"There", Max said, generally but for Anna. "There's something to look forward to."

And she smiled at him almost, but not quite, as if Adam's Hamlet had never happened.

Chapter 10

A little over a week later, Max and Adam, on the wagon-lit train from Vienna, woke up as a steward came into their sleeping car with two cups of coffee on a tray, a polite "Good morning, gentlemen", and the information that they would be in Venice in half an hour.

From that moment on, a magic—as of the summer of 1922 at Waldau—lit Max's soul for three weeks so that later, while he found it difficult to remember more than two or three actual days, or actual conversations, he remembered his time in Venice with Adam as one of the great blessings of his life.

Countess Zapolska and her new friend were staying on the Lido in the Grand Hotel des Bains.

"Death in Venice", Adam said, telling Max this on the train.

"What? Oh, the story."

Adam had lent the book to him to read when they were still at the Gymnasium. Max had disliked it very much, finding Aschenbach's obsession with the beautiful Polish boy embarrassing, and the creeping up of the cholera epidemic too clever a parallel. He had forgotten all about it till this moment.

"Tacky story", he said. "Very . . . grandly written, but, I don't know, unhealthy?"

"I thought it was wonderful then. But you're quite right. 'Unhealthy' is the word. But that was the whole point of Mann. He thought the world was mortally sick. It was just before the war. Perhaps he was right. *La grande décadence*. But don't worry. There hasn't really been cholera in Venice for years and years. And I've no doubt my mother stays at that hotel only because it's the most famous and the most comfortable."

Max could hardly believe that the journey on the little steamer from the station to the Lido in the early morning was real. He stood with Adam at the front of the boat. It zigzagged slowly from one side of the long curving sweep of the Grand Canal to the other, stopping often like a tram. People carrying briefcases or shopping bags got off, got on, bought tickets. In the softly gleaming light, not yet hot, the line of palaces on either side of the wide canal, each one different, carved, grey and pink and creamy, with their striped mooring posts for gondolas like sticks of sugar in front of them, looked insubstantial, conjured up, like something in a dream or a theatre. Narrow canals opened on either side, and wound away between tall buildings, mysterious, enticing, the first bridge over each of them, steep, carved, white, some way back from the Grand Canal because the palaces were all right on the water, making it impossible to walk beside the Grand Canal. As soon as people got off the boat, they disappeared into the city. He and Adam would be able to explore the narrow canals, the streets, the bridges behind the palaces: Max was lightheaded, almost dizzy. The boats on the Grand Canal, carrying supplies for the city—food, milk, crates of wine, newspapers in tied batches, fetching rubbish, delivering post, seemed more substantial than any of the buildings. Max saw go by, on boats with a puttering motor or rowed by a single oarsman standing at the back and bending to his giant oar, baskets and crates of vegetables and fruit, some kinds he had never seen before and had no idea of the names of, boxes of tiny silver fish smaller than anything ever eaten at home, and other boxes of bigger fish, some full of wriggling crabs.

An astonishing bridge appeared, low-arched with buildings on it and carving all its length.

"The Rialto Bridge", Adam said. "The market's along there on the right."

Their steamer chugged under the bridge, and the palaces became even grander and stranger. Round a further bend in the canal, a high wooden bridge was crowded with people walking to work. Then the canal opened out, with a large white-domed church on the right, steps, and a flat marble pavement with more people walking. After a few minutes and another two stops, a much wider stretch of water appeared.

"There's the Doges' Palace", Adam said. "A bit like a cake, don't you think? And the tower is the campanile of Saint Mark's. The church—you can only see the side of it from here—is more like a crab than a cake. You'll see."

The words went by, and Max felt his eyes almost aching with what they were seeing.

Then, leaving the city behind, they crossed a stretch of actual sea—a little disappointing because grey-green and obviously shallow—and arrived at the long, low Lido island with its palm trees, white hotels and striped awnings against the glare off the water.

The countess's new friend turned out to be a widower, a Transylvanian baron with a duelling scar and white hair, nearly old enough to be her father. ("Quite suitable, for once. Less embarrassing than usual, anyway", Adam said. "But I bet he gave her the swastika.") His only son had been killed in the war, and he had abandoned his estates in despair, finding them assigned to Romania rather than Hungary in the peace treaty. He was living in Vienna on the proceeds of selling his furniture and pictures, hoping that soon the postwar world would vanish and everything would return to normal. He was addicted to bridge, a fashionable English game; Adam's mother had applied herself, quite hard given her weak powers of concentration, to learning how to play it, and the pair of them, evening after evening at the Hotel des Bains, played cards with an English couple, two middle-aged German sisters, and an elderly American with a handsome twenty-five-year-old, "my nephew", in tow. What little conversation was necessary took place in a mixture of basic German and basic English.

"How can he stand the boredom?" Adam said. "At least Tadeusz played on the beach and didn't have to sit still for hours at a card table with a bunch of old people."

"Perhaps he really is his nephew?"

"Max!"

"Oh, I expect you're right."

"Haven't you heard of the collapse of morals since the war? But I'm all in favour of this terrible game. So good for my mother. Even some skill involved, one gathers, and it's much cheaper than roulette."

The German ladies and the Americans set off every morning on the steamer for the city with guidebooks, maps, and straw hats, the young man looking even sulkier than he had at the bridge table the evening before. The countess and her friend, and the English couple, stayed on the beach belonging to the hotel, lay on striped beach chairs under huge parasols, were brought iced tea and cocktails by waiters in striped waistcoats, and didn't read the books beside them. Sometimes the countess and the baron, with much preparation and with the countess in elegant clothes and a new wide hat each time, went to Venice in the hotel launch to have lunch in a smart restaurant, then came straight back to the Lido.

"We've seen Venice. And it's too hot for walking at this time of year, all those bridges, up and down, up and down, and the canals do smell in the heat. But you boys must do whatever you like."

After their first day, lazing on the beach, swimming and saying scarcely a word to each other, they did.

Every morning—they always caught a later boat than the bridge players—Adam had a plan. He had been to Venice twice before, but his plans were the result not only of what he remembered but also of a good deal of work with Baedeker, with Ruskin in a German translation (which he had found, left by some former friend, in his mother's house in Vienna), and with an Italian book on Venetian painting that he had borrowed from the hotel.

"There's so much in this city. It's important not to miss the real masterpieces. We may never be here again."

A few paintings Max remembered always. Tintoretto's enormous Crucifixion, in the Scuola di San Rocco, was so shocking, so compelling in its scale and immediacy, so close, so alive, so much an execution with its ladder and ropes and nails, that looking at it was almost to be present on Good Friday. On the same morning, because it was nearby in a big, light church, they saw Titian's altarpiece of the Virgin in a scarlet dress and a blue cloak being whirled to heaven on a cloud over the heads and rough, outstretched arms of the disciples in the shadow of the cloud.

"Look at that", Adam said, after a long few minutes in front of this painting. "How could any intelligent person ever have believed in that? It's wonderful, all the same."

"How do you mean, believed in it? What's meant to be happening?"

"Poor old Max, what a Protestant you are. It's called the Assumption. It's when Mary was taken, body and soul, straight to heaven. Look—she's alive. You can see. It's no more unbelievable than the Resurrection, I suppose. If you can believe that, you can believe anything."

"Can you? Believe in the Resurrection?"

"No, of course not. You know perfectly well I can't. Anyway, I don't."

"But did you ever, when you were a child?"

"When I was a child, yes, I did. But children believe what they're told. And some of the people who told me were not at all stupid, not at all simple-minded. And then there's old Fischer. One of your four really good people, the other night, I noticed. But I'm not a child any more, and now I can't—don't—believe in any of it. No. Certainly not."

A few mornings later, they went to the Accademia and stood for just as long in front of another Titian painting, a huge canvas still on the wall for which he painted it. A long flight of high stairs leading to the great door of a temple so big that most of it was out of sight. A crowd of people at the bottom of the stairs. At the top a tall priest with a white beard, a tall hat, and elaborate vestments, with another priest behind him, and a third behind them higher still and with a walking stick coming down more stairs to the door. Halfway up the staircase, alone and very small, a little girl, blue dress, in gold light. The crowd of watching people was as close, as vivid, as had been the stricken people watching the crucifixion. An old woman sitting by her basket of eggs could have come straight from the Rialto market. Max had no idea what the subject of the picture could be. The Accademia wasn't a church and clearly never had been. The tall priest was probably a Jewish high priest. He waited for Adam to explain, knowing he would.

"Now that", Adam said, "anyone could believe."

"What do you mean? What are they going to do to her, the little girl?"

"It's not what they're going to do. Far from it. It's what's going to happen to her. It's Mary again, at the other end of her life, the beginning. *The Presentation of the Virgin*, it's called. There's another great big painting of it, by Tintoretto, somewhere else in Venice, in a church, I can't remember where."

They looked at the painting for more time, in more silence. Some other people came, looked at it briefly, and went away.

"What did you mean, anyone could believe this? Believe what?"

"That she's already been chosen by God. Without her, there's no Incarnation, no revelation of the Trinity to the world, no sacrifice on the cross, no Resurrection, no Christianity. It's just as we were saying the other night, with Halpern. The adding of all that to Jewish belief, through God's choice of this Jewish child. This picture is of the very beginning of the new story."

"A story you think is only a story."

"And therefore not true. That's right. A story. Not exactly a lie but a kind of collective make-believe sustained by people who needed it, complicated it, and told it to other people down the centuries to cheer them up, to persuade them to behave better, to console them, to make them brave. But of course not true."

"So all these paintings"—Max waved an arm in the general direction of the museum rooms they had already walked through, full of Annunciations, Nativities, Crucifixions, Pietas—"all these churches, what they're for, what they mean or say they mean, are all false, well, perhaps not exactly false, but part of the making up of a story that's no more true than a folk tale, a fairy tale, like the stories in Grimm?"

"That's right."

Adam looked round the room, anguish of some kind in his eyes. Then he laughed.

"I know what it is. You're being seduced by a Catholic place, a Catholic atmosphere. You've never seen it before. Half the people in Breslau are Catholics, you know. Plenty of them are Germans, as well as the Poles. But they're so careful not to be noticed, because of Bismarck, that they're actually unnoticeable. Here ... well ... it's quite different, obviously. Be careful. Don't get carried away by a lot of beautiful churches, a lot of pictures. They're only buildings, only pictures."

"Is that what you really think? Like Nietzsche. If God is dead, he's never been alive. So all this, all these beautiful things, are just that, hundreds of years of clever painters and sculptors and architects making *things*, just pigment and canvas and egg white or marble and brick for us to look at and say, 'How lovely'. I don't think I believe that's all it is. Do you, really?"

"Oh, I'm immune. Inoculated when young. A little dose of small-pox so you don't catch it later. Come on. Lunch."

They must have spent an entire morning in Saint Mark's, and another in the Doges' Palace. Max remembered the darkness in Saint Mark's, the glimmer of the dark gold of mosaics almost impossible to see on windowless walls, the unevenness of the dark mosaics underfoot, the flickering candles lighting the feet of mosaic saints and the silver frames of icons, the smell of the incense of centuries, and the suddenly lucid enamels of the *pala d'oro* behind the high altar, in electric light switched on by a young man in uniform, with medals, who had to be tipped first.

Of the Doges' Palace he remembered only the heavy intimidating grandeur, the vast empty halls of a power silenced and gone, the pictures on every wall to impress every official—he thought of his ambassadors being dispatched all over Europe and received back with their reports—and every visitor with the glory of Venice.

One evening almost at the end of their stay they were standing together, as they did every day, on the steamer returning to the Lido. Each day, Max felt more melancholy as they went back to the hotel. So little time left. Less and less by a greater proportion each day, making each hour, each minute more painful to lose. Getting old must be like this.

That day, they had stayed for a longer time than usual at a café table in the Piazza, listening to the café band playing tunes from Verdi operas and watching the activity in the great square: the pigeons, the postcard sellers, and the sellers of corn for feeding the pigeons.

On the boat, Adam looked at his watch. "Just time to change for dinner", he said. "We're lucky dinner's so good. But we have to be civil to the baron and my mother."

"We certainly do. I'm more grateful than—"

"I have a plan", Adam said. "Tomorrow we leave Venice for a day and go to Ravenna."

"Ravenna? Where is it? What is it?"

"Ah. While you've been fussing over your ambassadors, I've been doing some prep. Ravenna was once the capital of the western Roman empire."

"What! I've never even heard of it."

"Oh, no one has. It's lost in the gap between ancient and modern history. Too late for old Fischer. Too early for that deeply boring man whose name I've forgotten who thought the history of Germany and therefore the history of everything began with Charlemagne. We're going there to have a look. It's not far, a couple of hours in the train, south of here, in the marshes. There are churches much older than Saint Mark's."

"Max and I are going to Ravenna tomorrow", he said to his mother at dinner. "We'll be back in the evening."

"I can't understand why you boys are so restless. I would have thought the beach would have kept you entertained, and the young people in Venice, in the hotels, the cafés in the Piazza ... so good for you both to meet young people less *démodés* than the university students in Breslau. I'll never forget—Istvan"—she turned to her baron—"you wouldn't have believed it, the scruffiness of the students—not Max, naturally—at Adam's play. And the producer! Taking a curtain call in shirtsleeves, without a tie! Where is Ravenna, Adam?"

"Not far. Down the coast."

"Ah, the coast! Is it the latest place for the young? Better swimming than the Lido?"

"It used to be on the sea, but it's silted up."

"Oh well, you must please yourselves, of course."

"You will at least", the baron said, "see something of Italy—Venice is hardly Italy—the new Italy of Signor Mussolini. The Italians are very fortunate."

From the windows of their early train, they saw little to suggest the Fascist good fortune of the Italians. There were national flags with laurel wreaths in the stations of the two cities, Padua and Ferrara, where the train stopped, and here and there a flag or a poster of Mussolini's large smiling, unreliable face in a village halt the train rattled through. But the country all the way was dreary, fields of maize, drainage ditches green with the scum of summer, rice growing in the wet flats towards the sea, almost no trees, and the farmhouses poor, with peeling stucco walls. Max felt miserable to have left behind the life and colour and now-familiar sounds of the Grand Canal on another early morning, to have left Venice at all when they had only two days remaining before they had to leave, Max to return to Breslau to earn some money looking after Dr Mendel's pupils, and Adam to go to Cracow to do, at last, some serious work on his thesis in the Polish state archives. So, there was today and tomorrow, and the next day there would be the night train to Vienna where they had to separate, for more than a month, until the university term began. Max looked across the carriage. Adam was sitting in the corner opposite, head back, eyes shut, but clearly not asleep. He opened his eyes.

"What's the matter?"

"Nothing. I wish we'd stayed in Venice. There's so little time left."

"It'll be worth coming. I promise."

The streets of Ravenna, with taxis, horses and carts, buses, motor cars, and a good deal of shouting and hooting, were another shock after Venice, where there was so little other noise that the ear got used to the sound of ordinary conversation, footsteps on bridges, and the occasional call of a gondolier rounding the corner of a canal. But after they crossed the busy road by the station and walked for five minutes in quieter streets—Adam, of course, had a map—they found themselves in front of a brick church with a tall, round brick campanile and a columned portico. "This is our first church", Adam said. Max thought it didn't look very interesting but said nothing. Adam put a coin in the outstretched hand of a blind beggar under the portico and pushed open the door. A grand, empty, pillared space stopped them inside the door: light pouring over white marble columns, a shining, empty white marble floor, and lines and lines of mosaic figures above the columns. White and gold figures, the mosaic sky gold against which they stood or walked, the ground at their feet emerald green with flowers of red, white, and gold: the processions of figures along the walls and the brilliance of the colours were so cheering it was impossible not to smile.

"They look as if they were done yesterday", Max said. "So clear and calm. The saints in heaven."

"Early in the sixth century. Theodoric the Ostrogoth. A barbarian warlord from Prussia, more or less. Trying to join in. Succeeding."

"Join in what?"

"Civilization. Christianity. The lot. *Rex Italiae*, he called himself."

"Like Mussolini."

"Exactly. Everyone, everywhere, always wants to be Roman. Caesar. The Kaiser. The Tsar. Even America has a Capitol Hill and a Senate."

They walked slowly up the church, keeping pace, as it were, with the mosaic figures, women on the left, men on the right as they walked down again, looking all the time, to the door.

"Virgins and martyrs", Adam said. "Those were the days. When it was clear how to live."

"You don't mean that."

"Don't I?"

They walked through the centre of Ravenna. In a pretty piazza that reminded Max of Venice ("No wonder. Venice ran this town for a bit") they sat for twenty minutes at a café table. They sipped little cups of very strong coffee and glasses of water. Adam was silent.

"What is it?"

"We take ourselves too seriously in the twentieth century. Why do we think we're right and everyone else has always been wrong? That would only be justified if things were getting better and better."

"They are, aren't they? Railways, the telephone, medicine, chemistry, electricity . . ."

"Are they? I'll grant you medicine. But people? Look at the war. It was worse by far than any war has ever been, and worse because of all the science. Nitro-glycerine. Poison gas. Submarines. Come on." He signalled to the waiter. "We're going to the church of San Vitale. Whoever he was."

From the outside, the church was a plain octagon, brown, made of thin bricks ("Roman, those bricks") with plain round-arched windows and a smaller octagon with more windows above, and terra-cotta tiles on all the roofs. A white path led to the door, which was opened for them by a black-suited old man who put his finger to his lips and pointed to where they should stand, at the back of a small, standing congregation of perhaps fifty or sixty people with a large space behind them. They were in dark clothes. A service had clearly just begun. Three priests in black and gold vestments and four altar boys were bowing at the altar. Many candles had been lit. A choir began to sing in Latin.

Max took all this in very quickly and then saw the coffin, in the centre of the church below the altar, black-draped, with four tall candles in silver candlesticks at its corners.

He whispered to Adam, "Should we leave?"

Adam shook his head. "Dante's funeral", he whispered. "Perfectly correct to stay."

The choir stopped singing. There were prayers and responses at the altar, and incense. The oldest priest walked back and forth in front of the altar with the incense, swinging it in a silver container on a chain, then handed it to one of the boys, who took it, bowed, and stood, swinging it gently. With a rush of tears to the back of his throat Max remembered the Requiems he had been to as a child with Emilia—for Freddy in 1914 and for his father five years later. He suddenly wished Anna were beside him, who had never been to a Mass, and who, he guessed—but guessed with a kind of certainty—would have loved the candles and the incense and the mysterious presence of God. But Anna was hundreds of miles away in cold and dangerous Vilna and, instead, beside him was Adam, who knew all this well and thought it nonsense. Didn't he? He glanced sideways at him, as they stood together, their straw hats in their hands.

Adam was looking straight at the altar, a set, concentrated expression in his eyes, a stillness in his face that was like—perhaps that *was*—the stillness of Hamlet in the last act before he turned to face the court.

Was Anna, far away in her father's house, thinking of Adam at that moment, or of him? He pulled himself together. Why should she be thinking of either of them? He tried to imagine her father's house and the streets of Vilna, but he had no idea what they looked like. The people in front of him were making a quiet gesture he didn't recognize, crossing the forehead, mouth, and breast lightly with the thumb of the right hand. The priest began to intone from his position at the altar. Max caught some words:

"Amen, amen, dico vobis, quia venit hora, et nunc est, quando mortui audient vocem Filii Dei: et qui audierint, vivent." Max looked at Adam. His eyes were shut.

Then, as the congregation sat, and he and Adam, without chairs, continued to stand behind them, he stopped trying to understand the Italian in which the priest was now talking about the dead man, an honoured husband, father, and grandfather. Etcetera. He looked about him and realized that he was standing in the most intricately beautiful church he had ever seen. It was like being inside a box lined with silk and enamels of green, white, scarlet, and gold. Grey and white marble columns and marble panels with watery swirls as of silk in the marble and above them mysterious arches and everywhere mosaic patterns and pictures: he couldn't see far enough forward to make out the bigger mosaic pictures. Perhaps later, when the funeral was over.

When the congregation knelt, so did he and Adam, on the marble floor. The Mass went on, with the bells Max vaguely remembered from the Waldau church, and the priest with his back to them raising at the altar first a round flat disc, the bread, and then a silver chalice, the wine. Adam's concentration was so intense that even to glance at him seemed like an intrusion.

At the end of the Mass, the priests came down to the coffin with the incense, more candles, and a heavy silver cross. As six men shouldered the coffin and carried it through the people, followed by altar boys, candles, priests, and then the mourners, the choir sang a chant that began with the words "Libera me, Domine, de morte aeterna." Adam turned towards the procession. So did Max. As the coffin passed them, Adam crossed himself slowly and deliberately. Hamlet.

When the church was empty except for the old man who had let them in, now snuffing candles and straightening chairs, Max turned to Adam to suggest looking at the mosaics properly, but he was not to be spoken to. Adam went and stood in the shadows beyond the marble columns and leant his back against a marble panel. So, alone, Max wandered about the church and looked at the birds and flowers and patterns and people in the mosaics. He didn't need Adam to tell him what was going on in most of them: the prophets and evangelists had their names in Latin, easy to read. So did Abel, dressed in skins, and Melchisedech, dressed as a priest, on either side of an altar, offering a lamb and a round, flat patterned loaf respectively, their hands lifted towards God exactly as the priest's had been in the Mass just finished. In the apse at the end of the church, behind the altar, two grand mosaic processions, one with a King or an Emperor and his court, Romans in robes, and one with a Queen, crowned and jewelled, and her ladies, moved as if towards each other and towards Max, standing and looking up. Above them was a youthful Christ, throned on a blue round world with a scroll in his hand, with angels beside him and two noble figures of men, one labelled 'San Vitale' and the other a Bishop carrying the very church in which Max was standing and looking.

"Justinian", Adam's voice said, very quietly. He was standing behind Max.

"What? I thought you—who?"

"Justinian. He of the Corpus Iuris Civilis we hear so much about. There he is." Adam, now beside him, pointed to the Emperor in the procession, carrying a golden bowl. "And that's his wife, Theodora. A formidable lady. A famous sinner in her youth. Later practically a saint."

Adam had returned, from wherever he had been.

"Weren't they in Constantinople?"

"Yes. They never came here. It's all assertion. Count Belisarius, Justinian's Moltke, conquered the Goths for him, for a bit. So this church is Justinian asserting imperial rule over Italy."

Max turned and looked back at the exquisite space and colours of the magical box that was the church.

"It didn't last. Naturally. Empires come and empires go. The Kings and the Kaisers disappear, as we know. Like the Habsburgs in Venice a hundred years ago. But the church ..."

"Yes, look." Max turned back and pointed up at the Bishop next to the angel, holding the brick church, his hands covered by his brown robe.

"We're there, in the mosaic, inside the church. You can't see us, but we're there."

Adam was in high spirits all the way back to Venice, but he said nothing about the Mass except to explain, when Max remembered to ask him, about Dante.

"He died in Ravenna. In exile from Florence. Not a bad place to be in exile. Perhaps his funeral was in San Vitale."

"When?"

"I don't know. Thirteen-something. More than halfway from Count Belisarius to now."

At dinner, the countess said, "Well, boys. How was your day at Ravenna? Did you meet anyone?"

"Not exactly", Adam said.

"Were you impressed by the new Italy?" the baron asked Max. ("He prefers you to me. Quite right. He thinks I'm frivolous. Claudius.")

"Ravenna seemed prosperous enough. But we were looking at old churches, very old."

"Theodoric the Ostrogoth", Adam said, "and Justinian the Emperor were running the Ravenna we saw. I don't think Signor Mussolini will make much impression on them."

The baron looked at Adam's mother with resignation.

After dinner they left, as they always did, the bridge party at two tables in one of the hotel's smaller grand rooms, and went outside. As they walked along the beach in the warm night, with the Adriatic lapping close to their feet and lights and dance music from the hotels spilling into the darkness, Adam said, "Tomorrow our last adventure. We take a boat across the lagoon to Torcello."

"Torcello's another island? I've seen it on the map."

"Torcello was once a city greater than Venice. It was where they first came, Romans in the collapsing empire, trying to escape the barbarians. This was fifty, a hundred years after San Vitale. There was chaos on the mainland. Venice overtook it centuries ago, so there's not much left to see, but Ruskin goes on about it. I think we should go there."

"You've never been there before?"

"Not glamorous enough for my mother. No one there who counts to notice her clothes."

The next day, in the middle of the morning, when the sun had lifted the last curtains of mist from the lagoon, the steamer dropped them at the little wooden dock labelled "Torcello" on a sun-cracked wooden board. No one else got off.

Adam put his hand on Max's arm for an instant. "Wait", he said. "For the silence." When the thump of the steamer's engine had faded completely into the green and blue indistinctness of the lagoon, there was, indeed, a silence different from anything possible in Venice, because it was a rural silence. There was a brick path beside a small canal like a country stream, a plain brick bridge over the canal, then another; grass, flimsy wattle fences, small fields with vegetables and vines, a few cows, the smell of hay, a faint scratching sound being made by an old man in a gleaming white shirt hoeing between rows of beans neatly grown on sticks, a butterfly, the unfamiliar call of a bird Max didn't recognize flying over their heads and out to the lagoon.

After a few minutes' walk they reached a wide grassy space, bounded by an ancient brick wall with an ancient fig tree growing against it. A great stone chair, the carving on it blunted by time and weather, stood on the grass, a throne waiting for an Emperor, or a god. There were four or five cottages, an old woman sitting at an open door making lace as gleaming white as the man's shirt, a couple of iron tables with iron chairs painted white outside another open door. A small boy, perhaps seven or eight years old, on a battered bicycle, head down, was bumping over the grass as fast as he could go, which was slowly.

"Good morning, signori", he said, skidding to a stop on the path in front of them. "Behold! The cathedral! The campanile! Santa Fosca!" For this self-evident information, since there, indeed, close by, were a large church, plain like a grey barn, a tall plain bell tower, and a smaller church with a dome, Adam gave him a couple of coins. He saluted and set off again on his bike.

The west door of the cathedral, its city, its Bishop, its people long since vanished, was open. They went inside. The silence changed, deepened to the silence of the ages. No one was there. In silvery grey light, dusty walls, cream and grey; ancient marble columns, pale green, grey, and white with white carved capitals; dusty mosaics; and marble pavement in patterns on the floor. The church seemed older than the jewel-bright churches in Ravenna, seemed to have risen of its own accord out of the island and the sea. In the nave were two or three untidy rows of narrow wooden chairs with old rush seats, a plain wooden kneeler folded down from the back of each. They walked together, as quietly as they could, stopping at the altar rail, a low marble wall, white, with thin columns and painted saints above the columns, and vines and peacocks carved in the marble, dividing the nave from the sanctuary. Max looked at Adam to see if he thought it all right to go through the opening in the centre. Adam nodded.

Under the altar was a heavy carved sarcophagus. "That's Roman", Adam said softly. "With relics of some saint. The Romans must have brought it with them." Behind the altar in the curved apse were another stone chair ("the seat of the Bishop; that's what a cathedral actually is") and a dusty stone bench round the curved back wall ("for his priests, like the apostles"). And there the apostles were a row of mosaic saints above the bench.

Max pointed upwards. "Look."

Still and quiet, above the heads of the apostles, was a mosaic Virgin and Child, her eyes looking down at them. Pleading, Max thought, and reproachful. Don't harm my child. You will.

"There. You see", Adam said.

They looked at her for a long time and then walked slowly back down the church towards the sunlight outside the open door. Covering the west wall, difficult to see because of the bright rectangle of the doorway, was a large, lurid mosaic of the Last Judgement, with a Crucifixion right at the top.

"That's pretty horrible", Max said, looking at the souls of the damned, nearest to him and Adam. "It's good that you can't see her and them at the same time." He turned back to look at the Virgin once more, her eyes, far away now, still on him.

"Ah. You have to. Not literally but in my mind's eye, Horatio. The court of the Lord is never closed. As Halpern said."

They sat at one of the rickety wrought-iron tables on the grass. The boy on the bicycle had vanished. Eventually a woman in an apron with a baby on her hip came out. "Signori?"

They ate bread and salami and big sliced tomatoes with oil and salt, and drank wine poured out of an earthenware jug. It was very hot. Their linen coats were on the backs of their wrought-iron chairs, their straw hats pulled down to keep the glare from their eyes. The silence of the church stayed with them. Not a single other visitor came from the lagoon.

Adam lit a cigarette and tipped his chair back. "Well ..." he said.

Max looked up. There was a smile in Adam's eyes, but an unfamiliar expression too, as if he were expecting Max to say something he wanted to hear. Max didn't know what it was: Adam was somewhere he couldn't follow him.

"What is it?"

"Nothing. Perhaps everything. How does one tell?"

Max waited.

"This is the most beautiful place I've ever seen." Adam waved a hand at the scruffy grass, the wall and the fig tree, the ancient throne, and the tall pale brick campanile behind the church. "Perhaps that's the problem. Or perhaps it's something to do with the solution."

He laughed.

"There are more things in heaven and earth, Friedrich Nietzsche, than are dreamt of in your philosophy."

Max waited again, and saw that Adam wasn't going to explain.

"I'm glad I'm going to be in Cracow for a bit", said Adam. "I don't think I could stand Breslau straight after Venice. It won't be so difficult for you. It's your city, after all."

"You'll come back?"

"Of course. I've got to, for the thesis. But in any case, Breslau is where I live now. And a month of Poland will probably be quite enough to . . ."

"To what?"

"I don't know. Restore my sense of reality. Facts rather than truth. All that."

For some reason, Max thought of the painting in the Accademia, the little girl on the great flight of stairs.

"Whoever does not receive the kingdom of God as a little child . . ." Max said.

"*What?*"

"I'm sorry. I was thinking of that picture. I don't know why."

"The stairs. I know. But we aren't children. That's the problem."

"We were. You were a child when you believed"—Max looked across the scorched grass at the church—"that what you were told, what you were given, was true. Now that you're not a child, you don't. But does it make the slightest difference to the truth, if it is the truth, whether Adam Zapolski or Max Hofmannswaldau believes it's true or not?"

"*I don't know,*" Adam said. "That's precisely what I don't know. And I don't know whether it matters, one way or the other. But I must find out. So must you. So must anyone with any sense of . . . proportion. Ach! Damn Venice, damn *Hamlet*, damn the whole damned thing!" He got up. "I'm going to see if they can produce some coffee." Then he disappeared into the cottage.

The next morning, they went to Saint Mark's and walked along canals and through dark narrow streets and open sunny squares and sat in the Piazza for the last time listening to Verdi. But there seemed to be too many people, too much pointless noise, too much dazzling light. They bought postcards and said almost nothing to each other.

In the afternoon, they packed. In the evening, they took the steamer to the station along the Grand Canal in the gathering dusk, and Max felt sadder than he had ever felt in his life except after his grandfather's funeral.

In the station in Vienna the next day, they parted, with a hand-shake. "I'll be back", Adam said. "In a month or so. I hope."

Chapter 11

"Well, that's it", Adam said, coming into the flat, bringing with him the frost from outside and flinging down on the sofa his briefcase and a pile of books. It was the middle of December, bitterly cold, and he was wearing his black boots, long leather coat, patterned mittens knitted for him by Katya (another case of unreciprocated passion, evident to Max from the first day she came to clean the flat), and a Russian fur hat. Max, who had never seen one, thought he looked like a Cossack, with the effect rather spoiled by the mittens. Adam went back into the hall to take off his outdoor clothes.

Max had been half-asleep in his grandfather's armchair by the fire, a book about customs unions and international law open on his knee. When Adam reappeared, rubbing his hands to warm them, Max said, "What's what?"

"I was told to wait patiently and to stay awake. Something would happen, something outside myself, to show me what I should do. It has."

"What are you talking about?"

Adam laughed.

"Max, dear old boy, I'm sorry. You know me so well that I always think you know what's going on inside my head even if I've told you absolutely nothing. How could you guess?"

"Well ... you haven't been ... as you used to be, since you came back from Cracow. Anyone could see that. Treuburg did. Anna certainly did."

"Did they? Did they. You never said."

"Of course not. I didn't want to trample all over ... whatever it is you've been thinking about. But it's been obvious. Music—you know how it makes things obvious. The Brahms upset you. I'd no idea why. You didn't want to play it more than once. More emotion sloshing about than you could cope with, I thought."

"Ah. You thought it was a girl."

"I thought it might be. I wasn't sure. Treuburg was."

"Treuburg would be. Treuburg was wrong."

"And you played the Trout quintet so well, so exactly right for Schubert, that we all ended up playing the piece, which should be quite light and cheerful, as if it were the saddest music in the world. That upset you too. I don't know why—you seem yourself only when you're playing Bach nowadays."

"Bach. Yes. Well, of course. Dear old fellow." Adam looked up at the portrait. "Keeping chaos at bay. Max, is Treuburg coming back to supper?"

"No. He left a note. He's staying at the hospital all night."

"Good."

"What do you want to eat?"

"Oh, never mind food. I'll open a bottle of Mosel."

Max shut his textbook, marking his place with a postcard of the horses of Saint Mark's, then put more coal on the fire and closed the curtains. Adam was back.

After he had poured two glasses of wine, Adam put his on the mantelpiece, went to the harpsichord, sat on the stool, and played the first page of a complicated fugue from the *Well-Tempered Clavier*, the parts echoing and chasing each other under his fingers. He stopped, closed the instrument, came back to the fire, lit a cigarette, and stood looking down at Max.

"Would you say I have a strong spirit?"

"What?"

"A strong spirit. Nietzsche says truth has to be fought for every inch of the way and that only strong spirits can do the fighting. He says in the same place that truth is always hard, ugly, and unattractive, and that belief—nothing to do with truth, according to him—makes people happy: *therefore* it lies. Quite a fight he set up, just by saying that. For me, at any rate."

"Is it truth you've been fighting for these last few months? I'm not surprised. It hasn't been making you happy, in any case. At least the fight hasn't. But yes, I think you have what Nietzsche meant by a strong spirit. Although you don't agree with him, do you? Not any more. About belief. Sit down, for goodness' sake. I can't talk to you if you're standing there looming over me like Halpern being a rabbi."

"All right." He sat at the far end of the sofa, stubbed out his cigarette, and put his untasted glass of wine on the floor. "You're right. You've always—and you were there in Venice, in Ravenna, in Torcello. Art. That was what that holiday was supposed to be all about. I don't understand how people can do it."

"Do what?"

"Go there. Look at the paintings, the churches. Regard it all as satisfying the senses, like a warm bath, a soft bed, a meal cooked by an expensive French chef. Halpern again. When . . ."

He stopped and sat still, looking into the fire.

"When what?"

"Have you heard of the Eastern Europe Institute?"

"In the university? Vaguely."

"They sent for me today. Five professors round a table. The chairman was a Viennese, Professor Übersberger, who knows my mother. That was the first warning light."

"Professors of what?"

"Oh, this and that. History, law, linguistics, archaeology I think."

"Why did they send for you?"

"Because of my thesis. Übersberger was very flattering about it, I must say. That was the second warning light. You know how sketchy it really is. Two of the others had read it as well. Anyway, they offered me a job."

"A job? You mean an academic job? But you won't get your doctorate for years, three years at least. What do they want you to do?"

"Research. Towards my doctorate, of course. But research in their institute, for their reasons."

"Research into what?"

"They didn't seem to mind. That was the third warning light. Choose your own subject, they told me, legal, historical, whatever appeals to you, as long as whatever you discover goes to show—ach!" Adam leapt up, found his cigarette case, and lit another. "It's really sinister, what's going on, you know. All right, all right, I'll sit down."

"I don't understand. What's the research supposed to show?"

"That the Germans, the bloody Aryans, are the ancestral people of the east, of all the old Polish commonwealth as far as Russia. That the Slavs are only nomads, here today, gone tomorrow, with no roots, who deserve to be pushed back into Siberia."

"Sounds like what Halpern says about Palestine. That's one of the reasons he's against it. It's ancestral for the Jews but not for the wretched Arabs."

"That was another thing, the Jews. You should have heard these professors, all of them chiming in. The Jews—Bolsheviks, the lot of them, push them east, let them rot in Russia where they belong. Übersberger got quite carried away. One of the others tried to shut him up—he could see I wasn't exactly agreeing with all this. But Übersberger assumed, no doubt because of my mother and her friends, that I was bound to think as he does. And they need reasonably bright people, educated in Germany but fluent in Polish, to do their so-called research for them."

"What did you say?"

"Nothing, for a bit. I was really shaken. There are plenty of good men in the university, after all. How can they let this kind of thing go on under their noses? There was a lot of stuff racing round in my head, so I just sat there, looking thoroughly stupid no doubt. Then one of the others said that if I would propose a suitable topic for my research and accept a place in their institute once it was approved, I could well find my doctorate advanced by a year, or even two."

"That's a bribe."

"Exactly. I almost said so. Thank God I didn't. They would probably have failed my thesis if I had."

"So what did you say?"

"I thanked them politely for their offer. Then I said that unfortunately I have already decided to pursue my studies in Cracow."

"You said *what*? But that was just something to say? A way out. Wasn't it?"

"Steady, Max. No, it wasn't. I meant it. I hadn't decided until that minute. But then I did. Now I have. That's why I wanted to talk to you."

Max felt the blood drain from his head. He got up, went to the window, and parted the curtains. Snowflakes were falling gently on the gaslit empty street.

"You'll break Anna's heart."

"Anna? What's she got to do with it?"

"Adam! You can't pretend you haven't noticed. She's been in love with you for months. Ever since *Hamlet*."

"But she's your—"

304

"No, she's not. I'm a kind of extra brother to her. Always there. Not as demanding as her real brother. She's fond of me. Full stop. You *can't* not have noticed what she feels about you."

"Mmm. Shyness, I thought. A shy child with not much idea of . . . and a bit of hero worship on account of the play. Damn. I'm sorry. I should have . . ."

"Should have what? Played the clarinet less well? Played the piano like Eva Grossmann? Not played Hamlet at all? It's no good, Adam. You couldn't have chosen—you can't choose—to be someone completely different. None of us can."

"Can't we? Can't I? Listen. Come and sit down. Please."

Max sat down again. He picked up his glass. His hand was shaking. He put the glass down.

"Don't go to Cracow, Adam. What would I . . . where would I . . . I can't speak Polish. Or only kitchen Polish." He saw Adam in the kitchen at Waldau, bending over Emilia's pan of jam, winning her heart in three minutes.

"Listen", Adam said, lighting another cigarette. "You must stay here, Max. Of course you must. This is your city, your country. Judging by what happened to me at the university today, Germany's going to need every intelligent person it can possibly find to understand what's going on, to fight for some truth to be saved."

"For facts? Or for truth?"

"Both. Both! That's one of the things I saw today. They want to alter the facts to suit their truth, because their truth is a lie. That is really terrifying. That's what Halpern says the Bolsheviks do—have to do—to justify sweeping whole categories of people onto the rubbish heap, 'the rubbish heap of history' they call it, since they allow history to have only one meaning, one direction. Facts are small, awkward; they arrive one by one to people's attention. So are—so do—human beings. So if the facts or the people don't suit the theory, the project you happen to have adopted as the truth—Marxist revolution, let's say, or the Germans to rule from the Rhine to Russia—then you alter them, get rid of them, redescribe them to suit the theory. You put the people in prison and shoot them and say they were trying to escape."

"But you could have understood all this, turned down their offer, and still stayed here, chosen your next topic, done the work honestly, properly, steered clear of their lies." Max looked at Adam, who was looking at the floor. "Couldn't you?"

"Yes. No. As it happens, I couldn't. Last year, perhaps. Not now. In Cracow, I understood some other things. About myself, and about my parents, both of them. Cracow isn't a city I know well. Lemberg was the city of my childhood, much nearer to Zapolsc. But Cracow is the real capital of Poland."

"What about Warsaw?"

"Warsaw, well, yes. The capital, the government, such as it is, and all that. I've never been to Warsaw. Our great poet Mickiewicz never went to Warsaw. He went to Vilna, certainly, a great Polish city, though I haven't been there either. Lemberg I love. But Cracow's the most ancient, the most venerable of the lot. To Poles like my father, Warsaw is practically a modern city. The Kings are buried in Cracow. The university is older than any of the universities in Germany: did you know that? Of course you didn't. But it wasn't just the city, the university, the library ..."

He stopped, looked straight at Max, then looked at the fire.

"The work you were doing, on Poland before the partitions ... was it that?" Max said.

"It didn't help. Or it did, depending on which way you look at it. Did you know that Frederick the Great said he took and ate the body of Poland eucharistically? A horrible remark. A horrible man. He doesn't inspire much enthusiasm for staying in Prussia, I can tell you."

"He was my father's great hero. He rescued Silesia from the Habsburg empire and turned it into part of Prussia. A thoroughly good thing, according to my father."

"There you are. Not that Breslau altogether seems like Prussia, even now. It's a friendly-enough city. There's still a bit of Habsburg soul here, I like to think. Or was. One or two of the churches. Cathedral Island. And once upon a time, it was a Polish city. A Polish city reasonably welcoming to the Jews, a thousand years ago. So much for their Aryan nonsense. But that was all a long time ago, before Poland became an incompetent shambles, the laughing-stock of Europe, as I'm afraid it's going to be again. If it weren't for Pilsudski taking a firm line last year, the republic would probably have disintegrated already. And look at where it is on the map. Between Germany and Russia, what hope is there for Poland? No. It wasn't all that. It was an accident, a coincidence. Or not."

He stopped again, and laughed.

" 'There's a divinity that shapes our ends, rough-hew them how we will.' Or there isn't. That *is* the question. More than to be or not to be, by far. Anyway ... one morning, one ordinary morning, when I'd been in Cracow about three weeks, I was sitting in the library rough-hewing away, trying to find perfect quotations, not too long, for my thesis, in a hefty great book in Latin about the ideals of the commonwealth. It was in seventeenth-century Latin. Old Fischer would turn green at the clumsiness of it. This book called Poland the serene republic. I didn't know it had ever been called that. The serene republic. Exactly like Venice. And they died, the serene republics—which were supposed to last for ever—within a couple of years of each other, wiped off the map at the same time by other people's will to power. So much for serene. So there I was, looking out of the window. The sun was shining. The bells of the Mariacki—that's the big church at the end of the market square, right in the middle of the city—were tolling. A wedding? Hardly, on a weekday morning. So I went to see. Anything to get away from the seventeenth-century Latin.

"The doors were wide open. Lots of people inside. A procession going up to the altar, the Archbishop at the back. The choir singing at full blast. 'Nos autem gloriari oportet in Cruce Domini nostri Jesu Christi, in quo est salus, vita, et resurrectio nostra, per quem salvati et liberati sumus.' We used to sing it with the monks. It was the feast of the Exaltation of the Holy Cross. Don't make that face. It's a standard Catholic feast, on the fourteenth of September. It makes you stop what you're doing and look up, at Christ on the cross high over us all. That's what we were told as children. You couldn't have it in a Protestant church, obviously. No crucifix to look up at.

"I stayed. You know the last time I heard Mass—Dante's funeral. You know that was the first time for seven years. Anyway, the Archbishop preached. Absolutely not about Poland, the nation, all that, but on two phrases from the Gospel for the feast. 'Nunc iudicium est mundi.' Halpern's court of the Lord—do you remember? But lit by Christ. 'Dum lucem habetis, credite in lucem.' He's a wonderful man, the Archbishop. Prince Sapieha. You wouldn't know, but that's a name that chimes through the whole of Polish history. So there I was, thinking as I'd been thinking more and more since *Hamlet*: either all this is nonsense, and that's a clever middle-aged man in fancy dress, hopelessly deluded and going through a ritual with bits of bread and a cup of wine that means absolutely nothing. Or it's the truth. Christ come from God into this world to save us and set us free. And if it's the truth, if Christ is the truth—the way, the truth, and the life—everything has to change. One can't just say, 'All right, it's true, so I'll go to Mass on Sundays.' It has to make more difference than that. *Now* is the judgement.

"Give God a chance, I thought. So after the Mass, I found an old priest lurking at a side altar and asked him to hear my confession. He just listened, the way they do. You wouldn't know about confession. It's as undramatic as anything could be. Takes one down a few pegs, I can tell you, when one's got used to thinking of oneself as interesting. 'Pride, my child,' he said, 'a more serious sin than all you have confessed, and driving all the rest. Think about it. Five Hail Marys.' Then he gave me absolution. 'And say a prayer for me.' And that was that. I felt nine years old. Which was good. As you said in Torcello that day."

"So who told you to wait patiently?"

"Oh, that was the Archbishop. I went to see him. I had to pull rank with his secretary to get an appointment, but that wasn't difficult. I asked him if he thought I had a vocation."

"Adam! What are you saying? That means ..."

"To the priesthood. Yes."

"What did he say? How could he say anything? He doesn't know you."

"That's what he said. He said he didn't know. And that I couldn't know, for a while. But God does know. Either God would leave me alone or he wouldn't. If he didn't leave me alone I would know that, and most likely there would be a fight between him and me, and one day something would happen that would make me certain, show me what I must do. And those professors today, round their mahogany table with their pipes and their glasses of seltzer, made me certain."

"But ..."

"But what?"

"I don't see why your decision has to be so ... extreme."

"Don't you?"

Adam looked at him, with the eyes that for more than five years had anchored Max's life in affection and understanding. Max met his look, but then had to look away.

"Perhaps I do. Yes, perhaps I do. If facts aren't worth dying for, they're not worth living for either. Is that it? More or less? You could say all those years of Nietzsche were extreme too. The other extreme. So either he's right or he's wrong. And if he's wrong, then all this follows? For you. But what follows for everyone else? Everyone else who can think, I mean. For me, for example. The consequences are so enormous, so complicated—and I don't know enough even to understand what they are."

He knew Adam was looking at him with more love than, perhaps, he ever had before. So he avoided meeting his eye.

"You're leaving me behind. In all sorts of ways. Aren't you? All these months since you came back from Cracow—I knew you were somewhere else. That was the fight, wasn't it? And now the fight's over. Won, but not by you, have you noticed?"

"Of course. That's exactly the point."

"So the victory doesn't prove anything. Couldn't it be that you lost the fight to other things, not to God? Why shouldn't Nietzsche be right? Why shouldn't the beauty of the paintings and the churches in Italy, even of Torcello, be just that? Beauty. A consolation in the desert of the truth. Why shouldn't you have been seduced, by all that beauty, by Shakespeare who seemed to have written God into Hamlet's soul somehow, by going to Cracow and rediscovering your father's Polishness, by what you were taught as a child in the world before the war? People of our age are always going to be in danger, all our lives till we're old, of thinking the world before the war is how things ought to be because it will never come back. Waldau will never come back. Paradise lost, old Fischer would say. And there's another thing. Old Fischer himself. You argued with him at school, practically every week. Was it because it would have been easy to agree with him, and you wanted to do the opposite, say the opposite, think the opposite, just because it was more difficult? Don't you see this could all be an illusion, a slipping into something that seems noble because it's giving up a lot? No academic glory, no fame in the world, no wife, no children— Adam Zapolski disappears into the priesthood and turns into a different kind of hero, the person in black at the party, Hamlet himself, Nietzsche's self-overcoming with a vengeance. Or is it a way of getting back at your mother? Punishing her for how she's behaved since your father was killed? Hamlet again. You know she wants you to marry some Viennese countess, princess, whatever, and cut a dash in drawing rooms, on yachts, on ski slopes. But you don't have to be a *priest* to avoid all that. Do you? You're perfectly capable of running your own life. You always have been, ever since I've known you."

"Max. Listen."

Max couldn't stop.

"No. I won't. I can't. Don't you see the whole thing could still be *false*? Just a story for children and the simple-minded, as you've thought for years? And even if now you're sure it's all true, why do you have to go away and be a priest? There are plenty of good Catholics who aren't priests—like Dr Fischer. Aren't there? And some of them even live in Breslau."

He knew Adam was still looking at him. He couldn't meet his look. Adam said nothing. So he blundered on.

"What I'm trying to say is, there can't be only two alternatives, being a Nietzschean and being a priest. There are many more ways, good ways, of being alive. Aren't there?"

"There aren't for me."

"Adam!"

Max got up and left the room. He went into the bathroom, slammed the door, and let the tears come. After a minute or two, he realized that he had shut himself in the bathroom to cry, as Anna had done when she couldn't concentrate because of Adam and was scolded by her brother. He blew his nose fiercely, looked in the mirror, saw the misery in his eyes, and made an effort to relax his face into its usual shape. If he was going to have to learn to live without Adam, then he'd better begin now. He blew his nose again, took some deep breaths, cleared his throat, and went back into the sitting room.

Adam was at the window, looking out into the snow. Max went up to him and put an arm round his neck.

"I'm sorry", he said. "It's a shock, that's all."

Adam turned and held Max by the shoulders at arm's length, making Max meet his eyes.

"I know. It's my fault. Springing this on you. I'm sorry. Sit down. Come on. Here's your glass."

Max sat. Adam threw some coal on the fire and sat down again on the sofa where he had been sitting before.

"Now listen. Please. Yes, the whole thing could still be false. That will always be so. All my life. All our lives. To allow it to be the truth is a guess, is taking a chance. But it's a more sensible, even a more rational, chance to take than the other one. And there are only two. It's taken me months to be sure of that, but that I now do know. There are only two. Either God became man to redeem the world from its own sinfulness. Or man is all of God there is, all the religions amount to nothing whatever, whistling in the dark, and the world is utterly lost.

"As for me—not that I matter very much. You don't think I haven't thought of all you've been saying, do you? All of it, and a good deal more. I have. Of course I have. I couldn't talk to you sooner. I had to reach a decision by myself. Also, for anyone not brought up a Catholic, even you, the whole thing is bound to seem crazy, so late in the day that it must be nostalgia, or escape, or revenge of some kind. Much as you've said. Also, I knew it wouldn't be fair to ask you for a view. We've been too much together all this time, since we were clever boys showing off— more mine than yours, the showing off, I have to admit."

"Too much?"

"Max! For goodness' sake! Not too much together, only too much for it to be fair to ask you what you thought."

"I understand. Sorry."

Max looked into the fire and made an effort to think himself into where Adam now was. He couldn't.

"I know I should be pleased for you," he said, "pleased that everything has become so clear. I will be, in a while, when I've got used to the idea. Or I'll try to be. But explain two things to me, poor stupid Protestant that I am, not that I'm even that, with Dr Mendel the only person who ever talked to me about God when I was a child."

"A highly intelligent Jew. I'm not sure that isn't the best upbringing anyone could have. As long as you don't let it rest there. One has to be a child and not a child. Be wise as serpents and innocent as doves."

"You know who said that to me once? Mendel. It was what he wanted Germany to be, after 1918. Not a chance."

"So what are the two things you want me to explain, Max?"

"First, why do you have to be a *priest*? Why not a Catholic *person*—a Catholic lawyer or a Catholic professor or a Catholic count, like your father, and saintly too if you've got to be a saint, like your grandmother?"

Adam stared into his half-empty glass for a long time before answering.

"I don't know why. But I do know it's the case. The Archbishop would say it's not my business to worry about the reason. God knows the reason. One day I may discover what it was. Or not. It doesn't matter. All I know now is that I can't stake a bit of my life on it being true, the story. If it's true it requires the staking of the whole of my life. And that's because it's not only a story, as you and I have always called it. It's something that happened in reality, to reality, and changed it forever. It's something that asked a question that, once we've heard it, we have to answer."

"I don't know what you mean."

"I know you don't. But you will. I'm certain you will, one day, perhaps soon."

"Do you mean that you think I'll have to become a priest too?"

"No. Absolutely not. Or not *necessarily*. Only that you'll hear the question, because you'll want to. You'll answer it, one way or another. But the priesthood's a different thing. If it's required of you, you'll know. As I know. It was because I didn't want to know what all the time—all the time at least since Torcello—I did know, that in the last few months I've been so ... quiet."

"'There's something in his soul'", Max said, "'o'er which his melancholy sits on brood.' I've thought of that often. Claudius was afraid of whatever it was. So was I. I was right."

"You needn't have been. This is good, not bad, or I wouldn't be doing it."

"It wasn't for you that I was afraid. Claudius wasn't afraid for Hamlet." Max looked into the fire again for a minute or two. "That's the second thing", he said.

"What?"

"Why do you have to go to Cracow to do this? There's a perfectly good Catholic theology faculty here, a seminary I'm sure, somewhere in the city. Some of the time perhaps, if you studied in the university a bit longer, you could still live in the flat. Couldn't you?"

"You don't know German priests. Some of them are excellent. But Bismarck made them nervous, so nervous of being thought not German enough that most of them are more German than everyone else except the brownshirts. One of the possibilities for research that a professor this morning asked me to consider was Church history. He's a priest himself. Do you see what that means? They want someone to prove that Christianity in Poland was always German, that the soul of Poland deserves to be organized by Germany just like everything else in Poland. I can't be part of all that. I can't become a German priest. I must learn what I have to learn in Cracow, and be a priest for the people in Galicia, where I belong—where the people, during the war and after it too, have had the kind of time no one in Germany has had since the Thirty Years' War. That's another thing I saw today."

"When ... when will you start?"

"I don't know. I'll go back to Cracow for Christmas, go and see the Archbishop, and do what he tells me to do."

"You might not come back, after Christmas?"

"Of course I'll come back. Even if they let me start soon—I hope they will—I'll have things to sort out here, with the university, and my stuff, in the flat . . ."

Max could say nothing. In the warm silence of Grandpapa's flat, a nest against the winter of the world, a charred lump of coal dropped in the grate, sending sparks up the chimney.

"Man is born to trouble as the sparks fly upward", Max said.

"What?"

"Mendel. One of his favourite sayings. He used to say it when I made a hash of an exercise. Or when my father was angry."

The silence regathered.

"Adam?"

"Yes?"

"What do you think I should do?"

"When I have to go? Or with your life?"

"Either. Both. They look the same. I suppose they're not."

"Keep going. With the law and the history. If ever Germany needed honest lawyers with a proper, educated sense of the past, it's now. The poor need defending. The republic needs defending. Stresemann has done well, but the enemies of the republic, noisy and stupid, are everywhere, waiting for their chance. There's plenty for good people, capable of telling truth from lies, to do in this country. You're one. Treuburg's another."

"Treuburg's going to be horrified. By you becoming a priest."

"Of course he is. 'There go the ridiculous Poles again. Superstition and nostalgia.' A joke. But he doesn't know me."

Adam jumped to his feet.

"There! Now, but not before, I can say 'good people, capable of telling truth from lies' and know that they are the same and that the words make sense. *Nietzsche was wrong.* You see how that makes all the difference to everything?"

"Yes. No. Do I?"

"You will. And another thing. Marry Anna."

"Adam! I'm nowhere near—"

"You will be. I'm going away. I've been getting in the light. I didn't mean to. Not in the least. But you're right. I have been, and once I've gone . . ."

"But Halpern—"

"You can deal with Halpern. He's only her brother. This is the twentieth century. And they're here, in Germany. For all its faults, things are possible here that aren't possible in Vilna, and have been for generations—look at your parents. Hope, that's the thing. Also faith, and love. Come on."

He pulled Max out of Grandpapa's chair as he had once pulled Anna out of the corner of the sofa.

"I'm starving. Let's fry something. Eggs, ham, bread, whatever there is."

They went together into the kitchen. As Max opened the larder door, Adam put a hand, for a moment, on his shoulder, and said, from behind him, "You'll be all right, Max. I know. And we'll never not be friends."

Adam and Max had agreed to say to Treuburg and the Halperns only that Adam needed to go back to Cracow for a few weeks to do some more work in the Polish state archives.

There had been in any case no quartet playing over Christmas. Halpern had very little free time because Jewish doctors in the university hospital always worked all through the Christian holidays to allow their colleagues to be at home with their families. And Anna hadn't been well. A few days after Christmas, Max called at Frau Schönfeld's with some chocolates for Anna and to ask her if she would like to come with him to a New Year's performance of Bach's B Minor Mass in the Century Hall. The old lady told him Anna was still feverish and shouldn't go out in such cold weather until she had completely recovered.

Max wondered whether Anna somehow had picked up, probably from him, that Adam's absence meant more than she had been told. She was ill because she was afraid. But then he told himself that was ridiculous. How could she know? People get the flu in the winter.

He went with Treuburg to the B Minor Mass, which he had never heard before, and they walked back to the flat through the icy city with piles of snow along the sides of the streets, saying nothing. He was grateful to Treuburg for his silence: he was thinking too hard to be able to say anything himself. Could this music, of such grandeur, such scope, be listened to in the same way as one might listen to—what? Other music of grandeur and scope? The last time he had been to a concert in the Century Hall, he had taken Anna, while Adam was in Cracow in September, to hear Beethoven and Mahler played most beautifully by the Vienna Philharmonic Orchestra and Furtwängler, who were visiting Breslau. They played Beethoven's Seventh Symphony—music grander than its slow movement didn't exist—and then Mahler's Sixth. On their way out of the hall for a breath of air during intermission, he and Anna heard a woman's penetrating voice: "We're going now, Magda. We only came for the Beethoven. Ferdl can't stand this Jew-music." They exchanged a look. So: tremendous music by Beethoven and Mahler, engaging the heart and, in its way, impossible to define or analyse, the mind too. But the B Minor Mass engaged something else as well. What? Those ancient Latin words, and Greek words too, *Kyrie eleison*, from long, long ago. And Bach, his face so familiar from the portrait, a good Lutheran, setting the words of the Mass. Could it be listened to like the symphonies, just for the music? If not, then what? Adam and the paintings in Venice? He pushed the connexions away. He didn't know enough to face them.

In the middle of January, on a freezing Friday afternoon, Max was at his grandfather's desk writing up notes on that morning's lectures, all of which he now had to listen to properly because he was alone. Treuburg was asleep in his room; he was on night duty at the hospital, and his alarm would wake him at seven in the evening, to get up, shave, dress, eat, and go back to work.

Anna was better, and that morning a note had arrived from Halpern suggesting that they might play quartets, if convenient, on the next evening, Saturday. Max had already replied, saying that he and Treuburg would be delighted.

He heard a motor stop in the street outside. He went to the window and rubbed clear a patch on the steamy glass. Adam, in his Cossack hat and long coat, got out of a cab, looked up to the window, which Max hadn't opened, and waved. Then he and the driver lifted out of the back of the car two large trunks. They were awkward, but light, clearly empty. This was it, then. Without giving himself time to deal with the realization, he left the flat with its door open and ran down the stairs to help Adam bring up the trunks. They were old, battered, and empty indeed.

"Where did you find these?"

"At the junk shop by the station."

"Treuburg's asleep. He's got night duty. You'll have to tell him as soon as you can."

"Yes, of course. But not as he's rushing off to work. Tomorrow."

"So you can start soon?"

"Next week. The seminary takes people from the beginning of the year. I'll have missed the first couple of weeks, that's all."

"I see. Tea?"

"Tea, yes. What we owe to your English governess—how am I going to manage without Earl Grey? There's only Russian tea in Cracow—everywhere except grand houses. Black stuff in glasses. Like Russian cigarettes. Black stuff in cardboard. Pretty horrible."

"Adam!"

"We'll get through this. It won't be so bad once I've gone."

"For you. Because it'll all be different. Here it'll be the same. Only empty. Sorry. I'll put the kettle on."

He did, while Adam pulled the trunks into his room and shut the door.

"Any quartets lately?" he said, appearing in the kitchen.

"No. But they're coming tomorrow."

"Then I can tell them and Treuburg at the same time. A united front of Baltic disapproval, that's what it'll be."

"They won't say much, Treuburg and Halpern. Because they won't have any idea of how or why you could do such an extraordinary thing, now, in 1928. They'll just think you've gone mad. Or been got at by some fanatic. That's what they'll think—a Polish nationalist fanatic got hold of you in Cracow and persuaded you to abandon everything, your German education, your German doctorate, your common sense, your part in the onward march of civilization Halpern's so sure of, for a bundle of old superstitions that holds the Polish people together so that when they're bullied by Russians or Germans they can at least think of themselves as martyrs. Like the Jews."

"Max! Treuburg and Halpern don't care enough about me—why should they?—to think any of that. But you. Is this what you think? Surely it can't be."

"No, it's not. Not when I'm remembering properly who you are. But I have thought it, yes, at three in the morning when I couldn't understand . . ."

"Let's have some of that tea."

316

Max poured two cups. Adam shut the kitchen door and sat down at the table with his tea. Max stood with his back to the stove.

"Listen", Adam said. "Poland is weak and frightened. How can it not be? Pilsudski has done a remarkable job, binding together bits of three empires to make a country, but he won't last forever, and everyone else quarrels—political parties, nationalists, socialists, enthusiasts of various kinds, the lot—as if Poland weren't just as open to attack as it was in the time of Frederick the Great and Catherine. Vengeance, German vengeance for 1918, is sure to be aimed first at Poland. And then there's Russia. There always is. It was a miracle, as everyone calls it, rightly, that the Polish army defeated the Bolsheviks in 1920. But Russia will never accept the loss of the Polish lands they ruled before the war, the richest part of the Russian empire by far. So you see: neither the Bolsheviks nor the Germans are going to forgive Poland for simply existing, for being there. And yes, I have a kind of loyalty to the hope that Poland can survive. But—you must believe me, Max— that has almost nothing to do with the truth, the Church, the priesthood. Not for me. All that's the reason for being in Poland, particularly in Cracow, where the old commonwealth tradition of forbearance, especially of moderately civilized treatment of the Jews, is strong because of the Habsburgs. But the reason for becoming a priest is entirely different. It has to do with the meaning of all of life, with the fate of the whole human race. It has nothing, nothing whatever to do with nationalism. You know how I feel about nationalism. Look at it here."

"All right, Adam. It's all right. I do understand. Or I think I do. I was hoping it might be a bit longer, before ... But I can see it's best for you to begin as soon as possible, now that you've made up your mind, or had your mind made up, whichever it is."

They heard Treuburg leave his room, go into the bathroom, and shut the door.

"Not a word", Adam said. "For now."

Adam was out most of Saturday at the university, returning books to libraries, sorting out his accreditation, and organising necessary letters of recommendation for his transfer to Cracow. When he came back, it was already nearly dark.

"What shall we play this evening?" Max said. The words seemed like stones. The last evening of music with Adam.

Silence.

"Oh, I think the Brahms", Adam eventually said. "It'll go better now. And it's a good farewell to the clarinet. I can't see the clarinet as a suitable instrument for the seminary. Frivolous, don't you think? In spite of Brahms."

"There'll be a piano?"

"There's bound to be. Don't worry, Max. There's always a piano."

Max got the music stands out, arranged them for the clarinet quintet, found the parts, and put them on the stands.

"I got some more beer", Max said.

"Well done."

Treuburg arrived at seven, changed into his usual crisp shirt and a clean pullover, and sat down at the kitchen table with Max and Adam. They ate—or Treuburg and Adam ate—tinned soup that Max heated in a pan, chunks of bread, and cheese.

"What's the matter?" Treuburg said. "Has somebody died?"

"Not exactly", Adam said.

"What do you mean?"

"Never mind. I'll tidy up in here. The Halperns will arrive in ten minutes."

Ten minutes later, they did arrive, punctual as always, and shook hands all round. Anna, white and thin in a plain dark dress with a white lace collar, looked questioningly at Max. He gave her an encouraging smile, feeling a traitor even to be smiling, knowing what was ahead.

They played the Brahms straight through, very well, Adam playing with a freedom and ease that he hadn't managed the first time they tried the piece. The Hungarian flourishes in the slow movement, flying above the dense, complex German accompaniment of the strings, struck Max as a perfect metaphor for—but the notes he had to play were difficult enough to need all his concentration. Anna missed a bar or two here and there: her brother, this time, let her mistakes pass without a word and without stopping the music. Or perhaps he too was for once held to the demands of his own line.

At the end, Halpern said, "That was very good tonight. Some beautiful playing, Zapolski. You must have practised in Cracow."

"I was practising, in a way, yes. I'll make the coffee."

When they all had coffee, and Treuburg had also brought the pewter mugs and the jug of beer, Adam, standing in front of the fire with his coffee, said, "I have something to tell you this evening. Max knows this already. I'm leaving Breslau next week, for good, I'm afraid."

Max was watching Anna. There was an almost imperceptible intake of breath, and then an absolute stillness as she sat beside her brother on the sofa looking at the patterned rug.

"I'm going to study in Cracow."

"Why?" This, of course, was Treuburg. "What's wrong with Breslau all of a sudden?"

"A good deal, as a matter of fact."

"You are right, Count", Halpern said. "I do not know how much longer, in conscience, it will be possible for me to stay here myself. Unfortunately, both medical knowledge and medical skill are here far in advance of anything that has yet been achieved in Poland. I should have thought that the same would be true in respect of the law. No?"

"I'm not going to Cracow to study law."

"Ah!" Treuburg said. "What, then?"

"Theology", Adam said.

Treuburg laughed. "Why would a Nietzschean study theology? To destroy its premises from within? Isn't that battle already won? And why Cracow? There's a perfectly good theology faculty here, two actually, one Protestant, one Catholic. Plenty of scope for the traitor within the gates, if that's what you intend to be. Is it?"

Treuburg, Max saw, was angry. Also, Treuburg knew Adam, not well, but better than Halpern knew him.

"No, it isn't", Adam said. "I've changed my mind about Nietzsche. I've come to think he was most likely wrong, deeply and fundamentally wrong, about practically everything."

"Well!" Treuburg said. "There's a surprise. The Polish count, educated by the Catholic Church, goes back to a Polish city for a few weeks, and, lo and behold, everything he's learnt in a modern German school, in a modern German university, is out of the window. What are you thinking of, Zapolski? Theology in Cracow instead of law in Breslau! The sixteenth century's over, you know. The Jesuits must be right—'Give me a boy till he's seven, and he's mine for life'—is that it?"

"Certainly not. Jesuits and Benedictines are not at all the same, you know. On the other hand, you're not perhaps altogether wrong. The land of my fathers—it does count for something."

"Ah! Blood and soil, like my father's ghastly Union of the Nobility. Sentimentality, that's what it adds up to. Pure sentimentality. Your father's dead, mine's alive—perhaps that makes all the difference. And if the

Prussian nobility are bad, the *szlachta* are ten times worse—sentimental to the last man. You should hear my father. Real Prussians never forget they were ruled by Poland for hundreds of years. I don't agree with my father about much, but he's right about the Polish nobility. As it turns out. I thought better of you, Zapolski, a lot better."

"Baron", Halpern interrupted, "the count is surely not going to Cracow to study theology in order to be a powerful nobleman, either in Warsaw or on his estate. If that were his ambition, it would be more useful to him to continue to study law, or to take up political economy, or modern agriculture, all of them more advanced in Germany than in Poland. I am correct, am I not, Count?"

"You are correct, Halpern."

Anna was now gazing up at Adam as he stood in front of the fire. He looked down, caught her gaze, then smiled at her so that she had to look away.

"Let me try to explain—to all of you", he said. "I'm going to study in Cracow because I am, when all's said and done, a Pole, or that's what I'm now choosing to be. A Viennese German, on the lines of my mother, is what, it'll surprise none of you to hear, I now definitely and forever choose not to be. And theology's what I'm going to study because it may be that I have a vocation to the priesthood."

Anna's gasp was this time audible. Treuburg jumped to his feet as if he might hit Adam, but he strode across the room to the other side of the piano and stood with both hands on its lid.

"There! What did I tell you? Polish sentimentality, sheer weakness, nostalgia for the superstitious rubbish of the centuries—Zapolski, how can you? You're the cleverest of all of us, with the possible exception of Halpern—and here you are telling us you're intending to do two inexcusably stupid things at once. Leave Germany for Poland—that's one. Poland can't survive. You know that perfectly well. We've often agreed, here in this room, that Poland's doomed. German rearmament is coming fast. Deals are being done. Even Stresemann, who's all for peace, has been pushing for rearmament, and the first target's bound to be Poland. There's no more a future for an independent Poland now than there was a hundred years ago. You know that, Zapolski."

"You may well be right. None of us knows what's going to happen; none of us here, now, in this room, has any real idea of where we'll be in ten years or twenty years, not even Max, whose own city this is.

Meanwhile, one has to live, get through each day as best one can, and I'd rather get through each day in Cracow than here. Come to that, if there's another war, I'd rather sink with Poland than swim with Germany, which is likely to win if there's another war, wouldn't you say?"

"It depends", Treuburg said. "If there is another war, Germany won't take long to mop up Poland and, if France is foolish enough to join in, will probably defeat France quite quickly too. Nobody believes France would stomach another Verdun. But Russia's a different thing altogether. Which side would the Bolsheviks be on? Ours? No thank you. They'll be on the other side, whatever that is. Who defeats Russia in the end? Russia is thousands of miles of forest and steppe and millions of poor, tough, drunk, brave peasants. Brave savages. I saw at the beginning of the war, when I was eleven years old—never mind. Look what happened to Napoleon."

"Exactly", Adam said. "The Poles, the people, will still exist even if Poland doesn't, and they may need more—what?—more faith and more intelligence, both, to cope with the Russians than to cope with the Germans, more than ever now that the Russians are Bolsheviks. Fifty, sixty years ago, a Polish poet said, 'Germany will destroy our body, but Russia will destroy our soul.' Now, it might. There are plenty of Bolsheviks in Poland, keen for it to try."

"So, Count," said Halpern quietly from the sofa, "you are committing your life to the soul after all, to the existence of the soul, which the scientific mind regards as a superfluous—indeed, as an entirely meaningless—concept?" He looked for an instant at his sister: she didn't notice. "I must say that, although I regard your decision as far from rational, I am impressed."

Damn you, Max thought. You want him to go.

"Yes, Dr Halpern. You are right. If the soul, then God. If God, then the soul."

"I'm glad", Anna suddenly said, and blushed.

"Thank you", Adam said, more quietly still.

Treuburg didn't hear or didn't notice this swift exchange. He leant forward over the piano.

"That's the second inexcusably stupid thing you've decided to do, Zapolski. Less excusable, and much more stupid than choosing Cracow instead of Breslau. Theology! What's theology? An intellectual structure like Euclidean geometry or quantum mechanics but, unlike them, built not on evidence but on sand. Discredited, Catholic theology most of all, by the eighteenth century. *Dis*-credited—not believed in because shown to be absurd. What's happened to your judgement, your critical intelligence, your trained mind? You owe your trained mind to Germany, you know—how can you abandon both of them, your mind and Germany?"

"Hold on, Treuburg. Slow down a bit. Perhaps I owe my mind, such as it is, or its training in any case, to Germany, but I don't owe Germany the use of my mind, the leading of my life. What have we that we have not received?"

Treuburg groaned.

"You mean from God? From God, who made the world in six days and sends us to heaven or hell? A fairy tale. Christianity's got no more claim to be true than Rumpelstiltskin, and you know it, Zapolski, you know it as well as I do, or Halpern, or Hofmannswaldau. As for the priesthood—how can you even consider it? Catholic priests in their silly clothes using spurious authority they've no right to and keeping people ignorant ..."

"Why does all this make you so angry, Treuburg?"

"Why does it?"

Treuburg stopped and looked straight at Adam, perhaps remembering that he liked him.

"I'm sorry. Why does it? You're right to ask. It's your life, not mine, after all. I apologize. But I do know why—I hate to see my father's prejudices proved to be entirely sound."

Into the silence, Halpern said, "It is interesting to me, Baron, that you talk, if I may say so, very much as I and my friends used to talk in Vilna, when we were students after the war was finally over. For us it was the rabbis, one of them my own grandfather, the orthodox scholars in Vilna with their learned followers as well as the Hasidic wonder-rabbis out in the country towns, who were, to us, old men in silly clothes using spurious authority to keep people ignorant. Now, although naturally I agree with you that it is no longer possible to believe that God made the world in six days, I would not any more mock the scholars or even the Hasidim. Ignorance, I trust, will be dispelled by education—I deeply believe, as you know, that it must be—but it may be that there is a wisdom in these teachers, possibly also in the Christian priests, at least in the best of them, which people also need in this dangerous world."

"There's a difference," Treuburg said, "a really important difference. The religious Jew is only told what to do. The religious Catholic is told what to think. It's taken centuries, Zapolski, for people to escape being told what to think—how can you give up that freedom?"

"The truth will set you free", Adam said. "I think we've been looking for freedom in the wrong place since the eighteenth century."

Treuburg groaned and sat down on the piano stool with his head in his hands.

Adam picked two or three big pieces of coal from the scuttle, put them carefully on the fire, took the bellows, and blew the embers under the coal into a low flame. Then he sat down on the rug, cross-legged with his back to the hearth. Anna watched him, but only until he turned towards her.

"It would not be possible", Halpern said, now at his most rabbinical, "for me to agree with you, Count, on that central point, considering that the freedom of the Jews, however partial and incomplete, was the result of decisions made under the rational auspices of the Enlightenment. Nevertheless, for the sake of all the Jews who are still religious and no doubt will remain religious for some time longer yet, it seems to me that it is time for some common cause to be made. Now that the Bolsheviks want to destroy all religion, those who believe in God should perhaps be allies rather than enemies. Do you not agree, Count?"

"I do. I remember in Galicia, not common cause exactly but at least age-old custom, common habit. They were all used to each other. That was then. I'm afraid it may have gone now, wrecked by the horrors at the end of the war. I gathered in Cracow—never mind. But you're right about the Bolsheviks, of course. And here, the Nazis ... Has any of you seen a book called *Mein Kampf*? Hitler wrote it when he was in prison in '23. I haven't read it all through, couldn't possibly. But someone left it on a desk in the law library here—who, one doesn't like to think—and I had a look at it. Mad, most of it, hysterical nonsense. But Hitler reckons his version of science, Aryan supremacy and all that, the elimination of Jews and Slavs by the survival of the Aryan fittest, is bound to destroy religion, not just Judaism but Christianity too, because Christianity comes from the 'poisoned root' of Judaism. And if Germany doesn't look out, the Nazis *will* destroy religion."

"I see", Treuburg said. "Well, if you're going to Cracow to be a German-educated priest, Zapolski, and Halpern's going back to Vilna one of these days to be a German-educated surgeon, what are we Germans, Hofmannswaldau and I, supposed to do? You're not saying Bolshevism, Nazism, and religion are the only alternatives. Are you? Perhaps you are. But if you are, you must be wrong. What's German culture been about for a hundred and fifty years? Something different from any of those alternatives, something more liberal, more humane, less dogmatic. In fact, not dogmatic at all, and very much the better for not being so. Surely?"

"Once upon a time that was true", Halpern said. "No one could more fervently hope that it might again be true than I myself. But I fear it is too late."

"Too late?"

"I will give you an example. For my Bar Mitzvah in Vilna three months before the war, successful secular Jews, friends of my parents, gave me beautiful copies, on india paper, bound in leather, of Goethe and Schiller, in many volumes. They disappeared—were burnt, stolen, I don't know—when we were forced to leave for Warsaw. You can see how we were brought up on German culture as well as religion, even in Vilna, a Polish city of the Russian empire, because the Jews have for a long time revered German culture. But since the war, with Bolshevism and this new Aryan religion so attractive to so many in Germany, we can see that culture will never fill the space religion leaves. Goethe and Schiller, and the string quartets we all revere: they do no harm, they identify no enemies, but also they do no good, except that they demand a little diligence, a little application from a few people. Bolshevism and Aryanism are as powerful as religion: they identify enemies, they direct hatred, they have done much harm and will do much more. The same is, alas, often true of religion; certainly it has often been true of Christianity, and even of Judaism, particularly when religion becomes confused with nationalism. It is easy for the chosen people to despise the unchosen: the history books of the ancient Jews are bloodthirsty indeed, and so are passages in the psalms and the prophets. But in religion, there is also very much that is good, as even the most secular, the most scientific, of us must admit, do you not agree, Treuburg? And if Germans are to 'look out', as the count says, to watch for untruths, for injustice, for bullying and violence against those who cannot defend themselves, then they will be relying on what religion has given them, even if they know God can no longer be believed in."

"So?" Treuburg said.

"So you, Treuburg, and Hofmannswaldau too, will stay, to be more necessary to Germany than I or Count Zapolski, both of us foreigners, could ever be. You will be a doctor, which is always and everywhere good. Hofmannswaldau will be an honest lawyer, which, if the laws are just and the courts are impartial, is also good. If the laws are unjust and the courts are biased, it is even better."

The rabbi had spoken. Silence for a long minute or two.

"You haven't said a word all evening, Hofmannswaldau", Treuburg said. "What do you think of Zapolski going to Cracow to be a priest?"

Max saw Anna's head go up. She looked at him, her eyes pleading for an answer that would help her.

"I think"—he hesitated—"I think it's sad for us, but not for him. Perhaps what he's discovered will be very good. Not just for him but for many other people too."

He caught a grateful look from Adam before he saw that Anna was going to cry. He saw Halpern see both.

"Come, Anna", he said. "It is time for us to go home."

"Let me just ..." she managed to say, getting up and gathering coffee cups and beer mugs. Max took the laden tray from her, leaving her the coffee pot to carry, and followed her into the kitchen. She put the coffee pot on the draining board as he set down the tray on the kitchen table. Her back sagged as she faced the sink, and then she turned and threw herself, sobbing, into his arms.

With her face pressed into his shoulder, she cried in despair. He held her close and stroked her hair.

"I know. I know", he said. "I'll miss him too. But he's sure this is what he must do. We can't persuade him not to go. We shouldn't even try. We'll have to be brave, both of us."

The storm of tears was fading, the sobs that shook her coming less often. She looked up at him, her face a mess. Once more he found his handkerchief for her.

"I'm not brave. I'll never see him again. I know. Not ever. Jakob doesn't understand."

"I think he does."

"If he does, he'll only be pleased." She started crying again.

"Shh, Anna. Try not to cry. You don't want Adam to see how sad you are, do you?"

This helped her to stop. She blew her nose hard, mopped up her face, and gave him back his handkerchief.

"Do you like skating?" he said.

Her eyes widened in surprise. "Skating?" she said, like a child. "Yes. Of course. I love skating. In Vilna—"

"Sunday", he said. "Not tomorrow, but next Sunday, when Adam's gone, we'll go skating in the park, when the band's playing. It'll cheer us up a bit. I'll collect you from Frau Schönfeld's at two. Now, come along. We'd better go back to the others."

In the hall, she managed to shake Adam's hand, though not to meet his eyes.

"Goodbye, Count", she said. She had never managed to utter his Christian name. "Thank you."

"No, Anna. Don't thank me. I should like to thank you, both of you, for coming here and playing so musically and so patiently. I have very much enjoyed playing with you. And luckily I'm the one you don't need. The quartet's the thing. A very fine quartet, you're becoming. You'll be playing late Beethoven any day now, and with old Mendel's blessing, Max. It'll be good to think of that, in Cracow. Good-bye Anna. Good-bye, Halpern. Look after her."

"I shall." Was there a note of relief in Halpern's voice? A faint suggestion that looking after her would now be easier? "And I wish you good fortune in Cracow, Zapolski."

"Thank you. Good night."

The following Wednesday, Adam left Breslau, on the coldest morning of the winter. Sharp, icy snow was blowing through the streets on a northeast wind from Russia. At nine o'clock, when the cab arrived to be loaded with the trunks, now full of books, music, and a few clothes, there was scarcely enough daylight for them to see each other's faces. Max was going to the station with Adam to see him on to the train. Adam and Treuburg, who had been on uncommunicative but entirely friendly terms since Saturday evening, shook hands on the sidewalk, Treuburg giving his brief Prussian bow a note of respect for Adam's future that pleased Max.

"Good luck, Zapolski", Treuburg said. "I shall always be glad to have known you."

Adam left his pair of clarinets in the flat. "Give them to Anna. She knows plenty of poor music students. Someone would like them. They're quite decent instruments."

Anna, Max knew, would keep them, probably forever. But he didn't say so.

326

They had got through the days briskly; Adam had a lot to do. Early on Wednesday morning, Max had come into the sitting room and found Adam, dressed and ready, looking round the room for anything else that belonged to him.

"That's the lot, I think", he said. "I shan't forget this room. You'll stay here, won't you, Max?"

"Of course. It's mine, this flat—in any case, where else would I go? I've asked Treuburg to find a medical student who needs somewhere to live close to the hospital. For your room. My grandfather would like that."

"Quite right. He would. I won't forget him either."

He looked at the harpsichord.

"Have it", Max said. "You know he made it for my mother. I can't play it as well as it deserves. Both of them would have liked you to have it, I know. I can have it packed properly and sent to Cracow."

"No, Max. Not in a seminary. Beautiful, eccentric, rare—altogether too personal. I couldn't. Perhaps one day, when I'm a priest in a presbytery somewhere. Out in Galicia maybe, where such a thing as a harpsichord has never been seen or heard of."

"I'll look after it for you. Keep it tuned. Let me know when it's possible for you to have it."

The drive through the snow to the old Upper Silesia station took fifteen minutes but seemed to take two. The Cracow train was standing at the platform. Steam, noise, people. With a porter's help, they loaded the trunks into the guard's van. Adam found a seat, left his Cossack hat on it, and climbed down to the platform. They stood side by side, not looking at each other, until the whistle sounded. Then a swift hug.

"Good-bye, Max. Pray for me."

Max couldn't speak. And then Adam was a figure at the window of the train, waving as it pulled out of the gaslit station into the grey daylight and the swirling snow. After it had gone, Max stood in what seemed a silent, empty space, though it was neither, looking at the gleaming railway tracks leading eastwards out of Germany to Poland. He went to the station café and asked for a schnapps, something he had never done before, and downed the small glass of spirits to shock himself out of crying like a child.

When he got back to the flat, he found on his bed Adam's battered copy of *Hamlet* from the production, with pencilled cuts, notes, crosses, and accents all over the text. On the flyleaf, Adam had written: "Max: III.ii.63–5. Adam." Underneath, in brackets, he had written, "But look it up in English." He did. Hamlet's lines said:

"Since my dear soul was mistress of her choice,
And could of men distinguish her election,
She hath seal'd thee for herself."

Chapter 12

On Sunday afternoon, Max collected Anna, as always, a little early. She was looking prettier than ever, in a long brown velvet coat with fur round the hem, the cuffs, and the collar, and a white velvet beret he had seen before.

"What a coat! You look—you look like Kitty in *Anna Karenina*."

"Do I? Max—it's kind of you to take me skating. I feel so much better now. The coat—it's not mine, of course. Frau Schönfeld has lent it to me—and she says I can have it, to keep, because it fits me. Isn't that generous of her? It's nearly fifty years old. She had it when she was young, in Minsk."

They went to the park, Max carrying over his shoulder Anna's skates, little brown boots with their blades in old leather cases, along with his own rough black boots, without cases for the blades, which were a bit rusty. The snow of the middle of the week had stopped falling, and the east wind had died down. Under a brilliant cold blue sky, with the sun striking stars from the snow, they sat on a bench and laced up their skating boots.

The lake had been frozen since late November, and on Sunday afternoons the military band from the barracks, the soldiers wearing fingerless woollen mittens on their hands, played for a couple of hours— waltzes, marches, two-steps for the skaters—in the summer bandstand with frozen snow on its roof.

They set off together, holding each other's gloved hands, among the tide of couples and children moving smoothly but quite cautiously in the same direction round the lake. In the middle of the wide expanse of roughened ice, lone skaters and a few couples were showing off skills that neither Max nor Anna had, jumps, loops, and turns like the pirouettes of ballet dancers. Looking at one young man, doing figures of eight at astonishing speed alone in the very centre of the lake, Anna missed a step in their sedate progress and tripped over Max's foot so

329

that both of them fell in a laughing heap. They got to their feet, untidily, still laughing, and skated on. The music stopped and, after a short pause, started again, this time a waltz. Anna looked up at Max.

"Shall we try? A proper waltz?"

"Let's watch for a bit. I need to see how it's done, with a girl."

Max had skated with Adam often, on this lake in the park, when they were at school. But waltzes had inspired them only to whizz round the ice, one long step to each beat, as fast as they could in time to the Blue Danube or some other Viennese tune. Max led Anna to another bench on the far side of the lake, and they watched as a few couples waltzed efficiently round and round like dancers on a ball-room floor, only more smoothly, while most just skated on as before. Max watched the efficient waltzers closely.

"It's not easy", he said, as a couple close to them, plainly dizzy, crashed to the ice and the girl sat, shaking her head to stop the world going round before she tried to stand up.

"We could learn", Anna said, turning to look at him, laughing again. "Well, we could try."

He leant forward and kissed her, lightly, quickly, but on her mouth. She gasped, as she had when Adam said he was going to Cracow, and her hand covered her mouth as if to protect it. Her eyes, looking at him over her gloved hand, were startled.

"I'm sorry", he said. "Anna—dear Anna . . ."

"No. Don't be sorry, Max. It's all right. You thought I would be sad, didn't you, about the count going away. So you thought skating would cheer me up. You're always kind to me—and I love to skate—but, you can see, I'm not sad. I thought I would be. Girls in stories, Russian stories, Yiddish stories, get their hearts broken, pine away. But it's better as it is, with him gone to Cracow, gone to be a Catholic priest. He can't marry anyone, ever, can he, now? He was a dream. Only a dream. Now he can always be a dream. I hardly knew him, really. It was *Hamlet* that was so—and his playing too, the piano and the clarinet."

"I know. I do know." He felt, after all, entirely alone with the loss of Adam. "You're a brave and sensible girl. You're able to be realistic. My old tutor, when I was a child, taught me that 'realistic' is a word of very high praise. He would approve very much of you."

"That's not Dr Fischer, whom I met for tea that day?"

"No. My tutor's name is Mendel. He's old now, but he still plays— he's an excellent violinist—in the opera house orchestra. He used to live in our house in the country, and he taught me everything until I came here to the Gymnasium when I was fourteen."

"Is he a Jew? It's a Jewish name."

"Yes. He comes from Alsace."

"Where's Alsace?"

"Between Germany and France. They fight over it every time there's a war."

"Like Vilna. Between Germany and Russia. Why are there always wars, Max? Do you understand why?"

He thought. It was a simple enough question.

"It's because of people. People are greedy, aggressive, envious, and competitive." He looked down at her for a moment. She was looking at him with a smile that he recognised as gratitude, to something, somewhere. "Particularly men", he went on. "They like to fight because they like to win. They like power. So they fight to get more—more power, more land, more wealth, more of anything they want."

"But then so many of them, even if they win, get killed, get wounded, or get sick and don't get better. And so do many, many people who aren't even fighting the war—my mother, my little brother. How is any of that any good?"

"It's not. It's dreadful, cruel, pointless. But when wars start, that's not what people think of. They think of victories and parades and being proud of their country."

"You said last week that you think there'll be another war."

"No one knows, Anna. There may not be. Herr Stresemann and Monsieur Briand have tried so hard to make sure there will be peace. Perhaps peace will last. People are also good, unselfish, kind, after all."

"Like you."

"Anna, you don't know me. I am very proud, revengeful, ambitious, with more offences—I can't remember how it goes on."

"What?"

She looked horrified. He laughed, gently.

"It's all right. It's what Hamlet says. He means we're not as good as you think we are, any of us. Men."

"No! You are not Hamlet. You are his friend, and you are alive at the end of the play, which is better."

She was pleased with this, and smiled up at him. So this time he really kissed her. After a moment or two, she pulled away.

331

"No, Max, no. Not yet. I don't . . . you frighten me . . . and Jakob would . . ."

"If Jakob brings you to Germany, he must expect . . . How old are you, Anna, now?"

"I'm nineteen. I was nineteen in November."

"Exactly. Nineteen's not so very young. And he allows you to come out with me. To concerts. To the park."

"Yes. Because he trusts you."

His arm was behind her, lying along the back of the park bench. He wanted to put it round her shoulders, to draw her back towards him, to reassure her, but decided not to.

"Anna?"

"Yes?"

"Do you think he trusts me because he thinks I'm Jewish? Because he doesn't know about my mother's family?"

"I'm not sure. I haven't told him. But perhaps he knows. I don't know."

"If he does know, and trusts me all the same, that's good, isn't it?"

"One day I'll have to talk to him. But it's for his sake too that I haven't. The quartet has been very good for him. He works so hard at the hospital, and he loves to play. Also to talk. There's nowhere else where he's able—German Jews, you know, in the hospital, in the university, he says they're so German they've forgotten they're Jews. The Grossmanns, for example. And the Jews from the east are so poor. Sometimes if they have interesting illnesses, they are sent to the hospital, and then Jakob, because he knows Yiddish, is called to interpret, to help to look after them. He loves them, of course, but they're patients, and he can't talk to them about . . . about anything of his own. That's why the evenings with you and Baron von Treuburg and—do him so much good."

"Anna. This is important. Do you think, by now, that your brother trusts me with you because he trusts *me*, a person he plays quartets with and knows a little? Or does he still trust me only because my grandfather's name was Meyer and everyone in the university knew my grandfather as a Jewish doctor?"

"Max—I don't know. I really don't know. But I'm certain that, in time, if he gets to know you properly, he will understand. He wouldn't ever trust the baron, because of Eva Grossmann. Jakob thinks all that . . . all that kind of thing . . . very . . . not wicked exactly but very . . . very un-Jewish, very . . . I don't know the right word . . . undistinguished?"

Max laughed. "Vulgar. Yes, he's right."

"And of course he wouldn't ever trust the count because he's a Polish nobleman with a mother who wears a swastika."

"You say 'of course'. But you know, don't you, that Adam can be trusted by anyone, because of who he is, not because of what he is. That's the point. That's what's important. And your brother is a clever man, too clever to prejudge people according to who their parents are or where they come from. Prejudice. Prejudging. It's all part of why people are taught to hate, or just despise, other people, because they're Jews, or Slavs, or Prussians like my father, or Catholics—my father despised Catholics—anything you like. It's part of why there are wars."

She thought about this.

"Why is the world so horrible?"

"It's because of people. As I said before. People can make a mess of anything, and they do. But they can also make things better. Your brother's a doctor. He would treat anyone, anyone at all, because the person was ill. Wouldn't he?"

"Yes. I know he would."

"So would Joachim Treuburg. He's a real doctor too. Sometimes I wish—it's so clear, being a doctor. But perhaps a lawyer may be able to do some good too. We have laws that are supposed to treat everyone the same, although ..."

"Although?"

"Well, in practice, they don't. When there are fights, meetings broken up, demonstrations on the streets turning into violence, that kind of thing, Stormtroopers beating Communists or Social Democrats, or the other way round, what happens? The courts are lenient with the Stormtroopers but are much harder on the Communists and the Social Democrats. The judges are on the right, politically—almost all of them are nationalists, conservatives—so they punish people on the left much more fiercely than people on the right who have committed the same offences."

"So one day you will be a more just judge, and punish people for what they've done, as a doctor treats people for their illness, not for who they are?"

"That's it. That's exactly it. You're a bright girl, you know, Anna, not just a good viola player, and very pretty."

"Max! Please don't!"

"Sorry. It's true all the same. It's all right." He smiled at her, and she smiled back. "I won't—don't worry—your brother trusts me, and it's for me to make sure you know he's not making a mistake. Are you getting cold?"

She looked round as if she had no idea where they had been sitting all this time.

"No. Perhaps a little. Look. The sun's going down, and the band's stopped playing. I didn't notice."

"Let's skate once round the lake as fast as we can without falling over, and then go and find some hot chocolate. With lots of cream."

Two weeks later, Max went to see Dr Fischer. "Come at six o'clock on Sunday", the old man had written in his reply to Max's request. "I try always to give myself a little break from work these days, at six o'clock; my concentration is not what once it was. I shall be pleased to see you." Max wanted to talk to him alone, and it was impossible to guess when he would have the flat to himself. Treuburg's hours at the hospital were unpredictable, and young Felix Stern, a second-year medical student from Prague who was now living in Adam's room, was often at home toiling over his textbooks for an examination he had to take at the end of March.

Stern was a shy boy, very earnest, with spectacles and an anxious expression, keen not to be in anyone's way, very grateful for the room. His family was Jewish, his father a doctor and his mother a nurse; he had been brought up with no religion. He didn't play any instrument, but on the one evening, two days ago, when the Halperns had come and they had played two Haydn quartets, he had listened with real attention from a corner of the sitting room, and Max saw him only just managing not to clap at the end of the first quartet.

That evening, while they were drinking their coffee, Halpern had said, "Dr Wolf is putting together a small orchestra to accompany the Saint Matthew Passion in England during April. The Bach Choir from the university has been invited to perform in, I believe, three English cathedrals, and a good orchestra is needed for the tour. He invited me—there will be only eight violins, I think. Naturally, I cannot accept the invitation, but I suggested that you might like to go. I vouched for your playing."

"Thank you." Adam, Max thought—how can I go without him? But he would tell me to go. "How soon do I need to decide? And will it cost a lot?"

"In the next week, you should tell Dr Wolf if you would like to go. There will be rehearsals, starting soon. It will cost you nothing. Someone is paying, the Ministry of Culture in Berlin probably. The plan, I have no doubt, is to demonstrate that German culture is still alive, that Germans make music as well as poison gas."

Max couldn't decide. England? Miss Wilson was the only English person he had ever met. On the other hand, Shakespeare. He didn't want to leave Anna for too long, and Halpern would never let her go to England, even if she were invited to join the Bach orchestra. Perhaps she had been asked, and Halpern had said no for her as well as for himself. Max would see what his old schoolmaster thought.

Dr Fischer lived in the ground-floor flat of a large terraced house in a nineteenth-century street not far from the school.

"Come in, come in, Hofmannswaldau. It's always a pleasure to see you. Ach! I see it's snowing again. Leave your coat and hat there, on the hook. I have a big fire in my study. Come in."

"Thank you, sir."

"Now, sit down. There, the other side of the fire. Would you like a beer? Or I have a very nice plum brandy from Bavaria. Would you like to try it?"

"Very much. Thank you."

Dr Fischer's study was as Max might have imagined it: a large, comfortable, dark, untidy room, with long red curtains over a window that perhaps looked out onto a garden, a light on the desk where two piles of exercise books sat on the left of a big leather blotter, a large Latin dictionary and a large Greek lexicon on the blotter's right, a standard lamp behind each of the two armchairs on either side of the fire, and books everywhere: lining the walls, on the desk, and on the low table between the armchairs. On one side of the mantelpiece was a bust of Homer, on the other a reproduction of Raphael's painting of Plato and Aristotle. Max recognised this because Dr Fischer had brought it into his classroom one day and told them not to forget that Plato was pointing upwards to heaven while Aristotle's gaze was fixed on the earth. Between Homer and the painting hung a crucifix, the figure of Christ white, perhaps made of ivory, the arms not straight out sideways from the body but nailed in the palms a little higher than the head, so that the sense of him hanging was strong, and also the sense of him blessing, almost greeting, the person looking up at him.

"So", Dr Fischer said, as he sat down with his glass and looked over the top of his spectacles at Max. "You have come to talk to me about Zapolski?"

He knew. For a moment, Max felt wounded, almost betrayed.

"My dear boy", Dr Fischer said. "Don't be upset. Or don't be more upset than you are already—and I quite understand that you are—because he came here to talk two or three times before he made up his mind. It would not have been fair for him to ask for your help, would it?"

"That's what he said, but . . ."

"Exactly. He was quite right. The prospect of saying good-bye to you, at least for two or three years, was one of the things making his decision difficult in any case. To have added to the possible loss, for you both, any expectation that you could have discounted your friendship in trying to help him through the struggle would only have confused both of you more than was necessary. One needs to be rather older than either of you to be able to put oneself in someone else's place, particularly when there is a tie of friendship such as you have."

"I see." He did. He thought he did.

Dr Fischer smiled.

"The young find it difficult to imagine—that is to say, to understand with the sympathy of their souls—being old. But it is not so difficult for the old to imagine being young because young is what all the old have been."

Dr Fischer filled his pipe to his satisfaction—this took some time—lit it and puffed away for a minute or two.

"When I was about your age, a little younger in fact, I thought I had a vocation to the priesthood myself. Those were glory days for the Catholic Church in Germany: Bismarck had done his best to bully the Church out of her loyalty to Rome by closing the monasteries, appropriating Church property, and refusing to allow the appointment of Bishops—all the usual tactics of a Protestant government determined to regard Catholics as inevitable traitors. The whole thing was a failure. Catholics showed with resolution that they could be as loyal to Germany as they were to Rome, and Bismarck, naturally without saying so, actually admitted defeat. The only time he did, I think. So, in a family with uncles and cousins in the priesthood, it seemed a sound patriotic project to become a priest."

He paused.

"But you didn't?"

"As you see." His eyes were laughing over his half-moons. "A wise old priest asked me what I thought my so-called vocation had to do with God. I didn't have much of an answer. Then he asked me if I was in love. I was, I said. There was this beautiful girl, but she and I had decided that renunciation, so that I could become a priest, was the noble path for both of us. Do you know what he said?"

Max shook his head.

"A lot of Wagnerian nonsense. That's what he said. You marry her, and find your way to God with her beside you. He was quite right."

Dr Fischer took off his spectacles, polished them, and put them on again.

"Now. Zapolski's story is very different from mine all those years ago. In the first place, the boy has a brilliance of mind, an eye for what is essential, that I most certainly did not have when I was young. In the second place, though it cannot be separated, his struggle has truly been with God, not just for the last few months but for years. In the third place, the world, since the war, has changed, I think forever, in many important ways. You boys who were children when the war began will perhaps never be able to grasp quite how much it has changed. The certainties within which people used to grow up have gone. Everyone now who has any education or reads a newspaper has to make up his own mind about everything. Of most people, that is asking too much, so they find ways of allowing other people to make up their minds for them, and they will choose whatever will make them feel better. The present is difficult—when, in reality, is it not?—so the promise of a golden future is what they're inclined to choose: this is the secret of the success of both left and right. The left promises the people's paradise on earth, a manifest impossibility, given the greed, laziness, and selfishness inherent in every human being. The right promises a new war that Germany will win, the restoration of throne and altar as if they were the same, or, more dangerous still, the triumph of the will translated into the triumph of the Aryan race—what nonsense! What wicked nonsense! As if we could—or as if God does—judge people according to their biological fitness! It's the soul which is judged, and also which judges, Christianity has always believed, and into each other's souls we cannot see."

Dr Fischer got up, stiffly, and picked up the bottle of plum brandy.

"A little more?"

"No thank you, sir. It's very good."

"You're right. It is powerful stuff." He poured himself a little more and sat down again.

The warmth of the fire, the brandy, and the familiar sound of Dr Fischer's voice explaining made Max feel better than he had since Adam left, except on his skating afternoon with Anna.

"In some ways the right, which uses and subverts Christianity for its own ends—flags and the Kaiser instead of God or, increasingly I fear, swastikas and Hitler instead of God, in both cases with plenty of borrowed talk of salvation, redemption, blood, and sacrifice—is more frightening, more evil I would say, than what you get on the left, which straightforwardly despises Christianity. Contempt is at least clear. Either way signifies death to the poor republic, death to the centre. It was inspired, you know, all those years ago, the choice of the Centre for the name of the Catholic political party. It was in itself a demonstration that it is possible for the centre to be principled and definite about some very important things. It was also a demonstration that the Church doesn't have to be, as she has always been in France, for example, on the right. But now, alas, the centre, not only the party but also the real centre, the only place from which sensible judgements, one by one, may be made, is becoming weaker by the year, by the month almost.

"And what has all this to do with the calling to the priesthood of Zapolski, who isn't even a German? A great deal, I would say. Everywhere in Europe since the war, God needs his priests to help people to understand that man is a fallen creature who can manage nothing good without the grace of God, and that the grace of God is always offered to him in the sacraments of the Church if only he will recognise his need of it, of them. You see, Hofmannswaldau, what is blasphemous about both the promise of the left and the promise of the right is that neither will acknowledge the fallibility of man, his dependence on God. Both of them suppose that man can do everything for himself and therefore that there was no need for the Incarnation, no need for Christ to come into the world and die and be raised from death. That is the heart of the blasphemy, because once man has no need of God and is permitted to do everything for himself, that is precisely what he will do. The self, what I want, what I can get at the other fellow's expense, what a few of us can get at the expense of the many, what the Aryans can get at the expense of the

338

Jews or the Slavs—the will of the self now has no bounds, and cruelty will be sanctioned on the right by the idea that the strongest have the right to prevail, and on the left by the idea that the strongest will deliver paradise to the weak. Which they will not.

"Meanwhile, there must be judgement, exercised every day, about small things and great, exercised in the light of Christ, with reference to the absolutes, the goodness, the truth, the beauty of God, and people must be able to look to the Church for help in making these judgements. And the Church more than ever will need priests with educated minds to give people with less ability, less good fortune, the capacity to make such judgements for themselves. God does not sleep."

"The court of the Lord is never closed, in the here or in the hereafter."

Dr Fischer looked sharply at Max.

"That is precisely right. Where did you find those words?"

"A friend of ours. Dr Halpern. He is Jewish—he's the brother of Anna, the girl you met when you came for tea. He says he doesn't believe that God exists."

"Yet this is the kind of thing he says to you?"

"Well, yes. He says all sorts of things."

"Of course. But the Jews have God in their bones. In Germany, with much encouragement, they have made great efforts to forget God, and many of them have succeeded. But your friends the Halperns are not from Germany."

"No. From Vilna."

"Exactly."

Max put down his empty glass on the low table between them.

"Dr Fischer?"

"Yes, Hofmannswaldau?"

"If Adam had asked me what I thought—you know, I wouldn't have tried to discourage him."

"It's easier for you to see, now, that you shouldn't have tried to discourage him. But it would have been a shock—as I'm sure it was when he told you his decision was made—and it's difficult to find the best in oneself to deal with a shock."

"Do you know what I feel most of all, now that he's gone? More than the loss of him. Envy. I envy him his clarity, his certainty. I envy all he knows, all he's been taught, that I don't have any real idea of."

"I wouldn't envy him too much. I can see that, now, as he begins his new, exciting life in the seminary, his certainty about what he's undertaking must look enviable to you, left behind with so much more to do at the university and perhaps no very strong conception of your life as a lawyer. But don't underestimate the difficulty for Zapolski, for a young man of his particular gifts and sensitivity, of what lies in store for him in the next few years. His notion of Cracow is very understandable: so ancient, so beautiful, so romantic, the old capital of the Polish commonwealth he's only recently learnt about. But a seminary, I'm afraid, is a seminary anywhere. Bleak. Bare. Very little music except for plainchant. Floor polish and bad food. Nothing to look at but the pious oleographs on the refectory walls. And his fellow students won't be easy for him to deal with: they'll be suspicious of his background, his German education, his talents, his brains—unless he's better than I suspect at hiding who he is. He'll miss you, I've no doubt, at least as much as you'll miss him."

"Poor Adam", Max said. Suddenly the whole enterprise looked quite different.

"Yes and no. If he has the courage and resolve to stick at it, to deal with the unhappiness and loneliness he's bound to meet, and perhaps above all with the irritation he's bound to be caused by men slower and stupider than he is, some of them his superiors, he'll make a very fine priest. Also he has in his character a useful streak of what the Poles call *polot*. It means lightness, insouciance, the ability to fly over, fly through hardship, as if it weren't so hard after all. Zapolski has that ability, without a doubt."

"So do you think he will? Stick at it?"

Dr Fischer looked at Max for a long moment before he answered.

"With the help of God, yes, I think he will. Don't you?"

"Yes, I do."

This time Dr Fischer got to his feet and filled Max's little glass without asking. When he sat down again, he said, "And what about you, Hofmannswaldau? How is Miss Anna?"

"She ... she was a little in love with Adam, like all of us in a way. But she's a sensible girl, and I think she's really ... proud of knowing him, proud of his having decided as he has. She is impressed by what he's doing."

"So her brother hasn't persuaded her not to believe in God?"

"No. He may have tried. Or perhaps not. Like Voltaire."

340

Dr Fischer laughed. "Safer to leave women benighted, you mean? He really was a terrible man in some ways, Voltaire. And you, and Miss Anna?"

"She's a lovely girl. She's nineteen, but—I don't know—very young in some ways."

"And you're very old?"

"No, of course I'm not. But ..."

"But nothing. You marry her, and find your way to God with her beside you." He smiled at Max. "I'm sorry. I'm quoting my old priest, long ago and far away. But it wasn't bad advice then, and probably isn't now."

"But ..."

"I know. She's Jewish. Her brother, whatever he may say about not believing in God, won't want her to marry a gentile. A Prussian count, my goodness!"

He gave Max another of his sharp looks. "But it isn't as simple as that, is it? You would say, would you not, that you have no religious convictions at present? Am I right? I imagine that you were brought up as a Protestant?"

"I went to church every Sunday with my parents when I was a child. They never talked about religion. There were long sermons I didn't listen to. I liked the hymns. The pastor came to the house sometimes, for lunch. My tutor, who was a Jew from Alsace, a musician, talked about God sometimes. All that was before my father died. Then I came to Breslau, so as to go to the Gymnasium. I lived with my grandfather. He and my grandmother—who had died by then—were Jews, officially converts to the Protestant religion. But my grandfather never went to church, or to the synagogue either, of course. He said he wasn't sure whether he believed in God or not. I thought he meant that really he did. So I know almost nothing about Christianity, except a very little I've learnt from Adam."

"You loved your grandfather?"

"Very much. He was a kind and clever man, good at all sorts of things. Adam called him Nathan the Wise."

"Have you ever been to a Catholic church, to Mass?"

"Twice when I was a child at Waldau, with my Polish nanny: when my brother was killed at Tannenberg and when my father died. My father was killed by the Freikorps in a riot in the village at home in 1919. And then Adam and I were at a funeral Mass—quite by accident—in San Vitale in Ravenna, last summer. Dante's funeral, he called it."

"Yes. He told me about that."

Max picked up his glass, took a sip, and put it down.

"If I wanted to find out more, sir, about Christianity, about the Catholic Church—because of Adam—what would you recommend me to do?"

"Ah."

"I don't like . . . being so left behind. I'd like at least to have some idea of . . . well, exactly what it is that has made him change his whole life. If it's true, he says, it makes all the difference to everything. I don't even know what he means."

"You know more than you think you do, thanks to Zapolski. There are plenty of people who call themselves Christians to whom it has never occurred that what you have just said is the case. It is."

Dr Fischer leant forward, with an expression on his face that Max recognised from long ago in the classroom. It always used to appear when a boy had asked exactly the question the old schoolmaster had been hoping for.

"All educated Germans, whether they know it or not, are, alas, pupils of Kant. They may have never read him, never even have heard of him, but somewhere in their heads they are certain that dogmatic Christianity has been left behind in the childhood of Europe, that no intelligent person can or should any longer actually believe that the assertions made by orthodox Christianity are true. It has a strong moral tone, all this. Kant said that anyone remaining in the condition of minority, refusing to become an adult, was to blame for his cowardice. Be brave enough to think for yourself, he said, and you will grow out of the errors of the past, of which orthodox Christianity is the greatest. He called the Middle Ages an incomprehensible aberration of the human mind: no one thought clearly between Aristotle and Descartes because Christianity didn't allow clear thought. The very term 'Enlightenment', of which educated Germans are so proud, implies that Christianity is darkness. You see? All this is entirely familiar to you, is it not, although I don't suppose for a moment that you have read Kant—any more than Zapolski had when he was trying so hard to impress us all as the schoolboy who had read everything."

"Yes, it is familiar, of course. One doesn't often think it out, but I remember my grandfather saying that when he was young he and his friends believed in science instead of God. He was a doctor, like Halpern, who thinks that education will solve everything. And no, I haven't read Kant himself—Adam and I did try, when we were about seventeen, but he was too difficult, even for Adam. We couldn't understand him. He did write a lot about God, though, didn't he?"

"Certainly he did. But his God is an abstraction, found to be necessary to the operation of pure reason, the only kind of thought Kant regarded as legitimate. Of the God who loved the world so much that he sent his only-begotten Son to rescue us from death, he says nothing, because the definite statement that that is what God has done, the dogmatic teaching of the Church down the ages that is at the very heart of Christianity, is an embarrassment to him. Christianity is not primarily a philosophy. It is about love, gift, grace, and the asking of a question to which we can reply only with love and praise or by turning away. It is about"—Dr Fischer looked up to the white figure on the cross above the fire—"Christ, who was crucified and rose from the dead to take us with him through death into the glorious life of God. Learn from me, he says. It is not about reason, it is not in itself philosophy, although it can always be thought about, once it is accepted as the truth, with proper philosophical rigour, with all the reason an intelligent person can bring to it. This was the great work of the despised Middle Ages."

"So it really is 'unless you become as a little child'?" Max said.

Again the keen look over the spectacles.

"That's right. But by no means does that warning imply that the adult Christian has to walk backwards into childhood, abandoning all, or indeed anything, that he has learned or that the scientists or the philosophers have taught us. Nothing that is true can be made untrue by the truth itself; the truth itself is that by which all other claims to truth are to be tested. The sea of God, a wise man said, is always shallow enough for children to paddle in and always deep enough for the cleverest philosopher to swim in.

"So you see," Dr Fischer said, smiling again as he leaned back in his chair and tapped out his pipe into a large wooden bowl full of ash and charred tobacco, "it's never too late, just as it's never too soon, to make a start. Now is always the time."

"Yes, sir. Adam said something like that", Max said. "But where—what—should I start with?"

"Well." He took out his tobacco pouch, from the baggy pocket of what looked like the very same shabby old-fashioned suit he had always

343

worn at the Gymnasium. "Here are three things for you to do. Go to Mass on Sundays, every Sunday for a while. I suggest you go to Saint Michael's Church. It's not far to walk from your flat, and it's a small church with a fine parish priest, Fr Görlich. If he asks you, say I suggested you should go to his church. Just turn up, listen, watch, and learn. No one will bother you or expect you to know anything you don't yet know. Second, before you get into bed every night, and before you get out of it in the morning, say the Our Father, without speaking the words but paying attention properly to every phrase and listening for what the words mean. They will mean more and more as time goes by. Third"—he put down his pipe without lighting it, creaked to his feet, and went to the bookshelves behind his desk—"read this book."

He gave Max a plainly bound, quite small book.

"You can keep it. I have the Latin text and several copies of this translation. Some very great men have never been parted from a copy of this book. It was written fifteen hundred years ago, by a man more intelligent than any one any of us is likely to meet and by no means a child in experience or understanding. He writes very much better than Kant did, and you won't find him difficult."

The book was called *The Confessions of Saint Augustine*.

"Saint Augustine—I'm afraid I know nothing about him."

"For that I am to blame. It has always been the custom in schools to read the Greek writers of the fifth and fourth centuries and the Latin writers of the two centuries either side of the birth of Christ, as if no one had written beautiful Greek or beautiful Latin later than those periods. This too is the fault of the Enlightenment. The later writers of both beautiful Greek and beautiful Latin were Christians, and so they belong to the darkness rather than the classical light. How foolish. And how sad. But examinations have to be passed.

"Augustine was the last great Roman writer, a Roman of North Africa, where he was for many years a Bishop as the barbarians approached, but he was by no means the last great writer of Latin. If you read that book, you will get to know him better than it is possible to get to know any other person in the ancient world. And he is worth knowing. The single most important idea in Augustine is not, however, in that book. It is in a book so long and rich that I wouldn't think of recommending it to someone of your age, with lectures to go to and theses to study for in the university. Although . . ."

"Although?"

"You are studying law, are you not?"

"Yes, sir. Law, and history."

"Then before you are very much older you should read *The City of God*. It's a book whose time has come again, because it doesn't belong to the Middle Ages, when everyone believed in Christianity: it came out of a world in which most educated people did not believe in Christianity. A world like our own, where people were inclined to think the state more important than it is."

Dr Fischer, who had been standing with his back to the fire since he fetched the book for Max, smiled down at him.

"I'm sorry, Hofmannswaldau. Once I start, I find it hard to stop. One gets spoiled in classrooms, where the boys have to listen politely for however long the old man chooses to bore on. Try the *Confessions*, and the Mass and the Our Father. You'll come to no harm. You'll be paddling at first, but my guess is that in a few months, perhaps in a few weeks, you will be swimming. Do you have a Bible?"

Max thought of the books in the flat—Grandpapa's, his own, a few left behind by Adam, Treuburg's medical textbooks.

"I don't think so. There was a big Bible at Waldau, in my father's library, with the family coat of arms on the front, but I never saw anyone open it."

"Buy one, a small, cheap one. Luther's translation of the Bible is a book no German should be without, although I'm afraid many Catholics are too afraid of it to have it in the house. Poor Luther, a most unattractive man in many respects. He started it all, of course, the disappearance of God into the abstractions of the philosophers, but it would have horrified him. It was Luther himself who said that without assertions, there is no Christianity. If only his entirely justified criticisms of the Church as she was then could have been met, if only his sense of the love and grace of God could have been contained as it should have been, things would have been so very different ever since. As it is, I was taught, long ago in the Gymnasium in Cologne, and no doubt you also were taught by Dr Hornberg, that German history has been a shining upward path from Luther to Bismarck. The shine is somewhat muddied now by the war, but soon the upward path will be resumed. Ach! A *downward* path is closer to the truth. There was in Luther, mixed with the good, so much violence and rage. Also the beginnings of Protestant nationalism. He was terrible, really terrible, about the Jews. Alas for Germany.

"But find yourself a copy of his Bible—Augustine will send you all over the Bible to look things up. If you want to read some of it for yourself, read Saint John's Gospel, or Saint Paul's Letter to the Romans, or the last five chapters of the book of Job. You will be astonished. Now—I must be getting back to my exercise books. Come and visit me again if you want to; I shall always be happy to see you. And Miss Anna—don't leave her out. It's possible that she has a stronger sense than you have had any opportunity to acquire of what it is to live in the presence of God."

Max got up, his book in his hand.

"May I ask you one quite different question. sir?"

"Of course you may."

"I've been asked to go to England in April, to play in a small orchestra for the Saint Matthew Passion, in, I believe, three English cathedrals. Do you think I should go?"

"Oh, yes! You lucky boy. Certainly you should go. I was in England for nine months in 1887. I was about your age. I was studying in Oxford, in the university. So long ago, it seems. That was when I first read Shakespeare in English, and Wordsworth and Keats. The English Romantic poets. So beautiful, and Oxford such a beautiful city. As for the cathedrals—we have nothing to equal them in Germany. Now, of course, the English are bound to be more suspicious of us. It won't be the same. But I can't believe it will be so very different. The English and the Germans were always allies, you know, until 1914. It was always France that was the enemy. Yes, you must go. England is an extraordinary country. It is a country of compromise and muddle—take its national church, for example—but the English have a mildness, a gentleness we should all learn from. Send me a postcard or two, of the cathedrals you play in. I should like that."

They were in the hall. Max put on his coat. "Thank you, sir. Thank you more than I can—"

"Good-bye, my boy. God bless you."

They shook hands, and Dr Fischer opened the door. As Max set out into the snow and looked back, the old man waved. Max took off his hat and waved it in return.

Despite the absence of Adam, which soon became an ache to which Max was accustomed, punctuated every so often by the pain of remembering that he couldn't tell him, ask him, anything any more, the rest of that winter of 1928 passed happily. In the mornings, he attended lectures and classes, mostly in the various branches of the law and of legal history, which were compulsory subjects for those intending to qualify as future judges. He had added a course in constitutional history given by a youngish professor from Prague who belonged to the political centre and was hopeful for the future of the postwar nations: Max's impression was that he was much disliked by the old, nationalist history professors in the university, who regarded him as suspect, foreign, an irritant who couldn't even be written off as belonging to the left. Because the professor admired the ramshackle structure of the Habsburg empire more than the Protestant establishment of Prussia, Max thought he might be a Catholic, but the professor was careful to reveal no religious loyalty, and his highest term of praise was "liberal", which had the right-wing students in the class exchanging scornful looks every time he used it.

Work was good because there was plenty of it: listening, reading, and thinking filled the day constructively, and as he thought harder about both the past and the present, it was becoming increasingly clear that the law and justice—what was meant by justice when it was said that "the Lord thy God is a just God"—were not necessarily the same thing and that lawyers would always be needed to make sure that they were as close together as possible. This began to seem at least as worthwhile a future as the medical career he had often regretted failing to choose when he was at school.

Meanwhile, the rehearsals for the Saint Matthew Passion—at first, two, then later four, evenings each week—were an exhausting delight. He was playing on the first desk of the second violins, his companion a mild, blond boy from Danzig who was studying chemistry and hardly spoke a word. They were still rehearsing without solo singers except for the tenor singing the Evangelist, who taught harmony in the university music school. The sorrow and glory of the music, pulling Max further into its depths as both choir and orchestra became more accurate, more disciplined, with each rehearsal, became a grand, secret accompaniment to the plain musicless liturgy of the early Sunday Mass at Saint Michael's that he now attended every week. He sat, stood, and knelt with the congregation, right at the back beside an old Polish tramp who turned up sometimes, more or less sober and more or less dirty, in many layers of ragged clothes against the cold.

347

He was now familiar with the pattern of the Mass—he had bought himself a basic missal without German translations but with the readings proper to each Sunday—and he listened carefully to the Latin of the Epistle and Gospel, grateful that he knew the language, and to the parish priest's homilies, which now, in the Sundays of Lent, were gathering in intensity towards Passion Week, Palm Sunday, Holy Week. The foreboding of these Sundays, of these names for the weeks before Easter, was new to him: Bach's music, the detail of which engaged all his attention evening after evening in the big rehearsal room at the university, became part of what he was learning to expect as real events, as if they had never happened before. He was going to miss Palm Sunday and Good Friday at Saint Michael's, because the Bach choir and orchestra wouldn't be back in Breslau from the English tour until the evening of what he had learned Catholics called Holy Saturday.

As his work occupied him more, and the rest of what he was doing and thinking and feeling made more sense of his work, he found himself alive and attentive to every bit of every day. And all the time, although they met only once or twice a week, when they could go for a walk or sit for half an hour in a warm coffee house, he felt Anna beside him, at the Passion rehearsals, at Mass in Saint Michael's, at his desk at home, in the university library. They had played quartets only twice since he had taken her skating: Halpern and Treuburg hardly ever had the same evenings free. Those evenings were different now, Halpern silent and preoccupied, although he played his violin with his usual restrained fire. Max hoped it was Adam's absence that had changed the atmosphere but feared it was Halpern's suspicion that there was more between Max and Anna than he approved of.

Anna's company, trusting, affectionate, sometimes serious, sometimes simply happy, occasionally wistful, even melancholy, lit both the hours he had with her and the days without her. He was careful not to frighten her. He kissed her lightly when they met and when they parted. They held hands in the park. He hugged her, once or twice, because she was happy, or sad. He loved her. He was more and more confident that she loved him.

He took her with him to Mass on a Sunday in March, when for the first time there was a little warmth, a faint suggestion of spring, in the misty early morning air of what was going to be a fine day. Halpern was away at a medical conference in Berlin that Professor

Grossmann had told him to attend on his behalf, but Anna was afraid, nevertheless, that somehow he would discover that Max had taken her to a Catholic church.

"He'll never find out. Don't worry. Look, we'll stay here, quietly at the back. There's no one here who knows us."

He was glad, though a little ashamed to be glad, that the Polish tramp wasn't there.

He didn't try to explain the Mass: he knew she would understand nothing except the homily. The Gospel was the story of Jesus feeding five thousand people with five loaves and two fishes. Father Görlich, to whom Max had not yet spoken, preached on the perpetual every-day miracle of the Eucharist. "You see," he said, "this was a sign for us all, this apparently impossible feeding of the hungry people, when so little became so much. And at just this time of the year." He looked down at the open missal and read, "Erat autem proximum Pascha, dies festus Judaeorum." He looked up at the congregation. "It was close to the Pasch, the festival day of the Jews." Jesus, in the feeding of the five thousand, is foretelling the Paschal mystery, the breaking of his own body for us at the Passover season, the very breaking of his body to feed us that will shortly take place at this altar, as it does at every Mass. We must never forget, in these times full of hatred and con-tempt for the people of Israel, the very people Jesus was feeding on this mountain, that, as he said himself to the woman of Samaria, 'sal-vation comes from the Jews'."

As the priest closed the book and moved towards the altar, and the congregation stood for the Creed, Max glanced at Anna. She looked at him, her eyes alight with surprise and pleasure.

After the Sanctus bell, they knelt side by side until the end of the Mass, when everyone stood for the last Gospel. He could tell that Anna beside him never took her eyes off the priest at the altar. As they were leaving the church, with silent people in their winter clothes crowding towards the dark door, Max felt a large hand on his shoul-der. He turned to find Dr Fischer smiling at him.

"Good morning, Hofmannswaldau. And Miss Anna. Good morn-ing, my dear."

Max saw him notice the panic-stricken look on Anna's face, saw him put a finger to his lips without a word, and watched him walk ahead of them down the church steps into the morning as if he hadn't seen them at all.

"It's all right", he said to Anna. "I'd trust him more than almost anyone I know."

She shook her head. "Max, it's not that ... it's ..."

She couldn't go on. He took her hand and they walked through the early streets, empty once the congregation from Saint Michael's had dispersed.

"Coffee", he said. "That's what we need. Coffee and rolls and butter and jam. That's what we deserve for getting up at six. What did Frau Schönfeld think?"

"She was still asleep when I left. She doesn't get up till nine o'clock."

"Good. Here." He took Anna into an old coffee house in the Market Square where they had been once before. It was smoky, beamed, and warm; two or three customers were drinking coffee and reading newspapers fixed into the café's wooden newspaper holders.

The waiter came, went, then came back. Max poured out the steaming coffee, halved a hot roll, spread butter and jam on the halves, as for a small child, and put them on Anna's plate. She took a sip of her coffee.

"Max, are you a Catholic?"

"No. At least not yet."

"Not yet?"

"Perhaps, in a little while, when I have learnt more ... Yes. I think I may ask them if I can at least start learning what you need to know to become a Catholic, quite soon."

"Why? Jakob will never ..." Her eyes filled with tears, but she recovered quickly, blew her nose, and shook her head. "I thought you agreed with Jakob that—"

"I wanted to understand what Adam has done. Also, if we decide that Christianity isn't true, we ought to know what it is that we're saying isn't true. I had no idea, before."

She wasn't listening.

She said, "It was so ... so quiet, and holy, in the church. Like the old synagogue in Vilna. The prayers—I didn't understand them because I don't know any Latin. I know hardly any Hebrew, so I didn't understand the prayers at home in Vilna. But they seemed, just now, the Latin, and the quietness, real prayers, for God, to God. Not like the German prayers in the synagogue Frau Schönfeld took me to, with the organ and the rabbi who doesn't even have a beard. I can't explain. And all the candles in the dark corners ... Max, did you hear what he said, the priest?"

"Yes, I did."

"But if that's what Catholics really believe, that salvation comes from the Jews, why have they hated us so much all this time? Why have they called us God killers? If Jesus was a Jew and he was feeding all those people just before Passover, and if the bread and the wine were the Passover bread and the Passover wine, which we still have, why is it all so horrible between us? Jakob would make me go back to Vilna at once, I know, if he found out I had been to a Catholic church with you. And those people just now, not Dr Fischer, but those nice harmless people, old ladies saying prayers with their beads, they would have thrown me out if they'd known I was a Jew, in their church with them, wouldn't they? I don't understand any of it. But I would like to understand better, and . . . and now I would be sad if I never went to a Catholic church ever again, because it was good, and God is there. I know he is."

"It is difficult," Max said, "almost impossible, all of it, to understand. So much history and so much hatred. Eat some breakfast, Anna. You're still thin and pale from your illness and the winter. Breakfast makes one feel stronger anyway. Go on."

Obediently, she ate some bread and jam and drank a little more coffee, waiting for him to explain.

"Catholics do believe that God is there, that Christ is there, in the bread and wine after the consecration, in the consecrated bread that's kept in the tabernacle, which is like a holy cupboard in the church with a lamp always burning in front of it."

"But that's just like the ark in the synagogue, a holy cupboard where the scrolls of the Torah are kept. It has a lamp too, just the same. And when the ark is opened, everyone stands up."

"The word of God. It *is* almost the same. I didn't know that, about the scrolls. The great, great difference is that Christians believe that the word became flesh, that the word of God came into the world as a man, Jesus."

"And he was the Messiah."

"That's right. That's why Jews and Christians can never agree: Christians believe the Messiah has come; Jews believe that one day he will come."

"Or not."

"Or not?"

"Jakob's friends, at home, used to talk and talk about the Messiah. They said the first superstition that Jews must give up is the hope

351

that the Messiah will come. They said that for hundreds of years it's kept the Jews in servitude in all the countries where they live, stopped them doing anything for themselves, anything to make their lives better. Some of them thought the revolution, first in Russia, then everywhere, would be better than the coming of the Messiah. Some of them thought the Jews living in Palestine would be the same as the coming of the Messiah, what it really meant. Either way, it's up to Jews themselves to achieve what the prophets meant by the Messiah. But now that Jakob's given up both those ideas, I don't know what he thinks the prophets meant about the Messiah. Nothing at all, I expect. Just wild men in the desert trying to make the Jews be good. And do you know something else?"

"What?"

"I've just thought—when the Messiah comes, there's supposed to be peace and justice in the whole of the earth, the reign of God—and look at the history of Europe since Christians were ruling everything! Jesus can't have been the Messiah, can he? Max?"

"Yes?"

Anna held her cup in both hands and looked at him with puzzled eyes.

"Was Jesus a Jew? A good, religious Jew?"

"Of course he was."

"Then how can he be still alive, when the prophets are all dead, when even Moses is dead?"

"Jesus died, he really died, as we all have to die. But at Easter, he came out of death into a new kind of life, which will one day be for all of us. I can't explain it. Perhaps no one can. But it makes all the difference to everything. It sheds a new kind of light into the darkness."

"Was it the new light from Jesus that the priest was talking about when he said salvation comes from the Jews?"

"Yes. I think it was. The light that came into the darkness which the darkness could not put out. That's from the last reading we had at Mass—but you wouldn't have understood that. Look. When Jesus was a baby, six weeks old, his mother took him to the temple to present him to God because he was a firstborn son. Do Jews still do that?"

"I don't know. I think very religious Jews still do."

"There was an old man there, a very good and holy old Jew, whose name was Simeon. He'd been promised by the Holy Spirit that he wouldn't die until he saw the Messiah. When he saw the baby in the temple, he knew he was the Messiah, and what he said to God shows exactly how salvation comes from the Jews."

"What did he say?"

"I'll read you his words."

Max got out of his pocket the Bible he'd bought in the same shop where he'd found his missal. Both were small black books with pages of very thin paper. The Bible he had carried about with him for the last few weeks.

"This is what he said. 'Lord, now let your servant go in peace as you have said, because my eyes have seen your salvation, which you have prepared before—to be seen by, that means—all peoples, a light to be the light of the heathen, and to be the glory of your people Israel.' You see, the Messiah, Jesus, is the way in which the light of God that the Jews already have will be spread to all the people of the world. That's what he's saying. There's an old woman in the temple as well, very holy, very old, and she knows who this baby is, too. She's called Anna."

"Really? Let me see."

He gave her the little book, his finger on the passage he had read aloud. She read it, shut the book, looked at the gold lettering on the back, *The Bible*, and gave it back to him.

"I've never seen a Christian Bible before."

"Most of it's the Jewish Bible. Look."

He found the beginning of the New Testament and showed her the open book.

"Only a quarter of the whole Bible's the Christian part."

"Could I ... could I read it, do you think? The Christian part?"

"Why not? I've been reading it myself for the first time, lately. It's not difficult to understand—at least the Gospels are simple in a way, and at the same time very mysterious."

But she shook her head.

"No. I can't. What would Jakob say, or my father? They would be really shocked, and very angry with me, and even more angry with you."

"All this anger. All this hatred. What can God think, the God of the Jews and the Christians? As for Jakob, if he doesn't believe the Messiah will come and doesn't believe the word of God means anything—that's what he says, at least sometimes—then how can he mind if you read the New Testament?"

353

"He would be very angry."

"He needn't find out. Here, take the book. I'd like you to have it. I'll get another one."

"I don't know ... I don't think ..."

She looked at the Bible in his hand as if it were a grenade that might go off.

Max laughed and put it back in his pocket.

"All right. It's too risky. Never mind."

"I'm sorry, Max."

"Don't be silly."

He put his hand on hers for a moment.

"One day, perhaps", he said.

She smiled back at him. "Yes. One day."

"Here's a plan", he said, sounding to himself like Adam. "Why don't you come to the last rehearsal of the Saint Matthew Passion? On Friday at six, in the university concert hall. With all the soloists. We're leaving for England the day after. You've never heard it, have you?"

"No."

"It'll be good for your musical education. Jakob's got no objection to Bach, has he?"

"No, but ..."

"But?"

"I wish you weren't going to England."

"Anna ... I know. But it's only for two weeks. I'll send you postcards. And I'll be back almost before I've gone."

They walked back to Frau Schönfeld's flat, hand in hand through the Sunday streets in the freshness of the morning and the spring.

Anna came to the rehearsal. Max saw her at the back of the almost-empty auditorium—a few other students were scattered among the rows of seats—with her spectacles on and a score of the Passion, which she must have borrowed from the library, propped up on the back of the seat in front of her. Then he had to concentrate hard for the more than two hours that the rehearsal took.

At the end, she was waiting for him in the dark, on the wide pavement outside the concert hall.

"Max!" She came up to him and stood for a moment looking at him with her shining eyes, as if he had composed the Passion himself.

Then she dropped her score and threw her arms round his neck, hugging him as he stood with his violin in one hand and his coat over his other arm.

"Max, that was so beautiful. The most beautiful music I've ever heard. And the terrible story—so terrible. But it won't be ... the end ... for long, will it? Because of what you told me. They're lucky in England, to be going to hear this wonderful music."

"Anna. I'm glad you came. I'll walk you home. Then I must get back to the flat—I have to iron shirts, and pack, and try not to forget anything."

"Oh, it's so far away. Such a long journey. I'm afraid ..."

"Don't be afraid. Everything will be all right. I'll be back very soon, and I'll tell you all about England." He picked up the score.

She put her hand through his arm as they walked back. Outside Frau Schönfeld's house, under the streetlamp, Max, who had felt Anna's excitement overtaken by sadness as they walked, put down his violin and his coat and the score and took her by the shoulders. She looked up at him, her eyes full of love and tears.

"Anna, one day when we're a little older, and I'm earning some money ... will you marry me?"

She looked up at him.

"Max. Dear Max. One day ... perhaps ... if I can ..." He saw her read the fear in his eyes that she was saying no. "One day ... when I'm a teacher and we can ... Yes, Max, I will marry you."

She put both her hands behind his neck and clasped them, pulling his face down, and they kissed, for a long time.

"Now," he said, "in you go, my darling girl. I will come and fetch you on Saturday week. Holy Saturday. Two weeks from tomorrow. We get back in the afternoon. I'll come at six o'clock. We'll go for a walk and I'll tell you about England. Good night, my love."

She clung to him for a moment longer.

"Good night, Max. I will marry you", she whispered. "Perhaps even soon?"

"As soon as we can. I promise. Here." He picked up the score from the pavement and gave it to her.

At the top of the steps to the door, she turned and waved.

PART THREE

Chapter 13

Max had lost his bench—his bench and Anna's bench—where they had sat often, for what in retrospect seemed hours although there was never enough time, watching the water, the ducks and the pair of haughty swans floating in and out of the shadows of the willows and alders and the moving reflections of their leaves. Across the old moat were not the hills of the Riesengebirge but the spires and towers of Cathedral Island. Nevertheless, the bench had been the nearest Max could get to taking Anna to Waldau.

In the hottest weeks of this last summer, the summer of 1930, the bench had become the haunt, perhaps the home if the empty bottles beneath it and the tattered blankets spread over it were anything to go by, of an unemployed man, tall, middle-aged, clearly a Jew, with the yellow armband of the blind, and also his dog, a mangy mongrel who wagged his tail hopefully at anyone walking along the path by the moat. The man sat on the bench with his eyes shut, a notice on a string round his neck with two words in capital letters, WARBLIND, WORKLESS. Apparently he sat there all day, because he was there in the mornings when Max, on his way to the law courts, walked past and was still there in the evenings when Max walked back. The man's cap was laid on the grass by the path. Max put a coin in it—the hat was always almost empty—every evening, for Anna's sake, who couldn't pass a beggar without giving him something. The man must sometimes have heard the coin clink. He never gave any sign of recognition.

There were thousands like him in the city. Every month the newspapers reported the numbers of the unemployed in the whole country to be still rising. People in what they hoped were safe jobs kept track of the rising figures with the same nervous disbelief with which they had followed the lunatic rise of the number of marks to the dollar seven years ago. Breslau, with its many closed factories and mills, and its slums, so easy to forget, where lived the poorest families, the fathers badly paid even when they were in work, had the highest number of unemployed after Berlin of any city in the country. No wonder the KDP, the German Communist Party, was doing better and better. So easy, it was now, to describe the plight of the poor as all the fault of the capitalist system. So easy, and perhaps also accurate. Yet Max was certain that Marx could not be the only answer to capitalism gone wrong. Dr Mendel, Dr Fischer, and lately his own reading of *The City of God* had persuaded him that any belief in the inevitable progress of history towards perfection crushed people into the ground and was bound to be false.

It was difficult to know what to believe about Bolshevik Russia. Some stories in the papers were too good to be true; most were too bad. It all depended on which paper you read. Treuburg said all the worst stories were probably true.

Max worried about young Felix Stern, still living in the flat and still quietly keeping as much as he could out of the way of Max and Treuburg. He had, though he said very little, become passionately interested in politics. He had gone to Social Democrat meetings for a year and a half; now Max suspected he had joined the Communist Party. "So?" Treuburg said. "Perhaps he has, perhaps he hasn't. It's glamorous. He's only a student. He doesn't know much apart from medicine. He'll grow out of it. All the students—you don't know the students any more—are either Bolsheviks or Nazis. Most of them don't know why, don't know what they're doing."

"There you are. He can't be a Nazi. He's a Jew."

"Of course. One forgets. He makes so little fuss about it. That's Prague. A sensible place. On the other hand, should a Communist be lodging with a count and a baron?"

"A doctor and a lawyer. Even utopia will be hard-pressed to manage without doctors and lawyers."

As Max walked back to the flat through the warm streets on a mild September evening, he thought of the conversation earlier that day in a restaurant beween the district judge who was his superior and the banker who had asked the judge and one of his Referendars, Max, out to lunch. The invitation was to thank them for the work they had done in a case to deal with a list of major defaulters the bank was tracking down. The banker held forth.

"This will get worse before it gets better", he said. "I was in Berlin last week, at a bank directors' meeting, and I'm sorry to have to tell you that there's no optimism whatever in the financial world at present. Of course the root of the trouble in Germany is that we have no strong hand on the tiller. Whatever you may say about Stresemann, such an unprepossessing man and much too friendly with the French for my liking, he did inspire some confidence that someone in Berlin knew what he was doing. A great pity he died when he did, and just before the economic crisis. Now what have we got? Brüning. Who's he? A Centre party man, a soldier—no doubt that's why old Hindenburg made him Chancellor in spite of him being a Catholic. Clever, they say, and knows something about business. But he's been running the country for nearly six months, and is anything improving? Thank the Lord for the Stormtroopers and the sense the Nazis are talking, otherwise the Bolsheviks would be having it all their own way."

Max hoped his boss, Dr Gerlach, would defend the Chancellor, or at least not agree with this praise of the Nazis, but it seemed to be Dr Gerlach's strongest principle that a judge should never express an opinion about anything, so Max was not surprised when he only nodded wisely and said, "Further austerity measures will no doubt be necessary." It was not Max's place to offer a view of his own. The conversation then petered out in a discussion of the gold standard in relation to deflation of the German economy, an issue that Max saw Dr Gerlach understood as little as he did himself.

When he got back to the flat, he heard, as he shut the door, Treuburg playing Bach. This was rare nowadays. Treuburg reached a cadence, played it with a flourish, and stopped as Max came into the sitting room.

"Good", Treuburg said. "I'm glad you're back. I want to ask your advice."

This was so unexpected that Max didn't manage not to sound surprised. "Oh. Fine. Of course. Where's Stern?"

"Out. Some political meeting, I imagine. He took off his bourgeois suit and put on his socialist overalls. Have a drink."

Treuburg poured them each a glass of wine and sat on the sofa.

"Sit down. Now listen. I think a good deal of your judgement, Hofmannswaldau, and I would appreciate your view."

This was all very unlike Treuburg, who was normally crisp, uncommunicative, and, though they had lived in the same flat for nearly five years, coolly impersonal. When for months of 1928 Max had been dealing with the loss of Anna so soon after the loss of Adam, Treuburg had never once shown him more warmth than the routine amiability of every day, though Max knew he knew something of what he was going through. Once the pain was less, he was grateful for this reticence.

Obediently he sat down in Grandpapa's chair.

"You know I've now qualified as a physician", Treuburg began, holding his glass in both hands and looking at the floor. "You also know that I was in East Prussia for summer manoeuvres in July and August, because reserve officers have to do summer manoeuvres every other year. This year I went home to see my parents. My mother was much the same as usual. She was looking a bit older, naturally—I hadn't been home for four years—but she's well and very busy. She's anxious about the peasants on the estate. They're always poor. You've never been to East Prussia. It's very different. Treuburg is only three or four hundred miles from Breslau, but the country's at least a century behind Silesia. No cars. No surfaced roads. No farm machinery of any description. Everything that's produced, and it's not much—potatoes, beets, sawn timber from the forest, reeds from the lakes—is produced by hard, grinding labour. Maybe there's a cow or two. Maybe there's a pig to last a family through the winter and another fattened to sell. Maybe there isn't. But now the peasants aren't just poor. They're starving. Prices are so low that it's hardly worth them taking anything to market. My mother does her best, with the children particularly, and the sick. There's a school in the village, but the teacher teaches in German and the peasants mostly speak Masurian Polish, so the children don't go. My mother teaches the girls sewing and how to look after poultry, how to make jam and cheese, that sort of thing, to make life a little better at home and possibly even earn a bit of money. There's one old doctor in the nearest town, usually drunk. Anyway, my father. He's changed a great deal since I last saw him. He looks twenty years older. Thin. Very pale. I'm pretty sure he has a cancer somewhere, but he wouldn't answer my questions or let me examine him. He's not that sort of man. He's deeply, bitterly angry. As if his whole life has been made worthless, meaningless to him. And he made such an effort to get the estate running again and the house sorted out after what happened at the beginning of the war. The Russians wrecked the house. They shot the eyes out of the portraits on the walls. And that wasn't the worst of it by a long way. There was nothing much left in one piece when they'd gone. Including any girls they found anywhere. We were hiding in the head forester's cottage. My mother was extraordinarily brave. They never discovered us. But they didn't know to look. They didn't find the cello either—it was hidden in the hay-barn because they were more likely to burn straw, useless as fodder."

Treuburg stopped and drank a little of his wine. Max saw he hadn't finished and said nothing.

"My father used to be angry because, according to him, we were told we'd lost a war we'd won, and because he couldn't accept being part of a republic run by Catholics and Jews. Now he's thought about it harder and longer—for years, in fact, all by himself because my mother's only interested in what's to be done each day—and his anger goes all the way back to Bismarck and 1870. The year he was born. He used to be so proud of that. Now he thinks it was all a hideous mistake. God never intended Prussia to be an empire. A King of Prussia—a King *in* Prussia like Frederick I—was quite enough, more appropriate. Königsberg and Berlin, honest Prussian cities. Protestant. The army, disciplined, honourable, Protestant. If Prussians got beyond Protestant Christianity, then they were clever, philosophical, rational. My father's proud of Kant, though he hasn't read his books and wouldn't understand a word if he did. Now it's all over, all a hideous mess because of the empire. The Hohenzollerns are copying the Habs-burgs, as if they were an example and not a warning. Rhinelanders, Bavarians, Württembergers, Catholics, soft southern Germans, all included and told that they're the German empire and that the King of Prussia is the Emperor. Not the fault of good old Wilhelm I. The fault of Bismarck, the puppet master who enjoyed his puppet show, making Europe dance to his tune and destroying Prussia in the pro-cess. The so-called Kaiser, skulking in Holland on a fat pension to stop him coming back: he was the worst disaster of the lot. This was the real change in my father. You know he was an imperial page as a boy—he used to talk as if he'd be loyal to the death to the Kaiser. Now he calls him an exhibitionist ass, a joke Emperor in fancy dress making ridiculous speeches twice a week cracking himself up as as some kind of mystical leader appointed by the hand of God for the providential destiny of Germany. Frederick the Great—who's still my father's real hero—must be turning in his grave at the stupidity of it all, the stupidity of the high-flown talk that got us into the war. It wasn't destiny that made the empire. It wasn't God. It was Bismarck, a clever man setting up something only a clever man could manage, and leaving it to be run by idiots. So Germany has destroyed Prussia."

Treuburg stopped. After a long silence, Max said:

"Do you agree with your father?"

"I see his point. My father's no intellectual, and needless to say, there's a lot of romantic nostalgia in what he thinks—feels, more like—about Prussia. All the same, he has a sharp eye for nonsense, thank God, or he might be one of the old Junkers who think salvation will come from the Nazis. There are plenty of them, and to his credit, they depress my father as much as anything else. Have you heard of something called the Union for the German Church? No, of course you haven't. At least Catholics aren't allowed to add new crazy ideas to the old crazy ideas they've always been told to swallow. Well, this Union says that Jesus Christ is really Siegfried—thoroughly German, you see, thoroughly ancient—and that he's there to break the neck of the Jewish snake, which is Satan."

"Poor Fafner."

"What? Oh, Wagner. Yes. He talked a lot of rubbish himself, but nothing to equal this. The extraordinary thing, my father says, is that he's met people, old Prussians like himself, who actually believe this tosh, the same people, naturally, who think redemption lies with the Nazis. If not Jesus Christ—since the King of Prussia isn't there any more to keep the church straight—then Siegfried. And if not Siegfried, stabbed in the back like Ludendorff and Hindenburg, then Hitler. Hindenburg, that's another thing. Senile. Quite incapable of intelligent judgement. Did you know he fought against the Austrians in 1866, before my father was born?

"So, Jesus Christ is Siegfried, and both of them are Hitler. So much for Prussian education, famous throughout the world. God in heaven! Where he should stay, by the way. And what gets my father down even more than his dotty friends is the peasants. Bismarck gave the peasants the vote because he thought they'd always vote for the right, for the Junkers against the liberal bourgeoisie. Now they're as likely as not to vote for the Communists. Perhaps the KDP will do something to improve their miserable lives, slaving in the cold and the wet for no money. There's plenty of propaganda, village meetings, bribes, new boots for the children, to tell them so. But on the other hand, the peasants are terrified of Russians, as terrified of Stalin as they were of the Tsar. So what will thousands of them actually do, next week in the election? They'll vote for the Nazis. There are Nazi posters all over the place—in Masurian Polish, would you believe? The Nazis despise the Slavs but buy their votes. Hitler's no fool. The posters say the price of potatoes will go up, that the peasants will make more money on their crop, if the Nazis win the election. That really is diabolical. These wretched people can't read *Mein Kampf.* Most of them can't read, period. They don't know that if Hitler ever got any actual hold on power, he'd do his best to wipe them out. Along with the Jews—whom they don't like much more than Hitler does but on whom, in different ways, they depend almost as much as they depend on people like my father. It's a complete mess and likely to get worse. No wonder my father's in despair."

Another long silence.

"Treuburg?"

"Yes?" He looked up, surprised, almost as if he had been talking in his sleep and had woken to find himself in an unexpected place.

"What did you want to ask me?"

"Oh. Yes. Sorry. I shouldn't have bored you with all this. But the change in my father is so ... marked ... and I would like to do something that would cheer him a little before he dies. I don't think he'll live long, and that's a medical opinion."

He drank some more wine.

"The army has offered me a regular commission. As a doctor, of course, but as a captain with immediate effect. I'd intended to find a small town, a set of villages, somewhere not too far from my father's estate, with no doctor or a useless doctor, and set up there. But I don't think that's affordable now. I would need a bit of capital. I haven't asked my father, but judging by the state of the house and the stables and all that, I don't think there's any money to spare. Then a third possibility cropped up. Old Schmidt, my consultant, who's taught me practically everything I've learnt in the last two or three years, told me last week that he'd recommended me to the research people in the university. He's a good man, and a very good diagnostician—I've watched him often just looking at a patient and thinking, and he's nearly always right—but he's an innocent. He sent me to a professor, not a friend of his but a senior man with a solid reputation in biochemistry, infection control, new drugs, that kind of thing. 'Ah, Baron von Treuburg', he said. Bad start. Schmidt has always called me Treuburg *tout court*. It got much worse. Do you know what he offered me? Have some more wine."

He got up, filled both glasses, then sat down again. Now he was looking at Max, for the first time.

"He offered me a research job in something called the Department of Racial Hygiene. I've never heard of it, but you can guess what it's for—proving that Jews and Slavs, my wretched peasants at home about to vote for the Nazis because they can't sell their potatoes at a decent price, are biologically inferior to fine upstanding Aryans like him and me, with our superior scientific training in proper methodology and respect for evidence. It makes you sick. It also shows how right my father is, though he couldn't know anything about this. The state that was Prussia—a state all this time for the Jews and the Slavs as well as for the nobility, my father's ridiculous old Eastern Marches Union—is being ordered to be part of the phoney nation of the German people, the *Volk*. I ask you, what does it *mean*? It means a hooray club for Hitler and his revolting doctrine of racial purity. And German science, the best of it Jewish, as we've often said in this room, is being compelled by some Gadarene instinct to abandon the principles that made it great, so as to give this 'hooray nation' some kind of veneer, some kind of varnish, of intellectual respectability that'll never be real."

"You turned him down?"

"Of course I turned him down. Wouldn't you have? He was very surprised. 'But Baron, you are perfectly placed for this work, work of such value, value that will be widely recognised in due course, I can assure you, with your medical skills and your unimpeachable inheritance, one of the oldest families in East Prussia.' He'd looked me up, of course, to make sure there was no questionable marriage, no dodgy name to rise up from the past and show that I'm unhygienic after all. I nearly said, 'My closest friend is a Silesian count who works as a lawyer for the Prussian state and is half-Jewish'—no, don't worry, of course I didn't. But I wanted to, just to see the look on his face."

Max was astonished and pleased by this but took care not to show it.

"So?" Max said.

"So, do I accept the commission and become a soldier as well as a doctor, with who knows what in store for the army? Or do I take a chance on making a living as a country doctor in the wilds of Masuria, where there's plenty of work to do but no money at all? If it weren't for—well, what do you think, Hofmannswaldau?"

"What would your father prefer you to do?"

"That's it. That's it exactly. He never wanted me to study medicine. Never wanted me to come to Breslau. Soft place. As near to a Habsburg city as makes no difference. Nothing wrong with Königsberg, he kept saying, though its medical school doesn't hold a candle to the one here. But now that I've done it, he would be so pleased if I became a Prussian officer after all. He thinks the army is the only place left for a gentleman, the last bastion of Frederick's Prussia. He thinks it can't be pushed around by the Catholics and socialists in Berlin and isn't infected with Communism or Nazism. Little does he know. But it would make a difference to what he feels about everything, I can tell—and if he's going to die . . ."

"Well, then. You've decided, haven't you?"

Treuburg looked at Max and smiled for the first time.

"Have I? I suppose I have. All the same, it helps, to—"

"How infected is the army?" Max asked, a bit too quickly.

"More than my father would ever suspect. Hardly at all with Communism. For ordinary soldiers in the east, Bolsheviks are Russians, and Russians are the enemy, and that's that: a lot of the NCOs fought in the war. But there's plenty of sympathy with the Nazis, although soldiers aren't allowed to be actual party members. It's not just in the ranks, as you'd expect, but among the officers as well, mostly the very young ones whose fathers were in the war, were killed perhaps, blinded, lost limbs. They envy the Freikorps, these kids. They even envy the brownshirts. And some of the older officers too, the stupid ones— always plenty of those—sounded pretty much like Nazis to me. They want the Kaiser back—that's harmless now—but everything's the fault of the Jews, all that, not harmless at all because it turns Hitler into their hero. Unbelievable, when you look at them and look at him— the scruffy Austrian corporal and the colonels brought up at Lichterfelde with their high collars and their monocles."

"How can you, then? Join the army. Disappear into the army and have to spend your time with a lot of Nazis. What about your cello?"

"Oh, I'll always have my cello. There'll be some officers' mess music, no doubt. Mostly rubbish on the gramophone, but there's bound to be one or two who can play. No, what I discovered in the army in the summer actually made me keener, if anything, to be there, to talk some sense into some of them. My father's right in one way. If everything else is collapsing, being corrupted, losing its sense of truth and honour—look at poor old Schmidt's professor—surely the army must be able to sustain some discipline, some sense of fairness and integrity."

"That's meant to be the business of the judges and the courts."

Treuburg looked at Max and smiled again.

"Yes. I'm sorry. Of course it's meant to be. Is it, though? Don't they always let off the thugs on the right and punish the thugs on the left?"

"Not always, no. And I'm there because I hope, like you ... You know something, Treuburg?"

"What?"

"You and Zapolski. It's exactly the same thing."

"What do you mean? I liked Zapolski, but I'd say we have practically nothing in common."

"It was the same. He was offered a research job too. Here in the university. Not medical, obviously, but in history—work for us and prove that Poland is ancestral German land and we'll advance your doctorate a couple of years. He turned it down, of course, and you know what happened next. It decided him, in a way. Decided for him what he should do with his life. You were furious with him at the time, weren't you? For reverting to the faith of his fathers, And what are you doing by accepting a commission in the army? Reverting to the faith of yours."

Treuburg winced and said nothing.

"Sorry", Max said. "That was no help."

"Zapolski's father was dead. Does that make a difference? Not much. Damn you, Hofmannswaldau, it *is* the same. How free are we? Is it all just biology after all, genetic patterns written in the brain? Zapolski bound to be a priest, a Catholic anyway, however much Nietzsche he read. Me bound to be a soldier, a Prussian Junker anyway, however much medicine I've studied. And"—he laughed bitterly—"it's even more the same when you think about it—coming out of the reserve who hang about in case there's another war, and taking a commission— it's exactly the same as Zapolski coming out of the vaguely Catholic flock who hang about so as not to panic on their deathbeds, and becoming an actual priest. So do we ever decide anything? Do we really choose? Or is all choice an illusion? Perhaps I should study racial hygiene to find out, damn their lying department and all the results they'll pretend to have proved."

"There, you see. You don't believe that what we do, what we choose, is determined by biology any more than you believe it's determined by history or class war or ownership of the means of production or whatever kind of Marxism happens to be the fad of the moment."

"Don't I? I don't know what I believe, to tell you the truth. I've been trained not to believe anything until the evidence proves it to be so. Theoretically, medical science may one day become so sophisticated that it can prove that everything we do is biologically determined, but ...."

"But you don't believe it will, any more than I do. I think freedom to decide, freedom to choose, is something we have to have faith that we have."

"*What?* I thought Christians had to believe that God knows everything, including whether we're saved or damned, so all we do is predetermined anyway, whether we realize it or not. So freedom is nothing but an illusion. Just as the Marxists say it is. Isn't that what you're supposed to think?"

"No. God's knowledge and our knowledge are entirely different. God's knowledge is in eternity. Ours is in time. The fact—better, the truth—that God knows what we will choose to do doesn't make us any less free to choose."

"I don't even understand that. But you're the philosopher. I just resent the very idea that somehow or other I was bound to end up as a soldier. It's only a profession—and my profession is medicine anyway. Faith of my fathers be damned. I don't have any faith in anything. Haven't had since I was about eleven. You know that."

"Oh, but you do. You believe truth is better than lies. That honesty is better than falsification. That honour is better than cowardice. That's faith."

"It's not. It's ...."

"What? You tell me what it is if it isn't faith."

"It's obvious. Everyone knows the truth is better than lies."

"No, everyone doesn't. If you wanted to win power over other people, particularly a lot of power over a lot of other people, you might easily think lies were better than truth."

"I don't. Want to win power, that is."

"No, of course you don't. That isn't the point. But some people do. And for them the priority, the absolute priority that trumps everything else, is what *works*. That *is* not having any faith. But you believe, you do actually believe, that truth is good and lies are bad, that Bach's music is beautiful and the latest dance record from America is less beautiful and that the beauty of Bach's music has something to do with both truth and goodness. Don't you?"

Treuburg looked puzzled and then laughed.

"I'll tell you something, Hofmannswaldau. The army's going to be a rest after you. You've been good enough the last couple of years not to badger me much with this philosophical stuff. When it was you and Zapolski, and once or twice Halpern too, I couldn't understand what you were all talking about half the time. Then the lab and the wards were a rest. You had me worried a minute or two ago. I thought perhaps I should change my mind, go for the village practice in Masuria, just to demonstrate to my own satisfaction that I *can* change my mind."

"Don't worry, Treuburg. You can change your mind. Freedom of the will is not an illusion. What shall we have for dinner?"

Treuburg took a moment to see the point of this and then laughed again.

"Thank you. I've decided, *I* have decided, not to change my mind. Dinner—let's go out. I owe you a decent meal after all that, and there's nothing much in the flat. A choice: we go out."

It was still warm enough to eat on a café terrace. They had a good meal, shared another bottle of wine, and talked about Waldau, Max's parents, Heinrich and Betsy: Max realised that after all these years, Treuburg knew very little about his life before he was a student. He said nothing about his grandfather or about Anna. Neither of them mentioned Adam again. They walked back, cheerful and relaxed, through quiet streets now lit with electric lamps. It was almost eleven, and there were few people about as they turned the corner into their own street.

"What's that?" Max said.

"What?"

"On our steps. Look."

"Oh Lord. A drunk, I expect. One of those wretched characters in the Market Square."

Treuburg walked a little faster, to the door of their house. He bent over the figure slumped face down on the steps.

"It's Stern."

"It can't be. He doesn't drink anything."

"He's not drunk. Look."

Treuburg turned him over gently so that he lay on his back. He groaned as Treuburg moved him.

"He's conscious, anyway. That's good."

Half of Stern's face was dark and sticky. Their house was between two street lamps, and Max at first thought there was mud caked on Stern's cheek. Then he saw a gash above the eye and another under it and realized the dark stickiness was blood. Suddenly he remembered the shot face of his father long ago at Waldau. He turned away.

"Come on, Hofmannswaldau. It's no use being sick. We've got to get him upstairs. I don't think it's as bad as it looks."

Max swallowed, shook his head, got himself together to help, and took Stern's legs after opening the street door with his key. They carried him upstairs, which, although he was very light, was surprisingly difficult. He was almost able to stand when they got him into the flat. Treuburg held him.

"Take the pillows off his bed. Cover it with something. A clean sheet."

They laid him on the sheet.

"Boil a pan of water. I need to sterilize some instruments. And make me some coffee. It looks as if his spectacles have been smashed into his face. There's glass in that cut, I think. I'll find a better light. It's all right, Stern. Relax. Don't move your head."

"Bricks", Stern said, in a whisper. "They were throwing bricks. I lost my ... I can't see ..."

"Yes, you can. You got home, didn't you? There's a lot of blood, but your eyes are fine. Go on, Hofmannswaldau. Boil water. And find a blanket. He's very cold. He's in danger of going into shock."

"Brandy?"

"Absolutely not."

When Treuburg had moved a light from the sitting room, he scrubbed his hands in disinfectant and sterilized tweezers, scissors, and a needle. He washed the blood from Stern's head and face and extracted several splinters of glass from the cuts, two of which he then stitched with surgical thread from his hospital bag. It was clear that Treuberg was right—Stern's injuries weren't as bad as they had looked, and his eyes were undamaged. Treuburg dressed Stern's face and bandaged his head to keep the dressings in place.

The military doctor, Max thought but didn't say. Dressing wounds on the battlefield.

"Sleep. That's what he needs. Leave his door open in case he panics in the night."

Over coffee at the kitchen table, Max said, "What about tomorrow morning—the hospital?"

"He needs a day in bed. I can get back at lunchtime. I'll make sure he has some soup or something. I'll say he had an accident, that he was knocked off his bike. That'll do. Silly fool. Perhaps this'll teach him a lesson. If he's going to stay here and pass his exams, he'll have to stay out of politics. Rough politics, anyway."

"This isn't politics. It's mindless violence. Stern wouldn't hurt a fly."

"Then he shouldn't have joined the Communist Party—if he has. He's got no idea. No idea about what the Bolsheviks want to do, have already done. No idea above all about Russia. Prague, Bohemia—the war got nowhere near them. And it's playing straight into the brown-shirts' hands, an obvious Jew going to Party meetings."

"We must try to talk some sense into him when he's recovered from this. They could have blinded him."

"They could have killed him."

"Treuburg?"

"Yes?"

"If you take this commission, when will you have to leave Breslau?"

"Soon. I'll need to report the first of October. I'm helping out Schmidt only for a week or two till his new registrar starts. Then I'll go home for a few days. To cheer my father a bit, I hope."

"I see."

Max realized how much he would miss Treuburg. He was used to him. He loved to hear him play. He said nothing.

He never had.

When Anna left Breslau so that their quartets suddenly stopped, Max said to Treuburg only that Anna had had to go home to look after her father. When, two months later, Halpern left the hospital and disappeared to Poland, it was Treuburg who told Max that Halpern had got himself a job as a surgeon in the leading Jewish hospital in Vilna.

One day last winter, Max had come home in the middle of the morning to fetch a brief he'd left on his desk in the flat. He heard a sudden cry, a woman's cry—of pleasure? of pain? of both?—from Treuburg's room. He shivered, standing in the hall, his papers in his hand, and saw Katya's hat and coat hanging on a peg. He left without a sound and never said anything to Treuburg. Katya was still coming to clean the flat. She had a ring on her finger and said she was engaged to a soldier, a Polish boy who would marry her as soon as he had finished his first year in the army. Whether or not—this Max suc-ceeded in dismissing from his imagination.

Treuburg's affair with Eva Grossman had waned long ago, in the autumn of 1928. It was, Max was certain, partly on account of music that Treuburg lost interest in Eva, though neither Treuburg nor Max ever mentioned Eva after she stopped coming to the flat.

When Anna had gone, Max went to see Dr Mendel. He packed the Haydn quartet parts into his briefcase and climbed the stairs to the neat, sunny flat he hadn't visited for several months.

"Come in, come in, Max. Herr Rosenthal is out, I'm afraid. Would you like coffee? We even have some cake—you remember my old weakness for cake. We haven't seen you for a while—I expect you are very busy."

"Busy, yes. I have law examinations at the end of the year. But I've been playing a good deal. Recently I went to England with Dr Wolf's orchestra and choir. We played the Saint Matthew Passion in three cathedrals there."

"Ah, that is excellent. You are now old enough to play Bach well, and Dr Wolf is a Bach scholar. I am delighted to hear this. What have you brought me here?"

"The quartets we borrowed. I'm afraid our quartet has come to an end. My—our—the viola player has had to leave Breslau, and her brother, our first violin, has too much work at the hospital now."

"Max, I am sorry. And all the more sorry because I never heard your quartet. You were always saying you needed to get a little better to play for me."

"I know. I'm sorry too. It was . . . it was most unexpected . . . that it all had to stop."

"Max, you are upset about this. I can tell. Was there a difficulty with your friends? A disagreement, perhaps?"

"No. No. Nothing like that. It's only a pity that the quartet . . . We played well together."

"But you must find other players, of course you must. There are many good players in Breslau. You still have your cellist, isn't that so? So you must find a viola player and a second violin—it's time you were leading a quartet yourself. Some of Dr Wolf's players, perhaps? He is very exacting."

"I don't think another quartet. Not yet, anyway."

"Well, what about trios? I think you should attempt the 'Archduke'. The challenge of a real masterpiece will encourage you, and Count Zapolski could learn the piano part: he is an excellent pianist, is he not?"

"He's left Breslau too."

"Ah, now I understand. His family needed him to return to Poland, no doubt. To lose your friend—that is serious. I am so sorry, Max."

"Yes. Well ... thank you, Dr Mendel." He could explain nothing to the old man, whose opinion of the Catholic Church he remembered vividly. "We—that is, Treuburg, the cellist, and I—do know a pianist. I've heard her play only once. Technically very proficient, but I'm not sure how musical she is. Perhaps we should try a trio."

"Ah. So good for your playing, to lead a trio. You should try the Schubert E flat, and even, as I say, the 'Archduke'. You will soon discover whether you enjoy playing with this young lady. Do you have the parts?"

"I think so, yes. My grandfather had a number of trios, I know."

"Take them, in any case. You can always return them if you don't need them."

They drank some coffee and ate some cake.

"Dr Mendel, how are you? I should have asked you before. Are you still playing in the orchestra? Still teaching?"

"Yes indeed. I am getting older, of course, but neither my ears nor my fingers are giving me trouble yet, and the opera house seems quite happy with my playing. My pupils—I have only four these days, as I get tired, you know—are good children and work hard. It is not such a bad life, and Breslau has been kind to me."

When he left, they shook hands, and Max, resolving to visit the old man more often, patted him on the shoulder.

It was a resolution he failed to keep; he had seen Dr Mendel only once in the last year, in the spring, when he remembered that he should return the trio parts. Then Dr Mendel had said, spreading his hands in a gesture Max remembered from his childhood, "I am afraid now, Max. Even here. This blaming of the Jews for everything that has ever gone wrong in Germany, in the world. Blaming them for the war, for losing the war, for the Bolsheviks, for the republic, for the crash, for the unemployment: how can all these things be the fault of the Jews? How can any of them? The Jews have no power anywhere. There is no Jewish conspiracy. How could there possibly be? Look at me, an old Jew who never wished anyone harm. There are thousands like me. Millions, probably. I am afraid now. I am glad for their sake that your mother and your grandfather, may they rest in peace, are no longer alive."

374

"You mustn't be afraid", Max had said. "This is Breslau. Jews have been welcome here for hundreds of years. The brownshirts only make so much noise because of the poverty and the unemployment. Things will get better. I'm sure you are in no danger. The opera house will take care of you, for certain. What does Herr Rosenthal think?"

"He agrees with you. He thinks I am a foolish old man jumping at shadows. We shall see. Max ..."

"Yes?"

The old man went to the big cupboard full of music in the corner of the room. He took out a thin, bound copy of something.

"Here. Take this away and learn it. When you know it by heart, come back and play it for me. Bach is for the end, you know."

It was the Bach Chaconne, and Max practised it from time to time when neither of the others was in the flat. It was very beautiful and very difficult, and he didn't yet know it by heart.

When he'd taken the trios home, Treuburg had asked Eva to come and play. She was coy about the invitation and said she would have to practise. She had the piano parts for several weeks before she announced that she was ready to try the trios. They played them through on two Saturday evenings, Stern listening in his corner of the sitting room. The notes were in place, the tempos, set by Max, as appropriate as he could manage, but somehow the music never achieved any vitality, any sadness, or any joy.

"Stillborn", Treuburg said to Max after the Beethoven, which they played on the second evening.

"I think it was mostly my fault", Max said. "Such wonderful music, and we let it down. I've got too used to following Halpern; that's the problem. He's a better chamber music player than any of us, better than the rest of us deserved. It was Halpern who made the quartets work."

"Rubbish", Treuburg said. "Halpern's good, yes. But you're good enough, and so am I. Eva's the problem. She just plays, loud when it says loud, soft when it says soft. There's nothing there. Perhaps because there is nothing there."

The trio idea was dropped, as was, shortly afterwards, as far as Max could tell, Eva Grossmann from Treuburg's life.

After two days at home, and with a new pair of spectacles Treuburg had managed to get out of the eye department at the hospital, Stern went back to his studies.

Five days later, the elections for the Reichstag, the national parliament for the whole republic, were held. By the afternoon of the next day, Max's colleagues in the judge's office were saying that the Nazi party had done much better than anyone had expected. The two junior clerks and the judge's secretary, a middle-aged war widow with a son at Max's old Gymnasium, were too excited to sit quietly at their desks and concentrate on their work. "Wonderful news, wonderful news. Only Hitler can save Germany." Max, pretending to be deep in some important documents, said nothing. He bought the evening paper on his way home. It was still unread, sticking out of his pocket, when he saw that the unemployed man on his bench, and his dog, but not his blankets or the mess under the bench, had gone. Where to? Why? How could he have left his blankets? Max was afraid for him, and for the friendly dog.

There was no one in the flat when he got home. He sat in Grandpapa's chair and opened the paper.

"My God", he said aloud as he read a short paragraph at the top of the first inside page and ran his eye down a list of figures. Not quite all the results of the election had been ready in time for this edition of the paper, but what he saw horrified him. The Social Democrats, the SPD, in most parts of the country still had more votes than any other party, but their share of the vote was lower than it had been in any election of the twentieth century. The Catholic Centre Party, for which Max had voted, had lost only a little ground, but voting for the centre-right parties had collapsed. The Communists had nearly half as many votes again as they'd had in the last election and would have the third largest number of deputies in the Reichstag. But the Nazi figures were astonishing. He read them again. And then again, finding what the paper recorded almost impossible to believe. The Nazis had jumped from less than a million votes two years ago to a likely six and a half million when they'd all been counted. They would have more than a hundred deputies in the Reichstag and would definitely be the second-largest party. Max put down the paper and thought of Dr Mendel. He also thought of Dr Fischer and what he always said to the class in the Gymnasium about the centre, how the republic would not survive if the centre did not hold fast. What would the Reichstag be able to do now, with so many Nazis and so many Communists pulling in opposite directions? Nothing. For the first time in his life, Max, putting down the paper and looking up at the portrait of Bach, felt afraid because of the news. During the inflation, he had been too young to be afraid, and the mad numbers in the paper every day, the mad bank-notes in wheelbarrows, had seemed only unreal. As eventually they turned out to be.

He heard Treuburg and Stern come in together from work. He went out into the hall, reminding himself of his father as he held up the paper, hitting it with the knuckles of his other hand.

"Have you seen this? The actual details?"

"The Communist Party's done very well," Stern said, "much better than we—"

"For heaven's sake, Stern! Where's your common sense? It hasn't done nearly as well as the Nazis have, and in any case, the better the Communists do, the more excuse the Nazis have for murdering them on the streets. Don't you realize how lucky you are to be alive?"

"Calm down, Hofmannswaldau", Treuburg said. "Calm down. Let me have a look." He took the paper from Max, went into the sitting room, sat down, and groaned.

"East Prussia. What did I tell you? Huge numbers of votes for the Communists. Huge numbers for the Nazis. My poor father. He'll think this is the end of Prussia, and he'll probably be right."

"But don't you see?" Stern said, coming into the sitting room, where Max was standing by the window, and taking up what was once Halpern's rabbi position in front of the fireplace. "It can't last. The Nazis aren't saying anything definite. They just give all sorts of different people a general impression that Hitler can make everything better. He's the saviour, the redeemer. It's all completely hollow, playing on old Christian reflexes."

"Higher prices for potatoes. Not hollow in Masuria", Treuburg said.

"It won't happen, though, will it? They're all empty promises. The republic's rotten to the core, and the Nazis are one of the rottenest things about it. Only a revolution can help the peasants, the unemployed, the factory workers on starvation wages. And only the Party can organize a revolution. The Party knows how to do it. It's done it before. This is the peak for the Nazis. They've got this far only because of the unemployment and everyone losing confidence in the republic but being scared of Communism. They can't get any further because they've got nothing substantial to offer anyone. People, ordinary people—not the rich, the bourgeoisie, the owners of the factories, railways, and mines, but ordinary people—they'll soon find out that the Nazis won't do anything for them, that only the Party is strong enough to make things truly better, truly equal, to deal with the corrupt capitalists, the corrupt banks, the slave-master landowners, the corrupt judges ..."

Max had never before heard Stern say so much at once. He was surprised at how angry Stern's reeled-out propaganda made him feel.

"That's enough, Stern. Listen to me. You're a medical student from Prague, a bourgeois German-speaking Jew, much as I am, except that I happen to be half-Prussian. Your parents have worked hard and saved money to give you a good education—the best medical education there is, very likely. What do you know, really know, about peasants and factory workers and the unemployed? They don't need a Bolshevik revolution, which would kill many of them as well as the capitalist monsters you caricature without knowing anything about them either. Do you know how many people were killed in the Russian civil war? Ten million. Most of them were peasants and poor workers turned into soldiers. Do you know how many Jews were killed in the pogroms the civil war made possible? If there's a Bolshevik revolution in Germany, what makes you think you'll be alive at the end of it?"

Stern, with a bandage still over his injured eye, looked startled, as if he had been expecting the others to agree with him.

"But ... I thought you both ... You can't be in favour of the Nazis?"

"Don't be a bloody idiot, Stern", Treuburg said from the sofa. "The Bolsheviks and the Nazis aren't the only options. But they're likely to become the only options pretty soon if the Communist Party—which calls itself German and has no business copying Lenin and Stalin— doesn't make some kind of common cause with the Social Democrats to keep the Nazis out of actual power. If Hitler is ever even close to being part of the government in Berlin, it will be the fault of the German Communist Party."

"How can you say that? The Nazis are fascists, like the fascists in Italy, and fascists are the class enemy of Communists everywhere."

"Well, then", Max said. "Why doesn't your party join with the Social Democrats as Treuburg says, at least so as to outnumber the Nazis in the Reichstag? If the Nazis are class enemies, surely the SPD are class friends? Don't you see, Stern? If the Communists refuse to join the SPD against the Nazis, they're in effect joining the Nazis against the SPD. The two extremes get stronger. They fight and throw bricks at each other, and worse, while the centre gets weaker. But the centre that Stresemann represented, moderate sensible government, peace not war—it's the only hope for Germany, the only hope for all of us."

"No, it's not. You're wrong!" Stern looked no more than fifteen as he said this. "It's Communism that's the only hope for all of us, because it's *true*. Marx said capitalism would destroy itself, and it is destroying itself. History is true. Anyone can see that! Here there are five million unemployed. In Russia, there are none. We can't support the SPD—they support capitalism. They're social fascists. I see that now. And there's got to be another war. If there is—when there is—all Russia's got to do is wait. The capitalist countries will destroy each other—they're all terrified of a Bolshevik revolution, which is why they've all got feeble right-wing governments where there isn't actual fascism—and then there'll be a great Communist victory on the Rhine for all the workers of Europe."

"Ah", said Treuburg. 'That's what Moscow says, is it? No alliance with the Social Democrats. Burn the house down instead. Of course. Let me tell you, Stern. If there's another war, it won't take long to defeat France and England. Then the great struggle will be with the Bolsheviks, and we shall win. The generals think it would take two weeks to defeat Russia. If the Poles could defeat the Russians just after the war—well! And another thing, Stern. How much do you really know about Russia?"

"When I've qualified, I'm going to Russia. To live. To practise. There are thousands of people in Russia, in the cities and in the villages too, who before the Revolution only saw doctors in the distance, driving past to take care of the rich. Now doctors are paid to look after the poor, but there aren't enough doctors. That's what I want to be. A doctor paid by the people to look after the people. You don't understand, do you? Russia is the future. I'm learning Russian. It's not so different from Czech. I'm learning it from another medical student. She's from Lemberg—Lvov, I should say. She has a Russian mother."

"It's a rosy picture, Stern. And a girl thrown in to make it rosier. Is she Jewish?"

The question stopped him for a moment.

"I don't know. It doesn't matter to the Party. Yes, she is."

"You'll take her with you, won't you? If she's stupid enough to go. It won't be rosy when you get there. When things get difficult, which they will because they always do, the Russians will turn on the Jews. You'll see."

"Treuburg's right", Max said. "When you've qualified, you should go back to Prague. To your family, for one thing. Or perhaps to Lemberg, though my friend Zapolski, who's from Galicia, said Lemberg had such a terrible time in the war that the Jews there now ... But Prague didn't. Have you ever been bullied in the street in Prague?"

"No, I haven't. But"—Stern sniffed and lifted his head proudly—"I refuse to allow my Jewish ancestors to dictate what I do with my life, where I live, where I work. Don't you see? That's to give in, to the Nazis and their bricks, to all this Aryan, non-Aryan stuff. The Revolution's put an end to all that. It's made people free. All religion is lies, invented by the powerful to keep the poor quiet. I don't believe in any of it. Jews believe in God. I don't. So I'm not a Jew. I don't become a Jew just because the Nazis tell me I'm a Jew."

"Ah, freedom", Treuburg said. "Hofmannswaldau and I were talking about freedom just the other day. We agreed that freedom isn't an illusion, that we *can* choose. People one by one can choose. That's entirely different from being told that history is freeing us from oppression. In fact, it's exactly the opposite. The Bolsheviks won't allow anyone freedom to choose. They can't, or history might turn out to be wrong. You be careful, Stern, that you don't exchange one set of lies to keep the poor quiet for another. The march of revolution, the workers' paradise—but if people get in the way, they must be crushed. Not much freedom for them."

"But it's quite different." Stern was nearly in tears. "Marxism isn't lies, like religion. It's scientific, proved, like medicine. Dialectical materialism is the key to everything that happens. Everything!"

"It's a theory. And you're told to believe it. You haven't done the proving yourself. Nor, as a matter of fact, has anyone else. It's not provable. So you're told to believe Marx, to believe *in* Marx, the same as Christians are told to believe *in* Christ. Isn't that right, Hofmannswaldau?"

"Yes. No. I see what you're saying, and personally, if there's a choice between Christ and Marx ... But there's one huge difference. Marxism is about power, and Christianity is about weakness."

"How can you say that, Hofmannswaldau? How *can* you?" Treuburg looked up at Max from the sofa, his blue Prussian eyes fierce like Max's father's eyes. "Think about the history of the Church, of Christian countries, Popes, Emperors, Kings—power, power, power all the way. Stern's got a solid point about religion telling lies to keep the poor quiet. Christianity's always done it."

"*People* have always done it. Christianity's about liberating people from the will to power, which, unless there is, really *is*, something beyond the human world that can rescue us from it, drives everything. Christianity's about liberating the powerful *and* liberating the powerless. The truth will set you free."

"Exactly. That's exactly what Stern's just said about Marx. Isn't it? But these so-called truths don't set you free, either of them. Either of *you*, come to that. You do what you're told, I've noticed, Hofmannswaldau. You go to church on Sundays and eat fish on Fridays. And Stern goes to Party meetings and gets bricks thrown at him by brownshirts. Both of you turn up when you're told to turn up and recite prayers to a God who doesn't exist. Dialectical materialism is more modern; that's the only difference. I bet a lot of Party members had a good religious upbringing. Christian. Jewish. Makes no difference. If you teach children one lot of nonsense, they'll all the more easily believe another lot later. The Messiah's not coming. Jesus the Saviour wasn't, isn't. So let's try Marx. Or Hitler. Look at the election."

"They're not all the same," Max said, "whatever you say." And then, to cheer Stern, who, deflated by all this, was now sitting in Grandpapa's chair with his head in his hands. "Better the Party than the brownshirts any day. At least there's something positive in what the Bolsheviks are trying to do, even if they'll never achieve it."

"All right, Hofmannswaldau", Treuburg said, looking at Stern. "I think we can agree on that. Time for a truce. My turn to cook. Pork chops, and it's Tuesday, so that should suit everyone."

Chapter 14

Two weeks later, Treuburg left Breslau. A taxi came early one morning to take him to the railway station. He had very little luggage after years in the flat—one large heavy suitcase, a medical bag, a briefcase, and his cello. Max carried the cello downstairs to the street for him; the driver put it carefully in the back seat of the cab. Max and Treuburg shook hands on the sidewalk.

"Good-bye, Max. Thank you. These have been good times."

"Good-bye, Joachim. Good luck."

Max went back up the stairs to the flat, close to tears. "Damn him", he said aloud because, after so long, of the Christian names.

He looked into Treuburg's room. It was as tidy and impersonal as a hotel room left by a guest after a single night and prepared by the staff for the next. He's right to be a soldier, Max thought. That's what he already is.

Stern had already gone to an early lecture. Max had almost an hour before he needed to leave for the law courts.

He walked slowly through the flat, into and out of every room except Stern's, which he knew was very untidy and which had once been Adam's. The September sun shone through the east-facing windows, which looked onto the street. The one in Treuburg's room was so bright that he must have cleaned and polished the glass yesterday when he was packing up. The two in the sitting room were streaked and fly-marked after the summer: Max was hardly ever in this room in the morning. He fetched a basin of soapy water and a cloth and cleaned the windows. As he tipped the dirty water down the sink in the kitchen, desolation of a kind he had not felt since the months after Anna left overcame him.

Why? He didn't depend on Treuburg for anything. Or did he? Holding the empty basin with both hands and looking across the sink at the familiar backs of the houses in the next street across the cobbled lane, he knew that Treuburg was somehow the last guarantee that it had all been real, the quartet, Anna, Adam. Ridiculous, he told himself, shaking his head; of course it had all been real, still was real. Anna was in Vilna, and Adam was in Cracow, and one day before too long perhaps ...

He put the basin away in the cupboard below the sink and went back to his own bedroom. In the top drawer of the chest of drawers, under the socks and under the paper that was under the socks, faded old paper cut to size once by Grandmama, were two letters. He hadn't looked at them for months, perhaps nine months. He had tried hard to forget them, though he knew them by heart, and he hadn't thrown them away.

He sat on his bed and smoothed out the old folds in the longer letter.

Monday

Dearest Max,

[Brave girl, to write that.]

I am writing to tell you not to come to Frau Schönfeld's on Saturday when, God willing, you get back from England because I won't be here.

Yesterday was a terrible, terrible day. Jakob made me promise not to write you a long letter, but I must tell you quickly.

I went to the church again, to the early Mass, because you were gone and I knew you would be singing the Bach in some great church that day and it would be like being close to you although you were far away in England. It was all different from the time we went together. There was a procession with palms—Palm Sunday, I didn't know—and they gave me a palm and I joined in the procession because it was easier. Then the Mass was very long, with the whole story I think of the Bach but in Latin, of course, so I didn't understand it until the sermon. The priest was a different one too, and what he said was terrible, that the Jews all cheered when Jesus came into Jerusalem, and then five days later they were all against him and made the Romans crucify him— and then I remembered the Bach and the shouting—and it was all their fault. Is this right, Max? It's not the same as what the other priest said when we were there together, is it? I wish I could ask you, but now I can't, because when I got home Jakob was there. He was going to be all morning at the hospital, I thought, but he had come back, and he asked me where had I been for so long. It was raining, and I was wet when I came in. I couldn't think of a lie quickly enough, which he saw, and so I told him where I had been, and he was very, very angry with me but even more with you. How could you take me to a Catholic church when you are half-Jewish and what he called a token Protestant? I was really afraid. I tried to remind him of what he said himself that night before the count went away, about Catholics and Jews being allies now. But he just got angrier and said being allies was one thing, committing apostasy was another, and didn't I realize that Jewish families had always regarded apostate children as dead? Then when I was crying because he was telling me I was a traitor to all my ancestors and he had been a fool ever to trust me out of his sight, I told him I didn't care what he thought because I love you and we are going to get married as soon as we can. Then he went white and cold and silent, and I was terrified. He said that proved I couldn't be trusted and that I was a romantic idiot to think a German count would ever marry a penniless Polish Jewess, that you meant to seduce me, that I was evidently too young to be away from home since I had deceived him and that he was sending me home to Vilna at once, tomorrow, that's today, tonight on the night train to Warsaw so that our father can talk some sense into me.

Max—I'm so sorry not to be here on Saturday. It must be Saturday when you are reading this. I don't know when I'll be able to come back to Breslau, but perhaps one day I will come back. Will you wait for me? Jakob says I must not write to you again after this letter. But I will. And you shouldn't write to me so I am not to give you our address in Vilna.

I love you, Max, always, whatever happens.

Your Anna

P.S. When you see the count, tell him I do not forget how beautifully he plays.

How young she sounded and how hopeful still. He hadn't heard from her again. Two and a half years, almost, and not a letter, not a word. He realized now that he'd been guessing all this time how she'd grown up, who she was now, how she looked, how she would smile and laugh as she used to, how she would run towards him one day and throw herself into his arms. He could feel her cheeks, her mouth, her hair, her narrow back, her breasts against his chest. But he had no way of telling whether any of this might be true—either how she had grown up and how she was now, or that he would ever see her, ever hold her again.

Treuburg had met Halpern once or twice in the hospital that spring, that early summer, on a ward, in a passage. A cold nod was the only sign of recognition he got from Halpern, and though he must have been puzzled by this chill, he told Max of these encounters only when Halpern had gone back to Vilna, some time in late June. Prussian reticence, Max thought. Even tact. In July Treuburg told him that Professor Grossmann had a new surgical assistant.

Reading Anna's letter again made him feel hot and tired as he had that wretched Saturday, Holy Saturday, standing out there in the hall before he had even taken his coat off after his long, impatient train journey from England. There had been so much he was looking forward to telling her. He had stood in the hall with the collar of his coat scratchy on the back of his neck and found it difficult to grasp what he was reading. He had never seen her handwriting before.

He went to Frau Schönfeld's, risking Halpern being in. "She has gone home, Count", the old lady said. "I do not know why so suddenly. I am sorry. The doctor will be in at eight."

When he got back to the flat, he saw his violin and the new suitcase he had bought to go to England on the floor in the hall, where he had put them down to read the letter. He looked at them as if they belonged to someone else, the young man who had carried them as he walked home from the station when everything was all right.

Now he was someone else again. Two and a half years had gone by. Had anyone asked him, he wouldn't have been able to explain how his memories and hopes, of Anna and of Adam, had kept him going, working hard, passing last year the examinations necessary for his job as one of Dr Gerlach's Referendars at the Breslau courts, able to get up in the morning and deal competently with each day. He had chosen a straightforward career in the law, several years as a Referendar and, after more examinations, as an Assessor in Breslau and then perhaps a more senior position in Berlin. Or perhaps in Breslau. He had chosen this rather than a doctorate at the university because if he were going to marry Anna, he needed a proper salary.

How, in a loneliness that he knew was backward-looking, he sustained his resolution to carry on through the months and then years of Anna's silence was not the kind of question that Treuburg would have asked. Dr Fischer, whom he visited from time to time, to report on his instruction in the Catholic faith, and who acted as his godfather when he was conditionally rebaptized eighteen months ago, on the Easter Vigil in 1929, probably, without asking, knew the answer.

Not for the first time, as he sat on his bed in the empty flat with Anna's letter in his hands, but more acutely than ever before, he realised that he had known and loved only the young girl who'd written it, scarcely grown up, with her fragile fingers on the strings of her viola, her spectacles that made her look so studious, Frau Schönfeld's velvet coat with the fur collar round her chin and under her ears, her gloved hands in his as they skated, her smile. Who was she now? He had made himself accept that she was very likely married. Perhaps she had a child? He bent his head lower over her letter as he faced once more the entirely familiar fact that he was very unlikely ever to see her again, and that if he did, she would in any case be lost to him.

He groaned aloud. How could he have been so stupid—this he had thought a thousand times—as to take an innocent Jewish girl, carefully brought up despite all the horrors the family had been through and despite all the repudiation of religion her father and her brother set so much store by, to a Catholic church, to Mass? It was on account of his stupidity, because she loved him and thought she was going to marry him, that she went by herself to Mass, was too candid to lie to her brother, and was sent home like a naughty child. He should have understood that she knew nothing of practically all the bits and pieces of his whole life that had taken him to that church, that her only reason for being there was him and what she felt about him, and that the scale of the difference between them, as he knelt beside her believing they were as one, hadn't then for a single moment occurred to him.

He had lost her through his own crass failure to think, to imagine, carefully enough who she was and what she was likely to do if he went away to England and left her alone with her love for him.

This he had realized at once. He remembered going to see Dr Fischer, a few days after that Easter Sunday. He'd been too shocked by Anna's letter—and, he couldn't yet see, had allowed his love for her to be too closely entwined with his just-beginning love for the light and colour and holiness of the Catholic liturgy—to go to the Easter Mass, although he had been looking forward to it with keener and keener expectation all through the rehearsals and performances of the Bach Passion in England. Sitting now in his bedroom holding Anna's unfolded, fading letter, he heard the last slow grieving chorus of the Passion, leaving the dead Christ to sleep in the Father's peace. His own sense of the joy and surprise of Easter morning had had to wait a whole year but then had become one with the exaltation of his first Mass as a new, a forgiven, Catholic.

He went to see Dr Fischer because he'd promised to give him a report about the expedition to England—or so he told himself. As soon as the old schoolmaster had let him into his flat and taken his coat, he stopped in the hall and looked carefully at Max.

"What is it, my boy? Something's happened, hasn't it?"

Max couldn't answer.

"Don't tell me what the trouble is unless you want to. Would you like a little plum brandy? Come in, come in. I should like very much to hear about England."

They sat in the armchairs on either side of the fire.

"Well? What did you make of the English? Were they willing to 'bury the hatchet'?" Dr Fischer said, in English. Then he smiled. "You don't know the expression. Were they willing to forget the war for a little while, for the sake of Bach?"

Max sipped his brandy.

"They were, yes. I was surprised. They treated us . . . very correctly, and in one house where I stayed, much better than correctly. Hundreds of people came to hear the Passion, and the people we met were polite, even kind, but . . . it's hard to explain. We're all too young to have fought in the war, and Dr Wolf's too old, but most of the English we spoke to couldn't help making us feel we were very unfortunate to be Germans—not that we all are Germans, but they didn't know that. It was as if they pitied us for losing the war but at the same time thought that that was what we deserved."

"I can easily imagine. There's an English word for it, 'patronizing'— it's inclined to be how they treat the rest of the world anyway, whether there happens to have been a war or not. English manners are too good for them to be offensive or unkind to a group of young musicians, but you'll have noticed the almost-universal certainty of the English that they are right and others are wrong, and it will only have been strengthened by the war."

"That's it, exactly. In the places we went to, I did see they have good reasons to be proud—the cathedrals were so wonderful. I had no idea. I suppose I thought that England, being a Protestant country, would have churches more like ours. I hadn't thought that the cathedrals would be great Catholic churches from the Middle Ages, taller and grander than any Zapolski and I saw in Italy, and made of such pale stone, extraordinary with the coloured light from the sun shining through the stained glass, and so much elaborate carving."

"Ah, the English cathedrals. They're so big and grand because there were so few Bishops in England. Twenty or so, I believe. Two hundred or so in Italy. You see? The cathedrals were once Catholic churches, of course, though now they're Protestant, but only up to a point." Dr Fischer took off his spectacles, polished them, and put them on again. "I would say that the Church of England will always be impossible for foreigners to understand. Which cathedrals did you visit?"

"We played the Bach in York—that was the first cathedral, the farthest from Dover, a long train journey. It's the largest church I've ever seen, and the windows ... I was amazed ... and then we went to Lincoln and last to Ely."

"Ah. I have seen Lincoln and York, and you are right. There's nothing to equal those churches in Germany, not even on the Rhine. I've never been to Ely."

As Max remembered the beauty of Ely cathedral, remembered looking up and up into the miraculous flying stone of the lantern, wishing Adam were with him and resolving to bring Anna one day to see this, he couldn't go on.

"Never mind", Dr Fischer said. "Tell me about Ely another time. The house you mentioned, where you stayed, where was that?"

"That was in Ely too, the last two nights before we began the journey home. In York and Lincoln, we stayed in cheap hotels, but Ely's a very small town to have such a cathedral, and families had offered to put us up while we were there. I stayed with a canon and his wife—that's a priest belonging to the cathedral, I think."

"Yes, we have them too."

"Do we? Do you? I'm sorry. I didn't know."

Dr Fischer laughed. "So like the Church of England, to have canons and to let them marry. In English, it's called 'having your cake and eating it too'. But go on—this canon?"

"They were an old couple, very friendly. There was also their daughter, widowed in the war, and her two boys, about twelve and fourteen. They had a tutor for the holidays, a student from Cambridge. And there seemed to be a lot of servants. They were all very old-fashioned. It reminded me ... This family, you'd imagine, would have every reason to dislike Germans, but not at all. The canon spoke good German and knew a lot about music. He produced the parts of a Mozart sonata and insisted on us playing it, him and me, in the evening—we'd rehearsed the Passion all the afternoon, and it turned out he'd listened to the whole rehearsal. He studied in Heidelberg for a while when he was young, in the eighties, I think."

"Like me in Oxford. He must be about my age."

"Yes. He seemed a bit older."

Dr Fischer laughed again. "Probably only because you've known me longer. A little more plum brandy?"

"Thank you. Well, the second evening, after the performance—he and his wife came to that as well—they all went to bed except him and me, I think because he was enjoying talking to me in German, which no one else knew. He loved the Passion and our much-smaller choir and orchestra than they're used to in England. We talked about all sorts of things. He told me that when he was a student in Heidelberg, he lived with a Jewish family, very civilized, very musical, and already there were anti-Semitic books in the shops and anti-Semitic articles in newspapers saying that the Jews are our misfortune. All that. He told me about Dreyfus, the officer in the French army who—"

"Yes. I know about the Dreyfus case."

"The canon's German hero is Heine. He said that Heine a hundred years ago foretold 1914 and foretold the Bolshevik Revolution as well. He also said Germans were at their best before Bismarck, when they weren't a nation but only a people, living in lots of different countries, like the Jews. It was all most surprising in an English priest. You would like him very much, I know."

"I'm sure I would. How fortunate you were, to meet such a man."

"And we talked about Shakespeare too. About *Hamlet* ..."

He was suddenly sitting beside a rapt Anna in the university theatre, with Adam in his black clothes alone on the stage. Again, he couldn't go on.

"Hofmannswaldau, what is it? You've heard from Zapolski? Some bad news?"

"No. Not Zapolski. Anna Halpern has left Breslau, been sent home to Vilna by her brother, and it's all my fault."

"Ah."

A long silence. Dr Fischer methodically filled his pipe, and lit it. Then he said, "I don't expect it was all your fault. Tell me what happened."

"She ... I ... we ... I'm afraid I didn't think."

"I saw her at Mass on Palm Sunday. I didn't greet her because I didn't want to frighten her. I can guess what happened. Her brother found out where she'd been and was angry with her and no doubt angrier with you. Was that it?"

"Yes. But worse. She told him we're going to get married as soon as ... But now ..."

"Congratulations, Hofmannswaldau. You asked her to marry you, and she said yes. That's excellent news. She's a lovely girl, pretty and musical and good. Poor little Miss Anna. So she told her brother the truth, about the Mass and about your engagement, and it would have been better to have said nothing. I am so sorry, particularly for her. If you feel this is all your fault, imagine what she must feel."

"She would have had to lie about the Mass. She couldn't."

"No, of course she couldn't. I haven't met her brother. Is he likely to remain angry with her, with you?"

"I don't know. He's a complicated character. Very clever. Very musical indeed. He played first violin in our quartet. I think I told you."

"You said he professes to be an atheist, but you don't believe him."

"Did I? Well, that's it. You can't predict what he's going to think about anything. We talked, all of us, on several evenings, and with Zapolski too. But I didn't really get to know Halpern. He's the most Jewish person I've ever met. Now he obviously thinks he's protecting his innocent sister—he's right, there—from a spoiled German nobleman who's out to seduce her. Wrong, as it happens. He agreed to play music with us in the first place, and to bring Anna with him, because he thought I was Jewish myself, Jewish enough. The grandson of Professor Meyer must be Jewish enough. He let me take Anna out, to the park, to Adam's play, skating. Now he thinks I'm only my father's son, and worse than that, taking his sister to a Catholic church—the Catholics in Russian Poland, Adam says, are horribly anti-Semitic. How could I have done such an idiotic thing?"

"You've done nothing to hurt her, remember that, nothing to reproach yourself with. Have you?"

A sharp look over the half-moons and the pipe.

"I've lost her." The sharp look persisted. "No. I haven't. Truly not. But I should have told her to stay at home on the Sunday I was in England. It never occurred to me that she might go to Mass by herself. But it should have."

"What about her parents in Vilna? Will they be as angry with her as her brother?"

"Her mother's dead. She died in the war, and so did Anna's little brother. The Russians . . . it's a horrible story. Her father is a doctor in Vilna. He's not religious, Anna says. But there's an aunt, and a synagogue Anna goes to. And Frau Schönfeld, the lady they lodge with here, a kind old lady, is a religious Jew as well. Anna's belief in God is very strong. Otherwise she wouldn't have come with me to Mass." Max looked up, straight into Dr Fischer's eyes, as all he had just said struck him as it hadn't before.

"I won't ever see her again, will I?" he said.

Dr Fischer thought for a long time, puffing on his pipe and gazing into the fire, before he answered.

"You may not."

He got up, poked the fire, put on a log and then another, and sat down again heavily.

"You may not. Now I see how difficult it would always have been for her, in another country, perhaps another faith, when her loyalty to her father and her brother must be very strong. I have no doubt at all that she loves you—and it's perfectly sensible of her, if I may say so—and clearly you love her. But you're both extremely young. If anyone is to blame in all this, I fear it is I, for encouraging you children and for not thinking hard enough about you both. A romantic old fool. That's what I've been."

"No, no—I was so pleased you liked her. And in any case, perhaps she will be able to come back, to Germany, to Breslau. In her letter— her brother allowed her to write me a letter before she left; it was waiting for me on Saturday when I got back from England—she says she will come back. She asks me to wait for her."

"Of course, of course. But it will be very hard for her, once she's at home with her father and her aunt and in the Jewish atmosphere of Vilna, which I expect you know is one of the great Jewish cities of the world. It may well be impossible for her, whatever she thinks, whatever she feels, now that she has had to leave you."

"I know."

"And there's one other thing."

Max looked up.

"In the weeks and months ahead, you're sure to be sad. Don't think too harshly of yourself or of Anna's brother or even of me. However painful at this moment is the loss of such a lovely girl, I suspect that the loss of Zapolski has cut more deeply, has left the more serious wound. But that loss is between him and God. No one to think harshly of there. And ..."

He knocked the charred tobacco out of his pipe and put it down, propping it in his wooden bowl full of ash and spent matches.

Then he stood up, so Max stood too.

"Remember that only love, human love, can teach us the love of God, and the love of God—his for us, ours for him—is, when all's said and done, the only thing truly worth learning. Now off you go. Be brave. You have plenty of courage, all three of you. I know. God bless you all."

Old Fischer had been right, Max thought, refolding Anna's letter. As the months and then years had gone by—and sooner than he would have thought possible, he became used to hearing nothing from her— Anna had become a kind of sacred memory, as if she were dead. He prayed for her every night and at Mass, that she might be safe and happy. He felt reasonably sure that far away in ancient Vilna—he had found photographs of the city in a book in the university library—she was indeed safe and happy because from all he knew of them he trusted her father and her brother to take care of her, and not, above all, to allow her to marry someone who wouldn't in his turn look after her properly.

After a while, he refused any longer to allow himself the torture of imagining her in bed with someone else; perhaps this was easier than it might have been because he knew her body only in his imagination anyway. He would always know her smile, her eyes, her hands. As time went by, he saw her across the distance of time and place, waving him good-bye from further and further away.

But missing Adam was entirely different, and he couldn't and didn't want to get used to it. Every single time he ran into, heard, noticed, or read something in any way interesting—good, bad, ugly, beautiful, funny, frightening—he wanted to talk to Adam about it, to see what he would say. It was of the essence of friendship, he often thought, that the other person was wholly present to you, wholly himself—or herself, but what he felt for Anna was not like this, he knew—but at the same time wholly unpredictable. Held in your love but free, that was it. He never knew, had never known since they were sixteen, what Adam would think or say or do. Hamlet to his Horatio Adam had always been. So that his absence was deadening, muffling, like a damp fog keeping the blue dazzle of the sky and the sunshine out of the grey streets of every day.

What would Adam say about how well the Nazis had done in the elections? What would he say about the disappearance of the beggar and his dog on the riverbank? What would he say about Treuburg's decision, about Stern and the brick, about Max's cautious judge, about anything, everything?

He unfolded the other letter he had taken from under the paper in his sock drawer.

Saint Stanislaw Seminary
Cracow
Low Sunday 1929

[Seventeen months ago already.]

Dear old Max,

You must wonder from time to time whether I'm still alive. As you see, I am. It was good to see from your envelope, handed to me by the prefect of discipline (I know I'm almost twenty-five, but that's how things are here) with some disdain for the Breslau postmark, that you're still alive too, and better to read that you've just become even more alive. The Catholic Church (human institution) is a collection of people who go all the way from wonderful to truly terrible, like any other collection of people, but the Catholic Church (divine institution) is nevertheless the only place to be. Alas, perhaps, but there it is. I'm glad for you and for me that you've dived into this ocean—swimming gets easier as you get used to it, and old Fischer will always throw you a rope if you think you're sinking.

Here I survive. I would have walked out several times—from rage and despair—if I weren't sure that this is what I have to do and that therefore these years here—only three more—have to be gone through. What can I tell you? Buildings: hideous, and in this beautiful city. Garden: lovely, very big, and carefully looked after, every blade of grass in its proper place and some very fine trees. I never knew gardens could be such a comfort. Library: pretty good, and we're allowed to use the university library, which is much better and a great deal nicer to look at. Music: not enough, but there's a reasonable piano here and another seminarian (dull) to play four-handed duets with. Plenty of music in the library. The seminarians are all so patriotic they want me to play nothing but Chopin, who's all right as far as he goes—which isn't far enough. I've been learning the big Schubert sonatas and the Liszt sonata—in memory of your mother, on account of her being pupil of a pupil—which is too difficult for me. Professors: mixed. Fellow students: mixed. See above on collections of people.

What else? Don't worry about me. It's all very much as I expected. In three years, barring accidents or gross misbehaviour (their phrase—I must say I do long for some gross misbehaviour from time to time, but so far so good), I should be ordained a priest. At last.

How strange to be writing German again. Essays are written in Polish here, of course. Not hard, any of the work, after years of old Fischer.

I think of you often (means prayers). Do the same for me. I'm so sorry you never heard again from Anna Halpern. A tyrant, the rabbi, but perhaps better for both of you in the long run. Another girlfriend? It's about time. Don't behave too well.

You'll come to my ordination, won't you? It will be with Archbishop Sapieha in the Wawel. More Polish you couldn't get but thank the Lord for Latin.

Hoops of steel, *Max.*

  Adam

This letter, particularly its last line, in English, and Adam's *dull* in its bracket, had cheered him often, and did now. Only a year and a half until Adam's ordination, not so very long.

He got up, put the letters back in the drawer, looked at his watch, opened the door of Treuburg's room once more on his way out, decided to move his desk and his law books into it because he could now afford not to find another student to share the flat, made a face at himself in the hall mirror but reckoned he was tidy enough for work, and left the flat.

Going down the stairs, he met Frau Hübner, who since the days of his grandparents had lived in the basement in return for dealing with the post, keeping the stairs and the hall clean, and polishing the brass knocker and letterbox on the front door. Her husband had lost both legs in the war and sat miserably in a wheelchair all day reading childrens' comics. She was a disagreeable woman, always with something to grumble about. This morning she was singing, loudly and badly, the song Max had recently heard marching brownshirts singing in the streets, over and over again. The Horst Wessel song. Horst Wessel, whose name had been everywhere in the papers for months, was a Nazi thug killed earlier in the year by a Communist thug. He was now reckoned by the Nazis as a "martyr", to go with the "Messiah"

Hitler, who had to be, as Treuburg had said, not just believed but believed *in*. Wessel—or someone—had written this anthem to the Stormtroopers, the swastika, and Hitler. It was meant to sound martial, confident, threatening. It did. Frau Hübner stopped singing and moved her dustpan and brush out of Max's way.

"Morning, sir. Lovely morning."

She never said anything positive.

"Good morning, Frau Hübner. Yes. It's good to see the sun."

"It's Hitler weather, that's what it is. The sun's going to shine on Germany again. That's what the paper says. It'll be like before the war, won't it?"

"Did you vote for the Nazis in the election, Frau Hübner?"

"Of course I did, and we pushed my husband all the way to vote too. The butcher's boy gave me a hand, carrying him up the area steps and all. He's in the Stormtroopers, the butcher's boy. People like us never voted before the war. Now we can show the government what's what."

"Yes. Well. We'll see."

Before he reached the street door, she was singing again.

When Stern came back from the hospital that evening Stern said, "Would you like me to leave too?"

"What? Why would I? Of course not. You're welcome to stay as long as you like—as long as you need a room in Breslau."

"I thought perhaps ... I see you're making Treuburg's room into a study. I thought you might like the flat to yourself now. And also— you're a Catholic, and I'm a Communist. You might not want just one lodger who—"

"I understand. Treuburg was neither, so that made it easier? Neutral ground between you and me. 'No man's land', they called it in the war. I sometimes think it's where we all live now. Poor old Treuburg. No, Stern. Of course you must stay. It's perfectly possible to disagree with somebody's ideas and to like them at the same time. It's certainly true in your case. But now that I come to think of it, I'm not sure it's always true. I discovered this morning that Frau Hübner and her husband, wretched man, stuck in that chair all day with only Frau Hübner for company, are keen Nazis. I don't think I could share the flat with a Nazi. Could one like a Nazi? I don't think so. Not that I'd like Frau Hübner very much if she were a faithful Christian."

"Oh, she is. She goes to the Protestant church at the end of the street every Sunday. I've seen her. But if she's a Nazi, she'll want me out of the building, won't she?"

"It doesn't matter what she wants. There's nothing she can do about it. All the more reason for you staying. Just try to steer clear of fights if you possibly can. Help me move this desk, there's a good chap. I've taken the drawers out, but it's still heavy and very awkward to get through the doors."

The weather changed the next day. Two or three grey, damp weeks followed. Max took his umbrella to work every day and felt middle-aged and low-spirited as he walked with the crowd of morning and evening office workers through streets that the rain made only dirtier. He thought, knowing it was probably an illusion, that there were fewer office workers and more resentful knots of the unemployed on the street corners with every week that went by. Mist, on increasingly dark mornings, took time to clear from the river and the old moat, so that the water's dull surface reflected nothing as he walked past, and even the ducks hardly bothered to move.

On Sundays he went to Mass, not in the church where he had taken Anna and where he might meet Dr Fischer, but at seven in the morning in the small Catholic church nearest to the flat, where he knew no one and where the early Mass had no sermon. A priest he didn't recognize at Dr Fischer's church, perhaps the priest Anna had heard on that Palm Sunday in 1928, had preached a sermon before the election recommending that the congregation not vote for the Centre Party, which Max thought almost all Catholics would always loyally support, but telling them to vote for the Nazis because "they're the only party that can save us from the Bolsheviks. The Bolsheviks want to destroy Christianity. That is their declared objective. What is more, Marx himself was a Jew, and all the cleverest Bolsheviks are Jews. The Bolsheviks are our enemy, and the Nazis understand that the Bolsheviks must be destroyed in Germany. My enemy's enemy is my friend. Therefore, a vote for the Nazis will be a vote in defence of the Holy Catholic Church."

After this, Max, who knew Adam's letter from the seminary by heart, went to Mass and bowed his head and his heart again at the presence of Christ in the world, prayed for Anna and for Adam, and avoided all preaching.

In the middle of October, there were a few days of wild winds and pouring rain and then a Sunday of sparkling, calm sunshine that met him when he emerged from the early Mass. He walked towards the Market Square, breathing the quiet Sunday air. Saint Luke's summer—the phrase, Emilia's, came back to him from his childhood: he had noticed in his missal that the feast of Saint Luke had been the day before. He went to the old smoky café where he had taken Anna on that Sunday morning before he lost her. He had some breakfast, drank a lot of coffee, and read the Sunday paper. Every week the news was getting worse. He winced as he read, in a long report on the assembly of the new Reichstag, of Nazi deputies marching and singing through the Berlin streets and smashing the windows of Jewish shops they passed. The actual meeting of what was, after all, supposed to be the democratically elected parliament of the republic had broken up in shouting, almost fighting, between the Nazis and the Communist deputies. On the same page there was the usual photograph of the Chancellor, Dr Brüning, looking grey, austere, and helpless among the reports that surrounded his picture. Max put down the paper in its long wooden holder and wished Adam were there in the flat, just getting up in his Sunday open-necked shirt and old flannels.

There was work waiting for him on his desk in his new, sunny study. Plenty of time for that. An empty day. He would probably play a game of chess with Stern in the evening, on the beautiful chessboard Grandpapa made, not black and white but squares of inlaid pale and dark wood, the grain going different ways under a surface of French polish as smooth and translucent as glass, and each of the chess pieces carved patiently with Grandpapa's small, terrifyingly sharp knife. Max used to play chess with Adam; mostly but not always, Adam won. Now he and Stern played about equally well, or equally badly. He finished his coffee and went out into the square, where a few people were walking—old women and one or two families on their way to church. A few others, beggars and young men in scruffy clothes, were hanging about or sitting on the steps of the market cross and the old city hall, closed for Sunday. A pair of policemen were standing by the post office talking to each other. Two tramps were lying asleep in the sun.

He walked to the old moat, to his bench. There was no sign of the man and his dog, or of his blankets or his rubbish. Max hoped to God, prayed for a second, that the man was safe somewhere and had

had some breakfast. Could he now sit again on his old bench, his and Anna's bench? Why not?

The water glinted in the sun, up to its old trick of reminding him of the river at Waldau. The remaining leaves on the trees, silver and gold on the willows, bronze on the alders, copper on one or two other trees, were sharp in the autumn light, their reflections in the water muddled by a bevy of ducks squabbling cheerfully. A single swan sailed out of the shade of a willow. Max thought of Adam singing the miller's song, "O river of my love, so full of mystery." Schubert and water. He remembered his mother's left hand rocking over the keys of the piano in the salon at Waldau long ago. Bittersweet, these memories. He smiled. More sweet than bitter. The swan sailed towards him and bent its neck as if acknowledging applause for its elegance.

"Max! Max! This way!"

A woman's voice, shattering the moment. He turned his head. In the road the other side of a band of grass, some nearly leafless cherry trees, and the sidewalk, was a white open car with a lot of shiny chrome, and in it, waving, a woman in dark glasses and a head scarf.

"Max! Over here!"

So few people called him by his Christian name. Eva Grossmann. He recognized her as he got up and went over to the car.

"Eva! Good morning."

"Max! I haven't seen you for an age! What a wonderful coincidence, on this lovely day. Get in—do you like my roadster? That's what they're called in America. I'll take you for a spin. Perfect! I was so bored I thought I'd drive into the country for the sunshine, and now you can come too. Or are you busy?"

"Busy? No. Not really."

He got in. The door of the car was long and heavy and closed with an expensive, precisely engineered thud. Eva took her right hand off the steering wheel, put her arm round his neck, and kissed him on the cheek. She laughed at his surprise, returned her hand to the wheel, and looked behind her for a second, and the car shot forward with a roar of its engine. He noticed her long, red, varnished nails, her long white fingers, relaxed on the wheel, on the lever as she changed gear.

Eva drove fast and expertly through the streets, nearly empty of other traffic except for some horsedrawn wagons and carts and Sunday morning trams with only a few passengers in them. She drove southwest out of the city, away from the river and towards the hills.

After half an hour, they were on a white country road among farms and small villages. She had to slow down to walking pace when a herd of dairy cows driven by a man with a stick, a small girl, and a dog filled the road in front of them. Suddenly the sounds of the country— the lowing of the cows, an occasional shout from the man, a peremptory bark from the dog, a late bird singing—were for the first time audible.

"Where shall we go?" Eva said. "It doesn't matter, does it, now that I've kidnapped you. Let's just drive till we see somewhere nice to stop."

The man opened a gate into a field to the left of the road and herded the cows into the field so that the car could pass. Eva waved in acknowledgement as she accelerated. The man shouted an obscenity after them.

"You get used to that", Eva said, loud enough for Max to hear her over the noise of the engine. "Peasants don't like women driving."

They drove for perhaps another half hour, mostly uphill on narrow lanes, and after a while through russet-leaved oak trees with the sun glancing down to autumnal bracken and brambles. In spite of the "let's just drive", Max could tell that Eva knew exactly where she was going. They emerged from the trees onto grassy meadows, a valley ahead of them, which, once they were driving downhill, turned out to have a pretty village by a stream at the bottom of the slope.

"What do you think?" Eva said as she stopped the car in the little white square in front of the church. "Shall we see if there's an inn?"

She knows perfectly well there's an inn, he thought, but stopped caring as she led him down a rutted lane between a row of cottages and the wall of a farmyard to an inn beside an old stone bridge over the stream. There were uneven flagstones, half a dozen hens and a rooster pecking about, a haystack behind the house, and four red cows in a fenced paddock. Through an open door, he saw a woman on her hands and knees scrubbing the wooden floor. Eva took off her scarf and her sunglasses, shook out her hair, winked at Max, and went up to the doorway.

"Good morning", she said.

The woman looked up, pushing her hair out of her eyes with a wet hand.

"Yes?"

"If my friend and I go for a walk for an hour or so and come back at about noon, would you be able to give us a beer and a bit of lunch? We don't want anything fancy."

"This is an inn, ma'am. It says on the sign. There'll be beer and something to eat, yes." She got to her feet and looked at Eva more closely. "It's Frau Winckelmann, isn't it?"

"You've got a very good memory. Thank you. We'll be back later."

As the woman turned away, picking up her bucket of soapy water, Eva looked at Max and laughed.

"Never mind. Life's rich tapestry, eh? Anyway, this is a lovely place."

"It is. It is." For the first time that day, Max saw Eva's eyes and was able to look properly at her face. He had forgotten the mischief in her face, the consciousness of charm, and her thick, short bronze hair the colour of the autumn woods in the sun. Her eyes—perhaps he had never noticed them before—were almost the same colour as her hair; tawny, like the eyes of a lion, he thought. A lioncub. Making you want to stroke it but dangerous. He thought of the long red nails. She had lipstick on her mouth, but it was faint, a faint coloured outline. He could imagine wanting to kiss those faintly painted lips. He shook all this out of his head as if to wake himself up.

"Max," she said, "it's so nice to see you after all this time. What a lucky day. Come on. Let's walk."

She set off ahead of him. She was wearing breeches, almost as if for riding, in the modern fashion—Max remembered his mother riding sidesaddle in a black habit—but closer fitting, probably designed for playing some game. Stockings, thin wool, perhaps—he was looking at her neat ankles and calves as she walked—and shoes in two colours with laces. Her jacket, tight at the waist, was dark blue, setting off her sleek tawny head. She was slim and light, as she had always been in the days of Treuburg and the green and gold outfit. From the back now, she looked almost like a boy, but her walk was not at all like a boy's walk.

She led him along a path, upstream from the bridge. The fresh mildness of the October air and the beauty of the valley, fields, and woods washed in the sun after the recent rain, scarlet berries on trees and bushes, the crunch of dying summer growth under their feet, made him realize how long it was since he had been out of the city. He stayed behind Eva, though he could have walked beside her. He didn't want to have to say anything and was grateful to her for simply walking, not even looking back to see if he was still there.

They met a gamekeeper with his dog and a gun over his shoulder coming towards them. The gamekeeper stood to one side of the path for Eva to pass and touched his hat when she smiled her thanks. He was dressed in old green corduroy, a feather in his hat, like a hunter in a romantic opera. He nodded to Max, who suddenly felt in his city suit and his city hat as if he had gone to sleep and woken up a hundred years ago. Then he looked at Eva's boyish figure, smart and brisk ahead of him: wherever, whenever, this was, she was with him, leading him. It was her place, her idea, her car, her fault, and all of it was wonderful.

The path was now through trees, difficult to follow, with rabbit holes and roots underfoot, and a little later it ended as the banks of the stream became sheer and rocky with water trickling blackly down the rock and small ferns, more brown than green, in the crevices here and there.

Eva turned and smiled. "Well. Shall we go back? I'm getting hungry. This is what one is meant to do on a Sunday in the country, isn't it? Walk until hungry. Eat in a village inn."

She looked round at the dark walls of rock. Trees with leaves still on the branches grew high above them, and only a few thin rays of sunlight pierced the gloom. "You know what I'd like to do here?"

"What?" Max was suddenly afraid.

"Paint a great mural on this black surface. Bright colours, squares and triangles, a surprise masterpiece for anyone walking this far. What do you think?"

Relieved and also horrified, he didn't know what to say. "I don't know. Isn't it perhaps all fine enough, dramatic enough, as it is?"

She laughed and put both hands, her thin white hands with the scarlet nails, on his shoulders. "Oh Max, I do love you. You're so old-fashioned. Let's go back for our lunch, and I'll tell you about what goes on nowadays at the Academy. I have teachers who would find ways of painting, or perhaps of making a sculpture, out in the wild just to make a gesture of solidarity with the wilderness. Do you see?"

He didn't. He did see that the beauty of their walk meant nothing to her. If he had gone to sleep and woken up in the past, she already belonged to a future he knew nothing about.

Her hands were still on his shoulders. She turned him round and gave him a little push. "Off you go. Be pathfinder. I've got to have a pee. I'll catch you up."

He set off slowly through the trees, flattered, confused, and, with a sudden acute pang, missing Adam.

Two young couples, clearly also from the city, had appeared at the inn when they got back and were sitting at a table in the scrubbed room drinking beer and laughing a good deal. Max and Eva sat in the opposite corner at a table with a red and white checkered cloth. The woman they had spoken to earlier, unsmiling, brought them beer, sausages, sauerkraut, and potato salad, all very good.

"So, Eva", Max said, for something ordinary to say. "How are you?"

"Very well, thank you, Count", she said, mocking. Then, "I'm sorry, Max. But we know each other better than that, don't you think? The Joachim year—that's what I call it to myself—seems a hundred years ago, but it was only two or three, wasn't it? No time at all, really. How is Joachim, by the way?"

"He's gone. Only three weeks ago. He left Breslau to take up a commission in the army, as a captain and a military doctor."

"Did he? That's a shame. I was very fond of Joachim, you know. Too stubborn, too Prussian for me, really, but so good-looking. He was a challenge. I like a challenge."

Her look across the sausages and sauerkraut made Max look at his plate.

"He didn't like my painting. But he didn't pretend to like it. So that was fine. Anyway, I've done doctors. Too many suitable doctors my parents would like me to like. Too many doctors who would like me to like them because my parents have plenty of money. It's a bore, all that. Marriage as a prospect is a bore altogether, don't you think? Children, servants, a house to worry about—not for me."

For a second, she reminded him of Adam, aged sixteen, finding practically everything "banal". But Eva was not sixteen.

"Do you still live with your parents?"

"Up to a point. Officially, of course I do. But I have a studio, high up at the top of an old house near the Academy. Wonderful, it is, white and light, perfect for painting, and if I don't want to go home, for one reason or another, I don't go home. My mother pretends not to notice. She's afraid of my father, and he actually doesn't notice. Luckily for me, it's my brother they worry about more. He's studying law at the university. He's joined a duelling club, heaven knows how—but he has got fairer hair than me and 'Grossmann' doesn't have to be Jewish, I suppose—and says he's a Nazi. What about that?"

"Eva . . ."

"What is it, Max? You look so serious. You always were such a serious fellow. We must do something about that."

"Have you or your father heard anything of Dr Halpern?"

"Oh, Jakob Halpern. Did you know him? I'd forgotten. I didn't like him. Too much the professional Jew—the sort of thing that gets us all a bad name we don't deserve. And serious—dreadfully serious, far worse than you. He wanted to go back to Vilna—a year ago? Two? I can't remember. My father thought he was mad to go back. Much better careers for good surgeons here. Anyway, my father helped him with references and all that, and he got a job in Vilna. Back where he belongs, in Russia or Poland or wherever it is, and a good thing too."

She pushed her plate away, put a white cigarette with a gold tip in a long black and gold cigarette holder, lit it with a gold lighter, and took in a deep draught of smoke. She blew the smoke out gently and smiled. Max resisted the smile just a little.

"Where he belongs", he said. "Do you think Jews belong anywhere?"

"Of course they do. German Jews belong in Germany. Like us. Like my family. Russian Jews belong in Russia, Polish Jews in Poland. And they should stay there. My father says all this anti-Semitism, which is becoming a real nuisance even in the university, even in the hospital though half the doctors are Jewish, even to people as senior as him who've been professors for years, is caused by the Jews from the east coming to Germany and expecting jobs, houses, charity. They ought to go back where they came from and leave us all in peace. They look so *obvious*, that's the trouble. They sound so obvious too, gabbling in Yiddish and not bothering to learn German."

"Eva, that's very hard. They have a terrible time in the east, a really terrible time, and worse than ever since the revolution in Russia."

"I thought the Bolsheviks were all Jews. That's what everyone says. It's their revolution. Let them get on with it and not come here to start a revolution in Germany."

"Have you ever met a religious Jew?"

"No, certainly not. I don't know anything about the Jewish religion. Or the Christian religion. All religion has ever done is cause trouble. We're much better off without it, don't you think?"

"Well, no, I don't. But—"

"Max." She laid on his hand her own, white, long-fingered, red-nailed, cool. "There you go again, being *serious*. Please—here we are, together as if by magic, on what was going to be a really boring Sunday—let's not talk about religion. Tell me ..."

She lifted her hand off his, and he managed to say, "What?"

"What happened to Adam? I know Joachim only asked me to play those trios because Adam had gone to Poland. Did he come back? Is he still in your flat? *So* attractive—did you know I knew him before I ever met Joachim? We were practically children then, of course. Very sweet, he was."

"He's still in Poland."

"What a waste. So are you alone in the flat now that Joachim's gone as well? And what do you do with yourself? Are you still at the university?"

"No. I'm a Referendar in the courts of justice."

"How like you, Max, to have such a serious job. I beg your pardon— such a serious *career*. Is it very dull?"

"It's pretty dull. But it's bound to get more interesting later."

"And the flat?"

"I share it with a medical student from Prague. His name's Felix Stern."

"A musician?"

"No."

"Oh, I remember. The quiet boy in glasses."

"That's right."

"His ears stick out. So you've got no one to play music with? I've got a piano in my studio. You could bring your violin. Wait till you see my studio—I'd like you to see my new paintings. I've been doing some modelling too—only clay so far, but the professor says they'll soon be good enough to think about casting. Not that I trust his judgement." She laughed. He saw she expected him to understand. "I am, well, perhaps a bit his favourite."

She stopped, making him look at her.

"Don't be embarrassed, Max. Have you a girlfriend?"

He shook his head.

"Good. Then it's all right to make you a little jealous. Come. Let's go back. As fast as the wind, don't you think?"

She paid for their lunch ("No, Max. This was my mad idea. Such a good idea, don't you think?"), and they got back into the car. Before she put on her scarf and her dark glasses, she put the back of her hand gently against his cheek and said, "Don't be frightened, Max. I drive quite well."

They drove back to her studio like an arrow that, once it has left the bow, nothing can deflect from its course. He tried to remember that he had always disliked Eva Grossmann. He tried to recall the slight revulsion he had felt earlier that day when he noticed her hands on the steering wheel. He tried to remember what it was that she'd said in the inn that he'd found chilling, shockingly selfish. It was all useless. He knew what was going to happen when they got to her studio, and he was fiercely, hungrily excited, expectant, thrilled by her hands on the wheel, thrilled by her ankles as she drove the car, her profile with scarf and sunglasses against the rushing air. Kidnapped, seduced, helpless—he wouldn't for all the world have been anywhere else but in this long white car beside Eva Grossmann tearing along the country roads back to Breslau on this golden afternoon.

He woke up in the dark wondering where he was, what had happened to him. There was some light from the street, but not the usual light, not the usual window. He lay absolutely still. There was a weight on his chest. He realized it was the weight of Eva's head, heavy, asleep. Her arm was across his stomach. How had this happened? When had he decided? Before he moved at all, he remembered the whole day. What was the time? Was it the middle of the night? Nearly the morning? Time to go to work? But before he moved his own arm to look at his watch— was there enough light to see the time?—she moved her arm, downwards, and desire stirred in him again. He forgot that he should find out what time it was. She moaned softly, "Max", and they made love again.

"Eva," he eventually said, "I must look at the time." It seemed somehow impolite to look at his watch, still on his wrist, without telling her.

She laughed. "Max, you are funny. 'I must look at the time.' So romantic. Such moving words. Of course you must look at the time. What is it?"

He could just see the hands on his watch.

"Nearly nine o'clock." He relaxed.

She laughed again. "There you are. The night is young."

She disentangled her limbs from his and sat up, looking down at him with her mischievous eyes. Her body was thin, white, perfect, her breasts small, rounded. He closed his eyes.

"Max", she said, gently. He basked in her voice. "How old are you?"

"I don't know", he said. "Yes I do. Twenty-five."

"And this is the first time you've ever slept with a woman. What a good boy you've been."

"How do you know?"

"One knows. You're not bad at it, I must say."

She bent over him and kissed his skin just below his breastbone.

"No", she said, twisting away so that she was sitting on the side of the bed. "Time for some champagne, I think."

She disappeared. He closed his eyes again and heard a door opening and shutting, water running, stopping, a different door opening and shutting, the pop of a champagne cork, glasses being filled. She switched on a bright lamp that lit a big painting of a stormy sea in dark blues and greys with bold white caps to lines of waves. She came back and sat on the bed.

"Here!" He sat up, pulling the covers over his nakedness. She gave him a glass, cold and slippery.

"To your very good health, Count."

She was wearing a loose silk dressing gown and smelled fresh and scented. She leant forward and kissed him lightly between his eyes. He shut them and opened them again.

"Eva, I don't—"

She put a thin, scented, scarlet-tipped finger on his lips.

"Shh. Whatever it is you don't, don't say a word."

She got up, crossed the room, and sat in a big soft black chair, looking at him, laughing.

"I know", she said. "You must get dressed, go back to your serious flat, and do some serious work for Monday morning at the law courts. Of course. I am only a woman, an accident, an incidental diversion. But there aren't enough of those nowadays, are there? You'll be back. What's your number?"

"What?"

"Your telephone number. Come along, Max. Don't tell me you have no telephone. This is 1930, you know."

"No. Yes. Only in the office, and I can't—"

"Certainly not. Loose women ringing you up in the office. Whatever next! No. Get a telephone in the flat. It's easily done. Now, get up. The bathroom's that door there. Your clothes"—she laughed again—"are about."

He was halfway home, walking across the old town through the silent Sunday evening streets, when it struck him that he had committed a grave sin. He stood still. What was he doing? Could he simply walk back into his ordinary life as if Eva had never called to him as he sat on his bench? His and Anna's bench. Anna. Had he betrayed his memory of Anna in a few insane hours? Or wasn't it the case that Anna was now too long ago, too far away, for her to be enough connected to him for loyalty or disloyalty to have any real meaning? And if Anna could no longer be betrayed—but she could be, she had been. Hadn't Anna all this time been his love, her imagined body in his dreams, his fantasies, his hot nights, his self-disgusted mornings? And Adam? Hadn't Adam years ago resisted Eva Grossmann as an easy temptation because that was all she was? But she was more than that. She was a person too, bravely keeping her spirits up, painting—had she painted that dark sea and its thundering waves? He would find out. Would he? Would he go back to that white studio, with its soft bed, its scented bathroom, its cold glass of champagne? Would he or wouldn't he? He would, he knew.

He stood and thought. And the sin? Fornication. What a word. A legal term, it seemed. Only a word. What bearing did it have on that excitement, that fulfilment? No harm done to anyone, surely. Yet it shut him out. He thought of the candlelit, almost silent, early morning Mass in the small dark church with the old women in their head scarves. It had been that very morning. He had filed up to the altar with them, and the priest had placed on his tongue the Body of Christ. A miracle, every Mass. A miracle that the little circle of bread was the Body of Christ, that he, the child of generations of Prussian noblemen and ghetto Jews, was there to receive it. It seemed a hundred years ago, that Mass, and somewhere on the other side of a chasm he couldn't recross. He could almost hear the river roaring far below him in the blackness. How had he got to this side of the chasm? Had he closed his eyes and jumped? When?

An old drunk stumbled down the street towards him. He found a few coins in his pocket, and when the drunk stopped unsteadily holding out his hand, he gave him the coins and said, "Get something to eat." "God bless you", the old man said in a thick Polish accent. Max watched him stumble on. He wouldn't get anything to eat, any more than now, after what had happened, after what—there was no getting away from it—he had *done*, God would bless him.

He felt suddenly very tired. He knew he had a great deal to sort out, in his mind, in his heart. But not tonight.

When he got home, Stern was reading a medical textbook with an empty cup beside him on the floor and the chess pieces set out on the board.

"I'm sorry, Stern. I got held up. We'll play another evening."

"Doesn't matter. I had some work to do."

"So had I. In fact, I must do a bit now. Stern?"

"Yes?"

"Would a telephone in the flat be any use to you?"

Chapter 15

On 31 October 1932, the morning train to Cracow pulled out of the grime of Breslau's Upper Silesia station into bright frosty sunshine. Max, alone in a second-class compartment, leant back in his seat and lit a cigarette—he smoked now, though not often, because he had caught the habit from Eva—with a sigh of relief and expectation.

He hadn't been out of Germany since he and Adam went to Venice, and now, five and a quarter years later, he was more pleased than he could ever have imagined to be leaving his own country, Germany, Silesia, even Breslau, if only for the inside of a week. Perhaps the atmosphere in Poland would be lighter, clearer, less overcast with the sense of foreboding and fear that was now stifling in the streets and squares of the city. From almost every wall there shouted some political poster showing a half-naked muscled bully representing Germany or the worker or Aryan triumph. There was always an election coming. As soon as one lot of posters peeled in the rain, a fresh layer was pasted on top.

In Cracow he would be a foreigner, walking streets he'd never seen, hearing people talking in a language he scarcely knew, and whatever the politicians in Warsaw were up to, he wasn't taking their wages.

Above all, he was going to see Adam, who, on the next day, the Feast of All Saints, was to be ordained with eleven others in Cracow Cathedral. He would see Adam for the first time since he'd disappeared to study for the priesthood, leaving Max behind. Adam had five days' holiday after his ordination before he was to start work in his parish in Lemberg, and he had asked Max to spend these days with him. Dr Gerlach had unwillingly agreed to Max taking this week off in the middle of the legal term. ("It's a very busy time of year, you know. But since you took no leave in the summer, which would have been more convenient, I suppose I must allow you to go.") Max had decided that if Dr Gerlach refused him this week off, he would resign.

Then he realized that he was devising an easy reason for resigning: was he hoping that the permission wouldn't be given, to save himself a much more difficult decision?

He groaned. He wasn't going to think about all that now, on his way to Cracow, to see Adam.

He had never been to an ordination. At the thought of the Mass, the crowds of people there would be, he winced. He should be used to this by now, his twilight life as an excommunicated Catholic. That was the phrase in his mind when he was being hardest on himself, not that any priest had given him any kind of verdict, because he hadn't asked for one.

For more than a year, since the shameful end of his shameful affair with Eva, he had been—what? Half a Catholic? An unforgiven sinner? He hadn't spoken to a priest, except to say good morning at the end of Mass. He knew that if he tried to, or went to talk to, Dr Fischer, he would be told to go to confession. He couldn't do that. He couldn't because what he felt about it all, at the very bottom of his heart, was relief. And that relief only compounded the sin, all the sins.

Since he stopped seeing Eva, he had been every Sunday to the early Mass in the cathedral. He liked the walk to Cathedral Island, over the moat, into the oldest streets in the city. He liked it best in autumn and spring, when early morning light caught the cobbles in the streets, deserted except for elderly women in black also going to early Mass. But the winter streets in the dark, with the lamps still lit, were beautiful too, especially if fresh snow had fallen overnight, and the not-yet-hot sunshine of summer with the odd café proprietor rattling up his shutters and boys on bicycles delivering newspapers had a promise that cheered him. Always, and more and more, there were tramps, beggars, the destitute of the city, in doorways, on steps, hoping for a coin or two. He gave a few of them something.

In the cathedral, he knew no one. He knelt at the back of the dark chapel, where the earliest Mass was said by any one of a dozen priests. No one even looked at him. No one to wonder why he never received Communion. Would Adam notice tomorrow? There would be hundreds of people, all the friends and relations and parish supporters of all the young men being ordained. He would be lost in a big congregation of strangers. Impossible that Adam would notice.

But later, in any case, he would tell him the Eva story. He knew he would.

One of the beliefs that kept him in the Church at all was his certainty, most of the time, that God knew the whole story and was able to judge exactly what in it was shameful, sinful, even wicked, and what was no more than confused, the result of the wide distance from each other of two people connected only by passion, two people who had the most intimate knowledge of each other's bodies and no knowledge of each other's souls. A second was his certainty that Anna, Anna whose soul he knew at least a little, while her body, except for her face, her hands in his, her mouth, he knew not at all, would want him to stay faithful to what he had been sure, what he was still sure—wasn't he?—was true.

Anna, a year ago, a little more, in September, had sent him a card, in Yiddish, Russian, and Polish, with the formal announcement of the marriage of Anna, daughter of Dr Samuel Halperin and his late wife Leah, to Rabbi Moshe Asher Heschel. So she had married a learned Vilna Jew. When he read the card, he heard something shut forever in his mind. But soon he was glad she was safe with God in her own faith, the ancient faith of which he wished he knew more. At the bottom of the card, she had written in German, "Dear Max, I am sorry. Remember always Anna."

Now, when he thought of her, as he often did, he was pleased that she and her even more obviously Jewish brother were safe in Vilna, where the marching bullies of the Nazi party couldn't insult or hurt them.

And he stayed quiet in his twilit condition also because he needed to pray. Every night before he went to sleep, he said the Our Father, making himself repeat it until he had concentrated some thought and feeling on each phrase, until he had understood again that the kingdom of God the Father could come only because Christ had come, making earth as it is in heaven in his life and death, and because Mary had said, "Thy will be done." This was a way of leaving himself out of his prayer. Forgive us our sins. He could not forgive Eva. At least in the last words of the prayer, he was there, present to God, along with everyone else facing the gathering menace he felt everywhere he went: deliver us from evil.

It was only at Mass that he found he could pray for his parents, his grandparents, Freddy, Emilia—whether she was still alive or on her way to heaven—Anna and her husband, her father, and her brother. And also and above all, for the soul of the baby, Eva's and his, the baby who had not been allowed to reach the daylight of the world. He knew that the souls of unbaptized babies were supposed to be in limbo forever, somewhere outside the light of Christ, but he didn't believe it. Hadn't Christ said, "Let the little children come to me"?

It was only at Mass, after the consecration, in the presence of Christ himself there on the altar in the candlelight of the dark chapel, that he knew his child, his three-quarters-Jewish child, was safe with God, safer perhaps than he—it was impossible, he didn't know why, not to think of his child as a boy—would ever have been in a world, a Germany, a Breslau getting more cruel and more frightening as every month passed.

He crushed his cigarette into the ashtray under the window and looked out at the last of the poor Polish streets to the southeast of the city. Then, after some untidy factory yards with coal heaps and trucks and wagons waiting to load or unload, there was a stretch of old forest with frost still on the pine needles, and then a few scattered expensive houses in a new kind of suburb, with young trees planted in what had recently been farmers' fields, and bright brick walls with the occasional tennis court. He thought of his mother's destroyed rose garden and wondered who had been playing tennis with Betsy in the summer gone by.

Not Heinrich.

He had seen Heinrich in the Century Hall—the Century Hall where he had listened to the B Minor Mass with Treuburg and taken Anna to hear Beethoven and Mahler—on that horrible evening in April when Adolf Hitler came to Breslau and yelled hatred to ten thousand people crushed together to hear him. They clapped and stamped and cheered their approval before, during, and—with loudest and longest enthusiasm—after the speech. Max and Felix Stern, who had come to see, were standing together by a closed door at the very back of the bottom level of the huge auditorium.

The week before, Chancellor Brüning had declared the brownshirts, the Nazi Stormtroopers, a proscribed organization. They'd been marching in white shirts for more than a year because of the Chancellor's earlier ban on political uniforms, which had produced only a change of colour. Now the organization was supposed to be banned altogether. But the Century Hall was crammed with men in white shirts, furious at the ban and determined to show Hitler their loyal defiance of the government.

Max looked at the people in the audience during the wait of almost an hour between the closing of the doors and Hitler's arrival. According to the Nazi functionary who appeared on the platform after the first ten minutes, the Leader was going to be late because, by popular demand, he had made three speeches already that evening, flying from place to place in an aeroplane because he wanted to see as many of his supporters as possible while he was in Silesia. A cheer. The men in white shirts then led singing, the Horst Wessel song over and over again and the "Watch on the Rhine", marching songs Max had heard in the streets. One song he'd never heard before had the chorus line "Hang the Jews and put the priests against the wall." Another seemed to be the Stormtroopers' own anthem: "Stormtroopers young and old, take weapons in your hand", it began. "For the Jew is wreaking havoc in the German fatherland." The chorus horrified Max—"When Jewish blood spurts from the knife we all feel twice as good"—but practically everyone joined in, as if this were a cheerful folk song. There were men and women of all ages and kinds in the audience: workers; the scruffy unemployed; students in their uniforms; old couples; old men by themselves, some with medals pinned to everyday clothes; and middle-class, middle-aged men in suits who might have been lawyers, doctors, school-teachers, or civil servants of any kind, and their respectably dressed wives and daughters, the girls more excited than anyone except the very young Stormtroopers.

At last the functionary reappeared, and in the instant silence that fell proclaimed the arrival of the Leader. A louder cheer. Then Adolf Hitler, an undistinguished-looking man surrounded by a small group of civilians and followed by a group of soldiers—not quite soldiers, because the black uniforms they wore were not quite military—entered the hall to shouting and stamping from the crowd and the waving of hundreds of swastika banners. Hitler climbed the steps to the platform. His guards lined up behind him as he stood at the microphone and the saluting crowd roared, "Heil Hitler!" Stony-faced, they remained standing while everyone who had a seat—the hall was much fuller than would have been permitted for a concert—sat down.

"What are they, the bodyguard?" Max whispered to Stern as loud clapping continued to flow round the hall though Hitler had so far done no more than salute the faithful. "Soldiers? Aren't political uniforms banned?"

"That's the SS. The uniforms are half the point. To hell with the Chancellor, the government, the law. Who's going to start arresting the SS? The police? Top-class protection for the Leader, that's what they are. In case anyone shoots him. Pity we haven't got a gun."

Max stared hard at the figures at attention on the platform.

"What is it?" Stern whispered.

"I think I know one of them. Knew one of them. Never mind."

He had read a bit about the SS in the newspapers. Unlike the brown-shirted, now whiteshirted, Stormtroopers who marched and sang and shouted insults at evident Jews in the streets and attacked people like Stern at Communist Party meetings, the SS weren't mere thugs, discharged ordinary soldiers who had fought in the war, unemployed labourers, or working-class boys whose fathers had been killed or wounded and who believed Horst Wessel was a martyr. The SS was more sinister, more educated, a highly disciplined weapon of the Nazi Party, its members picked from former officers and Freikorps commanders from after the war, and where possible from the nobility, the best Aryan families. Max looked across the crowd from the far end of the huge circular hall at the absolutely still figures in their black uniforms with a lightning flash, somehow more threatening even than the swastika, on the collar, and black polished boots. Perhaps he'd been wrong. They were a long way away. No, he knew he hadn't been wrong. What if they found out who Heinrich's mother was? He must have covered his tracks with care—and there were Betsy's father's millions to guarantee him as unimpeachably Aryan.

If Max had been told that Heinrich had joined the SS, he wouldn't have been surprised. But seeing him there behind the deeply unattractive figure of Hitler, who seemed almost mad with his staring eyes, his voice in a screaming crescendo of rage to which the audience was listening with open-mouthed adoring attention, shook him badly. He was glad they were dead, his mother, his grandfather. But also his father. Could this be what Prussian military honour and obedience had become? No. He thought of Treuburg. He hoped Dr Mendel would never discover that a boy he had taught, long ago in the peaceful schoolroom at Waldau, however resistant Heinrich had been to his lessons as he would have been to any lessons, now belonged to the SS.

Max tried to listen to what Hitler was saying, the words and sentences that the people of Breslau, though naturally only Germans had come to the hall, were finding so enchanting, so seductive. Contempt.

That was what the high-pitched, rasping voice, with its Austrian accent and frenzied delivery, was pouring out. Contempt for the republic, contempt for everyone who had tried to sort out a peaceful and prosperous life for the country since the war: "For fourteen years the ruling parties have driven us into the ground"—huge cheer—Bismarck, the hero who saved the German people, had been betrayed by the politicians in Berlin—"In fourteen years, they have destroyed not only their own efforts but the toil of generations"—another huge cheer. Only the Nazis can restore German pride and power and defeat the Jewish conspiracy. The politicians may try to ban Nazi propaganda, dissolve the Stormtroopers, dissolve the SS and the entire party. "They can terrorize us. They can kill us ... but we will never surrender!" Contempt and confidence, together. Hubris? No. Too noble a word. And hadn't Aristotle said that a tragic hero has to be a mixture of good and evil? How could there be any good in this man full of hysterical, contagious hatred and scorn?

An English phrase came into Max's head as Hitler reached the end of his speech, with the audience, all standing now, cheering and cheering and the SS guard forming up round him to escort him down the aisle between the most expensive seats. He stopped here and there to shake a hand, pat a shoulder. Women and girls sank to their knees as he passed. "Show scorn her own image." He couldn't remember where it came from and wasn't entirely sure what it meant. But he knew Hitler's face was the face of scorn and that this screaming, adored man was greatly to be feared.

It took them a long time to get out of the hall and away from the excited crowds in the streets.

"Well?" Max said to Stern as they walked back to the flat.

"I'm getting out of this country as soon as I can. If this is how things are going—it's Russia for me. I mean it, Hofmannswaldau. This time next year, if I can get through the exams in March, I'll be in Russia."

At home Max found on the bookshelves in his study, beside Adam's production copy of *Hamlet*, his own old school copy in English, with notes in his own handwriting taken down in Dr Fischer's class. He was sure that phrase was somewhere in the play, but it took him nearly an hour to find it. There it was—Hamlet talking to the Players. The point of a play, he was saying, "was and is to hold as 'twere a mirror up to nature; to show virtue her feature, scorn her own image, and the very age and body of the time his form and pressure." That was it, exactly. The whole evening in the Century Hall had been a play, a performance with Adolf Hitler as its leading actor and the SS taking walk-on parts to scare the audience with the threat of force—restrained, but for how long?—and hadn't it shown him, precisely, the form and pressure of the very age and body of the time?

He remembered now, because of his two vertical lines and a star pencilled in the margin of the speech, his private reminder to himself to pay particular attention to what he'd marked, old Fischer saying how it would have been easy, almost automatic, for Shakespeare to use the word "vice" as the opposite of "virtue". But he had chosen "scorn" instead. "Shakespeare makes all his really destructive characters scornful, driven by contempt. They despise people who can be taken in by lies. Then they deceive them, deliberately frighten them, and so acquire power over them. So contempt, power, and untruth become connected." Only tonight, Max realized, his old copy of *Hamlet* on the desk in front of him on top of a pile of legal papers he was supposed to be reading for tomorrow's meeting, had he understood what Dr Fischer was trying to tell the boys in the class.

He put the book back on the shelf. He would try to look after Stern, wretched boy, now asleep in his room across the passage. At least these student Communists weren't driven by contempt but by a hope, however forlorn, that somehow they could make the world a better place. What was the Nazis' hope? Destruction of every other hope but blind devotion to Hitler's hatred and scorn. And another war.

More than six months had gone by since that meeting in the Century Hall, and Hitler and the Nazis were considerably closer to real power. Brüning had gone at the end of May, the grim greyness of his rule making the Nazis seem only more colourful and glamorous with every grey week of more people out of work, more children going hungry, more resentment. "Watch out for *ressentiment*", Max remembered Adam saying in his Nietzsche period. "Drives the masses to their doom faster than anything." Wasn't it, precisely, resentment that Hitler played on, on and on, until the crowds who worshipped him believed that only he could smite—the right word, smite, straight out of the Bible—the enemies he identified for them, the government, the politicians, the "November criminals" who had unnecessarily given up the effort to win the war, the Communists, and of course the Jews all of them were said to be. Lies, a whole package of lies, but believed, apparently, by half the people in Germany as if they were the truth.

The presidential election, not long before Hitler's visit to Breslau, had been a shambles. Hindenburg had won it. Hitler had lost it. But Hindenburg—Max remembered Treuburg on the subject of Hindenburg, and that was two years ago—was now even older, even less connected to reality, even more a propaganda representation of a past that wasn't any use to anyone now, if it ever had been.

Max lit another cigarette as the train pulled into Brieg. A few people were waiting on the platform. No one got into his compartment. Good.

Perhaps Hindenburg was something like the tragic hero Hitler was too horrifying to be. There he was in Versailles in 1870, a young officer present at the hubris of the Hall of Mirrors. And here he still was, sixty-two years later. Present for the delivery of nemesis? The victor of Tannenberg having to depend on the votes of all the socialists in Germany to stop Hitler being elected President. That was a long way to fall for a Prussian field marshal. But even Tannenberg was a lie. Stern had told him that the famous battle in 1914, the battle that killed Freddy and made their father so proud, was planned by other generals, not by Hindenburg and Ludendorff, and had taken place twenty miles away from Tannenberg. They stole the name of a battle Teutonic Knights lost five hundred years ago, to show that Germans could, after all, beat the Slavs.

Was there anything Hindenburg could do now to prevent Hitler from becoming Chancellor? The Reichstag elections at the end of July had finally made the Nazis the biggest party. With the Communists as well as the Nazis resolved to make the Reichstag unworkable, it had been suspended after a single sitting in September. So who was governing Germany? The ancient Hindenburg, in theory—"presidential decrees", the new laws were called—but actually a collection of noblemen and generals, Hindenburg's inexperienced, incompetent friends, led by the new Chancellor, Franz von Papen, about whom Max knew almost nothing. At first the only visible consequence of the change of Chancellor had been that the Stormtroopers, no longer banned and in Breslau enlisting more and more men every week, were back in brown shirts. It particularly depressed Max that both Brüning and Papen were Catholics and had belonged to Dr Fischer's beloved Centre Party. What had happened to that?

He would have visited old Fischer to see what he thought about all this. But he couldn't talk about the twilight of Germany while he was so ashamed of his own.

He stubbed out his second cigarette. What a mess. What a bloody mess.

Suddenly it seemed to him, as he sat in the train travelling southeast in the morning sun—there was now a little snow on the ground—that truth was the only thing that mattered. And there was a war against truth going on in Germany. Newspapers kept being banned—not only Communist and Social Democrat papers, and not only single issues, but closures altogether of papers, some of which at least were attempting to tell the truth. Lies, meanwhile, flourished. Nazi speeches, Nazi posters, Nazi newspapers lied and lied, and people believed the lies. Otherwise they wouldn't have voted as they did in the Reichstag elections in the summer. In Breslau the Nazi vote had been the third-highest percentage in the whole country.

The worst lies of all were told about the Jews. You heard everywhere that there was a conspiracy of Jews throughout the world. What was said to be the purpose of this conspiracy could be anything anyone might fear: to run capitalism, to ruin capitalism; to run the League of Nations, to ruin the League of Nations; to run Germany, to ruin Germany; to run the universities, to ruin the universities; anything, as long as the secret machinations of invisible, powerful Jews were behind it. Yet Jews had no power anywhere and, according to Jakob Halpern, no inclination to unite in a common opinion about anything. Jews never agreed, Halpern said. They would argue till the coming of the Messiah and then argue about him. They certainly couldn't agree about Palestine, which some of them saw as the greatest hope for their future and others as the greatest disaster. Either way, the British had closed Palestine now, except to the rich. No more Jews were allowed in unless they had a thousand English pounds, a sum beyond the dreams of the people who were being most got at and frightened every day in Germany. How powerful were they, cowering in their shops night after night hoping their windows wouldn't be broken? Yet the conspiracy lie was so often told that many, many people—the millions, now, who thought Hitler was going to save them from it—believed there was a worldwide Jewish plot that had made them poor, had made them unemployed, had made them lose the war.

And not only uneducated people believed the lies. Two days after the Reichstag election, at the beginning of August, Dr Gerlach had invited Max to a party his wife was giving to celebrate the Nazi victory. He had politely refused. But Gerlach, however dull, and however professionally noncommittal on any political subject, was a clever man and a respected judge. How could he possibly allow his wife to celebrate what had happened in the election? Max soon discovered the answer.

Most of the discussion in the office in the summer hadn't been about the Nazis at all but about the Chancellor's decision to abolish the state government of Prussia. This was a move against the Social Democrats, who had ruled Prussia ever since the war. There was scarcely a murmur of protest in the city, even from the Social Democrats, now too frightened of the Nazis to make an evident fuss about anything. Dr Gerlach insisted that it made no difference to justice and to the efficient running of the law courts who paid the civil service salaries. Max's instinctive feeling was that it made, or might make, a very considerable difference, but he kept quiet. Until the Potempa case.

One night in August, the very night after the Chancellor had decreed a mandatory death penalty for political murder—this was aimed, of course, at Communists—a gang of drunken Stormtroopers had dragged out of bed, beaten almost to death, and then shot and killed an unemployed Pole, all this in front of his mother, in the village of Potempa, not far from Breslau, because they'd heard he was a Communist. Five of them had been arrested, tried, and sentenced to death under the new decree, in the town, the Upper Silesian town, of Beuthen. One of Dr Gerlach's closest colleagues, a judge he must have known for thirty years, had heard the case.

Max jumped to his feet and looked out of the train window. Here, or close by, it must have been. Signs of heavy industry were gathering along the track, smoke from tall black chimneys, old railway wagons on sidings, slag heaps in the distance, a huge brickworks, piles of rusting iron in cindered scrapyards. This was the Upper Silesian coalfield: mines, iron foundries, furnaces, steel, the area of heavy industry disputed in the plebiscite after the war, fought over for two scrappy years. The train must be still in Germany. No sign of frontier officials yet: perhaps at the next stop? Potempa, he remembered, was very close to the new border. As he watched the sullied landscape thicken, more snow now lightening it a little, he wondered how his father could have begrudged the Poles a share of this wealth, this grinding toil that represented thousands of jobs.

Then the train slowed, and stopped. Gleiwitz. A couple of porters on the platform were in familiar German uniforms. Still no one got into his compartment, and as the train, after a blast on a whistle, drew out of the station, he saw a smaller notice with an arrow pointing to a different platform, "For Beuthen".

That was it. Not on this line but not far away. Where the five murderers had been condemned to death, and where on the day of the sentence hundreds of brownshirts stormed through the streets, smashing Jewish shops and offices. Hitler and Goering had poured scorn on the "Jewish" verdict, praised the Stormtroopers, vilified the dead Pole, and leaned so heavily on the Chancellor that the death penalty was annulled. The brownshirt murderers were in prison, but if recent cases of Nazi violence were anything to go by, not for long.

Meanwhile, in Breslau, one week after the Potempa murder, a woman had been arrested for kicking a Stormtrooper twice her weight in the street. She was sentenced to fifteen months in prison. Max was at her trial, having had to prepare the prosecution's simple case. She would be given no reprieve.

Max knew perfectly well that justice was not being done in Prussia. He also saw terrible danger for the future in the fact that the judges were all now working according to the political whim of powerful people in Berlin rather than for the Prussian judicial system, which they had been brought up to revere for its incorruptible honesty. If anyone in the office shared his fears, they kept quiet.

So one day a month ago, he asked for a formal meeting with Dr Gerlach. Very nervous, he closed the door of the judge's panelled room behind him.

"Sit down, Hofmannswaldau. You have a difficulty?"

"Sir, it seems to me that the laws are no longer being applied justly in Prussia. We are trained to elicit from the evidence the truth about an offence, not about an offender. We are trained to deal without prejudice with those who are brought by the police before the courts. We may dispense justice according to the law without fear or favour, but now we see our sentences overturned and our decisions undermined by authorities altogether outside the system of justice, which exists to protect the equal rights of every citizen. People unjustly treated have no one to defend them except those who are trained in the law. Are we doing everything possible to ensure that justice is upheld in Prussia?"

He said all this too fast, but he said it. Dr Gerlach, for a long time, said nothing. He was looking down at his hands, turning over and over an ivory paperknife on his desk. At last he looked up and fixed his bleak eyes on Max.

"How old are you, Hofmannswaldau?"

"Twenty-seven, sir."

"Precisely. I am fifty-seven. And you are presuming to inform me that I am doing my job inadequately."

"No, sir. Not at all. It's a general point, a general anxiety. I was hoping that you might—"

"That I might what? Travel to Berlin and inform the Chancellor that one of my Referendars has concerns about the system of justice in the republic? I presume it is the Potempa case that is responsible for this lapse—most uncharacteristic, I'm forced to admit—in respect and decorum on your part. You may not be aware, Hofmannswaldau, that the evidence against the farmer was very strong. He was a Pole and a Communist, profoundly disloyal to the Reich—to the republic, I should say."

"But he was dead, sir. It was not his trial, his conviction, his sentence."

"It should have been. Perhaps you are not sufficiently informed about current affairs, Hofmannswaldau, to be conscious of the threat to us all in Germany from the Communist Party. The Communist Party here is aided and abetted with large sums of money from Moscow, where Bolshevik Jews are now in command of the Russian empire. The only political issue that matters in this country is the uprooting, the extermination, of Communists from our midst, and the only person able to undertake this essential service with any prospect of success is Adolf Hitler, soon, we must all devoutly hope, to be appointed Chancellor by the President. Have you heard of the Protocols of the Elders of Zion?"

"Yes, sir. They are a forgery put about by the tsarist secret police."

"That, Hofmannswaldau, is a Bolshevik lie."

Max felt slightly dizzy. It was Stern who had told him that the Protocols were a forgery. But of course, *of course*, they were.

"But sir, there is not and never has been an international Jewish conspiracy such as I believe the Protocols describe."

"Are you going to argue with me, Hofmannswaldau?"

"No, sir."

"May I remind you that, as a Referendar, you are in no position to argue with a senior judge and that your eventual promotion will naturally depend on the propriety—such as you have hitherto shown—of your behaviour in every respect. That will be all, Hofmannswaldau."

"Sir."

What could he do? Resign? He wasn't qualified to do anything else except return to the university, without a salary, and study for a doctorate. How could he afford to do that? And Stern had told him that half the students in the university were Nazis and the other half were terrified. If he could get as far as his appointment as a judge, wouldn't there be more he could do for the truth in the courts than he could ever manage at the university?

The train slowed again and stopped in a large, smoky station. Katowice, the signs said. Max knew this had been a Polish city since the plebiscite. There was a crowd of passengers on the platform.

Two Polish officials in different uniforms came into his compartment. One, with a pistol at his belt, asked for his passport in Polish, showed it to his colleague, nodded as he gave it back, and said, in German, "Thank you, Count". The other looked up at Max's suitcase and violin case on the rack and nodded in his turn. They both saluted and left the compartment. After another few minutes the people on the platform, who had been waiting until the passport and customs checks were done, surged, at a blast from a whistle, towards the doors. A family joined Max in his compartment: an elderly woman in black, with jet beads on her hat; a middle-aged woman, perhaps her daughter, also in black but less smartly dressed; and her sons, two tall boys, about eighteen and sixteen. The women greeted Max politely in Polish. The boys nodded. The younger one, catching sight of the violin case as he put his grandmother's bag in the rack, looked at Max again with a brief smile.

The old lady, alert and inquisitive, studied Max—he avoided meeting her eye—for a few minutes after the train left the station, and then said, in accented German,

"Are you travelling to Cracow, sir?"

"Yes, as it happens, I am."

"Have you been to Cracow before?"

He could see that the younger woman was embarrassed by her mother's questions, but he liked the soft, white face and bright, birdlike eyes. He smiled.

"Never."

"How fortunate you are. It is a most beautiful city. We are proud of it, you know."

"Of course."

"I was born and brought up in Cracow, and so was my son—the father of these scallywags."

She looked at the boys, now as embarrassed as their mother.

"But they are good boys, truthfully."

"I'm sure they are", Max said, hoping she would tell him more.

"Mother," the other woman said in Polish, although the old lady was her mother-in-law, "I think we should let the gentleman read his newspaper." Max understood this simple sentence. He tried a smile at the middle-aged woman. No response.

"Nonsense. He hasn't opened his paper." The elderly woman turned to Max. "Have you?"

He shook his head.

"Where are you travelling from, sir, if I may ask?"

"From Breslau. That's where I live."

"Naturally. And you are—let me guess—a doctor? An architect? A lawyer?"

"Yes. A lawyer. I'm a Referendar at the courts of justice in Breslau."

"There you are—I guessed right."

"Mother!"

"Don't fuss, Mathilde. The gentleman likes to talk. Yes?"

He smiled at her and saw the younger boy smile again. He was on his grandmother's side, probably always.

"We are travelling to Cracow for the feast day. All Saints, you know. Are you by any chance Catholic?"

"Well—yes, I am."

"You will know, then. All Saints. And then All Souls, when we shall pray for the souls of my son and his men. We always come, every year. We have to live in Kattowitz, you see, because my daughter-in-law's family took us in after the war, when Kattowitz was still in Prussia. But now at least we are in Poland. My son was killed in the spring of 1915, fighting for the city of Przemysl in Galicia, against the Russians, of course. He died for the Emperor, who was still alive then. My son was very brave."

"My brother was killed fighting the Russians too, at the very beginning of the war, at Tannenberg."

"I am so sorry. How tragic for your mother. Was he much older than you?"

"Yes. Eleven years."

"Are there any more children in your family?"

"One more brother, between us in age. He's married and has two daughters."

"That's good. Are your parents still alive?"

"No. My father died just after the war, and my mother four years later."

"May they rest in peace." She crossed herself, and her younger grandson, frowning as he tried to follow the German of this conversation, copied her. The older grandson was reading a magazine with a photograph of a sports car like Eva's on the front.

"You poor boy. How very sad. The world, now, is too sad. Why? I am old, I know, but that is not the answer. When I was young, my grandparents were not sad. The answer is the war. The war changed everything for the worse. I could not understand what the war was for when it began, and I cannot understand now why it had to be. So many deaths, and the world will never be as it used to be, will it?"

"Perhaps not."

He could see it didn't matter what he said. She was talking, not listening. Her daughter-in-law had taken a newspaper out of her large handbag and irritably unfolded it. She was now reading it so that Max couldn't see her face.

"Are you travelling to Cracow for a little holiday, perhaps? Or for the feast?"

"Both." He couldn't restrain the broad smile the question brought to his face. "A friend of mine, from school, is being ordained tomorrow, in the cathedral. And then we—"

"Oh, but my dear boy, that is wonderful news!" She leant forward, beaming. "So the world is not altogether sad, even now! Did you hear, Mathilde? The gentleman's friend is to be ordained tomorrow."

The newspaper was briefly put down.

"Yes, Mother. Very nice." The paper went up again.

"Is he Polish, then, your friend?"

"Indeed he is." He looked across at the younger boy. "His father, too, was killed in the war, fighting the Russians in Galicia. My friend came to school in Breslau when he was sixteen. We were in the same class in the Gymnasium."

"Is his mother still alive?"

"Yes, she is."

424

"What a happy day for her tomorrow will be. Now, I should like to ask you to give my best wishes to your friend when you see him after the Mass. Tell him I shall say a special prayer for him tomorrow. It is a great thing to be a priest, a very great thing, but easy it is not. He could do with an extra prayer or two."

"I'm sure he could. Thank you."

"Now look, we are almost in Cracow. I have so much enjoyed our little talk. Oh—is that a violin? Stefan plays the violin too, don't you, Stefan? And your friend, does he play?" she asked Max.

"The piano. He plays very well."

"Good, good. Music is such a comfort, I find, though I have arthritis now, in my fingers, which is most annoying."

"Mother, it's time to put your coat on."

"Yes, yes, of course. Thank you, Stefan, dear. Good-bye, my boy. I'm so glad we met."

She held out her gloved hand, and he raised it to his lips.

"Good-bye. So am I."

Just before Stefan followed the rest of his family out of the train, he shook hands with Max.

"Good-bye, sir."

Max let the family disappear onto the crowded platform before he climbed down the steps of the train and walked, suitcase in one hand, violin in the other, towards the daylight he could see dimly shining through high, dirty glass at the far end of the building. As in any big railway station, people hurried about, knowing where they were going, afraid of missing trains, a place in a queue, a taxi; or they stood waiting, either with expressionless eyes or anxiously searching the passing faces for an expected friend, a lost companion. There was the familiar station smell of smoke, soot, sausages, beer, unclean toilets, and poverty: here as in Breslau there were beggars sitting against dirty brick walls with their caps on the ground in front of them. One was playing a cheerful folk tune on a mouth organ. Max walked through and past everyone. It was good to be alone and to know where he was going, an old inn on the Market Square where Adam had booked him a room for tonight and tomorrow.

Out in the sunshine, he breathed in the cold, clean air. To ask the way to the Market Square, he chose an elderly man of vaguely military aspect who he hoped would know German. With great politeness and in perfect German that was probably his first language, the old man gave him directions, changing his walking stick to his left hand to point with his right and suggesting a route "that will show you a little of our ancient city, since I see you are a stranger here, young man."

"Thank you, sir. Thank you very much." He raised his hat, the everyday city hat he wore to work, and the old man touched his in return.

As he walked along wide boulevards of the last century and soon through narrower, older streets, cobbled and without trams or many cars, the sun shone on the roofs of buildings that had a thin covering of snow, perhaps the first snow of the winter—it had almost disappeared from the roads, sidewalks, and cobbles of the old town. There was a mixture of people in the streets, much like the Breslau mixture in the old centre of the city, but more, and more evident Jews, bearded, sidelocked and dressed in long black coats like the Jews of the Breslau slums, but clearly more prosperous and without the nervous, hesitant look of identifiable Jews in Breslau now. Why should these Polish Jews be afraid? There were no brownshirts in Cracow.

This was Adam's city, where he had lived for nearly five years—his city, his country, his language. After all this time in Poland, and all this time in the strange atmosphere of the seminary about which Max knew nothing, would Adam even recognize him? He shook his head to banish this ridiculous idea: of course he would.

And then he emerged from a cobbled street into a vast sunlit square, with buildings of different periods and styles on all four sides, cafés, shops, fine houses, and taverns; in one part of the huge open space of the square, flower sellers stood, gloved against the cold, with chrysanthemums, laurels, and branches of yew on their barrows; in another part were market stalls with more gloved and shawled women selling winter vegetables: cabbages, beetroot, parsnips, onions, and baskets of red apples; in yet another part were workmen hammering, putting up what looked like more elaborate wooden stalls, perhaps for a fair for tomorrow's feast. Standing alone was a tall, heavy medieval tower with an enormous clock; not far from the tower, a long imposing building crossed the centre of the square, brick and creamy stucco, with a grand gatehouse and a covered market arcaded with columns and arches; in more open space in front of this building was a statue of a bareheaded man in a nineteenth-century riding cloak, obviously not a King or a general, high on a plinth above deep steps on all four sides with other carved figures standing and sitting on them. Children were playing as mothers and grandmothers sat chatting on a circle of benches round the statue, and at the far end of the square, at an angle, he saw a large, elegant brick church, with two Gothic towers different from each other, a spire on one of them. It all reminded him of something ... yes, of course. Venice. Not so much the Piazza of Saint Mark as the big local squares with their buildings assembled over centuries, their fruit and vegetable stalls and children, their brick churches and their expanses of air and sunshine after the confusing geography of an unfamiliar city. But Cracow's streets were straighter and lighter than the twisting alleys of Venice.

He found his hotel, which looked as if it had been there since before most of the buildings on the square were built, and left his case and his violin in his room, which was low, dark, and warm and had a single window facing the clock tower. Downstairs, in his nursery Polish picked up from Emilia and Tadeusz, he asked the man behind the desk how far it was to the cathedral.

"To the Wawel, sir? On the hill, sir. Not far. Perhaps ten, fifteen minutes' walk."

The answer was in good German. The man, perhaps fifty or fifty-five, had a magnificent moustache and bushy eyebrows. His brown, downward-sloping eyes looked keenly at Max.

"You haven't been to Cracow before, sir?"

"No, I'm afraid not."

The man looked down at the register Max had signed only ten minutes ago, putting his finger on Max's name.

"Are you by any chance from Vienna, sir? You won't mind my asking, will you?"

"Of course not. No. I live in Breslau."

"Ah. Breslau. Never mind. I was in Vienna before the war, sir, for five years. A fine city, sir, a wonderful city. I was a sergeant in the cavalry, at the Emperor's barracks in Vienna. Those were the days, sir. I'm lucky to be here, mind. Most of the lads never got back. But you'll be too young to remember the war. Now, I see you're in Cracow for two nights. Very good. Cracow is also a fine city. But it's not Vienna. Never will be."

"I'm delighted to be here. I'm just going out now. I'll be back for dinner."

"Very good, sir. Anything you need, you ask me."

"Thank you."

Max thought the man might salute as he got to his feet with a smart bow, but of course not: he had a uniform on, but no cap. It was probably the "von" of "von Hofmannswaldau" that had had this effect, though he'd put no "Count" in the hotel register. Adam might have called him Count when he booked the room. Dear old Franz Josef, Max thought. Adam's phrase.

Outside, the afternoon light was gilding the square. It was freezing again. The statue turned out to be Adam Mickiewicz—of course. Who else? Adam's hero from childhood. The poet. The inspiration of all the risings against the Russians, the Prussians, even the Austrians for whom later Poles like the cavalry sergeant in the hotel had been happy to fight. Mickiewicz was the national hero who had never been to Warsaw. Adam had told him that. Had he ever been to Cracow? He was from Lithuania. A friend of the Jews. Vilna. He thought of Anna, with her rabbi in Vilna. Why wasn't Anna beside him now, in Adam's beautiful Cracow? He missed her suddenly, acutely. He never missed Eva, except in treacherous dreams.

He could hear Adam's voice in his memory as he walked towards the church at the end of the square. "Vilna, mother Vilna"—Adam singing in Yiddish. "Lithuania, my fatherland!"—Adam reciting in Polish, translating for Max. How did it go? This was Mickiewicz himself. "You are like health. Only he who has lost you may know your true worth." Those lines always made him think of Waldau. He remembered Adam declaiming in German in the schoolyard of the Gymnasium, in defence of a Polish boy in a junior form, whose not-quite-correct German was being mocked. "And Poland said, 'Who-soever shall come to me shall be free and equal, for I am Freedom.' But the Kings when they heard were afraid in their hearts, and said, 'Come, let us slay this nation.' Is that what you want to be? Free-dom slayers? Bullies? Now leave him alone, do you hear?"

Max went into the church, giving some small coins—he wasn't used to zlotys, but coppers were coppers anywhere—to a blind beggar sitting in the elaborate Baroque porch. The beggar heard the chink and muttered something. Thanks? A blessing?

The marvel of the interior of the chuch stopped him inside the door. The building soared, with many altars in the aisles, many paintings, sculptures, candles, people praying before them here and there. There was a lot of Gothic blue and gold, and in the middle, high above the crossing, was a tall crucifix with a white figure of Christ. Was this where Adam, that September day, had looked up, had knelt? At the east end of the church, above the high altar, under tall narrow windows with many small squares of stained glass, an astonishing carved scene glowed with colour, more blue and gold, and red, a group of men larger than life-size, concerned, anxious, miraculously caught by the woodcarver as they bent towards a woman who had sunk to her knees, who was perhaps dying, a simple woman with no halo, held in the arms of a man with a long beard and a sad, quiet expression. Of the others in the group, some were looking down at the kneeling woman, others gazing upwards to two smaller, sitting figures above them—Christ and his Mother?—from whom needle-sharp rays of light were shining down on the scene below. One of the men was looking right up past these figures—yes—to what must be the Father and the Son together crowning Mary in heaven. These figures were beyond the frame of the altarpiece, high above it in front of the central window, with an angel and a bishop to each side of them, still and quiet in contrast to all the movement below them. There were also heavy wooden wings, like the doors of a huge open cupboard, to each side of the altarpiece, and these too were carved with smaller scenes full of colour and life, three on each side.

It took Max a few minutes, as he walked towards the carving and then stopped behind a pair of nuns kneeling as they polished the brass communion rail, to realize that the main subject of all this vivid theatrical carving was the subject of the Titian painting in the big brick church in Venice that had so much impressed him and Adam. The Assumption of the Virgin. Then, Adam had laughed at Max's Protestant ignorance. At least Max had recognized the story here. He stepped back and stood in the centre of the choir so that he could see all the carving properly. He tried to remember the Titian. That had been about a miracle of swirling life, a woman of flesh and blood raised to the skies in a cloud of angels. This carving was much more about death. The apostles' faces and clothes, and most of all their hands, were full of grief. Mary had to sink and fail and fall asleep before she could be taken up to God, first to her Son, calmly sitting beside her, then to be crowned in glory in heaven itself. Death. He looked at the carved panels to each side more carefully. There was no Crucifixion here, but more sharp rays of light shone on Christ's Resurrection, on his Ascension, on an empty rock from which he had just disappeared, and downwards on Mary and the apostles at Pentecost. The Holy Spirit. He also saw the Spirit's rays on the Annunciation, the first scene on the left. Then he saw, radiating light over the Annunciation, God the Father holding the round world in his hand, the suffering world into which he was sending Christ to be born. God wasn't looking down to Mary and the angel but outwards, out of the frame altogether, to the misery in store for the world—Max remembered Anna's words— which the coming of Christ had not, because of the faithlessness of human beings, made a better place.

After a long time studying the altarpiece, he walked to the very back of the church and turned to look at it again, from far away. As tomorrow he would be looking at what was happening to Adam. Thy will be done. In Mary. God with the world in his hand and Mary accepting his gift to her, to the earth. In Adam, accepting God's gift to him, to the earth. And he himself? He could see all the way from the back of the church the twisted hands of the apostle at the back of the grieving group surrounding the dying woman—hands contorted in prayer, in pain, as if to keep out the rays of the Spirit.

He knelt at the back of the church. There were rows of tall, narrow chairs with rush seats, and rush kneelers that folded down from the chair in front. The light from the west windows behind him was fading. After a while, someone switched on more lights in the sanctuary—he realised then that the altarpiece had been lit all the time—and more people, not many, perhaps twenty or thirty, came in ones and twos into the church from the square and knelt many rows of chairs in front of him. A bugle call from one of the towers sang out. Then a bell tolled the hour. Five o'clock. Four priests appeared in the choir, in black cassocks, and Vespers was recited. He wished he had a breviary, to follow the Latin. The Vespers of All Saints. Of course. He prayed for Adam, somewhere in the city, nervous perhaps. He remembered *Hamlet* and how Adam had been sick. How different would Adam be? Max felt that he himself was exactly the same as he had been then, as if the whole untidy episode of Eva and his guilt and his relief hadn't touched the boy who had taken Anna to watch Adam being Hamlet. But that couldn't possibly be so. He shook his head to restore his attention to Vespers, here, now.

After perhaps a quarter of an hour of prayer, everyone stood for what he recognized as the Magnificat. He looked along the whole length of the church to the altarpiece again and saw the kneeling figure of Mary, stricken among the apostles, her hands not tidily together, not raised in devotion as they always were in painting, but limp, separate, drooping from her wrists as she gave up her hold on life. As he felt the resignation in her hands, he heard the words *fecit mihi magna*. Then he looked up, and further up.

He knelt for the blessing at the end of Vespers. Yes. He could at least be blessed. And if Christianity were not a paradox, Christ overcoming death through death, God overcoming evil through the suffering evil causes, then it was all nothing, meaningless. If Christianity were not the truth, then death, suffering, and evil were stronger than any goodness or beauty, because except in the God of the Trinity, goodness and beauty had nothing to do with each other or with truth, and there was no rescue for the soul. And compared to the scale of the truth that was in Christ, what did it matter what had happened to him, what he had done? And his child was safe in the hands of God, like the earth itself.

As he left the church, he saw a dusty table by one of the doors, with holy pictures, postcards with grey photographs of details of the altarpiece with broad white margins, and a small pile of single pieces of paper with accounts of the carving in Polish on one side and in German on the other. He picked one up, put the right coin in the box, and went out into the almost-dark square.

He was suddenly very hungry and walked, light-headed, light-hearted, as if he had shed a heavy load from his back, across the square, passed the statue of Mickiewicz—the women and children had all gone from the benches, and the last market traders were packing up their wares—and opened the door to the friendly warmth of his hotel. The sergeant, dealing with two other guests at the desk, unhooked his key without being asked. "Your key, Count." The couple who had just arrived looked impressed, as the old soldier had clearly intended.

The next morning, in more crisp bright weather, he walked up to the Wawel hill with an hour to spare before the ordination Mass at noon. He had read about the hill, the castle, and the cathedral in the Baedeker guide to Poland, which the night porter, clearly primed by his colleague, had produced with his key when he went up to his room after dinner. He had read that the church on the square was indeed the Mariacki and had been built by German merchants in Cracow when Cracow was a Hanseatic city trading with all of central

Europe and the Baltic. The German carver of the altarpiece was Veit Stoss.

Baedeker had told him that the Wawel was an acropolis, and it was. "What does 'acropolis' mean, Max?" Dr Mendel in the schoolroom at Waldau. "The high city?" "Good boy. The high city. The pride, the glory, the gods of the city, all on the hill, while everyday life, markets and houses and ordinary streets, are below on the flat land." Max walked round the battlements, the ancient walls of the Wawel, built long ago to defend the pride and the glory, the cathedral and the tombs of the Kings, and the castle of government, now a grand but rather dilapidated renaissance palace with turrets and a courtyard he was told he could not go into by a guard in medieval uniform. The cathedral had three towers, all different, and chapels of different periods along its south side facing the open space, with trees and paths, that was within the battlement walls.

He took in almost nothing but the height and the sunshine and the nine hundred years of Poland's citadel. This was the last hour of nearly five years of Adam's absence from his life.

When the bells of the cathedral began to toll and people, smartly dressed for the ceremony, old, young, children, and nuns and priests among them, began to gather at the west doors, he joined them and went with them inside the church, where an organ was already playing.

He knelt among them, among hundreds of them. He tried to pray, failed, then crossed himself and sat back in his narrow seat.

At last the organ stopped and everyone stood, turning to look back down the nave to the foot of the central aisle. A procession—candles; altar boys; servers; the thurifer, the boy with the incense; then a gap; then twelve young men in white cassocks. Yes. There he was, there he actually was, in the last pair, on Max's side of the aisle. Max saw him only briefly as he walked straight past him, beyond five or six of the congregation in his row, all peering at the procession. Adam was older, thinner, his eyes steady, looking straight ahead towards the altar. Max had never in his life felt such love for anyone or anything as he felt for Adam in that moment. And with his love came prayer: for Adam and his priesthood, for what would be made of him by God, for God, through what would happen to him in the sacrament about to be given him by—Max was still watching the procession, through a blur of tears—by, yes—he saw, behind sixteen or eighteen priests and then two deacons, who walked in pairs solemnly past, up the central aisle of the cathedral, the archbishop, with his jewelled crozier, his mitre, his white and gold vestments. Max looked at the fine-drawn, intelligent face, the strong jaw, the firm mouth, and the watchful eyes that he could see would be transformed by a smile. This must be Prince Sapieha. Adam no doubt knew him well by now.

What then took place in the cathedral, up in front of the high altar, was for Max, far back in the church and unable to see or hear clearly, a haze of holiness, music, incense, candlelight and obscurity, Latin and Polish, prayers, questions and answers, singing, and silence never silent because of the small children and babies in the congregation and the respectful mutter of apology as parents and brothers and sisters tried to see their own new priest through the crowd. Some of the sung Latin for the Mass of All Saints he recognized. *Gaudeamus omnes in Domino*—let us all rejoice in the Lord. That was the Introit as the Archbishop reached the altar. The litany of the saints he caught much of, sung when all the young men in white disappeared as they lay face down on the floor for what seemed a long time. Then—and this was easier to see because the Archbishop was standing—the archbishop laid his hands on each of their heads, slowly and with the deliberation of prayer, as they knelt one by one before him. Then for another long time, the figures at the altar were difficult to catch sight of as the Archbishop, sitting now, and with two priests helping him, vested the new priests one by one and, after the singing of the *Veni Creator Spiritus*, which Max could more or less remember, did something else to their hands—anointed them, then bandaged them; why?—gave into their bandaged hands a chalice and paten for an instant of prayer, and then went on to the next. During all this, Max couldn't see which of the new priests was Adam as they knelt in turn, stood in turn, each holding a lit candle and each presenting it to the Archbishop at the end—was this right?—of the whole sacrament of ordination. When all twelve of them lined up behind the Archbishop and his deacons, now facing the altar to celebrate the Mass, and the choir began the Offertory—*Justorum animae in manu Dei sunt*—Max couldn't tell from the backs of their heads which was the head he loved because they were all too far away.

Justorum animae in manu Dei sunt. The souls of the just are in the hand of God. And the souls of the sinful?

When the time came for Communion—and by now a number of mothers and small children and a few old people had left the church as quietly as they could—he saw gratefully that many others stayed in

433

their places. At the end of the ceremony, the Archbishop, sitting again, addressed the whole congregation in Polish and then stood to read the Last Gospel, which now, as every time Max heard it, reminded him of Anna standing beside him in that simple Mass in Breslau. And then at last the procession got itself organized again and came slowly down the aisle in the same order as before, the new priests in the vestments they were wearing for the first time looking to the right and left without moving their heads as they walked. Astonishingly, Max saw Adam recognize him, saw that Adam could neither smile nor wink, saw the quenched beginning of a laugh in his eyes as he passed.

It took some time to emerge from the cathedral because of the press of people and because the families and friends at the front of the congregation went out first. Among them he saw Adam's mother, dressed in black velvet, black fur, and diamonds, on the arm of a tall young man, this time certainly young enough to be her son. No Communion for them either. Not doing him much credit, Adam's supporters.

Outside in the sunshine, eventually, Max saw Adam and his mother and the tall young man standing with their backs to an ancient, crumbling wall. They were talking, the brilliant sky and half of Cracow behind and below them. Adam saw Max at the same moment and waved. As Max came close, he met Adam's laughing eyes for the first time today. Adam put a hand briefly on Max's shoulder. Then Max, naturally, had to greet Adam's mother. He took her hand and kissed it, with a bow. "Good afternoon, Countess."

"Max! Dear Max! How wonderful to see you! You haven't changed a bit—better-looking than ever. How very good of you to come—Adam said he thought you might. This is my friend Nicky Szecsen, from Vienna, you know." Polite handshake. "Wasn't that *long*? I don't think I've ever had to sit in a church for more than two hours! Now, Adam, can you take off those clothes so that we can all go out to lunch? Nicky and I are starving, and I expect Max is too."

Adam gave Max a laughing look. How had he got through all these years without him?

"I'll be five minutes."

After lunch in an expensive restaurant at the foot of the Wawel hill, the countess and her young man climbed into a taxi for the station and their train to Vienna.

"Lovely to see you, both of you. Good-bye, good-bye." She waved out of the taxi window. She had said not a single word throughout lunch about what had happened to Adam that morning.

They looked at each other, Adam now in a black cassock with a couple of inches of clerical collar at his neck. He gave Max a brief, warm hug. Adam looked down the street to where the taxi had disappeared round a corner.

"When I was twelve, she used to arrive at school with her latest friend and take me out to lunch with some other boy I'd chosen because I thought he had reasonable manners and wouldn't be shocked. *Plus ça change.*"

"Adam ..."

"Not now. Let's walk back. As you know because I booked you two nights in the hotel—I hope it's all right, by the way?—"

"It's perfect."

"I have to spend the rest of today and tonight in the seminary, celebrating, packing, and all that. Tomorrow morning at eight is my first Mass. In the crypt of the cathedral, among the tombs of the kings of Poland. Will you serve it, Max?"

He stood still, felt the blood drain from his face.

"Max?"

He shook his head.

"Never mind, Max. Doesn't matter a bit. Come anyway."

They walked back to the seminary in a silence full of what there would be time and opportunity later to talk about. At the door, Adam said:

"My mother has borrowed a car for us—you know how she has friends everywhere with boxes at the opera and spare cars polished twice a day by the chauffeur—so we'll set off after my Mass. Bring your stuff with you."

"How did you learn to drive?"

Adam waved an airy hand. "They teach you some quite useful things in seminaries, once you find out how to thread your way through the system. The director's secretary, another nice man, taught me to type. See you in the morning."

Chapter 16

Max was back at the cathedral by quarter to eight the next morning, carrying his case and his violin. The cavalry sergeant at the desk had asked him where he was going so early, and when he explained said, "Thanks be to God. I shall say a prayer for your friend the new priest. Good-bye, sir. It has been a pleasure to meet you."

The crypt was dark and mysterious. A few electric lights, with bulbs like candleflames, faintly lit the cavernous passages, off which were chapels with tombs and monuments and altars. At several of these there were priests, perhaps some of yesterday's newly ordained young men, already saying Mass with a few people kneeling in the shadows behind them. Max had to ask a passing sacristan with a chalice in each hand where he could find Father Zapolski. It was strange and wonderful to say those two words together, at the end of a question in his basic Polish. "The chapel of Saint Leonard", the sacristan said, and led him further into vaulted passages, showing him to an ancient chapel where candles were lit on the altar and two elderly nuns were already kneeling. Max knelt behind them.

Adam's first Mass was as different as could be from the grand ceremony of the day before. He appeared with a priest vested as a deacon to steer him through the liturgy, and with yet another old man with a magnificent moustache, this one a rugged peasant in cassock and surplice, to serve the Mass. In black vestments for the feast of All Souls, Adam said his Mass, simply and with dignity as if he had been at this altar at this hour every day for years. Max prayed, easily, for the souls of Adam's father and grandmother, for his own parents, brother, and grandparents, and for the baby who had not been born.

When Adam gave Communion to the other priest, his server, and the nuns, Max knelt on in the near-darkness and Adam didn't look, as Max knew he wouldn't, to see if he was there.

Afterwards the nuns blew out the candles and put away the missal left on the altar, and nodded and smiled as they left. A few minutes went by. Max, alone in the chapel, sat and looked into the shadows at the tombs on either side. Adam reappeared in his cassock, and they left the crypt.

"You've brought your fiddle. And some music? Good. There'll be a piano somewhere."

They set off in the borrowed car, polished indeed but not too showy.

"Who was the old man?"

"The head gardener at the seminary. Used to work on a big estate in deepest Galicia. The estate was wrecked by the Russians in the war, like mine. His daughter and granddaughter—never mind."

"And the nuns?"

"In charge of the kitchen and the laundry. Old ducks."

It was Emilia and the jam all over again.

Adam drove more carefully than Eva.

"Once we're out of Cracow, I'll know the way", he said.

"Where are we going?"

"Deepest Galicia. I want you to see my childhood. We'll find somewhere to stay. I'll bring you back here on Sunday. And return the car. On Monday I have to report for work in Lemberg. That's where my parish is. I've met the priest whose curate I'm going to be. A good old soul badly rattled by the war. He needs some help. The Archbishop's been kind, letting me start outside his diocese. Lemberg's more complicated than Cracow—lots of Greek Catholics and some Armenians as well as ordinary Catholics, and a very tricky atmosphere now. Bombs. Ukrainian nationalism. Partisans still fighting over this, that, and the other. A very poor Jewish quarter. The Catholic Bishop needs young priests. The Archbishop here has plenty, as you saw yesterday."

"What's he like, the Archbishop?"

"I love him. Never misses a trick. Careful with everyone but by no means a soft touch."

Once they had left the city, they drove for a long time in silence, on a main road in bad condition, white, stony, with potholes and ruts, but with very little traffic, a few farm carts, a few trucks, hardly any cars.

"How far are we going?"

"About a hundred and thirty miles. Perhaps a bit more. It'll be dark when we get there. It's more than halfway to Lemberg. There'll be petrol in Tarnow. And lunch. How are you for money?"

"I've got plenty."

"Good. I'm not supposed to have any now. Any to spare, that is. But my mother gave me a bundle of notes for this holiday, so we'll be fine."

"What does she think, really, about you becoming a priest?"

"She's got used to it. Plays it, I've no doubt, as a joker at Viennese dinner parties. 'My son, the priest.' She's not exactly nature's grandmother, so there's no problem there."

They had lunch in Tarnow, a large town with factory chimneys on the edges but in the centre a Gothic cathedral and a medieval town hall like the one in Breslau.

After Tarnow, in the golden afternoon sun, they drove through poorer farmland and forest stretching away to their left, farm buildings with dung heaps in their yards and hens often on the road, occasional villages, and wooded hills to their right with high, already snow-covered mountains behind the hills far away to the south.

"The mountains?"

"The Carpathians. Where did you go to school?"

By the time they reached Przemysl ("Say it again. Polish is impossible"), it was indeed dark. For a hundred yards there was a nauseating smell. ("The tannery. Still there.") Narrow streets, gaslit, not very effectively. Some derelict buildings. Not many people in the streets. They stopped for petrol in the marketplace. "This was the town we always came to if we had to go to a town. Twelve hundred years it's been here. My grandmother told me. One of the oldest towns in Poland. A famous fortress, the pride of the empire. Sacked by the Russians in 1915. Won back. Lost again. Here we cross the river. The San. A great river. No one west of Cracow has ever heard of it. We're going south now, towards the mountains. Not far."

At last, after a few slow miles on roads that were no more than farm tracks, they stopped in a large village square, unlit except for the glimmer of oil lamps from a few cottage windows.

"This is the inn. I hope. It always was. Leave your hat. Citified. I don't want to frighten them."

It was nearly seven o'clock, and very cold. The frosty air smelled of smoke and dung, with a stain of petrol exhaust from their car. There was a shout in the distance and the whinny of a horse; a cow mooed; ducks were quacking on a pond almost at their feet. It was too dark to see if anyone was about. Cracks of light were visible through the wooden shutters of the inn. Adam knocked on the door before opening it. They went in together and shut the door quickly to keep the warmth in.

Four women of different ages, some children, and a very old man with a long white beard and a black skullcap, with a faded quilt over his knees, were sitting round an old tiled stove, and in the middle of the room, three bearded men with battered peaked caps on their shaggy heads were sitting on benches at a long table covered with oilcloth. There was a single bottle on the table and three small glasses. Also a plate of pickled herring and gherkins. In the silence that had fallen as they came in, Adam said in Yiddish, "Good evening. Mrs Margolis, I wonder if you remember me. Adam Zapolski. As a child, I used to—"

A dark-eyed woman of about sixty-five, small, lively, straight-backed, with a shawl over her white hair, got to her feet as the men at the table growled in not-unfriendly surprise. The other women, all with shawls, one holding a baby, also got up.

"Well, Count! Is it really you? I can't believe it. After all these years! Come in. Come in and get warm." She spoke to him in Polish, or a version of Polish, with an accent Max found difficult.

Adam grasped Mrs Margolis' hand in both of his. "It's very good to see you. I was sure we would find you. And your father too. Good evening, Mr Katz."

The old man nodded and allowed his hand to be shaken but had either not heard or not understood who Adam was.

Adam took off his coat, still his old Cossack coat.

"A priest!" Mrs Margolis took a step back. "The count a priest! Well! You won't be wanting to eat here, to stay here, will you, sir? Perhaps with the priest? He's not been well, but I'm sure he would be pleased to ... You and your friend."

"No, Mrs Margolis, we should like to stay here, if you have rooms and something for us to eat."

"Oh, sir. Fancy having you in Zapolsc after all these years! We'll do what we can, sir."

"And this is my schoolfriend from Wroclaw. His name is Max Hofmannswaldau. He understands some Polish and a little Yiddish."

"Good evening to you, too, sir. Of course, we should be honoured. By tomorrow we could have killed a duck, but tonight ... I'm sorry."

"Never mind. We'll still be here tomorrow. Whatever you have will be very good, I know."

She said something Max didn't understand to the younger women. Two of them disappeared through the door into what was evidently the kitchen. The girl with the baby, an older woman, and the three small children, wide-eyed at the the strangers, stayed to watch.

"Sit down, sir, please. And you, sir, shall I take your coat? Some vodka?"

"Beer, please, if you have some", Adam said.

After supper, which consisted of herring and gherkins, a substantial borscht, sour cream and rye bread, and then chopped liver and groats, Mrs Margolis talked and talked to Adam, now in Yiddish, about his father and how she remembered him as a boy, a bit younger than she, riding an unbroken horse no one else could manage and shooting from the saddle a wild goose the horse had flushed out of the reeds, and about Adam's grandmother and how good she was, to the Jews as well as the peasants. Max, finding her Yiddish easier to understand than her Polish, followed most of this.

"It was a blessing that your grandmother died, may she rest in peace, before the war . . . Borukh, get your little bear to show the gentleman."

One of the children, a boy of about six, shot through the door into the kitchen and could be heard running up wooden stairs.

"Your grandmother never knew your father was killed, may he rest in peace, defending us all in the great battle. But it was no use, and no one was left to look after us when the Russians came. The Germans came through Zapolsc later, but they weren't so bad—even the common soldiers are never so cruel as the Russians—and the Germans were on our side, weren't they, the Emperor's side?"

The boy clattered down the stairs and reappeared with his bear. Mrs Margolis took it from him.

"Whose bear was this, Borukh?"

"It was Uncle Shloymele's."

"That's right. Look, sir. Your grandmother made him."

For the rest of the evening, Adam sat with the small plush bear in his hand. Borukh stood quietly, his suspicious eyes on Adam.

"It was terrible, sir. You wouldn't believe what the Russians did. They burnt nearly all the houses. Not this one because they wanted their vodka. Both priests' houses they burnt, and the Russians call themselves Christians. The synagogue was burnt out. The rabbi wouldn't leave, and they pulled him out and hanged him from a tree, and five other Jews too, for no reason. My brother was one."

"I'm so very sorry, Mrs Margolis. May he rest in peace."

She wasn't listening.

"But he was a hero, my brother. He got the holy scrolls and the menorah out of the synagogue the day the Russians arrived. The rabbi didn't want him to take them, but he saved them. He gave them to one of the farmers, a gentile, to look after, and the farmer hid them in straw and took them away in a cart. And after the war, he brought them back, and they're here now in the new synagogue. It's smaller than the old one, but there are fewer of us than before the war. And Jodok over there", she said in Polish, "is that farmer's son."

A nod from one of the men at the table.

"And the girls ... we hid them as best we could, but they found them. When the Russians had gone, in the next winter, that terrible winter, 1916, there were people living in the fields, in the woods, in holes they dug in the ground, with nothing but branches to keep them warm. And nothing to eat—the poor peasants, many of them died of the cold and starvation. And no one to do a thing for them. . . . In some places the count or the prince gave instructions for flour, salt, firewood, even medicines to be found ... Your grandmother, if she'd been still alive, she'd have done her best, I know. Your mother—well, she wasn't here, was she? Begging your pardon, sir. There wasn't a soul ... even the old bailiff, Jan—you remember him, sir? Of course you do ... he had nothing, could find nothing, after the manor had been burnt. Terrible times, they were."

"What's happened to the manor now? Is Jan still alive?"

"Oh no, sir. He died during the war, in 1917, that's right, the following winter when things had got a little bit better for us all. Only because the armies left us in peace, you understand. Your father's house, that beautiful house ... there's nothing much left of it, I'm afraid. It could be rebuilt, but now you wouldn't want ... now you're a priest ... would you, sir? We didn't know anything here. We didn't know you were alive. Some more beer, sir? No?

"Then, after the war, we were lucky. There was a lot of fighting. Poles against Ruthenes—Ukrainians, they call themselves now—stirring up the peasants round here with these fancy ideas about Ukraine as a new country. Russians against Ruthenes and Poles. Everyone against the Jews, as usual. But not here. We were spared the worst of that time. Before the war, we all lived in peace with our neighbours in Zapolsc. We still do, what's left of us. But every time someone comes home from the army, one army or another, or from prison or some camp in Siberia, they tell us that now we hate each other, now we have to fight. It was the Emperor who kept the peace, wasn't it, sir? And people like your father and your grandmother. Do you think those times will ever come again?"

"I don't know, Mrs Margolis. It won't be the same. But we must all hope and pray that better times, real peace for everyone, will come again."

There was a silence, in which perhaps some of the people in the room did pray.

"Where is your son, Mrs Margolis?"

One of the women who had prepared the dinner gasped and put a hand to her mouth. Mrs Margolis's face crumpled as if she had been hit. She sniffed long and hard to be able to answer Adam's question.

"We don't know, sir. The Russians took him with them—Shloymele and half a dozen others. They were young and strong, and the Russians took them away. We've never heard a word from him. We don't know if he's alive or dead. Masha there is his wife, and this is Esther, his daughter, and the baby is his grandson. Esther's husband is a scholar. He teaches the children in the daytime, and he's often in the study house till late. But Shloymele, peace be upon him—I believed for a long time he was alive and would come home one day. Now I ... Oh, sir. He was a good son."

"I remember him well. He played the fiddle, didn't he?"

Adam looked at the other woman and the children, Borukh and two little girls. Mrs Margolis understood.

"My daughter Rachele. That's her husband." She waved at the table, and another of the shaggy vodka drinkers nodded at Adam. "He's the cobbler and harness maker. I don't know where we'd be without him. He works very hard, bless him, and except on market day we don't have many guests at the inn now."

"Mrs Margolis, my friend and I have driven all the way from Cracow today. We'll be asleep on our chairs soon if we don't go to bed."

"I'm sorry, sir. I talk too much. They all tell me." The men at the table laughed, and even the women smiled.

"Now, you'll have luggage in your car?"

As Adam got up, Borukh held out his hand for his bear.

They were carrying their bags through the kitchen ("A violin, sir!") when the outside door opened again and a pale young man in a

442

gaberdine and a fur hat appeared. He carefully shut the door behind him and took off his hat. He had long hair, a skullcap, sidelocks, a youthful scruffy beard, and large black eyes.

"This is Hertz David, Esther's husband. You'll never guess, Dawidek, who's come back. The count. The count himself, and he's a priest. And this is his friend."

The young man bowed his head solemnly and shook hands with Adam and then with Max. Then, his face lit with a smile, he took the baby from Esther, kissed him, and muttered a few words over him. A blessing.

Eva. For the first time that day, the memory twisted inside him. Another world, but his own. He almost groaned.

Upstairs in a creaky wooden room next to Adam's, under a heavy featherbed that warmed him almost at once, he got as far as "Our Father" and the thought that the words were right, the Father of us all, before he fell asleep.

"Those are the gates. Look."

After scalding strong tea in glasses, more rye bread, and obviously precious jam in a polished brass dish, they had driven a mile from the village in crisp, cold sunshine. There was a heavy frost on the ground but no snow.

Adam turned off the engine.

"Padlocked. And anyway, look at the drive. The car wouldn't make it. Let's walk."

Cast-iron gates, ten feet tall, each with an elaborate roundel, at its centre a rearing horse, were leaning backwards on rusting hinges; a rusting padlock joined the length of chain fastening them together.

"Pointless, all that, by now."

Apart from hefty stone gateposts, still upright ("There used to be stone horses on top of the gateposts—worth something, I suppose"), the park fence was wooden, mostly fallen, and easy to step over almost anywhere.

There were trees either side of the drive, not regularly planted in an avenue like the limes at Waldau, but here and there, old oaks and chestnuts, a few leaves remaining, the rest stiff and silvered on the frosty grass. Their boots crunched as they walked up the drive, which was so overgrown as almost to have disappeared.

"Another few years, and the forest will be back. They used to clear the brush, the young birches, brambles, all that, from under the big trees. Now—over there. Look!"

A group of about a dozen deer, perhaps a hundred yards away, saw them as Adam spoke, lifted their heads, and bounded away under the trees. "Does and this year's fawns. You should see a big stag, with heavy antlers—but we won't. They're shy and go about by themselves."

They walked for a few minutes.

"I've never forgotten the first time I saw a stag shot. I cried for hours. My father thought there was something the matter with me. 'The child must be ill.' My mother too. The house was full of people. A shooting party—Count this and Prince that. Their valets and loaders were in the servants' hall. No wives, so my mother was in her element—you can imagine. I was sent to the nursery, to cry all over Nanny. My grandmother came upstairs to tell me she had never seen a stag shot without wanting to cry. I was about eight. Over there"—he waved a hand towards a ruin, brick walls overgrown—"was the stud farm, horses even more beautiful than the stags. My best friend was one of the stable boys. He was about fifteen, and he could ride the stallions bareback. There were two stallions, terrific creatures. There's the house. What's left of it."

The house had been very grand, much bigger than Waldau, with a classical portico on tall columns to the height of the roof. The pediment had collapsed with the vanished roof, and a long brick front remained, a shell now, with the stucco mostly burnt off and the tall windows, eight on each of two floors, all gone. Ivy and other weeds had already grown over the steps and some of the walls as far as the burnt-out window frames.

Adam stood and looked. Max put an arm round his shoulders.

"It's all right. I knew about this. Have known for years. Houses don't matter. Only people. And they didn't see this."

There was a wide space where the double front door once was. They went inside. Debris, charred beams, fallen bricks, and flakes of paint and stucco littered the cracked marble floor of the hall. Some of the ceiling, jagged and unstable-looking, was still there. In the back wall were bullet holes.

"Someone tried to defend the house. Died in the attempt, no doubt, whoever they were. May they rest in peace, as the Jews say all the time." Adam crossed himself, and Max followed suit.

"Like the Catholics", Max said. "A nice old Polish lady on the train—her son was killed at Przemysl, she told me—and the porter at my hotel who was once a cavalry sergeant both said they would pray for you. The new priest. I almost forgot to tell you."

"Thank you. Prayers are very welcome." Laughing eyes, but he meant it.

They clambered into the long room on the right. "This was the drawing room. Portraits. The piano." There was more ceiling left here, and still a faint smell of burning when Adam kicked a pile of wood ash. "Perhaps that was the piano." Another door, difficult to get to, led into a smaller room, its windows facing a wide grassy space with more forest trees on either side. A long way to the south, the snowy Carpathians shone in the sun. "My mother's sitting room. My grand-mother's was upstairs."

"This is like Waldau. Mountains at the back of the view, though these are higher and further away."

"There are wolves in those mountains. In the deep winter, they come down. You can hear them howling at night."

They stood side by side looking out of a paneless, frameless window.

"Was there a garden?"

"No. Not a real garden. No roses. My mother wasn't interested. But a big orchard, over there, look. Walled against the deer. Most of the walls are still there. My father was passionate about fruit trees—apples, plums, cherries." Then, in a whisper, "What's that?"

Someone was in the drawing room. Footsteps, uneven because of the debris, an irritated kick at a heap of something. A man appeared in the doorway. A large man, heavy eyebrows, spectacles, a coat with a fur collar.

"Good morning, Count. I apologize for intruding on your mem-ories. They told me in the village that you arrived last night—they are all excitement, of course. That I should find you here, I guessed myself." All this was said in correct but slightly stilted German, with a Vien-nese accent.

"I'm sorry. I don't know who—"

"Who I am? Naturally you do not. I am Franz Schickelmaier, your mother's agent in Zapolsc. I have not had the pleasure to meet your mother since she sent me here from Vienna after the war to save what could be saved and to collect the rents from the estate that I send to her bank every month. You owe me a considerable debt, Count, and I thought it correct to make myself known to you when I have this opportunity."

445

"Yes. Of course. Thank you. This is Count von Hofmannswaldau."
The man nodded.

"Shall we go outside, Herr Schickelmaier? I find it difficult to talk in the house."

They picked their way back to the other side of the house and emerged onto what had been the drive. There they stood in the cold in an awkward group.

"The countess informed me several years ago that you were studying for the Catholic priesthood and that therefore I should continue to deal with her rather than with you. However, she does not always reply to my letters. Therefore, I should like to have your instructions as to how we are to deal with the destitute peasants arriving on the estate from across the frontier."

"I don't understand. Zapolsc is a long way from any frontier."

"They are coming from Russia, Count, from what is now called the Ukrainian Soviet Socialist Republic. The Bolsheviks are starving them. They are the better, more hardworking class of peasant, but their bits of land have been taken and they have no means of feeding themselves. It is a Bolshevik policy. They come all the time further west, whole families of them, because so many are escaping from Russia. There is pressure on the Galician estates, severe pressure."

"I had no idea. They must be helped, of course, if they arrive here. Is there work for them?"

"I should prefer to move them on, Count. Some are troublemakers, agitators against the authorities, any authority. Some are Jews."

Adam's head went up, like the heads of the deer in the park.

"I don't suppose their wives and children are agitators, and in any case, it's difficult to make trouble in Zapolsc, as you will have discovered by now. As for the Jews—do you imagine they have been left in peace in atheist Russia? It's in the long tradition of the Habsburg empire and of the Polish Commonwealth before that to help those escaping from oppression. These poor people are to be helped. There are, God knows, enough abandoned houses, workshops, fields—I've seen them already—to give these families a start. They are to be helped. Is that clear?"

"It will cost the estate. The countess will not—"

"I shall ask my mother to confirm my instructions in writing. Good day, Herr Schickelmaier."

"Sir."

446

He turned and walked off down the drive, his solid back conveying disapproval, even anger.

They watched him.

"Oh, Max. I should be here. I should be here taking care of them, of everything. What a swine to leave in charge. Helping himself at every twist and turn, I've no doubt at all. What a specimen! The Viennese Jew on the make who despises Jews from the east. How could my mother appoint such a joke villain? Very easily is the answer. Max! I should have come back sooner. It's too late now. The day before yesterday it became too late."

"Adam, stop. Think. You gave up your life, not just the day before yesterday but nearly five years ago, for what is entirely good, for the truth, for God. You can't—you mustn't—regret what you've done. Far more people in your life will be grateful to God for what you've done than the people here in Zapolsc you could have helped—and could you have helped them? Could you have lived here, rebuilt this house, brought back the life that used to be lived in it? I don't think you could. I think it's too late anyway, whether you had become a priest or not."

"Max. Dear old Max." Adam took him by the shoulders. "You're right. Of course you're right." A friendly shove as he let go. "One day perhaps some Bishop will let me come back and be the Catholic priest in Zapolsc. A gentle job for an old man. Meanwhile, yes, I have to do what I'm told, and in Lemberg there's bound to be work worth doing. It's that much nearer the Bolshevik frontier, for one thing. Can they be starving hardworking peasants deliberately? It seems almost impossible to believe." He turned away from the house and shook his head. "Thanks. Now let's have a look at my father's orchard."

The brick walls were almost intact—nothing to burn here—and the rows and rows of trees, unpruned and shock-headed with unruly twigs, had nevertheless obviously borne much fruit.

"I hope Schickelmaier let the village have the fruit. I'll ask him. No, I'll ask them. They're more likely to tell me the truth. Why aren't there any apples on the ground? None at all. Ah—there's the answer."

Under almost every apple tree the ground had been recently roughed up, almost furrowed.

"Pigs?"

"Wild boar. The gate to keep them out has gone. They're never far away. Like the Russians. Wild boar. Wolves. Bears. This isn't Waldau, Max."

Outside the orchard, they walked until they had the ruined house directly behind them, stopped, and looked southwards towards the mountains. There was forest to either side of a wide, grassy space, sloping gently for half a mile down to a long, gleaming lake and a burnt-out boathouse, then away to their left were more substantial ruins, a considerable range of overgrown brick walls.

"That was the brewery, next to the distillery. It used to be the responsibility of the estates to make vodka that didn't poison the peasants. God knows what they drink now. Beyond the brow of that hill was—perhaps is—the brickworks. I hope it's still here: it employed a lot of people. That's why all these buildings aren't made of wood, like the village."

"It's very beautiful. The lake, and the fields and forest, and then the mountains."

"I was nine when I last stood here. One doesn't forget."

For several minutes they stood side by side in silence.

"Poor Poland. You know, Max, there'll be a war between Germany and Russia one of these days. How can there not be? Rathenau's treaty—probably got him shot—can't last. And where will it be fought? Here. What country will help Poland? What country has ever helped Poland? In 1920 when Poland—with the help of God, they all say in Cracow, of course—sent the Russians packing, what was the line in England and France? 'Hands off, Russia!' Can you believe it? England and France and the stupid Americans, with all that talk of redeeming the world and making it fit for free men to live in, were all for abandoning Poland to Russia *one year later*. They set up these weak countries and left Germany, which was supposed to have lost the war, a lot stronger than it was in 1914. No Habsburg empire to weigh against it, make it pause, just Poland, Czechoslovakia, Austria—I ask you? What's that? Run by a bunch of Viennese like my mother who would much rather be Germans—and later Yugoslavia. Easy meat, the lot of them. And Poland, as usual, is meat for both Germany and Russia. You should hear my fellow seminarians. Nationalists to a man. The empire forgotten as if it had never been. Poland the Christ among the nations and all that. What has the Pope ever done for Poland, the most Catholic country, etcetera, etcetera? In the November Rising—ever heard of it? No? That's a good German education for you—Poland rebelled against the Tsar. Not here. Russian Poland, but for the whole partitioned country. What did the Pope say? 'Authority must be obeyed.'

Even if the authority was Nicholas I. Hundreds of thousands of Poles were sent to Siberia. The Russians made the princes walk. All the way."

"Adam . . ."

"It's all right, Max. I haven't become a fire-eating Polish nationalist, even if yesterday morning I said my first Mass ten yards from Kosciusz-ko's tomb. You've never heard of him either. Napoleonic. Beat the Russians over and over again with practically no soldiers. Lost in the end, of course. Nationalism's all very well, but it makes people stupid. At the moment, they think Mussolini's wonderful—at least those who've heard of him do—and some of them even admire Hitler because of the anti-Semitism. The drive of the whole nationalist thing in Poland is terror of Bolshevism. That's fair enough. But fascism is not, absolutely not, the answer, and too many people think it's got to be one or the other. I'm afraid for Poland. Just afraid. There will be a war. If Germany wins, it will be bad; if Russia wins, it will be worse. This"—he swept his arm from left to right to take in all they could see—"will be in Russia then, Bolshevik Russia. What price a Catholic priest in Bol-shevik Russia? But perhaps that's what it's all been for."

A long silence.

"Max?"

"Yes?"

"What do you think? About another war. I've been out of Ger-many so long."

"It depends on what happens to the Nazis. It's terrifying how well they did in the summer. It wouldn't have happened if unemployment hadn't got so bad. At least that's what the liberal newspapers, what's left of them, the *Vossin* for instance, say. They also say the Nazis have got as far as they can get; they'll start losing votes and support when what they promise doesn't happen. They say the Nazis are a crazy flash in the pan. I wish that were true. I don't think it is. I went to see Hitler make a speech in the Century Hall. A most extraordinary expe-rience. He has an effect on a crowd you wouldn't believe, and yet he's so ordinary-looking . . . actually a lot worse than ordinary. He looks shifty, thoroughly unreliable some of the time, mad the rest. Staring eyes. He even foams at the mouth. What he says—shrieks—is mad too: the government's a bunch of traitors, everything's the fault of the Jews, the government's run by Jews, all Jews are Bolsheviks—complete nonsense, but they love it. Can't get enough of it. Thousands of people cheering and cheering, and women fainting, genuflecting as he goes by. And certainly not just poor workers and the unemployed—at least half bourgeois, that audience. My boss, the judge, an upright Prussian bureaucrat if ever there was one, thinks Hitler's practically the Messiah. You wouldn't believe—it's like a horrible mirror image of Christianity. No, it *is* a horrible mirror image of Christianity. Hitler's language is full of redemption, salvation, martyrdom ... Have you heard something called the Horst Wessel song? Not in Poland, I imagine—blood, sacrifice, and all the time Hitler himself is the saviour. It's really sinister, you know. People worship him."

"I know. I do know. Someone in the seminary got a couple of copies of a pamphlet a month or two ago, by a Capuchin priest, Naab I think his name is. It's in German, so nobody much read it. The pamphlet's called 'Is Hitler a Christian?' and the answer is absolutely not. Unless the Nazis are stopped, they'll be a catastrophe for Germany, and if it happens it will be partly the fault of educated Germans who call themselves Christians but have no idea what that should demand of them and in any case no courage. That was the point of the pamphlet. Do something before it's too late."

"But what? How? A wretched Polish Communist—unemployed, naturally—was beaten and then killed by Stormtroopers in Silesia in the summer. I passed the place on the train three days ago. The Stormtroopers were convicted and condemned to death. Then Hitler made a fuss, noble Aryans being executed for killing a worthless Bolshevik Slav, and, lo and behold, they were let off. Any fool can see the system of justice isn't working any more. I'm a lawyer working in Silesia for what's still calling itself Prussian justice, and what can I actually do? As far as I can see, nothing. I tried having it out with my judge, and he ticked me off like a naughty schoolboy."

"What's he like?"

"Caution personified, you would think. But then he goes and votes for the Nazis. And look at the government—more and more useless ever since Stresemann died. Useless chancellors, Brüning and now Papen, both of them are Catholics, and what have they done? Allowed the Nazis to get stronger and stronger. I don't see how Hitler can be prevented from becoming Chancellor now, with half the country behind him. Only old Hindenburg could stop him, and he's eighty-five, weak in the head and belongs to a world that doesn't exist any more. You should hear Treuburg on Hindenburg."

"How is Treuburg?"

"He's gone. Gone back to East Prussia to be a military doctor."

"Has he? Has he. With his cello?"

"With his cello. I miss him. He's not remotely interested in God, in the real reasons for thinking one thing rather than another, but his instincts are always right. Remember his playing? He's genuinely good and brave, and he might deflect some soldiers from thinking Hitler the saviour."

"And what about you, Max?"

"Me?"

"You. Do you realize we've been together for more than twenty-four hours after five years apart and you haven't told me a single thing about yourself?"

"Nor have you."

"Ah, that's different. I made it through the seminary. I've been ordained. This morning before you woke up, I went and said my Mass after the Zapolsc priest said his, in his freezing little church in the dark with two old ladies behind him. No need to tell you how often in the seminary I thought I was insane ever to have imagined I could be a priest. How furious I got sometimes, with the rector or the prefect of discipline or just the stupidity of some of my fellow students. How much I missed you, and the flat, and our music. It seems a hundred years ago, doesn't it, the Brahms and the Mozart quintets? What happened to my clarinets?"

"I gave them to Anna. She knew a lot of music students. But I expect she's still got them. She thought you were, I don't know, halfway between Liszt and Rudolf Valentino."

"Ridiculous. But she was a sweet girl. You told me what happened. I was so sorry."

"She got married last year. To a rabbi in Vilna."

Adam thought about this for a moment.

"That's probably good. Halpern has a very strong character, and she'd have found it difficult, if she'd married you, to choose your life wholeheartedly with him bitterly disapproving. Do you miss her still?"

"Yes. A romantic dream. But she's somehow safe in it. As if she'd died."

"Get thee to a nunnery."

"Yes."

"And are you by yourself in the flat?"

"No. I share it with a fellow called Felix Stern, a medical student from Prague. He came when you went to Cracow. He's younger than we are. He's a Communist. So he says. A nice boy. Clever enough but a bit naïve. He wants to be a village doctor in Russia."

"Has he been to Russia? No. But you, Max?"

"Let's walk for a bit. I'm getting cold."

"Down to the lake or into the forest?"

"The forest."

They crossed the still-frozen grass of the meadow in front of the house and then walked to the right across the slope of the long hill. There were more trees, then more still, some of them huge, venerable trees with roots as thick as heavy branches close to the trunk. There were young saplings, tall silver birches with a few gold leaves left at their crowns, and oaks with more leaves, russet-coloured, curled in the frost. The forest seemed ancient and wild to Max, quite different from the Waldau woods.

"It's always been managed for game," Adam said, "with timber taken out for the sawmill coming second." He looked back at the ruin behind them, now just visible. "Another fifty years, and you won't be able to tell there was ever a house."

"Is there a house down there? There's smoke coming from something." Max pointed through the trees, downhill towards the lake.

"Good heavens! That's where the head forester used to live. Can there be someone still there?"

Adam set off, got tangled in a low thicket of brambles, extricated himself, laughing. "Look out. What we need is horses. I used to ride in the forest for hours on my pony. I can't think how I didn't get lost and fall asleep on a pile of leaves like Hansel and Gretel. No Gretel, unfortunately."

"My pony was called Gretel."

"You know, Max, I think a happy, indulged, privileged childhood, at Waldau, at Zapolsc ... a lot of people would say now that it prepared us very badly for the horrors of the adult world. But wasn't it the garden of Eden? Doesn't it show how true the story is?"

"There were snakes about, even then, though, weren't there?"

"The snakes are always there, for every generation. Growing up is the problem. It's important for us, born in time to remember the war but not in time to understand anything about it while it was happening, not to regard it as having changed forever the nature, or—what?— perhaps the promise, of everything. People older than we are do that all the time, and if they're Germans, they end up voting for the Nazis because they're swept into the absurd belief that the Nazis can reverse the outcome of the war, can take us all back to 1914, when everything was wonderful. But it wasn't wonderful. It was a mess—not for us because we were nine, but for everyone in the adult world—the mess that human beings always make. If it hadn't been a mess, full of greed and pride and laziness and Nietzsche's will to power unrestrained by anything better, the war could never have been. Could it?"

"No. You're right. Of course. If we think of ourselves as a specially unlucky generation, to have lost our childhood worlds on account of the war, we're ducking the responsibility that everyone has to pick up. We're born fallible. That's not our fault. We fail. That is our fault."

"It's good to see you, Max. No one at the seminary, not one single person—look at that! There *is* someone in the forester's house. Smoke from the chimney. Hens in the yard. A milk cow. Geese ... come on."

The wooden house, one storey, perhaps four rooms, with the chimney in the middle, the shutters open, and clean curtains at the windows, looked like a house in a fairy-tale illustration. Like Hansel and Gretel. Perhaps it was made of gingerbread.

The geese, four of them, stretched out their necks and hissed in fury.

Adam knocked on the door. Loud barking came from inside, the bark of a large dog. An old woman's voice shouted in Polish. "Be quiet, you stupid creature! When did we have a visitor at this time of day? Who can it be?" More barks. "Lie down and let me go to the door." Then, "Come in. Come in, whoever you are. Blessed be the guest."

Adam pushed open the door. A woman, between fifty and sixty, worn with work, was holding an old, thin borzoi strongly by the scruff of its neck as it barked. Adam held out his hand, palm upwards, to the dog and gave it an order Max didn't understand. The dog dropped to the ground, laid its head on its paws, looked up at Adam, and thumped its tail on the floor.

"Now ... is it Mrs Sabok?"

"I'm sorry, sir. I can't ..."

Realising that he was between her and the light outside, he went further into the house and stood so that she could see him properly.

"Adam", he said. "Adam Zapolski. Do you remember me?"

She gasped, put her hand to her mouth, looked at him carefully, and then shrieked, "God in heaven be praised! It's the count himself!"

Taking both of Adam's hands and kissing them, she half-collapsed in a kind of curtsey. He pulled her gently to her feet and sat her down by the stove in what was clearly her usual chair, with a flattened faded cushion, a straw back, and a blanket of brightly coloured knitted squares over its arm.

"I'm sorry to give you a shock, Mrs Sabok. It's very good to see you looking so well. This is my friend Max, from Wroclaw."

Max bowed his head.

"You're very welcome, sir, I'm sure." She looked from Adam to Max and back for a minute or two, and tentatively touched Adam's coat as if to make sure he was real.

"This won't do", she said. She got to her feet. "This won't do. Sit down, sirs. Take your coats off and sit down, I beg you. There. By the table."

There was a chair and a stool. They did as she asked, Adam keeping his scarf wound round his neck. She disappeared through a door and came back with half a loaf of rye bread and a small pot with a lid—salt. From a cupboard she fetched a black bottle and three tiny glasses. The dog stayed where it was, gazing at Adam.

She poured a little vodka into each glass.

"To your very good health, sir, and to yours, sir."

"And to yours, Mrs Sabok."

They downed the scalding shots of vodka and ate a little bread with a pinch of salt.

"Now tell me, how is Mr Sabok?"

She crossed herself. "The Lord took him. Six years ago. But we were fortunate. The Lord took him, not the Russians. The Russians never found us here. My Pawel was too young for the war. You remember my Pawel, sir? He was two years older than you. He's a good boy. He works in the forest like his father. He's married, of course. His wife's a good girl, from the village. Her father was one of them killed at the manor, fighting the Russians. They live in Zapolsc. Pawel rebuilt a house the Russians burnt. They've three little ones now, but it's hard. That Schickelmaier—excuse me, sir, I know he's put in charge by your mother—doesn't treat us right. Pawel is paid so little—it's the Jews who did well out of the war, only the Jews. Pawel needs shoes for his eldest, who's seven, and the school won't have him without shoes—and that Schickelmaier's a Jew, and so's the shoemaker, and it's very hard. But Pawel looks after me too as best he can. He comes every week on a Saturday and brings me paraffin and candles and sugar. And I give him eggs if the hens are laying and cream cheese I make for the children, and at Christmas he'll kill a goose for us all. Oh, sir. We never thought you'd come back to Zapolsc. Have you seen the manor? Yes, of course you have, or you wouldn't be down here. It's a terrible sight. They did their best. But there weren't enough of them, with so many already away at the war. And the Russians—they're savages, sir. No better than savages. Will you stay, sir, now that you're back?"

"Mrs Sabok, I must tell you ..."

"You're the very image of your father, sir. When I first saw you ..." She turned to Max. "Isn't he, sir? Did you know the count, sir?"

"I'm afraid not", Max said.

"Mrs Sabok, I would love to stay. But it isn't possible. You see, I'm a priest now." Adam removed his scarf.

She looked at him in utter amazement.

"A *priest*, sir?" She leant forward and touched his sleeve again, leaving her hand raised as if she had touched something she couldn't identify. "Now, that is a miracle of God himself." She crossed herself. "Jesus and Mary—the count a priest!"

They stayed for an hour. She made them tea in an old samovar and talked and talked, telling Adam what had happened since the war to family after family in the village and beyond. Max couldn't follow all this in Polish. He watched their faces instead.

Before they left, Adam promised to see Schickelmaier and to do all he could for the foresters and the other workers on the estate.

"Where may we write, sir, if worse times come?"

"I shall be in Lwow. Not too far away." He took out a notebook and a pen and wrote on and tore out a page. "Here's my address."

"I'll keep it safe, sir."

They put their coats on. Adam got a couple of banknotes out of his pocket and put them on the table.

"That's for shoes for your grandson, and perhaps a Christmas treat for all the family."

"You shouldn't, sir, and you a priest now."

"I should. And much more. Thank you, Mrs Sadok. It's been a great pleasure to see you again."

Max shook her hand. When Adam gave her his hand she knelt, and he blessed her as if he had been blessing people every day for years.

They waved as she stood in her doorway to see them off, and walked up the hill in the sunshine. The frost had gone, and the grass was wet and green.

"I don't suppose she can read or write. But she'll keep the address just in case. The priest would write for her, or one of the Jews. I hate to hear that kind of talk about the Jews. I suppose the very poor will always blame the slightly less poor for doing a bit better. The Jews always have done better, because they teach all their children to read and they work harder and drink less than the peasants. As if everyone here hadn't suffered terribly in the war. Except Schickelmaier, of course. God knows whether I can get anywhere with him, but I'll try."

Early next morning, heavy-headed after the feast Mrs Margolis had laid on for them the evening before, Max, who had asked Adam to wake him in time, crossed the square in the dark with him and knelt through the Mass Adam said in the church after that of the village priest, who was middle-aged, lame, and overawed by Adam. They emerged into the grey light of the dawning winter day, warmer than the day before, windy, with rain on the wind.

"Why Borodino? So long ago, so far away", Max said. After the roast duck and potatoes and dumplings and stuffed cabbage of the night before, five or six villagers, invited by Mrs Margolis to meet Adam, had appeared in the inn. There were stories, toasts, and much laughter. An old soldier with a white moustache had gone out briefly and come back with a balalaika. He sang a couple of cheerful songs and then a sad soldier's ballad, in German, with a stamping beat and a tune still in Max's head. The song was about the graves no one dug at the battle of Borodino and the ghosts of heroes in the Russian snows.

Adam said, "There were Poles from Galicia fighting for Austria with Napoleon at Borodino. How long is a hundred years to soldiers learning songs from each other? German was the language of the Habsburg army. That old boy would have been shouting orders on parade grounds forty years ago in German. Of course, there were Poles fighting at Borodino for the Russians too. The usual story. Poor Poland. As always. Now Max—"

456

Max stopped and looked at him before they went back into the inn.

"All right. After breakfast."

After breakfast, Adam opened the door and inspected the morning. "It's stopped raining, and it's not too cold. The sun might come out later. Let's go up to the hills and have a look at the San where it's still almost a mountain river. Only fifteen miles or so."

Adam drove along farm lanes, stopping every now and then, so as not to frighten the horses, for a cart coming towards them. If they had to pass one going in their direction, he waited until the carter had seen them, driven the horse or horses to a good place at the side of the road, and stopped for them to go by. They saw not one other car.

"Extraordinary how one remembers the way. It's eighteen years since I was here. It could be yesterday."

"Paradise regained?"

"Certainly not. It never is. I'm not that boy. And the country round here's not really the same. It's untidier, less carefully farmed. Fewer animals, especially fewer cows. The fences and gates aren't repaired. There aren't enough people left to do the work—that's what it is. One farm in four, I'd say, burnt out and not rebuilt. And even the stetls—we just drove through one; did you notice?—are too quiet. Not enough children running about. Not enough dogs, hens, ducks. Silent ponds. No. It's not paradise regained. But it is still beautiful, isn't it? Let's stop here."

He pulled up the car on a bit of stony ground by the road. Through the silver and black trunks of birches and larches could be seen flowing water, its surface ruffled in the wind. They walked through the trees, the ground soft underfoot and golden with birch leaves and the fallen needles of the larches. The river, pewter-coloured under the cloudy sky, gleaming here and there where ripples caught the wind, was flowing quiet and full between wooded banks. They walked upstream, soon over slippery rocks with ferns growing green near the water, bracken dark brown on the miniature cliffs that were the banks. The distant roar of falling water grew louder and louder as they walked until the river ahead of them was swirling through rapids, broken into black torrents, with lumps of creamy foam stuck in pools and backwaters. A rank cold smell came off the water as they reached the rocky chaos at the foot of a high, wide waterfall, the trunk of a fallen birch across rocks rinsed black and shining.

"What a place!"

"The thing to do is to climb up the side of the waterfall. It's not difficult. I did it when I was seven. I'll show you."

The climb wasn't hard. It could be done far enough from the water for them to stay more or less dry, and it was possible to find corners of rock and roots to cling to while planning the next foothold. Adam got to the top first and held out a hand to pull Max up the last two or three feet.

"There", Adam said.

A mountain lake lay before them, its waters clear and cold, the lake absolutely still except for the wind sweeping changing patterns across its surface, though all of it seemed to pour, black, silky, and silent, over the straight sill of rock to become the din of the waterfall sounding behind and below them. Wooded hills, bare and golden-brown above the line of the trees, rose to either side. At the far end, two or three miles away, were more brown hills, and behind the hills the snow-covered peaks of the Carpathians. Not a house, a track, a wall, a plume of smoke, not a sound or sign of human beings.

"Good for the soul, empty mountains", Adam said. "How much do we count for? Nothing? A great deal? The fall of a sparrow."

"Adam," Max said, "I had an affair with Eva Grossmann. For seven months. It ended more than a year ago. That's why ..."

"Ah." Adam sounded not at all surprised. He said nothing for a while. Then, "But if it ended, then ... ?"

"If it ended, and it did, why haven't I confessed the sin, been absolved, returned to the fold? Sheep may safely graze. Because ..."

He couldn't go on.

"Describe", Adam said, looking not at Max but at the distant mountains. "You and I—I too, of course—what are we? A tiny smudge on the planet. Look."

The clouds to the south had cleared, and the sun appeared, gradually pushing shadow down the hills, spreading light like syrup over the brown slopes and the forests down to the lake.

It helped.

"Look at that", Max said. "When you left, it was the opposite, like the sun going. Then Anna left, and the greyness got greyer still. Eva seemed to light everything up. For a while. Electric light. I was obsessed with her. I thought about her all the time, though there wasn't much

458

to think about except her body, her brightness, the way she painted her nails, her eyes, her mouth—which was also, now that I come to think of it, the way she painted her pictures. That was her life, her work, after all. Bright colours with these black outlines, like mascara. Sometimes abstract paintings, squares and triangles. More often, paintings of people, heads, hands, people taken to pieces, fierce black lines and a kind of destructiveness, as if anger were the only feeling worth evoking, recording. I don't know. It's hard to describe. She took me to exhibitions in Berlin twice. I could see that the paintings were better than hers, but I liked them less. She painted a picture of me once. With a broken violin under my chin, all black lines and one huge eye open, the other closed."

"Did you play your violin with her? She's not a bad pianist."

"She *is* a bad pianist. Well drilled, but ... We tried the 'Archduke' with her, Treuburg and I, after you'd gone. It was hopeless. So, no. I never took my fiddle to her studio, though she asked me to. I didn't want ... This is hard to explain as well."

"It's not. I understand."

"I don't remember getting my fiddle out of its case all through those months, now that I come to think of it. And hardly since. She had a gramophone in the studio. We bought records. And she had a piano. She played ... Have you heard of Kurt Weill?"

"No."

"Berlin. Savage, hard-edged music, like Eva's paintings. There's an opera, a sort of opera, called *Rise and Fall of the City of Mahagonny*. Sex, whisky, and money. It could be America but is actually Berlin. The tunes are impossible to forget. The main singer is called Lotte Lenya—she's Weill's wife, I think. Eva could do an imitation of her at the piano, but the records—she played them a lot."

Standing by the lake in the sun, not looking at Adam, Max heard in his head the jagged beat of "Oh show us the way to the next whisky bar. Oh don't ask why. Oh don't ask why". He got his cigarette case out of his pocket—he hadn't smoked since the train to Cracow—and offered it to Adam, who shook his head. Max lit a cigarette and drew in comforting smoke.

He smoked the whole cigarette and flattened the butt with his boot before Adam spoke.

"How did the world look to you during those seven months? More beautiful?"

"Uglier. But much more exciting. You mean, was I happy? No. Yes, in a way. More alive. Drunk on her body, even on the thought of it. Happy, if that's the word, satisfied, every time. Never in the flat, by the way—I wouldn't let her come there. Partly because of Stern. But more because of—you can imagine. I suppose I was seduced by her whole atmosphere—her studio, white and bright, her short skirts, her records, not only jazz and Kurt Weill, Russian ballet music too, Stravinsky's *Rite of Spring*, the most extraordinary, thrilling music, and Negro singing, Paul Robeson—I've never heard such a voice, and whisky and cigarettes ... as you see. It made me feel alive, as if I'd been half-asleep all my life till then. That's what she said—how had I got to be so old without being young? 'You're not really a Prussian bureaucrat who only likes Brahms. You just look like one, talk like one, work like one. Take it all off with your clothes.' So I did. It was exciting, the double life. Pretending to be a Prussian bureaucrat in the day, punctual, thorough, reliable; pretending at night to be entirely free of convention, guilt, conscience, a modern man, or nothing but a man, maleness to, for, through her femaleness."

He heard Eva's voice in his head as he hadn't for months. Come on, Max, where's Mack the Knife? Every man should have a gangster streak. Every man does—but good Germans bury it under correct behaviour. He shook his head to banish the memory.

"Was I pretending all the time? It never struck me till now."

"Probably none of the time. There are a number of possible people in all of us, don't you think? You picked two. For the time being. One eye shut. Then the other."

"But neither of them was ... You think Eva understood?"

"Why not? Somewhere. Somehow."

This stopped Max for some time.

"Neither of them was who you want to be", Adam said. "Or who something deeper inside you has chosen to be. Or has chosen you to be. God, perhaps?"

"How does one know? How does one know anything? The word 'God' for a while meant as little to me, if I ever remembered it, as it does to Eva. I suppose I knew that neither of those lives was any good, even as half of a double life. But at the time, I wasn't capable of thinking even as far as that."

"Did you talk to anyone? Old Fischer? Dr Mendel?"

"How could I?"

"There, you see. Behind the two not-quite-real people you had chosen to be, you still knew where you couldn't pretend, in whose company you wouldn't be able to escape some truth. I suppose"— Adam hesitated for a moment—"you hadn't been a Catholic long when this began."

"A year and a half. I stopped going to Mass."

"There again. The same thing. Saint Augustine said—never mind. Did Eva know you were a Catholic?"

"No. That was part of the double life. She would have laughed. Ludicrous, she would have thought, by now, to *choose* to be a Catholic, a Christian. A Jew, come to that. Nothing to do with religion meant anything at all to her. I went back to Mass after ... it was over ... and that was good ... distant, from the back of the church, behind the faithful people, good all the same. But ... What did Augustine say?"

"'Love me either because I am of God, or so that I may become of God.' It's a kind of definition of human love."

"I couldn't ... I didn't ..."

"How did it end?"

Looking at the dying bracken, the coarse, whitening grass at his feet, he had not once met Adam's eye throughout this conversation. Now he looked up and away to the mountains, along the length of the lake. High in the air over the hills to their right was a large, a very large, bird, motionless.

"What's that?"

"That's an eagle. Wait."

After what seemed like minutes, the bird flew lazily away and disappeared against the brown of the hills.

"Some creature still alive that might have been dead", Adam said.

"Don't say that."

"How did it end, Max?"

He lit another cigarette.

"She went away for three weeks. She said she was going to Berlin to visit her mother's sister, who was ill. I didn't believe her. She came back, the same as usual. I didn't ask her anything. She said—this is exactly what she said—'I was pregnant. Idiotic, wasn't it? Don't worry. I got rid of it. Quite easy—a friend of my father's in Berlin.'"

Adam said nothing for a while.

"I'm sorry, Max. What I said about the eagle."

461

"Straightaway, I said that was the end for me. I couldn't go on with the affair. She had no idea what I meant, why I said it had to end. I haven't seen her since. But why I . . . what I . . . where there's something that can't be forgiven because I can't be sorry is that it was such a relief. There. Now I've told you."

"A relief that it was over? But also . . ."

"Yes. A relief that she'd done what she'd done. That is . . . that is to find it better for me that my child will never be born. How can I ever change that? Be sorry for that?"

Another long silence.

"Would you have married her?"

"Of course. And it's easy to imagine what being married to her would have been like. Remember Betsy. Worse, it would have been."

"Let's walk."

Without another word, they walked for an hour some way along the edge of the lake, over some difficult ground, sometimes rocky, sometimes boggy, sometimes with trees growing right down to the water, where apparently no one had ever walked before. Clouds came and went. The lake changed colour almost from moment to moment. The wind had calmed a little but still moved the surface of the water, stroking it into fields of ripples. They turned and came back. The lake was too big and the walking too slow for them to walk all the way round.

When they reached the waterfall again, Adam said, "Now listen to me, Max."

Max stood exactly where he had stood before and looked over the water to the mountains.

"Eros is the only sickness for which we volunteer. You are answerable for what happened between you and Eva, in a way that she's not, or not yet—no one knows what will become of her soul, what would have become of it, for example, if you had married her. What goes on in anyone's soul is known only to God, in any case. But what you have truthfully told me is that you understood the real quality of your passion for Eva only when its consequence—another life, not allowed to become a life—shocked you out of its everyday excitement. The idea of marrying her horrified you because there wasn't enough, there was hardly anything, of who you are in the connexion with her. What had you given her? Presents, I expect. And your body. How much of you is that? Your reaction to the abortion—I'm sorry, but the word

462

you avoided has to be used—shows that you know this. It also shows that you understand the self-indulgence, the distance from God, of the whole thing. You understood this all along. The fact that Eva didn't understand helped you to hide from the fact that you did. There was a word you never used in what you said. I used it, or Augustine did. You didn't."

"I loved Anna. I still do."

"Exactly."

"There was no sadness in Eva. How is it possible to love someone in whom there's no sadness?"

"Consider the possibility that you never saw it. Never looked for it."

There was another long silence.

"What I would like you to do is this. Tomorrow is Sunday. The village Mass is at nine. Come with me half an hour early and make your confession to Father Stanislaw. He's a good man—not that it matters what he's like. Tell him the simple facts. Be given absolution. Be given Communion. Pray for your child. Pray for Eva. And for me."

"Adam—"

"Not a word. We're going to find some lunch. Be careful climbing down here. It's much harder than climbing up."

The next morning, Max did what Adam had told him to do. After both priests had said Mass, they said good-bye to Father Stanislaw and to Mrs Margolis and her family. Her old father, with his long white beard, had not spoken all the time they were at the inn, though his frail hand had moved in time to the music on the night of the balalaika. When Adam bent to take his hand in farewell, he lifted his ancient head a little and said in Yiddish, in a faint voice from the ages, "Now you are a man. You must not forget."

They drove back to Cracow, saying almost nothing, eating as they drove the bread and cheese and apples Mrs Margolis had given them for the journey. It was dark when they arrived in the city. There was an evening train to Breslau.

In the station, Adam said, "I'll be back here tomorrow with all my books and stuff from the seminary, for the train to Lemberg." He took out his notebook and his pen, as he had for Mrs Sanok. "My address. Write sometimes."

"Good-bye, Adam. Thank you more than I—"

Adam put a finger to his own lips.

"I wish you could come to Lemberg and be a Polish lawyer. Alas. Things in Germany are going to get worse. Be brave. Good-bye, Max. God bless you."

Max climbed into the Breslau train with his suitcase and his violin, which he hadn't played with Adam. Never mind. Now he would be able to play again, he knew. He would practise the Bach Chaconne until he could play it for Dr Mendel. He would go and see old Fischer.

Adam had restored him to a place where the truth was steady.

Chapter 17

The ringing of the telephone in the hall woke Max from a deep sleep. Let Treuburg answer that, he thought. Blasted doctors. Then he remembered he was alone in the flat. Treuburg had left years ago. As for Stern, wretched Stern: not here either. The ringing went on. Max stumbled out of bed, switched on the hall light, and looked at his watch—twenty past six—as he reached for the receiver.

"Yes?"

"Count von Hofmannswaldau?"

"Yes?"

The voice was distantly familiar. He tried and failed to remember whose voice it was.

There was a long silence.

"Who is that?" Max said with some impatience. "It's very early, you know."

A shorter silence. Then, "I apologize, Count. It is ... I'm so sorry ... Count, there has been a tragedy."

As he heard the words, Dr Mendel's words on the day of his father's death, he recognized the voice. Herr Rosenthal's voice. He felt cold. "What's happened, Herr Rosenthal? Is Dr Mendel all right?"

"Would you come, Count? I am so sorry."

"Of course. I'll be there in half an hour."

As he quickly dressed, decided not to shave, put on his overcoat, and clattered down the stairs to the front door of the house, he was getting used to the idea that Dr Mendel was dead. Poor old Mendel. How old must he be? Max got into an early tram to save time. He had never been sure what year Mendel had been born. He must be at least seventy by now, but in good health surely, spry, not in the least deaf, the kind of man who gets thinner and drier with age. He seemed perfectly well when Max last saw him—when was that? Of course: in the middle of January, before—before the thirtieth, the day, not yet

465

seven weeks ago, when the whole of Germany had gone mad. Thank God, Max thought, as he sat in the tram between a stout lady clutching her bag with both hands, her hat fixed to her head with a large pin, no doubt on her way to clean some offices, and a boy with sleeked-back hair and a white shirt and black bow tie under his overcoat, no doubt a café waiter. Thank God he had visited the old man recently.

He had gone, at last, to play him the Bach Chaconne, so difficult, so beautiful, which he had set himself to learn properly when he came home from Cracow after seeing Adam, practising every evening before Stern got back from the hospital, forcing the fingers of his left hand to move, move again, move better, through the rapid passages and the remote keys.

"Well done, Max", Dr Mendel had said, exactly as he used to say, not often, when he was ten years old. "You must have practised for many, many hours. It's not all quite there yet, is it? But it will be. It will be. If you play it every day once, stopping only to correct the bars that don't go entirely right, and you do that for two or three months, you will be giving this great music the attention it deserves, and then you must come back and play it for me again."

There was no suggestion that he was ill. On the other hand he was uneasy, nervous. "Breslau, so good to me for so many years, has become a city I no longer care to live in. The streets at night: coming back from the opera house, we do not feel safe, Herr Rosenthal and I. We are shouted at. Once even stones were thrown. But I am too old now to think of going to a strange place. France would now be altogether strange to me. And we have our work. I still enjoy the work. And each of us has some good pupils, who encourage us to think that music in Germany will survive this politics of hatred."

Herr Rosenthal, his face white and strained, was waiting for Max at the street door of the house; it was five to seven, the gaslights fading in the grey morning light.

"Come in, Count, please. I apologize for telephoning so early."

Max followed the cellist up the many stairs to the top-floor flat. The door was open. Herr Rosenthal shut it behind them and took Max into Dr Mendel's small, tidy bedroom, which he had never seen before. The old man was lying in his bed, the sheet and down bedcover drawn up to his chin, his eyes shut. It was evident to Max at once that he was not asleep but dead. His face was the colour of old paper, a little blue round the mouth.

466

"I'm so sorry", Max said. "What do you think ... ?"

"I know. He left a note. It is cyanide. Because of what happened to us on Tuesday. And then an article in the newspaper yesterday. I had no idea he had bought cyanide. Excuse me."

Herr Rosenthal's voice had given way, and he left Max alone with the dead man. Max put his hand to his own throat in order not to make a sound, as he remembered Dr Mendel's voice saying across the red plush of the schoolroom table at Waldau, "Hannibal and Themistocles died in foreign countries a long way from home, not like heroes but old and sad, so that both of them swallowed poison." There was something else about taking from God the decision as to the day of death, but he couldn't remember exactly how it went. He bent over the body and kissed Dr Mendel's cold forehead. Then he stepped back, crossed himself with a prayer—Latin, he thought, for his old tutor—that God might give his soul eternal rest, and left the room.

He heard Herr Rosenthal rattling cups in the kitchen and went into the living room to wait for him. Max stood with his back to the door, looking at the Chagall picture of the violinist in his hat. He turned and took the coffee tray from Herr Rosenthal's shaking hands when he came in. He put the tray on the piano.

"What happened on Tuesday?"

"On Tuesday, the Jewish musicians in the opera house orchestra—that is, nearly thirty men—were told that our services are no longer required. German music, German art, German culture is henceforward to be Jewfree. Have you heard this terrible word? From the orchestras, the opera houses, the museums and galleries, the Jews are now purged, cleaned out and thrown away."

"Herr Rosenthal, that's appalling! Senseless! How can they run the orchestras of Germany without Jewish musicians?"

"Who knows? It is true, however. My old friend Mendel was as if broken by this news. I tried to cheer him. We have pupils, Jewish pupils. We can find more. Not all can be lost. There will perhaps be a pension, particularly for him, at seventy-two. But then yesterday, this."

Herr Rosenthal picked up a folded copy of the *Frankfurter Zeitung* and pointed to a short report on an inside page as he handed it to Max. It said that the great conductor Bruno Walter had been shut out of a rehearsal of his own orchestra—the Leipzig Gewandhaus Orchestra, no less—and had left Germany.

467

"He felt this as a mortal blow. To music. To Jews in Germany. He said in his note that he could see no light in the darkness and that I would be able to manage my life better without the anxiety of caring for an old man with a broken heart." Herr Rosenthal clenched his fists. "Excuse me, Count. I am angry with him." His bearded chin was trembling. "I hate to be angry with one who ... but he has made me angry. He did not give me the opportunity to care for him. Instead, he has taken himself away, taken away his company, his friendship. After fourteen years. He should have had more confidence in me. He chose to die alone. That is not Jewish. It is not right." He blew his nose. "Will you have some coffee? Please do."

"Thank you." Max poured the coffee and gave a cup to Herr Rosenthal, who sat down. "You mustn't blame him, Herr Rosenthal. It is ... it is the Nazis who have killed him. They are to blame, not him. And nothing ..."

"Nothing?"

"Nothing can take away your friendship, all the years ... your shared years."

Max sat down and allowed Herr Rosenthal to pull himself together. He drank some coffee. Herr Rosenthal put his on the floor, untasted.

"He said in his note that he would like you to have his violin. It is a very fine instrument, you know. Not a Stradivarius but Italian and probably from the eighteenth century. He was left it by his teacher in Strassburg when he was a young man."

Max swallowed rising tears and wondered briefly if Herr Rosenthal would need the money the violin would fetch, but said, "That is a great honour." Then he managed to add, "He taught me everything I knew before I came to Breslau, to the Gymnasium."

"He was devoted to you, Count, and to the memory of your mother. He said Kaddish for her in the synagogue on the Sabbath after her funeral. Ach"—he looked at his watch. "I must speak to the synagogue as soon as it is a proper time of day. And send for the doctor. He will know what else ..."

"Is there anything I can do to help?"

"The synagogue will see to the ... there is a burial society. You have been most kind to come here, Count. I am very grateful." He looked at the floor for a minute or two. "It would, as things are at present, be too much to ask that you should come to his funeral, would it not?"

"Of course I'll come. Is there ... is there anything I should be aware of? I've never been to a Jewish funeral."

"You will find it quite familiar, I think. You know, Count—or possibly you do not know—that in Jewish life the child of a Jewish mother and a gentile father is always regarded as a Jew."

"Really? Is that really so? But my mother ... never mind. I shall be there."

Max walked home. There was plenty of time to shave, change into a clean shirt, and set off for the office. Did Hitler also regard the child of a gentile father and a Jewish mother, although a fourth-generation baptized Christian, as a Jew? For the first time since the thirtieth of January, he felt not exactly afraid for himself but surprised into wondering whether it might be appropriate to be afraid. He pushed the thought aside easily.

The office was orderly, dull. Hard work, as usual. Max was now an Assessor, a properly qualified junior law official, having passed a set of examinations in December. He had assumed his work would become more interesting, more responsible. It hadn't.

In the afternoon, Herr Rosenthal telephoned to say that the funeral would be on Sunday afternoon, as tomorrow was the Sabbath. So Max didn't have to ask for permission to be absent from work.

The funeral took place in the Jewish cemetery, a nephew from Alsace, a middle-aged French dentist with little German, having travelled overnight to be there. Max joined a sombre group of orchestral players in the plain chapel at the cemetery for prayers in Hebrew and German and walked with them behind the coffin in a small procession headed by the nephew and Herr Rosenthal. The procession stopped seven times on the short path to the grave. It was a mild grey March day, damp with an intermittent drizzle, dirty thawing snow on the ground. It was also Max's twenty-eighth birthday. After everyone else, he took the shovel he was given to throw a little earth in the grave. Then they all recited a long prayer in Hebrew. This was Kaddish, the words Dr Mendel had prayed for Max's mother. Someone gave him a folded paper with a German translation of the prayer. It said nothing of death or mourning but praised the glory of God and prayed for his coming on earth.

Many times in the months that followed, Max remembered the last sentence: "May he who makes peace in his high places make peace for us and for all Israel."

There was no time, that spring, to mourn Dr Mendel as he should have mourned him, or even to think about his death with the attention it deserved.

The day after the funeral, on his way to work, Max went back to the local police station to ask again whether they had found any information about what had happened to Felix Stern. Behind the high counter, the policeman, a different one from last week's, shook his head after running a pencil down four pages of names, dates, and single-line notes, handwritten in neat copperplate in a large ledger he fetched from the desk behind him.

"No Stern arrested in this ward in the last three weeks. Jew, is he?"

"Yes, but he's not religious."

"Makes no difference these days. What's his age?"

"Twenty-three, I think."

"Occupation?"

"He's a medical student at the university. He has some very important examinations in ten days' time. He must be in Breslau to sit them, or eighteen months' work will be wasted. I do need to find him."

"What's he to you?"

"He's my tenant."

"Is he now? Name? Address?"

Max gave his name and address and then suddenly wondered if he needed to be afraid of any authority knowing Stern was his tenant. Too late.

"What would you be doing with a Jewish student for a tenant, sir? If you don't mind my asking."

"He's been my tenant for five years. A good tenant."

"Bolshie, is he? Demonstrations and that?"

"No. Certainly not."

"Well, if he's had anything to do with politics, Commies or Social Democrats, especially if he looks Jewish, you'd be better off asking the brownshirts. They're police now, you know, all the powers, since three weeks ago. They're much more likely than us to have picked up your friend. Poor blighter if they have."

"Where do I ... ?"

"Stormtrooper HQ. Behind the city hall."

Dr Gerlach's clerk was waiting for him in the office—he was ten minutes late—with a pile of paper.

"This is the prosecution brief for the riotous assembly case near the prison. Dr Gerlach wants it summarized—three or four typed pages, he says—for the presiding judge."

"All right. Put it on my desk."

He tried for the rest of the morning to concentrate on this straightforward task. By lunchtime he had produced something more or less coherent and concise for the typing pool. During the hour's absence from the office usually permitted for lunch, he went to the Stormtrooper headquarters in a building that he thought used to house the Silesian trades union council. Huge swastika banners hung from each window. Two brownshirts with rifles at the ready flanked the main door. They crossed the guns in front of him as he reached the top step.

"Your business?"

"A legal inquiry. I am an Assessor from the courts of justice."

"Pass." The rifles were uncrossed. "Heil Hitler!" the brownshirts said, as one. He did not return the salute.

Inside the building, several brownshirts with apparently nothing to do were talking to each other behind a long curved counter more like the reception desk of a smart hotel than the old police station counter of the morning. There were half a dozen bullet holes in one wooden panel of the counter. Max remembered hearing a couple of weeks ago that the trades union building had been stormed by brownshirts and that two officials were killed. Beyond the chatting Stormtroopers, three more were sitting at tables with typewiters, two of them copy-typing from papers beside them. One of those at the counter straightened up reluctantly as he approached.

"My name is Count von Hofmannswaldau."

As he said this, he noticed one of the typists turning his head towards him. The young man struck him as someone he had seen before. Where? When?

"I am an Assessor at the courts of justice, working for Dr Gerlach. I wish to inquire as to the whereabouts of Felix Stern, a Czech student living in the city, a medical student, who has not been seen at his home or at the university hospital since the second of March."

"Jew name, Stern. What's he to you?"

"His parents have requested our assistance. They are anxious as to his safety."

Lies. Implied lies. These days, apparently necessary.

471

"Are they, now? They might have to sing for it. The second of March, you say. Three days after the Reichstag fire. Communist, is he? Gärtner!" He shouted behind him. The boy of nineteen or twenty who had recognized Max's name got to his feet, still looking at him. Gärtner. Of course. Frau Gärtner's son. Max hadn't seen him since he was a child. "Fetch us the second-of-March list. And the third. Upstairs. Look sharp!"

The boy emerged from the far end of the counter and disappeared up the marble staircase, taking the steps only moderately quickly.

Five minutes went by.

Max had talked to Stern in the flat the night after the Reichstag fire. The streets that day had been full of police, brownshirts, even a marching detachment of the SS goose-stepping over the cobbles of the Market Square. The newspaper sellers were shouting: "Reichstag fire! Bolshevik plot! Bolshevik plot! Latest!"

"Was it a Communist conspiracy, Stern?"

"I've no idea. I wouldn't know if it were."

"Aren't you a member of the Party nowadays?"

"No, I'm not. I never have been. I'm not brave enough. Or first things first—that's what I tell myself. I want to qualify, more than anything, and once you're a member, they can send you anywhere, order you to do anything."

"Burn down the Reichstag, for example."

"No. I don't think so. It's possible, I suppose. But I very much doubt it. The Party isn't stupid. Who's going to benefit from the fire? Hitler. It's a perfect excuse for rounding up Party members everywhere. Social Democrats too, very likely. I wouldn't be surprised if the Nazis set fire to the Reichstag. They're not stupid either. If they did, it'll never come out. Not now."

"For heaven's sake, take care, Stern. No more Party meetings. It's just as well you're not a member. There's bound to be a crackdown."

"You're right. I've got to work every evening anyway. Less than a month to my exams."

That must have been on the twenty-eighth of February.

The next day, the first of March, Max and the other junior lawyers at the courts of justice were summoned to a meeting at which a state judge, with Dr Gerlach and three others beside him, sat at a table and told them that the government had deemed it necessary, in view of the clear threat—demonstrated by the atrocity of the Reichstag fire—from the Communist Party of Germany, and therefore from the

472

promoters of world revolution in Moscow, to suspend for the time being the constitutional guarantees protecting citizens from detention without trial. Freedom from arrest on suspicion, freedom of speech, freedom of the press, freedom of assembly, and freedom of the right to private communication by post or telephone had been declared to be in abeyance for the sake of protecting the security of the state.

Silence in the state judge's chambers. Then a murmur of approval from some of Max's colleagues, as he heard in his mind a door slam, the sound he had heard in his heart when he read the announcement of Anna's marriage. Now as then, something in him had closed for good.

On the following day, the second of March, Stern hadn't come home, and when, on the third, Max went to the university hospital and asked at the sister's office on Stern's ward whether he had come to work, the nurse shook her head. "And he's in serious trouble. Dr Feinstein likes to be told ahead if students are going to be absent."

The brownshirted boy—yes, Frau Gärtner's son—came down the marble stairs with papers in his hand.

"About time", the man at the desk said.

He ran a thick thumb down a long typed list. First page. Second page. Third page. There must have been fifty names on each page.

"Stern. Two here. Second of March. First name again?"

"Felix."

"Born Prague. Tenth of April 1909. That him?"

"Yes."

"Dead."

"*Dead*? How can he be dead? He's a perfectly healthy young man. There must be a mistake."

"We don't make mistakes. Look." The Stormtrooper turned the paper round so that it was facing Max and pointed to Stern's name, place, and date of birth. KPD, the entry on the list said. German Communist Party. Then three more capital letters that Max didn't understand.

"Shot while attempting to escape, that means. Should've kept his head down, shouldn't he?"

Max looked at him, stupidly he knew, for several seconds.

"But couldn't he have been injured? Not killed?"

"Shot while attempting to escape means killed."

"What about ... what happens ... the body? A funeral? He committed no crime. I know."

The man shrugged. "Shot while attempting to escape. End of story."

As Max left the building, he was aware of Gärtner saying something to the man at the desk.

Max went back to the office and made the riotous assembly prosecution an excuse for a visit to the law library, where he took some volumes of records off the shelves, opened them at appropriate pages, and read none of them until five o'clock. Then he walked home and ate some bread and cheese. Three hours, two glasses of wine, and five cigarettes later, he had managed to write a short letter to Stern's parents. He went out in the gaslit dark to mail it. When he got back to the flat, he took Dr Mendel's violin carefully from its ancient case, tuned it—which it scarcely needed—and played the Bach Chaconne, for Dr Mendel and for Stern, better than he had ever played it before. He put the fiddle in its case and, before he went to bed, went into Grandpapa's workshop behind the kitchen and remembered him turning tops on his lathe for Frau Gärtner's children on the Sunday Adam came to lunch. Nearly eleven years ago.

The next evening, he cleared up Stern's room, made a pile of books to take back to the medical library at the university, collected Stern's few clothes to give to the Saint Vincent de Paul Society at the local church—where he was now going regularly to Mass—and threw away an old copy of the Communist Manifesto, some KPD pamphlets, and all Stern's medical notes and papers. Five years of study. There was nothing worth sending to Prague.

At nine o'clock in the evening of the following day, the telephone rang again. Max had given up work for the night, leaving a pile of Dr Gerlach's documents almost dealt with on his desk, and was sitting in Grandpapa's chair smoking his first cigarette of the day and listening to a soaring, exhilarating performance—he had bought a gramophone and a few sets of records at Christmas for himself and Stern—of the Brahms violin concerto. He had chosen this piece because the soloist's name on the labels reminded him of the Halperns. Anna's brother had said, one quartet evening when even Treuburg had praised Halpern's playing, "I shall never believe that I play the violin well. There was a boy of my age when we were children in Vilna. Our violin teacher said he must go to Petersburg to be trained and that he would become the greatest violinist in the world one day. He will. Perhaps he has. His name was Jascha Heifetz."

Max had just put on the first side of the last movement and had resolved to get hold of the score and learn to play these wild, wonderful notes when he heard the telephone. He took the needle off the record and left it spinning.

"Yes?"

"Max, how are you?"

Eva. No. Absolutely not. His throat contracted.

"Max, are you there?"

"Eva. I don't think—"

"Max, will you take me out to dinner tomorrow? I'd like to say good-bye."

"I said good-bye to you a long time ago."

"Not that sort of good-bye, Max. A real good-bye. I'm leaving Breslau. I'm going to Paris. Next week. I'm going to live in Paris and paint in Paris. I'm saying good-bye to . . . to everyone, before I go."

"Not to me, Eva. I can't—"

"Max. You can. Of course you can. You'll never see me again. It wasn't nothing, between us, was it? You do remember. Have you another girlfriend?"

He couldn't answer.

"No? I thought not. So you can spare me just an evening to say good-bye. Of course you can. When do you get home from work? Still the same time? I'll come to your flat at eight tomorrow. I've packed up the studio. You'll be there, won't you? Max?"

"All right. Yes. I'll be here."

Max went back to the sitting room but didn't play any more of the Brahms. Heifetz and the Halperns and Dr Mendel's violin belonged to another world, the same world as each other but not Eva's.

He picked up that morning's *Vossische Zeitung*, which he had bought, as always, with his milk and fresh rolls at breakfast time, and later thrown on the floor. He looked again at a page with photographs, far more than usual. The day before, there had been a grand ceremony at Potsdam for the opening of the new Reichstag—the Reichstag for which yet another election had been held a week after the fire. In spite of the marches and the swastika banners and Hitler's voice crackling through loudspeakers on every street corner, the Nazis hadn't won the election. Less than half the votes in the whole country, they got, though more than half in Breslau. Not that their failure to win a majority signified any kind of defeat since there was no hope that the rest of

475

the parties would stick together long enough to hold firm against the Nazis on any single issue. So here was Hitler, dapper in his frock coat, bowing to Hindenburg, resplendent as an old portrait in his Prussian field marshal's uniform, his ancient face blank: this was meant to look as if Hitler were a mere functionary in an old-world conservative Prussian government. Side by side—the biggest photograph—the venerable soldier and the civil servant stood, reviewing a huge march past, army, Stormtroopers, SS, the lot. The flags of the Kaiser. Lies, all this. Lies to bury the war and the fourteen years of the failed republic, as if those years and all the efforts of moderate men to keep the republic alive amounted to nothing. The whole event had been staged to look as if 1914 were back, as if the war had never been lost and the Kaiser had never run away. At the top of the page was a photograph of a painting: the faces of Frederick the Great, Bismarck, and Hitler in a heroic row. Max crunched the newspaper between both his hands and threw it on the dying fire, where it briefly blazed and blackened into ash.

When Eva arrived, a few minutes late, she didn't kiss him but ran a gloved finger down his cheek. He kept still. He recognized her scent, with detachment.

"Thank you for letting me come. You look older."

"I am. You don't. You look very well. Do you mind if we go straight out? I have a table for eight thirty. Ten minutes' walk, if that's all right."

He had booked a table at a medium-priced restaurant where he and Eva had never been, near the river.

Against his stoniness even Eva soon gave up trying to talk about nothing in particular.

"So," he said, when their food was in front of them and each of them had a glass of wine, "why are you leaving Germany?"

"Max, really! Why do you think? The Academy's clearing out all the Jewish professors and all the Jewish students. Strictly speaking, I should have stopped being a student by now, but somehow I've managed to hang on. They don't mind as long as you pay. But the fun's over. I don't know how they know—do I have frizzy hair and a hooked nose? Have I ever been to a synagogue? I even joined the Party, as a disguise."

"Which Party?"

"Well, the Nazi Party, of course. What would have been the point of joining any other? But apparently even that's no use. My parents are going to France as well, but not to Paris, thank God."

"Your parents?"

"My father was told his contract won't be renewed. There can't be any other reason, can there? So they've sold the house, to a high-up Nazi—Nazis aren't squeamish about who they buy expensive property from, as long as they get it cheap—and they're going to the Riviera. They've always had a villa in Nice, and French hospitals seem to be quite keen on German surgeons in spite of everything."

"What about your brother?"

"He's in America. Studying economics or something at some university."

They ate in silence for a few minutes.

"What will you do, Max?"

"Do?"

"Count von Hofmannswaldau is a pretty good disguise, but it won't take them long to see through it. Has anyone asked you recently what your mother's maiden name was?"

"Certainly not."

"They will. Anyway, it's not difficult to find out, is it? Your grandfather was well known."

"My grandparents were Protestants. Buried in the Protestant cemetery. Not even converts. Protestants all their lives."

"Max—you know that's not good enough now. Half-Aryan is half-Jewish. That's what everyone says. So what will you do?"

Max drank some water.

"Come on, Max, you need to think about it. Why don't you come to Paris too? We could have a lot of fun, couldn't we?"

"No, Eva. I think not. I'm a German. A lawyer trained in the Prussian Code. That's all I know how to do. My life, my career is here in Breslau—they can't sack every lawyer who's Jewish or half-Jewish—and in any case—"

"I wouldn't bet on it."

More silence.

"This is very good. Eat, Max. You look thin, and tired."

A waiter refilled her wine glass.

"I'm looking forward to French food. Quite delicious. You've never been to France, have you?" She looked at him carefully. "Where's

your medical student? The boy from Prague? He does look Jewish."
There was nothing wrong with Eva's intuition.

"He's dead."

"How do you mean, dead? He can't be."

"He's dead. They arrested him after the Reichstag fire. He was mixed up with the Communists."

"Stupid of him."

"Yes. But he meant no harm to anyone. In fact all he wanted was to help people. They arrested him and then they shot him. They said he was trying to escape, but I don't believe that. He wouldn't have. He might have argued, but he'd never have tried to escape."

"Who shot him?"

"Stormtroopers. Since the day after the fire, they can do what they like. Officially. Detention without charge. Capital punishment without trial. It's all an emergency decree at present, with the fire as the so-called justification. But if this lasts, if it's made into actual law, then there will be a serious reason to leave Germany. A moral reason, for lawyers, for anyone."

"Isn't self-preservation a serious reason? Getting out of a country where Jews are being sacked from their jobs, bullied in the street—haven't you heard the kids shouting, 'Wake up, Germany! Let the Jew croak!'"

"Yes, I have. And harmless people, people with no harm in them, not an atom of harm, are being driven to suicide."

"Really? Someone you know?"

"Someone I knew. Never mind." He looked across the table at her. "No, I'm not leaving. Or not yet—not until things are clearer. Mere self-preservation isn't a serious reason."

"Well, I think it is. That's why I'm going to Paris. They like German painting there, or so I'm told. And—I'm not going alone."

"I didn't think you would be."

When they left the restaurant, Max said, "I'm sorry, Eva. I have to go back and do some work. I'll find you a cab."

They started walking towards a larger, better-lit street with more traffic.

"So soon? Oh, all right. I just wanted to see you once more to say good-bye." She stopped. "Max?"

"Yes?"

"I was very fond of you, you know. Apart from the obvious—we were good together, weren't we? The best."

"There are other things. More important things. How is your painting, Eva? Are you pleased with how it's going?"

"Kind of you to ask. I am. Yes. It's quite different now. There's a nastier world out there. Art has to change when the world changes. Wouldn't you agree?"

"Yes." He thought of the Bach Chaconne. "No. But I see what you mean."

"So why, Max? Why did you end our affair so suddenly? I didn't understand. I still don't. I thought it was going splendidly, much better than most such—"

"Eva, if you don't know the answer to that question, I'm more certain even than I was then that it was time to . . . to break the connexion between us."

"What a lawyer you are, Max. I've no idea what you're saying when you talk like that."

"The child."

"What child?"

"The child. Yours and mine."

"Oh, Max! Now I see. What a ridiculous fellow you are. This is the twentieth century, you know. That wasn't a child, that was just a silly mistake. Anyone's allowed the occasional mistake, wouldn't you say? Idiotic of me to tell you—if I hadn't, you'd never have known."

He began to walk again; she had to walk too. They reached the wide street with its noise, lit shop windows, traffic.

"There are plenty of cabs."

He hailed one, which stopped. He opened the door for her.

"Good-bye, Eva. I hope things go well for you in Paris."

She put a hand on his shoulder and kissed him on the cheek. "Good-bye, Max. Thank you for dinner. Good luck."

The next day, Friday, relieved of more of a burden than merely the obligation to take Eva out to dinner and be civil to her, Max overslept, had to shave and dress quickly, do without breakfast, and run for a tram to the office. Dr Gerlach was in court. Max saw only Hertz, who was another Assessor, and a typist in the morning and on his lunch hour took a different tram to Cathedral Island to buy, in the dusty old music shop he had known all his life, the score of the Brahms concerto. He would never play it with an orchestra, but with Dr

479

Mendel's fiddle that sounded so much better than his own, he was determined to learn it nevertheless.

He bought, extravagantly, a bound score, with the title of the work in gold lettering. He paid for it with a cheque. The elderly assistant looked at his signature and then looked at him over his half-moon spectacles.

"Now I remember you, Count. You used to come in with Dr Mendel, your violin teacher, I believe."

"That's right. How clever of you to remember."

"How is Dr Mendel? We haven't seen him in the shop for some time."

"I'm afraid he died—not long ago."

"May he rest in peace. He was a fine musician. I'm sorry, sir; I shouldn't have asked."

"Not at all. You couldn't have known. Thank you, and good day to you."

On Saturday morning, Max got up even later. The sun was shining into the sitting room: the dust on the piano and the harpsichord shamed him into fetching a cloth and dusting all the surfaces in the room while his coffee brewed. He opened the windows. Mild spring air. He felt as if the sun hadn't come out for weeks.

He went out in shirtsleeves and bought milk, croissants for a treat, and the paper. He opened the kitchen window too, poured his coffee, sat at the table, and spread out the *Vossin* as his grandfather used to at the same table.

Here was the actual opening of the Reichstag on Thursday, in a theatre in Berlin because of the fire. In the single large photograph Hitler looked quite different from the humble frock-coated figure at Potsdam two days before: brown shirt, arrogant lift of the head, outstretched arm, swastikas everywhere. No more imperial flummery. No lies now. But a brutal, a thoroughly Nietzschean, fact. The will to power as power achieved.

The paper had a long, detailed report on the single day's session of the parliament, on the speeches, the voting, the legislation passed. The report recorded the suicide, it slowly became clear as he read, of the republic as a constitution with checks to prevent arbitrary, absolute government. This is tyranny, Max thought. There is no longer any possibility of doubt, of hope. Backed by force, and not the constitutional force of the army. So much for bowing over the hand of the Kaiser's general.

Max drank some coffee, forgot his croissants, went to fetch his cigarettes from the sitting room. As he read, he felt for the first time
since Hitler had been appointed Chancellor—years ago, it seemed,
though it was less than two months—that there was no hope for goodness or justice upheld by the law in Germany, no hope for himself as
a lawyer even to work, even to earn a living, never mind to defend
what he had been educated to believe lawyers existed to defend: what
is right.

The purpose of the session was to pass an Enabling Act giving Hitler power to introduce laws without the approval of the Reichstag or
the President. That would mean the formal end of all the freedoms
suspended after the fire. It would also mean that in the future, Hitler
would be restrained by no legal or constitutional limitation of any
kind. So much for all the people who had said that putting Hitler in
a government that had only one other Nazi would neutralize him:
outnumbered in the cabinet, as Nazi votes were in the country, Hitler
would be powerless. Now he had in fact manoeuvred the only properly representative national parliament Germany had ever had into voting its own authority out of existence. Max read the numbers of
deputies, the numbers of votes, scribbled them on the edge of the
newspaper, added and subtracted them.

The Communist deputies, legally elected two and a half weeks ago,
had had their party abolished and weren't allowed to vote. Clever,
that. If they hadn't been allowed to put up candidates, there'd have
been many more votes for the Social Democrats. A third of the Social
Democat deputies weren't there. Why? Ill, terrified, in prison? Dead,
like poor Stern? The paper said that the auditorium of the theatre was
lined with Stormtroopers and SS men. That meant shouting and chant-
ing from the Stormtroopers; the silent menace from the SS; guns all
round. Hitler's speech was the usual diatribe against "the November
criminals" of 1918 and the Communists, but it ended with a straight
threat: vote for the Enabling Act, or there will be civil war. Otto
Wels, the brave leader of the Social Democrats, pleaded for the achieve-
ments of the republic to be remembered. Max thought of his grandfather and of Stresemann and of Dr Fischer's passionate loyalty to the
centre and the Centre Party. Finally, Wels, acknowledging that he was
now risking his life by making this speech, took his stand on what he
called "the basic principles of humanity and justice". Max at the kitchen
table almost cheered.

481

The vote came at the end of the report, the numbers given without comment from the paper: 444 in favour, 94—that was the Social Democrats who were there, all of them—against. This meant that every other party, *including the Centre*, had voted with the Nazis. How could the Catholic party vote away the republic in favour of Hitler as absolute ruler? How could they? Poor old Fischer. What must he be thinking, feeling, as he sat, alone like Max, reading this report, probably in the very same newspaper? Max should go to see him. He would go—but not till things at the law courts became clearer. He was too confused himself to talk to anyone yet.

He put down the paper, looked at his two croissants on the plate, and touched one. Cold. They'd been warm when he brought them home from the baker. He put them back in their slightly greasy paper bag. Tomorrow's breakfast.

He left the kitchen and stood for a moment in the hall where he used to help Anna out of her coat, where she used to carry the tray with coffee cups and beer mugs and smile up at him. He saw her smile as if yesterday evening she had been in the flat, concentrating on her part, frowning as she played, her spectacles on her nose, looking over the music stands to smile at him at the end of a movement. He walked into the first room, Treuburg's, once the dining room, light in the morning sun, now with Grandpapa's desk and his own law books on a shelf he had put up. Cardboard files with legal papers lay on the bed. The opposite door was to Stern's room, once Adam's, and before that, his grandparents' bedroom. A KPD election poster hung on the wall: he should have taken it down and thrown it away on Tuesday. He stood in front of it. A giant worker, at least fully clothed unlike the half-naked bruisers in most election posters, loomed over an official-looking table round which sat about twenty tiny politicians in top hats or uniform caps, one in a spiked 1914 helmet. The cabinet. Any cabinet since Bismarck. "An end to this system", the caption said. He felt a pang of pity for the little figures sitting round their too-big table with a small agenda paper in front of each of them except the general. Perhaps that was to show that the general couldn't read. Well, the system had ended now. And not because the wretched out-of-work workers—another pang of pity, for the giant in the poster—had smashed it. On Thursday in the Reichstag vote, the little figures had ended it themselves with the Nazis pointing guns at them, real as well as metaphorical. Could it have been saved if, a few months ago, all the other

482

parties had joined together, or just the Communists and the Social Democrats? Perhaps.

He was furious, suddenly, not with the workers but with the KPD itself, obedient Germans doing what Stalin in Moscow ordered them to do. They were to make no alliance ever, under any circumstances, with the Social Democrats. *That* was what had let the Nazis get this far. The better the KPD did, the more the Nazis could terrify everybody with the threat of Bolshevik revolution. The hundred Reichstag deputies the KPD had achieved in the November election, when Max had been in Zapolsc with Adam, had done more for the Nazis' popularity than anything before the Reichstag fire. He had read in the newspaper on the morning after he got back to Breslau, "One hundred Communists in the Reichstag! Is this a gift for Hitler or has the assault on the republic been repulsed?"

Which it had been was now entirely clear.

He pulled out Stern's thumbtacks. The poster fell to the floor. He crumpled it, then uncrumpled it, tore it into pieces and put it in the kitchen waste bin. He went into the sitting room, sunny, silent, inhabited still by the friendly ghosts of his grandfather, of Adam, of Anna, of Treuburg, of Halpern. He stood in front of the portrait of Bach and remembered, not for the first time, Dr Mendel standing behind him, hands on his shoulders, on his ninth birthday: "We cannot all be Bach, but we can all hope for faith, practise patience, and always work hard." As far as Max could tell, the old man had lived according to his own advice. A life not good enough for Hitler, but (if it were possible to believe in God) good enough for God. Which meant it was not possible not to believe in God.

Max couldn't stay in the flat. He went out, without a coat because it was the first day of spring, and walked to the places that had Anna smiling in them, the bench by the old moat, the university footbridge, and the park across the river, where the lake, with ducks squabbling and splashing, was no longer frozen for skating and where the bandstand, looking as if it needed a coat of paint, was between winter and summer deserted.

What was he going to do? For the first time in his life—or for the first time since he had so badly wanted to go to Breslau and the Gymnasium instead of to Lichterfelde—he had absolutely no idea. He wanted to join the Social Democrats, if only to demonstrate solidarity with their courage in the Reichstag on Thursday. They would want the

Catholic Count von Hofmannswaldau as a member of the Party even less now than when he and Adam years ago decided that no party worth joining would welcome either of them. And in any case, it was too late. Social Democrats were being rounded up by the Stormtroopers and taken off to concentration camps as if there were no difference between them and the Communists. He had heard in the office that an entirely respectable left-wing intellectual, a member of neither the KPD nor the SPD, an elderly man and a Breslau city councillor for decades, had been taken into what his wife, who had come herself to ask for Dr Gerlach's help, had been told by the police was called "protective custody".

Max picked up a stone and threw it as far as he could into the lake, scattering a few ducks. An old woman coming towards him with a walking stick looked disapproving.

"What did you do that for, young man? You might have killed a duck."

"I wasn't thinking."

"You ought to know better." She stumped on.

Protective custody: who was protecting whom from what? He must find out on Monday what had become of the councillor. What was his name? Dr Epstein? Dr Eckstein? He was Jewish, therefore, most likely, as well as a socialist.

And there was the most difficult question of all. As far as he had ever been able to detect, no one at the courts of justice knew that his mother was a Jew, at least according to the Nazi view that Jewishness was entirely a matter of race rather than religion. They could, as Eva had said on Thursday, have found out easily enough, but his name, his place of birth, his education, even his appearance, wouldn't have led anyone at work to suspect ...

He turned angrily away from the lake. He despised this thought, which struck him as both cowardly and itself Nazi.

He remembered his grandfather saying that although baptized as a baby and brought up as at least a nominal Protestant, he would never have accepted a job closed to an unconverted Jew. Out of loyalty to his grandfather, to his mother, to Anna—the people he loved best except for Adam—and out of loyalty also to Adam's clear thinking, shouldn't he be prepared to acknowledge his half Jewishness, to suffer whatever was in store for all those Hitler considered fit only to be persecuted, excluded, bullied, swept up like rubbish into "protective

484

custody"? Yet wouldn't acknowledging, announcing—how, when, to whom could it be done?—his Jewishness also be to concede to the Nazis that religion meant nothing and race everything?

He longed for Adam's help, for his intelligence and affection. Perhaps he would write to him, in his presbytery in Lemberg. How much would he be likely to have heard about what was going on in Germany? Might Adam's reply be opened, confiscated, used to prove Max was a Jew? He remembered the emergency decrees, now law. No. This was absurd. Why should anyone be suspicious enough of him to open his letters? Then he remembered Gärtner at the Stormtrooper headquarters. Would he tell Dr Gerlach that Max was Professor Meyer's grandson? That he, Gärtner, had forbidden his mother to work for Max because he had Jews visiting the flat? How could Gärtner know what he did, where he worked?

He stopped walking. Gärtner knew because he himself had told the Stormtrooper at the desk exactly that, what he did, where he worked. Damn. Damn. Damn.

Then he heard Adam's voice as if he were standing in front of him with his laughing eyes.

Pull yourself together, Max. Why should Gärtner bother? He was probably just boasting that he knew this count who'd walked into headquarters. What you have to do is wait and see. It's not your moral duty to provoke anything. If you can stay in the Breslau courts, stay on the right side of Gerlach who's always approved of you and is a snob in any case, and do what you can for anyone who's being treated unjustly by this bunch of gangsters calling itself a government, then that's what you must do. As far as Breslau's concerned, you're a Silesian count and a Catholic, and that's that. A little Machiavelli's what you need here. Not too much, but a little. Don't forget that not saying something no one's asked you to say isn't the same as lying.

Encouraged, Max walked home, noticing his own breathing in of the sunshine, of the gentle spring day, and started work on the Brahms concerto, a great deal more difficult than Heifetz made it sound.

The next day, Sunday, he went to the first Mass, at seven in the morning, at the local church. There was an elderly priest at the church and now a young curate: Max was pleased when the celebrant was the old man, who knew his name and greeted him after the Mass, as did three or four of the women who regularly came to the first Mass.

He knelt in an empty row of chairs towards the back of the church, propped his elbows on the back of the chair in front, and put his head in his hands, consigning to God the week since he last knelt here, the dead and the living and the betrayed republic and the danger he knew he was in. He heard again the sound of the earth on Dr Mendel's coffin as, one after another, his friends threw in a crumbly shovelful, with stones in the soil. Max knew that suicide was a serious sin, for Jews as for Christians, and he knew from long ago that Dr Mendel knew it too. So he prayed for his soul. And for Stern's: so hard, he was working, to become a selfless doctor for the poor peasants of Russia, and the Nazis had killed him too, no doubt as much because he was a Jew as because he had been to KPD meetings. May they rest in peace, he prayed, in the eternal light of goodness and truth, with the unformed soul of my child. And my child's mother: may her shell of confidence crack one of these days to let in—what? Some fear of God, perhaps, the beginning of wisdom? He buried his head deeper into his hands. Who was he to think he knew anything whatsoever about wisdom?

The clock in the small belfry chimed seven, and the old priest came in with a boy server ahead of him and knelt at the altar. The Mass began. At the end of the Gospel, the priest kissed the missal, muttered the usual prayer, and, instead of moving to the middle of the altar for the Creed—there was never a sermon at the first Mass—moved to the lectern and said to the standing congregation, "Please sit down for a moment." They sat. "I have an episcopal letter from the Cardinal," the priest went on, "directed to be read at every Mass today."

Max knew very little about Cardinal Bertram, Prince-Bishop of Breslau, except that he was the senior figure among all the Catholic bishops of Germany, and, according to Dr Fischer some time ago, had condemned the racial hatred encouraged by the Nazi Party as madness. Would he now condemn what had happened in the Reichstag on Thursday? No. Apparently not. The episcopal letter the old priest was reading, in an expressionless voice, said almost the reverse of what Max was expecting. It ended with the sentence: "Without revoking the judgements of our previous statements against certain religious and ethical errors, the episcopate nevertheless believes it can now cherish the hope that the previous general warnings and prohibitions need no longer be considered necessary."

As the priest put down on the lectern the paper he had read, he closed his eyes for a moment as if in prayer, or despair. There was a murmur of approval from the congregation, who stood, as the priest moved back to the altar, for the Creed.

What was this? Why was this? Surely the Cardinal must have understood what had happened on Thursday?

Max failed to do more than kneel through the rest of the Mass, his mind elsewhere. He didn't go up to receive Communion, nodded to the old priest as he left the church, and when he got home wrote a note to Dr Fischer asking to come to see him one evening. Old Fischer will always throw you a rope if you think you're sinking.

Before he saw Dr Fischer, the water had got rougher.

From that Monday morning, Breslau looked and felt different even from how it had looked and felt immediately after Hitler's appointment as Chancellor. Then the streets had filled with marching Stormtroopers, bands, flags, and cheering crowds. Frau Hübner had hung a portrait of Hitler on the door of the house and was standing on the pavement chatting to a neighbour when Max came home from work. "It's wonderful, isn't it, Count? Just like 1914!" But the next day things had returned more or less to normal, at least as far as one could see. Now there were suddenly huge swastika banners everywhere, fixed to all the public buildings, including the law courts, and many shops and ordinary offices had smaller swastika posters on windows and doors.

The atmosphere in the office was strained all week. Hertz, one of his two fellow Assessors, a year ahead of Max in seniority, was Jewish, as was one of the four Referendars on Dr Gerlach's staff. Hertz's father had been killed on the western front, and Hertz wore an enamel lapel badge, red, white, and black, signifying his loyalty to the Kaiser and the conservative cause. The Jewish Referendar, whose name was Goldstein, was two years younger than Max. He was a bright, cheerful fellow who had been at Max's Gymnasium and a pupil of Dr Fischer's. Once, in the autumn, they had been working together as juniors on a case of Dr Gerlach's in a country town in Lower Silesia, and Max had taken Goldstein out to lunch in a local inn and laughed a lot at his Fischer imitation, which was nearly as good as Adam's. Max had never heard the Jewishness of Hertz or Goldstein mentioned by anyone at the courts of justice.

Hertz on the Monday morning after the Reichstag vote came into the office the Assessors shared and said, "Well, Hofmannswaldau. I suppose you read the papers over the weekend. At least we all know where we are now. A good thing, I daresay. The republic's been dead for at least eighteen months. Time it was buried and Germany got back to being a decently run country. Don't you agree?"

"Actually, I think it's frightening, what happened on Thursday. It means Hitler can do exactly what he wants, and some of the things he wants haven't got much to do with a decently run country."

"Oh, most of that's just talk, to get the votes. President Hindenburg would never have appointed a Chancellor who was likely to do the real interests of Germany any harm, would he? What this country needs is some firm government, some consistency, the restoration of confidence, jobs, rearmament. All the things the republic was too weak and divided to deliver. Democracy's had its chance. Fourteen years of quarrelling and incompetence—quite long enough, in my judgement."

"Well, we'll see. But I don't think it's correct to say the republic didn't achieve anything. Stresemann—"

"Stresemann only stayed in the government with the support of the Social Democrats, and everybody knows they're practically Bolsheviks. Have been all along."

"That's not true."

"Don't tell me you're in favour of the Social Democrats, Hofmannswaldau. What are you doing working for Dr Gerlach, in that case?"

"My best, in the interests of justice, as a matter of fact. As I'm sure you are too. Since that's what both of us are here for, we'd better get on with something we're supposed to be doing, don't you think? Oh, by the way, is there any news on that city councillor Dr Gerlach was asked to find out about? His wife was here—do you remember?"

"Dr Eckstein? I don't think so. He's some kind of a socialist, isn't he? Doesn't seem to have done him much good."

On Tuesday a friendly note from Dr Fischer arrived in the post at the flat. He would be delighted to see Max, but he was going to be in Berlin for the weekend at his granddaughter's First Communion. Would Max like to come for a plum brandy at six on the next Saturday, April 8?

On Thursday afternoon, Hertz came into the Assessors' office and threw a file across the room onto Max's desk. "There you are, since you're interested. Eckstein."

A thin file. Three letters, two from Gerlach, or signed by Gerlach, requesting information on the whereabouts of Dr Ernst Eckstein, the second more peremptory than the first. Then a letter, dated yesterday, from Brigade Commander Edmund Heines, Chief of Police, Breslau, having the honour to inform District Judge Dr Heinz Gerlach that City Councillor Eckstein was in protective custody, being suspected of disloyalty to the state. He was, unfortunately, having difficulty responding to the conditions of his confinement and, since he was suffering from a disease of the lungs, was now in the hospital of the detention camp to which he had been sent, where he was being fed intravenously, as he had refused to take nourishment. It was regretted that since those in protective custody were under the direct guardianship of the police, they were permitted no personal access to a lawyer.

Max, cold as if someone had opened a door to a freezing night, put the letters back in the file.

"Brigade Commander Heines. Wasn't he the Stormtrooper boss who organized the sweep-up of Communists after Hitler's appointment, and again after the fire?"

"That's right. Coordination. Making him Chief of Police. Perfectly sensible, when you think about it."

"Sensible from the Nazi point of view. That isn't the only point of view there is. Yet. And it's very important that it shouldn't be—surely you can see that?"

"I'm not interested in theory. I'm interested in getting things done."

The next day, another soft spring day, Max walked home from the office. There were loudspeakers on corners and on the tops of Stormtrooper cars being driven slowly through the streets, as there had been before the election. Out of them came Hitler's voice. "From tomorrow, the first of April, a great day in the advance of the nation to unity and freedom, a boycott will begin of Jewish shops and businesses, of Jewish doctors and lawyers. All patriotic Germans will observe the boycott. Do your bit for your country! Germans, defend yourselves! Do not buy from Jews! Buy only at German shops! Do not consult Jewish doctors or lawyers. Defend yourselves from Jewish propaganda, Jewish conspiracy. Do not buy from Jews!"

The mad shouting voice seemed to be audible everywhere. It was difficult to tell, as people hurried home from work, as they queued for trams and crossed the roads in orderly groups—mothers with shopping bags holding children by the hand, and old people with walking sticks among the office workers—whether they were paying any attention, whether they were impressed or shocked or frightened by what they were being made to hear.

When Max got back to the flat, he went into Grandpapa's workshop and looked at his neat row of chisels, his lathe, his stone for sharpening blades, his vice on the edge of the carpenter's bench. Do not consult Jewish doctors. The instruction of the Chancellor of Germany. He was glad his grandfather had died when the Nazis were just a disreputable crew of fanatics disgraced in Munich. His grandfather never had to make the effort Max was making now, the effort to believe that all this was true, that it was the reality of the present day, the spring of 1933, in the same cities, universities, hospitals, the law courts that, not much more than a hundred years ago, had given Jews their opportunity to be educated, to be scholars and doctors and judges, to contribute to the civilization of which Germany was—until when? Until 1918? Until the murder of Rathenau? Until the death of Stresemann and the collapse of the republic?—so proud. So right to be proud.

He shut the door of the workshop and went to stand in front of Bach, the middle-aged composer in his eighteenth-century wig with his intelligent, forthright face, his slight frown. How much longer could he—should he—Count von Hofmannswaldau, hide behind his name, behind what they happened to know about him in Dr Gerlach's small world? What was going to become of Hertz, for all his conservative credentials? Or young Goldstein, whose father, Max remembered Goldstein telling him, was an ordinary family doctor in a poor district of the city? He was not now to be consulted by patriotic Germans. Max suddenly thought of old Dr Eckstein, being force-fed in a prison hospital. His stomach churned. His mouth filled with bile. He walked quickly to the lavatory and was sick.

The Stormtroopers must have been out all night with their posters and their buckets of paste. The first poster Max saw that Saturday was on the window of the newsagent where he always bought his *Vossische Zeitung*. "Germans! Defend yourselves! Do not buy from Jews!" A Stormtrooper, a tall boy no older than young Gärtner, stood outside the shop, smiling. Two housewives with shopping bags and a one-armed man were watching on the pavement to see whether anyone would go in. Max walked straight past them and the Stormtrooper into the shop. He bought his paper and said good morning in as every-day a voice as he could manage to the girl behind the counter. "Thank you, sir. Thank you very much." As he left the shop, one of the house-wives said, "Jew lover", in a nervous whisper. He didn't look back.

Later, he walked all the way to Cathedral Island. The Stormtroopers had done a thorough job. Shops and businesses all over the city—large and small, smart and modest, department stores, travel agents, corner tobacconists, perhaps one in ten shops of every kind—had posters plas-tered to their windows, Stormtroopers on guard, hesitant customers, mocking or anxious bystanders. He had decided to buy a big Bach score, the B minor Mass or the Saint John Passion, costing more than just the price of his daily paper at his local newsagent, as a gesture of defiance.

The music shop was closed, the ancient wooden shutters sealed with heavy iron bars, and the hateful posters pasted over the bars. Closed for today? Closed for good? The old assistant with his half-moons, Dr Mendel's friend, not being paid today, or ever again?

The next morning, Sunday, he went to Mass.

He opened his missal before the priest appeared. Passion Sunday—a fortnight of Lent was still ahead. The Introit struck him forcibly. *Judica me, Deus, et discerne causam meam de gente non sancta.* Judge me, God, and sort out my cause from a nation that is not holy. *Ab homine iniquo et doloso eripe me.* From the unjust and treacherous man deliver me. These desperate words were from a psalm, an ancient Jewish prayer for God's help. Yesterday, the start of the boycott, was the Jewish Sab-bath. Were they praying in the synagogues for God to help them against the unholy nation? It was Passion Sunday, Jesus struggling—he turned the page of the missal and saw the Gospel for the day—against the unbelief of the Jews. Max looked up as the congregation stood, and saw the curate coming in behind the altar boy to celebrate. When he saw, after the Gospel, that the priest, going to the lectern and grasping its sides with firm hands, was going to preach—never done at the first Mass—a sharp premonition told him to leave, now, at once, before the sermon began. He failed to leave. He sat down, like everyone else. As if he had to see, today as well, the reality of what had become of his country, his city, and now his church.

Max stayed in his place for less than two minutes. "How fortunate we are to be present, at this holy season of the year, at the resurrec-tion of our country, our nation. You see from today's readings from

Holy Scripture how Christ himself was deceived and betrayed by the Jewish people. They have not changed. No, they never change. We are blessed indeed to be given the opportunity by our leader, surely chosen by God himself, to escape the treachery and deceit of the Jews: we should support the boycott of their shops and businesses with all our heart and soul."

Max left the church, not trying to make as little noise as possible.

In the middle of the week, he began to wonder whether the boycott and the sermon had been as real as they seemed. Most of the posters had disappeared from the Jewish shops. Almost as many people as usual seemed to be going in and out of them, as if the boycott had never been proclaimed. Had the good sense of ordinary people prevailed in some unspoken way against the contempt of the Nazis? Would it be possible after all for the orchestras and the museums and the universities quietly to take back their musicians and curators and professors? Had Dr Mendel died unnecessarily?

On Friday it became clear that it was hope that was unreal.

At half past four in the afternoon, when the courts had closed for the day but all the lawyers were still at their desks finishing the week's work and preparing papers that would be needed on Monday, Dr Gerlach's clerk appeared in the Assessors' office.

"Gentlemen, the judge wishes to see you all in his chambers at five o'clock."

They heard him repeating this message in other offices down the corridor.

"What's this about? Do you know, Hertz?" said Hans Wittstock, the third and oldest Assessor, a Prussian from Berlin who was working for two years in Breslau because he had failed his last examinations.

"I've no idea. It must be quite important."

"The old boy's usually keen to get away as soon as possible on a Friday. It's a damn nuisance, whatever it is. I promised my wife I'd be back at five thirty. She's got some party we're going to. I'll have to telephone her."

They assembled five minutes early in Dr Gerlach's chambers, two junior judges, three Assessors, and four Referendars. The judge came into the meeting room from his inner office, not in the gown he wore in court but grim-faced as if he were about to deliver sentence in a trial.

"Sit down, gentlemen, please."

They sat round the polished conference table in the centre of the room. Max thought of the KPD poster, the little figures round just such a table, the giant worker poised with a raised fist to smash them. Dr Gerlach, no giant, sat at the head of the table and straightened the single sheet of paper he had brought in. He looked, as he had never before looked in Max's experience of him, embarrassed.

His eyes fixed on the paper in front of him, Dr Gerlach cleared his throat.

"I have to tell you, gentlemen, that the judiciary has been informed of a new law that has ... that has come into force today in the whole of Germany, as a ... a necessary component of the government's policy of national renewal. The directive I have received summarizes the salient provisions of the ... of the Law for the Restoration of the Professional Civil Service. This, gentlemen, is the designation of the current decree."

The judge stopped, took out a large, folded silk handkerchief, shook it open, blew his nose and returned the handkerchief to his pocket.

"The provision that ... that directly concerns us here, gentlemen, requires the ... the ..." He took the handkerchief out of his pocket again and mopped his brow. "The resignation of those officials of the courts of justice who are non-Aryan."

The quality of the silence round the table had changed, had frozen to a horrified stillness, but the judge, without pausing, went rapidly on.

"This provision, naturally, is part of the process of what is called coordination ... that is ... that has been put in train by the government. The ... the alteration in circumstances that it enforces on the lives of some of our ... some of our respected colleagues will, we trust, be limited. There are—are there not?—a good number of non-Aryan clients for ... for ... It may even possibly be temporary."

He looked up at last. Max, before he looked down himself, saw the judge fail to catch Wittstock's eye.

"That is all, gentlemen." He cleared his throat again. "Would ... would Dr Hertz and Herr Goldstein be good enough to remain behind for a few moments?"

And half of Count von Hofmannswaldau, Max thought, as he pushed in his chair, nodded to Dr Gerlach—shouldn't the judge resign in protest? Would it make any difference if he did?—and left with the others. The Aryans.

Chapter 18

"Come in, my boy, come in. Has the rain stopped? Good. Good. What a pleasure to see you."

But under the hall light, after Max had hung up his damp raincoat and his hat, Dr Fischer for a moment studied him carefully.

"You don't look at all well, Hofmannswaldau, and I can't say I'm surprised. Things at the law courts must be exceedingly painful at present."

By the fire, over the plum brandy, Max talked. Safe for the time being from the world outside, he told Dr Fischer about Dr Mendel's death, about Stern, about what had happened to City Councillor Eckstein, whom he had never met. "He's a distinguished man", Dr Fischer said. "So recently, Breslau was proud of such citizens. As it has been for generations."

Max told him about what had happened at the office the day before. "I don't know what they'll do, how they'll find work. We're trained in Prussian law. It can't be of much use in any other country, even if they can afford to leave Germany. Goldstein certainly can't. His father's a doctor in the slums."

"I'm sure you're right. Goldstein—a nice boy, I remember him well—would never leave without the rest of his family, and they are not wealthy people."

"Hertz—I don't know. Hertz's father got an Iron Cross before he was killed in the war, and Hertz is a conservative, all for the Kaiser and Hindenburg. Makes no difference, apparently. Parasites, lice, they're called all the time. Hertz. Goldstein. Dr Mendel. Felix Stern. People like my grandfather. When Jewish blood spurts from the knife, we all feel twice as good. Thank God Anna and her brother have gone home."

Dr Fischer puffed on his pipe, listened with all his attention, got up when Max stopped talking, and put more logs on the fire, more brandy in each of their small glasses.

494

"I don't know what to do, sir. I feel more Jewish than I've ever felt. Should I tell them? Is it a lie to go on turning up for work as if ... as if my father's name were some kind of Nazi passport? Or do I wait till they find out—which they will." He told him about young Gärtner recognizing him at Stormtrooper headquarters. "I thought ... I've thought ever since Adam went away that the law at least would make it possible to protect a few people, to defend people unjustly charged— that I would have opportunities to—but now ... do you know that Dr Eckstein isn't allowed even to see a lawyer? I don't understand what they're doing, this government, to the law, how it's possible for them simply to ignore it."

"You are right, of course, Hofmannswaldau. The law is the citizen's only protection against the state. But if the state is able to make what you and I can easily recognize as illegal laws—'when lawlessness makes law its instrument' (that's a line in *Faust*, you know)—then where is the citizen to turn? I'm afraid this terrible posssibility has been present in the republic since the beginning. So short a time ago. Fourteen unhappy years. The republic seemed to many of us so full of hope. There was no bloody revolution, because our good bureaucrats of whom we are so proud, our judges and administrators and honest servants of the government, stayed at their desks and did their work as always. The dear old Centre Party did its bit. We were proud that the first mayor of a great city to recognize the new republic was a Catholic, in my hometown, Cologne. Dr Adenauer—have you heard of him? No? Of course not, in Breslau. But look at the Centre Party now!"

"What happened, sir? How could they vote for the Enabling Act? I don't understand."

"What happened was that for the last couple of years, the Centre's been too useful to the extreme parties in the Reichstag, right and left, first one, then the other, and too preoccupied with the sole objective of safeguarding the Church. So the party's lost its footing on the rock and been swept into the waves. Believing Hitler's promises is being swept into the waves. Not that the Reichstag could have stopped him. The real problem has been that in the constitution they drew up in Weimar, the President was given too much power, the Reichstag not enough. It's as simple as that. We seem incapable of democracy in this country, so we give one man ultimate power. And now the President is too old to understand what he's done. Hindenburg makes Hitler Chancellor. Hitler terrorizes and cheats the Reichstag, taking all the

495

power to himself. And there you have it. The way is open to the Nazis to make illegal, or, more accurately and seriously, *unjust* laws."

Dr Fischer paused, out of long habit in his classroom, for effect.

"It is because you so clearly understand this that you must stay at your post. Germany must have some young men who one day, when we have all woken up from this nightmare, will be able to arrange things again according to true principles of justice, draw up perhaps a truly democratic constitution, making further Hitlers legally impossible."

"But nearly half the people in the country support Hitler and vote for the Nazis. I know more than half therefore don't, but since they can't agree about anything else ... What I don't understand is why. Why do so many people want Hitler to rule? Why do they turn out for him in millions, march for him, sing for him, when he's evidently mad? I saw him in the Century Hall last year, and he is actually mad. Dr Fischer, what is happening to Germany?"

More silence. More puffing. Max wished he were fifteen years old and about to be told that he must have been half-asleep when he did that week's Greek prose.

"That is the question", the old man finally said. "And I'm afraid the answer to it is truly terrifying. You're too young ... when were you born, Hofmannswaldau? In 1904? 1905?"

"In 1905, sir."

"There you are. So your memories will be of what I hope was a happy childhood before the war. Were you a small boy in the country?"

"Yes, in Waldau. It's a beautiful place. Lower Silesia. With a river. And you can see the Riesengebirge from the house." Max was nearly in tears.

"Exactly. And then the war. And the defeat. But I'm so old that I remember Bismarck's Germany well, the seventies when I was a boy, the eighties when France was defeated. A new empire. Industrial competition with England. Germany's turn in the sun. I was about your age when the old King died. Bismarck called him the Kaiser, of course, but the King didn't like it himself, and it never suited him, to his credit. If his son had lived even ten years, we might not be seeing what we're seeing now. Poor man—already dying when his father died. Dead in three months. Intelligent, with his sensible English wife, and quiet—an excellent quality in a public man. Herr Stresemann was quiet—compare the *noise* of Hitler—and Kaiser Friedrich was a liberal too, when his voice was occasionally heard. But he died, and so we had Kaiser Wilhelm, his fool of a son. And so we had the hubris and the war and the nemesis and the using of defeat for lies, even before the treaty. You know, Hofmannswaldau ..."

Dr Fischer took off his spectacles, polished them, put them on again.

"One of the most dangerous things in the twentieth century has been the catchphrase, the hitword, the slogan, whatever you like to call it. Politicians tell lies to the newspapers, a lie in a phrase, the shorter the better—the stab in the back, the Jews are our misfortune, the enemy within, the Jewish Question—and when they see them in print, they think they refer to reality. Then the newspapers use the phrase over and over again, and, lo and behold, words that originally referred to nothing outside themselves take on life, substance, the semblance of truth. There was no stab in the back in 1918; there was no enemy within when Bismarck invented the *Reichsfeinde*, the enemies of the state, to unite the nation. They were no one's enemies, just harmless Catholics and harmless Jews. And above all, the Jews have never been our misfortune—in fact, the reverse is the case—and there is in Germany no Jewish Question. Perhaps in Poland, perhaps in Russia, where the Jews are many and terrified, poor wretches, but not in Germany. Do you know how many Jews there are in Germany, Hofmannswaldau?"

Max was surprised that he had no idea. He shook his head.

"Less than one in a hundred of the population. Since almost all of them are good, law-abiding, patriotic Germans doing useful jobs, and since even in the KPD, for example, they're vastly outnumbered by what Hitler has taught us to call Aryans, much though I loathe the expression, where is the Jewish Question? It doesn't exist."

Silence while Dr Fischer puffed on his pipe and the burning logs shifted.

"A scapegoat. To carry the sins of the tribe. 'And the goat shall bear upon him all their iniquities unto the wilderness.' The transformation into a ritual of a cruel instinct as old as the sin of Adam, the instinct to find something—someone—*else* to blame, to punish. A culprit. So the Jews are to blame for the defeat, the treaty, the inflation, the corruption of morals, the depression, unemployment, everything. It is wicked. Wicked. There's no other word for it. Because there's no truth in it. Not a grain of truth. And yet millions of people have been persuaded into believing it. That is why, Hofmannswaldau, you must say nothing, do nothing, to provoke your judge to classify you as a

Jew. To do so would be to concede that this nonsense about blood—blood this, blood that, blood the next thing: more catchphrases turning into false truths—has some reality in it. It does not. Always remember that. You are a Catholic. A believing Christian is a Christian. A believing Jew, like little Anna, is a Jew. The category Aryan, like the category non-Aryan, is sheer nonsense. An unbelieving Jew is no different, in any sense that means anything real, from an unbelieving Christian. As you can see from the godless ideas of the nineteenth century, which have come together to drive the wickedness of the twentieth. Some of those ideas were invented and justified by people the Nazis call Jews: Marx, for example, and Freud. But their ideas are no more Jewish than they are Christian since these people altogether discount, indeed despise, God. Other ideas, just as destructive of what is good and true, were invented and justified by people the Nazis call Aryans: Hegel, Comte, Nietzsche. Now there's a witches' brew."

Max, back in a Thursday morning class at the Gymnasium, felt calmer than he had since the telephone rang on the morning of Dr Mendel's death.

"'The state is God walking among men.' Hegel wrote that. It's an idea of real evil, as Saint Augustine knew very well. Particularly so when only one state is meant. Hegel purloined words—catchphrases, yet again—not truths but words from Christianity, most dangerously 'spirit', 'the world spirit', 'the spirit of the age', so that people should believe that they were, that they always would be, with God's approval, on the side that was certain to win. March in step, gullible obedient Germans, good Christians as you are assured you are, to where the world spirit is inevitably taking you, and Protestant Prussia will rule Germany, then Europe, then the world. As the Bolsheviks, with a different inevitable history on their side, will rule Russia, then Europe, then the world. People are entirely right to fear the Communists but entirely wrong to think the Nazis better. They agree, after all, that anyone who gets in the way of the glorious future can be detained and then disposed of. Like Dr Eckstein, a good German citizen all his life; I fear he will not survive his imprisonment. Here we throw in a bit of Darwin for scientific respectability—the survival of the fittest means that those arbitrarily identified as the less fit can be trampled underfoot—and a bit of Nietzsche for spurious rationality—the will to power is the principle of all life—and what we get is Hitler."

Max thought perhaps the lesson was over, but saw it wasn't.

"Nationalism, my dear boy, has been the very devil for a hundred years, perhaps a hundred and fifty years. A people can think of itself as a nation, but you don't have nationalism until you have a state, or the prospect or the goal of a state. Before Hegel, before Napoleon—we haven't seen the end of the harm Napoleon did—the great virtue of Germans was that they were without nationalism. They had a language and a way of thinking and a good many books and most wonderful music—all of that held them loosely together—but where did they grow up? Where were their loyalties? They came from Prussia, Bavaria, the Rhineland, Sachs-Weimar, or Mecklenburg-Strelitz, or, come to that, from Salzburg, Basel, Prague, Sarajevo, and Saint Petersburg. It was a catholic kind of thing, being German in those days, in spite of Luther, Hegel's hero naturally, having launched the overvaluing of the state. Or, you could say"—he paused and looked keenly at Max over his pipe—"with some accuracy, a Jewish kind of thing."

He put down his pipe, signalling that the resounding conclusion of the lesson was to come.

"Then the triumph of Napoleon turned Prussia and its revenge into a religion. Napoleon was the devil, and God was practically pagan: the old faithful father-god of the Germans. Then Bismarck's wars created the German state. And now we have marching and hideous singing and hideous uniforms and the threatening swastika everywhere. Mommsen—you remember who he was, a great scholar and a defender of the Jews—said thirty years ago, 'Bismarck broke the back of the nation.' It was meant to surprise, that remark, since most people think Bismarck made the nation. But it was the state, with its scapegoat enemies within, that Bismarck made. Alas."

Max sat still in his warm chair, his whole body warm from the brandy, looking into the fire. There was something else.

"Dr Fischer?"

"Yes, my boy? I apologize. The old schoolmaster talking too much, as ever. What is it?"

"How can the Church approve of the Nazis?"

"Ah." Dr Fischer got heavily to his feet and stood in front of the fire, looking down at Max. "The Cardinal's letter."

"Yes. How can he say now that Catholics should approve of the Nazis? When these things are happening? And not just the letter. I left my church on Sunday in the middle of the sermon because a priest, an actual priest, was telling us that Hitler has been sent by God to resurrect Germany. Tomorrow is Palm Sunday. How can I go to church and sit quietly while I'm told that the Jews are still to blame? It was on Palm Sunday three years ago that Anna ... the time she went to Mass without me because I was in England and her brother found out and sent her home ... even then, a different priest, in your church it was, told her that the Jews—"

"Listen to me, Hofmannswaldau. I also was shocked by the Cardinal's letter. The reason for it, I suspect, is that Catholics who sympathize with the Nazis are deserting the Church for Protestant churches, where they sing the Horst Wessel song in their services and have pictures of Hitler on their altars. Catholics in Germany, as I've told you before, have been, since Bismarck's effort to drive them to the margins of German life—enemies of the state, you see?—desperately anxious to prove that they're good, patriotic German citizens. Furthermore, the whole Church has throughout history from time to time found herself supporting versions of authority that she would have done better to distance herself from. Too much Aquinas and not enough Augustine. I am certain, however, that at present it would be not only right but more effective for the Church to hold firm than to bend to popular enthusiasm.

"But the Catholic Church, thank God, is more than German; wider, older, and more resilient than Germany; and qualitatively different because she's a divine as well as a human institution. We are to believe—we do believe—that the Church is one, holy, catholic, and apostolic. At the same time, we know that as a human institution she is flawed, unpredictable, and imperfect, like everything else that's human. The bishops may feel that they have to go gently with this devilish government in order not to lose thousands of souls. Priests here and there may be carried away by an enthusiasm for the promise of better times, which has seduced so many into losing their balance, their judgement, and even their common sense—and if better times are delivered, more important things than prosperity and jobs are likely to get even worse. For a while. But all this will pass. Bishops and priests are not necessarily braver or wiser than anyone else, I'm afraid, though some are, some have been, and some always will be. And the Church will remain, a light and a reproach to the world, the presence of Christ and his truth in the darkness of all our lives. This we are to believe."

"But ... it's not easy, to hold all this in one's mind. Is it?"

Dr Fischer laughed.

"No one said it would be easy. Any of it. Except Christ himself. My yoke is easy. My burden is light. But it wasn't, was it? It wasn't for him and sometimes it isn't for us. Intelligent Christians, like you, have to learn to see things in two apparently conflicting ways at the same time. The Church is divine and will prevail. The Church is human and will fail. Faith is easy. Faith is difficult. There are times when it seems impossible. Faith is a gift of God we never deserve. Faith is of the will and we choose it. The paradoxes are infinite, and among them all we can do is our best. As you will, my dear boy, I have no doubt."

The next day, Max went to the cathedral for the Palm Sunday High Mass, for scale and anonymity and to regain something like the whole-heartedness of Adam's ordination Mass. And also because he was trying to hold on to the rope old Fischer had thrown him.

But there were Stormtroopers in uniform in the procession, their right hands holding palms, their left arms with swastika bands. *Plebs Hebraea tibi cum palmis obvia venit*, the choir sang. The Hebrew people come with palms to meet you. As the procession unwound in the cathedral and people were finding places in the nave, Max left. He went home and wrote to Adam.

In the middle of the week after Easter, he received Adam's reply.

> *St Andrzej*
> *Lwow (Lemberg)*
> *17 April 1933*

Dear old Max,

Your letter—I'm so sorry. Sorriest of all to hear of Dr Mendel's death. It's almost impossible to believe that Germany has suddenly become so stupid— Germans were always famous for their brains, at least out here in the barbarian east. To think that professors and lawyers and doctors and orchestral players are being sacked for no other reason than that they are Jews or that once upon a time their families were Jewish is a kind of national lunacy no one even ten years ago would have predicted. People like Grossmann are no great loss, of course—and people like Grossmann will always find customers to pay them lots of money in one country or another—but your young Referendar: what's he supposed to do with his life? And Mendel, poor old man. Try not to think of his death in too Catholic (or Jewish) a light. Roman in his case is more appropriate. Falling on his sword. Your mother loved him, didn't she? Too complicated for both of them, no doubt, but good that she's not alive to suffer this.

Old Fischer's right. You must keep going as an Assessor, doing what you can for truthfulness and justice—anything you achieve is better than nothing. And hope your name and your blue eyes and generally convincing Prussianness will see you through these horrors. They can't last. The failure of the boycott must be a good sign. It even made the Polish newspapers, which didn't know what to think of it all—plenty of anti-Semitism here too, I'm sorry to say, though it's not the law to persecute as it suddenly is in Germany.

As for Stern—if he wasn't going to go quietly home to Prague, his death may have been a blessing in disguise. You have no idea how appalling the Bolsheviks look from here. Actually, if you can believe it, they look worse than the Nazis. There has been an Old Testament famine all this winter in southwest Russia, what's now called the Ukrainian Soviet Socialist Republic. The famine was deliberately induced by Stalin in Moscow to force the miserable peasants into what are called collective farms and make them believe their socialist mission in life is to murder the farmers—some of them Germans, as you can well imagine—who have stayed sober enough to make a little money and buy a little land. Thousands and thousands of people have died. Perhaps millions. Thousands have turned up here so weak from hunger that many of them die as they reach the city. There have been collections of food for them for months. We do a bit to help—never enough.

Politics here is a complete shambles. This is supposed to be a civilized Polish city now in democratic reunited Poland. Most of the Poles here—our parishioners, for example—and most of the Jews (there are far more Jews here than in Breslau) try to live their lives as if this were true, but it's not. No one feels safe. No one has any confidence in the future. The bright young Jews want to go to Palestine and can't. The Poles think Warsaw is too far away and doesn't care (largely true), and the poor, especially out in the villages and farms, are mostly passionate Ukrainian nationalists who think Hitler wonderful because of what he says about Jews. So the Poles and the peasants are afraid of each other, the Jews are afraid of both, and all of them all the time are terrified of Russia.

I'm glad to be here, in spite of the above. Perhaps because of it. There's plenty to do, and the goodness of people surprises me as much, almost every day, as their wickedness. The priest I work for has lived in this city all his life, forty years since he was ordained. We talk a lot. He saw horrors beyond imagining here after the war. He's certain there'll be another war one of these days—hopes he won't live to see it—and he's probably right. Hitler wants

502

another war, doesn't he? If there is another war, nobody will defend Poland—why should they? Poland can't defend them. Like you, I'm sometimes afraid, sometimes depressed by feeling so powerless, sometimes angry that all that education and effort and work should only have brought me—us—to this sense of precariousness, as if we were condemned by some malign destiny to live until we die on the edge of a volcano that is sure to erupt sooner rather than later and will kill us when it does. But then I think, Fine. Isn't it only human life tuned up to a higher pitch than usual? Isn't everyone always closer to death than he thinks? 'Keep awake because the master is coming at an hour you do not expect.' Easter Day yesterday—but every day too.

Keep awake, Max. If you can't hold on to old Fischer's rope for the time being, never mind. You'll swim back to the land one day, I know. But keep awake.

Oremus pro invicem (= hoops of steel)
Adam

P.S. Yes, there's a piano here—a bit rocky as to condition but playable. The house is quite big but bare inside—the piano's in the hall, so it sounds better than it is. I play quite a lot. The old boy likes it. Excellent music library in the university. I wish I could hear you play the Chaconne.

On a hot Saturday morning in July, Max was working in the judges' library at the law courts. Half a dozen other lawyers were reading, taking notes, and occasionally getting up to find other books. They were sitting far apart at the long tables in the high, quiet room with shelves and shelves of legal volumes almost muttering into the silence the careful deliberations of Prussian legal history. Two or three of the tall sash windows were open a few inches.

Max was preparing a paper for Dr Gerlach. It was the only thing he had been able to think of that might possibly, one day, make a little difference. It had become clearer and clearer since Easter that the fundamental principle of equality before the law of all citizens had, without being explicitly abolished, evaporated from the minds of judges and the practice of the courts. The courts had been renamed "People's Courts"; the judges were now called "People's Judges": "people's" meant "Nazi". Definitions wavered: a street killing was a murder if the victim had ever belonged to a right-wing party, a patriotic act if the victim was a Jew or had had anything to do with the KPD or the SPD. Those guilty of the same offence were treated differently according to who they were, according to which group or political party or trade union they had ever belonged to or shown a passing interest in. The kind of death inflicted on Felix Stern never reached the courts at all. The number of Communists, Social Democrats, and Jews who had disappeared in Breslau alone in the last four months was a matter of hearsay, but Max, who often had to tell desperate families that there was nothing the law could do for them, guessed it was several hundred. It was known that a concentration camp had been established at Dürrgoy in a suburb of the city, that the regime there was brutal and sometimes killed detainees by torture, and that visitors were invited to watch the humiliation of prisoners from outside the camp fence. The older and frailer the victims, the louder the audience laughed.

About a month ago, Max had again asked to speak to Dr Gerlach. He began boldly, having rehearsed two sentences in his head.

"Sir, I am concerned that there is nothing we appear to be able to do to initiate any proper legal process to discover on what charge a number of Breslau citizens have been arrested and detained. I had always understood that according to the Prussian Code it is not lawful for any arm of the state to detain any Prussian citizen indefinitely without charging him with some offence."

He got to the end of his second sentence. The judge, looking down at the blotter on his desk, said nothing. After a silent minute, Max had to go on.

"Surely, sir, judges, as the custodians of the law, are alone able to—"

"Hofmannswaldau,"—Gerlach didn't look up—"the judges are custodians of the law only insofar as that law is framed and interpreted by the highest authority in the country. That authority has made it plain to the entire legal profession that every member of the profession must be firmly bound to the world view of the lawgiver. You must not forget that the Chancellor is no organ of the state but that he himself is the highest judge and the highest lawgiver. It is not for us, certainly not for an Assessor of a few months' standing, to question the interpretation the Chancellor has placed upon any law. Is that understood?"

World this, world that, Max remembered someone saying. Who?

"Sir", he said.

"Hofmannswaldau, if my memory serves me correctly, this is not the first occasion upon which you have seen fit to suggest in this room that I myself am in some respect falling short of the proper fulfilment of the obligations I have the honour to carry as a judge of the Breslau district court. I should like you to bear in mind that a third such suggestion may be regarded as insubordination by the bench of judges at these courts. That is all."

All right, Max thought—furious this time as he left Dr Gerlach's chambers—I'll make something useful out of all that education and effort and work—Adam's letter—and show Gerlach, and perhaps even judges senior to him, that taking meekly what they're told by Hitler as if he had the moral authority—where from? Hindenburg? The people?—to consign to the dustbin a hundred and fifty years of Prussian jurisprudence admired by the world is craven cowardice and the abandonment of all intellectual probity. If they sack me for insubordination or have me arrested for treason, then—precariousness being the true quality of every day—it will only be sooner rather than later, and I will have done something real for the truth.

This was the fourth Saturday he had come in early to the library, and he knew he was getting somewhere. He had looked up his student notes on the legal theorists of the seventeenth, eighteenth, and nineteenth centuries. He had read books he had neglected to read when told to by professors. He had borrowed from Dr Fischer, who warmly approved of the enterprise, books on Augustine and Aquinas that had given substance to his sense that the duty of a lawyer was to do everything in his power to close gaps between unjust law and the reality of justice itself. As he worked and thought, he felt both more Christian and more Prussian than a few weeks ago he had any idea that he was.

He looked at his watch. Half past twelve. Another half hour and he would stop for a quick lunch in the café across the square. The library stayed open till six, and there was a lot more he could do today.

He was suddenly aware of an argument of some kind beyond the door of the library, at the far end of the long room. The other readers had looked up at the same instant. The double doors, oak, tall, polished, opened, and the usher, silver-haired, backed into the library trying to tell someone that he couldn't come in. Max thought he heard his own name. Three SS men, a captain and two guards, pushed the usher aside and strode down the room, the noise of their boots on the old parquet brutal.

The officer stopped with his back to the window in the middle of the long wall and looked from one end of the room to the other.

"Count von Hofmannswaldau?" he said, in a voice that after the noise of the boots seemed quiet.

Max stood up.

"You are Count von Hofmannswaldau? Oh yes. I recognize you. Zapolski's friend."

Claudius. Claudius himself. With a perfectly sound left arm. With a monocle. With a duelling scar on his cheek. In the uniform of an SS captain.

"You are to come with us. You may bring your own papers. Leave the books, naturally."

Max opened his mouth.

"No questions here."

He screwed the top on his fountain pen, gathered his notebook and papers together and put them in his briefcase, neatly piled the three books he had been using, and pushed in his heavy oak chair. He walked down the library to the door, with an SS soldier each side of him and Claudius behind. Max was trying to remember his name. As they left the library, he heard Claudius turn and salute the remaining readers. "Heil Hitler!" There was a mumbled response.

At the bottom of the stairs, the small procession crossed the hall to one of the clerk's offices. A third SS guard opened the door and nodded Max inside. He was followed by the captain. The door was shut. They were alone. What *was* his name?

"Sit down."

They sat, the captain in the clerk's chair, Max in the visitor's, or petitioner's.

"What is the work upon which you have been engaged here on Saturdays during the last month?"

"I'm writing a substantive justification of the principle of equality before the law as grounded in the Christian tradition of natural law common to all mankind."

"For?"

"For my superior at the law courts, Judge Dr Gerlach."

"Has he asked you to carry out this work?"

"No."

"Haven't you understood that now that the regime of the November traitors is safely behind us, the law of the people takes precedence over the outdated codes of the past? And furthermore—I am also trained in the law, you may recall—that the sovereign state embodied in the

506

President and the Chancellor has the power to decide what is legal and what is not? You may not yet be aware that it is the view of Dr Goebbels and of all loyal members of the Party that whoever uses the word 'mankind' intends to deceive."

"A trained lawyer is bound to regard that statement as so alarming that—"

"Exactly so."

The officer—Manfred von Morsheim was his name, Max suddenly remembered—leant back in his chair and crossed his legs.

"It has come to our attention that there are also questions to be asked about your family. Your father, evidently—"

"My father was a Silesian Junker, as you can tell from my name. Waldau has been in my family for more than two hundred years."

"And your mother?"

"My mother, Antoinette Meyer, a concert pianist before she married my father, was the daughter of a professor of medicine in the university here."

"And a Jewess."

"My mother and both her parents were Protestants baptized at birth. My mother was married at Waldau in my father's church and buried beside him there. Both my grandparents are buried in the Protestant cemetery here."

Morsheim, with a patient smile of icy coldness, looked at him across the desk.

"Yes", Max said. "They were Jews."

The relief Max felt at saying these words astonished him.

"I am, therefore, in current terms, half-Prussian and half-Jewish. I am also a Catholic."

"Ah. A convert. How very convenient. Not, unfortunately, convenient enough. The truth will out. The minister of justice, Dr Frank, has decreed, as I have no doubt you are well aware, that non-Aryans are to be excluded from every aspect of the legal system. Your recent work in the library here is evidence enough of the wisdom of this policy. It is necessary for the future of the state that all positions of responsibility and influence in the courts of justice should be held by champions of the national cause and of the people. As a small privilege granted in respect of your name and title, you will be permitted to return to Dr Gerlach's offices on Monday to collect such items of personal property as you may wish to remove. Thereafter, it is recommended that you consider your position in this city and in the new Germany of national reform and coordination. You have means, I imagine."

"How is a Prussian lawyer—"

"No questions, Hofmannswaldau." Morsheim stood up. "This interview is at an end."

Saturday afternoon, evening, night. He couldn't eat, and thought he couldn't sleep, though he did, waking often. Sunday morning. Not Mass: he hadn't been to Mass since Palm Sunday. It was hot in the flat. He opened all the windows and played the last, hectic movement of the Brahms concerto, imagining the orchestra behind him filling the Century Hall. Then he turned towards the portrait of Bach, gave him a polite bow—he had often done this—and played the Chaconne, badly. He hadn't practised it for weeks. He made some coffee. Black. As always now. He had given up the routine of years—milk, rolls, newspaper—because the *Vossische Zeitung*, the dear old *Vossin* beloved of his grandfather, who used to say it was the oldest and best newspaper in Germany, had become almost Nazi since—when? Was it since Hitler's birthday four days after Easter and the loud, bright, marching, singing, beflagged celebrations all over the city? No. Later. The *Vossin* hadn't applauded the adulation on Hitler's birthday. Was it since the bonfires of books in May? The paper had kept quiet about this. In Breslau as in Berlin, as in all the university cities in Germany, the Stormtroopers had wrecked bookshops looking for the works of Marx, Freud, Einstein, Zweig, Kraus, any writer with a Jewish-looking name, and some famous sympathizers with Jews. A huge pile was made in the castle square, guarded by SS, and set alight by Stormtroopers. But the whole thing was a propaganda failure. No great crowds gathered to cheer the cleansing of German culture since most people in the city didn't understand the enterprise. Those who did stayed away in quiet despair.

Black coffee on an empty stomach today made him queasy. He knew it was time to think. What was he going to do? Where? How? With what? He couldn't think in the flat. Walking might help. The park. Anna's smile.

He walked all the way to the park, thinking not at all, except to know rather than to think that this city, since he had lost Waldau for ever, was his home. Breslau was not the most beautiful of cities—he thought of Cracow and of the unreal beauty of Venice—and not at its best in July, when it was too hot and too dusty, the leaves on the plane trees so dry and bleached that they looked as if they would fall long before autumn though the willows and alders were still silvery green by the moat. But Breslau was his own. Now it was not his own. Now it was infected with swastikas and photographs of Hitler in shop windows, with perfectly ordinary people in the streets greeting each other with the Hitler salute before shaking hands, with other people who had always lived here not in the streets but out of sight, sacked from their jobs, frightened, discounted as human beings, not knowing what to do any more than he knew himself what to do.

On the iron railings of the park by the main gates was a newly painted board. City of Breslau, it said. Scheitniger Park. Jewfree. No Jews admitted.

Had Morsheim hung a placard round his neck saying "Jew"? No. So, since he looked, and was, exactly the same as the Max von Hofmannswaldau who yesterday morning would have walked easily through these gates as to his favourite place in the city, why shouldn't he simply go into the park and pay no attention to the board?

Then he understood that the board had made up his mind without him having to think at all.

He was going to leave Breslau and Germany and find new work, a new home, a new life, somewhere altogether else.

The next morning, he took the usual tram to the law courts at the usual time. He had in his briefcase some unfinished work for Dr Gerlach and four books that belonged to the judge's chambers.

In the office, Wolfgang Lederer, the Assessor from another court who had replaced Hertz, was already at his desk. He looked up as Max came in, nodded to him, flushed with embarrassment, and looked down at once, writing something on the paper in front of him. Max put Dr Gerlach's files on his own desk with the four books beside them and went through his three drawers. He threw into the wastepaper basket most of what was in them, after piling current files on the desk with the others, packing into his briefcase only his spare white shirt, his spare fountain pen, two new pencils, the horn paperknife with a silver handle that had belonged to his grandfather, a round cherry-wood box for paper clips his grandfather had turned on the lathe in the flat and then inlaid with Max's initials, and a half-empty packet of cigarettes. He was weighing in his hands a file of notes for his essay on equality before the law, wondering whether there was any point in taking it, when the door opened and Hans Mackelroth came in.

"Heil Hitler!" he said, without a raised arm since he was carrying a briefcase and a pile of books. No one returned the salute.

"I'm sorry, Hofmannswaldau", Mackelroth said, putting his stuff on Max's desk. He pushed up his spectacles, as he had at fifteen, with his middle finger. "Dr Gerlach has asked—"

"It's all right, Mackelroth. I expect it was written in the stars."

Max shook hands with Mackelroth, who looked sheepish, surprised, and grateful. "Good luck and good-bye", Max said.

Then he shook hands with Lederer, who couldn't meet his eye. "Wittstock late as usual? Say good-bye to him for me."

Lederer nodded.

Max went into the typists' room and waved—one of the girls put her knuckles to her mouth and couldn't wave back—and then into the office of the judge's clerk and shook his hand. Down the stairs, out into the sunshine, his briefcase much lighter than before, Max felt better than he had since he climbed after Adam down the wet rocks by the waterfall in the Galician mountains.

When he got home, he realized it hadn't occurred to him to say good-bye to Dr Gerlach. He laughed out loud.

Then he sat down at Grandpapa's desk in Treuburg's room, with the morning sun streaming through the open window, and, on Grandpapa's headed writing paper, wrote a letter.

17 July 1933

Dear Canon Davidson,

Perhaps you will remember me from three years ago, when you kindly allowed me to stay in your house on the occasion of the Breslau Bach Choir's visit to your cathedral.

Because my mother came of a Jewish family, although she and both her parents were baptized Protestants, I have been informed by the Ministry of Justice that my work as an Assessor (a junior judge), the position for which I was recently qualified by examination, is no longer required. I have decided to leave Germany, not only because of my own dismissal but because of the shameful treatment of Jews at every level of society, which is now government policy here.

510

Therefore I am most respectfully asking for your help.

Naturally I understand that my training as a lawyer in the Prussian Code will be of little use in another country. However, I am, as you know, a competent violinist, and I have also worked as a tutor during school holidays since I was a student. I am able to teach Latin and Greek at a reasonably high level, and obviously German, and I have a fair knowledge of the history of philosophy and of French literature.

I understand that for the English authorities to allow a German Jew into England, it is necessary to have employment already promised. If you would be kind enough to enquire for me as to my possible employment as a violinist or schoolteacher or private tutor, I would be deeply grateful. I should have some money from the sale of my flat and my possessions here in Breslau to support myself for some months at least.

My skill in speaking the English language is not yet good, as you may see and as you know from my visit. I am capable and hardworking to learn quickly to speak correctly.

With friendly greetings to you and your family, and with apologies for the trouble I am afraid this letter will give you, and heartfelt thanks for any assistance you may find for me,

Max von Hofmannswaldau

A little more than a fortnight later, early in August, Max came round the corner of his street, light-headed and lighthearted having sold one pile of law books and another of his grandfather's medical textbooks quite well at a secondhand bookshop near the courts. There was a Stormtrooper car with a large swastika on the back parked at the door of his house. At the top of the steps at the open front door, Frau Hübner stood watching him walk up the street.

"A good job you're back", she said as he reached the steps, a very unpleasant smirk on her face. "Not so much the count now, are we? More the Jew Meyer. Just as well they made me block warden."

He took the stairs two at a time. The door to his flat was wide open. His new gramophone was sitting in the middle of the hall, on the floor. A young Stormtrooper with a broad grin came out of the kitchen, his hands full of spoons and forks. He stopped when he saw Max. The grin disappeared.

"Oh." He looked down at the cutlery, then looked up at Max. "Sorry, sir. Silver, isn't it? We're to go for silver if there is any. Orders is orders. Sergeant!"

An older, tougher Stormtrooper appeared in the doorway of the sitting room.

"Hofmannswaldau your name?"

"That's right."

"Mother's maiden name Meyer?"

"Yes."

"You applied for emigration papers?"

"Yes."

"Home search. That's us. Jews are not allowed to take valuables abroad. We'll take the gramophone. And the silverware. Anything else in the kitchen, lad?"

"No", the younger Stormtrooper said. "Just ordinary stuff. There's some good tools in a sort of workshop. Chisels and that. Other side of the kitchen."

"Fetch them out."

The boy went back to the kitchen.

"Jewellery? Clocks? Anything like that?" the sergeant said to Max.

"No."

"Come in here."

Max followed him into the sitting room. He heard the rattle of the tools being dumped on top of the silver.

"The piano must be worth a fair bit. We can send for that later." He got out a notebook, wrote something in it, put it back in his pocket, and stood, looking round the room. The boy came in.

"Nothing much else", the sergeant said. "Furniture shabby. Loads of books—worth nothing, books. What's in that chest? Turn out the drawers, lad."

The young Stormtrooper pulled out a drawer in the music chest, then another and another.

"It's all paper, sergeant. Music. Music writing."

"What! All of it?"

"Looks like it."

"Turn it out. On the floor."

When the boy, quite gently, had taken all the music out of every drawer and put it on the floor in heaps, the sergeant shrugged his shoulders.

"Well. That won't sell, will it? Leave it where it is. What else? What's this article?"

He thumped the harpsichord, which made a sound, a faint, hollow, reverberating discord, unlike any sound Max had ever heard.

"Oh, that's just a homemade piano. Like a toy. Not worth anything."

"And why've you got two violins? Those are violin cases, aren't they? And nobody else lives here?"

The violins were on top of the white bookshelves near the door.

"No. I have a good one for performing and a cheap one for practising."

"Which is the good one?"

Max picked up his own fiddle.

"Take that and put it with the other stuff."

The boy obeyed and came back into the sitting room.

"What about the picture, Sergeant? Looks old. Might be valuable."

"Well spotted, lad. Take it down."

Bach.

"Is there anything I can do to keep these things?"

"Not if you want the papers for leaving Germany, there isn't", said the sergeant.

"Couldn't I give you money instead, just for the picture?"

The sergeant looked hard at Max. Damn, Max thought. He thinks I care because it's worth a lot of money.

"No. Forbidden. We'll take the picture. And don't you try to sell the piano, or your papers might get unavoidably delayed."

They left, the sergeant carrying the portrait in one hand and a canvas bag with the silver and the tools in the other, the boy carrying the gramophone with the violin in its case on top. Max watched them go downstairs and then went back into the flat and shut the door.

He went to his bedroom. There was no mess. The young Stormtrooper must simply have opened the drawers and wardrobe and shut them again. He got the Canon's letter out of his sock drawer.

Dear Count,

I enclose a formal letter, addressed to whom it may concern, from the Cathedral School here, offering you a temporary post as a violin teacher from 26 September 1933.

You will be most welcome in this house as a holiday tutor for my grandsons at any time in August or September before the school term begins. I should be delighted, as would their mother, for them to receive some help with their Latin and for them to begin to learn some German. I enclose a further letter to this effect in English.

May I wish you courage and good fortune with your departure and your journey.
  Yours most sincerely,
    Philip Davidson

The letter had arrived that morning. He folded it and replaced it in the envelope with the two enclosures, slipped the envelope under the lining paper, where his letters from Anna and Adam still were, and shut his sock drawer. Then he returned to the sitting room, kept his eyes from the space above the fireplace, and knelt on the floor by the piles of chamber music parts in their cardboard folders. He should put them back, the piano sonatas and songs, the violin sonatas, the duets, trios, and quartets, where they had always lived, in the shallow drawers with the names of the composers in his grandfather's writing inside little brass frames.

What for?

He bowed his head over the heaps of music and wept for several minutes.

By the middle of August, he had sold his flat, for half its value—the "Jewprice", he discovered this was called—to a professor of metallurgy in the university who gave him the Hitler salute when he came to see the flat and looked surprised and then shook his head when Max failed to respond. Jews were not allowed to give the Hitler salute. A quarter of the money he received for the flat he had been required to pay to the officials stamping the papers giving him permission to leave Germany. This was the flight tax invented by the government in April.

The German official at the British consulate had studied his letters from Canon Davidson for two silent minutes before taking them away and returning with his superior, an Englishman with a monocle like Morsheim's.

"Can you speak English?"

"Yes, sir. Not perfect. Not perfectly, excuse me. But I understand much", Max answered in English.

"Where did you learn English?"

"From my English governess. And later in the Gymnasium, here in Breslau."

"After the war?"

"Naturally, sir. I am twenty-eight years old only."

"Remarkable. Have you money?"

"I have enough, sir. I have sold my flat."

"Strictly speaking, Jews are not to be given visas unless they have posts as domestic staff. However, since you are clearly"—he looked down at Max's passport, open in his hand—"only half-Jewish, and your father's family must be—yes, well, I daresay we can stretch a point. A tutor in some houses is treated more or less as a servant, in any case." He laughed, handed him back the canon's letters, and nodded to his official as he put the passport on the desk.

"Well, I suppose I should wish you luck."

"Thank you, sir."

The official stamped a visa in his passport.

He had bought his railway and boat ticket—several tickets, through Germany, Belgium, and France—to Dover and had spent considerably more money organising the packing, into two large crates, and despatch by removal van and train, of the harpsichord to Adam in Lemberg. Before the second crate was nailed shut, he wrapped Grandpapa's chess set in an old shirt and put it in among the packers' wood shavings. Different Stormtroopers had come with a large truck and packed and taken away, much less carefully, the piano. He had given the Meissen teapot to Herr Rosenthal when he went to say good-bye, and he had gone by taxi with the music from the chest of drawers in a suitcase to the shop on Cathedral Island and sold it for very little. Dr Mendel's friend who worked in the shop, the old man with half-moon spectacles, was nowhere to be seen.

Max had kept, to take with him, the scores of the Saint Matthew Passion and the Brahms violin concerto, and a few books. And Dr Mendel's violin.

He had written to Adam, and also, a much shorter letter, addressed to his home in East Prussia, to Treuburg, and a brief note addressed to Dr Jacob Halperin at the Jewish hospital in Vilna, informing him that he was leaving Germany for England and asking if he would be kind enough to let Anna know.

On his last evening, he went at six o'clock to say good-bye to Dr Fischer.

"Here are your books, sir. They made all the difference. And here's my essay. I would have had it typed at the office if I'd been able to stay a week or two longer. But I finished it and fair-copied it at home. Completely pointless to give it to Dr Gerlach. Do you know that one judge, only one in the whole of Germany, has objected to the so-called purification of the legal system? I'd like you to have the essay. Just in case it might be useful to some boy beginning a legal training—later—when this madness is over."

"Thank you, Hofmannswaldau. I look forward to reading it. A wise Englishman said that no serious piece of thinking is ever wasted. I'm delighted, by the way, that it's England you are going to, and not America. Sit down, sit down, my boy, while I find a new bottle of my plum brandy."

There were two wicker chairs and a small wicker table just outside the open window of the study, on a paved terrace. Then a few rose bushes, a small lawn, and two apple trees. The brandy was found and poured, the pipe satisfactorily lit.

"Yes, now, where were we? America likes to think of itself as innocent of all the evils of sinful Europe, but they took the evils with them. How could they not? All this wicked nonsense about race, breeding the perfect human being and so forth, is very popular in America, was popular there before Hitler got hold of the idea. They bought and sold human beings in America as recently as they did in Russia, and how they treat the descendants of the slaves, not to mention the Indians, whose home America was—all an example to the Nazis if ever there was one. Now tell me, your English clergyman. Has he found you a job?"

Max told him.

Dr Fischer laughed. "Ah! A schoolmaster. Not such a bad life, you will discover. I hope you will have the opportunity, nevertheless, one day to put your legal education to some use. Perhaps, as you say, when this madness is over."

He put his little glass on the ground and looked at Max through the pipe smoke.

"It will not be over soon. They are talking about an empire that will last a thousand years. Nonsense, of course. It's a phrase from the book of Revelation to convey the approval of God for what they're doing. There's no such approval, and all good men must hold firm to that belief."

"Adam Zapolski would say there's already been an empire that lasted a thousand years."

"Of course he would, loyal Habsburg subject that he is. The Holy Roman Empire of the German nation. Well, as I always say to schoolboys, it wasn't holy, it wasn't Roman, and a lot of it wasn't German. But at least it made some sort of effort to be Christian. I confiscated a book towards the end of last term, by a Nazi lunatic called Rosenberg. *The Myth of the Twentieth Century.* Have you heard of it?"

Max shook his head.

"It's in all the bookshops. It says that Christianity is Jewish. Therefore, it must be abolished, in favour of a true Germanness that will save us all. I had a letter from an old friend, a widower like me who lives near Munich, not far from my daughter's convent. He is on the committee that runs the Oberammergau Passion play—you have heard of it? They usually do it every ten years, but they plan extra performances next year for the third centenary. Some people on the committee, good Bavarian Catholics, want to stage the life of Hitler instead of the Passion of Christ. Worship of the state is bad; worship of the leader is the purest idolatry, the replacing of God by a sinful man."

"Sir?"

"Yes, Hofmannswaldau?"

"Do you think the people close to Hitler, the top Nazis, actually believe in him as a saviour, a divine figure? How can they?"

"Some probably do. Others, particularly those cleverer than he is—Dr Goebbels, for example—I imagine simply see that it works, his capacity to make millions of ordinary people believe in him. So staying close to him gives them power. And the will to power—Nietzsche was perfectly right—drives mankind as it drove Satan to rebel unless it is countered by fear of God, love of God, obedience to the truth."

"Why has Rome signed this Concordat with the Nazis?"

"Ah, the Concordat." Dr Fischer got up, went inside, came back with the bottle of plum brandy, and sat down again, stiffly, when he had refilled their glasses.

"Rome likes concordats. The idea is to protect the Church in each country from the inroads of the state, to safeguard the liturgy, Catholic schools, seminaries, all that. Rome has been trying to settle a concordat with Germany ever since the war, and probably even before that. Now they have one. At the worst possible moment, agreed with the worst possible government. They seem to think in Rome that Germany will be a Christian shield against Bolshevism, while the Nazis are basking in the warmth of a recognition from Rome that the republic never had. But the promises the Nazis have made in order to get it mean absolutely nothing, as I've no doubt we shall shortly see. Cardinal Bertram is now calling respect for the government a religious virtue. I despair."

But then he laughed.

"Despair is a sin, however, and hope is a virtue. A real one. There are good priests in the Church, good monks and nuns, and good laymen too. The Church will survive this madness, as you call it, because in spite of everything, she is the guardian of truth. She will never lose the grace to recognize evil for what it is, although individual churchmen may forget to ask for it."

He knocked out his pipe, put it on the ground beside his glass, and leant back in his chair. He smiled at Max.

"You are going to England. I have resigned my post at the Gymnasium."

"No, sir. You can't!"

"I can and I have. I am sixty-seven years old, Hofmannswaldau. I began to teach boys more than forty years ago. It is enough. All these years, I have tried to instil in generations of boys, some of them grandfathers now, a little classical learning, scholarly standards, a bit of Plato and Cicero, moderation, good sense, respect for the truth. Now that the truth is under daily attack in this new world of propaganda—the papers, the wireless, the loudspeakers with Hitler's voice coming out of them everywhere you go—I'm too tired to battle further for the minds of the young. I heard a class of junior boys the other day singing the *Lorelei*, as it's been sung in schools for a hundred years. One of them dropped his copy in the corridor. Under the title it said, 'Writer of text unknown.' Why?"

"Because Heine was a Jew."

"Precisely. 'Writer of text unknown.' A lie. Let us expunge Heine from the story of German literature, burn his books, blot out his name. Though he understood more than anyone else did in those days. He wrote that those who burn books will soon be burning people. I have been haunted by that line since May. And now another thing. A few days ago, a document arrived from the government. 'General German Teachers' Paper' is its elegant title. It orders us all to teach race, blood, the will, and above all, hatred of the Jews. It says—these are its exact words—'The idea that history should be objective is a fallacy of liberalism.' Time, you see, for me to stop."

"And the idea that judges should be objective, impartial, non-political—another fallacy of liberalism?"

518

"That's it, exactly. The Nazis want everyone to believe that these ideas, these good ideas that have their roots in Christian respect for truth, were invented by the Weimar Republic. The Weimar Republic has failed. Therefore, these ideas are false. Among other things, a diabolical—" He looked at Max.

"Undistributed middle."

Both of them laughed.

"Well done, my boy. Not all in vain, those years."

"Not in vain at all, sir. Really."

"Really?"

"In actual truth. Which you taught us to measure everything against."

"Thank you." He got out the usual filthy handkerchief and blew his nose vigorously. "So you see why I have resigned?"

"I do. It's why—or it's the good reason why I'm leaving Germany. The bad reason is that I can't think what else to do."

"No, Hofmannswaldau. You are leaving Germany because you are a young man who cannot stay to be carried with your contemporaries into the even worse times I am convinced lie ahead. You are right to leave. I would leave myself if I were your age and did not have children and grandchildren in Germany. You go, and take German civilization with you because it is not worthless, and here it is already almost completely lost. Teach English boys something about it, if they have any time left over from playing cricket. Now—"

He got to his feet.

"Now you must go. You have packing to do, no doubt. I have a couple of small books for you."

They were on the desk in his study.

"Pascal. Good for your French, and good for your soul. And the poems of Eichendorff because he was a Silesian nobleman, an intelligent Catholic, and a beautiful poet. Also because he was educated at our Gymnasium in Breslau."

In the hall of his flat, dark after the garden, he took Max by the shoulders.

"I shall think of you often, and of Zapolski too, struggling bravely with difficulties of his own—yes, he has written to me—in Lemberg, on the edge of another tyranny. What a world you young men have inherited. Good-bye, Hofmannswaldau."

He gave Max a bear hug.

"God go with you."

The Postcard

Adam, Count Zapolski, b. Vienna, September 1904; priest; tortured and killed in prison by Russian soldiers, Lwow/Lemberg, June 1941.

Joachim, Baron von Treuburg, b. Treuburg, East Prussia, January 1903; doctor in German army; July Plot suspect, hanged by SS, Berlin, August 1944.

Jacob Halperin, b. Vilna, Russia, April 1901; doctor and officer in Polish army; shot by Russian soldiers, Katyn Forest, Russia, April 1940.

Anna Halperin, b. Vilna, Russia, November 1908; shot with husband and children by SS Einsatzgruppe, Ponary Forest, Lithuania, July 1941.

Eva Grossmann, b. Breslau, Silesia, June 1906; died of typhoid, Ravensbrück concentration camp, August 1942.

Dr Alois Walther Fischer, b. Cologne 1866; refugee from Russian siege of Breslau, killed in Allied bombing of Dresden, February 1945.

Max Ernst, Count von Hofmannswaldau, b. Waldau, Silesia, March 1905;